The Initials of the Earth

A book in the series *Latin America In Translation /
En Traducción / Em Tradução*
Sponsored by the Duke–University of North Carolina
Program in Latin American Studies

The Initials
of the Earth

Jesús Díaz

Translated by Kathleen Ross

Foreword by Fredric Jameson

Epilogue by Ambrosio Fornet

Duke University Press   Durham and London   2006

© 1999 Piper Verlag GmbH, München

English translation © Kathleen Ross

All rights reserved

Printed in the United States of America on acid-free paper ∞

Designed by Heather Hensley

Typeset in Adobe Garamond by Keystone Typesetting, Inc.

Library of Congress Cataloging-in-Publication Data appear on
the last printed page of this book.

To Pablo,
who was born when I wrote
this book the first time;

to Claudia,
who was born when
I wrote it again.

but on the grip of his weapon of moist flint,

the initials of the earth were written.

—NERUDA

CONTENTS

Foreword by Fredric Jameson   xi

Translator's Preface   xvii

Brief Chronology of Events in Cuba, 1942–75   xxi

The Initials of the Earth by Jesús Díaz   3

Epilogue by Ambrosio Fornet   371

Afterword by Kathleen Ross   395

Notes   401

Glossary   425

Bibliography   429

FOREWORD: THE INITIALS OF THE EARTH

Fredric Jameson

It is something of a shock to find out how few literary works written in Cuba since the blockade have been translated into English. The exiles (not all of them dissidents) have of course been well served, but the American public, and American intellectuals not specializing in Spanish or Latin American studies, have very little in the way of narrative texts to help them into the experience of the Cuban people during these decisive years. Nor is it simply a matter of the foreign (and potentially exotic) nature of that experience, though one wants to insist that daily life in a genuine socialist revolution is radically distinct from life as it is led elsewhere, life which is normally and conventionally divided into public and private areas. In small-power countries, to be sure, the political and the international intersect with private life to a degree hard to imagine for the inhabitants of great powers (no matter how insistently some of us want to claim that everything private is in the long run really political). But in socialism—that is to say, in countries engaged in that endless collective project which is the construction of socialism, as Cuba has been for almost fifty years now—the personal is the political in a very special way, just as the political is always personal. How writers are to register this unique kind of experience we will examine in a moment. But it is also worth remembering that Cuba is not only unique, it is uniquely significant for us here in the United States. There has never been another successful socialist revolution in the New World, let alone one so close to the American super-state. Even in the world at large, the Cuban social experiment is unique, and utterly distinct from Soviet or Chinese practice. Meanwhile Fidel's great injunction—"Inside the revolution everything, against it nothing"—has made for a uniquely pluralistic cultural production of which we know little more than the films, the music, and dance.

This translation of *Las iniciales de la tierra* is thus an exceptional event, and a rare chance to experience Cuban revolutionary literature firsthand. Americans do not generally know that the revolutionary novel is a whole new genre that has emerged in Cuba since 1959 and that it boasts numerous practitioners and is part of the school curriculum. Not only is it not the socialist realism of other communist traditions (a mode of writing which in Cuba has become one among many), it has little enough to do with the forms of war literature and film which were so central in the Soviet Union for so long.

The Initials of the Earth, widely considered among the high points of the genre, is not limited to the period of armed struggle which culminated in Batista's overthrow, but, covering the whole of the 1960s (as well as the period of the protagonist's childhood leading up to it), gives a far more comprehensive testimony to the whole inaugural period of the revolution as a process (rather than a punctual event). It charts a movement whereby Carlos Pérez Cifredo's life, initially a private and sheltered one into which the political intermittently breaks like a thunderclap (or like that "pistol shot in the middle of a concert," as Stendhal defined politics in the novel), is gradually transformed, so that the formerly private—above all his experience of love and the drama of remarriage—becomes part of that public dynamic in which Carlos always plays a stormy part, alternating between withdrawal and commitment.

In that perpetual debate, then, about what the political is and indeed about what political literature is or should be, *The Initials of the Earth* has much to tell us. But it would be wrong to think that Jesús Díaz (1941–2002) was only a political novelist, or indeed that he was only one example of the Cuban writer and intellectual among others. In fact (as Ambrosio Fornet testifies in his epilogue to this edition), he was an extraordinary personality and a very distinctive figure—a passionately political militant (deeply involved in the Nicaraguan revolution as well) and a filmmaker of high quality, whose works also have something to teach us about the way films can be political and have political consequences. (*Lejanía* [1985], or *The Parting of the Ways*, in particular, is one of the few serious and successful meditations on the difficult personal relations between Cubans living in Miami and those living in Havana.) Nor is Díaz, a founding member of the exile journal *Encuentro*, to be assimilated to the garden-variety dissident (motivated by personal or professional interest), even though his exile from Cuba was occasioned by strong official displeasure with the 1990 film on which he collaborated, *Alice in Wonderland,* a critique of Cuban bureaucracy in the fictional small town of Maravillas. At that point, Díaz was on a research fellowship in Germany, where he remained. But it is certain that his initial position of critical sympathy with the revolution hardened into an implacable critique of Castro and the revolutionary state, as his exile lengthened (an exile tragically brought to an end by his premature death in 2002).

Whatever the meaning of this evolution (which was profoundly political and militant, as Díaz could not cease to be), it is important to avoid the omnipresent Cold War misunderstanding whereby any critique of socialism and bureaucracy is a sign of nascent dissidence. On the contrary, the critique of bureaucracy is one of the central vocations and distinguishing characteristics of socialist literature as such. It would be better to think of what we call culture and literature in terms of cultural revolution, in a social system in which the very function of the latter is not to safeguard already existing institutions or to promulgate ideological apologies for this or that status quo, but rather to participate in the great collective project of social transformation by the critique of current practices and attitudes whether the latter be observed in administration or in daily life as such. Cuban revolutionary culture worked hard at undermining and transforming gender and racial biases and stereotypes (as is apparent in films like *Portrait of Teresa* and *One Way or Another*). Such achievements should not be overshadowed by serious political mistakes, such as the imprisonment of the poet Heberto Padilla in 1971 (which alienated Cuba's intellectual friends all over the world); or the systematic persecution of homosexuals, for which recent policies and a film like Tomás Gutiérrez Alea's *Strawberry and Chocolate* (1996) only belatedly try to make amends. But the rectification of errors like these is also part and parcel of cultural revolution.

Nor are Carlos's self-doubts any signal of dissidence to come; but neither are they only the personal drama of his character or temperament, as it wavers between withdrawal and commitment, between the twin excesses of an overanxious self-interrogation and a temptation to overhasty or overzealous intervention. To be sure, the ingenious frame of the novel calls for judgment on precisely these tendencies, inasmuch as Carlos's whole autobiographical narrative (told in the third person) constitutes the background for his application for (re)admission to the party and the evidence on which his comrades will make their decision. Self-criticism (*autocrítica*) is in this sense the political or ideological equivalent to the process of psychoanalysis, which is today largely grasped as the conscious or unconscious story I tell myself about my life and psychic situation, foregrounded in such a way that this primal story can now, in the present, by my act or commitment, be decisively modified, and new desires substituted for older ones, new habits for those in which I have been paralyzed for so long.

But the novel is not to be reduced to such seemingly psychological issues: two further dimensions are implicit in Carlos's self-questioning and emerge from its tortuous paths. The first raises the question of class and the way in which a white middle-class youth can be expected to "identify himself" with the Cuban masses who actually make this revolution. Race and class cut deep into Carlos's childhood, as the opening chapters testify, and the leveling effects of the revolution are to be observed not least where a relatively sheltered individual is thrust into contact with people from more and more varied class and racial backgrounds.

Then, too, there is the politically central issue of the relationship between the individual and the movement itself. Carlos's initial hesitations, indeed, turn on the Soviet-style communist party (a distinct entity from Fidel's 26 July Movement until later on) and on his own reluctance to become the kind of camp follower or spear-carrier that he imagines political adherence to demand. But the same doubts come up in that reversal of this situation in which Carlos is called on to become a spokesperson and a leader in the student assembly (university politics always, and not only in Cuba, being both a microcosm of and a real force in the larger political world).

To be sure, like any traditional political or historical novel, *Initials* turns most centrally on its protagonist's relationship with the great political events, the official events of History: the resistance to Batista, the triumph of the Revolution itself, the Bay of Pigs (Playa Girón), the missile crisis, and finally, the disastrous gamble of the ten-million-ton *zafra*, or sugar harvest of 1970, which leaves the ending of the novel open. A historical chronology of these events is included in the present edition, and indeed it needs to be, since Díaz's approach to these events is far from direct and their intersection with Carlos's life and daily experience is often lateral and to be reconstructed by the reader after the fact.

History is in any case not the only raw material which demands commentary or explication, and the novel in its turn raises that old and new question about national literature as such and an international public (particularly today where an international dimension has mutated into globalization). To be sure, the translation of any genuinely national work (and even the distribution of national films abroad) demands a tacit background knowledge and a familiarity with local references that can often make the American reader uncomfortable. As a result of this distance from what is essentially an American or English-speaking public, and in a situation of multinational publishing monopolies, it has been observed that there is today emerging a new kind of international literature, sharply distinguished from what Goethe called world literature in the early nineteenth century, or from what Sartre meant, in the mid-twentieth, when he argued that the ideal situation for the writer was to have at least two distinct publics all at once. The new jet-set literature, however, is one which is first and foremost written *in order to be* translated into English, and it is accompanied by visible changes in the national language itself, which, if it is not altogether Americanized, is at least cleansed of its localisms and regionalisms and sufficiently abstracted from its national context and singularities to make it readily assimilable into the allegedly more universal public of English-speaking readers (themselves already standardized by American mass culture).

This is yet another reason why we have so few contemporary Cuban works in English. The literature of the Cuban exiles had gone through this transculturation process; that of Cuba itself, which remains fiercely nationalistic not least in its socialism and in its culture, has not, and the blockade ratified this isolation by sealing Cuban culture back into itself. In any case, Jesús Díaz makes no compromises with those onlookers who are the foreign readers to come, and this commitment to the specificities of the national situation is scarcely mitigated by the form itself.

Initials of the Earth, which covers a long and eventful period between the 1950s and 1970, is organized into a kind of historical slide show, in which "stills" of each historical moment succeed each other without explanatory transitions. Each chapter is its own in medias res, offering a rich humus of cultural materials which are not only multiple in themselves, but also demonstrate the deep relationship between Cuba and the United States, to which it is closer than any other Latin American country (perhaps even including Mexico). American cartoons (shades of Dorfman's and Mattelart's classic *How to Read Donald Duck!*), American rock, and Hollywood films here mingle with Santería, mambo, and the *Tropicana* in such a way as to demonstrate that the national is already transnational in and of itself. *Initials* thus continues the tradition inaugurated by Joyce's *Ulysses* in which the representation of daily life is saturated by a mass culture from which the individual lifeline can no longer be artificially separated and rendered in the style of introspection and pure subjectivity. Such works then stage a fundamental tension between the synchrony of the street and the collectivity and that diachrony of History from which—particularly in the Third World and very particularly in a socialist country like Cuba—the diachrony of the individual can scarcely be disengaged. We need more novels like this, which teach us not only about Cuba but about politics and literature in our own world.

TRANSLATOR'S PREFACE

The literary work of Jesús Díaz has been translated into many languages but appears here for the first time in English. Born in Havana in 1941, Díaz was a writer, filmmaker, and prominent intellectual force in Cuban culture until his sudden death in Madrid in 2002. Díaz was a complex character, a man who lived life with passion and even excess, a controversial figure who played an important role within the early Cuban revolutionary process and remained allied with it until the last ten years of his life, which he lived in European exile. To the international Cuban exile community, Díaz was a key fomenter of dialogue between disagreeing factions of various political stripes through the influential journal *Encuentro*, which he founded in Madrid; he has yet to be replaced in that exceptional role. Díaz's decision to leave Cuba in 1992 came as a surprise to many, if not most, who knew him. Ambrosio Fornet, in his epilogue to this volume, provides a view of those events from the perspective of a longtime friend who has remained on the island.

The Initials of the Earth, set in Cuba during the 1950s and 1960s, speaks eloquently to the controversial topic of the Revolution's numerous successes and failures. Originally written in the 1970s, then rewritten and published simultaneously in Havana and Madrid in 1987, it was the last book Jesús Díaz produced before leaving Cuba. Many critics consider this novel to be both Díaz's most outstanding work and the quintessential novel of the Cuban Revolution (Fornet's epilogue elaborates further on these questions of literary history and criticism). Through Díaz's narration of the coming of age of the protagonist, Carlos Pérez Cifredo, we are taken on a passionate journey that celebrates and criticizes with intense love Cuba's music, dance, history, racial mixture, humor, sexuality, struggle for independence, and, of course, language, the medium expressing it all.

To imagine revolutionary Cuba, as narrated through fiction by a Cuban for his compatriots, means that the English-language reader must make the leap to understanding from a Cuban perspective. With that goal in mind, I have left certain key words in Spanish throughout the translation; a glossary of those words has been included in the volume. These are words that cannot translate easily or neatly into English without losing a great deal of their meaning, and without taking a great deal away from the entire narration. I hope they will enhance the reader's sense of discovery rather than detract from his or her pleasure in the reading.

I have pictured the audience for this translation as a varied one. Some readers may have a great deal of knowledge about certain aspects of Cuban culture, music, for example, or leftist politics, or history. They may have read other works of Cuban literature in translation, or the writings of revolutionary figures. Other readers may approach this book with no prior knowledge at all. Some readers, then, may welcome additional information while others will not. Thus, while the text is followed by extensive endnotes explaining factual details, local references, and my own solutions to particular translation problems, there is nothing in the narration itself, whether numbers or asterisks, to interrupt the flow of reading. Endnotes, organized by chapter and page, are there for the reader who wishes to use them.

Readers will find three more aids: a bibliography and filmography of Díaz's books and films, as well as selected critical work on the author published in English and Spanish; a chronology of major events in Cuban history during the revolutionary period; and a map of Cuba, with locations pertinent to the novel indicated. In the firm belief that every translator should reflect on and write about practice, I have provided an afterword describing in greater detail my approach to the translation. Most importantly, Ambrosio Fornet's epilogue constitutes a critical evaluation of the novel's reception, structure, and placement within Cuban literary history, as well as a moving personal testimony.

TRANSLATOR'S ACKNOWLEDGEMENTS

The edition I have used for this translation is the 1987 text reprinted in 1997 by Editorial Anagrama (Barcelona).

Two research assistants contributed material that has been incorporated into this volume: Stephanie Kirk for the endnotes, and Alexandra Mandelbaum for the bibliography, chronology, and map. I wish to express my appreciation for their work.

My sincere thanks go to Enrique Del Risco, Ana Dopico, and Carol Maier for reading parts of the manuscript and for providing invaluable advice.

I owe a large debt of gratitude to Emanuel E. Garcia, who read most of this translation as it was being produced, and with whom I have enjoyed many conversations about translation issues both specific and conceptual.

Fredric Jameson originally suggested that I undertake this translation, and Reynolds Smith stayed with it through more than a few difficult periods. I thank them both for making this book a reality. I also wish to thank Ambrosio Fornet for bibliographical and historical consultation.

Finally, as with so many things, completing this project would have been hard, if not impossible, without the love and support of my family, Daniel, Ana, and Demian Szyld.

KATHLEEN ROSS
DECEMBER 2005

BRIEF CHRONOLOGY OF EVENTS IN CUBA, 1942–75

1942 Cuba declares war on Germany, Italy, and Japan.

1944 Ramón Grau San Martín is elected president for a four-year term and carries the Auténtico (Authentic) party into power.

The Communist party is reorganized and changes its name to the Partido Socialista Popular or PSP (Popular Socialist Party).

1947 Eduardo Chibás breaks with the Auténtico party to organize a new opposition party, Partido del Pueblo Cubano (Ortodoxo) (Cuban People's Party, orthodox).

1948 Carlos Prío Socarrás is elected president for a four-year term.

1951 Eduardo Chibás commits suicide.

1952 Fulgencio Batista seizes power through a military coup and ousts the Prío administration, thereby ending constitutional government in Cuba.

1953 Hoping to spark an uprising, Fidel Castro and 125 of his fellow anti-Batistas attack the Moncada barracks in Santiago de Cuba on 26 July. The attack fails (even though it is a harbinger of things to come) and survivors are sentenced to fifteen-year prison terms. Castro is sentenced to fifteen years on the Isle of Pines (now Isle of Youth).

1954 Running unopposed, Batista is elected to another four-year term as president.

1955 Batista proclaims a general amnesty in which Fidel Castro and other participants in the Moncada attack are released from prison on Mother's Day. The leader of the newly organized Movimiento 26 de Julio (26th of July Movement) departs for Mexico to organize armed resistance against the Batista government. In Mexico Castro meets Ernesto "Che" Guevara and together they spell out the philosophical foundations that become synonymous with Castro's revolution. Castro then travels to New York and Miami to raise money for the revolution, gather guns and ammunition, and campaign for support from abroad.

1956 In November, Fidel Castro, Che Guevara, and about eighty other revolutionaries set sail to Cuba aboard the *Granma* yacht and, after landing on 2 December, establish guerrilla operations in the Sierra Maestra mountains of southeastern Cuba.

Colonel Ramón Barquín is arrested for organizing an antigovernment plot within the armed forces. More than 200 officers are implicated in the conspiracy.

1957 In January, Fidel Castro leads the first successful guerrilla operation against the Rural Guard post at La Plata in the Sierra Maestra foothills. In March the Directorio Revolucionario (Revolutionary Directorate), led by José Antonio Echeverría, attacks the Presidential Palace in an effort to assassinate Batista. The assault fails and Echeverría is killed. In July a nationwide strike is called in support of the Rebel Army. In September a naval uprising in Cienfuegos leads to the temporary seizure of the local naval station.

1958 In March, Raúl Castro establishes guerrilla operations on a second front in the Sierra Cristal mountains in northern Oriente province. In the same month, the United States imposes an arms embargo against the Batista government. The attempt by the 26th of July Movement in April to topple the Batista government through a general strike fails. In May the government launches a major offensive against guerrilla forces in the Sierra Maestra. Government military operations fail, and the guerrilla columns mount a counteroffensive. In December guerrilla fighters led by Che Guevara take control of the city of Santa Clara in the center of the island, initiating Batista's fall from power.

1959   Shortly after midnight on New Year's Eve, Batista flees Cuba for the
        Dominican Republic and then to Florida, supposedly with U.S. $300
        million tucked away in his suitcase. A general strike in early January
        forces the military government to relinquish power to the 26th of July
        Movement. On 8 January, Fidel Castro arrives in Havana. The follow-
        ing month, Castro becomes prime minister and Guevara is appointed
        president of the National Bank. In May the government enacts the
        agrarian reform bill, which limits private land ownership. In an effort
        to end U.S. control of the island, the government confiscates foreign-
        owned industries. The government also outlaws racial discrimination,
        creates a low-income housing program, makes free health care and
        education available for all, and implements new policies in farming,
        sports, music, art, and defense.

1960   In May, Cuba and the Soviet Union reestablish diplomatic relations.
        In the same month Nikita Khrushchev presents Castro when the latter
        is invited to deliver a speech to the United Nations in New York. In
        June, the Cuban government nationalizes U.S. petroleum properties.
        In July, the United States cuts the Cuban quota. Between August and
        October, additional North American properties are seized, including
        utilities, sugar mills, banks, railroads, hotels, and factories. In mid-
        October, the United States imposes a trade embargo on Cuba. In the
        course of the year, a number of mass organizations are founded, in-
        cluding the militia, the Committees for the Defense of the Revolution
        (CDRS), the Federation of Cuban Women (FMC), the Association of
        Young Rebels (AJR), and the National Organization of Small Peasants
        (ANAP).

1961   In January the United States and Cuba sever diplomatic relations. In
        April the Bay of Pigs (Playa Girón) invasion fails, with some 1200–
        1500 CIA-trained expeditionaries taken prisoner.

        The Cuban government proclaims the "Year of Education," inaugurat-
        ing a national campaign to eliminate illiteracy.

1962   October 22–28: the Cuban Missile Crisis.

1965   The Communist Party of Cuba (PCC) is formed from the fusion of
        three revolutionary parties: the 26th of July Movement, the Revolu-

tionary Directorate, and the communist PSP. Che Guevara resigns from his posts in Cuba and settles in the jungles of Bolivia where he and fellow insurgents try to overthrow the government.

1967   Ernesto "Che" Guevara is killed in Bolivia, thereby dealing Cuban advocacy of armed struggle (*foquismo*) a serious and irrevocable blow.

1968   Fidel Castro tacitly endorses the Soviet invasion of Czechoslovakia, announcing the beginning of Cuban reconciliation with the Soviet Union and cementing the bond with this powerful ally.

The Cuban government launches the "revolutionary offensive," leading immediately to the nationalization of the remaining 57,000 small businesses and preparing for the ten-million-ton crop of 1970.

1970   The sugar harvest totals 8.5 million tons, short of the much heralded and symbolic target of ten million tons (*La zafra de los diez millones*). The economy falls into serious disarray.

1971   Poet Herberto Padilla is arrested and charged with writing counter-revolutionary literature.

1974   *Poder Popular* (People's Power) is inaugurated in Matanzas province, establishing local elections for municipal assemblies.

1975   The Family Code is promulgated, establishing a comprehensive body of law regulating family, marriage, and divorce.

The First Party Congress convenes.

Cuban combat troops participate in the Angolan war for national liberation against Portugal and the South African Army.

Sources

Louis A. Pérez Jr. *Cuba: Between Reform and Revolution.* New York: Oxford University Press, 1988.

Tony Perrottet and Joan Biondi, eds. *Inside Guides: Cuba.* Boston: Houghton Mifflin Company, 1996.

The Initials of the Earth

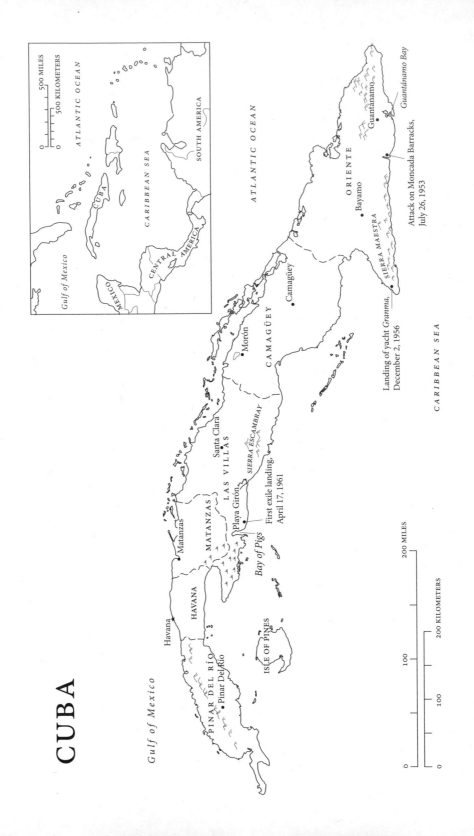

CUBA

Havana

Gulf of Mexico

Matanzas

Santa Clara

Morón

Camagüey

Bayamo

Guantánamo

Guantánamo Bay

Attack on Moncada Barracks,
July 26, 1953

Landing of yacht *Granma*,
December 2, 1956

First exile landing,
April 17, 1961

Playa Girón

Bay of Pigs

Pinar Del Río

Havana

ISLE OF PINES

PINAR DEL RÍO

MATANZAS

LAS VILLAS

SIERRA ESCAMBRAY

CAMAGÜEY

ORIENTE

SIERRA MAESTRA

ATLANTIC OCEAN

CARIBBEAN SEA

200 MILES

200 KILOMETERS

100

100

Gulf of Mexico

ATLANTIC OCEAN

CARIBBEAN SEA

SOUTH AMERICA

CENTRAL AMERICA

MEXICO

CUBA

500 MILES

500 KILOMETERS

He stopped reading, with the dark certainty of being trapped in a labyrinth, and then Gisela returned from her night on call dead tired, she said, and she leaned over the form, the simple *tellmeyourstory* over which Carlos had spent the night trying to reconstruct his past and asking himself why he'd done this and not that, why he'd almost never accomplished what he tried to do but rather what had been decided by chance, or fate, or go figure, as if life were an irreversible blundering and you always realized it too late, and now it accused him from that still-blank form, questioning and mute to Gisela's astonishment, as she encouraged him with a conspiratorial kiss on the cheek and walked on into the bathroom while he went back to the questions, to obsession and desperation, until he heard the hiss of urine like a call in the silence of the night, with the strange knowledge that he'd already lived that very moment. But no, that had been Iraida, and things could have happened differently; if, for example, he hadn't slept with her, he wouldn't have been expelled from the Communist Youth, or have hounded Gisela, or have suffered the torture of the black days that enveloped him afterwards; but where had he gotten the strength to go cut cane in the *zafra*, if not from that very desperation? There was no way around it, everything led into the labyrinth; even the ceasing of the hiss and the turning on of the shower, sending him back, he didn't know why, to the matter of José Antonio, maybe the greatest mistake he had ever made in his life, that zig-zagging trajectory that was crushing his memory now and at times seemed undecipherable. What would they ask him at the assembly? What would they criticize? He, who had wanted to be a hero and still aspired to be exemplary, what was he really? He had sung the same anthems, drank from the same cups, cried for the same dead as everybody else; he didn't have one single merit he could call his own rather than shared by all, or due to circumstances. He was just one among millions, he told himself; but this truth, which had the virtue of putting him at peace with himself, also made him fearful of failure. Maybe he aspired to more than he deserved, maybe he should just stop right now, leave the form blank forever, and, exercising his right, withdraw from the debate. But then how could he face himself in the mirror? With a start, he realized the noise of the shower had stopped, and picked up one of the five sharply-pointed pencils to his right. He had to make up his mind to concentrate on each one of those questions that disconcerted him in their simplicity. The final word—whether he was or was not an exemplary worker, whether he could or could not aspire to militancy—would be decided by his *compañeros* in a few hours. That was the unknown, the true question, and no matter how many times he went over it he couldn't imagine the answer, although in order to face it he had come back to Havana, to his old job and to that dark room, full of ghosts and fire, that Gisela was lighting up now with her naked body, making him wonder how it had been possible that once he wanted to kill her, while he felt again the queasiness of the labyrinth, returned her smile and tried to fit his bones, his smashed remembrances, together once and for all. There was a time to act, and a time to take stock: he was thirty-one, with no occupation, a daughter, and a wife he'd gone back to in defiance of memory's miseries, trusting that the future had to be better, so long as it didn't slip through his hands and turn against him as the past had done so many times, since all they had lived was part of them now and no one could change a single act or a single word, not even Gisela, who had struggled so hard trying, and now was pressing him because there were less than two hours left, my love, and he still had to shower and shave, while he nodded in agreement, looking at that wet skin illuminated by the unsteady dawning sun as by the fires of his childhood, and then at the empty form, where he would have to leave his skeleton bone by bone, like a leopard lost on a mountaintop.

ONE

From the snows of Kilimanjaro, Carlos looked into the jungle and yelled "Tarmangani!" three times, but neither Tantor the elephant nor Cheeta the chimpanzee nor the damned pigmies answered his call. Boredom overcame him, and he wished he had a Monopoly there, the game he'd gotten hooked on once he discovered the winning tactic: to buy up everything, Water Works, Electric Company, the railroads, Vermont, Illinois, Kentucky, where he'd build houses and hotels his opponents would land on, then they couldn't pay the rent, and they'd be ruined, go bankrupt, while he'd burst into stentorian laughter suddenly interrupted when he discovered an Apache girl watching him from the palm tree.

He decided to impress her and mounted his horse, Diablo, black with a white mane and a white star on his forehead. He did it in one jump over the croup, like Robert Taylor in *Ride, Vaquero*; from the side, like Alan Ladd in *Shane*; from a tree, like the Durango Kid, and jumped off at a gallop over the precipice, the cliff stained so many times with the blood of men and beasts. He was in the air, wrapped in a blanket, a hat, and a sheet of mist, firing his Winchester, letting go of the reins, and jumping over the abyss, better than Shane, when he heard her laughing. He pulled up the horse in the air and headed towards that mocking renegade who had just signed her death sentence. But the Indian girl ran away, losing herself along the banks of the Amazon, and she stuck her tongue out at him from the other shore before going into the terrible African jungle. It was impossible to swim across the Nile, the bare bones of a great prairie antelope revealed the presence of piranhas, and he didn't have a damned wounded cow to throw in as fodder to get them away from him, like John Wayne would have done.

He discovered a big white stone and dragged it to the banks of the Mississippi, sweating like a pig. It weighed too much to throw it into the water and use it as a bridge over the River Kwai. He sat down, thinking about putting together a Kon-Tiki with palm bark, but there was no bark on the ground. There was no other solution, he put his right thumb between his ring and little fingers, put the fingers of his left hand together and started jumping around the stone singing, "Pow-Wow, the Indian Boy." That would make him strong. When he'd jumped seven times, he picked up the stone and tried to throw it, but it almost fell on his foot. It was only then that he realized he had been tricked, the stone was kryptonite. He climbed up a liana and described the panorama with the voice of the No-Do newsreel: "We are in central Africa. Our expedition marches through the jungle. Yikes! What's that? Elephants over here, elephants over there! Jump, parrot, jump!" While the parrot jumped, he realized that the herd of elephants was led by Tantor. He yelled "Tarmangani!" again, but the stupid elephant was deaf. He looked for a thick vine, and swinging over the choppy Amazon, landed on his feet on the other bank of the Orinoco. Then he saw the Sioux again, but she turned out to be an impostor. She was wearing some ridiculous men's shoes, as if he didn't know that Indians don't wear shoes. He decided to give her what she deserved for making fun of him, a white man. He ran towards the reeds, but when he got there she was gone. He sniffed the air—nothing. He fingered the dust on the road—nothing. He put his ear to the ground—nothing. The laughter came from the river when he was among the reeds, from the palm tree when he got to the river, from the aroma when he reached the palm. He yelled, "Red ants, everybody run, the red ants are coming!" but the Stupid Girl in Men's Shoes didn't come out of her hiding place despite his warning of an invasion by the terrible killer ants. He sat down under the liana, and there, for the third time, the Cochise's evil laugh broke out.

He didn't chase after her. He had decided to hunt her for what she was, an Indian. He took out his knife. He opened it, holding the tip. He gave it a kiss. He threw it at the palm tree and watched it twirl in the air, tip, handle, tip, handle, tip against the trunk, stuck in. He walked over to the palm. He pulled out the knife. He turned around slowly and saw the Indian girl standing next to the orange tree, bug-eyed, as Grandfather Álvaro, his guide, would say. He held back his desire to run towards her. He showed her the knife, and she approached very slowly, suspiciously. When he had her close he thought how easy it would be to stick it into her aorta and then suck, like the bats in his nightmares. He showed her the knife, asking, "Do you want it?" and when she said yes he grabbed her wrist, bent her arm across her back, yelling, "Kreegor! Bundolo! Kill!" and put the blade to her throat.

He held her like that a few minutes, murmuring, "Stupid Blackbeard Girl! You're in the hands of Saquiri the Malay, none other than Saquiri the Malay!" and he kept her awhile longer so she'd feel the terror of finding herself at the mercy of such a bloodthirsty being. Then he let her go, but she made the mistake of trying to escape. He tripped her and fell on top of her, brandishing his knife with the evil murderer's laugh, "Heh heh heh, did you think you'd escape Saquiri, oh Stupid Girl in Men's Shoes?" She spit on him, and he dug his knees into her shoulders, to keep her from moving and to clean off his sullied face. "Ah, you swine," he yelled, "now you'll get what you deserve!" At that moment he realized she was crying sad tears like in Never-Never Land, and he started to let her go bit by bit, saying, "You Jane, me Tarzan" smiling at her and giving her soft, timid little taps on the chest while he repeated, "You Jane" and beating himself harder as he said, "Me Tarzan." But she didn't smile; she kept on crying even after he let he go free, showed her the knife, and murmured, "Here, you can have it." Then she stood up slowly, pointed towards a tree and warned, with a dry, faraway voice:

"The *daño*'s waiting for you under the ceiba." Then she ran off.

He couldn't manage to find her all afternoon, and at night he again felt the sad gnawing of nostalgia, telling himself that if his grandfather Álvaro were alive the plantation would be the best in the world, he'd be sitting on his lap asking what time is it, his grandfather answering seven o'clock, and Carlos asking again when would it be one, saying he wanted to be up at one o'clock. If his grandfather Álvaro were alive he'd send Chava into town to bring back sugar candy, and he'd tell him how Chava was just the same as when he met him seventy years ago. Chava was much more than a hundred years old and he was Grandfather's friend, and he'd been Great-Grandfather's slave, and Chava was never going to die. That was why they had fiestas at night in the old cabins, where the slaves lived before the Great War, when they went off into the swamp with Great-Grandfather against Spain. That was why the white hens, the beheaded roosters, and the U.S. copper pennies that showed up even when Weyler decreed his concentration-camp policy and everyone went hungrier than under Machado. That was why the red rags, the food left for the saints, the burned corn, the sugarcane brandy, the drums' monotonous call, the raw goat meat, and the *güijes*, goblins with liquid eyes that came out of the lake to frighten off the jinx; that was why, so Chava wouldn't die, because that black man had business with the devil.

Then Carlos would hide his head in his grandfather's chest and Grandfather would tell him no, Chava was a decent black man, and a decent black man would never do anything to a little boy. Chava was a decent black man, he had been a good *mambí*, and when the Great War ended he returned to what was left of the plantation to work for food. He was there when Grandfather was born, taught him how to mount and to rope, to hunt and to plant, but he was respectful, he never taught him his black things. Grandfather went with Chava and Great-Grandfather into the swamp for the War of Independence, and they spent three years fighting in Máximo Gómez's troop. Carlos liked it when his grandfather pronounced that name, Máximo Gómez, because he did it with a deep, proud voice, and then he cried, "The torch, damn it, the torch!" remembering the immense fires that turned night into day on the island, as happy as a kid riding horsy on a stool telling him, panting, about the fierce combat they fought for such a puny independence. Then he got sad, Great-Grandfather died in the war from a gunshot wound for which Chava's herbs could do nothing. Grandfather returned with Chava to what was left of what had been left of the plantation, an abandoned field of weeds, because his mother and sister had been sent to camps in town, accused of giving food to bandits, and died there of fever or starvation.

If his grandfather Álvaro were alive he'd want to go off to war again, he'd put him up on a horse and Carlos would shout, "The torch, damn it, the torch!" so that Grandfather would be happy again, would dig in his spurs and take him at a gallop through the burning cane fields of his memory to the ruins of what had been the mansion of the marqués de Santacecilia. They would make out the fallen walls, always wet, carpeted with moss dampened by the tears of all the wives and all the daughters and all the daughters of the daughters of the blessed lineage of the marqués, who had lost everything in the Great War, and fought again in the little one and the one for independence, and vowed still another war against the puny republic that had just been born, because there were too many dead with claims against it. The horse would be uneasy, sweaty, and Grandfather would make it bite at the bit, promising Don Antonio Santacecilia that someday, damn it, the fires would turn the night into day again, and then Cuba would be free forever.

If Grandfather Álvaro were alive he'd wake Carlos up by rubbing his mustache on his cheek, and telling him to keep quiet with a finger, he'd carry him out to the patio, and in the midst of that very white light coming down from the sky to the liana and then to his shirt, he'd say, "It's one o'clock, right now." Carlos would stay still looking at the lacy shadows and lights, listening to Grandfather saying, "It's a dead man's moon" surprised that the dead man's moon would be so pretty and one o'clock so radiant and dark.

But Grandfather wasn't there, he had died of fever, and without him the plantation was as boring as a Sunday afternoon. Carlos had to spend his vacation there because his father was saving up money and working like a demon to buy a new house, and he had left them, Jorge with Uncle Manolo and him here, asking why Carlos was crying when he'd always liked the plantation. Carlos tried to explain to him that what he liked was Grandfather Álvaro, but his father left without understanding, leaving him in those empty fields where nothing happened.

He missed Havana, that was where he had fun playing cowboys or Black-hawks or Cops and Robbers; there he could talk with Ángelo, the little black who knew songs and stories and how to make puppets for burning on St. John's Night, the one who brought a bat to the neighborhood and explained that it was a vampire, a bloodsucker, an animal that flew by night to bite the necks of white people. Carlos believed him, and the vampire settled in, living in his nightmares like a daily fright; but now he preferred that fear to this boredom, and finally he understood the answer his father and uncle gave when Chava asked them if they planned to come back to live on the plantation.

"Our plantation is Galiano Street," they said, "our country town, Havana, and instead of roots, we eat pork."

Chava became sad, murmuring that *niño* Álvaro was to blame for having separated his sons from the land, and Carlos didn't understand why his father refused to live on the plantation, it was so nice, or why Chava called Grandfather niño when he was so old, closed up in that gray box from which he would never get up again, according to what his mother had told him.

He told himself that Grandfather was sleeping and not dead, and when they led him into the parlor he slipped away toward the patio looking for that very white light in the branches of the liana. "It's one o'clock," he said. Grandfather didn't come and he, going back to the coffin, bent over his sleeping face, murmuring, "It's one o'clock, Grandfather," but now Chava, behind him, lifted him up off the floor to take him to the patio and sit him on his lap and let him cry. He felt better because being on Chava's lap was almost like being with his grandfather. Why didn't Grandfather talk? Chava looked at the very white dead man's moon and told him that niño Álvaro's soul had gone to his Lord in heaven, from where he would watch to see if niño Carlos was good and patriotic. Carlos wanted to ask Chava many questions but only voiced one:

"Do the dead watch us?"

"They watch," Chava replied, "and they'll always be watching, because the living betrayed their blood."

He liked it that his grandfather would be watching him, looking out for him, and he wanted to touch him like he was touching Chava, who was never going to die, right? Right, said Chava, one day he was going to go like niño Álvaro, however his gods were not in the sky but of the earth, and his spirit would be reborn as a *majá* snake or in a ceiba, and from there he would watch the living like niño Álvaro was watching them from his Lord's heaven.

Chava had gone, his light had gone out shortly after Grandfather's death, and his spirit had to be a ceiba or a majá, and Grandfather's a star or the moon, and Carlos felt lost on that plantation that his father and uncle had leased to Pancho José, a *guajiro* who only had time for work and now snored like a baby, while he fought not to sink into a sleep where the bat fluttered in the depths and despite everything clasped onto his blood, until the sound of a fingernail scratching the window brought him back to the light of day.

And there she was, with her old men's shoes, her little faded dress, her strange gray eyes. She said her name was Toña and she was from around there, she wanted to know who Saquiri the Malay, Jane, and Tarzan were, if they were from Havana, what did *kreegor* and *bundolo* mean, why did he drag around such a big stone, why did he jump while he sang, what was he singing, what was he laughing about so hard when he climbed up the liana. Carlos couldn't keep a mixture of rage and shame from making him run away, leaving her with yet another question on her lips. He mounted Diablo and galloped off ranting and raving against the Stupid Girl in Men's Shoes until he reached the cane fields, where he started to ache with the desire to see her. He turned tail thinking of answers for Toña, but she wasn't by the river. He began to cover the plantation and the surrounding area, felt like Diablo was too slow and decided to take the Batmobile, which made an enormous ROARRR! before rushing out of the Batcave. He went up and down all the roads through the cane fields, daring to go all the way to the ruins of the marqués de Santacecilia's house, where nostalgia for his grandfather attacked him again, but he didn't find Toña. Then he filled with courage and faced the dangers of looking for her in unfamiliar fields, where Spanish soldiers could be lying in wait. He was very tired when he discovered the huge iron weight next to the train track, in the middle of a solitary platform; a chain, battered by the wind, hit the metallic structure of the sad, empty transfer car, and for the first time he understood why grown-ups called those long months when there was no zafra the dead time.

He thought a lot about the dead during the unending hours that Toña didn't show up, and he asked Grandfather Álvaro and Chava to help him find her. They didn't, maybe because they had seen during their watch how he'd hit her, and he promised them he would treat her like Superman did Lois Lane and even better, because Superman tricked Lois by not revealing his true identity to her, and he was never going to trick Toña, he would treat her like Tarzan did Jane or Rodolfo Villalobos his sweetheart. The dead men heard his plea and promise, because Toña appeared in the same place where he had lost her, repeating her questions and gestures with such accuracy that he didn't know if time had really passed, or if he had only dreamed his punishment.

He kept pushing the mud on the riverbank around with a little stick while Toña asked her questions, but suddenly she finished, and he didn't know how to begin. The speech he had prepared got all tangled in his head, but nevertheless he had to say something so Toña would stop looking at him with her judging face. He talked about Tarzan and Jane, about Saquiri the Malay and about Chava, about the things his grandfather used to tell him and about how big the sea and the earth were; he said there were many ways to move around in the world, Batmobiles, boats, planes, submarines, and battleships, there was Africa, the West, and the stratosphere, piranhas, rhinoceros, and dinosaurs, Tantor and Cheeta, Superman and Scrooge McDuck, green-eyed Tony Curtis, black-eyed Rock Hudson, blue-eyed Doris Day, and there were people who didn't have eyes because they talked on the radio and you only saw their voice, like Raffles, the Gentleman Thief; there were languages, the Spanish they were speaking, the English people spoke in the movies, and the language of the comics that they only spoke in the comics, where things broke, CRASH!, cars raced, ROARRR!, earthquakes destroyed, RUMBLE RUMBLE!, pistols shot, BANG!, machine guns burst, RAT-A-TAT-TAT!, guys fell down wounded, AARGH!, got mad, GRRR!, cried, SNIFF SNIFF!, and fell asleep, Z-Z-Z, dreaming of sawing logs, waking up to African boys, little blacks with bones in their noses and heads, saying, DOOPA BOOPA UMT TOTA! Did she understand now?

She shook her head, confused, and he had to control a flash of impatience to keep on explaining, in the world there were Good Guys and Bad Guys, Superman and Lex Luthor, the Villalobos brothers and Saquiri the Malay, Mambises and Spaniards. Anything could happen, you had to be careful, and that was why he was never without his knife. You could trust only in Never-Never Land, but in the world, no. Nobody knew who anybody was. She, for example, could have had kryptonite in her shoes, that was why he had defended himself with the knife that he was going to give her now as a present, why didn't she take it? Toña didn't even look at the knife, he was the one who looked, confused, into those eyes that kept on questioning him, demanding an answer he didn't know how to give anymore. He asked her if she didn't go much to the movies. Toña continued looking at him in silence, and he yelled, "Haven't you ever read the comics?" She said no, shaking her head, frightened, and he contained his impatience again, remembering the promise made to Grandfather and Chava, and the gentle way Tarzan explained things to Jane. He picked up his stick again and drew, with great calm, a square in the mud. He tried to paint Superman inside but he'd never been good at drawing, so he had to settle for some lines, a mouth and a balloon in which he wrote:

Not very satisfied with his work, he said, "These are comics, what does it say there?"

She tried to start running away, but he held onto her arm and spoke softly, "Don't leave, come here, can't you see what it says there?"

Toña said no with her head, and Carlos shook her by the shoulders, yelling: "Chica, don't you know how to read?"

She said no again, and he let her go because this time he didn't have the strength to hold her back.

She didn't know how to read. It wasn't possible. Everyone knew how to read, even Ángelo. How could you live like that, with no movies, no radio, and no comics? She had run away out of shame, but she shouldn't be embarrassed with him, he wouldn't tell anyone, he swore it. He called her a few times and then suddenly became quiet, because he understood she would come only when she wanted to, and that the only thing he could do was wait for her under the shade of the liana, asking for forgiveness from his dead, explaining to them that he hadn't done it to be bad, that he'd be good if she came back.

For three days he told himself he didn't deserve that punishment, when he saw Toña's image reflected in the water and didn't dare to turn around, fearing that he'd break the illusion, until she was next to him, asking about the sea. He closed his eyes to remember and told her that the sea was made of water, a salty water as big as all the rivers in the world. It was beautiful, blue, Prussian blue, turquoise blue, or green, bottle green, emerald green, lime green, or sea green. It got angry in the wind and leaped up in great waves as big as two or three palms. It was worse than swollen rivers, much worse, it grabbed boats and split them in two, CRACK!, sank them, PHOOM!, swept them away, SMACK! Only the shipwrecked men were left, sending messages in bottles from far-off islands where they lived for years with no food or water, and they didn't die because in the end the boy got the message and saved them.

The boy was the Good Guy. In every film there was a boy who was strong and brave and good and who won in the end and got the girl. He faced all the dangers of land and sea, which were worse, because in the sea there were sharks up to fifteen meters long with three rows of poison teeth that gnashed together like this, CHOMP! There were whales capable of swallowing boats whole and then having the crew alive in their bellies for years, because whales blow a spew of fresh water from their backs. But the most important thing in the sea was the treasure, millions of chests with pieces of gold and precious stones that the pirates had stolen from the Spanish fleet. There were a lot of pirates, the Moluccan ones with their scimitars, the Crimson Pirate, just like Burt Lancaster, the Black Corsair, who was a woman in disguise, and above all Sir Francis de Sores, l'Olonoise, a Norwegian pirate who was the grandson of Leif Erickson, son of Erik the Red, brother of King Arthur, possessor of Excalibur, knight of the Round Table, and the chief leader of the Vikings. Sighting an enemy on the high seas, he would shout, "Ship ahoooy! Unfurrrrl the sails! All the way to port, helmsman, all to port!" He charged toward the middle of the other ship with the spur of the prow, ordering, "All on boooard!" His men jumped like wild animals onto the deck of the enemy ship and destroyed it completely. L'Olonoise always dueled with the Evil Captain, that one with his sword and he with his hook, Clang clang clang!, dueling and dueling and dueling *coñooo*, threatening the evil one, "Surrender, swine, or your damned body will be fodder for the sharks!" Clinkety Clink! But the evil one kept on fighting and cornered l'Olonoise by the aftercastle, crying, "This will be the end of your mischief!" It seemed the good one was going to die, nothing in the world could save him now, coñooo, and then l'Olonoise put his wooden leg on the evil one's chest, shoved him, "Ohhh!" threw himself at him, "You'll go to hell, vermin!" stuck his hook into the evil one's throat as he moaned, "Arrrgh!" until l'Olonoise lifted him up and tossed him to the sharks to put an end to his suffering. That's how it was, l'Olonoise's ship could duel with a fleet, with an army, and with the whole world. Against all flags except that of the Phantom Warship, which was a black ship, as big as those that anchored in Havana Bay and even bigger, and which was in all the seas and oceans at once, in the Pacific, the Atlantic, and the Panama Canal; in the Red Sea, the Blue, and the Yellow; in the glacial Artic Ocean, in the gloomy Dead Sea, and in the terrible Sargasso Sea. It brought with it tuberculosis and beriberi, leprosy and cholera, syphilis and scurvy, and all its sailors had always been dead, and dead they steered the awful ship that was as bad as the daño.

She told him he shouldn't talk like that. The daño was different from everything else. More evil than anything, and it was nearby, listening, in the lake and in the *ciguaraya*, in the *rompesaragüey* and the *abrecaminos*, in the marabou and the watercress, in the ceiba and the night-blooming jasmine, in the zebu bulls and the mares in heat that grazed by the cemetery, in the filthy buzzards and the worms that ate dead flesh, in the flowers and fruits, birds and plants, beasts and places of that world, sometimes as beautiful as paradise itself, other times strange and horrible like the depths of hell, where he who dares to go twelve times around a ceiba at midnight will be turned into a tormented soul, condemned to wander and wander around the cemetery walls. Carlos looked at her, both terrified and incredulous, and she promised to take him to see the eternal fire of the penitent souls burning in the graveyard, the headless horsemen who had to eternally retrace the same road, and the güijes, little blacks with big heads that popped out of the rivers with the greeting "Salaam alekim," to which you had to answer, "Alekim salaam," if you didn't want to be pulled down into the depths forever.

Carlos found it difficult to repeat that strange jargon and insisted that you could also answer, "Doopa boopa umt tota!" because that was how all little black Africans talked, and if she kept telling him he shouldn't dare to talk that way to a güije, it was because she didn't know how to read. He'd dare to do anything, he'd go twelve times around a ceiba at midnight, and nothing was going to happen to him because at just the right moment he'd yell, "SHAZAM!" to escape the spirits. Toña suddenly started walking, and he followed her in silence, and in silence they wandered over the plantation paths. Carlos thought she was going home, or to one of the places where she always went to hide, but he realized they were walking with no direction. He invited her to get into the Batmobile but she refused, he thought about forcing her but the possibility that her old dress would go RIPPPP! held him back.

Then he saw the bull, a zebu with long curved horns pawing the ground right in front of them. He hid behind Toña, who started laughing at his sweat and the cry that escaped him when the bull let out a terrifying roar and began to race as he watched in fright, expecting a deadly goring, but the beast passed them by in a cloud of dust and he turned and saw the cow who steadily awaited the charge, and he felt dizzy seeing the image of the animals steaming with sweat, as if the presence of so much force had suddenly weakened him, making him fall on the grass where he felt in his chest the brutal blow of the mount and the bellowing, and the savage beauty of the beasts yoked together.

Suddenly everything was calm again, and amid the quiet of grazing animals Toña's laughter rang out loudly, putting him into a rage and giving him back the strength to stand up, yelling, "Dummy!" at her, while she kept up her mocking and he started walking, hating the Stupid Girl in Men's Shoes whom he confronted at the crossroad, "You don't know how to read, dummy!" and whom he ran away from as fast as he could, never stopping his insults.

He felt shame and anxiousness, curiosity and rage in that land where the billy goats bellowed, the bulls roared, the stallions whinnied, ran, jumped with fury provoking that rush of blood to his face on seeing the she-goats, the cows, the mares awaiting their males with the same anxiousness with which Evarista opened herself to Pancho José in the early mornings, emitting a hoarse panting that he didn't want to hear, or stop hearing either.

He hid in the house, wanting Toña to show up so he could punish her with his indifference, and he didn't respond to Evarista's lamenting, that boy was going to do her in, always getting lost, wish they'd take him away, dammit. But Toña didn't show up, and he refused to eat lunch or dinner, and Evarista made him drink down some spearmint tea, telling him his trouble was a broken heart. He was grateful that Pancho José forbade him to leave the house, because that decision helped him find the strength he needed to keep to his plan. But there was Toña in the morning, playing hopscotch by the window, prettier than the sun, with some white flowers in her hair, whistling like a mockingbird for him. He had to wait until Pancho José left to escape, but by then she had gone, and he searched for her in faraway places telling himself he didn't want to see her, and informing Dick Tracy over the radio that he was doing a routine operation. He found her sitting by the lagoon, with her back to him, and he used telepathy to inform Dick that the suspect was eating yellow flowers. He climbed up a ceiba to punish the cannibal with his indifference, and from there he watched as she combed her hair in the water, heard her whistle like all the birds in paradise, and then he couldn't stand having her so far away. He began to climb down, slowly and quietly, at least to give her a scare, but she stopped whistling and said, without turning around:

"That branch is going to break."

He fell on his shoulder. Toña began unbuttoning his shirt, and he tried to stop her, because it made him feel naked, but she said, "Quit it," straddled him, and started rubbing his shoulder with warm, wet mud from the edges of the lagoon, producing in him a strange, animal drunkenness, a jubilant and different fear, a tremendous sensation of being like the roosters, the bulls, the feverish stallions on the plains.

Lying relaxed on the grass, they spent a long time watching the sky until Carlos told her the sea was just like that, what was the daño like? She couldn't manage to put it into one image, into one figure, one voice, and he said then the daño didn't exist. Toña stood up in fright, begging him to be quiet, and Carlos asked her if maybe the daño was like the dead. It wasn't like the dead, either, she answered, the daño was *in* the dead, especially in some dead people, and it was just simply the daño, that was why you couldn't see it all the time but only when *it* wanted you to, which happened sometimes on starry, calm nights and other times on stormy nights. To seek it out you had to be brave and have respect, would he dare to go with her to the cemetery that night? Carlos felt a chill up his spine as he said yes, and felt it again during the day every time he remembered their date, and felt it even stronger that night, when Toña scratched at the window frame. He had to repeat to himself several times that he was a manly man and that a manly man doesn't like soup or get scared by fear, so he could control his urge to urinate, and could escape in silence, taking advantage of Pancho José's being asleep. The very white light comforted him and the memory of Grandfather Álvaro, who would be watching over him from the world of the dead, instilled him with courage.

In the open fields, the light became spectral. It cut out the trees' silhouettes, created strange, curved shadows, became a borderless cavity for unexpected night noises. Carlos felt his courage leave him when they got to the grove, and went off to relieve the pain in his bladder, at least. He had started to let it out when Toña exclaimed:

"You can't urinate on the ceiba!"

He pointed his stream to the side, embarrassed that she was watching him and that he had profaned that majestic tree where Chava's spirit might be reincarnated. He asked forgiveness before entering the grove, but even so managed to go in only after taking Toña's hand and letting himself be guided like a blind man through that jungle, where the trees' frightful shadows closed around him like death, against which his humble attempt to invoke Tarzan fell apart. The Apeman didn't come to his aid, staying hidden back in his memory, refusing to come out into the shadows of an unknown forest, turning the formidable Tarmangani! he had planned to use to conquer fear into the timid tar-tar-tar of a sad stutterer.

On the roads through the cane fields, where the dust still preserved his grandfather's traces, Carlos felt more secure. He went trotting along, smiling at Grandfather's and Chava's spirits, who would be pleased with his bravery up there in the great beyond, and he kept on trotting down unfamiliar roads until he was startled by a little village, faded, vague, unreal amid the moon-washed mist. Toña went down an alley, stopped at the cemetery walls, and there she told him if he dared to jump over, he'd see the daño as a fire tormenting the souls of the dead, and if he didn't dare, he should wait for her, she'd be right back. He followed her, afraid to stay alone, amazed by the ease with which she cleared the wall he noticed was wet, dampened, according to her, by the tears of damned souls. He landed next to a grave, and again felt a sudden shiver that turned into trembling as he stepped on the ground of the dead, and that brought him to the verge of panic when he discovered, above the dust, the pallid flames consuming the condemned forever. He tried to start running but Toña held him back, and in that embrace they fell onto the ground, and there she pleaded with him, trembling, to please not run away, because then the daño would confuse them with tomb robbers, the ones who stole gold teeth from dead bodies, and they'd be condemned to the torture of toothless souls: to chew on thorns until the end of all time.

For the sake of his grandfather's and Chava's souls, Carlos withstood the sight of the flames until Toña decided they could now greet the daño by bowing their heads, like this, three times, and that this gesture of respect authorized them to go. When he got over to the other side of the wall, he started running as if he were escaping the devil. He crossed the night through the paths and the grove suspecting that the daño was lying in wait for him around every turn, that he was damning himself with that crazy race he wasn't able to halt until reaching the shelter of his bed. But there, too, he felt fear, something empty, dark, irreparable from which he couldn't escape because it was *in* his soul, like the daño was in the souls of the dead and condemned, and he sank down into sweat, tears, urine, until he fell asleep in a pool of terror, to dream of white fire in the cemeteries where the bat of his nightmares was screeching.

He awoke at mid-morning hearing Evarista's eternal grumbling, wetting the bed at his age, why don't they just take him away, dammit, and he went out to bathe in the Orinoco thinking he'd find Toña there. The colors of the countryside made him happy, and he decided to share that with the Black-hawks. He greeted André, the Frenchman, who, as amazed as Carlos at so much beauty, kept on repeating "Mon Dieu," while Olaf, the Swede, laughed at Chop-Chop the Chinese, who as always was crying, "Oh, wobbly woes." The Chinese was just an ugly toad, you didn't have to listen to him, the day was really wonderful, perfect for flying low over the soft green plain and the grove, full of *jiquis*, ebonies, *mahaguas*, lianas, ceibas, where all of a sudden he discovered the Secret Laboratory of the wicked Dr. Strogloff. He needed to act rapidly and cold-bloodedly. The wicked Dr. Strogloff was a genius of evil, who worked for a murderous semi-Asian power that intended to enslave human-kind by blackmail with the PLUTONIC WEAPON, a bomb that would put the Free World at its mercy because, if it exploded, it would end everything. As one more sign of his cleverness, the wicked Dr. Strogloff had located his Secret Laboratory in the West and he threatened to erase Civilization from the map if it was discovered. That was why such a risky mission had been assigned to the Blackhawks, the only ones capable of saving the planet. No one knew if the wicked Dr. Strogloff had finished his satanic creation, so the previous episode ended with terrible questions: Will the wicked Dr. Strogloff achieve his sinister intentions? Can the Hawks undo the grasp of evil? Will Civiliza-tion disappear from the face of the earth?

And now the Hawks were silently nearing the Secret Laboratory of the wicked Dr. Strogloff, guarded by a sinister cohort of masked thugs dressed in black leather, who beat a group of emaciated slaves condemned to work amid frightful moans. Meanwhile, the wicked Dr. Strogloff laughed, "HA HA HA!", leaning over the vessel where he was finishing up his creation of doom. There were only a few minutes left until Freedom on earth would die. "Slaves!" laughed the wicked Dr. Strogloff, "they will all be slaves!" Then the hoped-for cry of rescue was heard, "HAWKAAA-AAA!," and the heroic squad of the Guardians of Freedom attacked the lair of Evil, engaging in unequal combat with the bald assassins. Blackhawk knew the real enemy was Dr. Strogloff, who was feverishly pouring diabolical liquids into the vessel, and with resolve he went towards him. But a cruel bear, trained by the wicked Dr. Strogloff, cut off his path. It was the guardian of the guard! The Hawk began struggling in the mortal clutches of the beast. The wicked Dr. Strogloff hurried his diabolical work. Humanity only had seconds left, and the Hawk could only suffer, "ARRGH!"

Then he saw the thin figure of the good Dr. Walter, and he smiled. The good Dr. Walter was alive! Now he understood everything. The wicked Dr. Strogloff was an impostor. He had stolen his knowledge from the good Dr. Walter, who was tied to a board next to the vessel. He had to be saved! But that damned bear, with his beastly embrace, kept Hawk back. The wicked Dr. Strogloff turned on a gigantic saw that advanced towards the good Dr. Walter's chest, and he cried, "For the last time, Walter, what is the missing element?" Music sounded. The sharpened edge of steel continued its inexorable advance. It looked like the episode would end with new questions: Will the good Dr. Walter talk? Will the Hawk die in the bear's claws? Will the wicked Dr. Strogloff be able to explode the PLUTONIC WEAPON?

But the good Dr. Walter gloried in extraordinary heroism: "I will never tell you, you swine! Kill me if that's what you want!" Then the wicked Dr. Strogloff laughed once again, "No! You are too valuable. I will kill your daughter, idiot!" The Hawk cried when he saw her. The good Dr. Walter's beautiful daughter had suffered greatly at the wicked Strogloff's hands. She wore men's shoes and a little faded dress. He had made her a slave! The Hawk could not stand such an injustice. He heard the maiden murmur, "Oh my father, how you suffer! Speak, or I will die of pain!" and the blood boiled in his veins at the vileness of the wicked Strogloff. The good Dr. Walter was at the point of talking to stop the suffering of his beautiful daughter! The Hawk gathered up all his weakened strength and managed to push the murderous bear far away from him just a second before the good Dr. Walter revealed his precious secret. Then he ran to confront the wicked Strogloff. He delivered a terrible blow, SOCK!, another, POW!, gripped Strogloff's dirty, greasy neck and put it in the path of the saw, which meted out justice by lopping off the wicked head. Then Hawk turned to the beautiful daughter of the good Dr. Walter.

"We've saved the world!" he exclaimed.

The beautiful daughter of the good Dr. Walter looked at him gravely.

"Chico, sometimes I think you're crazy," she said.

Carlos sat in silence on a tree trunk, feeling as sad as could be. You couldn't play with that Stupid Girl, she'd never understand anything. It wasn't fair, he told her, that he would believe in the daño and she wouldn't believe in the comics. Toña defended herself, she didn't know anything about any comics, she had just seen him jumping around like he was crazy and yelling sometimes with a deep voice and then with a high one, as if he were possessed by different spirits, were the comics spirits? He felt impatience gnaw at him and had to control himself to answer no, the comics were comics like the daño was the daño. Toña reminded him he shouldn't compare them, the daño was something very great and the comics were nothing, and Carlos exploded with rage, yelling that it was the daño that was nothing, a puny little fire out there that she herself had probably made with old paper and dry leaves before taking him to see it. Then he felt Toña become remote, strange, challenging, asking if he wanted to see that night just how the daño entered the soul of a dead man, making him miserable forever.

As he answered yes he felt a shiver go up his spine again, and thought about some sudden illness that would get him out of his commitment. But at night when he heard Toña's finger scratching at the window, Carlos felt overwhelmingly curious to know how that episode would end, and he went out into the countryside. This time his fear didn't arise only from the moon and the shadows, but also from the story Toña told him in a low, choked-up voice. The noises they were hearing were the voices of the accursed dead, to which would be added tonight that of Fermín Préndez, whose throat had been slashed by José María Malo at the cockfight with the same razor blades Fermín had used to cheat his fighting bird out of a win. Fermín's brother, Nene Préndez, had killed Pepe María with thirteen machete blows, and they were going to have wakes at the same hour, and Toña swore that if Fermín was going to sit up in his coffin that night, if he was going to leave it, if he was condemned to roam forever along the borders of the cemetery, turned into a lament and a flame, it was because the Malos had cursed him with the daño, and the daño takes a good hold in the souls of dead cheaters.

Carlos walked all the way in silence, listening with his eyes as wide open as Fermín's when he felt the iron-like edge of the blade at his neck, and with those eyes, made to measure for the walking dead, he hid behind the ceiba and looked inside, into the house where Fermín Préndez had lived. From there he could clearly see the old women crying, the woman pouring coffee and handing it out to the men sitting on stools around the dead man, quiet in his rough, unfinished wooden box, so different from Grandfather's which had glass and everything. Little by little Carlos's fear abated and he became bored, while Toña kept clutching onto the ceiba's knots. He thought about sitting down and not watching anymore, it was all just a big lie, when Fermín Préndez sat up out of the blue in his box and opened his eyes with the thirsty, endless gaze of death.

He ran from the body and the screams, letting out howls that followed him even when he was out of breath, because Toña was screaming too while she ran beside him, screaming, breaking the gloomy silence with desperate sounds of "Ay!" which he answered, running with no direction in the middle of a night inhabited by souls in torment, headless horsemen, güijes, shadows of hanged men swaying from the ceiba branches, eternal fires, daño all throughout that unfamiliar path leading them to the dark cavern where the dead condemned to wander the hills reproduced their voices in the ravines and the gullies, forcing them to scream, to cry, and to scream again in a useless struggle to mow down the nocturnal howls of death that pursued them with its fire, calling them, encircling them, forcing them to join in an ultimate embrace screaming in each other's ears until they were deaf, without voice or strength to defend themselves against that irreparable emptiness into which, finally, they fell.

He awoke to an infernal heat, with Evarista's sweating face in front of him as she applied hot compresses to his neck. He wanted to shout, but managed only to produce a hoarse whine, while Pancho José kissed him as if he'd come back from the grave. He breathed in the peasant's warmth and hugged him, crying, slowly releasing the remnants of his fear. "Quiet now," said Pancho José, with the same affection he used when talking to his animals, it was all over, his father would be coming soon to take him to the doctor in Havana. God knew there wasn't one around there, but if he got some rest, he'd be well again, thank the Almighty. He'd been boiling with fever for two days, said

Evarista, and she made him drink down some honey and lemon, so he'd go to sleep on a warm stomach.

It was a very long and varied dream. For hours he floated, unraveled within a kind of torrid fog, through which he saw Evarista toiling with her compresses, hot drinks, and prayers to the Lord for the sick boy's health. At those moments he became delirious, seeing thousands of cold Coca-Colas in an immense tank full of crushed ice, just waiting for him to finally conquer the persistent fever turning him into a hot puddle under the blankets. He faded away, floating in the unbearable soup of boiling sweat, to wake up hours later with a biting, stabbing cold in his bones. He slept once again, and the face of Fermín Préndez's soul startled him, sitting up out of the blue, and the image of Toña fleeing from his screams.

Three days later Carlos awoke without fever, clearheaded, and tested his voice by asking for Toña. Pancho José, upset, told him to be quiet; Evarista asked God to send her to the devil; Pancho José told him how he'd spent an entire night searching for him with the hunters, desperate, until they found him lying there in the cavern, shivering next to that degenerate girl, who only had an old grandfather to cry for her; Evarista told him how through his whole fever he'd been calling for that shameless girl who'd put fiendish things into his soul, into him no less, the boss's son; Pancho José made him swear he wouldn't say anything to his father about how the daño had entered Fermín Préndez's spirit, those were truths for coarse guajiros like them, no one else understood, the boss might get mad and throw them out, that would really be bad; Evarista begged him never to talk to Toña again, because that little girl knew more than an old woman, and it was harmful.

Carlos swore it, he promised, he drank some steaming chicken broth, and he went out looking for her. He felt very weak, and exhausted his memory searching for a hero who had been sick at some time, but didn't find even one. Saddened, he settled on Superman, who, although he'd never been sick, felt weak from time to time, like now for example, because of the kryptonite the plantation was made from. He couldn't use his supervision, his superhearing, or even fly, so he put on his glasses because in reality he was stupid Clark Kent, slowly making his way to the offices of the *Daily Planet*. When he saw Lois Lane his knees shook as if she were made of kryptonite, too. He fell down, and lied to her, saying he'd been sick, because if he told her about his ferocious battle with Lex Luthor, she'd discover his true identity. As always, Lois played dumb, and she asked him if the reeds on his forehead were a remedy for fever.

"Come on, Lois, it's Clark," he answered irritably. "You know very well these are my glasses."

Toña burst out into crystalline laughter, and Carlos couldn't avoid the sudden sobs brought on by his weak state. He cried for a long while even though she apologized several times, she swore to him they'd play comics and withstood in silence the most brutal insults, dummy, dumb dummy, illiterate, degenerate, shameless, old lady, that stopped only when he had no more tears or resentment left. Then she begged him again to play comics with her, and he explained with a calm desperation that to do that, you had to know how to read. "Teach me," said Toña, and Carlos smiled, knowing he'd discovered a fascinating game. He took a stick and wrote MAMA in the mud. It took a bit for him to convince her that even if she didn't have a mama, they had to start there, because "old grandfather" was too complicated. At first he had to appeal to the memory of Álvaro and Chava to give him patience, but after repeating it many times Toña was able to start to read *My mama loves me*, and trembling he followed the effort in the muscles of her face, the tense concentration in her eyes, the slight throbbing of her lips, her tears of victory when she deciphered the sentence.

He had to reward his student, and since he couldn't find anything better he presented her with a guava he picked up off the ground. He began eating one, too, until the seeds getting stuck between his teeth bothered him too much. Then he said it was just dumb to eat hard guavas with seeds when you could eat guava ice cream that tasted like guava—it's soft, it's cold, it doesn't have skin or seeds, don't you think so? Toña threw her guava into the river, and Carlos knew for sure he'd made another mistake. She had never eaten ice cream. He said nothing, looking at the hundreds of guavas scattered over the ground, thinking how his had been, in truth, a poor prize for such a good student. Something grand would be to take her to the town's movie theater, providing her the happiness of seeing those heroes face to face, and buying her a chocolate ice cream afterwards. For that he'd need money, he told himself, going through his empty pockets. He thought about the movies again and suddenly shouted, "Eureka!" recalling the ad they projected onto the screen at the Maravillas: "This theater is cleaned with Eureka insecticide."

The guavas were the solution. It was as simple as filling up a sack and selling them in town. At first Toña was enthusiastic, she got the sack and helped him fill it with guavas. But then, when he had managed to get it up over his shoulder and was telling her about how good the movie would be, when, forgetting how much work it had been to pick it up, he let it fall to say goodbye Alan Ladd–style, Doris Day said to him, "Don't go." That was all. She didn't cry. She didn't argue with Alan's reasoning until he again picked up the sack full of gold from the mine. Then she confessed, crying, that she would give all the ice creams and movies in the world for the ice creams and movies he could tell her about, and Carlos felt sorry for Toña and wanted to stay with her, but being a hero, he had a serious problem, because heroes were hard types who didn't soften up to a girl's pleas.

"Take care of yourself," he told her. "I'll go report to the mine and come back for you. Remember, we're rich now."

He got to town dead tired, because the ingots were too heavy and on the road, in order to eat, he had had to kill the damned mule. He walked around the streets awhile, without finding anyone to buy the gold. There were only bandits who pretended not to have any interest in the merchandise, thus hiding their wicked plan to rob him. The worst thing was that the Winchester had no bullets left, not one, so he decided not to enter the saloon, in spite of his hunger and thirst. He sat down in the plaza and the church bells reminded him that he was in a miserable border town, full of disgusting, treacherous Mexicans. He felt better when he saw a law officer approach him.

"Hello, Sheriff," he said.

But the damned fellow proved to have sold out to the enemy, asking him what he was carrying in the sack.

"Guavas," he lied.

The sheriff inspected the load, believed the ruse, and asked for his name and address. He decided to go on with his deception.

"Carlos Pérez," he said, passing himself off as a Mexican, and carefully hiding the existence of a gold mine on the Dionisia plantation.

"Come with me," the sheriff ordered.

He went ahead towards the jail, worried because the guy had discovered his true identity and was blackmailing him, saying he couldn't understand why a nice white boy from a good family would be walking around town looking like that, what was he looking for? Carlos shrugged his shoulders and kept walking in silence until they got to the Seventh Cavalry. He felt smug penetrating the headquarters of that troop, covered with glory in the Indian and Mexican wars. The sheriff handed him over to two numbers mounted on fantastic horses so they could lead him back to the Dionisia:

"Take good care of this boy for me."

Carlos smiled, because in spite of his clothing, even the sheriff had recognized that *he* was *the boy*, and when they parted he confirmed it, there before the Seventh Cavalry:

"Goodbye, boy!"

It was a beautiful ending. He couldn't waste it. He started to sing a moving little tune, and hearing it, the members of his escort smiled, just as it should be before a good *The End*.

His film had come out great, but now another was starting in which he needed to get money to take Toña to the movies, and he didn't know how he could do it while a prisoner of two Spaniards, trotting along in silence through the rebellious Cuban countryside. His situation was desperate: the enemy had located the field hospital the mambises called "La Dionisia" in code, where there were only wounded, women, and children who, if taken by surprise, would be easy prey for Weyler's insanity. What was most annoying was that they were using him, Lieutenant Colonel mambí Carlos Pérez Cifredo, to mask their dishonorable intentions. But he wouldn't go along with the farce; he preferred death to disgrace. He had contrived the perfect plan: as they neared the hospital he would warn his people by shouting out, although it might cost him his life. Thus he calmly advanced down the road through that vast cane field about to be claimed by the torches of justice, determined to sacrifice himself at the altar of freedom like a true mambí.

The only thing was, something very strange was happening at the hospital. There was an old Ford there he knew only too well. Surely this was part of the occupation to impose that sickly republic, against which the marqués of Santacecilia was calling for war. From the ruins he could make out Mister Leonardo Wood giving orders, and he told himself he wouldn't respect them, not for nothing had he fought so resolutely for freedom. As could be expected, the Spanish soldiers yielded to the wishes of the foreigner, who shouted awful things at the Cuban peasants Evarista and Pancho José for letting the boy get lost. But not even the sensational fact that Mister Wood also recognized *him* as *the boy* could rescue him from his sadness. He could foresee reaching the end without carrying out his mission, that they would take him away without even letting him say goodbye to the girl, and he began crying with rage.

"Men don't cry. Let's go."

He paid no attention to his father's words and cried even harder, yelling, "Toña, Toña, Toña!" while they dragged him to the car, which suddenly started moving, lurching through the potholes in the road, amid a great cloud of dust.

TWO

On the fifth day of confinement, his father brought home a device to conquer their fear. It came sheathed in a kind of blue chamois cloth and it had to be very fragile, because José María wouldn't let anyone touch it. Carlos, Jorge, and Josefa watched him kneel down as if he were at an altar, put his hands underneath the chamois to operate some secret mechanism, and stand up like a magician, showing them the miracle of the lighted screen from which a very elegant gentleman advised: "Yes, you too can have a Buick!"

They hugged each other, open-mouthed at the magic of that first television set, and then sat down without taking their eyes off the marvel that allowed them to exchange their real-life fears for the delicious shivers of "Channel 6 Suspense." But that happened later on, when terror had free reign in the area surrounding their new house.

It was located in the Vedado district, across from a Protestant temple that read on the facade: "I am the way, the truth, and the life." Along the street, bordered by royal poncianas and parkinsonias, there were gardens with night-blooming jasmines and black princes, and at certain months of the year, like that one, the area seemed to burst into a whirl of colors. Behind the house there was a ravine, a crater extending the full length of the block, like an inexplicable cavity in the middle of the perfect set of teeth formed by the neighborhood's structures. They weren't allowed to go down there, and Carlos and Jorge spent hours looking at it, elbows on the fence their father had built around the patio on the advice of the Homeowners' Association. From there they couldn't see much, just the zinc or bark roofs of some hovel, goats, chickens, cats, and sometimes people, who never answered their hopeful greetings.

Their mother protested, they shouldn't talk to them, black people were the devil, didn't they hear the sounds of the *Bembé* at night? They played at scaring her, "The Bembé, the Bembé, run, the Bembé's coming!", and she fled, reappearing behind the kitchen window with the most beautiful smile on earth. The first time they heard the word, they thought the Bembé was a person, an old, scruffy black man on crutches, surrounded by dogs licking his sores, a lot like the one who came up from the ravine in the evenings with a dirty tin can in his gnarled hands, begging for food. Just that the Bembé had to be much bigger, huge, and the dogs would lick his pustules with fire, and their mother would never dare to take pity on him, or give him leftovers or alms, much less tell him he looked like St. Lazarus.

From the other side of the patio they saw the doors of the temple and the last set of stairs climbed by the faithful, men in dark suits, women in high-necked dresses with lots of buttons. Their mother didn't let them go into the temple either because, although it belonged to God, he was a false God. But once they managed to creep over to the door and there they heard, apprehensively, the pastor's formidable anathemas against sin, and they trembled before the idea of the Last Judgment, and they learned that the Bembé was not a man, but rather the very spirit of Satan.

From then on, no terror could compare with that of the nights when there was a worship service in the temple, and the Bembé sounded out from the depths of the ravine. There was no electricity down there, the blacks lit up the fiesta with fire, and the boys, from their window, saw deformed shadows dancing amid the flames. Fear compelled them to run to their father's room; there, feeling safe, they spied through the shutters in a tremble. From the street came the hysterical drone from the temple, "There is life, there is life, there is life in Jesus!", from the ravine arose the powerful clamor of the santeros, "Shola Anguengue, Anguengue Shola!" and their mother, terrified, prayed and made them pray, "Holy Mary, mother of God, pray for us, sinners!", and the repeated, harsh peal of the drums, and the chants of the Bembé fought in the night air against the tense Protestant petitions, and their mother's pleas sounded humble and helpless, and they seconded her remembering the pastor's terrible prophecy: the blacks would dance forever in the flames and never be burned, because they were the devil, and one day they would come with their fire up the side of the ravine to wipe out the white people's world, and that would be the day of Last Judgment, and woe to those who hadn't repented.

On those nights Carlos couldn't sleep. The war between the fierce hell of the ravine and the frenetic heaven of the temple produced in him a horrible, fascinating dread, and renewed his fears, mysteries he thought had been resolved and forgotten. The fires in the ravine were redder than the pale fires of the daño, and the chant of the Bembé, Shola Anguengue, wasn't it the same one Toña had used to greet the güijes so they wouldn't take her away? There were bats, güijes, daños, and penitent spirits down there, and he fought to stay awake longer because sleep was the dark cave where vermin would fall upon his soul, bringing Fermín Préndez from the great beyond to terrify him with the thirsty, endless gaze of death. Then he remembered, with relief, the explanation his father had given him to chase away the nightmares, when Carlos couldn't stand it anymore and told him what had happened. Fermín Préndez hadn't come back from the great beyond, the Malos had probably paid someone to tie his legs to his chest with a thin, wet rod, and when the rod dried, it shrank and made the poor dead man sit up in his coffin. That was what he and that girl had seen, did he understand? Yes? Well then, go to sleep like a man, the dead don't rise.

His fear disappeared over time, Carlos came to believe it was gone, and even was able to tell Jorge the real story of the dead man who sat up. But in the new house he discovered that fear was still sleeping in his soul, that he was drawn to the hymns of the worship service and the fires of the Bembé and that his father's explanation wasn't enough to chase it away. Then he would take refuge in Grandfather Álvaro and Chava, who'd be watching over him in death, Chava in the earth with the blacks and their fire, his grandfather in heaven over the whites and the temple, and he would sleep, promising them he'd be good and patriotic, telling himself that Fermín Préndez couldn't haunt him if he fulfilled his duty to the dead.

In the mornings, clear and happy, the temple would be open at the start of day. A quarrelsome black woman cleaned it. From the sidewalk, they liked to inspect the white-walled nave with its two simple wooden crosses. Inside, the air was slightly pink from the sun crossing through the stained glass, the parkinsonias, and the red poncianas. Over the door, the legend they had learned to repeat summoned up calm: "I am the way, the truth, and the life." But the depths of the ravine were still a mystery.

That was why they jumped for joy and fear on Christmas Eve, when Uncle Manolo invited them to go down with him. He had come with his whole family to the big spread his brother had organized to celebrate buying the new house and the birth of our Lord Jesus Christ, and for hours he had been making fun of the fears of his sister-in-law, who kept on warning how that night there would be a worship service and Bembé and that the family meal would be a disaster. For the boys, the neighborhood had gotten much better because Pablo had moved nearby, and Pablo knew as many tricks as Ángelo, the little black, and no party could be bad if Pablo was there. The parkinsonias had begun to drop their flowers and the poncianas their leaves, but there were poinsettias and a big Christmas tree full of ornaments and colored garlands. At its base was a crèche with a crib and the baby Jesus, a lot of cotton for snow, and threads of candied squash for ice and frost. At the top, with a little bulb, the star of Bethlehem shone serenely.

They went down into the ravine early in the day, with their cousin Julián, sticking close to Uncle Manolo's heels. Above, on the patio, Cousin Rosalina was left crying. Suddenly the landscape began to transform. The path snaked around, the house was lost from view, and high above only the temple's cross could be made out. The footpath was surrounded by brambles that caught your socks and by plants with white thorns like barbs. Beneath the squalid bushes you could see, at times, rocks that in other eras had been worked over by the sea, full of hollows. Carlos felt fear invading him and began to sing in a very low voice:

Tonight is Christmas Eve. Let's go to the forest, little brother . . .

The carol brought him an ineffable calm, but his uncle told him to be quiet. Manolo had a kind of bestial appearance, he had worked in a slaughter-house and retained the fierceness and the cow-butcher knife of his profession. He was tall, with a belly, according to him, full of beer, and his arms were muscular, like the haunches of a bull. Their father always held him up as an example: look at him, from slaughterman to owner of the slaughterhouse, he knew everything there was to know about business, nothing was beyond him.

When they got to the bottom of the ravine, Carlos and Jorge hid behind his back. Manolo turned around, roaring, were they mice or men? If they kept up that sissy crap he was going to find two little blacks to break their faces, they should learn from Julián, he was a real macho. Carlos thought how Julián was older, and above all, that neither he nor Uncle Manolo had ever heard the Bembé and they didn't know they were in the devil's house. The hamlet, made of rusty tin, rotten wood, old election posters, and palm bark, had a vaguely semicircular shape. In the center a bonfire was burning. Carlos approached it, fascinated, certain that that was where the sinister shadows danced at night. Behind the houses was a banana-tree grove.

"That's where they shit," said Manolo.

To the left were a few animals and a pile of yuccas. Not a soul was to be seen. Manolo took a few steps towards the fire and shouted:

"Hey, you people!"

They heard a noise. Turning around, they could just glimpse a little naked black boy fleeing towards a hovel. "He's more afraid than you are," laughed Manolo. Carlos thought that was true: the boy's eyes were bulging and bloodshot. He got up the nerve to approach the fire; there was nothing but boiling water in the blackened cauldron. They heard another noise. A fat black woman, dressed in white, came out into the clearing, scratching her head. Another, younger one followed, dragging the frame from an old bed.

"Good morning to you, sirs," said the old woman.

"Morning," Manolo repeated.

The young woman moved forward towards the fire. Carlos went to stand next to Jorge, without taking his eyes off of her. She was barefoot, with a yellow kerchief on her head and pustules all over her skin, like the old man with the tin can. She began pouring water from the cauldron onto the frame, producing a crackling sound from the metal wires.

A boy came into the clearing, playing with a goat.

"Lots of bedbugs?" Manolo asked.

"Lots," said the young woman.

The boy took off at a run and jumped clean over the goat, barely touching it with his left hand.

"*A la cholandengue!*" exclaimed Jorge.

The old woman turned around, astonished:

"White boy talking black?"

Manolo, annoyed, spoke to Julián: "Jump," he ordered.

Julián spit on his hands and flexed them. He was bigger and stronger than the other boy, and therefore heavier. He began running towards the goat and jumped over its side, supporting both hands on its back. Red with pride, he returned to join Manolo, who jovially tousled his hair.

The goat had started trotting towards a hovel with a double-framed door, the right side made from a rusty Coca-Cola ad, the pause that refreshes, and the left from political posters, faded by the sun and the rain.

"Is there a *toque* tonight?" asked Manolo.

"It's the Lord's day," said the old woman.

Carlos looked at her, surprised at her answer. At the door of the hovel the boy struggled to pull the goat back outside.

"If you break the radio, I'll burn your eyes out," said the young woman.

Carlos turned around towards the boy, who started to run again and jumped over the animal without touching it, like a cat.

"A la cholandengue!" shouted Jorge.

"You'll see what a macho is, dammit," said Manolo. "Julián," he ordered, "jump!"

Julián spit into his hands again, backed up, took off at an uncertain run. At the point where the other boy had begun his leap, he lost speed, didn't attempt the jump and stopped, panting, in front of the animal. The old woman fanned the air with her hands.

"It's your shoes," she said.

"And that one goes naked and he's just a tramp," murmured the young woman.

"Jump!" Manolo ordered.

The order was so sharp there were no more comments. Julián crossed himself before spitting into his hands. He began running with his eyes closed, jumped too soon, his feet tripped over the goat's back, and he fell on his face into a rusty chamber pot lying on the ground. The animal, frightened, spun all the way around. Julián stood up, crying, his pants torn at the knees and a wound over his left eyebrow, and went towards the same place where he had left his father.

But Manolo wasn't there anymore. From the very moment of the fall, he had begun moving cunningly towards the animal. Now he had it cornered in front of the hovel, and he spoke to it slowly, as if it were a dog. The goat, calmed down, let him come near. Manolo ran his right hand over its back, placed his left hand next to its eyes, and the goat licked his fingers while the right hand went from its back to its head, the left from its tongue to the knife, and they all scarcely had time to join their cries to the goat's last bellow as it fell, its throat cut. Carlos clung to the black woman's skirts as if he couldn't stand the animal's gaze, so very gentle, or the gush of blood oozing from its neck, or the soft fall of its front legs into the sticky puddle already forming on the ground.

The boy ran over to Manolo and began hitting him violently in the belly. The young woman disappeared, crying out. In seconds, dozens of men and women came out of their hovels, and began to surround them amid cries possessed by the devil. Manolo, in the center, took the blows, laughing. When the circle began to close, he threw the bloody knife into the cauldron of boiling water and shouted, "How much?" The force of his laughter redoubled as he pulled a roll of bills from his pocket. The advance stopped, not to begin again, and Carlos took off running up the path home, alone, certain that the boy's look of fierce hatred and the others' looks of hatred and greed would explode in the Bembé of the Lord's night, wiping out the white people's world.

Manolo returned home in good humor, telling of his feat while roaring with laughter. Carlos—his curiosity getting the better of his fear and disgust—dragged himself over to the living room to listen. His mother, Aunt Carmelina, and Aunt Ernesta got tangled up in an argument while they treated Julián's wounds and told Cousin Rosalina, who wouldn't stop making fun of him, to keep quiet. Jorge came, too, and sat next to his father, who listened spellbound. Manolo cleaned his fingernails with the tip of the knife and talked nonstop: If José María could have just seen, he stopped them with money, he bought the goat from them, then he paid them to season and prepare it; that night, besides the pork, they'd have a good *chilindrón*. If José María had only seen, they drooled over the bills, those blacks needed money, what did he think of lending it to them, huh? With interest, huh? At 20 percent, huh?

José María called out for two beers, wouldn't it be awfully risky? Manolo let loose a belly laugh and grabbed his bottle, drank half of it down in one gulp, did he think he'd gone down there just for fun? He wiped his lips with the back of his hand and made room for Julián to sit next to him, if José María could have just seen, those blacks even had a radio, was he going to spend his whole life on his cigar-seller's salary? A salary was just a salary, even if it was a good one, why didn't he make up his mind and do it? They'd go fifty-fifty, eh? Should they start with two hundred pesos as capital, a hundred each? José María drank his beer and shouted for two more, what the hell was going on in this house? Then he pushed Jorge to the side, leaning forward, and what if they refused to pay? What if they wanted to give them a hard time? Who'd collect from those blacks? Manolo slapped Julián's thighs and tapped his knife, he was a man ready for anything, José María, he had a cow-butcher that could also be a black-butcher, he had a small slaughterhouse with a few tough employees, and as a last resort the police were good for something, right? José María began to smile, drank more beer, and clinked his bottle against Manolo's, see boys? You should learn from this, your uncle's a sly fox, just like that, out of thin air, he'd invented a new business.

At seven o'clock sharp they brought the goat up from the ravine. Carlos and Jorge, anxious and terrified, had spent the afternoon telling Pablo and Rosalina about their adventures, along with the pastor's prophecies. Now, the image of that single file of blacks, bringing up a litter with the goat lying over large banana leaves, was for them like a procession, or a burial. A strange burial, because the blacks were singing. As soon as he could see the first faces, Carlos knew that the hour of vengeance had not yet come. They were happy, friendly, and it was a wonder the goat didn't fall back down over the cliff with their jumping around. As they entered the patio, the blacks became quiet, set the litter down on the ground like an offering, retreating respectfully back to the fence.

Carlos came closer, observing them. That confused expression in their eyes, could it be fear? Manolo plunged in among them with three bottles of rum in his hands. He drank straight from one, then gave them away to the newcomers, and began to pull off and hand out hunks of meat with his bare hands, exclaiming, "Come on, gents, you break it, you pay for it." Then José María joined the group and a real party began. The women stayed far away, inside the house. Only Cousin Rosalina stood spying through the shutters, where Carlos and Jorge always watched the fires of the Bembé burning in the belly of the night. They refused to eat goat meat, but they drank beer, ate fried pork, and noticed that the confused look was disappearing from the blacks' eyes, that suddenly they started talking about money and interest with Manolo and José María. The plans must have been going well, because there was laughter, embracing, toasts, until the guests said they were going, it was getting late and down below they had a toque. Manolo asked them to sing something first, in Spanish, not in their tongue, so he wouldn't be left feeling frustrated, and they said so long, *abairimo*, they'd sing on the way down, the *fiñes* should prick up their ears, the *guaguancó* would be a present for them. They left going downhill, beating out a rhythm on the bottles, with the goat's head held before them like a standard.

Carlos, Jorge, and Julián stuck their faces by the fence, and very soon, from the ravine, a song about their most beloved characters rose up:

> And here's the latest,
> here's the latest in the comics.
> Annie, the little orphan,

Jorge the Pilot, the one called Lard.
We're looking for the Phantom
and Dick Tracy's going to investigate.

The crystalline beat of coins against bottles had started up again when their father and uncle took them back inside. What they had seen was a business deal between men, but unless that was the reason, whites shouldn't get together with blacks, ever. Carlos and Jorge knew what the pastor said: blacks were the devil. Never, ever, did they want to see them playing with little blacks, it was a disgrace that in a neighborhood like this one that ravine existed. Their father finished his sermon, and his bottle. Down below, the guaguancó sounded again, far off:

And here's the latest,
here's the latest in the comics . . .

It stopped, giving way to the unmistakable sound of the drums announcing the toque. Carlos looked out through the shutters and saw the first torches being lit, and remembered the gaze of the goat, so very gentle, its empty eye sockets on the litter and the fervor with which the blacks had taken away its head, and thought about the mystery in that incomprehensible business. Then you couldn't hear the beginnings of the toque anymore, because Carmelina turned on the record player and Barbarito Diez's voice filled the house:

Virgin of Regla,
have pity on me, on me . . .

Ernesta called everyone to eat at the big table, with two extra leaves so the suckling pig, the goat, the rice, the black beans, the yucca with garlic sauce, the radishes, and the beer would all fit. They sat down as the *danzón* was ending, and in the space of six songs Manolo ate a quarter of the pig and another of the goat, drank fifteen beers, and now he was dancing with his wife, singing:

Ay, cry for Papá Montero
zumba!
canalla y rumbero . . .

Songs by Barbarito and the Antonio María Romeu Orchestra followed, briefly interrupted by a visit from Pablo's family, who came by to make arrangements to go together to midnight mass. Manolo danced with Carmelita, José María with Josefa, and Ernesta didn't dance because she was a widow, but she let Rosalina dance with the boys, who also danced by themselves, surrounding and bumping into anyone dancing with their cousin. They weren't allowed to drink rum, but beer was all right, as much as they wanted, and they gradually got happier, dizzier, more drunk, not realizing that worship services had started in the temple and from the depths of the ravine the Bembé's fire was resounding loudly. Around twelve midnight they all had their arms around each other, singing together in the middle of the living room:

> And if you go to the Cobre
> I want you to bring me
> a little virgin
> of Caridad . . .

That was when a horn honked insistently in the street and the adults left, still singing, for midnight mass. Their mother, before leaving, gave them a whole string of advice: they should lock the doors tight, turn off the lights, don't start looking out the windows, don't drink any more beer, go to bed and to sleep right away. Manolo yelled from the doorway, enough already, Josefa, weren't they grown men and women? The horn honked again, and their mother crossed herself before closing the front door.

There was something mysterious about the sign of the cross and the slam of the door, because suddenly the opposing roars of chants from the temple and from the ravine came into the deep silence of the living room, and with them came fear. They decided to go to bed right away, hoping the vertigo from the alcohol and the dancing would make them sink into drowsiness, escaping the threats of punishment and fire. Julián went with the boys, Rosalina headed for the servants' quarters. As soon as they undressed and laid their heads on the pillow, they realized it was impossible to sleep. The ceiling took on a spinning circular movement, it looked like it was going to explode right in their faces. The flames of the Bembé were reflected in the mirror over the dresser.

Outside, Rosalina was knocking feverishly at the door. Carlos looked for his pants, but Julián had already opened it and Rosalina ran in, diving into bed with them. She was trembling as if possessed, swearing she'd seen a ghost, the ghost of a huge man with wings who was trying to come into her room. Jorge showed her the lights reflected in the mirror, that was the blaze in the devil's eyes. Rosalina gave a cry, frightened, and for a second managed to fend off the chants at war on the Lord's night. But the music started again right away—"Shola Anguengue, Anguengue Shola!" "There is life, there is life, there is life in Jesus!"—and Jorge kept on saying they were the voices of the devil and of God, warning that they would come together to avenge the goat's death with blood. Then it was Julián who cried out, while Jorge kept on saying look how the eyes of the devil in the mirror were growing and growing. Carlos suddenly felt a warm wetness, thought about the blood gushing and the gaze of the goat, so very gentle, and also let out a ripping cry.

But it wasn't blood. There was only a hiss, a shriek from Jorge: Rosalina was wetting herself. Stunned, she was left watching the liquid flow out through her panties until it made a little golden puddle between her spread legs. They all felt a painful urge to urinate and decided to go together to the bathroom. Rosalina didn't want to wait for them outside the door. Inside, she turned her back as they all started urinating at once, noisily, with a lot of spume. Jorge whispered to them to look, Rosalina was watching. They didn't get to find out if it was true; although her face was turned towards them, her gaze was unreal, lost, her skin a bilious color, and suddenly her lower jaw opened forward into a retching she just managed to aim into the sink.

She was left very weak after the vomiting, pale, and they had to carry her back to the room, like the blacks did with the goat. Julián said she needed air, opened the window, and a stream of lights projected a huge fire onto the mirror, poked higher by the chants of the Bembé and the litany from the temple, echoing in the bedroom as if the voices and the drums were underneath the bed. Jorge changed the sheet and, transfigured, began his story again. Now the end was coming, the devil's eyes in the mirror were almost the same size as the devil's eyes, Cousin Rosalina needed air, air. He started pulling off her pajama top while she helped him, repeating between spasms, "Air, air." Carlos looked in absorption at Rosalina's little breasts, her dark nipples, and the obsessive way Jorge groped them while Rosalina, panting, tossed and turned, letting them do it to her, her tensed-up hand searching for something until she found Julián's between her legs.

Carlos jumped off the bed. He leaned on the wall and felt it vibrating with every drumbeat. Then he started to pray, he was witnessing the supreme kind of sin, he must already have the daño inside him because he let his voice, imploringly, run through the whole gamut of prayers from all the heavens and hells, "God save you Mary there is life in Jesus Anguengue Shola!" He must already have the daño inside because he docilely obeyed Jorge's cry, they all had to touch, they all had to touch the way of the truth and the life, they all had to touch cousin Rosalina's cholandengue. He was anxious as he began, Cousin Rosalina's breasts were hard and tense, and she was panting, "Oh my God, oh my God, oh my God, my God, what is this?" He must already have the daño inside because he heard the chants blending together in a new way, "There is life Shola there is life Anguengue there is life Anguengue Shola in Jesus!" Cousin Rosalina arched her back to the rhythm of the drums and the chants, and the flames in the mirror were reflected in her eyes with a diabolical joy, fierce and total, and Carlos couldn't resist the temptation to put his hand on that burning, wet cholandengue, or to shout out his mixed-up chant, which blended in the air with Rosalina's panting, "Oh God there is life Shola oh my God there is life Anguengue oh God what is this Anguengue? There is life Shola in Jesus my God!" and vibrated for a moment in the Lord's night, like the final statement of a condemned man on the day of the Last Judgment.

No punishment resulted. Rosalina, alone, sobbing, went to the servants' quarters refusing help, in spite of the continued sounds of the worship service and the Bembé. Carlos looked at the devil's eyes in the mirror for a long time, and seeing that they didn't grow, and that neither the fire nor the blacks were coming up the side of the ravine, he fell asleep, collapsing from exhaustion, before his parents arrived.

After that he gradually stopped believing in the pastor's terrible prophecies. The blacks doing business with his father became an almost permanent presence in the back patio. Sometimes when José María was in a good humor, Carlos asked them to sing the guaguancó about the comics. *A la cholandengue* turned into a customary phrase for the white boys in the neighborhood; riding your bike with no handlebars down a hill, getting a big hit in baseball, earning a good grade on an exam, it was all done a la cholandengue. Only on the nights when the Bembé and the worship services coincided did something of the old fear return, increasingly mixed in with the dark pleasure of evoking that night with Cousin Rosalina.

And when fear's atavistic fire was suddenly revived with the overwhelming force of the first time, there were at least four reasons that explained the change. One had to do with the gold objects the blacks started handing over to his father as payment for their loans: chains, watches, rings, bracelets, medals carved with names and strange magical symbols. Carlos liked looking at them, piled up in the top drawer of the display cabinet. The stones—rubies, aquamarines—combined their blue and purple reflections, the watches showed all different times, the bracelets and chains sent a message of love now for no one, the amulets, the saints' medals, could they preserve some kind of power closed up in there?

The terrible answer was given to them by their mother the day that Jorge, to show off, went out into the street wearing a big chain and a ring set with a ruby. Josefa broke down in a fit of crying, yanked them off his neck and finger, and for the first and last time in her life dared to raise her voice to her husband. They were going to kill them, José María, they were going to kill her sons, and it would be his fault, didn't he know those blacks? Didn't he know those stones and that gold were bewitched? He was involved in sinful work, robbing them, and would pay dearly for it. When he least expected it they were going to come in drunk through the patio to cut everyone's throats and take back their saints and their gold and their bewitched stones; or they were going to kidnap one of the boys in the street and drag him down there to the bottom of the ravine to kill him on a Bembé night; or they'd tie something onto his clothes and then they'd have the devil right inside the house without knowing it.

José María was in a cold sweat that morning, they could see the fear in his face. After a violent argument with Manolo, the stones disappeared from the house, the blacks didn't return to the patio. But he didn't give up the business, it made lots of money, he explained to them, so he'd gotten a little office with an employee, they didn't have anything to be afraid of, he was doing it for them, for their future, so they could enroll at the university later on. Their mother seemed to resign herself, but soon announced she was going to let go one of the servants, a black woman who worked like a bee and had a strange iron charm tied to her left ankle. Her name was Mercedes, and she had started working for no pay to earn back a big chain and a medal of the Virgin of Caridad that her husband had pawned. She stayed on because she worked long and hard, and because all she asked for in return was the leftover food for herself and her four children, some of the boys' old clothes, nothing more, and whatever amount José María decided to give her as a gift at the end of the month.

It got to where she was doing everything in the house, for nothing, and if his mother had decided to let her go, while crying for Mercedes's children, it was owing to the fact that the black woman had been another reason for the resurgence of fear. In those days Carlos picked up an abysmal guilty feeling, because he had been the first one to yell, in front of Mercedes, "A la cholan-dengue!" She turned around with the same expression of astonishment with which the old woman had looked at Jorge, hearing him in the ravine. Then she showed him a big chain, pointed at the image of the Virgin of Caridad carved in gold into the medal: look well, she was Shola Anguengue, Water Mother. Carlos felt that the first of a million mysteries of the ravine had been unveiled, and he asked questions and Mercedes told him the truth: the St. Francis of Assisi his mother had over the bed was none other than Kisimba; the St. Barbara Pablo's father had on a shelf in the living room was Insancio, Siete Rayos, the terrible god of thunder; the black man on crutches, St. Laza-rus, was Asuano, old Luleno, god of the sick; she herself, Mercedes, was the daughter of Tiembla Tierra, the warrior woman, goddess of mayhem and strife.

Carlos, frightened, ran out to tell Jorge and Pablo that their houses were being held by the terrible gods of the ravine. That afternoon, while he was again questioning Mercedes, Pablo's father told his mother and she decided to let her go. She did it almost silently, crying; she gave her a big bag of old clothes, the chain, the medal, and some money. Carlos asked himself if this was generosity or an awful precaution his mother was taking. He suggested that she remove the St. Francis, and she, as her only reply, took him to confess before God all the sins the blacks had put into his soul. This was extraordi-nary, because until then the Catholicism of their household had been limited to the stations of the cross during Holy Week, and midnight mass on Christ-mas Eve. Carlos and Jorge decided to conceal the sin committed with Cousin Rosalina, but taking Communion and the priest's words became the third reason for fear. The priest spoke in a way that was strangely similar to the pastor's, but the Catholic church was larger than the temple, darker, barely illuminated by weak candlelight. On the altars, knowing all about his sins, were St. Francis of Assisi, St. Barbara, the Virgin of las Mercedes, St. Lazarus. And who knew if, hidden in the same images, also lurked the evil spirits of Kisimba, Siete Rayos, old Luleno, and Tiembla Tierra. He could run from the pastor, able to think he was speaking in the name of another god, but the priest—voice made hoarse, eyes wide with fright before the hell he evoked—was the voice of Our Lord announcing the day of Last Judgment.

In February of '52, when the remnants of fear roared in the middle of the night louder than the Bembé, preparations began for war. The Homeowners' Association began promoting a campaign to move everyone out of the ravine, with the slogans of defending the family, morality, and religion. They proposed coming to a mutual agreement with the inhabitants of the ravine, whom they started calling the riffraff, giving them compensation so they would voluntarily go to live in other neighborhoods: Las Yaguas, Llegaipón, la Cueva del Humo. In the hollow, later on, perhaps there would be a park so the children could play without danger. Carlos, Jorge, and Josefa were surprised to see José María rabidly opposed to the idea: he would lose the blacks and his business, and besides, the riffraff weren't going to let themselves be kicked out just like that so easily, the neighborhoods they were proposing were dumps, he had it on good authority that if attempts were made against them, there would be a war.

The Homeowners' Association began the attempt; they took action through the city, in the provincial government, in the district precinct. The ravine mounted a rigorous defense; soon it was public knowledge that not even the police could dare go down. War, now imminent, was the fourth reason for fear. Rumors began to circulate that the blacks would attack by kidnapping little white children, making their tender hearts an offering for the barbarous gods of fire; that they would rape white women during the witches' Sabbath of the Bembé. The mothers, terrified, collected their children early, decreeing a virtual curfew in the neighborhood. Nights became a vast space where fear had free reign. They were black, like the riffraff who were going to come up impelled by their gods to have everyone's heads, as the priest and the pastor had warned.

Five sinister nights of confinement passed, and that was when José María brought home the television set to conquer their fear. The news went around the neighborhood like wildfire and the next night their living room looked like a theater: the children sitting on the floor, the adults on chairs, sofas and armchairs, all of them laughing at *Pedro's Tavern*, crying at *Divorcées*, becoming indignant at the crimes committed by Communists in Korea, as reported by *So Goes the World*. By the second night they had already forgotten the curfew. They were quivering from a hair-raising program, *Luuuchaaaa Liiibreee!* defined by the announcer as the clash of good against evil, the ground where the lowest passions entered into fierce combat against the greatest virtues. The announcer stopped speaking, expectations grew, then finally they saw that human mass: "Two hundred twenty pounds, the terror of the ring, the strongest, most traitorous man ever to fight, Boooone Breaaaaker, the Red Menace!" A tremendous booing followed this introduction of the monster, who spit in fury at the viewers. He was sheathed in a horrible mask, "that looks black to you," said the announcer, "but in reality is red, like Evil." He asked for silence, and in the other corner, "the Gentleman of the Ring, the best-trained wrestler ever known to the four corners of the Earth, the man who has come to our island to face the challenge of the international assassin. Our guest, a gladiator who needs no mask or pseudonym because he has nothing to hide. Here you have, dear viewers, especially presented by that great Cuban beer Hatuey, at one hundred eighty pounds, from Italy, Antonino Rocca!" Deafening applause, a commercial, and suddenly, Señor Joaquín Souza was pointing outside, shouting, "Look!" They became petrified by fear: the windows were completely filled by black people. In the dark night you could only see the orbs of their eyes. Mothers began shouting, hugging their children. Souza yelled for a knife, a machete, a revolver, and the blacks, on hearing him, dispersed and ran off running. Then the whites went out to the yard, finding trampled plants, urine, a stench, and decided to take the riffraff in hand, as Antonino Rocca was doing with the Red Menace.

The neighborhood awoke teeming with rumors. It was said that the riffraff had tried to attack the Pérez Meneses house, that blacks had gone so far as to pee in the living room in front of the ladies, that only thanks to the bravery of the men had tragedy been avoided. The boys organized gangs, talking about going down the ravine on white horses like Kid Durango, in a plane like the Blackhawks, flying like Superman, stretching like Elastic Man, in Batmobiles like Batman and Robin, and throwing flying kicks like Antonino Rocca to wipe out the riffraff a la cholandengue.

Carlos and Jorge couldn't join the gangs because their father continued doing business with the blacks. When the whites attacked and the war began they were considered traitors and cowards. Jorge suffered from this situation, but Carlos silently gave thanks because it allowed him to stay at peace with Chava's memory. The hostilities developed with unforeseen speed. Between both sides there tacitly emerged a simple code of war: the opponent at a disadvantage would be beaten until there was blood. The neighborhood boys didn't dare go down, they set themselves to stalking and hunting the boys from the ravine, who inevitably had to come up every day to run errands and do jobs and shop. The hollow's inhabitants compensated for their initial disadvantage with feline cleverness, slipping like snakes through the bushes, and if in the first days of the Gang War that preceded the Silent War they were caught at a disadvantage several times, and in the Homeowners' Association office they could boast that their sons had whipped those little blacks, very soon the situation evened up and blood sprang from both sides, when the riffraff adopted the tactic of going out in groups armed with sticks and stones. And since there were old debts to be paid in blood, they were collected by sending out decoys while the rest of the troop lay in wait, lying on the hillside. When the white boys attacked, the riffraff fell on them cursing in Spanish and their black tongue, yelling for Tiembla Tierra and for Shazam, giving flying kicks, beating them until they saw blood. Then the gangs from the neighborhood got together to hunt down the decoys and resist the counterattack. Things returned to an uneasy equilibrium until the blacks developed new weapons, slingshots and stone launchers, and began solo attacks from a distance. They enjoyed a natural advantage, their territory had thousands of uneven places practically invisible from above, they could hunt from close range those who dared to ride bikes or play ball in the street. The big gang of the whole neighborhood, held in check, planned a counteroffensive: on Saturday they would withdraw, and when the black boys came up in groups to do their shopping, they'd fall on them by surprise and destroy them in a final battle.

Carlos went to school in the morning, heard about the course of the hostilities in the afternoon, and watched television at night. But there were other sets in the neighborhood now, no friends visited them, considering them traitors and cowards, and Jorge spent every night protesting. For that reason Carlos was happy when his father's attitude towards the eviction changed radically a few days before the decisive battle. Manolo had come to see him, was José María dumb or what? The land! The association wanted the land! He took big strides around the living room, eyes glowing like a cat's, hands moving like paws, a park? Who was going to think about a park when the cost of every square meter was so high? A building! Fill it in, get financing, and put up a building! He shouldn't think it over any more, support the eviction, jump into the business headfirst. José María mumbled humbly, "But Manolo, I wanted a new car, to buy myself a Buick" and Manolo burst into laughter as if it were the best joke of the night, saying, "A Buick, so a Buick, huh," then became like a beast again, "Invest it, shithead!" José María looked at him, ashamed, "All right, Manuel, but how are we going to get involved if they haven't asked us?" Manolo fell back onto the sofa, spreading his arms wide in total astonishment, for God's sake, brother, who was controlling the blacks' debts anyway?

That night Carlos and Jorge enlisted in the Big Gang, which had decided to go for broke: they'd start with a formidable assault, no less than fifteen bicycles would take positions behind the big ESSO truck that Jimmy's father always parked in front of the house; they'd let the rabble come out of their cave en masse, get some confidence, for half a block the blacks wouldn't see anybody; suddenly the bikes would come out zooming downhill, roaring like tanks in war films. The tank drivers would have no mercy, the enemy's sole defense was rocks, but they would only have fractions of a second to use them, so they'd have to crouch down over the handlebars on the way down to frustrate the blacks' artillery and put them at the mercy of the tanks, which would charge into them and rout them, making them run like rabbits. The tank drivers would have to be fast, because two minutes after the clash the shooting would start. Nine rifles with flares, four shotguns with pellets, three with ball bearings, two U guns would be posted in the doorways. When Celso Henríquez fired his U, bombard the riffraff! Remember riflemen, the order was shoot to kill. Then they'd all come out with rifles, stones, bicycles, sticks, to rout them, stone them, shoot them, eviscerate them, to teach them with blood, a la cholandengue, really, truly, definitely, whose neighborhood *coño* it was anyway.

Carlos returned home agitated, would the saints of either side allow this? During the truce, many times he had thought of himself as the captain of military action, had imagined himself leading his men to victory and accepting the ravine's surrender, handed over by the black boy with the goat, who'd murmur with his head lowered, DOOPA BOOPA UMT TOTA! to which Carlos would respond ceremoniously, CHOLA ANDENGUE! so that blacks and whites together would chorus, ANDENGUE CHOLA! recognizing Captain Carlos Pérez Cifredo as King of the Neighborhood. Before, he had ordered that blacks not be killed in those battles, out of respect for Chava. But now the Big Gang was preparing a massacre that neither Grandfather Álvaro nor Chava would ever forgive.

There was no battle. That morning the parents carried out an exemplary search: not a bike, a rifle, a bullet was left in the boys' hands. José María yelled more than ever, it would be like grabbing a tiger by the balls, because then there'd be the law of the jungle, and in the jungle, who could hold back the riffraff? They *were* the jungle, hadn't they seen how they wallowed in it down there? Didn't they know they were going against civilization, progress, the building? Hadn't they heard the priest, the pastor, their mother? Didn't they realize that fighting with them was treating them like equals? That's why they would drive the blacks out of the neighborhood forever, before they made their way up to the street and got their smut all over everything.

From that day on, control of the hostilities was in the hands of the association, the boys weren't permitted any initiative whatsoever. The riffraff understood this as a truce and stopped attacking. Then the homeowners unleashed a Silent War: all the black women working in the neighborhood as maids, laundresses, and housekeepers were fired; no men at all from the ravine were allowed to paint a house, wash a car, build furniture; not one mamey, pineapple, or banana, not one lottery ticket or piece of peanut candy was bought from the peddlers; not one cent of credit was extended to riffraff families by the neighborhood groceries. Only one man from the ravine was given no trouble, and when the pastor howled against him in the temple, a tremor of unconfessed fear shook the neighborhood. No one dared to refuse leftover food to the Old Man on Crutches, who now went around three times a day with a big cart drawn by a goat and two boys, and looked more and more like St. Lazarus, Asuano, old Luleno, saint of the sick, cure for the ravine's hunger.

The Silent War was at its apogee when major news rocked the neighborhood: the Mulatto had staged a coup. Carlos thought for a few hours that maybe Kisimba, or who knows, Siete Rayos, had worked that miracle for the riffraff. Now a mulatto was president; the blacks held the cards now. All the fear stored up from the jewels, the confession, Tiembla Tierra, sacrifices of children, rapes of white women, the Gang War, and the Silent War exploded in those hours of anguish, making him ask Chava for God's sake to forgive him. But his father returned home radiant, Manolo said that if they just tightened up a little more everything would be resolved, Batista was their guy. Days later the association members laughed, agreeing that they'd gotten the idea from those words: to tighten the main valve that controlled the only pipes going into the ravine. Without water, the blacks couldn't last.

Amid the crowing about victory, fear vibrated through the neighborhood again: the Old Man on Crutches no longer came up to ask for food; during the night, from down below, you could hear his dogs howling. Their mother fell ill, trembling with fever and sobs, saying water was something you didn't even deny to animals, that they were committing a mortal sin, and they would have to prepare themselves to suffer the Lord's just and terrible punishment. Now Carlos had no more doubts, his mother had accepted the Old Man on Crutches as *something*: saint or demon, Luleno or St. Lazarus, god or devil, he was something supernatural, just and merciless, and he hated them with reason, and his vengeance would rise up from the depths of the ravine, awful like the plague that took away the sun at midday, deep like the barking of the dogs at night.

The miracle seemed to happen, not in the form of vengeance but rather as testimony to the infinite goodness of the saint of the sick. The May rainstorms started falling in April, torrential, and for the first time in many days there was a Bembé in the ravine. It was a terrible fiesta for the neighborhood, emerging from the darkness with the sound of chants mixing with the water's monotonous music, like a thanksgiving, proof of the powers of the demon over heaven. They weren't frightened because their mother was happy, lighting candles to good St. Francis of Assisi, singing softly to herself, *Que llueva, que llueva, la Virgen de la Cueva*, until on the third day her song and the expression on her face changed, as if the rising humidity had made the purple flora of her sadness burst. Now she was asking St. Isidro to stop the rain and let the sun come out, but St. Isidro didn't hear her. The rain had lasted four days and five nights when the first inhabitants of the ravine began asking for clemency. They came up the hillside, slipping in the mud, without a single flame, a single cry of war or vengeance, and sat down on the sidewalks like wet chickens. Down below, the water and the wind had wiped out the banana grove, lifted the zinc and the palms off the roofs, rotted the cardboard and wood of the walls and doors, drowned the animals. The bottom of the ravine had turned into a chocolate-colored lagoon where the remains of a shipwreck floated. It was still drizzling when Carlos and Jorge went out to see the victims of the flood, as the association called them. All their acquaintances were there: the boy with the goat, the fat old woman, the young woman with the sores, the singers who had negotiated with his father, Mercedes. They had managed to save just a few things, two radios, some furniture and animals, but they kept all their saints. The Old Man with the Crutches, terrified, feverish, lying on a cot, looked at that singular end of the miracles like a defeated god.

The newspapers and television ran the statements of the association president: it had been a lamentable misfortune of nature, perhaps a divine plan. The association was trying to get those unhappy people transferred to an appropriate neighborhood; then a park would be built there, or maybe a building, nothing had been decided. For now, the local Association of Catholic Ladies had begun a collection drive to aid the victims: clothing, food, medicine, everything was needed at this hour of suffering. The Homeowners'

Association had begun a cash drive and planned to organize a raffle, or maybe a big bingo game, nothing had been decided. That was all he had to say, gentlemen, please be so kind as to follow him.

For the neighbors, appearing on television was sensational, as if they had been able to be in two places at once: they were sitting in their living rooms and at the same time standing in their yards, before the eyes of the entire country, and they slapped their knees still amazed, "Can you believe it, fellows!" Carlos felt a sudden joy seeing his face on the lighted screen, smiling like an announcer's or an actor's, and he treasured that instant of joy among his most precious memories. If something spoiled the program, in the neighbors' opinion, it was that the blacks couldn't, or wouldn't, control their little black children and the latter spent the whole time stealing the camera, shoving and waving as if the television were for them. But the president of the homeowners read his statements without stammering, and the clothing, medicine, and food from the drive ended up being a whole mound, because during the broadcast several advertisers joined the humanitarian campaign, contributing donations that made the program into the neighborhood's great success. The last image was interpreted by all as an allegory of peace: to the left, the president of the Catholic Ladies; to the right, the president of the Homeowners' Association; behind them, the food, medicine and clothing in piles; in the middle, dogs and all, the Old Man with the Crutches, symbol of the ravine's surrender. The program was rebroadcast that afternoon. As one more proof of the spirit of harmony, the blacks were invited to watch television through the windows and for the first time Carlos accepted their surrender: when they saw themselves, "Can you believe it, fellows!" they reacted exactly the same way as the whites.

That peace was just a truce. When the weather cleared, the blacks started returning to the ravine, indifferent to the torrent of insults and threats that fell on them with greater force than the storms. The next day all the measures of the Silent War were restored. The Catholic Ladies suspended aid, the advertisers took back their contributions, the association transferred funds from the drive and the bingo into the down payment for construction of the new building. The main valve was kept closed. Within a few days, a penetrating stench reemerged from the bottom. In the neighborhood they no longer talked only about murders and rapes, but also epidemics and contagion. Vultures started flying over the Gang War, the confiscated shotguns reappeared, and at least three boys from the ravine were injured with pellets. The last Bembé sounded like a declaration of war to the death.

The riffraff's counterattack began far away, where no one would have expected it. On one single day five white boys, ambushed coming out of school, were marked with knives. The news report on television raised a racket. On the morning of the last Sunday in April the hollow woke up surrounded by police. White, black, and mulatto agents went down howling like beasts, destroyed the huts that had scarcely been rebuilt on the mud and, beating them, made the inhabitants of the bottom climb up. Beating them, they stacked them into trucks without allowing them to take a cot, a radio, a saint. Carlos, aghast, saw how they trampled Shola Anguengue's image, kicked Kisimba's, scratched Tiembla Tierra's. He saw the blacks attempting a desperate defense, and the police with their sticks splitting open the men's faces and heads, hitting the women with rifle butts, kicking the children, destroying the old man's crutches against the sidewalk curb, shooting at his dogs, throwing the old man into the floor of the truck as if he were a bag. He turned toward his mother, who was praying "Holy Mary, mother of God," felt an intense heat, a pestilent, thick smoke, and ran to the patio fence to see how fire was wiping out the remains of the ravine, kindled by the furious winds of Lent.

THREE

Maybe if Mai hadn't said, "Anyone who doesn't go is a fag," Carlos wouldn't have gone. But Mai said it, put his revolver in his waist, and stared at them with his big, blue eyes, gazing like Antonio Guiteras's did from the portrait Mai always carried in his pocket. The onlookers slipped away from the Instituto's entryway into the street, and the quick little game of Chinese charades that the Smartasses were playing in the yard broke up, leaving a riddle on the board: "From a rat it turns into a monkey / seated on his throne."

Carlos turned his head away, it was a drag that the demonstration was going to be that morning in particular. They'd organized a session of the Parapsychology Society for the afternoon, in which it was his turn to be the bait, and he had his act all ready. Maybe he'd get to touch some tits, they had invented the society for touching tits, and he had spent days rehearsing the slaughtered-lamb, dead-on-the-seashore look he'd have to use when Johnny Crime hypnotized him in front of the nice little rich girls.

"You are sleeping," Crime would whisper to him, setting his grandfather's watch into a pendular motion. "Follow the watch, you are sleeping."

Carlos would let himself be carried away thinking about nipples, and he would take on a lethargic, cataleptic state that would amaze the girls.

"He is ours," Crime would muse, turning off the lights.

Then you could hear the giggles of girls in heat, and Johnny, to make it all more realistic, would order him to say something in the tongue of his ancestors.

"*In hoc signo vinces,*" he would murmur, with Saquiri the Malay's voice.

"Under this sign you will win," Crime would translate, and the girls would be incredibly impressed, then he'd give them an order: "Put his hand on your heart, he doesn't feel anything."

That's when the whole bit would start and his chance would come, the heart was behind the tits, and the girls wouldn't have any choice but to let themselves be touched. But he'd have to stay calm, Crime had told him, spellbound until the girls started trusting in science, that way one day they'd be able to touch some little thighs and asses too.

He'd spent two hours trying to imagine what it would be like to be hypnotized, and suddenly he discovered it was like feeling swept along by Mai, hearing him say there would be shooting, and maybe someone's fate would be to *not* come back alive. What could he do? Like a shithead he had gotten *involved in something.* He vividly remembered the day Héctor had approached him in the bathroom.

"Go sell these," he said, and gave him some red and black vouchers with the legend "Don't cut cane with Batista. Liberty or Death! M-26-7," and he left, telling Carlos to be careful.

He couldn't refuse, Héctor was his pal, his bud, his batting partner on the Instituto baseball team, and during the last game in the dugout they had talked a lot of bad shit about Batista. Coming out of the bathroom, he had a feeling of danger that wasn't altogether unpleasant. From then on he began to walk like Joseph Cotten after the bank robbery in *The Naked City*. He would smile paternalistically at his classmates, hoping they wouldn't realize anything and at the same time that they'd notice he, too, was *involved in something*. He managed to worry Pablo, who came over to him: "Are you in some kind of jam, my man?" and seeing the vouchers on Carlos's desk, he became terrified. "You be crazy, *asere*! They'll kill you for that!"

He smiled, fascinated, almost not believing he was really risking his life, but he didn't try to sell the vouchers, fearing someone would inform on him. He hid them back in the corner of his room, along with the dirty books and the pamphlets from the Mexican Parapsychology Society. For two months he didn't spend a cent in the Casino, saved up the six pesos, and turned them over to Héctor with his best clandestine voice:

"Mission accomplished, mulatto."

Héctor gave him more vouchers. He took them in silence, resolved to continue his abstinence. Soon after, blinded by the sparks from Gipsy's hair, he thought about spending the money on her and betraying Héctor. But that didn't happen. Gipsy disappeared almost as soon as she arrived, like in fairy tales, leaving only a promise and a memory he was now trying to revive. He felt lost; maybe he'd never see the blond hair in Gipsy's armpits again, that down soft and exciting like a sex, because now he was walking towards the demonstration and no one could tell him if his fate would be to *not* come back alive.

At the university, he felt confused. From childhood he had learned to identify that place as the ultimate objective of his existence. His father used to take him and Jorge there to the base of the great stairs, and announce with a grave voice: "Someday you'll be going there, that's what I'm struggling for." And now Jorge was studying business and had the courage to keep away from craziness, while he was going off to war, telling himself he'd probably have time later on for touching tits, and he felt small and disoriented in Plaza Cadenas, surrounded by remote, harsh buildings, crisscrossed in every direction by groups of students who seemed to know exactly what to do on that cold November morning.

San Lázaro and L streets joined at the foot of the hill, forming a little plaza where the wide staircase started. Now Héctor was telling him they would go down it in search of liberty, or glory. Carlos breathed in the heroic morning air and felt he had the courage needed to lead his group down, acting as their chief and as an example in the way he would face the police thugs, bare-chested and bare-knuckled. And if he died in the effort, what did it matter? His name would be united with those that illuminated the altar of the motherland, from Carlos Verdugo to Rubén Batista, entire generations of students who had preferred to be martyrs rather than slaves and thus had achieved glory.

"There they are," said Héctor.

Carlos took his head from the clouds and looked toward where his friend was pointing. At San Lázaro and Infanta, two blocks past the stairs, the thugs were blocking the way with fire trucks and police cars. Remembering the eviction of the ravine, he began sweating intensely, thinking the police would treat them like they did the blacks, and even worse, and he told himself he wasn't black or crazy and it wasn't right to betray his father's dreams dying so young, for so little, with so little glory.

He went back to Plaza Cadenas. He sat down on a bench to relieve the sudden weakness in his legs, and tried to relax by examining the names engraved on the facade of the School of Science. After all, scientists *also* were heroes, it would be better to risk your life to save humanity from a scourge, like Finlay did with yellow fever. He thought about leaving, then stopped, remembering the contempt with which Grandfather Álvaro used to pronounce the word *runaway*, referring to deserters and cowardly types, and all of a sudden he realized that it was the monkey, the dictator, the murderous mulatto who was seated on his throne. At that point Mai arrived.

"José Antonio just arrived," he said. "Let's go."

The Hall of Martyrs was packed and they had begun the roll call. José Antonio would say the names of the heroes and they would all respond in unison: "Present!" Carlos was next to a photo in which Trejo looked very young, with a little thirties-style mustache, and he joined the chorus thinking how that man could have been his father. Little by little he let himself be won over by the invisible feeling of continuity floating in the air. Leaving the hall, fear had disappeared from his soul.

The group began concentrating at the top of the stairs while José Antonio, Juan Pedro, and Fructuoso unrolled a long banner with the slogan:

DOWN WITH TYRANNY! —FEU

Those in the vanguard held up a flag, a wreath, and a sarcophagus, and started the march. Carlos wanted to go back a bit, but the angry crowd pushed him forward, where he again felt defenseless. Many people were prepared for the clash, wearing rain hats or heavy coats. He, in contrast, had on only a little shirt. Suddenly Héctor dragged him towards the center. "Stay close to me," he said. The bells of the Virgin of Carmen church began ringing for mass and Carlos noted, with worry, that some people in nearby buildings were locking their windows. Then the hymn was heard. He began singing to give himself strength, made himself part of the chorus that turned its song into a war cry. Arriving at San Lázaro, the vanguard waved the flag. The police began slowly moving up the street, and the chorus of voices overflowed. Two squads of thugs came forward unleashing jets of water against the group holding the wreath, taking it apart: for a second, lavender, red, and yellow flowers were held up in the air against the misty white columns of water, fanned out by gusts of air, directed now at the chests of those carrying the banner. The demonstration stopped when the police concentrated their attack at the legs and knocked down those in front. Then someone cried, "Now!" Bunches of students broke away towards both sides of the street, and from the doorways, the dark entryways, and the roofs of the adjoining buildings they began throwing stones at the police. Héctor left Carlos and started running with Mai and Benjamín to join a group fighting to keep the flag held up. A rush of water reached Carlos. From the ground, breathless, head clouded by the curtain of water, by the lavender, red, yellow blur of the flowers' remains, and by the violent, shiny black of the asphalt, he could see the group holding the staff under the water jets and the flag waving, despite everything, in the air. "Under this sign," he thought, "under this sign, under this sign . . ." Then he made out a blur of blue to the right, a squad of thugs trying to surround the group and snatch the flag away from them. Héctor and Mai moved forward to mount a defense, and he stood up, running towards them: "Watch out, watch out, watch out!" He saw how Héctor fell to the ground with his head split open, how Mai punched a policeman with his fists, how another policeman unloaded a whip on his back, cornered Mai, knocked him to the ground, began kicking him. Mai grabbed the thug by the back, scarcely for a second: another policeman pushed him against the wall, landed a blow of the whip across his face, raised the whip again, and suddenly fell, his head split by a rock. A skinny guy with glasses dropped the rock, stained with blood, picked Héctor up under the arms, and shouted at Carlos to help him. They ran down San Lázaro with Héctor over their shoulders and sat him down in Plaza Mella, by the base of the stairs. The Moor was there, unconscious. "They'll be coming to get them now," said the skinny guy. "Let's go, there are more wounded."

But Carlos didn't move. The flag, wet, was barely waving in the distance, the skinny guy had plunged back into the crowd; and he stayed still, watching how Colonel Salas Cañizares was aiming at the demonstrators with a Thompson that spit out little yellow gobs. He became hypnotized, like an insect before the burning light of death, and suddenly he fled, feeling like a perfect target for the bursts of fire that kept on sounding behind him. He crossed Plaza Cadenas. Across from the Calixto García Hospital he was out of breath, but the swarm of ambulances there pouring out the wounded made him continue on. On Rancho Boyeros Avenue his run turned into a slow march, stubborn, anxious, and at a certain moment the colors of the morning went black and spun around faster and faster. On the ground, he felt his face burning, and his body soaked with blood, water, urine, sweat. He managed to sit up, saw sculpted into the facade of the National Library the familiar names of the motherland, and murmured, "Present." But now it was different, because Mai wouldn't be coming to tell him José Antonio had arrived.

FOUR

Around three in the morning Koch's Bacilli landed in La Victoria at the Kumaún bar, half a block from Otto's house, where according to Pablo a unicorn was working. Carlos shouted no, explaining that there were only Hottentots there, not even a miserable raccoon, but the others didn't pay much attention to him. Berto, Mister Cuba, started growling at the tiger on a sign showing its claws and fangs, yelling at it come down from there, you fag, if you dare; Dopico invited Jorge to tell him if that tiger was yellow with black stripes or black with yellow stripes, and Pablo challenged Dopico to decide if it was a male or female tiger, because you couldn't see either its balls or its slit. Then Jorge started singing their theme song, and the four of them entered the Kumaún like gunslingers in a Western going into a saloon.

Inside it was dark and cold, just a few spotlights creating a vaguely purplish atmosphere behind the bar. Ñico Mcmbiela, playing on a record, cursed some ungrateful, lying, and betraying woman, and Pablo declared that any woman would be within her rights to cheat on a guy who sang so badly, and Berto explained to him that the poor guy sang badly because the woman had cheated on him before, and Dopico said, if you please, catch that suffering platypus. They narrowed their vision in on the girl at the cash register, a mulatta with hair as smooth and hard as her thighs, combed through, with a little green light bulb lit up at her waist and nothing under her skirt, making Dopico say just catch that papaya, the pulp of that papaya, and they were looking, penetrating, eating up the girl at the register with their eyes, and they sat across from her still staring until Pablo asked if they realized that it was only an ad on a sign, and then they ordered three Burning Spains and one Polar beer.

The beer was for Carlos. The other Koch's went back to catching the mulatta through their glasses, through the golden mixture of hard cider and cognac in their glasses, and Carlos looked at the clock, calculating that he had to keep them there for at least an hour, cursing the moment he revealed Fanny the unicorn's existence to Pablo, yelling at him that he wasn't a man or a friend and thinking he'd kill the bastard who dared to mess with her.

For six months he'd been spending on Fanny the whole allowance his father accumulated temptingly, tenaciously, in the same money box Carlos had used to save money for Héctor's vouchers and newspapers. Meanwhile, Fanny changed her neighborhood, house, name, and price four times, and Carlos, obsessed, followed her from Polish Juana's whorehouse in San Isidro, to the House of Tiles in Colón, to Aunt Nena's in Los Sitios, to Otto's in La Victoria, and without complaining paid her one-fifty, two, two-fifty, three pesos, and called her Estefanía la Nueva, La Caliente, Madame Fannie, Fanny, and rolled around with her in her tiny, sordid den, in a dirty, oppressive little room, in a warm, pink room, and saw their trembling images infinitely repeated in the magical combination of round mirrors in the bridal chamber of Otto's house, and hid his passion from the Koch's as if it were a crime.

But that damned drunken night in a moment of weakness he had told Pablo, and the bastard had told Jorge, and Jorge the whole group, and from then on he, Carlos, had to bear the zigzagging that had gotten the Koch's closer and closer to Otto's whorehouse. Trying to explain to himself how he could have been such a shithead, he came to the conclusion that if the movies had been the cause of his happiness, they were also causing his misfortune. Since Gipsy left, with an uncertain promise of return, he remained obsessed, without knowing what to do, until he saw *Vertigo*. That was the solution to his anguish: he had to rediscover Gipsy, like James Stewart did with Kim Novak. He set himself to following women resembling his obsession, but none of them paid him any attention; more than once they threatened him with the police, branding him as crazy. His delusion had reached a climax when he discovered, in a miserable San Isidro brothel, a girl as frightened as a little animal.

Estefanía la Nueva vaguely resembled Gipsy. She was young and had the same long, slender, shapely legs, but her hair was light brown and her skin too white, almost milky. Her eyes were also green or blue, but they didn't change according to the color of the billiard table or the water's surface, rather with the intensity of Polish Juana's owl-like shrieks, or the number of men she managed to dispatch in a night. Carlos refused to put her at the level of dromedary, which was almost what fit her at that time, and had to recognize that Estefanía la Nueva would never be a unicorn. In honor of her eyes, he classified her as a fawn and called her Bambi at the moment of orgasm. In those days he hated intensely the disgusting den in the San Isidro neighborhood where Polish Juana even let blacks in; but now he was sure he'd never forget the Mondays in December when the place was almost empty, and Estefanía la Nueva told him how she was from Santa Clara or San Juan de los Remedios, the daughter of an unemployed man or a peasant, seduced by a hunter or a traveling salesman, the mother of a blond son named Esteban of whom all she had left was this photo, and, well, just put the one-fifty on the night stand because otherwise, Juana . . .

In the dark of sordid rooms with posts shoring up the walls, La Caliente resembled Gipsy a little more because she was blonde, but in the night lamps' weak glow the resemblance was a little less, because under the light there were telltale brown roots under the dye. During those days she developed the habit of singing, amid sobs, Mexican *corridos*, which gave Carlos goose bumps. The House of Tiles was the most famous one in the Colón neighborhood, and La Caliente, who got to be the most famous female of the house, sometimes allowed him to visit her in the afternoons to avoid the humiliation of waiting in line, and made him think, while he listened to her multiple sad stories, that between him and her there was something more than the shameful relationship of john and whore. She was from Santiago or San Juan, Puerto Rico, her stepmother had forced her to get a job in the governor's or mayor's house, and with that high-ranked person she had a blond son named Juan or Santiago, of whom all she had left was this photo. One afternoon she finished the story crying. Carlos tried to console her, and La Caliente started whispering obscenities in his ear. After that he stopped calling her Bambi at the moment of orgasm.

Aunt Nena was French. She went to Cuba, like many other celebrants, attracted by the heavenly music of the Dance of the Millions, and furiously wiggled her waist to its rhythm during the magic decade that ended one day in 1919. She was Yarini's lover, and along with him took part in the bloody War of the Guayabitos, which permanently did away with the dominance of French pimps in San Isidro. She attended the Big Fella's funeral escorted by the president of the Republic, and wagging tongues commented that she had, in reality, also been the lover and agent of Lotot, leader of the defeated French.

The police had always been certain that she was present at the murder of her close friend Rachel de Keirgester, but they never could prove it. By that time she had already become famous thanks to her mastery of fellatio, a buccal art she practiced to excess and passed on to her disciples until it became permanently incorporated into native Cuban erotica. She had never returned to France, but boasted that her house was like a Montparnasse café. In that fake boîte on Trocadero Street, where all you heard was French music played by an albino violinist, Aunt Nena presented her outstanding pupil, Madame Fannie, who laughed a lot while circling around her tutor, lifted her skirt, showed her behind, tra-la-laed "Pigalle" and "Mademoiselle de Paris," used colored ribbons and laces, charged two-fifty, and didn't see anyone in the afternoons. She was the descendant of French people who had come to Cuba just a sliver of time ago from New Orleans, Louisiana, or Haiti, and had been initiated into adult life at age twelve by an uncle or a cousin. With him she had a blond son named Jacques her family had sent to France, of whom all she had left was this photo. Carlos would have classified her as a platypus if her linguistic virtuosity hadn't suggested a rattlesnake instead.

The first time he saw Fanny dancing in the bar at Otto's house he thought he was looking at Gipsy. That woman, so incredibly blond, with cinnamon-colored skin toasted like layers of puff pastry, eyes blue like the dazzling spotlight falling on her, or green like the crème de menthe she was getting drunk on, that woman was definitely a unicorn. She went around wearing gauzy green bikini shorts and a lamé blouse, and she liked playing Little Richard's "Rip It Up" over and over on the Victrola, dancing to it until she appeared exhausted and then putting on "Rock Around the Clock" by Bill Halley, to get the johns all fired up before dispatching them one by one. Carlos desperately hated that waiting line and pleaded with Fanny to allow him to come in the afternoons, but that can't happen, my baby, because this is an American house and tine ees monee, no? He consoled himself thinking that going to bed with Fanny beneath the mirrors of the bridal chamber was a trip multiplied in circles into infinity that cost only three pesos. She was from Miami or Key West and used to make her living as a singer or a waitress in the bar on the *Floridita* ferry, until a mafioso or the captain mixed her up in a drug trafficking or white slavery deal and they expelled her or deported her from the United States. Back there she had a blond son named John of whom all she had left was this photo. One night Carlos asked her for the portrait that was on the nightstand, and for five pesos, Fanny dedicated one just like it to him, where she appeared alone, naked, and sad.

He told Pablo that story only for the pleasure of saying that he was the James Stewart of little Cuba the beautiful, but the big jerk repeated the story between giggles, and Jorge's eyes shone like a cat's when he said that night all the Koch's would lay their eyes on Fanny, so Carlos would learn not to fall in love with a whore. The threat had dissolved in alcohol, and Carlos's suffering would have ended, if it hadn't been that the bars they went to got closer and closer to Otto's house. Now they had been at the Kumaún for a while and had gone into a dangerous silent patch, into a vacuum, into the moment when all the alcohol and smoke consumed returned in a great hungover weariness, and it was possible Jorge would start provoking him again, so Carlos decided to gain some time.

"So tomorrow you're finally going t'hell," he said.

Jorge smiled for a long while before saying t'hell no, t'Yunai. Dopico told the girl at the cash register that his brudder was going up north, and the mulatta, spreading her legs a little more, asked him to take her along.

"This dark girl sure knows what life is all about," commented Dopico. "Hey, catch that, why don't you take her along, my man? What a catch, partying it up with the mulatta in Yunai."

The mulatta smiled and spread, closed, and spread her legs, yeah, take me along, I sure know how to earn a living. Pablo said with what you have in the bank, and the mulatta:

"No way, sonny, with my knife, like this." And she ran the tip of her index finger between her thighs as if she were slashing up to the navel. "Go on, boys, it's on the house."

Dopico suddenly went white, yellowish, and looked at the mulatta with a stupid grin.

"Let's go," said Jorge.

"Where?" asked Carlos.

Outside there was a sticky, wet heat and a drunk sitting on the sidewalk, talking to himself. Seeing them, he tried to get up, but slid softly back down to the curb.

"Adversity," he said. "One by one I'm going to get rid of them all."

"Where are we going?" Carlos insisted.

Jorge didn't answer. In the distance you could see the gray ramps of the new Carlos III Market, huge, orderly, and as clean as a big drug store. On both sides of the street, for blocks and blocks, the whorehouses of La Victoria were lined up. Carlos tried to think how there were still dozens of opportunities for the Koch's to go wrong, and stayed quiet. In the middle of the second block, Jorge pushed open a big red door, as if by accident: they had arrived at Otto's house.

The girls were in the patio in the back, and Dopico called with a high-pitched voice, oh little girls, come out front, the Americans are here, until some of them came around with all the weariness of the night reflected in their faces. From there, Carlos could see Fanny get up from one of the high bar-stools and start dancing "Love Me Tender" with a john. Pablo asked him which one she was.

"That one," he said, feeling himself blush pointing her out.

"A unicorn," approved Pablo.

Carlos smiled, annoyed. The john was entwined like a snake around Fanny, and it was as if he could feel his sour breath on her neck. He'd witnessed that scene a thousand times, but it had never irritated him as much as now, in front of his pals.

"My man," he asked with a tense voice, "don't go to bed with that dame."

Pablo automatically started fixing the knot on his tie and saying, all right, asere, but first he had to confess something, he was into that whore, he swore he was like a dog in love with that whore. Jorge joined the group with a drink in his hand and said, not with that whore, Nose, you've got to treat her nice, that dame was his brother's honey. Pablo agreed, he had to treat her nice, he stopped fooling with his tie and put his finger on Carlos's nose and asked him to confess if he was in love with his honeythewhore.

"All in all, that's a man's business," said Carlos.

Jorge clapped him on the back and began singing "A Man's Tears." Carlos slipped away to the sofa where Dopico was creating strange figures with a young black woman, docile and slender. At the bar, the song had ended, but Fanny and the john were still groping each other under the spotlight. Pablo had started harmonizing with Jorge and now they were bleating with all their might, "a man's tears / too bitter to show / since they're condemned / never to flow." Otto, the matron, burst into the room with hands on his hips, ready to impose silence, but seeing Berto he was left stunned.

"Oh, goodness me, just who do we have here?"

Berto instinctively stepped back, and Otto undressed him with his eyes. The matron was a short, corpulent mulatto, his kinky hair straightened, shiny, greasy, and with an intense odor of perfume. He was known for being bellig-erent, a morphine addict, and an intimate of the precinct police captain.

"Why it's Mister Cuba himself, in person, just like I saw him in a maga-zine," said a redhead who hadn't left Berto's side for a second.

The other girls swirled around Berto, raising a ruckus, asking him to take his jacket off. Fanny came over, hearing the cries, followed by the john; she recognized Carlos, let out a little cry of joy, and threw her arms around his neck.

"How's my sweet little harasser doing?"

"More or less," said Carlos, kissing her on the cheek without taking his eyes off the john, who came towards them defiantly:

"Hey, hey, hey there!"

"Leave her alone or I'll kick you out!" ordered Otto with the look of a tigress. "Let me see that boy!"

The john stopped, confused, retreated, and leaned against the wall, watching them. Berto had taken off his jacket before the continued, insistent admiration of the girls, but he refused to take off his shirt.

"I dare you to arm wrestle me," said Otto. "Bet whatever you want. If I lose I pay double."

Berto stuck out his chest with an almost automatic reaction. He was much taller that Otto, and had better defined muscles.

"Go on," said Dopico from the depths of his black woman, "you'll get rich."

Berto remembered he had no money. Dopico lent him five pesos and Jorge five more, they'd split it.

"Place your bets," said Otto.

"A hundred," said the john from the darkness.

"On me, or him?" asked Otto.

"I always put it on the macho," said the john.

"You mean the one who's with your woman now?" asked Otto, pointing at Carlos, who had Fanny on his lap.

The john looked towards them again. He had the baleful, dull, vague gaze of a drunk.

"A hundred on the macho," he repeated.

They all went into the small inner room, barely lighted by a reddish glow. The girls put a small, black table under the altar to St. Barbara, Changó, Siete Rayos, goddess of sword and thunder. Candles in offering to the saint were stuck into little glasses bloodred in color, almost wine, and they gave off a wavering, diabolical light.

"Your money," said Otto.

Berto placed his two five-peso bills on the table, and Otto put two tens. The john staggered over and let fall a pile of one-peso bills, dirty and wrinkled.

"Eighty-nine," he said.

"That's not a hundred," Otto replied. "You're missing eleven pesos."

The john turned his pockets inside out. A key and a few cents fell. With much difficulty, he crouched down to pick them up.

"It was for her," he said pointing to Fanny, to the money, and smiling for the first time. His teeth were set in gold.

Otto counted the bills, smoothing them out, before putting his on the table. Berto recounted the total slowly.

"You're missing a peso."

"No matter," said Otto. "How much?"

"Two nine six," replied Berto.

"Which adds up to seventeen," said the redhead, "St. Lazarus."

Otto took off his canary yellow shirt with dozens of little mother-of-pearl buttons on the chest. He greased his torso with a smelly, shiny pomade.

"Snake oil," he said, offering it to Berto.

The latter shook his head. He leaned against the wall, doing a series of exercises supporting himself on his fingertips, then stretched them, making them crack.

"Ready," he said.

Otto traced a straight line down the middle of the table with red chalk. They sat down, placed their elbows, opened their hands, took a tight hold.

"Go," said Berto.

At first they were in a stable, sluggish equilibrium. The pressure barely produced a slight change of color in Berto's fingernails; he was looking only at their ensnared hands. Otto's nails were covered by a coat of pink polish and shone under the winy light of the candles. Slowly, stubbornly, Berto went in the opposite direction. His biceps sprung out under his shirt, which looked like it was at the point of bursting. He gained a millimeter. He produced something like a smile, and for the first time took his gaze off their hands to keep watch on the money. Otto at no time had looked either at their grip, or the money: from the beginning he had been stalking Berto's eyes, continually seeking a meeting that Berto seemed to avoid. Their arms moved in Otto's favor one, two millimeters, and the john let escape a muffled, dying exclamation, but soon a counterattack began and Berto wound up recouping lost ground. Now they returned to equilibrium. Berto's white arm looked like a statue's, and Otto's a solid, polished ochre log. Berto's face started to reflect a sort of stupefaction, as if it weren't possible for someone to hold out against him for so long. He stared at Otto's wrist, much wider than his, and then, for the first time, at his enemy. He was left dazzled. He made a pathetic effort to pull his eyes away but couldn't. Otto was undressing him again, now face to face, and Berto lost his strength, gave way terrified by Otto's laugh as if it were the devil's, and suddenly left at a run.

"Let him go," said the matron, throwing down the money. "He's a kindred spirit."

Standing before the altar to Changó, he looked like a little idol made of fat.

"Pepilla," he called.

A mulatta consumed by her years, barely a small framework of skin and bones, dressed in white from her shoes to the scarf on her head, came out of a room and placed herself by his side.

"White boy," said Otto, with a childish, trembling voice.

"Cheater!" yelled the john, as if he had just come out of a trance.

"I'm going to see about Berto," said Pablo suddenly, running out.

"Cheater!" repeated the john.

"Shut up!" ordered the old woman.

Her voice was deep and cavernous. The john didn't dare open his mouth. The old woman took Otto by the hand and led him towards her room, slowly, like a guide leading a blind man.

"That's it for tonight," said the redhead. "The couples can stay."

Dopico began to walk towards a room followed by the black woman, yelling that he was a tanker, a Greek hundred-thousand-ton oil tanker, Aristotle Socrates Onassis. Jorge took the money Otto had left on the table with a furtive, thieflike movement. The john put one of his last coins in the Victrola and the beginning of a guaguancó was heard: "If in this, in this, in this beautiful Havana, León, where I met her . . ."

"You going to take care of business?" asked Fanny.

Carlos didn't answer. He was enjoying that vague wine-colored drowsiness, just having Fanny seated on his lap, without hurry, without fear of any other johns coming in, as if she truly were his girl.

"You going to take care of business?" Fanny insisted.

The technical term annoyed him. He wasn't just any john "taking care of business" with her.

"My honeythewhore," he said, and began to follow the guaguancó.

"My honeythewhorer," said Fanny, and she stuck her tongue in his ear.

When they got up the rumba was starting, the moment when the gua-

guancó builds and becomes intense, repeated, and obsessive, and good dancers respond to the call and answer of the *quinto* by intensifying the sexual
chase until they reach the point of the *vacunao*, that violent, definitive gesture
directed towards the female's sex. But this guaguancó was a recording, lasting
for three minutes, and the rumba lacked the rhythm and the flavor of the
drums that can only be achieved with a *güiro*, and Fanny was there with her
haunches up, waiting, because Carlos hadn't done the vacunao and the music
had just suddenly disappeared beneath her feet, when Jorge went over to her,
his face pale with alcohol and weariness, and said, listen whore, leave my
brudder alone, all right? enough, all you are really is just a nice bitch.

"He's my brother, Jorge," Carlos explained, "he's drunk."

Fanny turned around towards Jorge, took a long, pantherlike step, as if she
were advancing over the trumpet's harmony in one single *son*, pulled him over
by the hair pretending she was going to whisper a secret to him, and then put
her tongue into his ear, moving it like a snake.

"She's a bitch!" screamed the john.

Carlos smelled the cognac and cider on Jorge's breath and softly pushed
him away, leaving Fanny with her tongue in the air. Jorge stumbled backwards, she's a bitch, brudder, ran into the wall, didn't he realize?, slowly slid
down to the floor, should he show him?

"You show him good," said the john.

"No one asked you for your two cents," replied Carlos.

He turned to Jorge, who had put his finger to his lips, asking the john to
play along quietly with him.

"Come on, chico," Carlos said, helping him stand up, "you're as plastered
as hell."

He smelled again the unbearable odor of cognac, cider, and sweat, because
Jorge lost his balance and fell onto him; if he wanted him to go he would, but
if not he'd prove that whore was a bitch, did he want him to?

"No," said Carlos. "Let's go t'hell."

Jorge shrugged his shoulders with a defeated gesture and started waving
goodbye with his right hand, like a polite little boy.

"Wait a minute," said Fanny. "What if I want to?"

Carlos moved towards her, then towards Jorge, and finally wound up next
to Pablo, who had just returned.

"Yoyi," he said.

But Jorge was going towards Fanny, listen good to what I'm going to tell
you, that guy over there was his brudder, did she know what a brudder was?

"*Hermano* in English," answered Fanny, mockingly.

Jorge smiled, satisfied, that dame knew everything, well, just for her information, there was nothing, nothing that would fuck over his brudder more than if he slept with her, wasn't that true, asere?

Carlos formed the words *my bro* with his lips, but didn't emit a single sound. The john let out a cackle.

"Let's go," said Fanny.

Hey wait, little bitch, Jorge called after her. He'd do his duty right there, he added, pulling down the zipper on his fly. Fanny smiled, got down on all fours, and started towards Jorge's crotch.

"Bark," said the john.

Carlos threw himself at them, but Pablo held him back and dragged him towards the door, he wasn't going to get into trouble with his own brother, that dame was a real bitch, didn't he see?

Berto was in the car, his skin ashen and a remembrance of fear in his eyes. Did Carlos feel bad? He should just vomit it all up at once, look, like this, sticking his finger down his throat. Carlos called Pablo, and they sat down on the curb. Across the street, the sign at the Kumaún was turned off.

"All right, explain, mulatto, go on."

Pablo handed him a handkerchief, chico, don't think about it, OK, what do you want, that's life. He talked without taking his eyes off the handkerchief, made of linen with a blue border. That's what you get for being a jerk and falling in love with a whore.

"And if I kill her, what happens?" asked Carlos, wiping off his snot.

"Then you're really done for."

"I'll stick a knife in her throat," he said, and started hitting his head against his knees. "I'll stick a butcher knife into her."

Suddenly he retched and vomited, loudly and abundantly. Pablo took the handkerchief from him but couldn't manage to keep it from getting stained. He put his hand on Carlos's forehead to hold his head, that's it, mulatto, spread your legs apart, watch the pants, easy, feel better now? Carlos vomited again and looked, cowlike, at the thread of drool falling from his mouth to the vomit, dissolving down into the whirlpool of the sewer. Then he wiped his lips with the back of his hand and stood up.

"Maybe I will kill her," he said. "If I feel like it."

Berto put his head out the car window, who was he going to kill?

"Your mother," said Pablo. "Come on, give me a cigarette."

Berto shook his index finger no, he didn't smoke, mulatto, that's why he was *strong*. Pablo leaned down over the sidewalk and picked up a butt; I'm saved, he said, like Pancho Vivo in the comics.

"You're a pig," murmured Carlos.

The light from the corner streetlamp turned bluish in the smoke. All of a sudden there was a brief, sharp bang, then the noise of shattering glass.

"A bomb," said Carlos.

Pablo took him by the arm, smiling, turn up the juice until they fry, friend. They heard the wail of two police car sirens.

"Zone two, zone two, zone two," Carlos repeated. "Corner of Toyo, corner of Toyo, corner of Toyo."

Berto came out of the car, shouldn't they get moving, fellows? This was going to be a bad scene, why didn't they go get those folks?

"You go," said Pablo, throwing away the butt as he felt his fingers burn. Berto didn't answer right away, then he clenched his fists and said he didn't want to see that fag again ever in his life, not even for a million pesos, that guy had horrible eyes.

"I'll kill her," said Carlos, "I'll whip her ass."

Pablo told him to be quiet, you're being a pain, mulatto, let it go. Berto asked himself what would have come up in the numbers and started to repeat cat, ass, death.

"With my own brother," sighed Carlos.

Two shadows turned the corner and came weaving in S shapes down the middle of the street. It's our folks, said Berto, should we give them a hand?

"As far as I'm concerned, they can fuck themselves," said Carlos.

Pablo held up Dopico, Berto almost carried Jorge and put him into the car, saying he couldn't drive, he was half-dead.

"I'll drive," said Carlos.

He went towards Jorge, who was letting out strange guttural sounds. He started going through his pockets looking for the keys, and found them along with the money. Rapidly, he hid the bills.

"Bitch, whore, and shithead," he said in a fit of rage.

He had kept up the illusion that Fanny's motive was stealing. But feeling the money, he realized it was all there, and he thought how Fanny had done it purely and simply for no reason, just to fuck with him, like Jorge, that bastard who still smelled of cider, sweat, cognac, vomit, and who now was also going to smell of saliva, the pasty saliva Carlos was letting fall onto his face.

He felt a violent yank on his shoulder and suddenly found himself knocked down onto the car seat. Pablo held him down, no, not that, mulatto, you can't do that, that man was drunk and was his brother and it was total shit to spit on him, here and anywhere else.

"Let go of me," said Carlos.

Berto Mister Cuba started wiping the saliva off of Jorge with a handkerchief, listen, Charliechaplin, do you hear me? Let me tell you so you'll get it right where you deserve it, what do you think you're doing spitting on your own brother? Leave him be, said Dopico, he threw a fit because Jorge got his little bitch to cheat on him.

"The one who got fucked over was Berto, not me," Carlos replied, starting the car.

Dopico, looking at Berto, had started singing *Caballito de San Vicente, tiene la carga y no la siente,* when the sudden lurch made him tell Carlos hold on, hold on mulatto, did he have his license on him?

"Yes," Carlos lied, speeding up.

Berto tried to keep Jorge's head by the window so he'd get some air, why did he say he'd been fucked over, coño?

"Because you lost almost three hundred bills."

Berto smiled, don't be a jerk, at most, at most, he'd lost seventeen pesos on the machines and now he was going to get them back, should they go to the plaza and see what was coming up in Castillo? Carlos agreed with a nod, turning onto Carlos III. Dopico started singing, imitating Barroso, "What came up in Castillo? / What came up in Campanario? / What came up in La China? / What won it?" Suddenly he stopped with a jolt, hey wait, hey wait mulatto, who'd taken the money that fag had gotten from Berto? Wait, coño! Carlos braked across from the Pepsi-Cola bottling plant, from which a constant dull noise emerged.

"I don't know," he said. "I think it was Jorge. Take a look."

Berto turned to Dopico, what money? But the latter was feverishly searching Jorge.

"Fuck!" he said, "there's nothing but change here."

Pablo knelt on the seat, look through the other pocket, asere, for God's sake.

"Don't be such shitheads," said Carlos. "I already searched him. There's not a damned cent left."

Dopico slapped his knee, fuck, he repeated; shitty little thief, they'd have to go find her and drag her, son of a bitch, yank her out of there, Pal, why hadn't he said something before?

"She doesn't sleep there," said Carlos, "who the hell knows where she is now?"

Berto started asking what was this money when they heard screeching brakes. The police car's doors opened, and three policemen came toward the car, guns aimed at them.

"Get out!" ordered the sergeant.

Carlos, Berto, and Dopico obeyed. Pablo tried to get Jorge out.

"Hands up!" yelled one policeman, waving his pistol.

"What's with that one?" asked the sergeant.

Pablo tried to explain, but the sergeant shoved him onto the sidewalk.

"Hands on the wall," he said, "legs apart."

Behind them, their fingers taking hold of the wall, they heard Jorge's body falling onto the asphalt. Carlos turned around automatically, and the third policeman stuck a pistol into his ribs.

"This one's hurt, Chief," reported a policeman.

"He's drunk," said Dopico.

Another policeman grabbed Dopico by the hair and hit his head against the wall. They heard the crackling of a Thompson over the monotonous noise of the bottling plant. The squad car moved around until they were focused in the headlights. At an order from the sergeant, the police started frisking them, rapidly and violently, from head to toe. The lights created an enormous, yellow circle against the wall, which vibrated to the rhythm of the factory's machinery.

"Look this way!" ordered the sergeant.

Turning around, the violent light forced them to close their eyes, and the image of the police, the cars, and Jorge was just a confused black blur. Carlos felt intense thirst and a painful need to urinate.

"Drunk as a skunk, Chief."

"Search the car."

They heard retching, Carlos opened his eyes and for a second saw Jorge vomiting in the middle of the street and the policeman searching the car, and the one who was pointing a Thompson at them, and he closed his eyes because he couldn't stand the light, or the idea that those black blurs could be announcing his death. Suddenly he felt great relief, a hissing, a wetness, and only then did he realize he had started urinating on himself. The sounds of the search speeded up. The liquid cooled off rapidly and his pants leg stuck to his skin. He felt an enormous desire to pull off his tie, as if he were choking, but he didn't dare move.

"Nothing, Chief, not even one little knife."

"Move away from there!" ordered the sergeant.

They came forward not daring to lower their hands. Coming out of the headlights' circle, their sight returned painfully. Dopico's right cheekbone was black, like a beat-up boxer. Jorge, sitting right in the street, watched the scene in silence, with the eyes of an idiot.

"They pissed on themselves like dogs," laughed the sergeant.

Under the circle of light the urine had made a puddle. Carlos looked at his pants legs, all wet, and raising his eyes met those of a policeman who said, with a fake Mexican accent:

"Less choot theem, *mi jefecito.*"

"So less choot theem then," laughed the sergeant.

"They're whorers, Chief," said the one who had searched Jorge, "look at this."

He handed over to the sergeant the picture where Fanny appeared alone, naked, and sad. Carlos made a gesture, and the sergeant caught a glimpse of it.

"You know her?" he asked, showing it to him.

"Yeah," he said, "she's a bitch."

The sergeant indicated he should lower his hands. Carlos felt a slight cramp in his fingers.

"Give me your license," the sergeant said.

"I don't have it," Carlos murmured. "I . . . he was drunk."

"Say viva Batista!" a policeman shouted at Berto.

"Viva Batista!"

"Get out of here," said the sergeant. "Some day when we see each other you'll buy me a drink, ok?"

They got into the car without looking back, as carefully as if the sides of the car were electrified. Jorge got in by himself, asking in a low voice what had happened. There was no answer. Carlos continued, very slowly, down the street where the police car had cut them off. They made the rest of the trip in silence, repeating mechanically, every time one of them got out, "At the airport tomorrow, mulatto." Half an hour later, Pablo, the last one, was dropped on the street bordered with parkinsonias and royal poncianas, and Carlos put the car in the garage. His father was sleeping, the snoring gave him away; but the light on the night table made all their caution, the shoes they carried in their hands, useless.

"Boys," said their mother, and they saw her shadow as they passed her room, "it's past five."

She found them in the kitchen. Jorge was drinking water and Carlos milk, right from the bottle.

"Use a glass. Where were you? It's almost daylight, what have you got there, Jorge?"

"Don't bug me, Mom," complained Jorge, pushing her away softly.

Carlos sat down to hide the urine stain. The kitchen, enameled in white, smelled clean. The only thing standing out was the red surface of the pantry counter.

"Did you have a good time?" their mother asked, her face wilted by insomnia, going over to Carlos and stroking his head.

"Fantastic," he said. "A really great night. Come on, fry me up a steak."

FIVE

Then his mother started shouting at him that he was crazy, and opening the door wider, he said you are too, and she, yes, crazy, and for good reason, he was going to kill her with a heart attack the day they came to tell her they'd found him out there like those poor wretches, with two bullets through the head.

"But what have I done?" he asked.

"The same as them," shouted his mother, "being young. Running around out there at night."

How could he make her understand he couldn't take being cooped up any longer? She went back to harping on her old worn-out questions, and yes, Mamá, he knew, but that torture and those killings didn't have *anything* to do with him, he'd sworn to her a thousand and one times that he wasn't involved in anything, on a stack of Bibles, he only wanted to go over to the Casino and listen to a little music, *some other* music, you know? Because he was fed up already with that same old tune.

He couldn't fool himself, going out was a betrayal, and totally crazy; but he had a furious need to see Gipsy, the remote hope, during that sinister, torrid autumn, of meeting her and shutting himself up with her to make love, listen to jazz, and smoke mariguana. He promised himself unimagined pleasures if Gipsy were there waiting for him by the Casino's swelling waves, if she'd received that frenzied message he'd never found out where to send, if while crossing a deserted street in her town she'd *sensed* that only she could deliver him from his anguish. Then he'd be happy again, like in the summer of '56, when Gipsy had shown up, barefoot, bronzed, and bossy, at the pool table, ordering him: "Teach me." He had felt an intense hatred for her because she was pretty and she knew it and she gave orders as if everyone were her servant; that was why he kept on practicing the five-fifteen combination, refining the unusual shot involving a kiss, a bank off the cushion, the ball, and twenty points. That was why, and because, if they both started to shoot, they'd have to pay for the table, and he really had no desire to degrade himself by explaining to her how all the money he had, and whatever he could pillage, beg, or find, he ought to put in the box where he was saving up to pay for Héctor's vouchers and newspapers. And so he kept on shooting without answering her, hearing those feet sliding across the floor, watching how Gipsy's dirty naked feet, buttocks, back, and blond hair went off and out of sight.

From then on he set himself to stalking her silently, like a cat. He watched her playing tennis, white, agile on the clay court, and he was happy when she lost, because then she was a capricious little beast, vomiting out obscenities in English, and that image excited him as much as the blond down in her armpits; he watched her on the green squash court, running between the three huge walls of the green squash court, chasing the ball like a dog amid the furious echo of the players' cries and the points being scored on the green squash court; and then he followed her along the seawall, and was sure that her eyes were green like the felt of the pool table, and blue like the clear, calm waters of the Caribbean in the summertime; he watched her do three flips off the high board over the swimming pool, and thought how her bathing suit was as tiny and as blue as a drop of water between her breasts and her thighs, and anxiously he followed her to the foot of the stairs leading up to the solarium, and imagined her whole, perfect, full, and absolutely naked lying beneath the sun, like a goddess made whore.

That exercise went on for months, tense, frustrating, and pleasurable like masturbation, and Carlos was certain that the Bacilli knew about it and made fun of him, and that Gipsy was playing with him like a cat with a mouse, and he promised himself again and again either to move off, or to move in on her, and the promise only lasted until the next time he saw her, always barefoot and aggressive, and he couldn't help following her like a dog. That was how he felt, alone, scorned, and in love like a dog, when on the next to last Sunday of September 1956 she showed up at night for the first time. The tea dance was smooth, the Hermanos Castro orchestra was playing "Boom-she-Boom," and he was trying to get close to Florita, struggling against the determined, starchy resistance of Florita's many net crinolines, when Pablo announced that the cops had arrived, and Berto and Jorge and Dopico asked where, and Pablo pointed into empty space, towards what at that moment was empty space for Carlos, saying take a look, please, at that insane platypus, and Carlos pressed Florita until he managed to make a turn against the beat, and there she was: a white silk dress, and the unshaven blond down in her armpits, and her skin copper, cinnamon, toasted like layers of puff pastry.

He decided to do nothing, to firmly resist that traitorous attack, that violent break with the delicate rules of the hunt he'd been carrying on for months, to put up with the teasing of the Bacilli that Pablo started, saying go on, hell, don't be a dope, go get her, and Jorge continued, the little girl's all alone, are you a man or a mouse? and Dopico and Rosendo and Berto Mister Cuba had the nerve to say to Florita don't hang around like a third wheel, give Charliechaplin a chance, that's the love of his life over there. Florita got nervous, you're all a real pain, leave us alone, and he ordered her to shut up with a look and a pinch mentally aimed at Gipsy, but which made Florita cry and forced her to bite her lip while Gipsy went on alone, dancing a slow blues, forcing him to come up with new justifications for his fear. He couldn't just move in on her with the Casino technique, pointing at her, pointing at himself, and waving his index finger in the air as if he were stirring a Cuba Libre; she wouldn't understand anything and he really had no desire to degrade himself by explaining that he couldn't buy her a drink because all the money he had, and whatever he could pillage, beg, or find, had to go into the savings he should use to pay Héctor for the second bunch of vouchers and newspapers. So he did nothing, nothing at all. He kept on watching her and hating her until the Orquesta Sensación arrived and Barroso's drunken voice proved why Barroso was, would be, will always be Abelardo Barroso in little Cuba the beautiful, and he reminded them all how since 1920 he'd been plucking those chords, struggling with those sounds, *negra*, and nobody never come close to me. That was when the Rueda started up. Now Carlos was in his element. Gipsy kept on dancing alone, and he entered the outside circle, thinking that she might know how to do three flips from the diving board, but she was incapable of doing even one turn on the granite dance floor, and if she got it wrong, if she dared enter into the Rueda, if by accident she snuck into the middle of the triple circle of couples, she was going to be screwed, because there he was king and he was ready to spin her, defeat her, and humiliate her in front of Barroso and the Bacilli.

The Rueda was wild that night. The sixty couples had divided into three concentric circles—ten in the first, twenty in the second, thirty in the third—and the small circle turned to the right and the middle one to the left and the outside one to the right, and you had to dance without looking to the side so you wouldn't get dizzy, because now was the bikini, a step as delicious as mamey ice cream, the bikini and then the double bikini and you had to turn yourself around and dance to the beat, go in and out and back in, not with Florita now but with Bebé, and get a glimpse of Bebé's nice breasts before letting her go and entering back in with Maggie Sánchez and with Mayra and with Nydia and with all the girls who had been sweethearts, or were, or would be, as if they were dancing at once in space and time over the smooth, sinuous *montuno* of the *son* that turned into the image of Gipsy, that aroused unicorn who was marching toward the center showing off her teeth and her skin against the stars, as if there were anyone who could stand that image without hating her. Berto said, "Kim Novak, my man," and began humming "Moonglow," but who the fuck could keep on humming "Moonglow" when Juan Pablo Miranda was creating ambrosia with his flute, ambrosia, nectar, and pure tamarind pulp with his flute, and someone had to accept the double dare of the notes and of that woman who didn't have any idea what she had gotten herself into, and Carlos said, "I'm going, my man!" said, "Leave her to me!" cried, "A la cholandengue!" and went out like a cock to the center of the ring.

The Bacilli took the party aside, held back the rhythm of the Rueda in favor of the sacrifice, and grouped all the couples into one big circle that roared its approval of the way Carlos began to dance around Gipsy, taking it to the limit, supported by Barroso's hot leathery voice, so that the orchestra and the chorus and the sixty couples called out, *Ay, mira, mamacita de mi vida!* and Barroso came back in, asking, pleading, demanding, "Give it to me mama!" while Carlos gave it to her smooth, gave it to her dirty, gave it to her like an alley cat, young and excited by the hot song of the chorus, "For God's sake squeeze me!", gave it to her proposing a cross, a square, a corner, a kite, and a drumful of steps to which Gipsy didn't know how to respond, gave it to her certain that she couldn't get away because no one left the center of the Casino Rueda until Barroso or Faz or Benny said so, and Barroso wasn't going to say so, Barroso was good that night, slightly drunk, smooth, deep into the atmosphere that got lewder and lewder, playing with the double meaning of the phrase that had only one for the dreams of everyone there, *Ay mama, mama, mama, mamacita de mi vida!* while she resisted, barely dancing, impatient, perhaps waiting for the chance to slip away, the same chance Carlos wasn't going to give her because this was the end and he had to lead her with his back turned, then attack frontally, playing, chasing, fucking in the air until the chorus was brought to a climax singing feverishly, "Mamá, mamá, mamá!" so that he could humiliate and step on a Gipsy who suddenly rallied to the assault, sang, "Mamá, mamá, mamá!" like one more of the vast, delirious tribe; she invited, lured, opened her thighs slightly, fit it in, joined tongue and groove, showed that down, blond, sweaty, obscene, that took him, would always take him into a deep delirium, full and complete, marked out by the sonorous beat of the tumbadora closing the *son*'s perfect square.

She smiled for the first time at him, not at the stars, and she left, and he happily received the excited greeting of the tribe and joined the conga line that left the club singing "*Mamelá-mamelá-mamámelavarropaconFab.*" In the street, the Bacilli lifted him up and went off the winners, as Pablo was saying to him, "Asere, if she comes on Sunday, you'll make it with her for sure, asere," and Jorge, "She won't come, she just did it to get you hot," and Dopico, "She'll come," and Berto, "She won't come," and Roberto Correa slipped in, "I think the one who came was him," and they all burst out laughing and went towards Fifth Avenue together, singing their theme song:

> We're the tuberculars
> we have the most fun,
> we spit the most blood,
> we do the least work,

and, producing a noisy onomatopoeia of throat clearing,

> Koch, Koch, Koch's bacillus,
> Koch, Koch, Koch's bacillus,
> spreads all through our lungs.

The next Sunday, the last in September, Carlos arrived at the club feeling afraid: if she was there and he didn't make it with her he'd look like a fool. He decided to passively leave it up to fate. The Bacilli were together by the swimming pool. Pablo wanted to see what Berto's biceps were like, show them off, a dromedary's coming. Berto went to the edge of the pool, lay down on his side, placed his arm in a triangle between the wall and his forehead, and pressed until the muscle swelled up under the skin and began moving in spasms, uncontrollably. The dromedary, a new girl, short and shaped like a Coca-Cola bottle, smiled when Pablo said to her, "Beauty, please have a look at the beast," and kept on going. Berto said no luck, but Pablo went on amusing himself, asking Berto to stick out his dorsals and starting to shout all around the pool, "Behold Zampanó, the world's biggest brute!" Then Bebé Jiménez and Maggie Sánchez arrived and began to squeal that Berto was wild, fantastic, a total monster, and Berto, purple from the effort, smiled in contentment.

Dopico proposed going over to the tennis courts, because behind them there was a door leading to a corridor leading to another door leading to another corridor leading to backstage at the Blanquita Theater, where the Follies Bergére chorus girls might be rehearsing with no clothes on. Pablo agreed, all those French women had to be platypuses and unicorns, and Berto clarified that no, there were some dromedaries, too. Rosendo and Jorge bought the idea, those women were the best in the world, and Carlos said no, he preferred staying in case Florita came. The Bacilli didn't believe him, he was looking for the blonde, and Carlos, no fellows, honest, and Pablo, "Pinky says the blonde goes to bed, ring finger says she doesn't, middle finger says the blonde goes to bed, pointer says she doesn't, fat finger says: the blonde goes to bed, asere!" So then let's leave him alone, conceded Berto, going off at a run down the seawall followed by Jorge, Dopico, Rosendo, and Pablo, who was yelling, "She's going to bed, asere, fat finger said so!"

He watched them go off, wanting to follow them, imagining his luck being so bad that the stuff about the French women with no clothes might be true. He hadn't stayed behind because he was waiting for the blonde, but rather precisely because he was afraid of meeting her on the courts, in front of the Bacilli. He felt an urgent need to move, went over the edge of the wall, dug in his toes, bent his knees, and leaped into the void. He did a swan dive, and in the air, while he arched his back, he spread his arms and imagined himself enveloped in a clear, deep, unlimited blue, remembered fleetingly the moment when the policeman beat Nelson, and he was scared, and he wished that death would be the exact, infinite repetition of a happy moment, as full as that one, as his body penetrated the sea heading for the bottom, intoxicated with the blur of his hair and of the legs of some woman walking along up there, high up. He surfaced, kicking slowly, gently, looked for the stairs and sat on the wall thinking about not thinking, struggling to get rid of Héctor's image and the knowledge that he was about to commit a betrayal, because that unicorn in a bikini who was coming down along the wall was her, and he knew absolutely that he was incapable of saving anymore, and he cursed himself for not bringing the money from the box.

"You're a good diver," she said, "quite good."

She lay down next to him and he didn't know what to answer and they breathed for a while in silence. She had a strong odor of something very clean and very clear, and he couldn't escape the image that obsessed him: her pubic hair had to be blond, he'd never seen a woman with blond pubic hair. He followed his line of thought with his eyes and calculated that if he moved his head a little more he might be able to see her nipple, and he thought he could glimpse a dark border, a kind of dark cherry, but he couldn't be sure where his imagination ended, and where the spots that the dazzling sun kept making him see began. On her belly, slightly protruding, began a soft line of down that died, or was born, there where her bathing suit bulged a little, next to the strong tightly held thighs, bronzed, tanned, shining with drops of sweat or salt crystals. Then he thought he glimpsed a provocative, small movement that obliged him to slide his gaze towards her legs, to control the urgent desire to bite her.

"Finished?"

She smiled, with a look exactly midpoint between provocative and mocking, and he thought the right thing to say would have been, "Still have the feet left," but he knew he wouldn't be able to pronounce a single word. He wanted to close his eyes, do a swan dive towards her, and sink himself in.

"Open your eyes."

Now it was an order, a fabulous order that he began to obey; his expression changed, thinking that death could be nothing else than the exact, infinite repetition of the instant when he kissed her.

"That's not allowed."

At first he didn't understand. He broke off the motion, impossible to continue after that grotesque pronouncement, and looked up with all the hatred of a man searching for the one who's clubbed him without warning. Standing before them was the club's police sergeant, a kind of uniformed red gorilla. Behind him, a group of swimmers observed the scene.

"Kissing in the club area is not allowed according to the rules," the sergeant informed them. Then he gave Gipsy an obscene look and went on his way.

"Forget it," she said, holding Carlos back as he tried to get up. "That's always how it is here."

"And where wouldn't it be?" he asked, looking sadly at the open sea.

"Up there." She pointed north. "You can do whatever you like, and no one bothers you."

"That's what my brother says."

"Has your brother been up there?" She opened a plastic cigarette case. "They're Kools, you want one?"

He silently accepted, drew close to light up, and the sun created a bright stab as it hit the lighter.

"No, he's just talking."

"And you?"

"I haven't been there either."

"How strange."

Carlos pulled off a splinter of cement loosened from the wall by the waves, and threw it into the sea.

"You go often?"

"I live there," she replied, inhaling the smoke with a gesture that seemed masculine to him. "My father works there and here, in the aviation business, Aerovías Q, in Fort Lauderdale. My mother's American. I'll only see you during the summers."

Carlos mentally repeated what was a type of order, but didn't dare express his annoyance. She turned over to expose her back to the sun.

"I want to get dark," she said.

"You *are* dark," he commented.

"Black," she said, "I come here to get black."

Carlos turned over, too. Their faces stayed very close, magnetized, and he saw the blue sea in Gipsy's eyes, which suddenly shone with a forbidden spark.

"Have you done it with black women?"

"What?"

"*It*," she repeated.

"No," he answered, "never."

Gipsy gave a hint of a disappointed smile, threw away her cigarette, and closed her eyes.

"I want to sleep," she said.

She turned her head away. Carlos thought of leaving, but now he had Gipsy's blond head of hair like a blaze before his eyes, and just by leaning on his elbow, he could look at her back that narrowed at the waist and rose up into round buttocks. "She's got a black woman's ass," he thought. He looked at her for a while and was dreaming about having her when she sat up with a gymnast's quick movement.

"I have to go see Helen," she said. "She has dyspnea."

"Who?"

"Helen, my mother."

"She has what?" he asked, sitting up and lifting a knee to hide the bulge in his crotch.

"Nothing. She invents illnesses because she doesn't like it here. She hates the heat, the humidity, the language, the blacks."

"And you, you like it?"

"*So-so*," she replied, standing up.

Her legs were spread apart, with her navel in Carlos's face, while she made her hips swivel lightly and bit her lips.

"See you at the dance," she said. "*Bye.*"

He closed his eyes, let the cigarette fall, kissed the air, and heard a chorus of fluty voices sounding out the syllables: "Skin-ny-son-of-a-bitch!" He recognized Dopico, Pablo, and Berto.

"That's always how it is here," he said.

He stood up thinking how he didn't have a goddamn cent to pay for Gipsy that night, and suddenly felt himself in the air. The Bacilli had lifted him up and were running with him on their shoulders along the wall, to throw him into the water. He didn't have time to spin in the air and took a burning blow on his side. Up above, the Bacilli were singing:

> We sell lots of chamber pots,
> We sell lots of chamber pots,
> We sell lots of chamber pots,
> And give a Christmas bonus!

When he saw her again he had a headache because he hadn't had lunch or dinner, to save the peso in his pocket. Now he knew he was a traitor. He'd break the piggy bank and wouldn't pay Héctor for his vouchers or his newspapers, and all the money he could find, pillage, beg, would be spent on that woman in the center of the ballroom, stopped there on the northeast of the compass card, wearing a beige dress so close to the color of her skin that it made her seem naked. When he joined her, the Bacilli struck up their anthem, and the only defense he had was to take her far away from the orchestra to dance. Then he realized the long lament splitting the air was the beginning of "You and You Alone," and it was her singing in a slow, fluent, somewhat hoarse English, playing a slow game with the orchestra, slipping her left hand behind his neck and hotly fitting herself along his body. Up to that point it was a great blues rhythm, but then the orchestra broke into "Naricita fría," a big cha-cha-cha for the band that played out the explosive capacities of the brass to the limit, and the Rueda started up and she wanted to join and he had to say no.

He had bet his whole hand, because Gipsy was a lot more explosive than the brass in the orchestra, but there would have been nothing worse than taking that dare. The Rueda was a brotherhood, a sect, a kind of dance religion in which only the cardinals could participate, or some opportune victim, some unhinged female who would risk involving herself in the carnival, where she would be made into a sacrifice, nailed, raped, burned, branded with the flaming iron of the *son*. It had gotten started by accident, in the area around the orchestra, a circle that penetrated into the western edge of the big ballroom like the prow of a little boat. Sunday after Sunday a founding brotherhood met there, imitating in their dance and walk certain lewd, elegant, and rhythmic gestures of Havana's blacks. Little by little they went on inventing a style that wasn't that of the blacks anymore, wasn't as free and spontaneous and fresh as that of the blacks at the dances at La Tropical, but was still beautiful, a bit spectacular, choreographic, arranged, and in its own way lovely, sensual, and savory like the *son*.

When the four hours of tea dance became too little, they started meeting around the Victrola behind the billiard room; first they went on Saturdays, then on Thursdays and Saturdays, later on Tuesdays, Thursdays, and Saturdays. The old cha-cha-cha moves—the *yerro* and the *tirapaquí*—for them became obsolete. They started to double-step, maintaining the basic three-step dance structure, but stepping twice on each one, thus achieving an adjustment in the rhythm that was perfect, sensual, and hot. They made up a new center move, the *cuadrao*, which had ins and outs and allowed a couple to cover the room chasing each other through the counterpoint of rhythm with harmony, like cats in heat. When anyone asked what kind of dancing that was, they invariably replied: Casino style. On Sundays they had an audience, the initial success inspired imitation, and several groups of couples started combining their efforts to make up figures. One night twelve of them got together and started improvising; that night Benny was singing.

Benny was cool, submerged in alcohol, he said, with no teeth, he said, and he smoothed out his long, wide jacket, like a *chuchero*'s, and looked like a golden bird as the huge band sounded out the *primera* and he said, "All right!" and realized that the dance floor had a team he could work with, and he started pressing his tribe hard, giving more and asking more of the dancers, to take them flying with his *son* all the way to the *icuiricuiricui*, he said, higher with every number, until he got to "Castellanos" and "Mi son Maracaibo," which came out brilliantly, hot like the center of the sun, of the *son* that he, that very Benny Moré himself in person, conducted, danced, sang with that smooth voice, all crystal, steel, and copper, forcing the team to follow him, through the congas, through the horns, to let go turning, playing, inventing steps that later on would be called the bikini, the double bikini, the let-it-go-and-don't-let-go, but that back then were only Benny's moves, answers from the dancers, that unified body, sweaty, knowing, delirious, and happy up to the moment when the congas gave the last sounds of the *son* and Benny's tribe started gathering up their pieces.

That night the Rueda was born. Carlos, Jorge, and Pablo called it the Toque for a while, because from the start, it reminded them of the flaming nights in the ravine. Sometimes they were transported back to those days, and they liked playing a number by the Orquesta Aragón over again on the Victrola:

> Oh divine Being,
> Tiembla Tierra,
> pray for both of us.

But all that reminded them, too, of the police, and the fear, and other people thought that Toque sounded too black, and the Rueda kept being the Rueda, a superior and enviable level of the dance religion that could be aspired to by initiates only if they mastered the seven secrets of Casino style, and if they punctually attended the dance masses on Tuesdays, Thursdays, and Saturdays, the musical vessel where, week after week, concoctions were distilled to start off Sundays. That was where they invented the circles, when the Rueda grew so much it threatened to burst, and the collective, universally approved decision emerged to put the limit at sixty couples. From then on, the Rueda grew in depth, not in breadth: whoever made a mistake on Sunday had to accept the disgraceful punishment of being expelled in front of everyone, and giving up his place to a new couple. That was a disaster Carlos couldn't have happen; he'd done enough by going off alone to teach Gipsy, a liberty he could allow himself the luxury of taking, despite the Rueda's mistrust, as a member of the powerful brotherhood of the Bacilli.

It was a problem that didn't worry him much, because Gipsy was a good dancer, Gipsy was music, and in two, at the most three months he'd have the pleasure of rejoining the Rueda with a golden unicorn on his arm. Now they were off by themselves, they were dancing to "Cicuta tibia," traveling through the four cardinal points, sheltering in the protected ports of the compass card, and going out again into the sea of that danzón, of that knowing musical poison of Ernesto Duarte, when someone, a woman, made a face at Gipsy from the door, and she shouted, "Go to hell!" in English and dragged him by the wrist out to the seawall. He sensed he shouldn't ask any questions. They sat silently for a long time, looking at the long coastline, the slow lights of the eastern beaches that suggested the beginning of another city, far away, in Coney Island. She started singing a lament, a plea, a kind of earthly mass that narrated a nocturnal story, tender, painful, and happy.

"What's that?"

"It's Ella's 'Summertime.' "

The sea was dark and calm. A boat hauling sand dragged slowly along the coastline. Inside the ramshackle wooden cabin, by the light of a bare bulb, you could see the owner, alone.

"Who do you think that man could be?" asked Carlos. "What's his name?"

She pulled him to her without answering, and kissed him.

"Look for me the next time," she said, before running off.

It took many Sundays for Carlos to convince himself that the next time was next summer, next year. It was then that he first began to grasp the idea of time, and the ambiguity of words: the next time really meant something immensely far away.

During that time he got more involved in the struggle, but one fine day the shootings, the beatings, and the fear he felt at a student demonstration distanced him from everything, and he withdrew into himself. After that he found Fanny, had her, and lost her, and then he ruminated on his ruin by the violet winter sea, prepared to wait until May, or until never, which was what he thought sometimes when he got sad and the club seemed painful and gloomy. Everything was going wrong. The Bacilli almost didn't exist. Jorge had left. His father had kept him from going back to classes. Héctor was in jail, and Mai was underground, maybe armed by now. Fanny was a bitch, but even so, he couldn't manage to get rid of her disgusting memory. The only thing he had enough of was money. The building was doing well, and between a raise in his allowance and Berto's cash, he had more than 250 pesos, which he carefully saved to spend on Gipsy.

One Sunday in March of '57, he was walking along the seawall with what was left of the Bacilli, when he saw two girls coming towards them from the opposite direction; she was behind them. She was smiling, as if she'd been following him silently since he walked onto the beach. He started running, forgetting about the moss the sea makes on the cement, and he slipped. He could hear her laughter before falling on his back into the water, going under, and coming up, dizzy, with the sharp taste of salt in his throat, doubting until he saw her again, still laughing, the very image of joy outlined against the sun. Suddenly he lost her, and she reappeared in the air, and submerged like a goddess, and came to the surface with some seaweed in her hands.

"Go down," she ordered, "swim through my legs."

Under the water, while he oriented himself towards that undulating body, Carlos thought about all the time he'd spent finding a simple, appropriate greeting, like *hi* for example, only to have it all be worthless facing Gipsy. Now he was touching the blurry edges of her legs, giving a slight push to bend them and slide between them, but when he had, Gipsy closed them tight, forcing him to push against her sex with his head, and with his elbows into her thighs. The pincers started to open, and Carlos understood that he could, that he should, flip himself over, that she desired as intensely as he did for his body to make the turn it had started to make, that ended when she trapped him again and there was no other way out than to grasp her buttocks and drive himself through, rubbing his chest along her sex, his sex along her sex, until she grabbed him by the hair and pulled him to the surface. Up above, the sergeant was banging the edge of the wall with his stick.

Carlos wanted to swim west to avoid the policeman, but Gipsy insisted on coming out by the stairs and going along the wall.

"Give me your cards, both of you," said the sergeant.

"*What are you talking about, you dirty cop?*" she muttered, without looking at him.

She gathered up her cigarette case, her radio, her robe, and glasses, and began walking away, followed by Carlos. At first the sergeant stayed glued in place, then he tried to make a gesture, a grotesque move that blended respect and courtesy, as if to help her, but she stopped him cold:

"*Go to hell, bastard. Leave me alone, will you?*" And then, while lying down on a lounge chair: "That's how you have to treat them here."

"And up there?" asked Carlos, doing the same.

"There they don't mess with you, if you're white."

"My brother's there."

"Really?" she asked, very happily. "Tell me about it."

"Nothing to tell," he said. "He left."

Gipsy turned on the radio, a little Zenith with a very long antenna.

"Where is he?"

"In New York."

"I'm from the South," she noted, without moving the dial. The radio emitted a high, earsplitting whistle.

"What did you do this year?"

She took out a cigarette. The case was new, made of silver, with a lighter in the top. Vicentico Valdés started singing "Mambo suave" on the radio.

"Helen didn't want to come, she says this country's in an uproar, I had to force her."

Carlos shuddered a little and took her hand.

"She invents illnesses," she added. "I don't know why she doesn't just die."

He brought her hand to his lips and kissed it. They didn't speak for a while. Across from them the Biltmore's crew was practicing, its oarsmen maintaining even, obsessive strokes. Orlando Vallejo started singing "Serenata en Batanga."

"Shit!" she yelled suddenly, pulling away her hand and turning off the radio.

"It isn't shit," he replied, "it's music."

"Jazz is music," Gipsy said quickly. "Do you know jazz? Have you heard Satchmo, Ella, Bessie, Duke, Charlie the Bird?"

"I've heard a little of them," he said vaguely.

"Well then, *that's* music."

"Benny Moré is music too."

"Chano Pozo is music," she said vehemently, as if Carlos had declared the opposite. "Chano Pozo was the only one from here who changed jazz a little."

"Pérez Prado is music!" shouted Carlos.

Gipsy, confused, moved around in her lounge chair.

"ok," she conceded, "mambo."

The oarsmen picked up the stroke, and the boat turned into a black dot on the horizon. Carlos took her hand again and brought it to his face.

"I was in jail," he murmured. "They tortured me."

She looked at him, terrified.

"They snuffed out cigarettes on my back," he added with a bitter smile. "They pulled out my fingernails."

He smiled to see her moved, unsettled, starting to touch his back, then his hands, finally holding him with tenderness.

"Now you're mine," she said, "now you're with me."

And she started to talk to him about snow, which sometimes was dirty, sometimes blue or golden, you could never know, you had to see it. One day they'd go together from Fort Lauderdale north, all the way to the St. Lawrence River, without Helen. He was following her words, seeing the snow, blue, golden, white, traveling from the heat towards the river with her in a convertible, when at the mention of Helen he noticed intense hatred on her face. She had to go see her, they'd find each other later that night, *bye*.

She showed up walking along the small pathway surrounding the saltwater swimming pool. The Hermanos Castro Orchestra was playing "Even Queen Elizabeth Does the Danzón" again and the Rueda had started turning, but they didn't want to go out onto the dance floor. They stayed by the sea, lighted by the full pale moon.

"What did you think about while they were torturing you?"

"About not talking, about the compañeros. It's better to forget about that."

He leaned against the railing and passed her a packet of mint-flavored Adams gum. She took five pieces.

"I like Double-Bounce better," she commented.

"Since you were smoking Kools . . ." he murmured, a little put off.

She blew a bubble that burst, covering her lips like a membrane.

"Take it off me," she said.

He started pulling it in as if he were smoking her lips, then he passed it back to her and got it back again, purged of any flavor but the one he was imagining. The Orquesta Sensación had started their set, and Barroso's voice opened up like a cave, an owl, a train, a flag against the border of night:

> I painted a hazy Matanzas,
> the cave in Bellamar,

"It's beautiful here," she said.

> but I still needed
> to paint the owl's nest.

"In Cuba? Say it."

> I painted the crossing
> where a lovely train goes by,

"It's beautiful in Cuba."

a machete and a rifle
and a gunboat,

"Say it again."

and I didn't paint the flag
for which I will die.

"Cuba," she said against his lips, and they kissed for a long time, licking each other, biting each other, inspired by the montuno's obsessive repetition, *Chupa la caña, negra*! and by the excited chorus from the Rueda that reached the sea like an order: *Chúpala! Chúpala! Chúpala*!

Suddenly she pulled away and stared at him.

"Did you kill someone?"

"Yes," he answered with a terrifyingly cold voice. "I killed."

"Sometimes I'd like to kill Helen. She wants to leave."

When they started kissing again Gipsy was crying, and the kiss was long, wet, and salty, and her eyes, close up and blue, were the perfect image of death towards which Carlos felt himself descending in a shudder, when she pressed his sex through his pants, and he felt it move and vomit like a wild, dying animal.

"Take me in to drink," she ordered. "I want to drink rum."

He spent all week remembering how intense things got between them, the hard way Gipsy drank, her systematic refusal to see him anywhere but at the Casino, her stubborn insistence that he didn't know Helen, didn't know what Helen was capable of, didn't know who Helen's friends were, and above all, her sinister certainty that she'd wind up killing her. When the tea dance ended she was pale from the alcohol, knocked out, and he didn't know what to do because she refused to give him her address. Carlos headed for the door, Dopico's advice following him, he had money, didn't he? So take her to a hotel. Then Pablo's protests, who was going to deal with José María if this guy didn't go home to sleep? And Berto's suggestions, put her in a cheap hotel, give it to her a couple of times, and leave a note for the attendant: "Her name is Gipsy. She's American. She's drunk. Please take care of her." He got to the door feeling like everything was a disaster, carrying her on his shoulders, and suddenly an elegant young man commented with a bored tone, "Again?" and asked Carlos to please take her to the car, pointing out a blue Triumph TR2.

Now he was remembering how he had obeyed without asking questions, because it was obvious the man had something to do with Gipsy. But today it was Sunday again, five in the afternoon, and she hadn't shown up. He wandered along the beach like a zombie, feeling a dreary sense of defeat. There was another Gipsy, unknown, alien, and therefore enemy, into whose world he would never enter. He found himself thinking about some foolproof way to kill Helen and the guy with the car and her father so they could be alone, together forever: she would appear in the middle of the big ballroom absorbed in some game, some complicated, strange operation, staring at the spot that was now the sun, the sky, the sea, the clouds high, dense, deeply red. Then he would encircle her from behind, from a distance, in silence, while she went forward under the scarlet summer sky, jumping from one point to another on the great compass card, navigating among the signs, escaping the reefs, the storms, and suddenly she would stop under the one last, tenuous, reddish ray of sun, and call him to start the journey together, slowly following the long coral reefs, unfurling only those sails whose colors would inexorably resemble the bottom of the waters encircling that far-off northeastern island where they would live, for ever and ever.

"Are you Carlos?"

He nodded, startled and confused. The guy handed him a note. He was the same one who had taken Gipsy the previous Sunday.

"She says you should come," he said, leaving.

Half an hour later Carlos stopped in front of the door to an apartment in Miramar. Gipsy opened it before he rang the bell, as if she'd been watching for him. She took his hand, whispered, "Helen is here," and he thought he caught her smiling like someone planning a macabre joke. He let her take him along; suddenly he tightened up, seeing two blurred figures in front of him. Then he almost started laughing, it was the two of them reflected in the huge, sepia-toned living-room mirror. They were submerged in the afternoon penumbra, and Carlos could barely make out the green granite floor. On the far wall you could guess at a terrace, and past it the pine trees on the street and the wind whistling through the branches and the monotonous sound of the sea.

Gipsy led him to a short, side staircase that went up to a hallway lined with doors. They went through the last one. The penumbra in the room was torn by lights filtered through the glass doors of another terrace, reflected in a side mirror. "A closet door," he thought, while he automatically flattened himself to the wall, as if seeking protection. Now she was a shadow, curled up in a ball on the bed.

"Why did you do it?"

"What?" he asked. "What did we do?"

"The attack at the palace," she said. "Now Helen wants to leave, and Helen's going to go."

Carlos went towards the bed, murmuring:

"And you?"

"Helen's taking me, I'm Helen's prisoner."

He searched for her face, trying to figure out if she was crying, but she shied away from his hand. Then he felt his way over the mattress as if he were swimming, until he reached the lamp and turned on the light. She wasn't crying, she had a fierce look.

"It wasn't my group," he said.

On the nightstand there was a bottle of Johnnie Walker Black Label, a glass, a plate with the remains of an anchovy fillet, and a pair of panties. She poured herself three fingers and drank them down in one gulp. When she bent her head down her hair covered her face, and she smoothed it back, exposing her unshaven armpits.

"Helen's there, downstairs," she said, with a resentful smile.

He automatically looked toward the door. There were some dirty blue jeans on the knob. On the wall, a picture of someone he didn't know.

"She won't come up?"

"She's off in the clouds. We gave her a fix."

"A fix?"

Gipsy pulled her skirt up over her thigh, imitated an injection, a brief moment of pain, an intense rubbing, and a sensation of brutal, unbridled pleasure.

"Helen shoots up," she said.

Carlos asked her for a drink, and the hot, dry taste of the whiskey helped him conceal his shock.

"Daddy hides it from her, and Helen goes crazy and starts tearing everything apart. John and I found the hiding place, and now she leaves us alone if we give her a fix."

"Do you shoot up?"

"It scares me," she confessed, drinking again. "Once I injected myself with water, but not with drugs, it scares me. Doesn't it scare you?"

"I smoke."

"Marijuana?"

"Guana. Mari-guana."

She moved forward on her knees over the bed. Her face reflected the same interest as when he talked to her about torture. She got to the edge and sat in an Asian position, with her buttocks on her feet.

"Did you bring any?"

"No."

"How do you do it?"

He remembered the way he'd seen the sharps smoking at the Arco billiard hall, across from the Instituto; he held a cigarette between the tips of the index finger and thumb of his left hand, so it was covered by the palm and the other fingers, brought it to his lips, and took a puff.

"Then you pass it around," he said, passing it to her.

She repeated the operation with impressive skill. The closet mirror returned their images and Carlos thought about the room with round mirrors and Fanny.

"How does it make you feel?"

"Like you're being kissed," he said. "When you really smoke, you feel like you're being kissed."

"Listening to jazz," she remembered. "I'm going to teach you about jazz."

When she jumped off the bed to look for the records, he got a glimpse of her blue panties and a dark blotch, thought about how his obsession was there, and asked her to sing "Love Me Tender." She started singing, and the song was a call, a slow howl of desire that lasted as he went towards her, gauging their images in the mirrors so that when they started dancing, tearing off their clothes and making love in a primitive, immediate way, they saw themselves repeated to infinity, as if they were all the couples of the world.

They ended up lying on the cold granite floor. The wind howled at times through the edge of the glass door, like a wild animal.

"Help me to kill her," she asked. "John's afraid to. It's easy."

"How?"

"I give her more and more drugs, and . . . who's to know?"

He looked at her, terrified. Beneath the tenuous light of the night lamp, her face had a sinister innocence.

"Who is John?"

"Helen's friend. You met him. Do you want to see her?"

He refused, thinking she meant going down to see Helen on drugs, but now Gipsy was coming back from the night table and showing him two postcards. Helen was Gipsy twenty years older, and she was still very lovely, a little heavier perhaps, taller, and she was completely naked in both photos.

"Give me another drink," Carlos asked.

Gipsy laughed as she passed him the bottle, roaring to see him fake indifference to the photos, and he decided to take a long, drawn-out drink, and then calmly take a careful look at them. In the first, Helen was more or less sideways, recreating a fake gesture of surprise, her lips forming an O, her fingers covering her nipples and her left leg squared across, covering her sex. In the second she was facing the camera, squatting, with her arms, legs, and sex obscenely spread open.

Gipsy threw out a little laugh, short and hysterical.

"You like them?" she asked, before starting to roar with laughter.

"She looks like you," Carlos replied. "Don't you have any of you?"

"No," she said, "I haven't had any done yet."

"You're just like Fanny," he murmured.

He watched her go over to the phonograph. Her skin had the warm, toasted color of certain woods; she put on "Stardust," and the melody seemed to slowly wrap tightly around her buttocks.

"Is Fanny black?"

"No, she's just like you."

"John likes black women. He goes off with black women and Helen can't stand it, and I have to shoot her up."

"Oh," said Carlos.

"John says I'm like a black woman," she said, drinking from the glass.

She was giving off an arousing odor, vaguely sour, and her armpits, and surely her crotch, too, were sweaty, and now the melody had exploded and the piano wrapped around her breasts and the trumpet penetrated her sex, that great yellow blaze to which she forced him to descend, and submerge himself amid the most obscene, delicate, bestial words of love.

Then there came a long drowsiness, and sleep, and he woke up dizzy. The phonograph needle was scratching the record over and over, and the clock showed three in the morning. He tried to wake her up with little slaps on her cheeks, and she murmured, "*Oh John, John, go to hell,*" and turned her back to him. The wind howled through the pine branches. He thought he heard a noise downstairs. He stayed still, lying in wait, but the noise did not repeat. Could it be his nerves? Two, three cars passed by on the avenue and he always confused their motors with John's Triumph. He decided to leave. He left a note: "I'll see you this Sunday, or next time. Carlos."

But the summer of '58 was devoured by fear. Gipsy didn't come, and Carlos gradually plunged into a perpetual feeling of terror totally different from that of his childhood or adolescence, without a drop of magic or mystery, as primitive and brutal as being arrested because you were under thirty, whether you were guilty or innocent, and for that they would pull out your fingernails, put out your eyes, cut off your balls, and throw you in some barren place. To protect himself or to protest, he never really knew which, he stopped going to class, and carried out a strict code of the Three Zeros—zero shopping, zero movies, zero clubs. He withdrew inside himself, until he went crazy remembering Gipsy, with an intolerable suffocating feeling he decided to break, despite his mother's stubborn opposition and his knowledge that it was a betrayal and totally crazy, that torrid October night when he walked around the Casino just to confirm that the Bacilli no longer existed, that no one was dancing the Rueda now, that Gipsy had never gotten the message he never sent to her in Fort Lauderdale.

As he went out, he was pondering his frustration and fear, when a car stopped behind him. He thought of running, but suddenly he felt weak, flimsy like a rag. In a heartbeat he felt this was the end, that Héctor or Mai, ground into pulp in some torture chamber, had given his name.

"Carlos."

He almost cried on recognizing his father's voice saying nothing is wrong, get in the car. But something was wrong. His mother was inside and she held onto him, trembling like a little leaf. They moved forward in silence until they got to the Línea tunnel, with fear settling into the car like a fourth passenger. Then his father said:

"They shot a boy across from the building."

"Dead," murmured his mother.

She spoke without emphasis, and for him that made even more terrible this revelation that, for the first time, touched him so closely and began the final phase of his confinement. But not even stuck at home could he escape fear's domination. One night he woke up sensing someone in the room and saw his parents peeping out the window. Two patrol cars were parked across from Pablo's house. Three police thugs were talking inaudibly, in low voices. The door was open. "We have to warn them," he murmured, then went silent realizing the stupidity of what he'd said: the other thugs were already inside, searching the house. They stayed there, without moving, for almost an hour, his mother muttering prayers, he and his father with the secret hope that her unending plea could somehow help their friends in misfortune. Suddenly

Carlos broke out into a cold sweat: Héctor's vouchers and papers were in the night table. He didn't even dare to move away from the window, any little sound could attract the attention of the attack dogs. He started praying for himself until Pablo's father came through the doorway, surrounded by four policemen, followed by his wife and son, and got into the backseat of a patrol car that left without the slightest sound, sliding down the hill. Then his father crossed the street and a few minutes later came back with Pablo and his mother, while Carlos, locked in the bathroom, burned Héctor's vouchers and papers.

They were dark times, his father's business took a dive, but he never took even a cent from Rosario, who left Pablo with them while she set out on a pilgrimage through the precincts and jails. Pablo was terribly depressed, and for Carlos, the masters of the night continued to be fear, longing for Gipsy, and a sadness barely broken by the exploding bombs that made the city tremble, and the encouragement of Radio Rebelde, and that announcement that Consuelito Vidal repeated night after night on the television: "You have to have faith, everything comes in time!"

A bloody Christmas season came. For the first time that Carlos could remember, there was no celebration at his house. The family gathered in a somber ritual. His father informed them he was going to go back to his old job as a cigar salesman, business was bad, no one could pay what they owed, he was thinking . . . He went silent, looked at Carlos's mother with unusual tenderness, and then, speaking to him, "about sending you north with your brother, because today in this damned country it's unlucky to be young."

Carlos jumped for joy thinking he'd finally be able to see Gipsy, sleep with Gipsy, come back to life with Gipsy, but how? he suddenly thought, if that country was so big and maybe Fort Lauderdale . . . ? Ten minutes later he was leaning over a map, looking for that sacred town, now so close, calculating in inches how far it must be from New York, telling himself that Jorge would help him, startled when three bomb blasts went off and Rosario, as was her habit, crossed herself giving thanks to God.

The poor woman's nerves were in shreds, she ranted and raved in public against the government and ended up cheering for Fidel, even when she could see nearby police, who, for some unknown reason that made Carlos think about the Old Man with the Crutches, always kept on going, limiting themselves to branding her a crazy woman, as he himself was at the point of doing when he opened his eyes that New Year's morning and saw her wrapped in the flag, waltzing around, tra-la-la-ing and laughing between uncontrollable sobs while he kept repeating, "What's going on, Rosario?" certain that anguish and fear had completed their work, that they'd all been living too long in terror for such a fragile woman not to wind up in a breakdown. And then his parents and Pablo came in, transformed, and he asked himself if the impossible could have happened, if he finally could be happy with Gipsy, if they could have been freed once and for all from fear, and from wanting it so much he *couldn't* believe it, and he shouted "No!" "Yes, boy, yes!" exclaimed his father, and Rosario opened the window and stuck her head outside, "Down with Batistaaaaa!" and his parents and Pablo, at the top of their voices, "Dooooown!" and then he knew that yes, it was true.

And it was as if the whole world had gone mad, or as if Rosario had been sane all along, since the tragic days, now incredibly far away, when she cheered for Fidel right in the street. Now they were all doing it, they hugged and kissed each other all the time, learned to sing the 26th of July Anthem and surrounded Pablo's father, who came back as thin as a wire, the marks of torture still fresh, to guarantee, compañeros, that from today on everything in Cuba would change forever.

Carlos had to wait for a whole unending month before the Casino offered a Great Freedom Tea Dance, and then he headed for the club preparing himself not to find Gipsy, telling himself he'd have to wait for the summer. But now, when the Banda Gigante began to practice and you could hear the sounds of alto and tenor saxes, and the trombone bellowed, roared softly, and the trumpets scarred the cold, pale night air, and now it was certain that only a few minutes later, when fireworks burned the night, Bartolo, Belisario Moré, el Benny would say to a woman, would sing softly into her ear, *vidaaaaaa . . .*, precisely now Carlos began to dream again of Gipsy, taking Benny's words to recite to Gipsy, since I met you there's no one else but you; now, when Don Roberto Faz's great head passed under the canopy and Pablo and Berto and Dopico came out of the car and found tons of friends and acquaintances and everyone cursed that damned '58 and in a flash they put together a colossal chorus right there in the street, cheering the 26th of July and Cuba Libre; now all that was missing was to see her there, waiting for him, for the world, *his* world, to be complete.

Everything promised to be the same as before and even better, because fear had disappeared, being young was all the credential you needed, and his father couldn't keep him from going out at night. From the street you could see the ballroom decked out in flags, and Carlos ran inside greeting everyone with slaps on the back, shouts and smiles to friends and acquaintances. He went through the ballrooms, the pool, the courts, the billiard room, the seawall, and stopped at the purple winter sea, crying like one of the converted. He breathed in *her* smell and turned around trembling, with no time to think about hallucinations, because she herself, Gipsy herself was there, laughing, kissing him, dragging him into the ballroom and saying all in a jumble that Helen "*was fine,*" Castro was "*very nice,*" Cuba was "*a many splendored thing,*" and that now, yes, now they were really going to have a terrific time.

When they got to the large ballroom, the manager, López, was ending his introduction of the Freedom Tea Dance amid a cascade of fireworks and a wave of applause that grew to a frenzy when Faz came onto the stage, and nodding his great head, greeted them and attacked "La sitiera." The applause was a tribute to the Sonerito, the player of the *son*, to the times when the Sonerito had taken them, with his voice, to the very gates of heaven. The Bacilli started up a simple, relaxed Rueda, and Carlos took very close steps so that Gipsy would get it, and he was sure that this was the start of a whole new story. Very soon she'd be able to participate in the Rueda, and then Sunday after Sunday he'd be hanging out with the people he loved most in the world, his buddy Pablo and his brother Jorge, when Jorge returned. He had money, everything he'd saved up for two years. If that wasn't happiness, then there was no happiness on earth.

Now Faz had gone into "Castellanos," changing the words, making fun of himself with "Roberto Faz, how badly you sing" which parodied the sound of Benny's band, forcing the dancers to react, to rise to the challenge, to form a large, expanding Rueda, Robertísimo Faz and his group hitting that rich *son* right on the mark, and a trumpet sounding out like a great golden phallus, and Benny, called by the music, recognizing the tribute in all this, because "Castellanos" was a piece where Benny would say, "Benny Moré, how well you sing," and Roberto was playing with that, calling him, and Benny responded with a subtle second voice, knowing and distinct, that grew like a thin stream to spill out over Faz, who understood, saluted him, went into the background, happy to be there, together with Benny, possessing the night with their voices.

The duet had ended and the Banda was warming up when Baby Sánchez asked the Bacilli to come with him, there were some guys trying to crash the party, they were going to ruin the dance. They quickly followed him, indignant, and on the way to the door joined with other groups also ready to defend their right to enjoy themselves in peace. An argument had started under the canopy, in a horseshoe-shaped narrow street. The entryway was packed and from there you couldn't see exactly what was happening. Carlos elbowed his way through and Gipsy and Baby and the Bacilli followed him, until they got to the edge of the half-moon formed by the crowd. On the other side of it was a strange scene. On the street, head to head, were the manager and a Rebel Army captain. Behind them, the squad of club police; around the captain, a dozen soldiers.

"They're trying to crash," announced Baby.

The captain had a long blond beard, and next to him was a black lieutenant, with a tangled beard. The majority of the soldiers were mulattoes with messy, reddish kinky hair. Inside, Benny had started "Pero qué bonito y sabroso," and the music could be heard clearly at the door, where the captain and the manager were still arguing.

"It's not within my powers," López was saying.

"Then have them call whoever has the authority," the captain ordered.

López, a little man as wrinkled as a cork, let his arms fall over his belly and said something to a club policeman, who went into the building. People kept arriving, the half-moon started spilling out over the sides. With the pushing coming from behind, the Bacilli went into the street, winding up on the front edge of the semicircle. The captain took a few steps back and looked behind him several times, until he was sure there was no one there.

"Compañero, what's going on?" asked Dopico.

"We heard Benny, and we want to go see him, and they won't let us," said a rebel soldier. "They'll let the captain in, but not us, and the captain says all of us or none."

"Why won't they let you in?" asked Pablo.

The rebel soldier rubbed the back of his hand with his index finger, and Carlos shouted that this was bullshit. Pablo assured them that he had an idea, called Florita over, said something in her ear, and Florita responded that yes, anything for the rebels, and went walking over to another soldier who was dancing a few little steps alone, and asked him something.

"What's going on?" said Gipsy.

"They're black," explained Berto. "They won't let them in because they're black."

"It's a bunch of sissy crap!" said Carlos.

"What?" asked Maggie Sánchez.

"They should let them in," said Berto.

Florita had started dancing with the rebel soldier. She was somewhat uncomfortable, tense, their styles didn't fit together well. She was the best female dancer of the Casino, the queen of the Rueda, and she twirled in a choreographic way, rallying to the orchestra with the purest club style, as if saying, "Look at me, by God look how lovely I dance," and the rebel didn't understand all of that, he let himself be carried smoothly by the *son*, effortlessly, as if the music were a wave and he a fish, someone who'd always lived there and who thought it was really good, really nice and delicious, as if saying, "It's so lovely, Lord, enjoy it, *compay*," and he was so far gone that he almost didn't realize it when Berto pulled Florita away and stood in front of the group with superior hatred in his eyes.

Pablo leaped over to where the manager and the captain were and started to say, choking with rage, that this was unbelievable, compañeros, what they were seeing was, was, was, didn't they have blood in their veins? How could they dare allow this to happen? Those guys there were the compañeros, they were heroes, heroes, coño! Everyone into the club, goddammit! Twenty thousand Cubans hadn't died so that things would stay the same! Everyone into the club with the compañeros! He headed towards the door, but the captain stopped him. Baby Sánchez pulled out a pistol, a rebel soldier armed his Garand rifle, part of the crowd withdrew shrieking, others blocked the door, and the rest joined the rebels who surrounded the captain and obeyed his order:

"Put down your weapons, coño!"

Carlos had tried to go over to the group surrounding the rebels, but he stopped, stunned, when he felt Gipsy holding him back, saying: "If you go with them, you'll never see me again." "What?" he asked, and she, "You heard me." Baby had stayed by the door with his pistol in the air, shouting, "No black is going to dance here!" and suddenly a tough, mellow voice said, "No white is going to dance to my group," and Roberto Faz came out of the club and Berto asked him why, if he was white himself, and Benny, coming behind him, said he was going to sing in the street because he was white like the captain, and black like the lieutenant, and mulatto and free like Belisario Moré in Cuba Libre, and the manager said, "Cubans, Cubans, Cubans," and asked the captain for calm, telling him they could go in, watch a little, keeping some order, please, gentlemen, compañeros. Carlos desired with all his soul for the captain to go in and for his world to be at peace again, but the captain thanked the manager, they could eat their club in a cellophane wrapper, they were going, and now Benny was singing "Pa que tú lo bailes, mi son Mara-caibo" in the street, and the crowd started breaking up, some with the *son* and some into the club, and Carlos felt Pablo and Benny on one side, and on the other Gipsy's warm, wet breath, and he stood without moving, as if those pieces of himself, as they separated, were ripping him permanently in two.

SIX

"*Play it again*, Sam," said Pablo, and Carlos reread RENTS LOWERED BY 50%, while Pablo hummed *Casablanca* and the vendor kept shouting, "It's true, the poor people have been saved, this time for real," and a couple argued violently over the new law at the door of the movie theater.

Carlos felt a sudden sensation of joy that was quickly interrupted when he thought of his father, who now, without a doubt, really would have a heart attack. The first warning had taken place two months earlier, two months that seemed like years, because so many things had happened that time had acquired the strange quality of becoming instantly far in the past, overtaken by new, unforeseen, thunderous events. So the remote times that he was now remembering in actuality had to do with the night, still not so long ago, when they watched Fidel on the television at home, all sitting comfortably on the sofa, amazed by his frankness and totally unprepared for the words he pronounced with calm emphasis: "Don't pay back the moneylenders."

José María took perhaps a minute to react, his left eye blinked spasmodically two or three times, and suddenly he jumped out of his seat and turned off the television. Carlos stood up intending to protest and encountered his father's face, purple and with the large vein in his forehead pulsating like a blue snake.

Now Pablo was green, dancing under the light of the Capri marquee with Lauren Bacall, *bacán*, as he was saying, like Hunfry Bogar, he was saying, and Carlos invited him to go together to Central Park thinking about the color of memories. The ones that had to do with his house were gray, like his father's ill face, and like the ratface of their family doctor when he said: "Don't go against him. A heart attack would be fatal. It's your responsibility." It was obvious that the doctor was gray because he was scared, with an uncontrollable fear expressing itself in the sticky sweat on his hands and his stuttering when he told them he would be leaving the country. The rebels were a bunch of melons, green outside and red inside, this was nothing but Communism, Com-mu-ni-sm, he repeated, opening his eyes wide to illustrate the enormity of the fact; how else to explain the conflicts with the Americans, the firing squads, the constant assaults on capital? On ca-pi-tal! he underlined, before narrating the tragic odyssey of his parents, who fled from barbarism halfway through Europe, always followed by the *specter*, as Karl Marx himself would term it; rampant in the somber Moscow of the fearsome Lenin, reborn in the horrible Budapest of the execrable Bela Kun, stalking the convulsed Berlin of the Jew Rosa Luxemburg, howling through the streets of Rostock, made red by the insatiable Karl Liebknecht, his two parents finally managed to embark on a packet with no destination that brought them, only God knew how, to the shores of this paradise that very soon, mark his words, would be hell.

Carlos shivered from that horrifying account, but the prediction seemed absurd to him; it had nothing to do with what was actually happening. His father was a moneylender, and he remembered all too clearly that business, and knew that the Revolution had liberated the poor from the pressures of loans, after burning down the smoky slum with the fires of justice and turning over to its inhabitants a whole new city, almost a resort, full of sun and surf. Clearly, he concluded this could *not* be Communism.

But it was *politics*, and that simple word was enough to bring on a bile attack in his father.

"What are you going to get from getting involved in all that shit?" he would say. "Where's it going to get you, huh? Don't you realize that in revolutions, the sharp guys always come out winning and the fools lose? Don't you realize my grandfather went to war in '68 and my father in '95, and that I was in the literacy campaign in '30, and we lost it all and not even one of those damned promises was kept? Don't you realize that revolution is the business of operators? That in this country, anyone who can't be a doctor, a lawyer, or mayor, or senator, starts shooting a gun to do business with the dead? Don't you see how the only thing that politicians do is take advantage of shitheads like you to get themselves into power? Come on, tell me, what did Batista do in '34, and Grau in '44, and Prío in '48, and Batista again in '52? You see? You can't answer. The only reason this fucking island hasn't sunk is that it's made of cork, goddamit, otherwise by now we'd all have been eaten by sharks!"

The thought of his house paralyzed him; it was still gray because the doctor ordered it shut up tight, saying that José María had been particularly clear-thinking when he turned off the TV, they should warn their friends and not buy the newspaper, or listen to the radio, any news from outside could raise his blood pressure to an intolerable level and provoke a fatal outcome. Now that news was here, and the worst thing was that it was just, too just not to get to his father somehow. The cancellation of debts through usury had caused him to lose almost five thousand pesos and his business, but the income from the building allowed him to ride out the situation without having to resort to the savings put away in a box he had moved from the pawn shop to his house, following Manolo's suggestion. Now, suddenly that income was reduced by half, and that could not be hidden from him. Nothing would stop disaster, except for Jorge's arrival. His father was waiting anxiously for him, and so was Carlos, sure that Jorge would help him make the old man understand that with the tyrant's fall, a new and different country was being born, the one his letters from New York greeted with such enthusiasm.

He was filled by a sad envy thinking how Pablo's father, co-owner of the building, supported the Revolution, and Pablo could be happy without reservation, while Carlos preferred to hide in the movies. That was where he had taken refuge to forget Gipsy, and he had wound up becoming as addicted as an alcoholic. He had a tumultuous romance with Marilyn, he saw her in exclusive cinemas and sordid little theaters, in ecstasy over her legs, her breasts, her smile, hating the lights that always frustrated his illusion, until he stole from a neighborhood movie theater the picture showing her with her skirt blown up by a gust of air, legs apart, displaying an expression of surprise both ingenuous and wicked, before which he masturbated dozens of times until the picture was yellow, and Kim Novak's green gaze dragged him back to the memory of Fanny.

He couldn't say when he succeeded in freeing himself from that nostalgia, or how Roxana's sweetness entered his soul until it became a habit. He'd started studying with her to recoup the time lost in '58, and imperceptibly he'd gotten used to her company, her intelligence and her dreams. They liked to watch the boats go out and imagine they were on deck, saying goodbye, until one day they decided to leave after they got married. It would be a beautiful wedding, she would dream, with a *ring boy* and *flower girl* and Schubert's *Ave Maria* and many, many pictures in the social pages of the *Diario de la Marina* and a *honeymoon in Mexico*. Carlos came to share the illusion, seeing himself in a tuxedo in the Carmen church with a chic smile, like Cary Grant, while

Roxana waited longingly for him in the vestibule, à la Elizabeth Taylor. But soon afterwards the *Diario de la Marina* showed its true colors, and he told Roxana he'd rather die than see himself pictured in that newspaper that was so oligarchic, a stylish little word that reminded him of lunatic, and then and there they wound up in an argument that turned out to be the beginning of the end. From that point on they broke up and got back together several times, never regaining the sweetness of their first days, until life submerged them in its whirlwind and Carlos went back to burying his loneliness at the movies.

Now he was with Lauren Bacall, giving himself a real Bacall bacchanalia at the Capri's retrospective, and he used code to force Pablo to change the subject, saying, "*High Sierra*, my man, I've got *The Big Sleep*," to which Pablo replied that's what you get for eating a *Maltese Falcon* in a *Casablanca* restaurant, and Carlos hummed the theme that had taken the place of the Bacilli's song, to keep up the gibberish and word plays that let them go on for hours communicating with each other through titles, music, phrases from movies. But all it got him was Pablo saying that now even *Casablanca* had its rent lowered, Sam, and following that line, even the *Casa de Usher*, Sam, interpreting Carlos's silence as capitulation when in reality it had to do with the return of his sadness about the problem he was trying to avoid, hidden now in the sanctuary his buddy was profaning, adding that even Father de las Casas himself, and Elia Kazan's pictures and Víctor Casaus's poetry and Kasabubu's atrocities and Alejandro Casona's plays and Martínez Casado's acting, and even things at the Kasalta coffee shop, would be cheap, Sam, although not for the *casatenientes*, who'd present casuistic arguments for cassation, but the judges would send them goddamn packing off to their castles, and what was it with this silent castigation, what was on his case anyway? It wasn't *High Noon* yet, Carlos commented randomly, and Pablo answered OK, enjoying his winning thrust, *Corral*, he said, looking over at Central Park, which was filled with students, tonight there'd be some tremendous gunfight there.

Before crossing the Paseo del Prado, Pablo pointed out the lighted sign over the Manzana de Gómez, your thing is *Mission Impossible*, Sam, even the little doll in the ad was diving head first into the water. At that moment the doll touched the neon wave, above her twinkled JANTZEN, and then she pulled herself out, going back up onto the diving board with funny little leaps that didn't make Carlos laugh. He thought how Pablo was right, you had to dive head first into the water with your clothes on, becoming part of the river of

Revolution, but he was paralyzed thinking of his father, and not knowing coño which way the current was going to flow. Since he'd gone back to the Instituto, ashamed to look at the heroes of the clandestine fight, he had gotten involved in a whirlwind of discussions that made him forget his classes and that had begun to compete dangerously with the movies, but he hadn't gotten anything clear. At first they were one big family, neither Héctor nor Mai ever reproached him for his cowardice, and he even started to imagine he'd kept on fighting. But very soon, raging polemics started over topics too abstract for him to be able to take a position. Everyone was for the Revolution, but they divided into the left and the right, and then subdivided like amoebas, the left into the 26th of July Movement, the Revolutionary Directorate, and the PSP, the right into the Auténticos and the Catholics, the Catholics into progressives and reactionaries. Each subgroup was, in turn, subdivided by unspoken fine points or questions of leadership, except for the Communists, and for Carlos this was their only, unsettling virtue. On the right he was attracted by the progressive Catholics, but he couldn't stand the reactionaries, on the left he liked the 26th of July but was afraid of the Communists. He was literally in the center, or even worse, on the fence.

They got to the area of the park where debating went on, and Pablo said, look at that, my man, the *3:10 to Yuma* was coming with Mai at the engine to climb up *The Hanging Tree*. He silently watched Mai climb onto the left bench to nail a poster into the tree. The day before, Nelson Cano had nailed the first poster over the right bench, and now Mai had brought a reply, rolling it out after securing the top edge with a dagger, and jumping back down. There was a muffled murmur of amazement, the posters looked exactly the same. They both had a photograph of a child in the center, the same child, neatly combed and innocent, and below, slogans. On the right:

WILL THIS CHILD BE A BELIEVER OR AN ATHEIST? CUBAN, YOU DECIDE!

On the left:

WILL THIS CHILD BE A PATRIOT OR A TRAITOR? CUBAN, YOU DECIDE!

Carlos never knew at what moment shouting took the place of the murmur, or who was the first to say, "You people are paid by the Vatican!" or "That's money from Moscow!" or how all the other words had disappeared and all that was left was "Moscow!" "Vatican!" "Moscow!" "Vatican!" thrown out from both sides as the worst of insults, while he and another group went over to a third bench, towards which the other two quickly went, ordering them with threats to take sides, until Roberto Menchaca answered for all:

"This is a neutral bench, No Man's Land."

He felt horribly confused, Roxana was calling him from the Vatican, Héctor gave him a sad, understanding look from Moscow, and the gunslinger Roberto Menchaca boasted loudly about No Man's Land. He thought of running away, even though they all might turn against him, but curiosity held him back. That night the left and the right would put into practice the only agreement they had reached, the inaugural meeting of the José María Heredia Circle for Intellectual Proposals, with the stated intention of turning the park debates into constructive, serious dialogue. Carlos knew—and this was what interested him—that the real objective of these debates was to measure each other's strength and gain allies for the next elections of the Student Association, when who was going to control the Instituto would be decided. There, he would listen to all of them, without shouting or anger, he'd think a lot, by himself, and he would decide whom to vote for.

The leaders left the park, dragging their groups behind. Pablo asked him, so where's the *gunfight* gonna be, my man? and started to hum the music from *Duel of Titans*. Carlos shrugged his shoulders, whatever he replied would be *The Damned Lie*. He remembered the long council meeting about a headquarters, because no organization wanted to accept a location proposed by another. Now it seemed they had come to agreement on a place, but without informing anyone else. Along the way the little bands had begun to disperse, left and right talked among themselves with a tense kind of politeness. Carlos gave into his desire to find Roxana, and was surprised by an ironic "Hi, No Man's Land," which made him answer, "How are you, Vatican girl?" while he looked away in another direction. Then he decided to say something friendly but suddenly stopped in amazement: they were entering the National Capitol building.

They moved forward silently along the long, darkened hallways and stopped in front of the six doors to the Senate meeting room, stunned by the spectacle. All the light seemed to come through the stained glass windows, green, red, with yellow flowers, and to rise up serenely to the ceiling, where they could make out several levels. On the outer edge, a vaguely Greek kind of business with matte-gold figures, then gold scalloping, an arch with gold and black marble, great gold leaf designs against a blue background, and towards the center, lavender rectangles that framed gold rosettes against an illuminated red background. The leaders went in with ceremonious silence. Carlos followed Roxana, until he discovered that the armies had divided again, and that she was offering him a seat on the right. He acted like he didn't see her and sat next to Pablo, who was on the right of the left and the left of the right, exactly in the center, in the calm vertex of that concealed cyclone.

He looked around the place, asking himself how they had gotten permission to use it. It had two floors: above, the boxes formed a semicircle supported by marble columns, flanked by red and gold drapes, lighted by heavy bronze lamps; below, the comfortable green armchairs were lined up before mahogany tables shining like mirrors. He saw how Roberto Menchaca took out his pistol and put it on the table, and how those on the left, the right, and even in the center defiantly did the same. Pablo pursed his lips before saying, asere, it looks like the *gunfight* is for real and we don't even have a *Winchester '73*, but Fernández Bulnes proposed a point of order on behalf of the Socialist Youth: to surrender all weapons. Nelson Cano concurred as spokesman for the Catholic Students Association, and since the two extremes were in agreement, the problem was solved. Big León Morales, a progressive Catholic, collected all the weapons and sat down by himself, with the arsenal in front of him. The left yielded the floor as a sign of good will, and Juan Jorge Dopico stood up on the right to open the debate.

Dopico spoke well, with the calm then emphatic rhythms of a public speaker, and Carlos smiled, content that his Casino crony was turning into an orator of surprising resources, which he displayed by saying how he hoped the debates would not be interrupted by those who were afraid of ideas. Benjamín el Rubio interrupted him, "Meaning what?" and Dopico didn't lose a beat, he turned toward Benjamín saying, exactly that, meaning those who are afraid of ideas, provoking a wave of applause on the right, which Carlos joined enthusiastically for the quick jab to the Communists. Afterwards, Dopico said that they should democratically elect a session president that evening and choose a topic for debate, and thanked the audience.

Mai stood and responded on behalf of the left. He recalled Heredia, the poet in whose name they were gathered, who said that Cuba united the beauties of the physical world with the horrors of the moral one, horrors, compañeros, that the Revolution was banning. The left began to applaud, with the center and the right joining in either from conviction, or contagion. Mai raised his voice and proposed that a poet preside over the debate, a heroic poet of our clandestine struggle, compañero Héctor. Dopico was opposed and proposed Nelson Cano, Benjamín was opposed and proposed Fernández Bulnes, León Morales was opposed and proposed Dopico, Fernández Bulnes was opposed and proposed Héctor again, and Héctor was opposed to himself, at which point they fell into an expectant silence. Everyone knew he was on the left, he said, the important thing is to find an impartial comrade with some standing, therefore he proposed compañero Carlos, all those in favor raise your hands.

Carlos stuttered a protest, he didn't know how, compañeros, he'd never done anything like that, he couldn't possibly accept . . . but no one seemed to pay any attention to him. A zone of silence was created, crisscrossed by winks, elbowing, nods, passed notes, and following the leaders' hands, all others were raised. Pablo gave him a clap on the shoulder, now you're *The Man with the Golden Arm*, my man, and he began humming the theme song from the film, while Carlos went down the stairs leading to the central desk of the semicircle, amid a round of applause. He sank down into the red leather armchair, finished with the seal of the Republic in gold relief, and felt it to be extraordinarily cold. Pulling the microphone towards him, he noted the sweaty fingerprints he left on the base. "So," he said, his voice sounding exaggeratedly high—for a moment he thought the curtains and the lamps were moving— "now we have to choose a . . ." but he contained himself in time, because what he was going to say was nonsense: he was the president. He felt his face on fire and said nothing until Roxana's refined voice came to his ear, whispering, "The topic." "The topic," he thankfully repeated, "the topic for debate." He hadn't finished the phrase when he saw Dopico's and Mai's hands raised. Who had been first? It was impossible for him to determine. He had to be impartial, and make a quick decision. He looked again at Roxana's soft smile, illuminated by the candelabra next to the black wooden door, and was surprised to hear himself say: "Dopico."

Roberto Menchaca cried foul and there was a threat of disorder on the left, which Mai cut off by saying in compliance, "The president decides." Dopico waited with a studied calm, then proposed: "Communist conscience versus Christian conscience."

Rubén Permuy jumped up to his feet, that was a divisive and counter-revolutionary proposition. What are you saying? said Nelson, waving his arms in the air, what are you saying? Prove it or else the Catholic Students Association would withdraw from the debate. Dopico disavowed Nelson, the CSA wasn't going to withdraw just because a Communist . . . Who's a Communist? shouted Permuy, who? Benjamín ordered them to shut up, coño, and Johnny Crime demanded some respect for the compañeras in the room, while Héctor's voice rose over the din, demanding that the president impose order. Carlos took advantage of the silence to ask for silence, discovered his face reflected in the polished surface of the desk, and it seemed like that of a stranger asking for him who wanted the floor.

Johnny Crime asked that Nelson withdraw the accusation that Permuy was a Communist. Dopico demanded that Permuy withdraw the accusation that Nelson was a counterrevolutionary. Benjamín shouted that Juanito's proposition was impossible, since being a Communist was an honor, and Carlos surprised himself, beating Héctor to it by banging the table, quiet! Let's vote on Dopico's proposition, compañeros, said Soria el Negro, taking advantage of the silence. Fernández Bulnes asked for a point of order and spoke against Soria's proposition: it was incorrect to choose a topic with no alternative, he said, he proposed that the right support its idea, and that the left present and support its own, then they would try to reach a consensus, and if there was none the president would decide, could they agree to that? They all approved, and Carlos gave the floor to Nelson Cano, wishing he wouldn't have to decide anything.

Nelson argued that the need to discuss the topic "Communist conscience versus Christian conscience" came from the urgency of the moment. Rubén Permuy, for example, had said it was a divisive topic, but he maintained that it was a unifying one, the topic of unity of Revolution in Christ. Who among them did not believe in Christ the King? Well then, in a short while there would be an election, the cross and the sickle would come face to face, Cuba against Russia, and they should all know that anyone who collaborated with the Communist campaign would be committing apostasy. He ended, starting up strong applause on the right, while the left protested with a droning "opposed, op-posed, op-posed." Carlos demanded silence and gave the floor to Mai.

Christ, began Mai, was a carpenter, and he said it would be easier for a camel to go through the eye of a needle than for a rich man to enter the kingdom of heaven. He stopped in silence, looking calmly at Nelson Cano, whose eyes blinked when he asked, What do you mean by that? Mai continued, still looking at him, Just what you heard, the majority, including the Communists, agree with the true Christ, the one who kicked the merchants out of his house, with sticks.

"With a whip," noted Nelson uncomfortably, "from the temple."

So much the better, continued Mai unperturbed, therefore it was divisive to oppose Communists to *that* Christ. The applause from the left and the center included part of the right. Mai asked for silence, compañeros, he was going to propose a unifying topic for discussion.

"Imperialism and revolution."

The applause grew, the right was taken aback, Nelson, Dopico, and Roxana started whispering, and suddenly Nelson agreed, and asked for the floor to reopen the debate.

He congratulated Mai for his idea, imperialism was a rich topic for discussion, so much so that they would need years to go over it, since from the very beginning of the world there had been imperialisms: Assyrian, Babylonian, Chaldean, Greek, Mayan, Roman, Etruscan, Aztec, Spanish, French, Dutch, English, etc. Therefore he proposed discussing only one, the most voracious imperialism, the one presenting the greatest threat to the Cuban Revolution, that is, compañeros, Russian imperialism. He succeeded in turning the situation around, now the applause included the center and a sector of the left. Carlos was thinking about that specter going through countries devouring everything, when he received a note from Pablo, "I was a Communist for the FBI" and he thought how that smartass would never stop screwing around. But he couldn't stop to answer, Fernández Bulnes had asked for the floor.

Nelson's opinions, he began by saying, although learned in form, had been profoundly false in content. Almost none of the examples he had given referred to imperialism, but rather to co-lo-nial-ism. From that point on, Carlos couldn't understand his dry reasoning about the export of capital, concluding in an explosive idea: Russian imperialism was like God.

"Why?" shouted Nelson, standing up.

Fernández Bulnes answered, without raising his voice:

"Because neither one of them exists, compañero."

Carlos could not control the chaos that resulted. He received a note from Roxana, *They're making this into a joke. Are you with us or not? See you later at the soda shop. R.* He smiled at her and left the note next to Pablo's, because Héctor had said that he disagreed with Fernández Bulnes's words, thus creating, for a second time, an expectant silence: now the left was publicly divided.

Carlos got excited, hoping someone would finally express his political ideal: the 26th of July Movement without priests and without Communists. Héctor began in a low voice, without rhetoric and with curse words, saying that he didn't give a damn about debating the existence of God or Russian imperialism, since neither one or the other had any fucking thing to do with the country at this moment, and believers from both sides would have to forgive him, and Mai also, he said, but the topic "imperialism and revolution" was insufficient, they had to define which revolution, he exclaimed, leaving the word in the air and then repeating, out loud, the murmur that had spread all over the room, yes, the Cuban Revolution; but he didn't ask which imperialism, rather, who was it, coño who had pissed on Martí's statue, and when he heard someone yell, "A Yanqui" he said there you have it, "Yanqui imperialism and the Cuban Revolution," that was the topic, compañeros, that was the topic *here* and *now*, the rest was crap.

Carlos joined the round of applause thinking that the point had been decided by acclamation, but Nelson, Dopico, and Soria let their hands fall to their sides, thus silencing all the right and a small part of the center. Then Carlos stopped applauding and reassumed his function. Now the Communists and the 26th of July were reunited, and his chum Dopico put him on the spot:

"The president decides whether it's Russian or Yanqui."

The left was taken aback for a minute, but Héctor took charge of a decision without consultation. "Agreed," he said, and Carlos was left hanging in the air, knowing that both the left and the right were sure he would decide in their favor, that now he was forced to jump off the fence, to leave the center forever with a phrase that suddenly seemed to him the only possibility, which was why he said, with an unexpectedly serene voice:

"We will debate Yanqui imperialism."

SEVEN

"They're going to move in at twelve," said Maí.

On getting this news the group in the old Senate room got stirred up: war between Washington and Moscow was inevitable.

Roberto Menchaca let go of the blade he was using to carve a woman's figure into the mahogany table, and took up his Luger.

"How did you find out?" he said.

Maí smiled. He was short and blond, with big blue eyes, and didn't move them off Roberto Menchaca's pistol while he pulled out his own revolver, a .38-caliber bulldog.

"We found out," he said.

Roberto Menchaca slowly took his hand off the Luger, wrote a note, and passed it to Azeff the Moor, avoiding using Carlos as intermediary.

"Now we'll see who on the left is a leftist," said Héctor.

Carlos pressed the spring that made the silver ashtray attached to his chair start spinning, and asked himself if he ought to take part in a clash between two groups he didn't identify with. He was on the left, but he had made clear a thousand and one times that he was not a Muscovite. What should he do, then, when the right tried to destroy the wreath of flowers that Mikoyan was going to place on Martí's statue? Who was correct—Héctor when he declared this wasn't a problem about Russia or Communism, but rather a reactionary attack on the Revolution? Or the Moor, replying that this was the business of pinkos and holier-than-thous and anyone who went would just be getting used? Or Fernández Bulnes, saying that all the problems of the modern world were basically between communists and anticommunists, and that anyone not participating in it was participating anyway?

There was no consensus, and Carlos left the Capitol without knowing what he would do. He went along with Mai's and Hector's group through the Arco del Pasaje, a sordid alley connecting Paseo del Prado with Zulueta Street, in the center of which was a banner of the United Left:

YES TO AGRARIAN REFORM!

VOTE FOR THE REVOLUTIONARY STUDENT MOVEMENT!

Halfway there, they were startled by the sound of loudspeakers. The United Student Bloc had started transmitting.

"Bastards!" said Mai, looking at his watch. "They started three minutes early."

The strident harangue reached them from an amplifier placed over the billiard hall.

"Students, don't let yourselves be fooled! For freedom with bread, for bread without terror . . ."

"It's Nelson Cano," said Rubén Permuy, "that dirty little creep."

". . . vote for the United Student Bloc, the BEU!"

Carlos lagged behind, listening to that voice, distorted by amplification, which was shouting exactly the opposite of what he himself would shout half an hour later.

"Juan Jorge Dopico for president! Nelson Cano for general secretary! They will give Christian direction to our future!"

Héctor stopped to wait for him at the Zulueta arcade, and when Carlos got there, put a hand on his shoulder.

"What did you think of the meeting?"

"Not much," he said, looking at the tips of his shoes. "There's a shitload of a lot of things I don't understand."

"Against Communism: vote for the BEU!"

"But you're going to go, right?"

"For the family, the motherland, free trade and the 1940 Constitution . . ."

"I need to think it over."

". . . vote for the BEU!"

"Think what over?"

"To save Cuba or sink it: that is the question! God or the Devil! Marx or Martí!"

"Everything," he said, shrugging his shoulders and looking distractedly towards the Instituto. A long line of students was waiting for a turn to vote.

"Students: don't let yourselves be confused by crypto-Communists, proto-Communists, philo-Communists!"

"OK," said Héctor, "think it over. Ciao."

"Ciao," murmured Carlos.

"For a Christian bloc: Dopico and Cano! For a Cuban bloc: Dopico and Cano! Students . . ."

Carlos crossed the street like a robot. At the corner of Zulueta and San José, Nelson Cano's metallic voice was scarcely a buzz. Two students coming out of the Payret coffee shop started taunting him.

"Trai-tor! Trai-tor! Trai-tor!"

"Your mother's a traitor!" he shouted, putting his hand to his waist under his shirt, as if he were going to pull out a pistol.

The boys, frightened, changed direction and went towards Prado. He quit following them, crossed San José, and sat down on Havana. Across from him, Washington was deserted.

Several elderly people were resting in the park. There was nothing to indicate the imminence of the battle. He told himself he wasn't obligated to take part, and felt a gentle sensation of freedom that he almost immediately realized was a false door, a knot, a riddle, a high gray wall. He really didn't have the slightest wish to go with either Washington or Moscow, but nevertheless, something definitive would happen today, tomorrow the world would be irremediably another, and if he didn't go, who would he be in that world?

He followed a sparrow's flight until he saw the poster, nailed like an insignia onto the tree shading Washington:

CUBA IS, AND BY RIGHTS SHOULD BE, FREE AND INDEPENDENT

JOINT RESOLUTION, CONGRESS OF THE UNITED STATES—1898

And he repeated, with a murmur, the reply nailed by Havana on the tree behind him:

I LIVED INSIDE THE MONSTER

AND I KNOW ITS BELLY

AND MY SLINGSHOT IS THAT OF DAVID

Those posters had been the high point of the arguments between the left and the right, the axis for the regrouping of forces and the origin of new names for the battling groups. Until the day that Nelson Cano nailed up the one about the joint resolution, the right bench had been called the Vatican and the left one Moscow, but when Héctor saw the new poster he shouted at the rightists that it was unbelievable, they were nothing but open and declared agents of Washington. Nelson replied that was a great honor, because Cuba owed its freedom to Washington, as was proven by the text of the joint resolution he had nailed up high, so the people wouldn't forget it. He could relax, relax, relax, Héctor repeated, the people would never forget the Platt Amendment, or Guantánamo Base, or the Yanqui support of Batista; they would never forget that Martí called them imperialists because he lived inside the monster and knew its belly, or that a marine had pissed on the apostle's statue.

From that day on, the right bench began to be called Washington and the left one Havana. But the Vatican and Moscow stayed alive in the constant activity of the Catholic Students Association and the Socialist Youth, who picked out other benches where they developed their own arguments before participating in the general debates. The whole mess was linked, in some way, to the decision Carlos made as president of the first and only session of the circle, but the disputing groups saw significance in his act that went far beyond his intentions. For the Vatican he was a traitor, for Moscow a fellow traveler. He asked himself what he really was, and a whirl of words exploded in his head: Martí, Marx, Christ, Lenin, God, Devil, Washington, Moscow, Vatican, Havana, Believer, Atheist, Patriot, Traitor.

He thought about Pablo, who would surely have helped turn his anguish into a joke if he weren't out in the Sierra, being a volunteer teacher, serving the Revolution with something necessary, concrete, and certain, while he, Carlos, had stayed in Havana being useless because his father was still threatened with a heart attack. He felt desperate waiting for Jorge, whose influence might help ventilate that house where the word *revolution* couldn't even be mentioned, forbidden by the doctor, who stood his ground even on the day when Manolo arrived foaming at the mouth and told them, tears in his eyes, that the Communists had stolen the Dionisia from them and given it to that ingrate Pancho José, and that now they didn't have even a little bit of land to die on. Carlos took pleasure in Manolo's furious sobs, his torn voice crying out to heaven against so much injustice, saying that if his father were alive he'd have died all over again from shame or rage. But Carlos knew that if Grandfather Álvaro were alive, he would have been a captain in the Rebel Army, and also that the Agrarian Reform reached even a little plantation like the Dionisia because his father and uncle had exploited Pancho José for years, violating the principle that the land belongs to the one who works it. That's what he had said in the debate, when the Washington spokesmen accused him of being a Communist, like Manolo had accused his mother; she crossed herself twice, but refused to upset her husband with the news, she wasn't going to tell him anything, they'd work it out, she said, after all they'd been born naked.

"Will this child be a patriot or a traitor?"

Carlos jumped, and smiled to see Roxana sitting next to him. She had on the burgundy skirt and white blouse of her uniform, and the monogram with the initials IH embroidered in red fell exactly over her left breast.

"Let's go look at the sea," she said.

A silky, soft line of hair began above her knees; her right inner thigh, a little exposed, was white and firm, and the pink ribbon on her bra left a subtle mark against her skin that he saw through her sleeve, asking himself what this woman could be up to, coming on suddenly like this.

"No," he answered, "I don't jump ship on my people."

She took his hands in hers.

"Carlos," she said, "are you a Communist?"

"I'd rather die first," he answered, returning her gaze.

"Are you . . . working for someone?"

"Yes."

He brushed her cheek with his lips, and she let him touch her, then suddenly pulled away, afraid. It was as if they had put themselves into a bell jar until they were separated from the world, and now the world suddenly entered with the honking of the number twenty-seven bus, the cries of a newsboy, the fluttering of a flock of sparrows.

"I love you," she said, "and I trust you . . . we'll get together after all this is over." She stood up silently, and looked to both sides. "Watch out with Soria," she murmured. "Ciao." And she blew him a kiss.

Carlos was left in a daze. He saw her cross the street and kept watching until she was nothing but a little black dot at the Centro Asturiano arcade. He got up humming "Amor bajo cero" with a euphoric feeling, clear and sweet like an orange. Suddenly he fell silent. Soria? Why had Roxana mentioned him? What did he have to do with that black traitor? He clapped his hand to his head: Soria wasn't a black traitor, he was a confused black, a Vatican black; it was a funny thing, but Soria was like him, a confused white, interested in spite of himself in a Vatican girl who had come to think of him as a Muscovite.

He returned through the Payret Theater arcade, thinking about how to convince Roxana that he was at the same time an anticommunist and an antiimperialist. In the dark little room that the MER, the Revolutionary Student Movement, had rented in the Pasaje Hotel across from the Instituto, there was a stale odor of sweat, cigarette butts, and coffee dregs. When Carlos entered, the Smartasses were playing a quick little game of Chinese charades: "From the nuns to the big fish, no one wants it at night." He stopped to translate, from five to ten, so the saps would bet on eight, dead; but Chicho Thick Lips wasn't so generous that he would give away the game like that, and if the Revolution hadn't forbidden gambling, Carlos would have bet on the turtle or the elephant, who were good for nothing at night.

"You can't play in here," he said.

Thick Lips protested, so then what was there for them to do? He was a short black, fat and a wise guy, whose principal, almost sole, occupations were playing the tumbadora drums and gambling forbidden games. During the elections, he had led the MER conga band, but today, the day of decision, he was on reserve duty because the pact with the BEU prevented musicians from going out.

"Read," said Carlos.

He threw a pile of books from the end table over towards the Smartasses: *The Fable of the Shark and the Sardines, The Communist Manifesto, The Great Fraud,* and *The New Class.* Johnny Crime caught the avalanche of paper and dust, saying that here they had culcha, stoopid, but Emiliano Mateo exploded: Washington was transmitting with nine loudspeakers, three cars, and RCA equipment.

"Yeah," commented Carlos, "their master's voice."

"Of course," said Emiliano, "but all we've got is three loudspeakers and shitty equipment, and on top of that, you know, they've stolen like half an hour of transmission from us. Why don't we start right now, and get back five minutes?"

Carlos went out onto the balcony without answering. He grabbed onto the side bars, made of wrought iron in a treble clef shape, and did a chin-up. Starting five minutes early implied they were also breaking the pact, but neither Héctor or Mai was there to consult, and he couldn't decide alone. He went back into the room with rust-stained hands. The Smartasses were passing books around, where they'd surely been marking down numbers and verse. He was going to scold them when Roberto Menchaca came running in, shirttails open to show his Luger. He dragged Carlos out onto the balcony; Carlos followed him tensely, eyes glued to his hands, ready to strike first.

"Asere," he said, his voice sounding more disagreeable than usual to Carlos, "watch out. They've got your wagon covered. They're following you."

Carlos picked up the direction of Roberto Menchaca's gaze, and turned around at exactly the moment when Roberto told him not to. Soria was on the opposite sidewalk, watching him.

"You're like a fish on a plate," said Roberto.

"What?"

"Eyes wide open, but without seeing, asere. Watch out with Soria. Abairimo."

Roberto left at a run. Carlos kicked the metal sheet covering the edge of the balcony and made a clanging sound. He didn't understand a goddamn thing.

"Turn it on," he said when he went back inside.

Johnny Crime asked, smiling, if they were going to break the pact, but Carlos didn't respond. He needed noise. He took the microphone, said testing-one-two-three, and began reading.

"Student, compañero! White, black, Chinese, Jew, revolutionary Cuban! Don't let yourself be fooled by the shady reactionaries! Catholic, freethinker, Protestant! Don't pay . . ." He stopped talking because a word was filling the room, amplified by the BEU's equipment: "Me-lon! Me-lon! Me-lon!" The damned accusation choked his call for unity, jammed his improvised reply, and made him say, without even turning the audio off: "Now they're screwed, let's go rumble."

He plunged down the stairs followed by the Smartasses, armed with tumbadoras and ashtrays, who went along banging, beating out, and singing *The Yaaanquis*, so Chicho Thick Lips could lead them, *are losing their pants*. It was like a call, lots of students joined in the chorus, *The Yaaanquis*, went into the street and followed Chicho, who turned up Zulueta, *we're breaking up their dance*, in a long conga line that turned around, *The Yaaanquis*, and doubled over on itself, *can't even advance*, until they surrounded the BEU's car and beat out on the body, *The Yaaanquis*. Then Nelson Cano's reaction, "It's a Communist betrayal!", the conga line redoubled its chant, *we've got them in a trance*, Nelson shouted, "Melons, green outside, red inside!" and the metallic sounds of the loudspeakers entwined in a duel with the congas' leathery voices, *The Yaaanquis*, "We will not be held responsible for the chaos that the Communist betrayal . . ." *Are just a hill of ants*, ". . . may bring our school . . ." *The Yaaanquis*, ". . . a low and sneaky betrayal . . ." *haven't got a chance*, ". . . that proves who they are . . ." *The Yaanquis*, " . . . the ones responsible for the difficult times . . ." *they're fags who only prance*, ". . . our unfortunate country . . ." *The Yaaanquis*, ". . . is now going through," yelled Nelson, and the Instituto's director grabbed the microphone from him, saying: "That's enough!"

What bothered Carlos the most in the meeting the MER had, after a discussion with the director and the BEU, was Mai's distrust when he asked why Carlos had broken, without consultation, a pact that benefited the left. It was evident that his decision left the MER at a disadvantage: with the pact that established fifteen minutes of alternating transmission per candidate broken, the BEU would dominate with its powerful equipment. But there was something hidden in Mai's reticence when he put off the discussion until after the confrontation with Washington.

"I mean, you're going, right?"

Carlos felt harassed, and looked at Mai, knowing that the tilt of that strange balance on which his personal standing was being weighed depended on his answer, then said: "No."

After that he felt better. If his anti-imperialism, demonstrated at the circle, and his participation in the left's campaign weren't enough for them, too bad. He wouldn't give them any more. He wasn't a Communist and never would be one. He was afraid of those irritating types, methodical and stubborn, who the right accused of being paid by Moscow's gold, although the truth was that they never had a cent and were always, always asking for money; but when they were around you couldn't touch Russia even with the tip of a feather, and now they wanted to impose an exotic, Asiatic, antilibertarian ideology in Cuba . . .

The Russian Bolshevik anthem broke into his reflection. He looked out the window. In Central Park, the OK Corral of his game with Pablo, the ceremony had begun. Mikoyan went up to the base of Martí's statue and placed a wreath of flowers. Suddenly you could hear a duel of cries: "Down with Russia!" alternated with "Down with Yanqui imperialism!" at an accelerating pace. He was in agreement with both slogans, and punched the wall with rage; to be on both sides in a war was craziness. Washington came out ahead in the battle, about a hundred guys from Villanueva University moved in from Neptune Street and the BEU leadership did the same from San José. Muller shouted, "Agrarian Reform?" and his people responded, "NO!" as the photographers' flashes went off. The left had situated a small group around the wreath, and it was evident that the right was going to surround it, when dozens and dozens of people came out of the arcades, businesses, and coffee shops shouting "YES!" For a couple of seconds there were three concentric circles that made Carlos recall the Casino Rueda. Suddenly someone threw a punch, and the two larger circles mixed it up in a huge fight splashed with insults and moans. But Carlos could make out only a tangle of movement and words—*imperialism, down, Agrarian Reform, Russia*—until the police arrived and ended the clash.

Shortly after Mai came in with his bulldog in hand, asking if anyone had called. Héctor followed.

"No one," replied Carlos, smiling to hide his nervousness, and then he realized that Héctor had a wound on his forehead.

"Ok," said Mai. "Let's get this straight. What happened with Roxana?"

His mouth opened in amazement. The attack had come from a new direction, unexpected, incomprehensible. He looked to Héctor for support, but he seconded Mai.

"She was with you in the park," he said with a neutral tone. "What was her proposal?"

He didn't know what to answer. It just wouldn't come out, the humiliation of telling them his story with Roxana. It seemed incredible to him that his buddies in the 26th of July would have been spying on him.

"Nothing," he said.

"Read this," replied Mai. "Let's see if your memory clears up."

He took the little piece of paper and recognized Roxana's handwriting: *They're turning this into a joke. Are you with us or not? See you at the soda shop. R.*

"Did she send it to you?" asked Héctor, while Mai handed him a second little paper.

"Yes," he said, before reading: *I was a Communist for the* FBI.

"That was your answer," murmured Mai. "You're a rat."

A thick, bubbling fury kept him from speaking. Who had stolen those papers from him? When? How could Héctor possibly believe that craziness?

There were three knocks on the door, the bell, and then three knocks again. The shape of a figure was sketched against the frosted glass. Mai took up his bulldog before opening. Rubén Permuy entered, saying:

"The BEU gangsters beat up Soria. Are we going to war?"

"No," decided Mai. "Get one gangster, just one, and bring Soria here."

Rubén Permuy left without saying goodbye.

"They have a rat infiltrated among us," said Mai, "and I think it's you."

"What about Soria?" shouted Carlos.

"He's with us," Héctor commented.

"And Roberto Menchaca?"

"Also ours," said Mai.

Carlos made an effort to concentrate his attention on the flies lighting on the electric cord of the fan, but he couldn't keep from exploding, that was enough, who the fuck did they think they were? He was a man through and through, he'd rather die than be a rat, the Revolution had cost him his father's money, and his father's plantation, and his father's building, and his father's health; he was on the left because he had balls, but he wasn't a Communist nor was he going to explain any goddamn thing about the notes, and if they believed him, good, if not, too bad.

"Sit down," Héctor said to him. He didn't, and Héctor continued calmly, "You have to make some effort here, Flaco; first, we lost the pact because of you; second, you didn't go to the fight with Washington; third, you're still involved with a Vatican girl; fourth, the notes; fifth, the right blew Soria's cover. Let me finish, Flaco, I didn't say you were a rat."

"So what then?" asked Mai.

"The right has another plan for Flaco," said Héctor, touching his head as if it ached. "They use Roxana to make him resign. Get it? On election day, the spokesman for the MER accuses Havana of being controlled by Moscow."

"Maybe," Mai murmured.

"Maybe, my ass!" yelled Carlos, banging his head against the wall.

The bell rang with the secret code. Héctor opened the door, and Soria entered, holding onto Rubén Permuy and Johnny Crime. The black was dragging one foot, with his mouth split open and his eyes almost shut from the beating. Héctor helped him sit down.

"Talk," said Mai.

"They sent her to win him over," murmured Soria, very slowly. Moving his swollen lips was difficult.

"Give names!" shouted Carlos, piling himself on, but Soria continued his efforts as if he hadn't heard.

"She says that he says he's working for someone," he raised his head to look at Mai. "But I couldn't get proof, they fucked me up first."

"Go ahead," said Mai.

"The Catholic Youth gave them a thousand pesos and they have a plan . . ." He went silent and pointed to Carlos, but Mai had him continue. "To steal the ballot boxes tonight, if they lose."

"There you have it," said Mai.

Suddenly, Carlos felt very tired, and went to the door, which Rubén Permuy had blocked.

"Let him go," ordered Mai.

"This guy?" murmured Rubén, amazed.

"Be careful," said Mai, and Carlos turned around, because he needed to see his eyes while he listened. "If the right finds out we know about the ballot boxes, you're the rat."

"Go to hell," said Carlos.

He went slowly down the stairs. He felt very weak. He crossed the park without knowing which way to go. The Communist wreath was at the base of the statue, there was no one on Washington or Havana. At San José you could hear the war of declarations, dominated by the BEU's power. He had to make an effort to figure out who was transmitting for the MER, and finally recognized Benjamín el Rubio: they had picked a Communist to substitute for him. Why? Until now the Communists had stayed on the margins of that business, unless they were manipulating it off the books. But who, coño, could be manipulating Mai? He had to see Roxana.

He went into the soda shop and quickly looked over the booths. Roxana wasn't there. He decided to wait five minutes, if she didn't come, he'd go find her even if it meant going to BEU headquarters. He had to get this situation straight. If Roxana could convince him that this story about a conspiracy was nonsense, he'd resign tomorrow, when the election results were public and his action couldn't hurt the MER. He would have liked to order a shake, but he didn't have enough money, and he had to settle for a Coke. The metallic sound of a car with speakers on it invaded the place, warning students not to let themselves be fooled by crypto-Communists, philo-Communists, proto-Communists. Carlos started making fun of the didactic style of Fernández Bulnes, the secretary of the Socialist Youth.

"Compañeros," he asked himself, "where does the money come from to pay for those cars, those printing presses, those gunmen? It comes, compañeros, from the ones who used to rule us, the big owners, the land gobblers . . ."

"Boy, you tark arone."

José, the Chinese employee, was next to him. Carlos smiled awkwardly at him and suddenly let out a laugh, remembering Rubén Permuy's answer to Fernández Bulnes, "Pal, you want a land gobbler, I've spent my life eating dust."

"Carlos, you member MER?"

The boy was short, with Indian-like features, muscular; one of the little Smartasses who drummed on the table with his index finger, waiting for the *yes* that Carlos pronounced without enthusiasm.

"You resign?"

Carlos jumped to his feet yelling what the fuck, and the little Smartass pulled back, and said:

"Mai send me."

"Well, tell Mai I'm not a faggot!" he yelled, and the little Smartass started running.

Strange things kept happening. Fernández Bulnes would explain them as manifestations of the class struggle, but what, coño, was a class? Had the Gang Wars been a class struggle? Were the Bacilli a class? Suddenly he started to hum in a low voice, "Koch, Koch, Koch's bacilli . . ."

"Boy, you sing arone, you tark arone, you raugh arone, you clazy, boy."

He was trying to smile at José when Nelson, Dopico, and the BEU gang came in and came over to his table.

"Hi," said Nelson.

"What's up," he answered. "Where's Roxana?"

"She'll be here soon." Nelson rubbed his eyebrows with his fingers, in a gesture of fatigue. "But we know about everything, the pinkos have been playing dirty with you."

"Yeah," admitted Carlos. "Who told you?"

"Oh, someone," said Nelson, moving his hands as if he were waving away cigarette smoke. "You should resign."

"Maybe so," murmured Carlos. "Maybe tomorrow."

"Tomorrow's no good," argued Nelson. "You have to resign *today*."

"No," said Carlos, and he tried to go. But the gang had blocked his booth. "What the fuck is this?" he asked.

"Calm down, Flaco," Dopico told him. "Calm down and think, you're not a pinko, but the pinkos are using you. You have to resign, pal."

"I'm leaving," said Carlos.

"No," replied Nelson, "you're not leaving. You may be crazy, but I'm not, and we've already announced your resignation."

Carlos shoved a gang member, got a punch in the stomach, and fell back down into the booth.

"Over there!" someone shouted, and Carlos recognized the little Smartass. He led a group over to the table. Mai pushed his way through the gang, and sat next to him.

"What's the deal?" he asked.

"It's a lie," said Carlos. "These people . . ."

"These people are leaving this minute," decided Mai, stroking the bulldog he had just set on the table. "Stay calm, this dog's nervous and besides, we have more than seventy boys outside."

Nelson Cano stood up and said, looking at Carlos:

"You decided, you made your own decision." And he started to retreat, without turning his back.

"So, who's the rat?" asked Carlos.

"I don't know," murmured Mai, holding his gaze. "Sorry, chico, that's how it is sometimes with politics."

Carlos bit his lip, not knowing then that Roxana would tell him something similar two hours later, in a fury at the Centro Asturiano arcade, when she decided not to see him anymore.

EIGHT

The coffin didn't weigh much, but it was hard to carry it on his shoulder and also follow the conga beat of the Smartasses and the river of young people emptying out into the whirlpool that was Central Park. It was annoying to see a second coffin, because he was proud of the idea he'd proposed as secretary for press and propaganda of the Instituto's Student Association, and he'd expected to score a big hit winding around the street with that black box, whose replica he now saw on the shoulders of the cigar makers from the Romeo y Julieta factory. At the end of the park he saw a third one, then a fourth, and stopped counting because the coffins were multiplying like loaves and fishes, making him doubt whether the idea had been his, or if he'd responded to some order no one ever identified, and that he, like the rest, took from the partylike atmosphere in which the coffins swayed to the chanting beat, dancing with the huge puppets that spun over the multitude, attracted by the delicious conga:

> Hey, friend, don't be scared when you see it,
> hey, friend, don't be scared when you see it,
> the scorpion screwing the Yanqui,
> the scorpion screwing the Yanqui.
> That's what happens in my country, brother . . .

The people joined in with the montuno, "*Sí, sí,* screwing the Yanqui," and a puppet that depicted a crying Uncle Sam asked the Instituto's coffin to dance, and Carlos and Rubén started stepping in time, responding to the fellow working the puppet, a fellow who could conga well, did the *guaracha* with style, and moved the strings of his puppet to the beat, shaking like a skeleton doing the rumba while an enormous tear rose and fell from his cheek to his chest, where the words were written: "It's all over!"

While he danced, Carlos tried to forget the problem causing his grief, but when the puppet left with its music, he thought he saw Jorge and hid his face behind the coffin. He spied out from there until he was sure it was someone else, but he couldn't get back into step with the conga beat and gave up his place under the coffin to Benjamín el Rubio. He felt depressed in the midst of that huge bash, as if he couldn't get loose from the atmosphere of disaster ruling his house, where his father counted his money three times a day, then put it in the safe, and sat up all night with those damned papers, as if they were a dead child.

Carlos gradually took on a growing pity for his bitter, defeated figure, more and more alone. The world he had succeeded in building was in shreds, he had brutally rejected his Fidelista friends, like Pablo's father, and the *gusanos* that came to the house to give him the "latest" had been leaving, fleeing, and now they sent postcards from Miami telling him of their impressive financial success. The last one to go was the doctor. He visited the house the very day of his departure, left a plan with all possible measures against disease, and took advantage of the moment when José María went to recount his money to talk with Carlos and his mother.

He was thin and ruddy, and especially excited that afternoon when he began by saying the end had come, they were seeing the fulfillment of the millennial prophecy. Fidel, unknowingly, was the Messenger of the Latter Days, the day was nearing of a holocaust that Christians called the Day of Final Judgment and the Jehovah's Witnesses, Armageddon; they should save their souls and flee to the Promised Land before the ire of the Unknown One was unleashed on the Evil Island. Carlos smiled, realizing that this guy liked to hear his own voice, and recalled the words Manolo said before leaving, knowing that they held the key to the doctor's verbal diarrhea. Manolo was disgustingly earthy, and his only virtue was that he never tried to hide it. That was why he confessed to Carlos that he was pulling out, nephew, the Yanquis weren't going to allow stupid little revolutions here, so now you had to go there, to return later on with the victors. Carlos especially recalled his last guffaw, "Nephew, I always bet on the macho, and in this fight, the macho is the Yanqui."

During those months, Carlos had discovered an unexpectedly independent judgment in his mother, and he sensed that behind her obstinate silence and her stubborn insistence on waiting for Jorge before making any decisions, she cherished the secret hope of convincing her husband that the Revolution was making into law the basic precepts of simple Christianity, which constituted the deepest truth of her soul. Thus, without making any references to the disturbing fact that Jorge had stopped writing to them, she woke up fresh as an Easter lily on the morning they went to pick him up at the airport. Carlos felt a sudden tenderness overtake him as he recognized on that suffering face a smile just like the one that had lighted his few moments of happiness, when they played hide and seek and would say to her, "Run, run, the Bembé's coming!" to then see her reappear in the kitchen window with the most beautiful smile on earth.

He was observing her when she closed her eyes and started talking about herself. He gave into the impulse to close his own eyes, so as not to see the streets the car was going down. He had just discovered, to his horror, that he'd never listened to his mother, that maybe no one had ever listened to her, that they'd all gotten used to her taking care of their wounds and drying their tears in silence, the house and the clothes all clean in silence, like an automatic mechanism that had ceded to the simple need to talk, making him feel guilty and wanting to redeem himself, as if he were seeing a revelation or a miracle.

She recalled her childhood at the sugar mill, saying how it was so painful knowing that her mother had died giving birth to her. She'd been scared to have him, because she suffered the same disease. It hadn't been so much the fear of dying, she swore to that, but rather of leaving him, Jorge, and José María alone. She got quiet then suddenly said, "*Lata*," as if she were remembering something very valuable. "*Lata*," she repeated, caressing the word. When her father had wanted to teach her to read *mamá*, she would say *lata*, she recalled, laughing in a pitiful way. Her father, what was her poor father going to do, may he rest in peace, a carpenter left alone with two daughters, other than farm them out with the hope of going back to get them some day, to keep the family together? She repeated the last phrase, and Carlos stroked her hands, soft and unexpectedly cold, while she murmured, "It was never together again, never," and recalled how she bumped around from one house to another, separated from Ernesta, waiting for her father who came, when he could, to take her a handful of sugar candy. Her voice sounded slightly terrified when she asked, as if inquiring about the fate of a beloved one, what ever happened, Lord, to sugar candy? Carlos looked at her, sobbing, her lips trembling with the thought of that sweetness, lost in memory, hand to her head as if she had a bad headache.

He didn't dare interrupt the placid silence into which she sank, just limited himself to sending her tender thoughts: Mamá, he understood why she had put up with and supported Papá, despite the moneylending and Uncle Manolo, whom she had never managed to hate; he knew, Mamá, that she was unable to hate; he loved her so much that he had learned to understand her silences; he admired, Mamá, her silent way of loving the Revolution and of not hurting Papá by saying so; he wanted to tell her that if he was a revolutionary, above all he owed it to the sense of justice she had instilled in him with her actions; but she shouldn't worry, he wasn't going to hurt Papá, he swore it on his love for her: the family would stay together, all he wanted was for her to be happy for once.

At the airport, he thought many times of that vow, and turned it into a commitment. There were dozens of families there, all saying goodbye with a searing display of anxiety, bitterness, misery, sobs and lack of understanding, reproaches and renunciations, and he couldn't keep her from witnessing that tragedy because she insisted on roaming around, drawing near to those who argued, cried, or kissed each other for the last time with a stubborn curiosity, almost disrespectful, absolutely improbable in such a shy person. Carlos followed her attentively, and felt the situation had reached an extreme when she went over to a beautiful girl, alone and crying inconsolably on a column, and stroked her hand over the girl's wet face, asking what was the matter. "He's not coming," answered the girl, looking out into space, "he's not going to come." "Go look for him," his mother advised her, "don't you leave," and kissed her before continuing on.

Carlos was working up the strength and the reasoning to make her sit down when she virtually put herself in the middle of an argument: a little boy was yelling that he didn't want to go and was crying to go back to his grandmother's house, while a woman was yanking him by the arm. The boy managed to get free and by chance took refuge in the arms of the intruder, and she started to stroke his head, saying to the woman how could she be doing this. Carlos had to intercede to keep the woman from hitting his mother, he apologized, said, "Mamá, please," while an aseptic voice announced, "Pan American Flight 443 to Miami now boarding at Gate Two," and his mother watched powerless as the woman dragged the boy away, while the girl by the column, looking back over her shoulder, went towards Gate Two, and she leaned on him, defeated.

Those accompanying the passengers left, downcast. They went over to a bench in silence. At that moment Carlos reproached himself for not having been brave enough to tell her about his tender feelings. She was sad because in the nearly empty lounge there floated an aura of tragedy that just would not disappear; she was nervous waiting for Jorge, and kept wringing a little linen handkerchief between her fingers. The magical halo in the car was missing, and he thought he might be able to create it if he dared to ask her something really important, and suddenly he said, "Did you ever love Papá?" He felt angry at himself because at the crucial moment, some unknown mechanism kept him from asking if she had ever been in love, as if being in love, those beautiful words, were something obscene between his parents. She looked at him in fright before murmuring, "Of course, son, what kind of question is that?" and he knew that in his mother's fear, and in his own inability to formulate the true question, was the answer he was seeking: she had never had the chance to really be in love with a man, she had to be content with serving him. He felt a mixture of rage and pity, and struggled to think about something else, because suddenly he found himself coming to the conclusion that his mother had never known physical pleasure, and he felt he had stepped into territory where he had no right to go.

He concentrated on the people waiting along with them, immediately identifying them as belonging to a different class. It was evident, for example, that the ones leaving were wealthy, members of the bourgeoisie, and the ones returning were emigrant workers, for whom the Revolution was making repatriation possible. Suddenly he asked himself a question, was Jorge part of the proletariat? He answered no, and didn't know where to place him. The son of a moneylender, a usurer, would he be part of the petit bourgeoisie?

He was thinking through pros and cons when his mother squeezed his hand, exactly a couple of seconds before Cubana announced the arrival of its Flight 339 from New York and Miami, as if she had sensed the exact moment when Jorge touched the ground. They glimpsed him immediately, among the first to come out, decisive and elegant. She didn't let go of Carlos's hand during the entire time Jorge was going through entry procedures, as if she were afraid of falling. She watched Jorge, nodding briefly in greeting, until she had him next to her and started putting her hands to his face, like a blind woman, in the same way and in the same place where she had said goodbye to him two years before. Carlos knew she would pull him towards her, too, without letting go of Jorge, and would unite them, she was uniting them under her wings, squeezing them with an unexpected strength, fighting to postpone the question Jorge anxiously voiced, "Where's Father?" while Carlos recalled

Fanny, the charades, the police that frenetic night before he left, and embraced his brother ready to reveal the truth to him about that money, to love him and explain to him the abysmal distance separating those times from the new world they were beginning to build.

But Jorge didn't allow him to organize his words. He was very excited, jumping from a question about the Revolution to a story about his success in the North to worries about the state of his father's health. For a few hours the chaos kept them from noticing that they were having an argument; then they tacitly agreed to maintain peace in public, and finally they closed themselves up in their room, with a bottle of whiskey on the night table. They drank hard from the start, toasting the Bacilli, the great times they'd had screwing around in the old days, remembering the dames, the music, and the jokes that made them die laughing, pissing, literally doubling over with laughter before clinking glasses and feeling themselves mellow, affectionate, happy to be there, dammit, brothers, coño, over and above everything else on this earth, said Jorge, and on the other, added Carlos, and Jorge agreed, on the other, did he remember that joke? He began telling the joke, which was really good, really great, said Carlos, crying with laughter, watching his brother through the light film of his tears, feeling how much he loved him, as much as that inevitable guffaw after which flowed new tears that kept on coming by themselves, uncontrollably, consoling, why not, coño, Yoyi, he wasn't sad, he wanted to tell him something coño, he shouted, knowing he had finally found the words to strip himself bare to his brother, to tell him how he'd taken the money from his pocket the night of his going-away party and how he'd spit on that face that now he looked at ceaselessly, asking Jorge to spit on him now if he wanted, feeling a sweet calm in his humiliation, like a person confessing.

Jorge started wiping away his tears, how many times did he have to tell him that men don't cry? and kept on looking at him with as much love as Carlos felt inside himself, while he heard his brother saying that all that didn't matter, all that was *out*, and he saw him extend an arm into the air repeating *out*, like a baseball umpire sending a player off the field with that hand that suddenly fell over his shoulder, squeezing him affectionately, he'd done the right thing, he'd done the right thing to spit on him, because after all he'd slept with that whore Carlos loved so much, but did he know why he did it, huh? Did he know why? He didn't wait for Carlos to answer to say to fuck him over, pure and simple, to fuck him over and show him he was too good, too much of a shithead, too idealistic about life, and you couldn't be idealistic in life, because life, *shit*, he said forcefully, *shit*, he repeated, *shit, shit, shit*! he yelled so insistently that Carlos forgot his wish to answer even before Jorge concluded, *mierda*! Did he understand? Get this through your head, brother, you can't go through life being a dumb ass!

They went back to drinking in silence, slowly, with an unconfessed awareness that all the old cards had been used up, and there was nothing else to do but play as hard as the look they suddenly gave each other, before lowering their eyes, ashamed of the distance that had gotten into the love, of the remoteness that made useless the speech about the Revolution's virtues that Carlos had taken such a long time to prepare, but now kept quiet, realizing that the real topic was the one Jorge brought up, with a crudeness barely veiled by fatigue, how much money is left? He went back to snapping his fingers while Carlos gathered the strength to answer, "Almost nothing," watching with desperation his astonishment. "Almost nothing?" and suddenly Jorge burst out laughing like an idiot, repeating, "Almost nothing, nada, finished," and he kept on laughing when Carlos, becoming animated, started telling him all that had happened and even dared to include in his story comments about the justice of the Revolution, that had abolished debts, lowered rents, and carried out agrarian reform to benefit the poor, the dispossessed, he almost shouted, because Jorge had interrupted him, "And the plantation?" and he couldn't answer just like that, he needed to talk about poverty, about Pancho José's state of neglect, looking all the while at his brother, who repeated, "And the plantation?" then received a jumbled explanation about Grandfather Álvaro's true ideas, drowned out by the cry, "I'm asking you about the plantation, coño!" while Carlos tried to tell him about Toña, the little illiterate peasant girl who now would start to live like an, an . . . choking now, because Jorge had taken him by the neck and was tightening his grip, "The plantaaation, goddamit!" collapsing when Carlos whispered, "We lost it," and then raising himself up over him, spitting on his face and giving him a head butt on the mouth that Carlos received like a penance, wiping off the blood and saliva saying in pain and joy that now they were even-steven, and feeling within his rights to return the punch that Jorge threw at him. They fought while talking to each other, swearing that their parents weren't going to find out and wishing each other dead while they hit more and more slowly, with less force, until their mother found them at dawn, asleep in an embrace.

That day they began a useless struggle to forget, and in front of their parents they pretended things were fine. They were happy they'd been able to hide so much bitterness, and were amazed when their mother sat them down, asking what had happened. After the first babblings, they understood it was useless to keep on lying, because in some strange, deep way she knew everything. Then began the speeches to convince her of their respective truths. Jorge, that the Revolution was hell and that the only possible future was to leave as soon as his father could travel; Carlos, that she should tell Jorge the truth, her truth, that she was a revolutionary, that she knew the revolutionary laws were just and that the only possible future was to stay and for them to convince his father together. She listened anxiously, and when they started repeating themselves, ordered them to be quiet with an authority that satisfied Carlos and surprised Jorge, to whom she said, now listen well, that old man counting his sacred money in the other room was his father, and he was sick, and she wasn't going to take him to die in a strange land. At that moment her voice broke, and Carlos stroked her hand, certain that she would tell Jorge the whole truth, that she'd talk about her childhood at the sugar mill, about the misery she'd suffered that was being banned from this country; so he was surprised when she turned to him, ordering him not to talk anymore about politics between those four walls, and he looked at her astonished, trying to discover some hidden message in her eyes, but he found only a terrible strength in her threat: I will never forgive the one who divides this family.

From then on, Carlos felt more and more depressed and ended up abandoning his political activity. He saw his mother suffering for him, but he told himself she was to blame for that suffering. He took dark pleasure in not getting out of bed, dreaming of the moment when they would all realize that great injustice and would crowd around the bed to say come on, get up and get going. Meanwhile, he thought about the barbaric explosion in the harbor, the row he had with Nelson Cano, which he won in spite of everything, and the argument with Héctor and Mai, which he lost in spite of everything. After the right attempted to falsify his declaration and the left won the elections, Nelson Cano wouldn't stop provoking him. At first, the MER opposed the fight because the left was governing and they should be doing it responsibly, without rows, but the signs that had appeared in all the bathrooms, saying "Carlitos is a little melon," suddenly had added to them "A little fag" and that was too much to tolerate. Even the Communists, champions of coexistence, were in agreement that an example had to be made. Héctor offered to face off with Nelson, because he thought it outrageous that such a slimy guy should fight Carlos, but Mai didn't agree, the one who was being affected had to make his manhood clear.

Nelson Cano was almost the same weight and size as Carlos, but he was famous for his aggressiveness and his knowledge of boxing. Because of that, the Smartasses didn't agree with Mai, the fight might seem fair, said Rubén Permuy, but when they started chewing him out Carlos was going to turn chicken, and that would be a loss of prestige for the left. "Loss of prestige, my ass!" shouted Carlos, before going out to find his rival. He felt an urgent need to get through this ordeal, which he had known for months was inevitable, as if the Instituto had become a wild-west town not big enough for the both of them. Until that moment he had shielded himself behind the MER's opposition to avoid the encounter, but now Mai's and Rubén's words had blinded him with rage, making him leap past his fear, and he entered the Instituto ready for whatever damage had to be done, so long as he could hold his head up high.

He continued on into the Physical Education patio, because Nelson wasn't in the entry hall. He saw him at one end, his back to the parallel bars, perfect for whamming him by surprise. But hitting from behind was not a manly thing to do. "Nelson Cano," he shouted, "you piece of shit, fuck you and your fucking bitch of a mother!" Nelson turned around scornfully, sure that Carlos wouldn't attack, and received a punch that split his lips. "Left, left, left, always the left!" shouted dozens of students, urging Carlos on, as he hit again and felt a short, unexpected punch to the stomach. He took a step backwards while hearing the enemy shout, "To the right!" He threw a left that Nelson took, so as to hit him low while saying, "You pinko dog." Carlos couldn't stand that insult, he let go with his right and Nelson's face shuddered. But in return Carlos received two hooks to the stomach. "Kill him!" shouted Dopico, "Give it to him!" He felt like he'd lost his wind. "Cover yourself!" Mai shouted to him. "To the right!" shouted his enemies, and immediately his side responded, "Left, always the left!" Nelson didn't hurry himself, he moved around calling him pinko and began to hit below, leaving his face open. Carlos concentrated his attack there before receiving a hook to the stomach that made him fall back amid shouts of "To the right!" Then he advanced with a whirlwind of blows that disconcerted Nelson, and he heard "Left, always the left!" while Nelson rallied with a combination of jabs and hooks, and the shouts melded into one absurd chant, "Left to the right!" He felt dizzy, he could hardly see the face of his opponent, who kept on giving it to him below at the moment when he shot out a solid punch to the jaw that made Nelson fall back, and he grabbed him in a clinch looking for air while he heard Héctor, "You'll lose it by boxing, Flaco, wrestle him!" and with a stumble he dragged Nelson down and the two of them rolled on the ground, the chorus shouting left, right, and suddenly there was the sound of a colossal, deafening explosion that made the students run for the door, while the two of them stayed there entwined, unmoving, until, without saying anything, they let go and went to see what had happened.

No one knew anything. On Zulueta Street people were hugging each other with emotion, sensing some enormous catastrophe. In the distance ambulance sirens sounded. A man went by shouting, "The gunpowder, the magazine's exploded!" When they all looked at each other disconcertedly Mai shouted, "Viva Fidel! Down with Yanqui imperialism!" and the shouts of "Viva!" and "Down!" flattened the right which retreated in fear, because there was a strong smell of vengeance in the air. Mai hugged Carlos and was going to tell him something when another explosion, even bigger, shook the street, breaking shop and automobile windows. Many people started to run crazily, without direction. Others grouped around Mai demanding that they go to help, but Mai burst into a rage, replying that he didn't know where the catastrophe had happened. "Over there!" shouted Héctor. A thick column of smoke rose up over the buildings in the direction of Atarés. They started running down Zulueta; when he got to Monte, Carlos ran out of breath, because Nelson's blows had had their effect, and he began to lag behind, lost among the thousands of people arriving at the scene, running into the ones coming back who advised them not to go further, you couldn't get through, there were more than a hundred dead, more than a thousand wounded. "Where?" shouted Carlos, "where?" "In the harbor," replied a woman crying spasmodically in the middle of the street, "a ship with arms and bullets exploded." In the distance unending bursts of fire sounded, as if thousands of machine guns were all firing at once. A man returned from the left direction, shouting, "Blood, they need people to give blood!" Carlos started running towards the harbor, but by the railroad station he lost his breath again. The smoke, the shooting, the shouts, the sirens, and the car horns had created total confusion. He went on as far as Egido and in the distance could see, burned and black, the iron pieces of what had been the ship's frame, sinking into the sea like the convulsing hand of a shipwrecked giant. He stopped before the image of that fanciful sculpture of death, and a Rebel Army soldier pushed him.

"Go back, compañeros, there could be another explosion, compañeros!"

"It's Che!" someone shouted.

Carlos turned around and saw Che crossing the security barrier, going towards the scene where they were pulling out pieces of destroyed men, arms, legs, torsos, that filled the street with guts, bones, and blood as he sat down, on the verge of vomiting. There he heard again, over the sirens, cries, and shooting, the voice saying, "Blood, they need blood!" and he stood up to head for a hospital shouting: "Blood, they need blood!"

He never got to give it, the whole city seemed to be spilling into the hospitals with the idea of donating, the workers and activists discouraged people, "There's no room, compañeros, come back tomorrow, compañeros, go back, please," and he decided to go home where he spent hours consoling his parents who cried about the catastrophe, happy that he was safe and sound. The next day he attended, with the Instituto, the burial of the victims of the La Coubre explosion, of the detonator or time bomb or acid placed among the weapons that never arrived at their destination, that the enemy had marked with its bloody sign in some remote Belgian or French port. And there, amid the bodies destroyed by shrapnel, Fidel melted and merged the fury and sadness, the shouts and silence of the people, turning them into one sole voice, when, for the first time, he gave them the slogan that all would repeat as a guide and banner in the many battles to come: "*Patria o muerte!*"

That night Héctor and Mai congratulated him on his bravery during the explosion and against Nelson Cano, and they told him he'd won the right to know the truth: in the struggle of the Revolution against imperialism, the bourgeoisie, and the landowners, in the struggle of the poor against the rich, in the hard struggle of life, through fighting, studying, and thinking, they had become Communists. Carlos wished the earth would swallow him up. How was it possible? Communism was a foreign doctrine, antilibertarian, Russian, that was against property, the family, and the motherland, that threatened the free world with secret weapons and had bloodied whole countries like Lenin's Russia, Bela Kun's Hungary, and Rosa Luxemburg's Germany; how was it possible? Héctor smiled, somewhere between understanding and irony, and showed him a sticker that he had put on the cover of his notebook. There, framing the face of an Indian, it read: ARE YOU A SIBONEY? BECAUSE IN THE FINAL ANALYSIS THE LAND BELONGS TO THE SIBONEYS.

"But not the ideologies, my friend," said Héctor. "After all, the Siboneys weren't Catholic, and the pope doesn't live in Havana, the Taínos didn't know shit about private property, or the starving people a fuck about freedom. What you said was baloney, ignorance, and an ignorant person is just a guilty one, with balls."

He ended almost shouting, and Carlos avoided his gaze, because he had no arguments to offer and he wasn't willing to accept Communism, the word alone still produced in him a visceral repulsion. He had to say something, Héctor and Mai were waiting.

"Fidel's not a Communist," he murmured.

"And if he were?" asked Mai.

He considered that possibility and smiled for the first time, as if he had just discovered what he had heard so many times on the street.

"If Fidel's a Communist, then sign me up."

"Here, start getting the picture," said Héctor, and extended a little book that he took, feeling like it was burning his hands.

For days he didn't dare to read it. A new challenge from Mai made him decide: "Real men aren't afraid." His curiosity stirred with the first sentence: "A specter is haunting Europe: the specter of Communism." He thought how what the doctor said was true, Karl Marx himself had described Communism as a specter, and he kept reading until he found the explanation of class struggle, where he stopped, fascinated and uneasy, because he felt like the book was talking about them, about the torment in which his country, his family, and his life were tearing at each other. That same day he abandoned his reading, scared of continuing his slide towards the abyss. But as it turned out, he inevitably recalled those pages trying to explain to himself the continual battle in the streets, the open and hidden positions of groups and newspapers, his father's attitude, and at night he returned to the book feeling an unmentionable mixture of joy and fear, a persistent excitation that kept him from sleeping and made him ask himself many times if he himself, to his chagrin, hadn't become a pinko.

From then on he felt an uneasy ambivalence, because politically he still considered himself not only different, but also distant, from the Communists, whose almost military discipline irritated him. But when the depression following the fight with Jorge turned into boredom, he started missing his responsibilities, feeling like his sleeping was an obscure kind of betrayal, thinking that maybe he could go back to the struggle without his family finding out. Thus he was overjoyed when his mother asked him to visit Aunt Ernesta and his cousin Rosalina. They were revolutionaries, and he interpreted the request like a coded message, a kind of secret authorization for him to keep on feeling what he was sure his mother also felt, deep down.

The meeting with his cousin moved him greatly: she seemed to know everything, feel everything, she had been everywhere. She was thin and rather small, but she grew as she told him how the people had risen up against the blows of the counterrevolution, which had set fire to cane fields and stores, did he know about that? Carlos didn't say anything, ashamed of not knowing, but she didn't let him dwell on his shame, now she was laughing, telling him about her daily routine in the militia, and she laughed about how she kept pace during the exhausting marches, one, two, three, four, eating shit and tearing up her shoes, her laughter turning into anger because in the OAS there was a maneuver being plotted against Cuba, and again laughter when she told him how Roa had described the Yanqui secretary of state as "a viscous concretion of all human excrescencies." You see what's happening, cuz? she asked, touching his shoulder, getting upset again because the American companies refused to refine Soviet oil, convincing him about the Revolution's right to nationalize them, and what had they done? Cut back the sugar quota to strangle Cuba with hunger, ah, but the Revolution was going to counterattack, and how! Would he go to the ceremony in the Cerro stadium where Fidel was going to announce new measures, huh, would he go? Carlos said yes, of course, feeling stupid and emotional with his cousin, who was now predicting the future, the Yanquis would attack, they still had to figure out if it would be with Eisenhower or after the elections, with the next government, but they would attack, and they'd get their teeth broken in by the people's rifles.

During the ceremony in the stadium, he never stopped feeling grateful for Rosalina's enthusiasm and Ernesta's silent complicity. Thanks to them, he had returned to life along with his compañeros from the Instituto, who accepted his explanation of illness without asking too many questions, because time seemed too short as they listened to the Colombian leading them with his accordion:

> The Americans say
> that Fidel's a Communist.
> The Americans say
> that Fidel's a Communist,
> but they don't say that Batista
> killed twenty thousand Cubans

and joined with the multitudes who filled the stadium:

> Cuba yes, Cuba yes
> Cuba yes, Yanquis no

feeling, as they sang the chorus, that it was the earth singing with the voice of ancient justice, as necessary as life, with the united voice that suddenly started to repeat the name of he who had won the right to speak for all because he represented the hopes of all, Fi-del! Fi-del! Fi-del! like a cry of victory, a flag that kept on waving over the silence of that unique moment in which Fidel could not speak, and Raúl spoke first, before he resumed that speech in which the motherland became everyone's forever. And it was also a chant, in which Fidel would say, "Cuban Telefón Compani," and he didn't pronounce it *cueban*, but rather *koo-ban*, nor did he say *telephone* but rather *telefón*, and the people picked it up on the fly and started singing in unison, "Done gone!" and the chant was as happy as a *son*, delightful and delicious like a *son* in which the multitude took up the phrase of the mambís and turned it into a montuno, reclaiming the voices of those old heroes in Fidel's, saying "Unite Frui Compani," and in the people's, chorusing forever, "Done gone!"

In that atmosphere, Carlos had the idea of building a coffin to bury imperialism in the party that was improvised that night and that still continued, more than twenty hours later, in the colossal rumba that went down Misiones Avenue singing:

> And here's the latest,
> here's the latest in the comics,
> the end of the Yanqui
> Superman is screwed.

The rumba dancers wound around with torches and big puppets of comic-book characters. Under the firelight there came crying Superman, Dick Tracy, Tarzan and Jane, Donald Duck, Batman, Reddy Kilowatt, and Rin-Tin-Tin, with a dying Uncle Sam, more coffins, fireworks, rockets and firecrackers that sounded like a gigantic shoot-out and covered the sky with red, green, and yellow lights under which Carlos, for the first time in a long while, felt happy. He was enjoying the rumba, happy to have been brave enough to have gone from the stadium to the Instituto with Héctor and Mai, who told him that Johnny Crime had been the rat infiltrated into the left during the elections, and added, "He did it for the money, poor guy." Carlos felt embarrassed to have such a hardened leader as Mai apologizing to him again, and told him, "Cut it out, my man," while he joined in with the sawing, nailing, lining, drumming, and dancing, because the coffin was finished and the Smartasses' conga line made a path towards the street, pulling along a river of young people with him at the head, the coffin on his shoulder.

Carlos went winding along, sometimes crazy with joy and other times somber, almost alone, like now, when the obsession ambushed him again: Jorge would hold up these twenty-odd hours away from home as proof that he had been the one to break the delicate balance imposed by their mother. Just then, a black woman who had been coming along doing the rumba stopped, looked at him, took him by the arms, and started asking him wasn't he José María's son, without waiting for a reply, because she was sure he was José María's son. "But boy, I can't believe it, you here with us, Tiembla Tierra, damn, ain't that something!" she said, shaking Carlos out of his surprise because the saint's name suddenly gave him the clue to that face still looking at him in surprise. "Mercedes!" he said, and the black woman answered, "The very same," amid a belly laugh of rejoicing, he remembered her, damn, is the family fine? "Fine," he said, and it was almost impossible for him to recognize the timid servant from his home, who now invited him to rumba while she wiggled and said all right, all riiight when Carlos responded to the beat and she let her buttocks loose to the rumba's *son*, laughed and hugged him saying she was so glad to see him on the side of the Revolution, but she had to go be with her people, and she said goodbye, abairimo Tiembla Tierra, damn, to blend back into the rumba and wind along, invoking the gods who invaded Carlos's memory wrapped in the whirlpool of the enormous Bembé that sowed fear in his childhood nights, stirred up by the terrors of the pastor and the priest, which now were true, now it was rising up from the bowels of misery to wipe out the world of the rich with fire, and in that world there was room for blacks and whites, St. Francis and Kisimba, Alvaro and Chava, Luleno and St. Lazarus, everything in a mix, Carlos, Toña, and Mercedes who disappeared now in the multitude invoking Tiembla Tierra while he felt nearby the low boom of the drums and the voices that made true the saint's name: the earth was trembling beneath the dancers' feet and the torches' fire illuminated the night until it turned it to day, making him recall, The torch, damn it, the torch! and he understood that they were finally winning his grandfather's war, that this was the true Judgment Day, and he felt a shiver of joy and wound along like a possessed man, shouting "Armageddon!" until he heard how the Smartasses turned his cry into a conga, *Armageddon, pucutún, Armageddon,* and he went back to his place under the coffin to respond to Superman's challenge as the puppet danced, trying to fly with no success, making an attempt and going down to the ground displaying a sign on his buttocks, "Oh woe is me!" while the conga guys chorused:

> Little Cuba has kryptonite now,
> you've got kryptonite, my beautiful little Cuba

and started to move towards the sea, where the end of the party started and the people threw Tarzan and Jane into the water, with Uncle Sam, Dick Tracy, Donald Duck, and Superman himself, who flew one more time before sinking under, and Carlos felt wonderful as he shouted, "Armageddon!" and helped with all his strength to toss into the illuminated water the first of the hundreds of coffins that the Caribbean began to smash against its rocks.

NINE

G etting to the corner, he felt a shyness bordering on fear. He didn't know anyone there, nor had he gone to earlier call-ups because he wasn't in the militia, and he wasn't sure he had the right to set out on the trek. Before leaving Ernesta's house he told himself, and they told him too, that no one would notice him, that all he had to do was get in line and walk, thus winning the right to start a new life. But now he imagined that everything could be dangerously different. Maybe they'd ask him who he was, what he was doing there, when he'd been called up . . . Something worse could happen, some militia member from the Instituto could recognize him and accuse him of having abandoned the struggle. Then they'd expel him without a doubt, shouting at him : "Cow-ard! Cow-ard! Cow-ard!" like that strange crow did with deserters from the Sierra.

He stopped at the camp entrance, under the sign LA COUBRE MARTYRS, calculating the consequences of possible disaster. By leaving his house, he'd escaped a confinement that had been strangling him for months, taking him to the verge of madness. Rosalina suggested that he enlist in the militia, where they were admitting all volunteers able to prove their loyalty to the cause by walking sixty-two kilometers in one day, and he accepted enthusiastically. Then it had all seemed so easy, but now he was terrified at the possibility of being turned away because he didn't have anywhere to go, and he knew he was capable of anything, no matter how crazy, rather than returning to the craziness of being holed up. And so he commended himself to God and Tiembla Tierra as he slowly entered the camp.

A handful of lieutenants were struggling to organize thousands of militiamen into improvised squads, companies, and battalions, and Carlos realized he'd committed an irreparable error by asking where to go, instead of just standing anywhere. For a second he imagined how his expulsion would now unfold, but the young lieutenant he had asked shouted a phrase at him that afterwards he would tire of hearing: "Step lively, militiaman!" and placed him at the front of a squad because of his height. It was so simple that it made him laugh, although he immediately stopped, afraid the lieutenant would mis-interpret his happiness. "That corporal, he be crazy," said someone behind him, and he laughed again and kept on laughing because he wasn't only a militiaman, he was a corporal in the militia, he was *someone* in the Revolution, just like that, as if by magic. He turned around towards the squad to say something to the men under his command, but he couldn't come up with anything better than a greeting. "What's up?" "Here," answered a young, smiling black with the surname Kindelán, "just bob-bob-bobbin' along," and then turning towards his neighbor and saying, pointing at Carlos, "I'm tellin' you, he be crazy."

Carlos found Kindelán's kidding around annoying, as he kept going on to his neighbor, whom he called my mate Marcelo, about the disadvantages of going to war commanded by a crazy. He told himself he should do something, and replied, "All in all, asere, to each loco his own," to clearly establish, with the initial phrase and the watchword *asere*, that he wasn't just some little white private-school boy. It worked, because Kindelán whispered to him imme-diately, "Got it, got it," and started telling him stories about crazy people. Within a few minutes he had traced out a fantastic idea of what he called his personal crazy house, through dozens of stories in which the sole reigning purpose was to make them laugh to delirium in a carnival of guffaws that didn't stop when the march began, but rather when the crazy in a story started to sound out a beat with his mouth, making a delicious rumba with his mouth, intoning:

> Fifitaaa the militia girl
> in the early morning
> Fifita's calling me.

Carlos joined in the chorus, remembering the Smartasses' conga, thinking how this guy was as good a rumba dancer as the Smartasses and asking himself where the hell they might be now. He laughed again, for the first time in a long while he wanted to see his buddies, without being hounded by shame and fear. He felt like a part of that multitude walking in the night along the Managua highway, secure in his uniform, wanting to make this march that would give him a permanent place in the world to which he had returned, where now they were singing to him *He be crazy, pucutún, he be crazy,* and a lieutenant interrupted the chant, what is this, militiamen? The army isn't a rumba, after forty kilometers they'd be allowed to dance, let's see who can handle it then.

Kindelán told him they'd have twenty-two kilometers left to party, and the lieutenant said he'd give them that and went off to put some order in the rear guard. The march had gotten disorderly as it advanced. What mattered was making it to the end, the lieutenants were only concerned that the men kept walking, not with their formation, and Carlos recognized with some sadness that he himself, joining the rumba, had added to the disorder in his squad. He couldn't pull it back together, Kindelán just said, "What squad you talking about?" when Carlos asked for his help, and he went around a few times trying to recognize his men's faces until he was convinced that the rumba dancer was right, there were no squads anymore, just a very long column where each one advanced at his own rate. Nighttime even made it hard for him to locate Kindelán. After approaching several marchers in vain, he thought how in the darkness all blacks looked alike, and went along on his path alone, singing the guaguancó about Fifita in a low voice.

The song took him back to the Armageddon rumba, and the perfect alibi he had invented to keep Jorge from accusing him of breaking the pact their mother had imposed when he got home. His voice didn't even shake as he murmured he'd stayed overnight at Ernesta's and Rosalina's house after watching TV, but Jorge's smile started making him nervous. He was secure with the story, because he'd gotten Ernesta's complicity on the phone, but Jorge kept smiling until his mother couldn't stand it any longer and said, "Show it to him." He lowered his head; it was obvious she had some proof of his lie, and he wasn't capable of looking her in the eyes. Jorge put before him a copy of *Revolución* where there were several photos of the celebration. He smiled involuntarily as he recognized Superman and Donald Duck, then followed Jorge's index finger, which had started moving slowly down the page until it got to a photo where he recognized his face, doing the rumba under a coffin. There was nothing he could do. He looked at the photo, lamenting that his old wish to have his picture in the paper would come true like this. He read the caption, "Popular joy spills over" and felt weighed down by the fatigue of so many hours of rumba dancing, sad, without even the strength to respond to Jorge's brutal assault, "You were dancing with your father's coffin," ashamed by his mother's unending anguish. "I waited up for you for hours," she said, "we heard shooting, rockets, firecrackers, shouting, chanting . . . It all sounded like a Bembé, and your father started saying it was the riffraff, paying back their eviction with fire, and he asked where you were and I fooled him with the same lie you just told me now, knowing you weren't at Ernesta's house, that you were God knows where, but certain you'd come home to sleep, like you promised me. But you didn't come, we spent the night waiting up for you, and you didn't come. I had to give your father sleeping pills before going out to look for you with your brother. At the police station they told me no one could find anybody on a night like that, and they were right, everywhere there were drums, rumbas, puppets, coffins . . . I almost went crazy, and you, meanwhile, were dancing with death. Just let me cry! Give me a kiss. Eat something. Rest. And promise me you'll never do it again."

"Militiaman! Do you hear me, militiaman?" He looked in surprise at the lieutenant who was shaking him by the shoulders. "We gave the order to be on your feet! Step lively!"

He stood up with a jump. His right leg had gone numb, and he stumbled until he regained his balance and joined the column. Behind them they left a little town asleep. Some men began asking about the goal, but the lieutenants smiled ironically, the goal? What are you thinking, militiamen? You're just getting started, now you're going to find out what creampuffs are, move your hides, dammit, move your hides and light a fire. Carlos cursed himself for sitting down during the rest period against the lieutenants' instructions, they shouldn't sit down, their bodies would get cold, then afterwards it would be harder. Now he had proof that they were right, he felt a cramp in his leg and decided to run a little to warm up. He gained speed imperceptibly until he'd gotten near the vanguard, where a lieutenant advised him, "Walk, militiaman, it's a long, loooong way." He stopped and then realized that his boots were starting to bother him, especially on the left foot, but it was really nothing, he said to himself looking at them, a minor detail. They were new and shiny, a present from Rosalina along with his backpack, canteen, and uniform, which Carlos valued as a symbol that Ernesta made into a commitment: "The most important thing is that you get there." That didn't worry him, he felt physically fit, a little discomfort in his left foot, and very hot. Not a leaf moved on the trees bordering the curb. He opened his canteen and several militiamen immediately surrounded him thirstily. He passed it around after taking three long swallows, and only had the courage to ask for it back when he realized that the guy drinking from it was carrying his own. A lieutenant passed and advised them not to drink water, militiamen, they should just rinse their mouths out and spit, if not it would be worse. The guy returned his canteen with a smile of Iscrewedyou that sent Carlos back to the times when Jorge had accused him of being a shithead. It was almost empty. Just as well, he told himself, now it weighs less.

After a while marching, that day seemed much longer than others to Carlos, and he joined the rumor of protest that began running through the column, were the lieutenants sleeping? It was time for a rest, wasn't it? What was going on? The end, the end, were they getting to the end? But the lieutenants answered, Quiet, militiamen, move your hides and light a fire, the end was in the back of beyond. He needed to urinate. He decided to do it before they rested, because now he wasn't sure when the stop would be. He went off the path and saw a group competing to see who could wet the trunk of a ceiba the highest. He urinated on the curb, unable to do it on the tree, annoyed at having lost his place in the vanguard and by the heat that made his shirt stick to his back.

He made a push to return to his position. He didn't want to be walking alongside the old men, the fatties, the slowpokes spontaneously grouped in the rear guard. He passed by an asthmatic who advanced in the midst of an attack: his face convulsing, his hands struggling to hold his atomizer to his mouth, open in a muffled, silent cry. Carlos left him behind, trying to forget that sad figure bent on an effort that seemed tragic; the asthmatic knew, he had to know that he wouldn't finish. He kept up the pace until reaching the middle of the column, but there he had to slow down to reduce the discomfort in his foot. He put his hands to his back trying to raise up his backpack and lessen the weight on his shoulders, which had started to burn. The movement forced him to walk with his head down, looking at the asphalt. In that position the order of "Halt" startled him, shouted by the lieutenants who made the "t" function like the crack of a whip. He stayed on his feet to avoid letting his body cool down. He let his backpack fall, threw his head back to loosen up his neck, and then, suddenly, he discovered the sky. Involuntarily he opened his mouth, stunned, with vertigo from the serenity of the infinite, it seemed incredible that he'd let himself be blinded for so long by the despicable city lights.

He looked at his astral mother, the moon, shining like a great circle of quicksilver illuminating his path, and it seemed like a good omen. While he was holed up, depressed, he'd killed time with Monopoly and Chinese checkers, which proved themselves almost immediately to be empty pastimes. He became a chess fan, fascinated by the strange moves of the bishops, the unpredictable jumps of the knights, the names of defenses and openings: Sicilian, Spanish, King's Indian, suggesting powerful women, traitorous and naked. One night, tired of beating himself, he took a magazine open by chance to the horoscope section and smiled at the subtitle: "The stars impel, they do not compel." There he read that the presence of Pluto in Libra during the past few years had been the reason for drastic changes in the lives of those born under his sign, Cancer, and then, intrigued, he got involved in the labyrinth of prophecy.

"All projects and unions that have not solidified will end. Pluto is considered to be a kind of Shiva, destroyer of all foundations that are not solid. This year Saturn is found in Libra and will form a quadrilateral with Cancer, therefore the next two years will be characterized by an unending task, in which all things concerning these natives will be tested. Anything not valid will not pass the tests, and all things overcoming these times will develop rapidly and will become solid, lasting projects."

It was all obscure, and at the same time, it all seemed to make sense. What was coming to an end, his union with the Revolution or with his family? Which foundations was Pluto disturbing? What would the unending task be? Which tests? He feverishly read the brief description of his sign to help him figure out the enigma: "The sentimental Moon children are the creators of the family, of togetherness, of tradition, of patriotism, of love for the place where one is born, of the family to which one belongs." The riddle, then, became even more painful. What should a moonchild do when loyalty to the place where one is born implied leaving the family to which one belongs?

The questions obsessed him for a long time, even when he repeated to himself that the stars impel, they do not compel. Now he set out on the march again, asking his astral mother to continue illuminating his path, shortening it a little, if she could; asking the stars that they impel him to keep going, telling himself that they had heard him and that he was walking on the soft, black carpet of the sky, where his feet couldn't hurt him, amid the freshness of the sky, where he wasn't thirsty, or hot, or bothered by that dust, "Stardust," he thought, evoking the trumpet sound that Gipsy had liked so much, because it was she who accompanied him now from star to star, to the very center of the compass card, there where neither the stumble, the fall, or the "Buddy, are you dumb or what?" directed at him by the militiaman he had bumped into were real.

He leaped up, irritated at having made a fool of himself, and by the "Step lively, militiaman!" that a lieutenant shouted at him. Going forward he felt pain in his right knee; he had torn his pants, he was limping. The first deserters had started to stay behind on the curb and one of them said to him: "Keep going, *cojo*!" and kept insisting, "Cojo!" to which Carlos responded, "*Nudo*!" with the result that the third time the words sounded like one, *Cojonudo*! which helped him keep advancing without having the knee pain give way. He began fooling himself by setting partial goals. He would look at a tree, one of the huge ceibas lining the highway, and think that mysterious plant was the end, if he got to it he could rest by the great knots of its powerful trunk, under the branches through which clear moonlight would filter down. Arriving there, he would tell himself that actually this wasn't the ceiba he'd picked out, but rather another one much further away, under which he would stretch out to take off his boots and relieve the pain in his feet.

He was walking, hoping that the real end would come by surprise, when they started making out in the distance the lights of a town where that endless march had to end. He picked up his step adjusting to the rhythm of the column, which now advanced more rapidly, drawn by the lights of the end. But disillusion began in the vanguard and immediately spread all the way through the troops, ratified by the lieutenants' voices, what were they thinking? Move your hides and light a fire, they weren't even halfway, the best was yet to come, the La Ruda Slope. He got to that damned town that wasn't the end anymore, making a painful effort to keep up the pace. Behind him he could hear the dying breath of the asthmatic and he didn't want to get there after him. When they gave the order to stop he let himself fall, and then he heard someone calling him, "Hebecrazy." He greeted Kindelán, amazed that he still had the energy to improvise a little rumba, "Loony, loony, crazy as a loon."

He gave in to the desire to lie down on his back despite the continual warnings of the lieutenants, but he couldn't concentrate on the mysteries of the sky. For the first time he was afraid he wouldn't make it to the end, his astral mother seemed like a dead man's moon, he could feel how new aches were showing up in every muscle and every bone, and to his chagrin heard what someone was saying about the La Ruda Slope, better known as the Militiamen's Cemetery, because they fell there like flies, without the strength or the courage to conquer the trek. The asthmatic was nearby, standing up, his chest sounding like a useless bellows. Carlos admired his anguished, stubborn image. "Have a seat," he told him, and the other declined with a gesture, as if by not speaking he were saving his strength. Now Kindelán was telling the story of a crazy militiaman who had done the trek playing the trumpet to the moon, pal, tatata, tatata, tatatu, and the story had two endings, in one the crazy turned into a wolf and went running to the finish, where he became a man again, pal, and was the first to get there. In the other, the crazy went along playing tatata, looking at the moon, tatatu, until he fell down, pal, splat bam, and stayed sitting there in the Militiamen's Cemetery. And now, every time a man stays in the cemetery, the crazy's voice yells at him, "Splat bam." Carlos felt that the second ending, so like Pablo's story of the birds, alluded to him. He'd have to invent a third ending, he told himself, because he wasn't going to be the first, nor the last one either.

The lieutenants gave the order "On your feet!" and the idea of not being the last one helped him make the stubborn effort he needed to stand up. His body hurt as if he'd been meticulously beaten, without leaving any little bone, any little tendon, or any miserable cell untouched. He advanced slowly, like an old man, until he rejoined the column. "You feeling bad, corporal?" Next to him was a man with gray hair who must have been part of his old squad. "Just fine," he answered, annoyed, and the man confessed he was wiped out, but he had to make it, he said, because his son-in-law had made it and he couldn't lose face with his daughter. "Move your hide and light a fire," commented Carlos. He'd been sizing up the La Ruda Slope and it didn't seem so terrible, a belt of white dust, full of curves, in the middle of uneven country. But the pain was biting at him, especially in his knee and foot, and the continual chatter of the old man made him dizzy. He quickened his step, obtaining some pleasure from overcoming the pain, until he joined a little group led by Kindelán. In spite of the effort it took to maintain the pace, he felt better in that outfit of jokers who made fun of everyone and everything, reminding him of the Bacilli and the Smartasses. He joined Kindelán when the latter questioned a man sprawling out on the curb. "Splat bam, madman?" The guy responded, "I'm not going on," and Carlos shouted at him, "Coward!" using the same high-pitched voice with which, according the Pablo, the big ugly birds in the Sierra screeched the word.

He would have liked for Pablo to see him advancing across the La Ruda Slope in spite of the weight of his backpack and the thirst, heat, and dust, his hurt foot and wounded knee. He would have liked that, because he suspected Pablo didn't think he could do it, and in his wish there was both challenge and gratitude. He would never forget that Pablo was the one who pulled him out of the lethargy that followed the crisis with his mother, made up of pastimes and indecipherable omens. That simple message "Pablo wants to see you" was enough to make him jump out of bed and be left speechless with admiration and envy at the beard and uniform of the friend who returned and wasn't the same anymore, in spite of his embrace. From the first he felt they were separated by a distance as great as the one between his pajamas and that literacy teacher uniform, between his closed-up room and the mountains. That feeling kept growing during their conversation, in which Pablo didn't want any rum because he had stopped drinking and smoking, and Carlos felt he was pure and distant, like a hero. Now he thought that maybe, when he finished the trek, they could talk man to man, but at that moment he had perceived himself too small and miserable, and Pablo too sure of himself in his monologue about the swollen rivers he had crossed during unending downpours, about the mountains with hillsides of steep ravines you had to go over through really dangerous passes like *Los Monos* or *Las Angustias*, not much more than a string of rocks between two abysses, on the other side of which was Turquino Peak, where he had carved his name into a trunk with a knife.

Carlos felt even worse when Pablo told him how that mission had been carried out by thousands of people, since not only the literacy teachers were in the Sierra, but also the Rebel Army recruits, the cadets, and above all, the Five Peaks, hundreds of kids, almost children, who had responded to the call from the Young Rebels Association. He concluded with fury that he was the only one shut up in his room, only he was a stupid shit, and he felt an urgent need to talk, to tell about something, anything to redeem himself to Pablo, and he started exaggerating the story of the Armageddon rumba, which nevertheless came out sounding weak, pale, measly without the glow of magnificent madness it really had and that he was incapable of communicating, and so he called up the old fraternity, the old codes, and he said it was great, Sam, something wild, *Ten Days that Shook the World*, Sam, and Pablo smiled, nostalgic, but didn't pick up the game, just asked, and then what? leaving Carlos with no more story to tell, fucked, with a sudden need to hurt this person who knew perfectly well what had happened next, he said, months in

144   Jesús Díaz

that room, without doing anything for the Revolution, hear me? Closed up reading horoscopes, got it? Horoscopes! Because he was a shit, and if that's what he wanted him to say now he'd said it, he, Carlos Pérez Cifredo was a shit, so now he could go back to his little schoolhouse or way the hell away, he didn't care.

He would have preferred it if Pablo had yelled at him, if he had left, anything but that measured, calm reaction, underlined by the little phrase, "You're still so green." He laughed with rage, it was like he was comparing him to a banana, and he wasn't a banana, he said, not ripe or green. Pablo repeated his little phrase, along with a "don't you see?" that for Carlos was absolutely intolerable. He covered his head with the sheet to avoid the next volley, and then another phrase hit him like a slap in the face, "This is ridiculous." He thought that was true, he was doing something infantile, stupid. He took the sheet off his head and found the adult Pablo, whom he had just met that day, asking him, "What's the matter with you, Carlos?" He felt that if Pablo had at least called him pal, asere, my man, buddy, or Flaco he would have told him about his sadness, but he'd called him Carlos, as mature people undoubtedly do, and he didn't have the slightest wish to open up to him. Thus he answered, "Me? Nothing. Go ahead, keep telling me about you."

Pablo reluctantly agreed, and Carlos felt he was treating him like a child, or a crazy person. He decided not to pay much attention to that strange history that was the counterpart of his Armageddon. A gray counterpart, he thought with a certain scorn, because Pablo told how he'd spent the night closed up in a warehouse on the outskirts of Havana, along with dozens of literacy teachers, watching the ceremony on television, to which Carlos commented that he'd missed the best part, on television you couldn't see anything, and Pablo went on saying of course, they were all really mad about being held there, because it wasn't fair that after so much time breaking their asses in the Sierra they'd put them there without knowing why or what for, without even taking them to the stadium where the course of history was being changed. That confinement, he said, generated a sort of competition between different groups of teachers who said they knew the reason; according to some, they had been made into a guerrilla column that would have as its mission the overthrow of Trujillo in Santo Domingo; according to others, they'd be leaving for the Soviet Union to become MIG-17 pilots; the rest said don't be shitheads, they were just literacy teachers, the next morning they'd be given a pass and then they'd go back to the mountains to teach.

None of them were right, added Pablo, they spent the night arguing and none of them were right, because at dawn a rebel commander came to inform them that the Revolution had decided to place in their hands the assets that the people had just nationalized during the night. Carlos didn't understand, and he felt better when Pablo told him he hadn't understood either, not even when the commander called his name.

"Aleaga, Pablo. Cunagua Sugar Mill, Camagüey, former property of the Tuinicu Sugar Company. You leave immediately. Any questions?"

"No," Pablo said he had told him, surprised, but then he corrected himself. "Yes, excuse me *comandante*, but what am I supposed to do?"

"Boy," the commander had put an index finger on his chest, "you are the ad-min-is-tra-tor of the Cunagua Sugar Mill!"

Now Pablo was asking him how about that, and Carlos said, wow, and repeated, wow, to the story of the demonstration the workers put on at the mill offices to receive Fidel's administrator, and to alert him to the snares the Americans were planning, and Carlos felt his Armageddon rumba was irresponsible and ridiculous compared with the mountain of problems Pablo was telling him about, that his crisis was absurd beside the huge task of reliving the fear and ignorance he was forced to conquer every day, in the face of enormous unknowns. The Americans had left millions of pesos of debt they owed the tenant farmers, who now demanded their pay and claimed their rights to certain lands the Yanqui administration had stolen from them; the workers were asking that four work shifts be established to combat unemployment, a measure that was socially just, but economic suicide; the cane cutters, the *macheteros*, were leaving for the cities and towns looking for new sources of work and escaping their slavelike task, which was also just, but left a huge gap in the canefields; some ass-licking technicians and employees were conspiring and attempting sabotage, and with all this he had to complete the zafra, and maintain the level of past sugar yields, and start studying to see if he could master that complicated technology, in which the majority of the terms— *shaker screens, pol in cane, pol in bagasse, imbibition water*—were Greek to him.

"Inhibition water," murmured Carlos, nostalgic at having gotten a good phrase for the word game that wasn't going to start up, because words weren't a game anymore for Pablo. Now they were something just a serious as that volcanic world he evoked, even more distant than the mountains themselves from the boring stupidity of his room. It was incredible, his buddy Nose, the whoring Nose, administering a huge sugar mill in the legendary Camagüey plains, to which he had to go back the next day, pretty down because he didn't have a wife or any way to get one: he worked eighteen or twenty hours a day, he didn't mind that, but during the four hours he spent in the mill boarding house he felt as lonely as a dog. Wasn't there anyone he could go out with tonight? Even some skinny little toothpick?

Now Pablo had collapsed, imploring him, and he felt a dark kind of calm seeing him like that, without being able to help: he was alone, too, fucked, as he could see. Pablo stroked his beard in silence and Carlos jumped out of bed shouting, "Rosalina!" and ran to the telephone, inspired by his clearest thinking. Pablo and Rosalina, damn, how perfect, he said to himself after everything for the date that night was arranged, and Pablo thanked him, curious, yeah, he remembered a little, Rosalina? and Carlos clarified that his cousin was a revolutionary, and skinny, but she had a nice ass. Pablo snapped his fingers, happy, and asked Carlos to tell him about his problems. Carlos spoke movingly, expecting his friend to hug him or at least put a hand of solidarity on his shoulder. But Pablo was cold, distant, almost annoyed, and spoke without reference to the story he'd just heard, not even to accuse him again of being green.

"In the Sierra," he said, "a guy wanted to leave, scared by the downpours, the treks, and the hunger. He tried to slip off in the dark so he wouldn't have to face us. The rest of us suddenly started hearing some very strange cawing, went to see and found the guy running away, followed by a flock of birds screeching what all of us repeated: 'Cow-ard! Cow-ard! Cow-ard!' After that anyone wanting to desert had to do it in the light of day, and face it."

The moral of the story was all too clear. Carlos felt a fierce hatred for Pablo, that bastard incapable of helping a friend in trouble, and he cursed himself for having gotten him a date with his cousin. That night he felt painfully, sweetly sorry for himself. He felt more alone than Pablo in the loneliness of his dark little room at the mill, because he didn't have anything to do the next day, except to keep on being alone, and he again slowly caressed the idea of suicide. But in the middle of the night for the first time, birds' cries assaulted him, he woke up trembling and couldn't get back to sleep until dawn. The next afternoon, his mother woke him up with his lunch and some news: Rosalina and Pablo were getting married, just like that, without a ceremony or an engagement, to go live in Cunagua, and Ernesta had agreed and was happy; that's all there was to it, the world had gone mad.

Carlos took a few seconds to comprehend and then had a rush of joy, those two would make a great couple. Suddenly he felt darkly depressed, Pablo had killed his solitude with one shot while he would stay solemnly solitary, as his mother always said, even more alone than the silence of the room where he'd put up with the insults of that bastard who wasn't even in love with his cousin. He went to get some coffee while his mother talked about finding the money to buy a gift. Jorge was in the kitchen, feeding birdseed to his canary. They let weeks pass without talking to each other, Jorge involved in his business and Carlos in his bed, thus he passed by his brother without greeting. He was pouring his coffee when he heard Jorge say:

"What do you think about this wedding?"

He didn't answer. The coffee was cold and bitter, and he began looking for sugar on the shelf.

"Getting married to a whore," murmured Jorge.

"She's not a whore," he retorted, happy to contradict him.

"A huge whore," Jorge insisted.

Carlos took his coffee, now too sweet, and turned around to tell Jorge to wash his dirty mouth out with hydrochloric acid before talking about Rosalina. Jorge wasn't ruffled.

"All in all, you've always liked whores," he said. "You want me to tell you why Rosalina is a whore?"

Carlos came over to him and could see his brother's sneering face up close.

"Because I touched her ass and so did you!"

He hit him frontally, a short, crushing blow that threw Jorge into the wall, but couldn't stop his cry, "Julián touched her ass too!" as he came forward with a stick at Carlos, who picked up a knife and then let it go, seeing his mother's terrified face.

He refused to explain, went back to his room trembling and was there for hours, assaulted by bird cries and the murky memory of that Christmas Eve when they touched Rosalina, measuring the split second that kept him from stabbing Jorge, certain he'd kill him if he couldn't escape that confinement once and for all, where he lived in hate like a bulldog, despising himself, apart from everything that had ever given meaning to his life. He could calm down only by dreaming he was leaving, that he was outside, free, allowing himself to be pulled by the river of Revolution like Pablo. But that euphoria soon dissolved: he had no place in the process, he'd lost it by betraying his compañeros at the Instituto, abandoning them at the most difficult moment, even refusing to see them when they went to visit him during the worst days of his depression. He *had* to leave.

And to join the Combat Battalions now, he *had* to pass the test; only afterwards could he look at his old compañeros again without embarassment. But the Militiamen's Cemetery merited its name many times over: the uneven slope made the march as grueling as a shortcut maneuver, and he managed to advance only in fits and starts through that hell that didn't even offer the consolation of a tree. He told himself it wasn't a question of strength but of balls, because he'd been exhausted for a long time already and he kept on going forward, his left foot and right knee all bruised up, limping in both legs like St. Lazarus, evoking the dear Luleno of his childhood and imagining himself supported by his crutches, overcoming the difficult tests that the somabitch Saturn was submitting him to, for going around in confluence with Libra and forming quadrilaterals with Cancer; and he repeated to himself that he was a *cojonudo* who could make it to the goal and thus win for himself a space of his own, from which he could again take up his reflections on the ideology of the proletariat. Only now he didn't have books, or a home: he'd decided not to return to Ernesta's to avoid encountering his mother, and even any eventual contact with Rosalina or Pablo, promising himself he'd only see him again when he'd become a man on his own. That decision, made with an air of heroic solitude, made him feel proud; but now he couldn't stop asking himself where the hell he'd go when the trek ended.

The black wind of La Ruda had stirred up a dust cloud that dried out his throat. The trickle of water left in his canteen couldn't relieve his thirst. He ran his tongue over his lips, and it tasted like dirt. He felt how rough it was, filled with the dust that continued whipping the road, getting into his mouth, eyes, nose, making him silently curse and see absurd sights: now the black Kindelán was white, as if dusted with flour, and he looked like one of those whites who paint themselves with shoe polish to act the part of the *negrito*. He wanted to tell Kindelán that, but felt like he didn't have enough saliva to articulate even one sentence. The marabou tree where he set his next goal was white, too, with its bent trunk and fluttering branches, like the body of a shipwrecked man he should save, because if not, he told himself, the poor guy would drown, and the poor guy was him, advancing through the dust in the middle of the night. For the first time he longed for his bed, he evoked with painful force the sweet stupidity into which he'd plunge for weeks, the ineffable pleasure of sleeping for fourteen or fifteen hours, then getting up, bathing, and going back to bed on clean, fresh, just-ironed sheets that lulled him to sleep with the celestial music produced by the lightest layer of starch his mother gave them. She, standing at the foot of the bed with a breakfast tray, and him yelling at her, "I don't want it! Let me sleep, you hear me?" Her saying psalmlike, "Don't sleep so much, moss will grow on your bones." But that unending march wasn't a dream, he wasn't dreaming that he was walking, but rather walking so much he thought he was dreaming, hallucinating, dissolving into the white dust clouds and the tortured forms of the marabou trees and the screeches of bats and the infinite column of shadows and the pain and the thirst and the hunger and the terrible fatigue that would end up conquering him if he wasn't able at least to get to that plant, a little more, even after the lieutenants' Halt and Kindelán's Hebecrazy, until he touched the marabou's trunk and let himself fall down exhausted, breathing heavily, as if on the sand at the beach.

He thought about taking off his boots, gave up the idea for fear that he wouldn't be able to get them back on again, and tried to massage his knee; it was inflamed, sensitive even to touch. He gently pulled his shirt away from his shoulders, freed from the weight of the backpack, but couldn't lessen the burning. He ran his tongue over his cracked lips and again felt it rough, like sandpaper. He threw himself face down, with his face on his backpack, and was startled by the smell of a steak sandwich that Ernesta had made him. He made an effort to pull it out, gave it a bite, and felt like he was chewing sand. A coughing fit shook all the aches in his body. He touched the canteen, empty. He let go of the sandwich, closed his eyes, and the coolness of the earth sent a vague drowsiness into his body, in which all the aches became intolerably sweet. Thus the "On your feet!" surprised him, deafened by his drowsy fog. He was aware that the column had begun to march again, and he didn't move. In a minute he'd stand up and he'd join the ranks. No, maybe in two, maybe in ten . . . He felt incrusted into the ground, he'd managed to dissolve the noise of the column's march in his fatigue and now it was as if nothing was happening, except that delicious dream. He stayed there without moving even after the first "Cow-ard!" which was rapidly followed by others. It had been awhile since he'd heard that cry, which he had made part of this ordeal, and now the militiamen were repeating it, making him think not of Pablo's story, but of Kindelán, who sounded in his ear a "Splat bam?" making him sit up without intending to, frightened and with an awful pain in his back: he was crazy Carlos, sprawled out forever in the Militiamen's Cemetery. Then he grabbed onto Kindelán's hands, which were white now and hauled him up like a crane, putting on its feet the useless collection of aches that was his body.

He walked rigidly, scarcely even moving his joints, like a rusted robot.

Kindelán had gone further ahead, to support his mate Marcelo, leaving Carlos in the rear guard, from which he could not manage to detach himself. He thought about how freeing himself from that torment would be easy, as easy as walking more and more slowly, until he had allowed the column to go far, far, far away . . . Then he'd be alone on the road and no one could shout cow-ard; in reality he hadn't chickened out, just walked slowly, very slowly, more and more slowly, when the lieutenant in charge of the rear guard yelled alongside him, "God almighty couldn't stand this!" and continued walking next to him, "Move your hide and light a fire, militiaman, are you a cojo . . . ?" "Nudo," whispered Carlos. The lieutenant acted like he was deaf. "Shout it, militia-man, a cojo . . . ?" "Nudo," repeated Carlos. The lieutenant seemed un-satisfied, "Shout means shout, militiaman, a cojo . . . ?" "Nudo!" voiced Carlos, to get him off his back, and the shout felt like a brisk shower for his muscles and the lieutenant's mood, as he repeated with a hoarse, powerful voice, "Cojo!" and heard the echo, "Nudo!" and they went along like that until the lieutenant made the game plural and extended it to the rear guard, from which it took over the whole column, which advanced through the night shouting that that's what they were, cojonudos.

Carlos made a desperate effort to get out of the back of the rear guard and gradually left behind the old men, the fatties, the slowpokes. He kept going until he made out the asthmatic, who was walking stubbornly, with short, even steps, thirty meters away. Carlos imposed an anxious march on himself, telling himself he was a cojonudo and seeing how he slowly was nearing the back of the asthmatic, who did not change his rhythm even when Carlos passed him, forcing him to move aside: the guy walked without looking at anyone else. On reaching the head of the rear guard he knew he'd committed a serious mistake by setting out on that stupid competition, where he'd wasted the strength that had come from the shouts that he couldn't even repeat anymore. He stopped setting goals. Each step was just a step, and he took it not knowing if he could even make it to the next. How was it possible that at twenty he was weaker than men of forty or fifty, or even the old men, the fatties, the slowpokes in the rear? Getting there, he repeated to himself, was not a question of strength, but of balls. Many young men had dropped out on the road, while others, almost little boys or almost elderly, were still in the thick of it. But he was pulverized, destroyed, and he thought his mother had been right: moss had grown on his bones. Moss, why hadn't he realized sooner? Moss was something slippery, spongy, that made his body flimsy like a rag and took away his strength and the resolve to move, even when he heard behind him the anguished breathing of the asthmatic, who passed him as if in a dream from which he could not wake up. He wanted his bed, he was in his bed dreaming that passing by him were shadows, shadows, shadows that soon would stop passing to leave him at last to sleep in peace. He said, "Huh?" and again, "Huh?" when the chief lieutenant of the rear guard gently pushed him forward: "The camp is over there, militiaman. Just a little more effort, move your hide and light a fire."

He was the last man of the column to arrive in Managua, the little town they had left behind so many hours ago, and he understood that they'd made a long loop in the trek, a loop of sixty-two kilometers that could take the world by the throat and strangle it. A diffuse pink light wrapped around the column that arrived in the main street of the little town, where the inhabitants were waiting, cheering for Fidel and the militiamen, bringing them water and bread. Carlos discovered how long the column was when he saw it stretched out, covering blocks and blocks. He picked out Kindelán and made an effort to get over to him, halfway there his knees gave out and he started to slide down until he was on all fours, then on his back, sprawled out in the middle of the road. He was destroyed, but he had made it. Suddenly a hand slid under his neck and a woman who could have been his mother started pouring a stream of water between his lips, gave him a piece of still-warm bread and told him she had to go take care of other militiamen. Carlos sat up, overcoming a persistent pain in his back, ate the bread chewing slowly, like an elderly man, and gave in to the wish to take off his boots. His feet were swollen and it required great effort to get them off. Then he tugged on the green socks that were now black, and torn, and stuck to his blisters. He laid down again, and only then did he notice he had left his backpack on the road. He shrugged and wiggled his toes with the endless pleasure of feeling them free. Later on he'd find a bag for carrying his things to the boot camp. He wondered if he should talk to that lady and ask her if he could spend a couple of days in her house until they called him up for training, but he didn't have the energy to stand up and, wrapped in an aching sleepiness, he heard the impossible shout, "On your feet!" He thought he was suffering from hallucinations, one of his recurring nightmares, while the militiamen protested, no, it couldn't be, they'd walked maybe a hundred kilometers; and the lieutenants, "Sixty, militiamen! You finish sixty-two at the camp! On your feet!" and into that nightmare came the murmuring and the commotion of men getting up, the shouts of the rear guard chief and Kindelán's voice, more and more urgent, "Come on, Hebe-crazy!" He opened his eyes because Kindelán wouldn't stop shaking him, said, "Shaker screens, Pablo talked about shaker screens," and babbled, "I can't," stroking his feet, his tumescent knee, while the vanguard resumed the march and he felt incapable of putting on his boots again and taking another step with those blistered feet. It wasn't fair. It wasn't fair that after an effort like that, they'd leave him there, beaten, swallowing his anger while he watched the vanguard leaving and heard Kindelán's words of encouragement. He felt an immense tenderness towards the black man and murmured, "Go on without me, buddy," which provoked in Kinde an explosion of rage before he lifted Carlos's body up in one yank, incapable now of walking, unmoving, rigid, leaning on Kindelán, who stumbled under the weight shouting, "I need a man here, dammit!" A robust, blond militiaman put his arm around Carlos under his armpit and over his shoulder, making a lever with Kindelán, who said, "Looking good there, Gallego," and Carlos felt like they were making him walk like St. Lazarus with human crutches, like Christ on the cross with two friendly thieves who had performed a miracle, and he thought it wasn't fair to the others, while Kindelán encouraged him, "Go on, get walking," and right away he perceived the beat of a guaracha hidden in the phrase, with which he improvised a moribund little rumba: "Go on, get walking / get walking, Juan Pescao . . ." Carlos felt like the rhythm helped and started putting his feet on the asphalt, sometimes stepping firmly, but eighty meters further he couldn't stand the burning of his blisters and had to hang onto his crutches again, who now had named each other Lumumba and Gallego, shadows which only I see, he said to himself, thinking about his two grandfathers, Chava and Álvaro, on whom he was also leaning to go forward. Kindelán had left a riddle hanging in the air, why, in Cuba, were the Gallego and the black man brothers from even before the Revolution? Easy, he said, because they had the same last name: Black Shit and Gallego Shit. Carlos didn't laugh: he was saving up his strength to let go and continue by dragging himself, if necessary, when the last row caught up to them, seven haggard militiamen advancing towards them, lean-ing on each others' fatigues and shifting their weight towards the end, where the lieutenants marched. Joining that line, Carlos knew he was saved. Now they were too weak not to make it, his pain leaned on the others' moans and on the irregular breathing of the asthmatic, who was the first to notice the goal from which the vanguard's and the center's cries of victory came. They sped up the pace, or maybe only thought they did as they stumbled like drunks, inspired by the voices of encouragement of those who had already made it, by the applause and the cheers with which they were received, like heroes who only collapse at the goal.

Carlos fell down next to Gallego and to Kindelán, who had recovered his joy and didn't quit calling him "Hebecrazy," trying to convince him that being crazy was an honor, since only true crazies were capable of voluntarily doing such an outrageous thing; his mate Marcelo, for example, was sane, that's why he'd stayed behind on the road, but they were demented, wacky, nuts, cracked, loony, dazed, with their wires crossed and a few loose screws, that's how his dear little crazies were, he was saying, his little lunatics, he was saying, provoking a spasmodic laughter in Carlos that was suddenly interrupted by the inconsiderate way in which that Red Cross girl started cleaning off his foot, making him yell like crazy, said Kindelán, while the girl kept working on the dried blood and the pieces of woolen socks, pulling off strips of his skin, requesting him to please be quiet, militiaman honey, it's not such a big deal, just sixty-two little kilometers that's all, leaving him amazed at the nerve with which she talked about his heroic deed and laughed at his pain, with which she asked him, teasingly, for his other little hoof.

TEN

He leaned his left arm into the mud and lifted his head above the guinea grass. He looked behind him; the men in his platoon were still lying flat. "They look like ghosts," he thought, seeing them covered in mud. He let himself fall back down on the black, viscous earth, calculating that they'd probably been sunk in there for more than half an hour. He breathed his own intolerable smell for a while. He brought his head up again. The vast grassland seemed deserted. "They're going to fuck us," he said to himself, scrutinizing the palm trees in the distance that marked the visible end of the field.

"Liaison," he called, "liaison."

Remberto Davis's agile and thin body approached, splashing in the mud.

"At your orders, sir," he said.

Carlos stroked his rifle's muzzle brake.

"I'll bet my balls they're over in that grove."

Suddenly they heard one long whistle, three short ones, and then there was only the breeze blowing over the tips of grass. "They're going to fuck us," he murmured. A group of buzzards flew over the field, spattering the slate-colored sky with fleeting marks.

"It's going to keep on raining," he said.

"Or else someone died," commented Remberto Davis.

He calculated the distance. It was too far away, but if he managed it, the enemy was done for.

"Tell the corporals we drag ourselves to the palm grove," he ordered.

He started to secure his rifle strap. Remberto Davis was still next to him, frightened.

"What's the problem?" asked Carlos. "I mean now!"

The liaison instinctively put his right hand to his eyebrow and justified his nickname, Blacksquirrel, as he dragged himself through the grass. The men started to move forward, protesting in low voices. Carlos leaned on his left elbow to calculate their range. "You can see them a league away," he thought, picking out the muddy, sweaty faces, "or is it just that I know where they are?" Twelve meters to the left, the buttocks of Zacarías the Stutterer clearly stood out over the field. He threw a rock, the stutterer pulled his ass down for a moment, and put it up again as he continued the advance. Carlos started crawling. Blacksquirrel had caught up to him and moved forward without talking his eyes off Carlos.

"Look somewhere else!" he shouted, thinking that maybe Remberto Davis was right, attacking was crazy, but he couldn't stand it there any longer, sunk in the mud like a motherfucking frog.

It started to rain, and the grassland turned into a mire. Suddenly, Corporal Heriberto Magaña's shouts filtered through from the enemy camp amid the noise of the rain.

"One, three, five, seven!"

Carlos crouched down instinctively, wondering if they'd been discovered.

"Fifteen meters!"

He armed his rifle, thinking that if the corporal had discovered them they were done for, but if not, he was going to go right into the very heart of enemy command to fuck half the human race. Numbers two, four, and six of Heriberto's squad lifted their rifles over the grass to cover the advance of their compañeros, while Carlos thought that the fight would be decided right then and there.

"Hit them!" ordered the corporal, starting to run. His four men followed him, spread out, and passed the platoon to the left without discovering it.

"We fucked them," Carlos told himself, dragging himself on his elbows over the puddles. The enemy was unprepared. Through the downpour he could see the black Tanganyika's huge blue body. Twenty meters more, two minutes, and he'd be done for by rifle fire.

"Tell Kinde to go towards the left," he ordered without stopping.

Blacksquirrel turned to carry out the order. Carlos indicated to the Barber that he move his squad to the right and took charge of Gallego's group to attack from the center. "Not even God can save them," he told himself, waiting desperately for his men to finish spreading out. When he was sure, he shouted, "Hit them!" and his platoon emerged out of the mud, running towards the enemy command. He felt huge, advancing across the open field hearing his own bursts of fire. "Rat-a-tat-tat! Rat-a-tat-tat! Rat-a-tat-tat!" He knew his men were attacking, he was the leader of that hard, experienced troop, capable of fighting in the rain in spite of the mud, or the fire coming from an enemy who had realized the strategy too late, and now attempted a desperate defense with small weapons. "Bang! Bang!"—as if that would be enough to stop the march of the platoon—Carlos swept along shouting, "Attaaack!" while he ran in a zigzag to evade the lead buzzing by his temples, "Zinnnng!", closer and closer "Zinnnng!", until he reached Tanganyika, whom he commanded:

"Surrender, goddammit!"

There was great confusion. Tanganyika and his squad would not surrender, Carlos and his platoon proclaimed themselves victors, from the other side of the field there also came shouts of victory and protest; then Lieutenant Aquiles Rondón shouted, "Here!" and everyone ran towards him, forming a semicircle to analyze the exercise. Carlos was all excited by the cleverness with which he'd managed to enter and lay waste the enemy camp, and by Tanganyika's refusal to surrender, a position he considered childish and which had infuriated him, so when the lieutenant asked who had won, he responded:

"We did, Lieutenant, the reds."

The second officer gave the order to sit, and the lieutenant shouted a furious, "On your feet!" Carlos made a ridiculous move and fell down trying to carry out both orders. He stood up thinking that something must have gone wrong. The lieutenant gave the second officer a demerit and asked him:

"You tell us the reason why yourself."

Cristóbal Suárez looked at the mud before responding, "Improper attribution of power," and stared at Carlos, who felt confused as the lieutenant invited him to speak.

"Go ahead, tell your compañeros how that victory happened."

Without a doubt, something hadn't worked right, but he didn't know where the error was, and on top of everything, he was thinking again about the nightmare.

"Cat got your tongue, militiaman?"

He was speechless, his mouth hanging open. Aquiles Rondón gave him a demerit for hesitation, and Carlos began to explain, he hadn't said anything because he was reconstructing the exercise, they won when his platoon dragged themselves across the entire area and occupied the command post of the blue group. Aquiles Rondón looked at the field, nodding his head slightly.

"Yes? And what else, militiaman?"

Carlos looked at the men in his platoon for help, they surprised the enemy, Lieutenant, some twenty meters from their post they leapt into attack and entered firing, he himself emptied his shotgun clip.

"Silence, militiaman! What did you fire, what did you empty, what's the name of your weapon?"

Carlos watched the gesture, the wide, open, callused, muddy hand with which Aquiles Rondón had underlined the words, and he felt overwhelmed, if he got another demerit God himself couldn't save him from all-night duty. Mechanically, he apologized and explained, they had fired a live round, emptied the magazine, his weapon was called an automatic rifle, and the error he had just committed, inadequate terminology.

Aquiles Rondón ordered the second officer to explain his point of view about the exercise, and Carlos felt safe from more demerits, thinking that in actuality they had won. But the second, leader of the red group, was brutal and accused him, chief sergeant of platoon two, with violating the order he had been given to protect the red command post, so that the blue enemy had won with superior power.

"Respond," Aquiles Rondón ordered.

Carlos tried to control himself and to speak slowly, precisely, because the demerit and the night duty depended on his answer: the problem had been, Lieutenant, that he spent more than half an hour sunk in the mud with his platoon doing nothing, so he had the idea of dragging across the field, going around and surprising the enemy post from the rear, something he'd accomplished in the downpour, winning without opposition by numerical superiority; but the enemy, with an attitude he'd rather not characterize, refused to surrender.

Aquiles Rondón listened to him in stormy silence, then suddenly let loose in condemnation.

"He refused to surrender because your side had already lost! I let you go ahead to see what the hell you were going to do! And what were you going to do, what were you doing, what did you do? Running in a zigzag, firing with your mouth like in a children's game! But this isn't a game, militiaman, this is preparation for war! Real war, militiaman, where people kill and die! The blues entered by the flank you left uncovered when you disobeyed, *disobeyed*, militiaman, disobeyed an order! You have four demerits against you: hesitation, inadequate terminology, insubordination, and apologizing; give your number to lieutenant Permuy!"

Carlos replied "Elevenfortyfour" and went into a coughing spell. He was trembling, duty that night was more than his nerves could take. He felt furious, ridiculed, discredited, wanting to resign from the platoon leadership. But in the militia you couldn't resign, apologize, move, or even talk without permission, as had been made clear to him from the first day of training, when he arrived, disoriented, along with Gallego and Kindelán at the huge enclosure where orders cracked like whips. Looking for compañeros who might have made the trek along with them, he accidentally came upon Rubén Permuy. He had a fit of laughter seeing the leader of the Smartasses his very self, dressed as a lieutenant, giving orders like a general, and Carlos put his hands over Rubén's eyes, shouting: "Guess who, you faggoty mulatto!"

At that moment Aquiles Rondón appeared in a fury.

"What is this, militiaman?"

Carlos started explaining to him that he was greeting a buddy, a total somabitch, an old friend. But the lieutenant didn't let him speak, he ordered him to run to the camp entryway and come immediately back. Carlos asked why and what for, and received a categorical reply.

"That's an order, militiaman!"

While he ran he heard a guffaw of mocking laughter behind him. He felt annoyed with himself for not having responded to that bully as he should have. He decided to do it on his return, to tell him, "Listen, Lieutenant, don't think you're going to slap me around, see?" and then to say to the ones who had laughed at him, "And not you either, see? Because I'm ready to mix it up with anybody." He'd say something like that, the point was to make his manhood clear, not to let them hit him below the belt. Halfway there he felt better, his body was responding, he almost didn't feel the blisters from the trek. Maybe he shouldn't be so hard on the lieutenant, he could be more polite, keeping in mind that the guy's level of culture was low, explain to him, "Look, compañero Lieutenant, you shouldn't talk that way to the militiamen, you ought to win them over with intelligence, understand?" He liked that way of dealing with the issue, and he thought about Rubén Permuy. Now that was news, the mulatto who used to gamble, rumba, screw around had been sent by the Instituto to the Militia Officers School and now he was a lieutenant. He had changed a lot, he didn't have kinky curls over his ears anymore, or long pinky fingernails, or nail polish on them, and the lack of those three details made him at once the same person and another. Carlos remembered having had that feeling before with Mercedes and Pablo, as if the struggle could change even the way people looked.

He touched the entryway and returned at a walk. A group of militiamen went past him running. "Why?" he asked them. "For laughing," replied one; "At you," added another. He liked that, the officer had been tough, but fair, the correct thing to do would be to give him a simple, polite explanation. Inside the enclosure, orders kept on cracking. He was amazed to realize that in such a short time the officers had succeeded in organizing into squads, platoons, and companies that mass of militiamen who were still wandering around the area, disoriented, when he began his run. A guffaw came up out of him when he discovered something unbelievable, comical: the men had started shaving each other's heads. The wind pulled locks and locks of hair over the grass. He was still laughing when a shout startled him, "Step lively, militiaman!" He kept on walking slowly, in spite of it being obvious that Aquiles Rondón was talking to him.

"Run, militiaman, I said run!"

Carlos started to run because he thought taking so much yelling in public was really intolerable, and he decided to give the stupid little lieutenant a piece of his mind. He made it back to where the officer was, saying, "Listen, don't think you're . . ." and received a "Silence!" that made him go cold. The lieutenant was furious. Carlos held his gaze, reassembled his own rage, and said, " . . . going to abuse me . . ." But Aquiles Rondón withered him again with his eyes.

"Silence, I said! The motherland takes away your right to protest, the right to discuss, the right to complain! The militia isn't a labor union! Here orders are carried out and are not discussed! Understood? They are not discussed! Got it? They are carried out and are not discussed! Is that clear?"

Carlos bit his lip as he murmured, "But this is voluntary," and Aquiles Rondón replied:

"Voluntary means you stay or you go, militiaman! You can leave if you want! Are you leaving?"

Carlos felt himself redden with hatred for that abuser who insulted him in public, using his power as blackmail, and he told himself he would never abandon the militia on account of a bitter man who now shouted again at him:

"Answer, militiaman! are you leaving?"

"No," he murmured, before hearing another order.

"Shout it, the loudest you can!"

He vented his ire in a "Nooo!" stentorian and unending, that seemed to please the lieutenant, who commented with enthusiasm:

"You have a good voice, you're hardheaded. Good, you're the platoon leader I still needed."

He felt a strange mixture of rage and gratitude. He was still red with ire from the lieutenant's excesses, but thanks to him, he was a sergeant, he had twenty-four men under his command.

"Have a seat, sergeant," said Kindelán, who had been named squad corporal and was happily brandishing an ancient razor, with which he carefully scalped him.

Carlos, still perplexed, was thinking about the incident when he began to feel a strange sensation of cold on his skull. He touched his head and realized with horror that his hair had almost totally disappeared. He was going to protest when Rubén Permuy ordered a general guard duty, he wanted to see the area clean of hair immediately. Carlos asked him for a mirror, and Rubén left him stunned.

"Forget the mirror, militiaman! Lead your platoon, clean up the hair!"

He crouched down grumbling his anger at Rubén, he'd turned into a bully too. He picked up a few locks and didn't know what to do with them. He felt awful, stupid, he hadn't gone into the militia to clean up hair. Aquiles Rondón passed by him.

"Step lively, militiaman, command your men!"

Carlos looked at the area where several militiamen were passing the time talking, and delivered his first order:

"Platoon, clean up the hair!"

They gathered up great piles, grey hair, kinky hair, black, blond, red locks, then put them in a pile and set fire to them. When he finished, Carlos had a bothersome back ache. He was going to sit down and rest when Aquiles Rondón formed the unit to lead it double-time to the place they would sleep. He ran, thinking he'd be able to lie down a while in a bed, or a cot, or at least in his hammock. It started to rain. "Sergeant," Kindelán said to him, "the devil's daughter is getting tired." "Silence!" shouted Rubén Permuy. "No talking in formation!" Carlos cursed that shithead Rubén and the stupid devil's daughter who had brought about the union of the sun and the rain, perfect for giving him a cold. He responded willingly to the order to speed up the pace, eager to arrive in the area and take shelter in the barracks. The downpour worsened, forming a dense gray wall in the distance. Suddenly, the formation began to dissolve, the men stood underneath the trees, some trying to cover themselves with tarps. Aquiles Rondón reacted with surprise, what is this, militiamen? The rain won't hurt you, back on the road, militiamen, at a run. They returned in silence, turned to the right, and entered a clearing surrounded by trees.

"Gentlemen," said Rubén Permuy, "this is your home."

Carlos stood motionless, looking in vain for a roof over the open ground. "Hebecrazy, hurry up," Kindelán called to him from the place assigned to their platoon, where he'd claimed two pairs of trees to hang up hammocks. Carlos went there murmuring, "There's no roof here," but no one paid any attention to him. Each of them was concentrating on setting up his own crazy house, as Kindelán said, talking to themselves. Carlos tied his hammock before putting up the tarp that was supposed to cover it, saw how it was getting soaked by the fat drops filtering down between the leaves on the trees, sat down thinking that in any case, it was done, and felt himself fall slowly to the ground, from which Kindelán picked him up, murmuring, "A clove hitch, Hebecrazy, a clove hitch." Two or three men laughed at him, and Carlos, ashamed of his uselessness, looked away from them, joining Kindelán to braid those incomprehensible knots that finally readied the tarp and the hammock where he stretched out, only to be shaken with a start.

"On your feet! Hammocks don't get hung up during the daytime, militiamen! Take them down! Two minutes to form!"

He insisted that Kindelán not help him. He arrived late to the formation, where they assigned him a number that he had to repeat immediately, "Elevenfortyfour," because they had given him two demerits, one for hesitation and another for standing without asking permission.

"But that isn't fair," he protested.

Aquiles Rondón gave him a third, for answering back, gave demerits to other militiamen who arrived late, and took the unit double-time to the classroom area, another open ground bordered by a narrow highway. The sun followed the rain and the rain the sun, while they received rules and procedures of shooting, tactics, military courtesy, and infantry in a session interrupted only by five-minute periods between classes, that had just now finished. Now they were marching again on the narrow highway, dead tired, toward the combat-engineering class that had excited Carlos's imagination, making him think about mathematical calculations during which he could rest his tortured body and make function his overheated, wet head, in which the strange "A-ran, oh-oo, heh, ara! A-ran, oh-oo!" with which Aquiles Rondón paced the march mixed with the rudiments learned in the afternoon. He got excited when the lieutenant had the platoon turn off to go with him and get the instruments. They would work on creating a very efficient defense system, he said, called double French apron. Carlos arrived at the warehouse, a vast space made of planks, thinking about theodolites, compasses, complex military maps.

"Here they are," murmured Aquiles Rondón, moving like a cat in the darkness, "all nice and new." He turned on a light and showed them a hundred picks and shovels, so small they seemed made for midgets. "Let's go," he ordered, "four each."

Five minutes later Carlos was panting and cursing that little mountain-climbing pick coated with a muddy layer that he had to keep removing, as if he were digging with his fingernails. He smiled, thinking about Gisela. She'd make fun of his backache and his shaved head, of his illusions about combat engineering and his anger about that picking which seemed like nonsense to him, of his desire to complete boot camp and how perplexed he was by the discipline, the rain, the sun, the mud, the lack of a roof and a bed, the orders and the permanent rush-rush that had left him in a daze, missing the calm of his house. She'd make fun of him, like always; making fun of him, she'd tended to his feet at the end of the trek, and she'd nicknamed him Cinderfella when he committed the stupid error of telling her he'd lost his boots on the march. At that point Carlos was broken by fatigue, incapable of taking even a step with his wounded, uncovered feet, with nowhere to go and no one to share his victory. When Kindelán went over to help him, asking where he lived, Carlos told him all this, but didn't count on Kinde being crazy, getting really upset, saying "Good gosh!" sorry he couldn't give him a hand, because he lived in a single room with his crazy woman and his five little crazies.

Carlos was saying, "It's ok, brother," when Kindelán jumped up, shouting, "This is a job for Superkinde!" and went over to Gisela saying, Princess, as you can see, Cinderfella lost his dancing shoes, and on top of that he hasn't got a palace to stay in, that is to say, he hasn't got the goods. Carlos thought he was going to add that he was a no-good, but Kindelán did something worse by asking, would she invite the wounded man to her mansion? He began to protest, that was going too far, but Gisela paid him no attention, she laughed at Kindelán's craziness, called Carlos militiaman honey and offered him her home, which she also made fun of, describing it as poor, but honorable, and she laughed again showing her teeth like a cute rabbit, which provoked a sudden interest in Carlos and made him accept the invitation, thinking how maybe that little rabbit could put some sugar on his carrot.

The ambulance raced dizzyingly, siren sounding, roof light on, and Kindelán, lying on the stretcher next to Carlos, was having loads of fun, saying to the driver, "That's it, asere, that's it, you be crazy, sir!" and imitating the sound of the siren, "Ooeooeooeooe!" cutting it off to shout, "War wounded! War wounded!" when they had to stop for a traffic jam or a stoplight. Carlos imagined he'd been wounded in combat, and smiled proudly at the looks of admiration and the words of encouragement given them by pedestrians or drivers of other cars who let them pass, but he was annoyed by Gisela's constant flirtation with the ambulance driver. A few blocks later, she put her hand through his hair asking how he was feeling, and when they got to the house, Kindelán helped him get up onto his feet at the little doorway and said goodbye to Gisela, who had kissed the driver on the cheek and now came to the door with key in hand, opened it, had him go in, and began doling out kisses to the little children who were asking, "Auntie, auntie, who's this soldier with no shoes?"

Behind the nieces and nephews came the siblings, brothers- and sisters-in-law, parents and grandparents. Gisela introduced him to them as a friend who would spend a few days in the house until boot camp started. Carlos wanted the earth to swallow him up, he thought about leaving and going to dock at Ernesta's house, but he was ashamed to go out into the street with no shoes, afraid of his mother seeing him in that state, and he allowed himself to be overcome by the immense fatigue that the trek, and life, had dumped onto his shoulders. He accepted the bath, the meal, and the bed that Gisela's mother, a fat, prematurely aging mulatta, offered him with the simple phrase: "This is your home, my son." He spent three unforgettable days there, and nonetheless never managed to adjust to that numerous, noisy family, where mocking jokes were a way of life and there didn't exist the least sense of privacy or decorum. Several times he was surprised in his underwear by Gisela or her sisters, who made fun of his modesty or his skinny legs without giving it any importance. Now and then he got them mixed up with each other, since in that house clothing belonged to whoever could use it, and he himself wore the best things from her father and brothers. Sometimes arguments came up about a blouse or some pants, voices were raised, the atmosphere became heated, it seemed like the world would end, then suddenly everything leveled off, like boiling milk removed from the fire.

Gisela tended to his feet three times a day, in the mornings, after coming back from the Red Cross, and at night. Carlos could never get used to those sessions in which she set herself to the task, making fun of the size of his toes or the shape of his arch, while someone danced to the music on the radio and the kids made a racket in front of the television, each with a plate of food in their hands, ignoring the aunt who threatened them while she kept on strumming her guitar and answered the greeting of some neighbor who'd just come in without calling with a pleasant, "How's it going, fellow?" Carlos withstood the scene and the jokes in silence, thankful, wanting the moment to arrive when he'd get going, used to seeing Gisela as a friend, a cousin, a teasing little sister. He felt liberated from an indefinable pressure when Gallego and Kindelán came to get him. Andrés, Gisela's father, had made him a gift of a complete outfit, uniform, beret, boots, backpacks, hammock, tarp, underwear, and socks. "So you'll do something for the motherland," Gisela had teased, and as he left, Carlos told himself he'd treasure that instant in his memory, he said goodbye to the family members one by one saying to them that he didn't know how, he had no way of thanking them. "By doing your duty," replied Andrés embracing him, while Gisela dragged him to the doorway and gave him a kiss on the cheek. He couldn't figure out what to say, he felt an immense tenderness toward that mulatta little sister who'd saved him from the very edge of failure. He confined himself to lightly caressing her temples, her beautiful curly hair. She teased, "You know how to write, little militiaman?" "Bunny rabbit," he joked, to banish a sudden desire to kiss her. She stared at him. "Write me," she said. And Carlos knew that for once, she wasn't teasing.

But now, what he longed for exactly was joking around, the ability to laugh, the lack of inhibition that would help him turn into humor the sharp pain in his kidneys, the trembling in his legs, the burning in his blistered hands, the memory of his house, the rage against that camp where they hadn't even seen a rifle, the repulsion with the orders that cracked at twilight, "Steponitsooooldier!" so that the unit wouldn't arrive late for the retreat where the captain in chief asked for reports and the lieutenants responded that the staff officers, the Mortar Battery, the Sapper Platoon, and the First, Second, Third, and Fourth Special Infantry Companies were present, creating an atmosphere of power and organization, of protection and force within which the Bayamo Anthem started and the lone-star flag was lowered, cut out against the red sun of the evening, and before it Carlos promised his grandfather to find the courage to toughen up the miserable stuff he was made of and become a patriot worthy of clenching the weapons that, as the captain informed them, would be delivered to them immediately after dinner.

The dining hall, like everything at the camp, was an open clearing. A few spotlights created small zones of weak light, insufficient to illuminate the food served on tin trays, which they consumed standing because the ground was a muddy swamp, with a tin spoon as the only flatware. Reaching the Third Company area, the lieutenants handed out new tasks. Carlos reacted with enthusiasm, in spite of his backache, because his platoon had the job of carrying the crates of rifles, while the others had been assigned work he supposed was unrewarding and hard to figure out, gathering big rocks like for bonfires, bringing dry firewood, dragging in barrels, and filling them with water. "It must be for getting the bath water ready," he said to himself, taking up his position next to a sledge loaded with crates, at the start of a human chain that would transport weapons to the quarters. The idea of a hot bath cheered him up, he had a whole day's worth of mud, sweat, and dust on him. "Heads up!" they shouted from above. He received and passed along the first crate, thinking that maybe his own rifle was in it, the first rifle of his life, a real rifle, clean, new, oiled, that they'd hand over to him after the bath. "Heads up!" He automated the movement of receiving and passing. The crates were heavy, but he told himself it didn't matter, "Heads up!" as long as they got them quickly to the quarters, opened them, took up arms, "Heads up!" which he would use to fire, become a soldier, prepare himself for a necessary war, "Heads up!" respond to the voices of his dead, who only then would rest in peace, "Heads up!" not to let himself be taken meekly, to sell his life at a steep price, to give it up if that was needed, "Heads up!" for the motherland that had taken away his right to protest, his right to discuss, his right to complain, "Heads up!" about the pain that was splitting his back, his arms, his legs, "Heads up!" which he had to conquer, because those crates were exactly the same, "Heads up!" as the ones he'd seen destroyed in the harbor when, "Heads up!" the La Coubre explosion happened, "Heads up!" and alongside them there had been torsos, legs, arms that no longer could clench rifles, "Heads up!" and he had to continue, because his swollen arms were carrying in place of those others, "Heads up!" grandfather's, Chava's, Toña's, Mercedes's, and even, "Heads up!" his mother's, about whom he preferred not to think because, "Heads up!" he couldn't let you down, Gisela, done gone, he had to, "Heads up!" take it to the end cojones patriaomuerte goddammit here comes the last one, "Heads up!"

He ran to the area without thinking about his tiredness, he'd earned his rifle and he expected to receive it immediately. He stopped before the five bonfires burning in the field. The fires lit up the night, and distorted shadows of armed militiamen moved around them. To the left, in a dark zone where they had put the crates, Aquiles Rondón handed out rifles. He went over, feeling his hands sweaty, trembling as he stretched them out, and said, "What is this?" on receiving the weapon. It was slippery, dirty with mud, as he thought before he recognized the texture of grease, a thick grease lubricating the rifle from end to end. "Step lively!" shouted the lieutenant. He didn't know what to do, but he left with the feeling that a doubt, a question, a delay would lead to a new demerit for hesitation, and the demerit to a penalty duty, as they had explained in the military courtesy class. He went towards the fire, vainly trying with his hands to take the grease off the rifle. Coming closer, he felt how the cold suddenly turned into hell's vomit, he found himself wrapped in a cloud of smoke and sparks that, jumping from the crackling wood, singed his arms. He stepped back, watching how the men, bathed in the brilliance of the bonfire, took the greasy rifles by the muzzle brake, dunked them in the boiling, blackened water, pulled them out, and flipped them over to take them by the still-steaming buttstock, and stick them in top down to clean out the barrel; then they gave them to others who dried them with burlap, took off the remainders of grease, and left them gleaming by the fire.

Carlos thought he'd ask for the burlap, set himself to the easiest job, but Gallego called him from the other end of hell and he went forward towards the huge tub with his eyes turned away to avoid the smoke, that in any case made him cough and his eyes tear up. He sunk the rifle into the boiling water, pulled it out streaming wet, and looked at it while he waited for it to drain, fascinated by the pistollike grip and the shiny buttstock, by which he took it to sink it top down and clean out the barrel with fire. This time he didn't let it drain, he pulled it out grabbing it as if he were going to shoot, he held it firmly in spite of the water burning his still-greasy fingers, managed to read its number by the firelight, twentyfiveninefortyeight, and he hid it by the tree. Two hours later he returned for it, after having cleaned dozens of rifles, his eyes reddened by smoke and lack of sleep, his arms singed by the sparks and the water, feverish from so much back and forth from cold to fire. He set himself to cleaning it slowly, meticulously, until he saw it shine. That night Aquiles Rondón congratulated the company and annulled all demerits given out before classes. Kindelán helped him set up his hammock, Carlos felt he couldn't leave his rifle alone, hanging from a tree, out in the open, and he slept next to it, watching the burning embers and thinking that it had been worth it after all.

Reveille sounded at 5:15, still nighttime. Everything was wet with rain or dew, but there was no water to wash your face or teeth. The toilet was a latrine whose dead-dog stench put Carlos at the verge of vomiting, making him feel miserable, incapable of defecating standing up, until he stopped trying, thinking he still had to lace his boots, tuck in his shirt, untie the damned clove hitch, run in ranks shouting at his men to follow him to have the platoon ready, and then report that the number two was present. Rubén Permuy performed the inspection and demerits rained down on the latecomers, the ones who joined ranks after the order was given without asking permission, or had a button undone on a grimy shirt. Then they went double-time to the dining hall, where they swallowed down, while standing, a mug of scalded milk and a piece of bread. Then the rush-rush of classes continued, not ending until nightfall, except for the ones who got demerits and went to do night duty, where they'd lose two of the six damned, insufficient, absolutely necessary hours of sleep.

On the fourth day, Carlos discovered that his fatigue didn't accumulate. He felt stronger after so much coming and going, his back was looser, and calluses were forming over the blisters on his hands, allowing him to hold a pick with confidence. He regained the speed of his baseball-playing days and that gave him prestige with his men. He succeeded in tying a clove hitch, repeating from memory the names of all the pieces of the FAL, putting it together and taking it apart with his eyes covered, directing the ditch construction crew. But he was annoyed by the dust, the rain, the mud, the cold, the hammock that always sagged, the stinking latrine where he had to defecate standing, the dining-hall clearing where he had to eat standing, the impossibility of bathing, of brushing his teeth in the morning, and through the chink of that annoyance began to filter through the memory of his house, the yearning, the nostalgia for his mother's warmth and care, the shame and feelings of guilt for not having even told her where he would be, the desperation of imagining her looking for him like on Armageddon night, reproaching him for his lack of love, suffering from it, flooded by sadness, imagining him tucked into his bed, where he himself was imagining he was when he heard a cry that either came out of, or sunk into, the depths of his memory, "Cow-ard! Cow-ard! Cow-ard!"

He accepted discipline as an irrational imposition. It irritated him to be

Elevenfortyfour, a number, an element, one of the FAL personnel, according to that jargon that was more like a new language where a shotgun was a rifle, the bullets rounds, the trigger a release, and in that way old habits were broken, another vision was shaped by fire, a new order, where every effort seemed insufficient and any error implied a fright, a demerit, an extra duty, pissing someone off. He kept his distance from Rubén Permuy, whom the men nicknamed "The Whip," with the suspicion that he and Aquiles Rondón demanded more from him than from the others, they prodded him, always making him go further than his limit. He confirmed this in a class on shooting rules and procedures, he was enraged about the moment when Aquiles Rondón, at the blackboard, explained that it was necessary to aim at the center and the lower edge of the target, and with the chalk divided the circumference into two and concluded, vaguely, "This little line here." Carlos said, "It's called the diameter," and he almost hadn't finished when Aquiles Rondón was ordering him:

"On your feet! You have one demerit for speaking while seated, another for doing it without permission. Now tell me: what is the diameter?"

He responded immediately to avoid a third demerit for hesitation.

"The longest of the chords, Lieutenant."

"Chord! I'm going to hang you with a chord, militiaman!" shouted Aquiles Rondón. "Don't you realize that for these men, a chord is a piece of rope?"

That night, during his extra duty, Carlos recalled the laughter of his compañeros. He didn't blame them, but rather himself and the lieutenant. It began raining. He hung up his rifle barrel-down and covered himself as well as he could with the tarp. The dampness disgusted him, that impossible-to-grasp water that created a light greenish patina on your boots and underwear, on your pants and spoon. He had the urgent need to touch something dry, but it was impossible, there was not one dry object for a hundred leagues around. He looked upwards: his poor astral mother also looked greenish through the rain. He felt homesick. Homesick. His grandfather had used that sweet word at some point, that now gently pushed him towards the warmth of his house, towards the dry, white toilet bowl at his house, towards the dry white sheets on his bed, where he could sleep tomorrow, if he could just get up the courage to recognize what was evident, he couldn't stand any more, he couldn't take the discipline, Aquiles Rondón, the guard duty, the damned dampness. Moreover, he didn't want to, he just simply didn't want to. The next morning he would go to the staff office and request a discharge. The unit would find out later, as had happened in four earlier cases, and no one would be able to shout cow-ard to his face. Then suddenly he realized that before leaving he'd have to hand in his rifle, his twentyfiveninefortyeight, and automatically he armed it, taking pleasure in the sound of the cartridge entering the chamber.

That night he dreamed his father had died. The wake was like Grandfather Álvaro's, but he, Carlos, wasn't there. His mother was asking his whereabouts, no one knew, and he saw her crying and looking for him, and saw his father dead in the Armageddon coffin. He shrieked and woke up shivering, the tarp had slipped, the hammock was completely wet. He sat up, afraid to go back to sleep. He greeted Asthma, who was also awake, wrapped in his blanket, struggling from an attack with his atomizer. He put on his boots, moldy from dampness, and went over to him, did he need anything? Asthma gave a hint of a smile that became lost in another bout of choking, his eyes were sunken, a desperate resignation emanating from his sad expression. Carlos returned to his hammock, Asthma only needed solidarity and air. He'd given him the first, the second wasn't in his hands. Asthma had to keep on struggling alone with his bronchial tubes, like Carlos with his nightmares. Why was that man there? he asked himself. Why didn't he go home? Where did he get the strength to face, after the tremendous effort of the trek, the permanent trials the camp imposed? What was the source of his madness, or of his stubbornness?

He recalled Che advancing towards the twisted iron on the La Coubre's dock, the stories about his asthma attacks during the invasion, and that last word sent him back to Grandfather Álvaro, crossing the burning cane fields with Gómez and Maceo to bring the necessary war to western Cuba. He felt ashamed of his nightmares, of his hesitation, and murmured, "I'm not a worker," telling himself that maybe it was a question of class, wanting that to be the total explanation for the problem, to feel himself relieved of responsibility. But there was something more, because two of the four deserters were workers, and while it was true that almost all in the company were too, there were also unemployed men, self-employed laborers, office workers, students, technicians, and even a well-known professional, the Doctor, an engineer who, according to Kindelán, was a Communist. "And you?" Carlos had blurted out on the night of the confession. Kindelán laughed at the implicit tension in the question and answered yes, he was a Communist, too, because the Communists were crazy, can you imagine, wanting to change the world? Wanting to end misery, hunger, and destruction? They were flat-out crazy. Carlos smiled while Kindelán kept on talking, everyone at the camp was a

Communist, some of them knew it and others didn't, but all of them wanted the same thing, to change the world, which was a piece of shit, and moreover to change it big time, that's why they were crazy, how else could they stand the rain, the cold, the trek, the guard duty, and the crap and the stupid nonsense? Preparing for what? For a war against the Yanquis, the most somabitch empire in the world, which was right there around the corner? Flat-out crazy, brother, forget it.

Now Carlos told himself that perhaps that was where he got messed up, he wasn't crazy enough, his screws were in too tight from the months of comfort and doing nothing between Armageddon and the trek. He watched his men sleep, thinking about what they would say if one day they woke up to reveille, in the rain, and found out their leader had deserted. He felt a shiver imagining the anger and the insults, faggot, asshole, gusano, and he was moved by the phrase Kindelán would say, without laughing: "Sane, damn, that bastard was sane." He had a coughing fit. The downpour had turned into drizzle. Asthma smiled at him from his hammock, he'd managed to control his attack, but he didn't lie down, maybe from fear it would happen again. "Shoot, guard, shoot!" Carlos turned with his rifle in hand, but immediately let it rest on his thighs. It had been Zacarías the Stutterer, who also suffered from nightmares, cried out and talked during the night, but never stuttered in his sleep. He was very slow physically and mentally, and the men poked fun at him during the very short rest periods. Zacarías laughed at himself after all the others had already done the same, and gave the impression that he wasn't aware of any of it.

Next to the Stutterer slept Library, a worker whom everyone respected because he'd won an argument with the Doctor, who couldn't hold back his surprise at the bookish volley thrown out by that long, slightly hunched-over mulatto, who seemed to know everything about Victor Hugo, Bakunin, and Garibaldi. "You're a walking library," the Doctor said to him, and the mulatto explained that he was nothing more than a cigar maker who had been at his work for twenty years, listening to all the world's books being read. Further away, in a triangle made by royal poncianas, were hung the hammocks of Asti and Chang the Chinese, between whom there was a snoring war. Closer in, next to Gallego, lived Remberto Davis, Blacksquirrel, almost a kid, scarcely a hand taller than the FAL. On the other side of the trees slept the rest of the platoon. Twenty-four men, among whom there were all kinds: whites, blacks, Chinese, and mulattoes; young and old; well-built and rickety. From the command post came the sharp sound of reveille. The men turned over in their hammocks amid muffled protests, snores, yawns, and began to get up in the night, in the rain. "Forget it," he said to himself, looking at them, "flat-out crazy."

That morning, during breakfast, the chief cook militiaman informed the second officer and the platoon leaders that the next day the Third would have the right to use the underground post, a clandestine system of communication with the outside put together by the militiamen supply-truck drivers. The second officer then reminded them that Aquiles Rondón would have a birthday during their training, as Permuy the Whip had mentioned at some point, and he proposed taking up a collection to buy him a gift through the underground. Carlos was not enthusiastic about the idea, but he agreed when all the other leaders were unanimously in favor. Kindelán, happy with the possibility of writing his crazy woman and little crazies, imitated the question from a radio program when the word *birthday* was heard, "Want me to bake you a *kaaay?*" The joke settled the idea, the present would be a cake, for which the men contributed willingly. During the day's rest periods they wrote to their families and talked about the legend of Aquiles Rondón, whom they'd started calling Panfilov, for the legendary defender of the Volokolamsk Highway. His story had reached them in a fragmentary, apocryphal way, and they went about reinventing it in the same manner. Aquiles Rondón was likely from Camagüey, probably had cut cane with his father and eight siblings from the age of ten, and would have left during the off-season to pick coffee in the eastern mountains. His father's name would have been Aquilino Rondón, murdered by the rural police during the 1954 strike over the sugar workers' pay. Aquiles had fled to the mountains and wouldn't have returned to the plains until Comandante Juan Almeida's forces accepted him as a messenger, at the beginning of 1958. When the Revolution triumphed, he would have been seventeen years old, and illiterate. But his will and his natural intelligence would have allowed him to better himself to the point of becoming the first graduate of the first Rebel Army Cadet School. The scar he displayed when he removed his shirt probably hadn't come from an operation, but from a bullet. And who could say how many years must have passed since he celebrated a birthday? It was almost certain that there had never been a party for Lieutenant Aquiles Rondón, and it seemed he was never going to blow out candles, unless he came back from the dead for another life.

Listening to that story, Carlos imagined a similar one for himself, while he hung up his wet hammock. He'd have faced down the forces of tyranny in the city, alongside Héctor and Mai, carrying out fantastic acts of sabotage that put the tyrant on the rack. Because of an informer, he'd been wounded and captured after an unevenly matched fight. Submitted to brutal torture, he would not have said a single word. After a sensational escape, he'd have reappeared in the Sierra to participate in the invasion, along with Che. Now he would be the captain in chief of the camp and with his valiant militiamen, he'd have saved the motherland from an artful enemy attack, thus winning recognition from the staff office and the devotion of his men, who would take a cake to the hospital where Gisela, deeply moved, would be taking care of his terrible combat wounds. The thought of Gisela interrupted his daydream. Should he write to her? He'd spent the day trying to decide whether or not to write his mother a letter, and had come to the sad conclusion that it wasn't possible. The underground post worked at dawn, it would be disaster for a militiaman to show up at his house at that hour. Jorge might receive the letter, he might show it to their father, perhaps his father was already dead.

He lay down in the hammock. All his compañeros were finishing their letters, and he didn't have anyone to write to. Except for Gisela. She had put paper, envelope, and a pencil in his backpack, and now he recalled her rabbit teeth, her curly hair, and her breasts, and he felt a desperate need for her to kiss him on the lips, take care of his cold, love him. He took the envelope and wrote out the address, then stopped, looking at the paper. What if she made fun of him? What if she showed the letter to her family? What if Andrés thought it was disrespectful? No, better he shouldn't write. The decision calmed him down for a few seconds, until the liaison for the underground began collecting the platoon's letters. Then he felt alone again, torn, and he thought about writing her a friendly letter thanking her for everything. But those words sounded to him like an ending, a breakup, and he was left paralyzed once more. The liaison came over to his hammock, asking for the envelope. "Just a second," he said. He looked at the paper, and the liaison's hand. Then he wrote: *I love you. Patriaomuerte. Carlos*, and handed it over, without realizing he was sending his first love letter.

Doubts began immediately, he wished he hadn't done it, he realized that he hadn't even written Gisela's name, and he wanted all at once for time to race by and not to pass at all, for the following night never to come and to come right now, to read and not to know the answer she would send him. He ran to the center of the area, where Aquiles Rondón had assembled the ritual formation before the words "you may retire, break ranks" that sounded like a bolero, asking his watch not to give the time, because he was going to go crazy, telling himself she'd be gone forever by the next dawn, reporting "present" when his turn came, desperate to return to his hammock where he'd hear her purring in his ear I'm yours because you taught me how to love. But that night they didn't go all the way back to their hammocks. They stopped midway, by a carob tree that had the pink cake underneath it, with blue meringue writing that said, *Congratulations Lieutenant Aquiles!* They picked it up and went back running and singing: "Happy birthday to you, Lieutenant, happy birthday to you . . ."

Aquiles Rondón did not react immediately. He kept on looking at the cake, surrounded by the men, who kept on singing even after curfew. The leaders of platoons three and four brushed off the leaves stuck to the meringue. Black-squirrel and Zacarías licked them before throwing them away, awakening in Carlos the memory of a sweet, faraway taste, and Cristóbal, the second officer, explained that this was just a simple tribute, a gesture of revolutionary affection from the entire unit for their dear leader. The sharp "Silence!" ordered by Aquiles Rondón broke up the burst of applause and cheers and made the men automatically come to attention, feeling a storm coming. But it didn't explode immediately. Aquiles Rondón looked at them sadly. "You haven't learned anything," he said. Then, in the same soft tone, he asked whose idea this had been. Carlos knew that calm would be followed by an explosion, a punishment, and he looked angrily at the second officer, thinking he was a bootlicker and a coward.

"Whose idea?" the lieutenant asked again, taking long strides in front of the cake, which was getting covered with leaves. Then the second officer said, "Mine, Lieutenant," and Aquiles Rondón stood directly before him, telling him this was bad, bad, bad, because a cadre in command could not make certain mistakes. Carlos admired the second's reaction in spite of himself, but didn't join the scattered voices claiming responsibility for everyone, which didn't change Aquiles Rondón's opinion, that was much worse, he told them, much worse, much worse, much worse. Didn't they know, hadn't he told them a thousand times that any agreement made by more than three militiamen without the knowledge of the leadership was, technically, insubordination? How had they gotten this thing into the school? Didn't they know that their location was a military secret? What kind of post? Underground? What was it, how did it function, since when? But this was serious, Second Officer. You realize? Serious, serious, serious. To start with they would all have guard duty that night. Tomorrow he would discuss it with the leadership.

Carlos began his new guard duty grumbling with rage, thinking that lost sleep did accumulate and that at this rate he wouldn't be able to stand it. Moreover, he was obsessed by certain disaster, the underground post would be shut down, he wouldn't be able to receive Gisela's reply to the letter that maybe he shouldn't have sent. He asked himself where he should go, what he should do when the training was over, and the answers ran him into a wall of new questions that he resolved in his dreams, his father would be alive, Gisela would say yes, Jorge would have changed, his mother would be proud of him, there wouldn't be a war, he'd marry Gisela, and they'd go together to Cunagua. At that point his dream was interrupted, Gisela was a mulatta, and even if his father were alive, Jorge changed, and his mother proud, they'd never accept her into the family. Suddenly he felt a bayonet point prodding him in the back and a voice saying, "Surrender." He didn't know if he was asleep or awake, or if it was a joke or an attack, until he saw Lieutenant Aquiles Rondón in front of him. "You sleeping, militiaman?" He answered no, thinking that now he really was fucked, that surprise could have come from the enemy, his negligence merited another extra duty that he couldn't stand. "Elevenfortyfour," he said, bowing his head.

Aquiles Rondón did not take down the number, he looked at him calmly before asking, "Are you all right, militiaman?" "Yes, Lieutenant," he responded, surprised. Aquiles Rondón kept looking at him while he slowly shook his head and asked who could be all right in the rain, covered with mud to the bones, dead tired and with no sleep, far from his home and his family, who, militiaman? "No one," answered Carlos, brought back to his dreams by the nostalgic rhythm of the questions. Suddenly he suspected he might have made a mistake to let himself be carried away like that, but now Aquiles Rondón assented, no one, and put his hand on his shoulder while explaining, No one wanted it, none of them wanted it, and nevertheless, it was being imposed on Cuba; it was for her, to defend her—he continued as if he were talking about a woman—that they had to stand all this. War would come soon, did he realize? Carlos answered yes again and Aquiles Rondón again said no, they didn't realize, they were still civilians giving cakes to their leaders, betraying military secrets. He kicked the mud, mumbling to himself, "Underground post," and went on, saying that two weeks wasn't enough, but the Yanquis didn't leave time for more. "For Cuba," Carlos murmured, while Lieutenant Aquiles Rondón, without saying goodbye, slowly disappeared into the night.

The memory of that conversation turned into his shield and spur during the most difficult moments of the days that followed. As he expected, the underground post was shut down. The replies to the letters from the Third Company were kept in the staff office; they would be delivered only after the training ended. The cake was served the next day for breakfast, and there wasn't enough for the Third. Many men woke up in a foul mood, mumbling criticism of the lieutenant. Carlos stubbornly defended him, in spite of the fact that the post's closing kept him from knowing if he could go back to Gisela's house, and above all to Gisela herself, and this brought him again to the verge of a breakdown. Then he got into the habit of fixing intermediate goals, as he had done on the trek. Three objectives excited him: the practical shooting exercise, where he would finally shoot with a real weapon; the infiltration range, through which he would have to drag himself one hundred meters, avoiding mines and negotiating wire fences, while thirty inches over his head bursts of machine gun fire whizzed by, loaded with live rounds; and the great tactical test, in which the blue and red groups, each one made up of three platoons, would face off in an exercise very similar to combat. That would be the last day of training. Afterwards, he'd figure out what to do with his life, and his tragedies.

But now they were there before him, inescapable. The great tactical test had ended with his group's defeat, which Aquiles Rondón was analyzing meticulously, almost desperately, repeating to them over and over that they still weren't soldiers and they had to understand, militiamen, understand that imperialism was going to force a war on them and they had to prepare themselves to face the future, while Carlos was asking himself what he was going to do tomorrow with his own, when he left those compañeros who were forming in the rain, with whom he'd spent two intolerable weeks that were beginning to seem beautiful to him, now that the end was taking him once again to the verge of emptiness.

He set out on the return path anxious to recover the time, and its signposts. He passed by the double French apron system, finished now, remembering the moments when the ditch's hole was so deep that it covered them completely, and taking out the mud from the bottom with the little shovel became an interminable, painful task, which he now recalled with pride, breathing the humid evening air, without traces of the exciting odor of gunpowder that burned in his memory as he passed by the shooting range, where he could see himself stretched out, trying to glue his heels to the ground, pull his elbows in close, avoid sneezing, and get rid of the damned drop of sweat that clouded his eye when the order came: "With a live round: Load!" He had held his breath and was wondering what firing from a real rifle would sound like; it wouldn't be BANG! because that's how small weapons sounded; ZINNNG! would it sound like ZINNNG? Then Aquiles Rondón pronounced the order that took away his doubt: "With a live round: Open fire!" and on pressing the release, he suddenly felt the indescribable thunder of one hundred rifles firing at once, and a kind of kick in his shoulder. He cursed himself for not having adjusted the gas cylinder correctly, that's why the FAL's butt end was kicking like a rearing horse. He went back into the fray thinking he'd have to take ten kicks, ten thunders. He did, and at the end he stood up with the rifle held high, marked by the noise of the firing and the pain in his shoulder, happy to have gotten four out of five on the test, drunk with the odor of gunpowder, the memory of which now put him at the verge of vomiting: they were passing by the infiltration range and he remembered Asthma's death, his own fear on coming out of the trench beneath the bursts of machine-gun fire and Asthma's death, his desire to flee from the hell of bullets, mines, wire fences, and above all Asthma's death, besieged by his bronchial tubes right there in the range, struggling to breathe, standing up, and then receiving the bullet that filled them with desperation, with powerlessness, and with rage because it had ripped away from them their best compañero, as the captain in chief of the camp would say when they buried him with the honors of a officer killed in action.

The captain was right, in his humble way, Asthma had been the best compañero, and it was only right that they were dedicating the final retreat to his memory, delivering to his widow the green beret and the books he had earned with blood. Now they were being called, the platoon advanced single file towards the platform, and Carlos led their march until he stood at attention before Aquiles Rondón and received his green beret and his books, *Panfilov's Men* and *The Volokolamsk Highway*. The widow had placed the beret on her little son, who smiled as if he'd gotten a toy. Making a half turn, Carlos recalled his own father, thought about his father's possible death, and was afraid of the solitude awaiting him during that night's duty, the last one before facing the answers that life would have already given to his questions. Now, back in his place, he kept looking at the smiling boy, at the mother fighting to keep from crying, at Asthma's daughters who cried beneath the slogan that presided over the evening:

PATRIA O MUERTE!

Then the Bayamo Anthem began, the woman started singing amid her tears, the battalion joined together forming a huge, uneven chorus, and he sang for Asthma, for his stubborn march during the trek, for his moving figure during night duty, for the thud of his coffin in the earth, which suddenly reminded him of his grandfather and made him imagine that perhaps it held the remains of his father, while he finished singing, envying the boy who had inherited that beret, earned with blood.

ELEVEN

He told himself the solution wasn't in the psychiatrist's authorization of his return to the unit, but rather in knowing how his compañeros would receive him. His mood was dark as he hid behind a tree across from the ridge of hills where the Third Company's forces were spread out. He didn't dare let them see him. He decided to watch from where he was until he saw Kindelán, then ask him what people thought. The scandal he'd made on the night of his final guard duty, shooting until the magazine was empty and they had to send him to the hospital and sedate him with sleeping pills, made him feel ashamed. He woke up looking at the psychiatrist, a short fat guy with a captain's bars, a beard, and a hat, who introduced himself as a Chinese detective.

"I'm Chan Li Po," he said. "Tell me everything, absolutely everything."

The nutty nut doctor inspired his trust, and he poured out all the details of his crisis. The doctor listened, stroking his beard, asking brief questions, with his eyes closed. After Carlos finished he stayed silent, as if he were asleep. Suddenly he said, "Put on your uniform and let's go."

They got into a rickety Willys jeep the psychiatrist called Gilberto, and bumped around over narrow local roads until they reached a military camp. Above the entry, a sign: *The Rebel Army is the people in uniform. Camilo.* Carlos went inside, asking himself what they were doing there, why the soldier on duty had called the doctor Archimandrite and the latter had responded with the sign of the cross. The doctor guessed what he was thinking.

"I've got them fooled," he said. "They don't know I'm Chan Li Po."

"Archimandrite!" called a lieutenant from the headquarters.

"Shock therapy," replied the doctor, making the sign of the cross without stopping.

Carlos's body contracted, imagining what that treatment would be like. They came to a little room behind the camp. At a distance, atop a fence, were hundreds of bottles.

"Now they'll bring the instruments," said the doctor.

He thought about a dentist's drill, an electroshock machine, an enormous hypodermic needle, and he saw the Archimandrite smile enigmatically, saying he wasn't going to put up with any craziness. The lieutenant entered with a rifle in each hand and gave one to Carlos. He was looking at its number when he heard a blast: the doctor had opened fire on the bottles.

The smell of gunpowder, the noise, the image of the jumping bullet casings made him shudder, but the doctor had finished and was saying to him, "Come on, I dare you." He leaned on his elbows in the window, loaded the rifle, and shot, feeling how the FAL moved in his hands as if it were a living thing, capable of making him remember his madness while breaking it into pieces, like the bottles' glass. He started liking the noise and the powder, and the Archimandrite laughed, handed his own rifle over to him and laughed, "Shoot, goddamit, shoot!" and he unloaded his fury with those shots that were relaxing and sedating him, allowing him to guide the cadence of the shots, getting three, five, or seven cartridges into each blast, according to his own sovereign will, euphoric, playing with the rifle as if it were a big conga drum, pulling a five-note beat out of it, tan-tan-tan, tan-tan, confirming that the piece of shit didn't make a ZIING or a BANG or a RAT-A-TAT-TAT, but rather a *piquitipá*, with a *son*, coño, with music, cojones, like a cowbell or the drums.

One week, seven conversations, and two thousand shots later, the doctor showed up with a deck of Spanish cards.

"I'm going to put the cards on the table for you," he said, and began turning them over and pointing to them with his finger. "These are the gold coins your father lost, these are the batons he wants to beat you with, here's the bitter cup of life, and look, here comes the sword of justice."

He looked at the cards, fascinated, and the doctor asked him to keep on turning them over. He put his hand on the pack, took one, and before turning it over the doctor asked him what it was.

"The queen," he said.

"She doesn't exist in the Spanish deck," the psychiatrist remarked, as if he had confirmed something. "You're talking about your mother, she wants to keep you sheltered under her skirt. Turn that card over."

He trembled as he uncovered it, as if before a decisive bet, and stared at the knight of swords.

"That one is you."

He looked at the psychiatrist: now he was saying not to pay too much attention to the cards, they had been fixed, but to pay attention to life, where one step could lead to another that couldn't be fixed. And listen well: he had found out that his father was alive, in stable condition; but on the other hand, the whole country was on the verge of war, waiting for an invasion. This was the moment of truth: he could go home and shut himself up there, or go back to his battalion and fight, what was his decision?

Carlos was remembering now the moment when he said, "To the battalion," and also the embrace of the Archimandrite, who was certain that his compañeros would receive him with bells and whistles. But he didn't dare let them see him, and Kindelán still hadn't shown up. He heard a noise and hid until he recognized Remberto Davis.

"Liaison," he called, "liaison."

Blacksquirrel ran towards him, and on seeing him opened his arms wide, yelling, "The sergeant! The sergeant's back!"

Carlos returned his embrace and ordered him to be quiet, to look for Kindelán and bring him there without saying anything to anyone.

Remberto Davis gave a military salute as he left and another when he returned with Kindelán, who couldn't believe it, Hebecrazy, that he was back with his people again, coñoooo, that's great, he said, embracing Carlos and giving him a letter. He opened the envelope thinking, she loves me, she loves me not, as he had done when he pulled the little leaves off on guard duty, during his madness, and he closed his eyes as he took out the paper. He unfolded it blindly feeling how his hands were sweating, thankful for this gesture from Kindelán, who nonetheless could be the bearer of his downfall. He placed his right thumb between his ring finger and pinky, closed together the fingers of his left hand, opened his eyes, and read: *Me too. Venceremos. Gisela* and he felt like all the colors of the world were changing: the greens grew vivid, voracious; the reds exploded like flares; the rainy grays took on an unexpected shine. Now his misfortune could go to hell, the Yanquis could attack, the war could start, it didn't matter. He picked up Kindelán to free the force of his enthusiasm and began going around in circles, "She loves me, *negro*, she loves me!" while Kindelán laughed, waved his arms, dedicated his highest compliment to Gisela, "Crazy, asere, she's fucking crazy!" and invited him to the big party all the squad leaders had planned on hill twenty-four to ring out the year.

He stopped spinning and let go of Kindelán, shocked that it was December 31, to have spent Christmas Day without realizing it, not to have been with his family. But now Kindelán and Blacksquirrel were walking, telling him the men were going to be so happy, and he followed them with a furious nostalgia for the holiday, breathing in the yellow smell of tamales, the amber smell of *buñuelos*, the smell from childhood of his mother frying up chunks of marinated pork. Suddenly, a bleating goat coming down the side of the hill made him see Manolo, knife in hand, and hear the anxious words of his cousin Rosalina, who right now would be in Cunagua with Pablo, seeing in the new year. He went nervously into the thatched hut of headquarters, but his compañeros greeted him with smiles and nods, without stopping what they were doing, setting up four bits of candle at the corners of the cot where the second was lying, his face sharpened by the livid light of the tapers, while the Doctor intoned a litany sung in chorus by that troop where everyone seemed to have gone crazy, like Kindelán and the Archimandrite.

"Exemplary soldier. Oro pro nobis. Second, our good pal. Oro pro nobis. Goddamn great guy. Oro pro nobis. Anti-imperialist. Oro pro nobis. And even a Communist. Oro pro nobis. Huge Marxist. Oro pro nobis. Really tough. Oro pro nobis. And really fucked. Oro pro nobis. Hard to crack. Oro pro nobis. And about to pack. Oro pro nobis." The Doctor stopped the litany with a gesture, raised the second's head, gave him a tablet and a potion. "The body made aspirin, the blood made decoction, will save you from the diabolic cold. Get behind me, virus!"

Kindelán started beating out a rumba on the metal cot and the glass bottle, inventing his own scale, *The second can't get up, ooora pro nobis, cause he hasn't got the stuff, ooora pro nobis, and who'll give the second a look, ooora pro nobis, when this thing of his won't work, ooora pro nobis,* and one by one the men danced out with their weapons, embracing and kissing them while Kinde kept up the inspiration, trilling with a voice nostalgic with rum that recalled old prison guaguancós for missing lovers, *Xiomara why, Xiomara why, Xiomara why are you that way,* creating a happy, sad, and desperate mood like his music, that used only love and his hands to cry out for that woman, whose name was now Fifita because the soldiers were dancing and they had invented her, one and many in Kindelán's voice, that Fifita who called them in the early mornings to accompany them in the solitary trenches and the combat fire, *Let them* come to Cuba, just let them touch the ground, we'll blast them with our Pepechás, till we've turned them clear around, and also to see in the new year in the thatched hut, in whose center Tanganika was working wonders dancing a *columbia*, touching his balls and his chest with his Pepechá and leaving the dance floor free so that Carlos, with the rifle Gallego handed him, could come out singing and leading the chorus towards a journey back to the source, a return of the rumba to its origins. *The second's head is on the moon, ooora pro nobis, he hates dancing in the room, ooora pro nobis, the second's mind just isn't right, ooora pro nobis, gentlemen it's twelve midnight!* Kindelán yelled at the moment when dozens, hundreds, thousands of shots into the air could be heard that made them go out of the hut into the night, crisscrossed with the yellow sparks from tracers shot off by other squads, companies, battalions with which they joined, shooting into the sky as well and singing the Bayamo Anthem.

The next morning, the battalion leader, Lieutenant Permuy, called a meeting of the seconds and squad leaders, which Carlos attended along with Kindelán, who insisted on giving him back his post. Permuy began by saying awful things about the shooting and Carlos thought the mulatto's head was still swelled with his own importance. But the lieutenant was nervous, almost desperate about the lapse in discipline, lamenting that Aquiles Rondón had had to stay at the boot camp to train other men, yelling that it was unbelievable, compañeros, they had spent thousands of cartridges for nothing, for diddly squat. Carlos joined in the general laughter that Permuy cut off, saying please, this is serious, men were leaving to go home and returning whenever they pleased, construction of the trenches was not moving forward, reporting infractions, giving salutes, or following orders wasn't even in the picture. He knew all too well, compañeros, as they all knew, that a negative expression was going around, "Orders go out but aren't carried out," and what kind of war were they going to fight with the troops in this state? Well, war might just come tomorrow. He had called them together to order them, like the leaders they were of the people's army, to return to their units with the instruction to impose discipline. Patriaomuerte, compañeros, they were dismissed.

"It's not so simple," said Kindelán when Carlos commented on the way back that they would need to take people into hand. At that moment he decided to take back command of the squad. He couldn't understand the discouragement of Kindelán and the rest of the leaders, nor was he in agreement with their thoughts about how the men were tired of working with picks and shovels, of not seeing their families, and that they left because they needed to. He was moved by Permuy's desperation and by the title "Leaders of the people's army," which made him the equal of the legendary combatants of Panfilov. He had reread the book in the hospital, impressed by the forcefulness with which it treated the same drama they were living now: becoming soldiers. If lack of discipline kept on undermining the battalion's base, he told himself, after that general fear would enter. It had to be stopped. He, a leader of the people's army as hard as Momish-Uli, was the one to do it.

Given the passivity of the squad leaders and the second's illness, he decided to take over command of the company. During a lightning-quick tour through the unit's area, he prohibited all leaves, set an immediate date for finishing the trenches, demanded that they salute him properly. Returning, he informed Kindelán that everything was done, but Kinde was still skeptical, telling him that to change the situation something big was needed, a Yanqui invasion for example, or real leaders like Aquiles Rondón. Carlos decided to teach him a silent lesson; it was enough for someone to learn from Panfilov's example, for an inflexible Momish-Uli to emerge to put things in their place, and he had emerged as that Momish-Uli, soon they'd be realizing it. He straightened up the line of the double French apron system and spent the day digging, opposed to reasoning that the battalion's area was far from the sea and in the case of an attack they would be mobilized towards the coast, so it didn't make sense to kill themselves opening up useless trenches. At night he made a surprise inspection, but they were all in their places. "They go out during the day to take care of problems," Blacksquirrel informed him. He decided to repeat the check in the morning and set himself to making rounds of all the posts.

He didn't sleep that night, feeling it wasn't possible to end his rounds, the discipline learned in boot camp seemed to have been erased by the rain. No one said halt three times as rigor demanded, when they heard a noise they simply shouted, "Halt three times!" and armed their rifles, or as they said, forgetting military vocabulary in addition, they put a bullet in the punch. Some did guard duty sitting on their hammocks and fell asleep. Carlos set himself to reporting men without any precise idea of how to punish the infractions afterwards, guard duty wasn't an option because they did it every night there, and prison was more like a prize, it meant sleeping under a roof in headquarters without being obligated to use the pick and shovel. He was thinking about that when he lay down in his hammock at dawn. Two hours later the sun woke him up. Remberto Davis was watching over him with a mug of milk in his hands, in the distance the monotonous striking of picks could be heard. He sat up missing the hot shower in the hospital. The uniform the nurses had washed for him was beginning to get incrusted with dirt and the milk was scalded.

"Shit," he said.

In the area around the trenches the men were working slowly. He counted them with his eyes three times, feeling that now he really had something big on his hands, Corporal Nemesio Martínez, alias the Barber, was missing, and if he had left, as an officer he'd be doubly responsible. Carlos turned half around, making up his mind to inform Lieutenant Permuy in order to create an example. He felt excited as he went towards headquarters, he was going to denounce a flagrant lapse of discipline, the kind Momish-Uli or Aquiles Rondón utilized to fire up their troops. Hearing someone running after him he turned around.

"What's the matter?" he asked Blacksquirrel.

"Don't say anything," Remberto Davis requested. "He's out on the road, but don't say anything."

Carlos changed his direction, telling himself it was preferable to catch the Barber at the moment he was leaving. He ran up and down the hill across from the road. He hid in an acacia tree, beset by its thorns, and made an effort not to swear. The Barber was at the curb, talking with a woman. He had decided to come out and give him a piece of his mind when two children playing near the acacia went over to the woman and asked her for some water.

"I'm talking with your father," she said, annoyed.

The boys disappeared among the bushes. Nemesio and the woman argued, she was saying it couldn't go on and he was yelling it couldn't go on, but it was clear to Carlos that they were talking about different things.

"Bang! I killed you!" shouted one of the boys behind him.

He motioned for him to be quiet with his finger, but Nemesio had heard and was heading towards him.

"They're mine," he said, coming near.

Carlos stroked the head of the younger one, who just then asked him for a bullet. They were thin, with scars on their legs from falls.

"They're hungry," commented the woman in fury.

"I've got to take off, Sergeant," said the Barber, looking at them. "I'll get them some food and come back."

Carlos stayed on the curb without moving while the Barber went off with his family. What would Momish-Uli do faced with a problem like this? The Barber was a self-employed worker and didn't benefit from the law that obligated employers to pay all militiamen in the field their entire salaries, he had to go and Carlos had to let him go, he had let him go making himself an accomplice to a lapse in discipline. That smartass Kindelán was right, it wasn't so simple. He returned to the camp thinking about his mother, shocked at having spent a month without seeing her. Suddenly he caught himself wondering, "And what if I left, too, like the others?" He nurtured that idea for a second and rejected it immediately. "I'm Momish-Uli, what the fuck is going on?" he murmured, bending over the trench.

During the afternoon he was worn down by sleepiness and fatigue, but kept on struggling to maintain a rhythm while he repeated a tongue twister he'd invented to boost his spirits.

"The company's got a Momish-Uli / who's really momishulisized / and demomishulisizing him / would take a great demomishulisizer."

"You crazy," he heard someone say behind him.

He stood up, almost not seeing Kindeián against the red light of the sunset.

"A Chinese guy told it to me once," he answered, while he went back to counting the men and then stopped when he saw the returning Barber, who greeted him with a nod and took up his place in the trench.

At night, Remberto Davis made an effort to convince him to sleep, but Carlos insisted on making his rounds. He suspected that Zacarías, the Sorcerer, and Roberto the Dwarf had something up their sleeves. It took him three hours to discover the watch trick: Roberto and the Sorcerer set theirs ahead and did an hour and a half of guard duty, while Zacarías did three. When he took Gago to the thatched hut to sleep and ordered the others to cover until dawn, he felt that he'd achieved something concrete, and could finally go to sleep. On the way to his hammock he passed the posts of Kindelán, the Doctor, and Library. Kindelán was still on duty, the Doctor was snoring in his hammock.

"And Library?" he asked.

"His wife is giving birth," Kindelán answered simply, "and Libe went to the hospital."

"And you let him go?"

"Look," said Kinde, "the squad's got a Kindelán who's really kindelanisized, and dekindelanisizing him would take a great dekindelanisizer, get it?"

He didn't reply. He owed Kindelán too much and now wasn't the time for challenges or tongue twisters. He collapsed into his hammock and thought so intensely about Gisela that he wound up dreaming: she was putting her breast near his lips, and he was trying in vain to bite that bewitched nipple that moved further and further away until it dissolved into a mist.

On awakening Carlos thought again about leaving, but gave it up; it was Gisela's obligation to come see him, like his compañeros' wives did, like women had always done. That day he worked half-heartedly. Library hadn't returned, Gallego had gone, and he didn't know what to do. He decided to consult Permuy. He wouldn't give any names, but he'd explain things clearly. Maybe the mulatto could help him, he hadn't been his old pal for nothing. On arriving at headquarters he stood at attention before Permuy, who responded with a tired, somewhat distant salute. Carlos started talking about discipline and soon realized he was repeating Permuy's words, but he kept going until he got to *Panfilov's Men* and the examples of Momish-Uli and Aquiles Rondón.

Permuy had gotten more relaxed. He confessed to Carlos that at boot camp, he'd had reservations about his attitude and had even come to think that the shots he'd fired on that last night had been a trick to escape. So it was exciting to hear him valuing so highly the attitude of Communists like Momish-Uli and Aquiles Rondón, but the situation now at the barracks was different from that of the camp, or a war. The men were near home, they had needs, they had gone a while without seeing their families. What was significant wasn't that they left now and then, but that they returned voluntarily. Nevertheless, things were improving, after New Year's they hadn't fired guns anymore, the trenches were deeper, and what else could he say? That Carlos should keep on being an example, that was the duty of Communists. When the contradictions of imperialism intensified, the disciplinary situation would modify radically, that he could be sure of.

Carlos left militarily and returned to the unit disillusioned, uncomfortable with Rubén's vocabulary: reservations, value so highly, significant, intensified contradictions; Aquiles Rondón had never talked like that, but now he turned out to be as communist as Kindelán and the Doctor, as Héctor and Mai. It seemed like everyone was becoming a Communist, but that wasn't his problem right now: he had more urgent things to think about. Taking off, for example, pulling together the courage to take off at dawn keeping in mind that what was significant was to return voluntarily. The only problem was his clothing, he didn't want to show up at his house dressed like a militiaman, carrying a rifle. He could go to Gisela's house, see her, and change clothes, but he simply didn't want to give in on that point; she was the one who should find out where the battalion was and come see him. He lay down on his hammock thinking about starting his rounds later on. He tenderly considered the idea of seeing his mother, wondered how his father was, if Jorge would still hate him, what to do when this time in the barracks was over, and he fell asleep in a sea of contradictory answers.

Kindelán's shout awoke him: "They broke off, Hebecrazy!" Carlos stuck his head under the blanket because he was too sleepy and didn't give a fuck that someone had broken something, but Kindelán kept on shouting, "They broke off!" lifted up the nylon, the blanket, pulled him with wet hands, making him sit up. Carlos did so swearing about the cold, his acid stomach, his sleepiness, and he spit before reading in the copy of *Revolución* that Kindelán had spread open in front of his face:

Viva Cuba libre!

The U.S. breaks off relations with Cuba

Venceremos!

Meanwhile, the Doctor was explaining how that old smartass Eisenhower wanted to deliver the blow before Kennedy came in, because the Democrats were just like the Republicans, replied Library, but no one paid them any attention. Kindelán was singing *Let them come to Cuba*, dancing with the company towards the trenches, and Carlos joined the conga line thinking about the war that he now supposed was inevitable, imminent, although incapable of stopping those lunatics who tackled the work of the trenches with a rumba, as if suddenly the situation had given meaning to Asthma's death, the boot camp and the barracks, the cold, the loneliness, and the fatigue.

But he had something to do before the war started, and that atmosphere of euphoric madness paralyzed him. He knew the battalion wasn't capable of mobilizing in less than two hours, and that was enough time to get to his house, where they'd have to accept him armed, or never see him again. He'd decided not to go find Gisela, he'd die without her or he'd return a solitary hero, and he'd never ever forgive her for having abandoned him. But what could he say to his men, how could he explain to them that Momish-Uli had personal problems, how could he take off at the moment when discipline was returning, before the imminence of combat. He had only one answer, to stay, and then what would he say to his mother, how could he explain to her that he was more responsible to the motherland than to his family, how could he not see her again, see his father and Jorge, how could he not see them precisely today, the last day of peace that could also be the last day of his life.

Half an hour later he was working with a pick at the same ferocious rhythm as his compañeros when Remberto Davis whispered in his ear, "Sergeant, there's a dame looking for you." He gave his pick to the liaison and turned command over to Kindelán, he'd be right back, he was just going to the road for a moment, and he started running with his rifle slung over his shoulder. Only one person in the world could be looking for him and he started shouting her name when he got to the top of the hill, and shouting he ran towards her and picked her up and started whirling her around and kissing her, while Gisela laughed, "My God, my boyfriend's crazy," and then he let go of her, "Say it again," and she said, "Crazy," and he, "Boyfriend," and she, "Crazy," and they kept going like that until she started kissing him in an naive, open kind of way, paying no attention to the things people on buses were shouting at them, or the horn that was still honking even after he turned his head around towards the ambulance. "I have to go," she said, "why didn't you tell me where you were?" Carlos kicked a tree and Gisela started explaining that the Yanquis had broken off relations and the country was on a war footing, that she'd spent a lot of time looking for the battalion and she had to go back to the hospital. He listened to her impatiently, he knew or could figure all that out, but he didn't want her to go, and then she said, "Your father's pretty bad" and left him confused and surprised, and she apologized for being so stupid, she was going to explain. She'd looked up his number in the telephone book, and she'd asked his mother, that was all, and she turned around towards the ambulance driver who was honking the horn. "He had another heart attack, did you know? He's in the hospital, at Calixto." Suddenly she burst out crying in his arms, God she didn't want to go, God she'd been looking for him for hours . . . Why? she looked at him, leaving the sentence unfinished, like a little girl asking why about all the terrible things between heaven and earth, and at that moment he decided to go see his father before combat began, and he kissed her without allowing her to ask again, because the only answer he could give her was his love.

TWELVE

"José María Pérez Meneses," he said, drumming his fingers on the wooden counter behind which the woman at the information desk leaned over a sort of account book, in which credit corresponded to the names of the sick people and their bed numbers, and debit to the state of their health, as if it were a matter of gains and losses for death. He'd taken off an hour and a half ago, it was totally impossible for him to return to the company at the hour he had planned when he left, and he cursed the very slow, dizzying passage of time, again and again moving the safety catch on his rifle, while he watched the woman's index finger go down the credit column and he wondered if his father could have died, if the Yanquis could have attacked, if by now the battalion would be mobilizing and he'd be considered a deserter. When Gisela took him as far as the Diezmero district by detouring the ambulance, he thought he'd have time for everything. He even spent some time looking around in the street: it seemed incredible to him to be walking around among civilians who went on with their lives as if nothing were happening. But almost immediately, he realized that was a false impression, people were continuing their routines, however one detail showed that *something* was happening, and that detail was him carrying his FAL and two hundred rounds, in campaign uniform, proud to be getting looks from the girls, encouraging words from the old ladies, fascinated stares from the children. He let himself be admired until a newspaper vendor passed by shouting, "War's here, the war is coming!" while he displayed the newspaper Carlos had seen at dawn. He asked him which bus route went by the Calixto García Hospital, and between shouts the vendor said none of them, he'd have to get on the dead man, get off somewhere in Havana, and ask there. It seemed to him a sinister coincidence that the route that would take him to his father should be the eight: the Chinese numbers were turning against him the same way the cards and the horoscope had done. He traveled along in that agonizingly slow death, making useless turns down alleys, roads, unknown streets, until finally he got off by a park he'd walked through at some point with the Bacilli, where now a crowd was chanting: "Fidel, we're with you, give the Yanquis what they're due!" The woman speaking to the group picked him out, invited him to say a few words to the women of the rear guard, and he understood it was impossible for him to refuse, he looked at the faces of those sweethearts, wives, mothers of men in combat and he assured them, compañeras, in the name of all militiamen, that the island would sink into the sea before we'll consent to being anyone's slaves, and he ended with his rifle held high and a feverish "Patria o muerte!" to which the women responded, "Venceremos!" while he went to go take the bus on a less ominous route, the twenty-three, steamship, which would take him to the known land of the Vedado and Calixto García Hospital.

Finally, the woman found the name and took his hand, as if something irreparable had happened. "Tell me," he murmured in a surprisingly low tone, thinking that the omen of the eight had been realized. But the woman answered, "Critical," and he closed his eyes murmuring "God," while she added the name of the pavilion and the bed number, which was twenty-five, gemstone, and he made up a cabala sending him back to the gemstones his father got through the loan business, something he would have preferred not to remember at that moment. He entered, almost running, and felt lost in that fortress, vaguely neoclassical in style, noticeably municipal, silent like a vast pantheon. He asked directions from a nurse who insisted on guiding him herself, convinced he was going to visit a comrade wounded in combat. When they got there, she suddenly said, "And is there going to be a war?" He looked at her sadly, the question had been naive and playful. "Yes," he replied, "thanks."

In the entry hall, the same clean, somber smell of the hospital where he had spent the time of his madness startled him. It evoked the Archimandrite's cards, but now the old king of batons was dying, with no strength to hit anymore, and he knew the queen of cups would fight with the immense power of her tenderness to file down his sword and to reunite, sheltered under her skirt, the three suits in her deck: gold coins didn't interest her, and that made her demands all the purer. He also knew that putting away his sword there would be equivalent to suicide, and he started climbing up the steep stairs with the conviction that he was heading for a game where his destiny was at stake. He understood the reason behind his obscure rejection of visiting home since the day he'd escaped: he was afraid of hanging up his weapon and staying. Against that temptation he had fired the night of his last guard duty at boot camp, and against it he would return to fight now, telling himself that the island was under siege and that his grandfather, the king of swords, was watching over him from death reminding him that the place for weapons was in combat. He wondered what strategy Jorge, the ace of batons, would follow; Carlos remembered the desperate moment when he'd been on the verge of killing him, and told himself that this time he'd let down his guard with his brother, let him give him a piece of his mind and have the last word, because Jorge's victory, to throw him out, would also be his, to go.

Suddenly he discovered a martial figure reflected in the mirror on the landing. He'd never seen himself like that, and he stayed there, held by that image both lamentable and heroic, dirty, bearded, and battle-hardened, with his mouth slightly open from the amazement he felt on recognizing himself as different from the way he remembered. "I'm someone else," he murmured, trying to touch his rifle in the mirror.

Maybe he shouldn't have come dressed like that, but he had no alternative other than forcing them to recognize his true face. He gained entry to a large rectangular hall, painted white, divided into two rows of beds. There, he felt both the sick and their companions looking at him with the same admiration as the people in the street, and they directed him to keep going, as if they knew who he was, and where he was headed. "He slept better last night," the old man in bed thirteen told him, and Carlos cursed the number while realizing that they recognized him because of the family resemblance which his father had always pointed out with pride. He stopped at the end of the corridor, across from the cubicle of bed twenty-five: his father was covered up to his chest by a sheet, from which his pale right foot was sticking out; Jorge was looking out the window into the void; his mother, sleeping in an armchair, suddenly raised her head as if she had sensed his presence, murmuring, "Son." Carlos gave her a kiss on the forehead and went towards the bed. His father was breathing with difficulty, through his mouth, they had taken his teeth out and his gaunt face prefigured a skull. "He's better," she murmured, taking his hand. He turned around to kiss her, and for the first time since they had been on the verge of killing each other, found himself facing Jorge. Their mother gave them a gentle push, Carlos embraced his brother, gave in to the desire to caress his hair and his back, felt him crying and saying, "He's dying on us," and also cried in silence. His mother gently took away his rifle, like someone taking a visitor's cane, and on doing so hit the barrel against the leg of the bed, producing a metallic noise. Then his father asked, "Who is it?"

The rifle was against the wall, his mother leaning over the bed, and he knelt down unarmed beside his father, replying, "Your son," while he kissed the consumed face that seemed to come back from the dead to smile at him. "Carlos," said his father with unusual sweetness, opening his eyes. Light transfigured his face with the beauty of life, and Carlos knew that the knight of swords had done the right thing, and remembered calmly the child with the beret, not wishing for himself any other father than that old grouch with whom he'd never been able to get along. Now he loved him as much as in those few moments of his life when he hadn't been scared of him, thinking how it was a shame he hadn't grown up sooner, to find with maturity the courage to sit across from him and invite him to remember his grandfather's story together. Maybe he'd still have time, if he came back from the war alive, to take care of him, convince him, or at least give him the growing tenderness he felt, looking at that defeated image.

There was a white peacefulness in the room, his father was smiling at him, Jorge put a hand on his shoulder, his mother began stroking her gray hair across his cheek while gently intoning that he was dirty and thin, that he should eat and take a bath, and he suffered the sweetness of return, let himself sit on the armchair feeling that he was losing the game; the batons and the cups caressed him, gold coins hadn't been mentioned. He recalled the king of swords to pull together his strength, but the king wasn't there, his Grandfather Álvaro wasn't there to avert his father's sad gaze, which dragged him towards the unmoving vortex of the cyclone.

Shortly afterwards the doctor came on his rounds, and they went out into the corridor. His mother had a plan: she and Carlos would go home, he'd bathe and eat, rest a little, and they would come back to the hospital to relieve Jorge, who had been there with his father for a week, almost without any sleep. Carlos looked at his watch, only eleven minutes of his initial two hours were left. Two, eleven: cock and butterfly. "The cock turning into shit," he thought. "No," he said, "I have to leave right away." He was sorry he'd been so brusque, but it was done, and now his mother was torturing him, reminding him of the sacred obligations of family. He couldn't find the calm to reason, and almost shouted that all the country's families were threatened. Jorge's imperturbable voice condemned him once more, "It's all right, Mamá, I'll stay," and he tried to give a desperate explanation about how war was imminent. At that moment the doctor came out, his mother turned red, he couldn't know if from embarrassment or anger, because she had turned her face towards the doctor who seemed optimistic, he'd left him sleeping, completely out of danger, it was best that he rest, he said, and he withdrew with a little bow while they thanked him all in a jumble.

"Let's go," said his mother, heading for the room. He followed her and took his rifle. Turning around he saw Jorge distracted, looking out the window; his father slept and his mother was looking at him with a love that for the first time seemed to him resentful. He covered his father's right foot with the sheet and ducked his head between his shoulders, ready to escape. He'd already gotten to the door when she said, "Come here." He knelt down by his mother, unable to withstand her tender, hardened gaze, let his head fall into her lap, and felt her hands, soft and unexpectedly cold, caressing his neck. Suddenly he knew he had to leave at that very instant, or he would never be able to do it. He leaned on his rifle to overcome the resistance of that magnet attracting him with a dark force, and escaped into the light.

THIRTEEN

Now the sky was clear, reddish, almost amber, and he couldn't stop looking at it from the flat roof of the Beca, the large residence hall. He was waiting for the war, he knew it was about to break out, had broken out, or was breaking out that very dawn of 16 April. He looked at the sky somewhat frightened, because now it was hiding a latent threat and during those days it was rare to see it so clean and pale, the stars becoming lost into the light like dissolving icicles. Only three weeks ago he had discovered the roof, a kind of ideal lookout from which, according to the Coachman, you could see all the nymphs of Vedado naked. Their successes were fleeting, limited, far-off, and undecipherable, but he stayed in the habit because he'd rediscovered the splendid magic of the cloud game. Suddenly he was the master of a ship, an elephant, or the rifle he'd lost when he abandoned the battalion, and his possessions were blue, gold, reddish, and ethereal, and always ended up dissolved into the wind, or silently swallowed by the unfathomable darkness of the night.

Then the stars came out, and Roal Amundsen Pimentel Pinillos, better known as Munse the Indian, would offhandedly share with them his knowledge, which he used to call galaxicology. Carlos—the Dude to his university classmates—quickly shared his enthusiasm and learned that not only Ursa Major and Minor existed, but also Giraffe, Hunting Dogs, Chameleon, Crow, Crane, Toucan, a whole bestiary of constellations. The firmament (Munse hated the word *sky*) was not even remotely filled by those animals. There were plant constellations as crucial as Hydra and Hydrus, mythological heroes like Hercules and Perseus, and also many instrument constellations: Microscope,

Compass, Sextant. Although they couldn't make out more than a few with only their eyes, Munse always talked about the machine constellations, like the Furnace and the Air Pump; Carlos, for his part, felt a feverish inclination towards Berenice's Hair, the Painter's Easel, and Bird of Paradise.

In public, they always said their favorite constellation was *Cochero*, just to bother Osmundo Ballester who, owing to his legendary ugliness, was called Frankenstein's Coachman. Francisco Urquiola, known as Pancho the Ghost, liked to add "Tripleugly as his master," and Osmundo defended himself, "Tripleugly but white," and declaimed some verses learned from his father's lips: "To be white's a career, / mulatto, a profession, / black, a sack of charcoal / you can buy just anywhere." And that's how they were going along, ironic, enthusiastic friends, the day that God's Gift to Man surprised them with the news:

"The Russians put a man in the sky."

There wasn't time to explain to a guy like God's Gift that you didn't say Russians, but Soviets, or sky, but cosmos. They preferred running up to the lookout to see the blue that guarded the immemorial questions of its constellations, and they went up again in the evening, after classes. Munse, deeply moved, began to explain that man had crowned the legendary dream expressed in the winged myths of Icarus, Pegasus, and Chullima, in order to initiate a new phase in history, the Cosmic Era, while the Ghost beat out a rhythm on a case of sodas:

Yuri Gargar-in,
Yuri Gargar-on,
I'm headin' for the cosmos
In a rocket made of tin.

The Indian interrupted his explanation, how the hell did he dare to make fun of the Cosmic Era. "Because I'm inventing the Comic Era, asere," the Ghost replied, and they all started laughing about the cosmocomic and stopped on seeing the fire that suddenly broke out in the east, over El Encanto, and that grew with dizzying speed, devouring what was now no longer the most beautiful department store in Havana, sweeping it away and reddening the sky in the distance, as if it were burning the Bird of Paradise's song.

Twenty-four hours later the bombardment started. In the west, the sky blew up in explosions resembling the kinds of stars whose existence Munse had explained, wandering, binary, triple, multiple, shooting, fixed, with a deafening, sinister noise. The Coachman went down to get the news and returned, saying that airplanes of unknown origin were attacking the air force hangars in Ciudad Libertad. Carlos joined the cries of *Patria o Muerte* and felt sorry for the invaders, certain that this wasn't just a diversion like that of four months earlier: this time war had started.

He tried to rejoin his old battalion and was denied permission. He was a university student, the university would decide when and how to mobilize its units. He was thinking about breaking this absurd rule when they were informed that the compañeros killed during the bombardment would be laid out in the administration building, the Rectorado, and it would be their job to maintain order. On seeing the closed coffins, he thought about the La Coubre: now, too, the bodies would be charred or destroyed. He recalled Chava's warning, "The dead are watching," and cursed himself for leaving the combat battalion in order to accept a scholarship to the university. With the scholarship, he'd also gotten a place to live in the Beca, thus overcoming the fear in which he'd been living since leaving home and joining the militia. But now that war was going to break out, had broken out, was breaking out perhaps that night, now that the nine hundred comrades in his battalion were risking their hides for the motherland, he thought that the cost of his decision had been too high and realized he'd made it impulsively, out of anger because he'd been sanctioned for having left.

Life in the Beca meant a return to the lost paradise of normality. In the tall building, so like the one his father once owned, he shared a room with his buddies, had a bed, sheets, towel, a tiled bathroom with a blue toilet, and also received a stipend. On the first afternoon he went to the movies with Gisela, and on rediscovering the dream of life in the play of light and shadows, came to think that his life in the militia had all been a dream, and evoked the cold, the thirst, and the fatigue with the joy of someone who had awakened. From there, he went on to the hospital, giving his family's rigid customs as a reason not to take Gisela with him, and when he was alone, he felt like a heel. His father's old Buick was across from the pavilion; Jorge had stuck a decal on the windshield: I AM RELIGIOUS. IN CASE OF ACCIDENT CALL A PRIEST. He read it with a bitter smile, thinking how he could stick next to it the reply that decorated the car of the residence-hall director: I AM A REVOLUTIONARY. IN CASE OF ACCIDENT CALL A DOCTOR, or he could take Gisela along to visit, put her right in front of Jorge, and say to him, "Take a good look: a militant and a mulatta." Nevertheless, he'd kept her hidden, because he was a coward, as if her beautiful curly hair was a stigma. Rejoining his family, he calmed down. Jorge was still distant, but his mother thanked him with a kiss for his decision to stay and take care of his father, who smiled, happy that his two branches were there, next to their old trunk.

From then on, he lived intensely happy and sad days. Soon Gisela would leave with the Literacy Campaign, she'd spend a year far away, living with the peasants, and he was proud of her decision and encouraged her, telling her Toña's story, but at the same time wishing the day of her departure would never come. They'd go to the movies, dreaming that the show would last an eternity, while they discovered each other's bodies in the darkness. Going outside, they rediscovered their faces in the twilight, and Carlos would break off their happiness by making up unusual reasons for not taking her to visit. He would walk toward the hospital ruminating on his misery, telling himself that tomorrow he'd end his hypocrisy once and for all. But looking at his father's ever more-consumed face, he'd think he'd done the right thing, that he had no right to assure his own happiness by showing up with a black woman and hurrying death: because for his father, there was no such thing as a mulatto.

The nights he stayed to take care of him, Carlos felt a confusing happiness. Jorge wasn't there, and he wasn't obligated to make up friendly conversations about nothing under his mother's tender, inflexible gaze. His father had improved slightly, he spoke in a very low voice, said please when he asked for things and didn't make any wounding comments about politics, as if the nearness of death had sweetened his character. Carlos took advantage of the peacefulness in the room and the night to treat him tenderly, attentive to his urine, excrement, and sores, discovering the body that had engendered him as if he were discovering that of his own son. He would have liked to bathe and shave him, but didn't try because his mother would never give up that privilege. He contented himself with tickling him lightly on the chest, to see him smile, hear him murmur, "Cut it out, kid," feel him close, a buddy. But one night his father didn't respond to the tickling, took Carlos's hand to his chest and said, "I'm scared." "Of what?" he asked, ready to ask for help. His father held on to him with a tenacious anguish, repeating the phrase, and he too felt something empty, irreparable, dark, from which he could not escape, because it was *inside* his soul like the daño, and he knew that it was the final, inexplicable fear of children and the dying, and he told himself he had to be a man, and kissed his father's forehead murmuring, "Cut it out, kid, cut it out," before calling the nurse, who leaned over that emptiness against which neither doctors nor priests could do a thing.

He remained sunk in a strange stupor, in a fog resembling sleep or fatigue, surprised at not feeling a desire to weep. He telephoned his mother, told her simply, "You need to come," and she responded with a mutilated cry. But when she arrived she didn't weep, she asked permission to be alone with the body for five minutes, and Carlos consoled Jorge, who was sobbing like a little boy in the corridor. Hearing the bang of the door, they turned around. Their mother had emerged dressed in black, a dry suffering in her eyes, ready to take care of everything. During those hours, Carlos admired more than ever her practical sense of life, her natural capacity for work, and told himself that therein lay the source of her wrinkled beauty.

When they arrived at the funeral home it was dawn, a strange lilac light was floating in the room, they still hadn't brought the body. Little by little, distant friends of the family or of Jorge's arrived, greeting them by saying "My deepest sympathies" or "My thoughts are with you," to which Carlos invariably replied with a subdued "Thank you," while he watched them milling around his mother or his brother, and felt more and more alone. He asked himself if he had the right to call Gisela; if his father, so understanding after seeing the face of death, would have accepted her. He answered himself that he shouldn't do it without consulting his mother. Carlos was afraid that Jorge would snub her in a way he wasn't willing to put up with, he preferred to suffer through his solitude in silence; but then he'd never be able to convince Gisela of his love. He needed some advice, his buddies from the university still hadn't arrived, Pablo was in Cunagua, his battalion comrades in Escambray, his father dead.

A growing murmur startled him awake. Jorge was gesturing to their mother, and Gisela, Pancho, Osmundo, and Munse had paused at the threshold of the chapel. Carlos went towards his mother, almost running, and got to hear the last of Jorge's words, ". . . who are those people?"

"She's my girlfriend," he replied, with too loud a tone.

"Bring her here," his mother said, making Jorge stay beside her.

Carlos turned towards Gisela, who now had blended into the crowd, gave her a kiss on the cheek, and led her towards his mother, who gently caressed her face, kissed her forehead, and gave Jorge an order:

"Say hello to your *cuñada*."

Jorge held out his hand unable to control his resentful gaze, Gisela responded to his greeting with her head bowed, murmuring "My thoughts are with you," and a funeral home employee approached them.

"Señora Josefa Cifredo?"

His mother nodded her head yes.

"Please," said the employee, with a serious voice. "Who will dress the deceased?"

She looked at Jorge with a sad desperation, then at him, and replied: "His sons."

Carlos went down the stairs first, in silence, feeling a sudden shiver that turned into trembling on reaching the penumbra of the corridor, which got darker and darker. He entered the shadows remembering a night inhabited by souls in agony, the daño all along that unknown path that took him to the dark cave where for the first time he heard the echoes of death, which now sounded like his own footsteps as he headed towards the pale light at the end, under which his father lay naked, yellowish, poor, and able to put love in the place of hate and fear, to make him share with his brother the task that they carried out methodically, serenely, sobbing in silence.

And now, at the entrance gate to the Rectorado, he watched the relatives of the victims of the bombardment, thinking that they hadn't even been given the chance to dress their dead, to see them grow old, or to close their eyes. He felt like part of the wide human sea that spilled out over the wide staircase and the street, clamoring for vengeance. Across from the coffin where her boyfriend lay, there was a girl who refused to eat or to sit; she didn't weep, nor did she respond to the pleas of her family that she rest; she simply stood there, looking at the wood. Carlos searched for her eyes, to tell her silently that he was with her, but when their gazes met he felt it was useless: the girl couldn't see him. He asked himself where Gisela would be, in what remote place in Pinar del Río, maybe right there where the war would be starting, where other militiamen would protect her from death, like she had protected him from the loneliness into which he had plunged after the burial. Then, he had left the cemetery fearing that his mother would reinitiate the battle to shut him up at home with Jorge, knowing that precisely at that moment it would be impossible for him to say no. But on reaching the door of the house, she looked at him as if trying to memorize his face, before kissing his forehead and saying:

"Go live your life."

Hours later, waking up in his room, he felt as desolate as an orphan and ran to look for Gisela. They walked in silence along Avenida de los Presidentes, followed the seafront promenade, and sat on the wall, backs turned on the sad March sea. Across from them, in the gardens of the Hotel Nacional, next to the rusting cannons of Spanish times, three antiaircraft batteries guarded the afternoon.

"I'm leaving tomorrow," she said.

Carlos didn't answer, her departure fit perfectly into his sadness; everyone was leaving, to teach, to Escambray, to Cunagua, or to die.

"I want to give you something."

He thought how a picture or a lock of hair wouldn't do any good.

"I know it's not the right time," she said, "but I'm leaving tomorrow."

Carlos turned around, ready to receive whatever it was, forcing a smile. Gisela was tense, especially beautiful, set against the reddish sky like the blaze of a fire.

"If you don't want to, then, no," she said, and he took a second to understand that she was offering herself, just like that, for nothing, and he told her no, love, no, later on, when she came back, they'd get married.

"But I want to now," Gisela insisted, like a little girl. "I want you now."

The cheap hotel room was gray. Gisela didn't know what to do, and Carlos realized in horror that he didn't either, that Fanny and Gipsy had done everything, while he tried to find a dignified way to take off his pants and struggled to overcome the idea that he couldn't, that it wasn't the right place, or day, or hour, that his member wasn't going to respond because he was committing a sacrilege. Gisela had lost her self-assurance, her moment of madness, she took off her clothes in silence, head lowered like someone accepting punishment; she sat down next to him on the bed, turned her back to him, and asked him to help her. He thought he had no way to do that, and was going to say so when he realized she wanted him to undo her bra. But his clumsy fingers, damp with sweat, couldn't solve the mystery of a clasp that was neither a button nor a snap, but a sort of inexplicably complicated hook that she herself suddenly opened, turning around to take refuge in Carlos, who kissed her, feeling her small breasts fluttering against his chest, hearing her say, "Come" while she dragged him towards the bed and he felt his sex burning on contact with that warm skin, and his right hand and her left managed to pull off her panties leaving her open, waiting, and Carlos moved onto her and penetrated her and felt her cry and those serpent-like contractions devouring him, making him spill over in the very essence of pleasure.

"Finished?" she asked, and he burst out crying. He felt like an orphan, guilty and a failure, and he cried over the stupor of the hospital, the sadness of the funeral home, and the loneliness of the thud of his father's coffin in the ground. She let him cry on her breasts next to her warmth, breathe the scent of her hair, hear the beating rhythm of her heart, feel running on her groin that unique blend of blood and sap, harbor the marvelous, terrible thought that he, too, could have engendered a son. That was how he wanted to remember her the next day, when he said goodbye at the train amid the jubilation of thousands of literacy teachers and their relatives, and she murmured after kissing him:

"You are my husband."

But now, alone in his lookout, watching the almost completely blue sky, waiting for the war that was going to break out, had broken out, or was breaking out precisely then, he recalled her in the open train car, dressed in her uniform, with a backpack, a primer, and a huge cardboard pencil, radiant amid the racket of her compañeros, while he tried to cut a path through the crowd of relatives, the farewell committees, the music band, the vendors, and the locomotive's hoarse puffing, the departure whistle, and the vibrating crash of cymbals sounded, and he yelled a useless goodbye and saw her disappear behind the cloud of steam, singing in chorus with the crowd:

> We're the Conrado Benítez brigades,
> we're the vanguard of the Revolution . . .

And now, he mechanically repeated that goodbye on the roof, from the rear guard, feeling that something wasn't right, because in the movies, in books, in songs, it had always been the women who said goodbye to their heroes.

"Dude, your *pura*'s downstairs."

He didn't need to turn around to identify the Ghost, no one at the Beca managed to talk like that, although many tried. He went towards the elevator wondering what his mother might want. She'd never come to the Beca, it wasn't likely that she was sick. After his father's death, Carlos had taken her to the Archimandrite, who had found her hard and flexible, like a cedar branch. She had smiled, pleased with the diagnosis and even more with the prescription.

"Medicines will make you sick, my dear. Drink an infusion of jasmine, lily, or orange blossoms so your stomach won't be jumpy anymore."

Since then she had remained calm, resigned, telling him to bring her his dirty clothes and to come eat more often at the home that was as much his as his brother's, offering him half the money his father had left in the safe. Carlos gave her this pleasure only when Jorge wasn't there, because arguments with his brother had gone back to being about politics and it was almost impossible for them to talk without shouting. He knew that Jorge had kept the car for himself and was also trying to get the house and the money, saying that Carlos lost all his rights when he abandoned the family, but it didn't matter. He had a picture of his father in his wallet, he didn't need anything more.

When he found her sitting at the other end of the dining hall, he thought that the Ghost's obscure idiom was as clear as day: dressed in black, leaning slightly over the bagasse-board table, illuminated against the sunlight, his poor mother was the image of purity. He went forward without taking his eyes off her. She hadn't noticed his presence: through the glass wall, she in turn looked out at the street, where some militiamen began to move into formation to head for the burial. Carlos believed he knew the motive of her visit, she had come supposing that he'd be going to war, and he told himself that the fact that he wasn't going, that he was part of that stupid unit with black berets and cartridgeless rifles, would at least have the advantage of calming her.

"Hello," he murmured, kissing her on the cheek.

Startled, she turned around, anxiously taking his hands.

"Your brother's been arrested," she said.

"I warned him," murmured Carlos, shaking his head.

"He didn't do anything," she said, with conviction.

"I don't know that, Mamá, and neither do you."

She bit her lower lip, looking at him imploringly.

"Talk to your friends," she said.

He started to kick the floor with his boots, asking himself if his mother was able to understand that he didn't have any such friends, nor was he willing to intercede on Jorge's behalf, nor would he find anyone who would listen.

"I can't," he said. "There's a war on."

She wrung her small linen handkerchief over and over, as if saying a rosary. The Coachman rapped on the glass with his knuckles, Carlos made signs to ask them to wait for him.

"Are you going?" she asked, with a defeated anguish.

"No," replied Carlos, looking into her eyes.

His mother stood up, pulled him to her, kissed him on both cheeks, and murmured thank goodness, while she opened up her inevitable black pocketbook with a gold clasp, from which she took out a grease-stained roll of paper.

"Here, take it," she said. "I brought you a steak."

FOURTEEN

Behind the dark leaves of the cane palm, the outlines of an inexplicable gray mass appeared in the night mist. Startled, he took aim at it. Only then, running his tongue over his lips and finding the taste of dirt and gunpowder, did he recall that it was a tank, broken down in the road. He closed his eyes, but kept on seeing the brutal bomb explosion and the crazed running of the militiamen: the image pinned to his retina like fatigue to his bones, like napalm to the skin of those who screamed and ran, like fear to his nerves and hate to his combatant's heart; he let his head drop down to his chest and the image of his mother was imposed over that hell, as if her stooped figure had the power to erase the fear, the pain, the death, the anger, before disappearing behind the window of the Beca while he was leaving for the victims' burial through streets galvanized with fury, thinking he wouldn't go to war, feeling himself outside that colossal mechanism that the Doctor called the Wheel of History, ashamed when he saw the combat battalions. He gave in to the wish to look for his own, to greet his compañeros before they went off; he handed over his old, cartridgeless rifle to Munse and took off walking down Twenty-third Street, amid waves of unknown combatants; he passed Tenth, big fish, and got to Twelfth, whore, from which he saw the sea of militiamen merging into the Caribbean behind the hill that he descended, feeling depressed, down to Twenty-first, snake, Nineteenth, earthworm, that he kept going down, irritated by that despicable cabala, until sighting in the garage on Seventeenth, moon, Library's unmistakable humpback, and running, sure that his astral mother would help him, had helped him in that unexpected conjunction of Chinese numbers and the horoscope. There were

Blacksquirrel, the Barber, Library, and Kindelán, who was the first to see him, "Coñoooo, Hebecrazy!" sounding the alarm to the squad that surrounded him with embraces and questions, while he, in turn, "And Gallego and Zacarías?" and all the joy suddenly ended in a tumultuous silence that made him understand: the strongest and the clumsiest had died in the Escambray Cleanup, while he, the most cowardly, was studying in Havana; he couldn't reconstruct their faces, even by closing his eyes, and he felt Kindelán's arm around his shoulders and thought about his other crutch, that Gallego who had died like a man, said Kindelán, spitting lead and yelling patriaomuerte, he added, giving Carlos a shiver: the phrase had acted like a charm that unleashed the gigantic "viva" with which the militias saluted Fidel's arrival on the platform, making the lieutenants give the order take your places, and leaving him disconcerted, out of place: the militiamen had run to form ranks and he remained on the sidewalk, like a nuisance; Kindelán and Blacksquirrel called to him from the formation, but he didn't dare, he didn't have a rifle, or any right; Lieutenant Permuy approached, checking the lines, discovered him and stared at him like an apparition, before shouting at him, "What are you doing there, militiaman? Fall in!" and he took Zacarías's place, thinking of the cabala: number three in the third squad, sailor sailor thrown into the sea of workers, yoked to the waterwheel of his memory, remembering his clumsy dead friend, raising his arms without a gun amid the wave of rifles that went up when Fidel said once and for all, what the imperialists couldn't forgive was that we made a socialist revolution right under their noses, and the explosion of joy made Carlos yell patria o muerte and venceremos before getting up on the trucks, to the beat of a multitudinous chorus: "Marching we go towards an ideal / knowing we will prevail." And he felt worthy of Gisela, heroic in the farewell of the people bunched up on all the sidewalks of all the streets of all the cities, villages, hamlets, mill towns, railroad crossings they went through after leaving the camp where he recovered his rifle and was seized by anxiety: Zacarías was the one who carried ammunition for the seven-point machine gun and he wasn't used to the ammo boxes that knocked against his ankles when the caravan entered the little snaking highway, alongside of which dust shrouded the scattered cane palms, *yagrumas*, and black twisted mangroves that sprouted up from the spectral ground of that swamp with the same name as the cemetery street, Zapata, twenty-nine, "Rat," he murmured in light sleep, realizing that the cemetery was at the corner of rat and whore, that death is a rat and an unforgettable whore when you've seen her face in war. Now she returned to his memory riding on the plane, with the smile the gunner in the rear cockpit must have been giving them while they waved, trusting the insignias on the ship that made a full turn and fired on their heads, vomiting a line of white and yellow lights that blew up the road, forcing him to throw himself into the ditch, pounded by the rockets' noise and by the cyclonelike explosion of the bomb that was still resounding in his ears when the broad wave of a second line of rockets announced that a third would explode exactly there, in the mud where he had buried his face. He raised his eyes, convinced it would be for the last time: the sky was empty, blue, cloudless, and only then did he realize he had urinated on himself and that in the road, life and fury were exploding; it smelled of powder and fire and the lieutenant was demanding, "Report losses!" and there were small craters and "Who?" the second was asking, "Who?" and the bomb had unleashed a blaze in the nearby forest and "Don't look," the Barber was saying to him, and he saw the remains of Corporal Heriberto Magaña, the blue and pink guts of Corporal Heriberto Magaña, which he now was seeing again in the shrill nightmare where he was descending towards a dark sea, leaving his father's corpse behind, and he woke up weighted down with terror, happy to be alive, able to imagine that Gisela was letting him rest in her lap, breathe in the scent of her skin, listen to the regular beat of her heart, wishing that she were pregnant, that a male child engendered by him was being born in her womb so he wouldn't die completely from a bazooka blast, a bullet, a grenade, or a bomb like the one that he managed to erase from his memory with Gisela's singsong voice teaching a little girl to read *my mama loves me*, on that same gelatinous swamp mud, bitten by the mortar fire he hadn't identified until then because he was lost in his fear, remembering the contempt with which Corporal Higinio Jiménez put the ammo boxes for the seven-point in his hands and said, "Take these, you pissed on yourself and dropped them," thinking about Heriberto Magaña's intestines and about Asthma's death while he waited for another plane, took off running with everyone else, and only after the first explosion realized that those whistling sounds were the descending mortar shells that stopped the commander's jeep cold, forcing him to jump out onto the road, blood on his left arm and his face, and to order, "Shoot, goddammit! Spread out!" while Carlos threw himself behind a tree stump, fired off a burst, and the FAL jumped in his hands as if alive: he had shot into the ground, Higinio and his squad weren't anywhere in sight, from the road came the din of a column of tanks, he fired again and was changing the magazine when he heard the

Sorcerer calling him: he had a wound like a fishing line, a horrible tear, bloody in the center, black from the powder on the destroyed edges of his shirt. Tanga's seven-point had gone into action with a rhythmic sound, hot and rich like the sound the Sorcerer knew how to get when he beat out a rumba, but the Sorcerer was gasping with his mouth open, pleading coño, for the love of his sweet mother, that they cover his burn with the gelatinous mud where now the little girl was reading *my mama loves me,* Gisela observing with a tremble the tense concentration of her eyes, the slight beat of her lips when she deciphered the phrase, and now he could put mud on the Sorcerer's wound, hear his cry and the lieutenant's voice asking for a squad behind each tank, dream that Toña was watching him through time and distance, "On the way!" running hunched over under the bullets to the road, taking cover behind a T-34 from where he fired against the circles of light from the Fifty, which kept on firing until the tank stopped, the turret spun on its axis, fired twice, three times, and the enemy machine gun burst apart like a firecracker while the commander yelled, "Now, militiamen! Patriaomuerte and cojones, militiamen!" and he advanced behind Tanga, halted now by the fire from another Fifty and saying, "Ammo! Ammo!" before Carlos gave him the boxes and threw himself into a hole with a bunch of militiamen hearing Lieutenant Teodoro Valdés, "Fan out, I said fan out!" when a blast from the Fifty tore him in two and the tank destroyed the Fifty and a bazooka stopped the tank and it got dark and the fires from the mountain allowed him to see the lieutenant's contracted face from which he now tried to escape, calling his mother and the corporal who had died without fighting, while Asti offered him urine and the Barber a liquid just a little less thick than the mud, and he remembered the murmuring of the march that had pulled him out of his torpor, making him move and touch the rack on the destroyed tank, while he heard the commander positioned for ambush in a thicket: "Where are they now?" "Beating it out of here," responded the Barber. "And where will they be tomorrow?" "In their mothers' whooziwhatsis," yelled Metro. "And what's our motto?" "Patriaomuerte and cojones," voiced Tanganika while Carlos, rejoining his squad, took the ammo boxes and they all continued down the road that at midmorning the mercenaries had covered with crossed lines of fire from two Thirties positioned amid the bushes, and his squad received its first concrete mission of the battle: Squirrel said that the second said that the commander said that they cover his squad, he was going to take up position to the right, on the low hill, to remove the Thirties; that was what Squirrel said before he crossed the embankment at a run and fell into the ditch, while they alternated the FAL with the seven-point to keep the lead constantly over the pintos, and with the militia's mortars whistling the second yelled, "Fuck, they're beating it!" and as he advanced Carlos stopped next to Squirrel who was lying down as if asleep in the ditch, and the commander pushed him, "Forward, militiaman! To the sea, goddammit, militiaman!" and he thought that yes, now with a big push they'd flatten the mercenaries and then he'd be able to think in another way about Higinio, about Heriberto's guts, and about Squirrel's pinhead, whose kinky hair, of the blackest cotton, now floated in that terrain located between dreams, imagination, and memory above a body so soft it too seemed made of cotton, as if boneless, and yet it had steel, maybe moon silver, and he was looking at him, calling him sergeant, calling on Chava and his grand-father to see how well he fought against the tank that attacked them at kilometer fifteen, with a frightening noise at which Carlos felt a stubborn fear, overcome by the Barber's "Nobody behind!" the FAL's rattling, and the artil-lery blows that broke the Sherman, leaving it in the middle of the road like a dying beast while the enemy flanks gave way and the commander started the march to kilometer seventeen, where artillery preparation against San Blas began and they went back to the rear guard and finally he ate, drank, sent someone to tell his mother he was alive and collapsed under a yagruma while everything happened over again in his memory or in his dreams like an endless movie where he didn't get to act the hero, the fear returning with the night, coming back at dawn in the noise of a plane, a noise so implausibly real it made him open his eyes: the big bug was in the air vomiting fire and he looked for a second at the double line of death lights with the certainty that he had already lived that moment, before starting to run, confused, without finding anywhere to go until he felt the antiaircraft thunder and ran towards it: the four tubes of the fourmouth blowing out shrapnel at the plane which answered with the eight .50-calibres on its wings, trying to silence the machine gun, while Carlos was overtaken with the feeling of being in the wrong place, of being in a rat hole wanting to flee and not able to move, fascinated by the craziness of the shirtless artillerymen going at it with bravery and balls against the bug, whose discharges, nearer and nearer, had turned the earth into a blaze that would take them all to hell when the plane got a little bit closer, but at that moment black smoke started flowing from its left motor and an orange flame exploded under its wings and the artillerymen kept on going at it with bravery and balls and the bug started losing altitude and, burning, passed over the antiaircraft that kept up the punishment until it was completely out of range: then there was an anxious silence, artillery and infantry following the descent, the fall, the death of the bug in the swamp mud, exploding into a multiple, crazed embrace made up of tears, laughter, and the "Fucking shit!" repeated three times, like a spell, by the artilleryman Carlos had embraced, a little blond guy as young as Blacksquirrel who was now returning to the base of the antiaircraft while a captain ordered the battalion to follow him, there were rumors of a new disembarkation and now the pintos were going to find out what it meant to get the full treatment, and Carlos went back to the road, walking in place of Roberto the Dwarf who had stayed behind with the wounded, and he asked himself where the hell were Permuy, Kindelán, and the rest of the compañeros in the special squad for which he hadn't been picked, how the whore had behaved with them, if she'd taken many of them to bed, and he continued going forward under the sun, hands wounded from the handles of the ammo boxes, the bipod starting to weigh heavily on his back, Tanga explaining to him that he shouldn't worry if he didn't know how to load the machine, telling him he'd give him belts when needed and asking him where might Aquiles Rondón be fighting, without receiving a reply, because Carlos didn't want to say what had happened: Aquiles Rondón had a hero's halo and heroes die young, like Blacksquirrel, except that Squirrel didn't have the look of a hero, but of a boy, and Zacarías looked clumsy, and Heriberto Magaña like an old man, "And Aquiles Rondón is alive," he said, and Tanga looked at him with surprise and continued walking in silence under the sun, now heated up, which Carlos felt burning on his shoulders under the bipod's tack, and on his forehead, flooded with sweat he couldn't wipe off because he was carrying the damned boxes: he was doing the work of two men and felt a growing irritation with Tanga, a black man as strong as the trunk of a ceiba, who carried only the seven-point and two bullet belts crossed over his chest, who moved forward showing no mercy nor worrying that his ammo carrier was loaded down like a mule under the sun at its zenith, which now forced him to stop, to wipe off the sweat before the first shots sounded and he threw himself to the ground: Tanga spitting with fury that he was missing the bipod, firing on his feet, enormous and almost invisible against the light until Carlos dragged himself over to him; they positioned cover with Metro's FAL, and Tanga made music with the machine: the belt of yellow cartridges passing vertiginously into the mechanism, the barrel vibrating, reddened by the flames, the dark little mountain of mercenaries bitten by lead until suddenly some underwear floated out on the tip of a stick and the captain's unappealable "Hold your fire!" was heard, after which there was silence and seven pintos appeared with hands behind their heads, saying they had several dead and wounded, making him think that the cabala was right, seven, ass, when the captain decided to transfer the wounded and the prisoners to the rear guard, leaving the dead for later, and three militiamen seized the moment to say goodbye to the shrapnel that was sounding in the distance, towards the sea, and he thought they were saving their hides and Tanganika put the bipod on his back, the boxes in his hands and continued the advance without giving him the option of retreat, returning him to the thirst and the resentment that made him take refuge in Gisela: now she was at his side, toning down the torture of the march, softening the sun, shortening the distances, making the dustiness breathable and disappearing as suddenly as she had come: the noise had increased in the direction of the sea, the captain ordered the pace doubled, the grimy column began to advance more and more rapidly, now almost running, pulled by the thunder from the coast where they would need reinforcements, and he fought to keep up the pace, hands wounded by the boxes' ring-handles, the bipod and his rifle hitting against his back, the surprise of the "Aiirplaane!" the captain shouted out before Carlos threw himself head first into the ditch when the big bug passed over the column spraying fire, and now it was coming back to drop its bombs and rockets while he, once more with his face in the mud, waited for the explosions that didn't happen: the bug kept on circling and firing its eight machine guns against a new, far-off target that allowed him to turn himself faceup; now there were two airplanes, one enormous and slow and the other small and fast, flying in opposite directions as if they were going to hit, the B-26 vomiting fire at the T-33, which suddenly moved out of the trajectory of the shots, accelerated and banked to the left, climbing, leveling, coming back, banking at ninety degrees, and opening fire on the bug, which spun violently while the T-33 passed by its side like a tornado, climbed, reduced power, and came back to the attack, small and persistent like a kingbird, and Carlos got up on his feet, yelling, "Now, coño! Rip his balls off, coño!" when the T-33 dove at the bug, fired, chased it as if it wanted to bite before the crash that now seemed inevitable, and suddenly dodged the discharge that shook the sky, the bug's yellow tracers chasing it, the kingbird stabilizing itself up high while the B-26 fled, diving into the sea, and the column continued its advance shouting at its fighting cock, and Tanga averred, "No matter how far the buzzard flies, the kingbird will always bite it" and Carlos, "It's biting, cojones, it's biting!" because the T-33 had climbed over the B-26 again, touching it with fire, dislodging its cabin, making it smoke, biting it and pecking it until the blaze reached its motors and the bug leaned to the side, exploding in the air, raining down sheets of steel and sinking into the sea under a great circle of fire, which gave them the strength to make it all the way to the coast, to see the mercenaries trying to reembark in a furious fit to reach the lifeboats, and to see their own little plane and the artillery on the coast bombarding the lifeboats, sinking them, setting ablaze the transport vessel, breaking it apart and making the pintos retreat and surrender to the same units that had pushed them to the beach and that now led them, single file, to the trucks while the captain ordered the battalion to stay on guard until further notice, and Carlos collapsed in fatigue by the sea, which now was calm, as it should have been on a spring afternoon.

FIFTEEN

He took the little box on the night table and counted out the pennies inside. Five. With anger he let them drop, it wasn't possible that all weekend long Roal Amundsen, Francisco, and Osmundo had said only five curse words. They were still a bunch of smartasses. He stopped at *smartasses*, he hadn't said it out loud and therefore didn't have to pay for it, but he had thought it and that was a serious sign of lack of control. He had to be careful, he wouldn't be satisfied until he had interiorized a correct, clean, pure, absolutely communist way of thinking. In this case, for example, he should have thought that his compañeros (not his buddies, or his pals, or his aseres, or his bros, or his chums, or his men, or his mates, much less his homboys) were just immature. He still was, too, in a certain way. During the weekend, annoyed by the objective conditions created by Benjamín el Rubio's plotting, he had let out six curse words: three *coños*, two *fucks*, and one *fag*. Only the fact that they were compañeros had saved him from also saying *somabitch*, thus freeing himself from two errors, since the word wouldn't only have been a curse, but badly pronounced. The correct thing would have been to have said *son of a bitch*, although thinking about it, could there really be correct curse words?

He left that troubling question unanswered. The story of the mysterious five cents was that Roal Amundsen and Francisco, the most filthy-mouthed of his roommates, had not made the appropriate deposits. They were still immature. Osmundo, on the other hand, had indeed adopted the correct way of thinking, as his five cents proved. It was always ironic that Osmundo, a petit bourgeois who studied with the Marists, would be so consistent with revolutionary ideas, while Francisco and Roal, from poor backgrounds, one black and the other mulatto, persisted in their messing around and lack of discipline. Was *messing around* a correct word? In this case, yes, because it didn't mean an obscenity, but just disorder. The explanation could be that Osmundo had practiced the negation of negation on himself, succeeding in turning religious values, intrinsically negative, into positives. Negative values? Didn't that phrase hold an internal contradiction? No, because the word *negative* erased all value, reducing the expression to nothing. So therefore, could nothing negate itself and turn into a positive value?

He again left the question in the air, he had to study more, go deeply into these intricate theoretical problems. But now he had to devote himself to practice. He deposited six cents into the little box and made the entry in the account book. The subcolumns agreed. Debit: one hundred eighty-seven curse words; Credit: one hundred eighty-seven cents. With just thirteen more curse words they could buy a new book. But in this case the internal contradiction was evident, the acquisition of books would depend on crude thoughts. Could pureness and filth be poles of unity and struggle between opposites? Probably, and that contradiction had to be overcome to bring about development. Only then could a new type of money collection be put in place. One hundred eighty-seven was an enormous amount for one trimester and that was only half the real story, surely three hundred sixty-four curse words had been said, which was terrible. Starting the next day he'd put in place a new method, each entry would have to be made individually, that way no one could cover up his errors. To let off some tension, with determination he set about cleaning his pistol.

He took it apart it with the skill that had won him so much admiration from his compañeros. Lovingly, he polished every piece. He was checking the state of the barrel grooves when Osmundo entered the room and stopped short, not daring to interrupt him. Carlos continued at his task unperturbed; cleaning the pistol required full concentration, Osmundo would wait. He looked at him without seeing him through the barrel, in which, as it turned out, there was a lot of powder. He started cleaning it with a rod and suddenly ceased the movement: putting in and taking out the rod from the hole was a profoundly obscene gesture. But there wasn't any other way to clean it, the objective justified the means, obscenity was just a phenomenal appearance.

"Hey," said Osmundo.

Carlos looked at him in surprise, with that slightly disdainful expression he had perfected, until he made Osmundo bow his head. Then he kept on cleaning, the damned powder seemed like it was incrusted. Osmundo was a good compañero, and precisely because of that he could not permit himself the slightest weakness towards him. Benjamín, Francisco, or Roal would have left, but Osmundo waited with discipline, as he should. Only when Carlos was able to see him through the untainted barrel did he murmur:

"What?"

"The Hardliners changed José Antonio's testament," said Osmundo, in a low, broken voice.

Carlos had to make a great effort to control himself. This was very important news, and if he, president of the School Student Association and floor leader at the Beca, didn't know about it, Osmundo, his subordinate, shouldn't know about it either. He found himself with a new contradiction: he needed to inform himself, but he couldn't reveal that he wasn't informed. He maintained the facial immobility he had gone to so much trouble to design for occasions just like this one. Osmundo shifted around uneasily, it was clear that he didn't know if Carlos knew or not.

"They took out God's name," he said, and kept scrutinizing his face. "Did you know about it?"

Carlos nodded in silence. Osmundo let out a little mouselike laugh.

"I'll leave then."

"Wait!" Carlos ordered, looking into his gray, watery eyes. He couldn't lower himself to finding out details, but he had to assure his victory. "Remember that's classified information," he said, "*top secret*, OK?"

"Yes, of course," murmured Osmundo before leaving.

He stamped on the floor. Did Osmundo know he didn't know? Was there something in his eyes, in his smile, something like a background of mockery? No, it wasn't possible. Nothing had happened, he was just very sensitive because Benjamín was plotting against him and Roal and Francisco refused to accept his authority. Osmundo was different, not for nothing had he brought him that serious, key news. Was it correct to modify the testament of a hero? No, the Hardliners had gone too far. It was a terrible thing to alter the last wishes of someone who had died fighting and had no way to defend himself. But the very exceptional character of the decision left one thinking that those who made it had very powerful reasons to do so. Apart from the intentions that José Antonio would have had at that moment, the mention of God would be damaging for new generations and that was also unacceptable. So then? Thinking it through, it was the future, not the past, that should serve as a guide for action; the risky decision of the Hardliners was a necessity of the struggle and a political line. Interpreted in the context of the battle that he was carrying on with Benjamín, it meant a ratification and a development of his own point of view. He would support it with all the weight of his prestige, a virtually mythological halo, as the Peruvian had affirmed with devoted admiration on finding out that Carlos had walked down an endless road in the middle of the strange, misty night when the B-26 passed over him, burning the darkness with the phosphorescent lights of death: the noise of the shots, the bursts of the rockets, the cyclonic explosions of the bomb, his orphan's shriek, and Osmundo's icy hands, waking him up.

"It was horrible," he said, and told about him the horror.

The next morning Osmundo wanted to know more and Carlos discovered the pleasure of talking about a war that is over, the nearness of a now inoffensive death. During those days the Beca was the supreme place for messing around, the slobs blocked up the toilets with paper, crowned the heads of sleepers with toothpaste, and frequently stole sheets, soap, towels. Carlos didn't meddle in any of this. He had returned from the war ready to concentrate on his studies and maintained a haughty silence, a rigid discipline against the chaos. But after the conversation with Osmundo, he began to feel unsatisfied with his passivity, offended by the disorder, and when the boot battle broke out he decided to intervene. The first one hit the window over his head, waking him up. It took him a few seconds to realize it hadn't been a shot, that he wasn't dreaming again about the war, that the huge boot before his eyes didn't hold the foot of an enemy or a comrade. The second one hit the Ghost. "Who's got such an aim? Who's got such an arm? That you hit me in the dick, and your mother in her twat?" shouted the victim before throwing a boot against the aggressors, who responded that night with boot-sown fire. The Ghost organized the defense, ordering his troops to use mattresses as shields and to take over the inside door to the bathroom, to gain an exit to the hall and surprise the enemy between two lines of fire. The bathroom door turned into a beachhead where the boots were landing like bombs when Carlos turned on the light. The combatants, taken by surprise, froze unmoving as if in a photograph: the assailants had painted their faces, the black ones white with toothpaste and the white ones black with shoe polish; next to the door opening into the room they had an arsenal of boots and pails of water. The defenders, hidden behind their mattresses, took a few seconds to stick their heads out. Then they started laughing and it spread to the assailants with painted faces, who made expressions like clowns until Carlos yelled that he couldn't believe this, coño, that paste, that polish, those boots, those mattresses, all of it paid for by the people, and starting today, compañeros, the partying in the Beca was going to stop.

It didn't stop, and Carlos began to feel that impotence was eating away at him. When the assembly to pick candidates for the presidency of the Student Association took place, he wasn't thinking even remotely about being nominated; that was why he spoke in favor of Benjamín el Rubio, who had been a Communist since high school, "when I," he said, "was still navigating a sea of profound ideological confusion." He was very surprised to hear that the Coachman, as he then called Osmundo, was proposing Carlos himself, naming him as a hero. That word seemed to him totally out of proportion and he interrupted the Coachman to reject it. But the latter took his rejection as proof of modesty and told the saga of Carlos in the Playa Girón battles, where he dueled hand-to-hand with the mercenaries, compañeros. "He, compañeros, who came from a petit bourgeois family, whose father, recently deceased, had never been integrated into the revolutionary process! But that didn't prevent him from carrying out his duties as a son and a Communist. That's why I propose him, compañeros, because he is first in war, first in peace, and first in the hearts of architecture students!"

An ovation followed Osmundo's words. His compañeros demanded that Carlos stand, and doing so, he felt himself floating. Benjamín el Rubio withdrew his candidacy and supported that of compañero Carlos, who also, he said, had been a combatant against tyranny and an outstanding student leader in high school. The wave of applause surged again and the sensation of floating became real: Munse and the Ghost had picked him up and were carrying him on their shoulders to the podium. On the way everyone congratulated him, shouted "viva!" wanted to touch him. The leaders of the FEU embraced him when he arrived, the students chanted, "Speech! Speech! Speech!" and he asked for silence because nothing else occurred to him. But suddenly there was silence, and he felt the terrifying pleasure of having obtained it with a simple gesture of his hand. Now he had to speak, he had to be worthy of that unmerited honor.

"I will have to be worthy of this unmerited honor," he said.

He knew he'd gotten it right, and promised to devote all his strength to advancing the Revolution at the school. In the midst of the new round of applause you could hear the Ghost yelling:

"This cat can cook, asere!"

Carlos was left confused, you didn't talk that way in public, he had lost his concentration, he didn't know what to say.

"I'm sorry, compañeros," he said. "I'm very moved."

The emotion spread through the room in frenetic applause, over those who shouted "Patria o Muerte!" to which the students responded "Venceremos!" while the woman acting as MC went up to the microphone to announce that with the music of the National Anthem the assembly would conclude.

Outside, he was surrounded by students congratulating him. The Peruvian asked him to please tell about the battles, about clandestinity, he too someday would have to fight, brother, he needed experience. Carlos said he'd see him later, at the Beca; a stunning dark-skinned woman had asked him for five minutes, and he wanted to talk with her. But he found it very difficult to make his way towards her; on his brief path, the students reminded him about the need for textbooks, of a cafeteria for the students who weren't on scholarship, and the presence of gusanos among the faculty; they asked him for sports equipment, new dates for the exams, his autograph . . . When, finally, he got to the dark-skinned woman, he felt overwhelmed.

"Did you want to discuss some problem with me?"

"No," she replied, separating him from the group. "I just want to be with you, that's all. I like men who are leaders."

They went down the wide staircase in silence. Was this woman crazy? Now she was holding his hand, purring at him like a cat. It wasn't right for him to be going around this way, cheating on Gisela, who was surely going through who knows what difficulties with her illiterate students. But that woman, crazy or sane, had phenomenal tits and she was dragging him through the turbulent lights of La Rampa until she pulled him into the conspiratorial darkness of the La Zorra y El Cuervo Jazz Club, where she started kissing him with an insane voracity that took him to the very center of pleasure, she said, of a real good time, she said, while he put his hand inside searching for that invisible center, which she stopped with, "No, I've got the curse," leaving him frustrated until she unzipped his fly. "Don't think I'm just going to leave you like that," she said, and dove down in the darkness to unleash a sucking synchronized with lustful rock music, until she raised her head and looked at him with the most innocent of smiles: "Did you like it, sweetie?"

He went back to the Beca with a persistent feeling of uneasiness, almost as if he'd been raped. Entering the room, the Peruvian looked at him devotedly.

"Brother," he said, "your life is almost mythological. Osmundo told me: clandestinity, torture, ideological struggle, your father's death, the war . . . You're like Aeneas, brother."

Carlos looked at him suspiciously. Aeneas? Aeneas was a character in the comics, the sidekick of Benitín, a tall guy, skinny and slightly stooped over like he was. Is that what the Peruvian was saying to him? Could he be making fun of him? Carlos didn't think he was capable of that. But then, who was the other Aeneas? He decided not to ask, a guy who was almost mythological couldn't be ignorant. What tortures had the Coachman been talking about?

"That's all a lie," he said.

The Peruvian's eyes lit up as he murmured the word *modesty*.

"I'm sorry," added Carlos, "but I can't stay with you, I have guard duty."

Entering the room to put on his uniform, he heard the Peruvian talking about his enormous sacrifices. During guard duty he began to harbor the suspicion of being involved in a terrible confusion. It was as if the person for whom his compañeros had voted wasn't him, but rather someone heroic, modest, capable, and self-sacrificing. Should he resign? And leave the Beca and the school in the hands of irresponsible people? That would be an unforgivable cowardice. He had to study and work, fight, grow as much as he could.

The next day he learned, thanks to the *Pequeño Larousse*, that Aeneas was the protagonist of an epic poem in which were narrated the dangers, the tribulations, the deeds accomplished by the hero in his constant wandering from conquered Troy to Roman lands. He felt depressed, the Peruvian's comparison was so hyperbolic it was absurd, and could be hiding a joke on him. He was consoled to know that the other Aeneas, the one in the comics, didn't even appear in the dictionary. But he had to be on his toes with the Peruvian; no one made fun of Carlos Pérez Cifredo, the candidate. Conversations with him convinced Carlos that his admiration was real, but it was based on an immense confusion. Osmundo had talked about his life in such a way that the result was a legend. Carlos himself felt so moved when he heard it that he wasn't capable of explaining to the Peruvian what the precise limits of the truth were.

"It's all a lie," he said, disheartened, "don't repeat it."

But his prestige kept on growing and he won the election with 92 percent of the vote. The next day he presided over his first meeting in the school's FEU, from which he left satisfied and worried. Benjamín was a great vice president and Osmundo a very efficient secretary, both with the additional virtue of knowing how to work as subordinates. But there was a mountain of urgent tasks, he took responsibility for all of them, and having made that decision he turned into a galley slave. His days lasted between eighteen and twenty hours, he didn't have time to visit his mother, or to go out with the dark-skinned woman, much less to play clouds and constellations with his friends. That devotion to work inspired Osmundo and the Peruvian to tell over and over his legend, which from then on was repeated by an ever-larger number of students, who added onto it new tribulations, dangers, deeds. The truth could only be established in a general assembly, and that was totally impossible. He couldn't accuse Osmundo, who'd been so good to him, of being a liar, or disillusion the Peruvian, or the hundreds of students who had placed their confidence in him. It was his obligation to let his legend keep on growing, for the good of those same people who believed it.

For a few days this situation made him suffer; he withstood it by telling himself that this was the price of responsibility and that it had two decisive compensations: to permit him to do good for others, and to give him the instruments to act, with the certainty of being an extraordinary personality. When he attended his first plenary of the FEU, he learned that it could serve him for even more important things. The meeting really confused him, it had *tendencies.* One hard, inflexible, implacable, and the other soft, contradictory, perhaps too reflective. Although he felt his immediate leaning to be towards the Hardliners, he was annoyed by the existence of that useless infighting. For him things were very clear: revolution and counterrevolution, good and bad, period. Fuck the rest. There wasn't any space for those shadings and dancing around, in that sense even the Hardliners seemed soft to him. But he didn't intervene. The leaders of both tendencies were skilled, they had a long history, they knew a lot of philosophy, and they weren't impressed by him. For them, he was still an unknown. Nevertheless, they had taken positions: the Hardliners considered his presence to be a defeat, they would have preferred Benjamín el Rubio, a proven Communist; the Reflectives, in contrast, received him warmly; it was evident that they lacked cadres, and they opened up space to new people in the hope that they would join. In time he would make sure he showed them that with him they'd been mistaken; although it might seem the opposite, he was harder than the Hardliners, and he had no commitments to anyone.

On leaving, he headed for the bookstore of the Havana Libre hotel. He needed to study philosophy; a few weeks back, recalling the fantastic experience he had had with the *Communist Manifesto*, he read Hegel's *Philosophy of Right*; he didn't understand beans and when he asked for help, they told him he should also read a very long list of German philosophers, English economists, French socialists, and a miscellaneous group of thinkers who ended, or began, with Democritus, Anaximander, and Anaximenes. But he didn't have the time or the head for that, and he bought five of Mao's pamphlets that were brief, basic, and bargain-priced.

He headed for his house, got there saying he had to leave very soon, he was in a huge hurry, they had elected him president. His mother sang a litany of reproaches as if she hadn't heard him, he was thin, nervous, he looked sick, why didn't he stay and eat?

"Because they elected me president," he insisted.

"That's fine," she retorted, "but I have tamales."

Carlos banged on the table, annoyed.

"Don't you realize they elected me president?"

"Yes," she said, inviting him to follow her into the kitchen, "and that's why you have to eat."

She raised the lid on the tamale pot and a golden smell spread through the room, making him sit down. His mother smiled.

"President of what?"

He began to tell her about the assemblies, the applause, the responsibilities, and the honors, and he saw her nodding with her timid smile while she moved about, and suddenly he gave in to the desire to kiss her. She caressed his face with a damp hand that smelled of onions.

"You almost never come here anymore," she said.

And she didn't give him time to justify himself, she continued talking and moving about, food was scarce, there was speculation and a black market.

"Those are rumors, inventions," he said.

"No," she replied, "I've seen it with these eyes that one day will eat the earth."

Carlos was just about to ask her if that bastard Jorge had made her a gusana. Then suddenly he breathed easy, now his mother was asking Fidel to finally impose rationing so that everyone would get the same thing, protesting and grumbling with that surprising ability, for him a bit irresponsible, to say whatever came to her lips.

"The committee will help with this," she concluded. "It makes me want to join the CDR."

Carlos thought of Jorge, his mother would never join the CDR so as not to hurt him, preferring to silence the Fidelista inside her who had just spoken out, and she asked him about his girlfriend and the Literacy Campaign.

He told her about Gisela's last letter and all of a sudden felt overtaken by the kitchen smells and by the confused memory of a word: *lata*. "*Lata*?" he asked himself. "Where's that from . . . ?" But just then his mother hit her palm on her forehead.

"Boy, do I have something to tell you, Pablo and Rosalina got divorced!"

Carlos didn't want to believe it, such a lovely couple, so revolutionary.

"Revolutionary and all," she said, while she served the food. "Imagine that poor girl, divorced and with a little boy. Go ahead, sit down and eat."

The taste of his mother's cooking made him forget that surprising news. The meal was frugal, but it tasted of the best memories of his life. She watched him eat anticipating his wishes, water, bread, salt, telling him she was very proud they had elected him president and complaining that there was no meat to offer him. He closed his eyes to concentrate on the delicate flavor of the tamales and the *mojo* sauce, and invented a game of discovering which flavors were there, and which ones weren't. There was the tender texture of the corn, and that was enough for his palate, accustomed to the insipid macaroni at the Beca, but the lovely acid of lemon juice was missing. On the other hand, he sensed the hot flavor of onions and the excitation of a little clove of garlic, after which, unfortunately, did not follow a crispy pork skin. He was yearning for it, recreating it, when he felt a strange tension. He opened his eyes and saw Jorge standing in the doorway. His mother had stood up, looking at them with a desperation that only gave way when he said, "Hi," and Jorge answered, "Hi." He hadn't seen his brother since their father's funeral, he was thinner, with a bitter, nocturnal look in his eyes. Carlos thought of asking him about prison, but controlled himself, tried to find another topic of conversation, didn't come up with one, and knew, in some unclear way, that the same thing was happening to Jorge. They looked at each other without speaking until Jorge turned around and went into his room.

He finished eating in silence, in a rush.

"I've got to go," he said.

His mother started to softly caress his arm, he could come whenever he liked, she murmured, it was his house too, and his money, and his Buick, why didn't he ever use it?

"Private property is robbery."

He wished he hadn't said it, his mother had taken it as a personal allusion to his father. He tried to explain that he was referring to social classes, not to individuals, but she made him stop with a kiss on the forehead.

"Come on," she said, "I'll walk you to the door."

On the way she gave him all the expected advice, and then stayed standing in the doorway, waving goodbye with her hand, like a little girl.

Carlos observed her lighted image, skirted around the building, and the memory of the ravine got him thinking about the boot battle. The students acted like children, except that now it wasn't blacks fighting with whites. But that key difference still wasn't sufficient; tossing, stealing, breaking, playing with the people's property was a crime and he was not willing to allow it. Thus he would pressure Munse until he did his duty as floor representative. It was a shame he'd spent so much time away, at least if he had his father's Buick he'd make it back to the Beca quickly. But he could not give in on a matter of principle, although it might hurt his mother: private property *was* robbery, there was a reason that all the biggest thieves were property owners.

He arrived back at one in the morning, tortured by a long wait for the bus and the terribly slow trip. Munse was in the little yard, playing an old Elvis Presley song on the guitar, surrounded by a group singing along with him. Carlos approached indecisively; did he have the right to interrupt? They had agreed to meet at eleven and he was the one arriving late. He sat on a little wall to wait until the song ended. Perla, the dark-skinned woman with the defiant breasts, went to his side and put her hand on his thigh.

"The pearl of the Orient," Munse improvised.

"And what a Pearl!" the Ghost chimed in.

Carlos felt oppressed by the laughter. What was he doing there, wasting time as if he were just one more of them? He was the president, coño, and Munse knew very well that this was the day for preparing an offense against lack of discipline. He violently pushed Perla's hand away, ready to take Munse away from there.

"Indio," he said.

"Later, asere," replied Munse, passing without a transition from the slow blues to a blasting rock. "*You ain't nothing but a hound dog, crying all the time.*"

The chorus shrieked with enthusiasm. Carlos hit the wall with the Mao pamphlets, he was not willing to keep wasting time and prestige in that place, where to top it off they were singing in English.

"Roal Amundsen," he insisted with an authoritative voice.

Munse didn't even look at him, he hammered the guitar sending the hound dog somewhere else with his fleas, and Carlos shouted:

"Hey listen, dammit, I'm talking to you!"

Munse stopped playing, hugged the guitar like a woman, and said:

"Not now, asere."

Carlos sensed that he had made a mistake by lowering himself to arguing in public as an equal. Any way he would lose; even if he won the argument or the row they could always say that the president went around getting into fist-fights, acting all cocky in front of the girls, the compañeras. He looked at the group, making an effort to transmit in his eyes the certainty of revenge.

"All right," he said.

Now in his room, he vented his anger with two kicks at the wall. How the hell did that shithead dare to challenge him in public? And how could he have been such an imbecile by accepting the challenge? He had to learn, his best argument would have been silence, not shouting, a gesture, not a word. He had to remember that he wasn't just a regular guy, to always position himself at the level of his legend. Now, for example, he was obligated to contain his rage and to continue the plan to sleep only four hours a day. He took a pill to conquer sleep and sat down with the Mao pamphlets, his Chinese artillery. From it he'd obtain knowledge of the general laws that govern nature, thought, and society. He'd be able to interpret and predict everything scientifically. The Chinese *charada*, the horoscope and the cards, tools for the unseeing, were behind him now; left behind were the bembés and the beliefs of his childhood, substitute knowledge for the unhearing. And when he read the first line of *On Contradiction*, he felt, deeply moved, that he had entered the kingdom of truth.

The next day he had a rigorous regimen of volunteer work approved in the assembly, with the goal of having the students contribute to the quick finish of construction of a cafeteria for the students not on scholarship. After the first few days of work he began to be called a Hardliner by the little cliques in the Beca. The news reached him through the Coachman, because its originators didn't have the courage to say it to his face.

"They hide," Osmundo told him, "because they envy you."

Carlos savored the word *Hardliner*; it was true, no one, ever, could accuse him of being soft. That was why he worked more than anyone at the construction site, taking advantage of his experience in the militia to be the best with the pick and shovel, as he also was in his studies; and afterwards, when the rest of them wasted time, talked nonsense, spent their energies on women or their families, he devoted his life to advancing the university reform project, preparing files for the purge, rounding out a strategy for struggle against lack of discipline, creating agreements for the printing of textbooks, and still, while he traveled in the bus or ate, strengthening himself ideologically by reviewing his Chinese artillery.

The first book printed under the new agreements had a symbolic name: *Material Resistance*. He picked it up from the shop at night and took it to the Beca as proof that he had carried out a task many considered impossible. When he arrived, Osmundo was talking about what Carlos, in turn, had been weak enough to tell him: that Carlos had renounced his father's money and car because private property was robbery. He told him to be quiet, showed the book, which to the Peruvian seemed like another feat worthy of Aeneas, then felt a lash like a whip when the Ghost said:

"Run, run, he's got to piss bad."

Osmundo replied:

"Don't you think that's disrespect?"

"The more they suck me, the bigger it gets," rhymed the Ghost.

Carlos had to make a great effort to contain himself, controlling his expression was the hardest part of his new personality, but he already knew he wouldn't get anywhere by lowering himself to the common plane of shouting and curse words. Therefore he looked contemptuously at the Ghost until he made him bow his head, and felt happy with his triumph over the others and over himself.

At dawn, when he finished studying *On Practice*, he felt he'd earned the right to rest a few hours. On his cot he found a little note: "There's a lot of self-satisfaction here, but no self-criticism or automobile." He gave in to the furious wish to rip it into pieces, now when no one was watching. He couldn't understand how his efforts could produce such ingratitude and mockery in the ones who had been his buddies. But this was no longer a joke, the masses had delegated authority to him, and he was going to exercise it. If Munse and the Ghost wanted a war, they'd have it. He'd give them a response that was organic, complete, capable of institutionally establishing the path to the most rigorous discipline, taking over as floor leader, although that would imply raising his quota of sacrifice.

Two days later, the representative from the Beca called an impromptu meeting where he proposed the need to replace Munse as floor leader because of his bad work, and obtained approval from the majority, previously convinced by Carlos, Osmundo, and the Peruvian. Munse protested, how come he knew othingnay about it? "Because you never wanted to meet with me," answered Carlos, before asking for nominations. The Peruvian mentioned him with a decisive argument: how could anyone else be the leader where Carlos lived, and therefore be Carlos's leader? When the representative asked for more names, Osmundo said it wasn't necessary, they all wanted Carlos. The representative couldn't get another candidate to come forward. The vote was made by a show of hands so no one could shield themselves behind an irresponsible anonymity. Carlos smiled on confirming that 99.9 percent of the students voted for him openly. Only Munse, probably moved by an insane attachment to the position he was losing, had the nerve to vote no, the cynicism to look him in the face while he did so, the unbelievable daring to say, once the count was over:

"The Peruvian's a shithead, the Coachman's an opportunist, and you, Dude, are power-hungry."

Carlos controlled the desire to punch him, that second public challenge was a great opportunity. He had to give the irrefutable answer that his admirers were expecting. He had one, he'd prepared it in case Munse was irresponsible enough to oppose him. It was simple and deadly, a sort of open checkmate in the political arena. But he had to take his time, to first show his authority with silence; he looked to both sides, and then at Munse, before saying categorically:

"Prove that. Demonstrate it."

Munse stayed silent, livid with rage. When everyone understood that he had no more argument than his stubborn conviction, Osmundo shouted that such irresponsibility should be severely sanctioned, but Carlos decided to pardon him.

"Leave him be," he said. "Practice will teach him to be more profound."

Then he presented for the assembly's consideration the *Plan for Regulations for the Internal Order of the Floor*, explaining that it was a pilot program that would later on be extended to the entire building and even, where pertinent, to the university itself. He had written it all in one shot early one morning when he felt especially offended at finding an obscene expression dirtying the wall of the luxurious floor bathroom. Basically, it was a gloss on the regulations that already existed, although more rigorous and precise in defining infractions, responsibilities, and sanctions. It went so far as to set expulsion from the university and the Beca for cases of theft, and made the students on guard duty responsible for all irregularities they could not prevent. Moreover, it included a new, "Insofar as: thought and language form an indivisible unit, obscene expressions, nicknames and the like are a manifestation of impure thought, incompatible with our situation as revolutionary students; Therefore: the public or private, oral, or written use of said expressions, nicknames and the like is rigorously prohibited, and whoever commits said errors must voluntarily pay a fine of one (1) cent, as recognition of his error, if the latter is oral, and twenty (20), if it is written. Moneys thus obtained will be earmarked for the purchase of books for the floor library." "Is anyone opposed to this?" he asked, as he finished reading. No one. Carlos looked at the shaken face of Pancho, who would no longer be called the Ghost and who was now institutionally prohibited from saying his dirty little verses; he searched for that of Roal Amundsen, but he was no longer in the room. He adjourned the assembly, and while the others went towards the dining room, he went to his room to get the papers for an urgent meeting. Munse was on his bed, crying.

"What's the matter with you?" Carlos asked him.

The Indian lifted his face, red with rage.

"Asere," he replied without stopping his crying, "what I need is to have it out with you, asere, let it all out in a fistfight with you, asere."

Carlos felt perplexed. Munse was on his guard now, furiously mad, and Carlos didn't want to fight.

"Why?" he asked.

"Because you're a hard-line guy, and at the same time you're a shit," replied Munse, without letting his guard down.

Carlos noted the internal contradiction, but didn't have time to stop and think about it.

"Right now I can't," he said, looking at his watch. "I have a meeting with the dean."

"This afternoon?" Munse asked anxiously.

"We have classes," replied Carlos, "and after that I have volunteer work, a follow-up with the printer, and a meeting about the reforms . . . Can you make it at one in the morning?"

"At any time," said Munse, and then, almost pleading with him, "Don't stand me up, asere."

For the rest of the day Carlos lost his ability to concentrate, he couldn't figure out the root of Munse's craziness. He needed to remember that the

Indian (whom he shouldn't continue to call by that name, or Munse either, but rather Roal, Roal Amundsen) had accused him in public of being power-hungry, something truly vile, to convince himself that Osmundo was right: his motivation was envy. Then he felt like breaking the balls of that ungrateful Indian fag. He slapped his hand against his forehead, he'd thought two curse words. He struggled to control himself and to imagine correct expressions, but the "On your guard!" that came to his lips seemed ridiculous, useless as a response to the insults he'd been subjected to. To accuse him—him, coño!—of being self-satisfied and power-hungry was the height of ill will and envy, in short, it was faggoty crap. And now he was having base thoughts because he was responding to baseness. But he wouldn't let himself be dragged down by this provocation, he'd break Roal Amundsen's face in silence. In the early morning he went looking for him, excited by a day of draining battle on behalf of the collective good, and when he had his enemy before him, a "What the hell's going on with you?" rose up from his heart, to which Roal replied in an unexpected way, his eyes feverish and bulging, his arms hanging down by his sides: "I can't go at it with you, asere, I . . . coño, you were at Girón and you were my buddy." He couldn't contain a sob and he embraced Carlos, who let him continue, "You were a good guy, asere, and now you're wrong right down to the core," while he fought to keep Roal from noticing that he, too, was crying.

That night he slept badly. He got up late, annoyed by the tenderness of his dreams, and without allowing himself the luxury of having breakfast, went out to shovel mortar at the cafeteria construction site. He was weak, there were dark rings around his eyes from hunger and insomnia, but he had to set an example for those who were slacking off in the shade, and for Roal, who insisted on working on a par with him and who, perhaps ashamed of his crying the night before, was shoveling like the devil, challenging Carlos in an unacceptable show of arrogance. There it was, patently evident, the sign of resentment and immaturity; Roal Amundsen had transferred to the work arena the argument in the assembly and the anger that, in the final instance, he hadn't had the courage to express, with the intention of surpassing him, ridiculing him in front of the group. But Roal had forgotten he was competing with him, who neither gave nor asked for quarter. By midmorning everyone had noticed the rivalry, they followed it without wondering why the two of them didn't stop even for a second, and even formed camps (Roal supported by a ridiculous entourage of insubordinates led by Francisco; he, with the warmth of a circle of compañeros who followed Osmundo; the ungrateful majority neutral and expectant) before which he would make his opponent bite the dust of defeat. Except that the cement dust was killing him (the opportunistic Amundsen had masked himself with a handkerchief, he looked like a cowboy murdering Indians, but Carlos couldn't lower himself to imitate him), it made him cough all the time, making him shudder, enervating him, while the sun cruelly punished his pale face (Roal was a mulatto—how the hell could he look like a cowboy?, or in any case an Indian, that's why they called him that), making him drip with briny sweat that got into his eyes (the somabitch mulatto, meanwhile, with another kerchief on his forehead and shining eyes), and he, clouding over, his vision blurred, confused, and the sun suddenly dark and the voices, "Get him to the Policlinic! To the Policlinic!" and the Ghost's macabre joke, "To the Polinesio! To the Polinesio!"

When he woke up he had an IV in his arm. The doctor prescribed balanced meals that he should eat following a strict schedule, frequent trips to the beach, sports activities, a minimum of eight hours of sleep a night, reading for pleasure, music, dancing, and a considerable lightening up of his responsibilities. What planet was this man living on? Was he crazy or did he have ideological problems? He was going to answer back, but the doctor ordered him to be quiet and left him alone with the sudden awareness of his defeat. That faggot Munse had achieved his goal: to ridicule him. For three hours he tortured himself with that idea and with the slow drip of the IV. When the nurse accompanied him to the door, he felt depressed, but as he opened it, his eyes misted up with tears of joy: in the large waiting room of the Policlinic the masses were waiting for him, almost three dozen compañeros who shouted "Viva!" when he came out waving, still pale and trembling. How could the doctor not realize that the best medicine was the virtue of sacrifice? How could he have prescribed the loss of his precious time in frivolous diversions? How did he dare order him to lower the intensity of his submission to the cause? No, compañeros, he wouldn't say anything out of modesty, but all of you who had waited for him and now followed him on the way back to the Beca could be sure that your president will not fail you, that he will continue to be implacable with himself, and from the height of that unstained morality, also implacable with anyone else who doubted. Now, for example, he would have the courage, the moral will, the discipline and the humility of self-criticism. "Compañeros," he said on arriving, "yesterday, a fateful day, I committed a series of errors over a series of problems when I argued with Roal Amundsen over a series of issues. We were at the point of punching each other, compañeros. I violated the regulations when I said and thought a series of obscene expressions, evident remainders of a past we should overcome. I criticize myself, I pay twenty cents in fines, and I invite Roal Amundsen to do the same as proof of remorse."

Days later, when there was enough money in the little box to buy the first book, he asked his compañeros democratically what title they should purchase, and Roal proposed *Don Quixote*. Carlos was annoyed because he expected the question to be returned to him, so he could suggest ten pamphlets by Mao. But Roal was excited by the possibility of buying the first book edited by the brand-new National Press, and he had managed to add on the Peruvian, who solemnly said, "It is the most important work in the Spanish language," as if with that, his own language were made important. Carlos weighed the circumstances, this was a secondary contradiction that in no way should be elevated to principal rank, and in silence he accepted the proposal.

That night he understood that he'd fallen into a trap. Francisco and Roal were waiting for him, dying of laughter, while Osmundo was serious, frowning. Carlos put himself on guard, that was a bad sign, laughter always had a corrosive background that threatened order and took away the strength needed for larger tasks. "What's going on?" he asked. Francisco extended the book to him amid guffaws. "Get a load of this, my man, get a load of Miguelito." Carlos took the volume; his eyes, guided by Francisco's index finger, came to an incredible word: *somabitch*. He read it as if taking a slap in the face, as if that unspeakable expression had been directed at his mother by the felonious Francisco, who kept on laughing as he shouted, "But what a somabitch that Miguelito was!"

He had to control himself, political problems couldn't be reduced to the personal sphere.

"You're fined," he said.

"But the one who wrote *somabitch* was Cervantes!" replied Francisco.

That was true, but he had to find a response to that challenge to his prestige. Francisco, emboldened, asserted that Cervantes had been in Cuba and that when he heard how we speak Spanish, he was left *manco del espanto*, crippled with fright. Everyone was laughing when Carlos found his response:

"Perhaps Cervantes wrote that obscene word, but no one could prove it; you, however, have said it twice, so pay up."

Francisco ended up crushed by authority, he paid, and the group broke up because Carlos was telling them with the look in his eyes that if they wanted to waste their time, that was their choice, he had to study.

When everyone was asleep he put down his textbooks and took up *Don Quixote*. He wasn't planning on reading the whole thing, it was too long and after all it was a novel, it couldn't teach him anything about life; he simply needed to become informed so he could argue about it. He skimmed through several random chapters and was left in growing confusion. The hero turned out to be an ugly, skinny, ridiculous guy, who sometimes made you laugh and other times made you sad because he was always mistaken (in reality, he wasn't a hero, he *put on airs like* he was a hero) and he fought for justice without knowing the laws of history, or taking into account the masses, or objective and subjective conditions, or the correlation of strength between the exploiting and the exploited, and he mixed up antagonistic contradictions with nonantagonistic ones, principal with secondary, internal with external, because at base he didn't even know what a contradiction was, and therefore, couldn't understand the inevitability of periods of accumulation of strength, he was incapable of transforming quantitative change into qualitative change, making the leap, and exercising the negation of negation over the historical process to promote a spirallike development; he was, finally, a petit bourgeois (a pharmacist, or rather, a druggist) who hadn't been able to commit class suicide, and maintained his anarcho-individualist character by trying to take justice into his own hands. He believed he was a hero, but he didn't have the slightest sign of humility, modesty, or self-critical spirit. He even had a servant! All of this was due (as the author himself naively confessed) to a mountain of badly assimilated reading that had made him go mad, and at the end, when he recovered his sanity, that very same Cervantes recommended the prohibition of those tomes. And what about his own? Couldn't *Don Quixote* also do incalculable damage to new generations? Then why had they printed more than a hundred thousand copies?

There was only one answer, the publishing houses were mined with old people (or people with old opinions, same thing) incapable of understanding that the revolutionary task consisted in wiping out the past, destroying false idols and values, and creating a totally new, proletarianized, pure world. Excited by this idea, Carlos opened the drawer with his Chinese artillery and rooted around among the many papers where he amassed weekly news reports from Xinhua and Mao's pamphlets, until he found the little book on the talks at the Yenan forums. There was the entire truth on the topic of art, set out in thirty pages. It was that capacity for synthesis, that ability to liquidate in a brief, simple manner the most complicated problems (or apparently complicated, since the bourgeoisie twisted them to fool the people) that fascinated him in the Chinese theorists. It must have been very late, but his enthusiasm was so great that he stayed up studying until dawn.

He woke up at midmorning, head aching and with no time to eat breakfast. He had to run to the Student Association's headquarters to approve an exhibition of paintings that the Reflectives wanted to mount at the school. The paintings confused him even more than *Don Quixote*. He didn't understand a thing. Simply, sincerely, honestly, not a thing. Stripes, stains, women with four eyes. He was silent for a while, struggling to find the possible sense in that nonsense, and he didn't find it. (Even such an ideologically weak guy as Francisco made fun of it, risking a fine: "What a face!" he said, "What a being! What the fuck am I seeing?") But Carlos couldn't laugh, he had to make a decision and he decided that the association could not sponsor that craziness. The press and culture secretary (a Reflective so self-satisfied that he had the nerve to use the word *commissar* to describe his role in the exhibition) challenged him with a question:

"You don't like that painting?"

Carlos looked at the canvas he pointed out, it was an eyesore; the future could never ever be reflected in that manner.

"No," he said. "Who ever saw a woman with four eyes?"

"But it isn't a woman, it's a painting!" yelled the other, before charging at him: "Do you know you're prohibiting Lam, Portocarrero, Antonia Eiriz?"

The yelling attracted a dozen students, whom Carlos looked at with the confidence that he was in the right.

"I am prohibiting the past," he said.

He was surprised to learn that the FEU had approved an agreement (proposed by the Reflectives with the silent complicity of the Hardliners) criticizing him for having prohibited the exhibition that, according to what the agreement itself stated, would be mounted in the Rectorado as redress for the glories of national culture. He attempted to fight it through the association, but for the first time Benjamín opposed him, keeping him from getting a consensus.

"He envies you, too," Osmundo whispered in his ear, as they returned to the Beca. When they entered the room, Francisco started proclaiming:

"Look at what *Al Mamarte* is saying!"

"You're fined!" yelled Osmundo.

"No!" replied Francisco, "I said *Alma Marte*, Mars, the Roman *orisha* of war."

Carlos yanked the copy of *Alma Mater* away from him and kicked them out of the room. In the centerfold of the organ of the FEU there was a commentary full of praise for the blessed exhibition, illustrated with some photos of the paintings, even more horrible than the originals. This was a serious ideological problem, and he had to face it head on; so that very afternoon, with Osmundo's help, he placed charges of Chinese artillery in key points of the university. That night he presided over a meeting of the school's FEU and gave an impressive report on the activities carried out: the establishment of discipline at the Beca, the printing of two dozen textbooks, a decisive push for construction of the cafeteria . . . Benjamín tried to belittle his extraordinary efforts by bringing up the delay in supporting the reforms and in the purging process, but Carlos defended himself with an evident truth.

"I work twenty hours a day, I almost don't sleep or eat, what else do you want?"

"Lead the way you should," responded Benjamín.

Carlos smiled, el Rubio had exposed himself. Osmundo stepped into the breach and attacked him, supported by the rest of the compañeros who praised the report, leaving Benjamín isolated, very small compared to the hero's saga that Osmundo evoked. Carlos took the floor to make mincemeat of el Rubio, but it became evident to him that this was a nonantagonistic contradiction, and that wouldn't be the correct method for resolving it. So he put the report to a vote. It was approved, with votes against from Benjamín and Romualdo, the secretary of culture. Suddenly he thought his condescension could be confused with weakness, and he decided to leave a slight threat in the air before going.

"Very well," he said, "I'll pose a question that should be answered at the next meeting: are there compañeros among us with ideological problems?"

He headed back to the Beca and made a tour of all the rooms on the floor. Everyone was asleep. The application of the regulations had been so successful that the council had decided to extend them to the entire building. Thefts, waste, and breakage had disappeared after the first expulsions. Only the level of obscene language continued to be alarmingly high, even though many never paid the fines. He decided to begin a master book to record the payments and to make a radical change in the situation. He was worn out, but felt he didn't have any right to sleep. In only ten days Gisela would return, and he, exhausted by responsibilities, had written her very little. She complained bitterly, because she didn't know that her boyfriend was no longer just any regular student. So now was the opportune moment to tell her everything. He began evoking her while he wrote and allowed a desperate feeling of loneliness to overcome him. He even wrote that he couldn't go on without her, that he needed her to meld their lives in the great battles that were to come, in which they would die for the motherland or arrive together at the red dawn of the future. The sun was coming up when he wrote at the bottom of the page: "Patria o Muerte!"

The next day, with the stipend he had saved up for months, he bought a pistol. For the first time in his life he didn't go to class. He spent the afternoon in front of the mirror, admiring how good it looked at his waist; giving imaginary reports on great battles, gravely serious invasions, and imminent dangers; finding Gisela amid a sea of literacy workers or being found by her, wounded, dying and happy, after winning the last combat without letting go of his pistol, now empty.

Two days later he was able to arm and disarm it blindfolded, prompting the admiration of his compañeros and a really bad little poem from the Ghost: "I went by your house / and you tossed me a pistol / Now I've got it with me still." Carlos put the pistol to the Ghost's head, achieving the miracle of a black man turning gray, almost white. "I don't like bad jokes," he said, while the others laughed. His obsession with work and the pistol made his wait for Gisela tolerable for a few days, but his anxiety grew as the decisive day approached and now he couldn't calm himself down at the station, packed with young people looking for their families in the red evening air, where he thought he saw her and was mistaken and then made the same mistake again, and then stopped in confusion when he felt those fingers covering his eyes, and let out a yell that she silenced by kissing him.

The first days were a marvelous succession of emotions that culminated in a gigantic ceremony on the Plaza de la Revolución, where Fidel raised a flag with the slogan that made them clap and shout in a frenzy:

CUBA: The first country in America free of illiteracy

But later, when they sat down on the seawall, now dressed in civilian clothing, she started reproaching him for not visiting her family for a whole year; her father, her mother, and her siblings were all seething against him, they considered him uncaring and ungrateful, and they said he wasn't in love with her. Carlos reacted with annoyance, if she was going to be his wife she should know right now that he wouldn't have any time for niceties. His life was totally, fully, absolutely, and definitively given up to the Revolution.

"You could have gone on a Sunday," said Gisela, "or some night."

Carlos sighed, who did she think she was talking to? He didn't have any Sundays, or nights, and anyway, what for? To waste time? He'd done enough by missing his duties for a week to be with her.

"And that's something I should have to thank you for?"

"If you like," he murmured, looking away.

He was surprised by the inconsolable sound of her sobs and gave in to the desire to hold her. Gisela pulled away, this is what she got for being so stupid, to be so stupidly in love, writing him letters that the little boy didn't even take the time to answer. Her mother was right, coño, all men were the same, this is what she got for being a shithead. Carlos controlled his desire to reproach her for the curse words, hadn't she gotten his letter signed in blood? Gisela shook her head no, impressed, and he took advantage of the moment to explain to her that he loved her, he loved her very much, but it wasn't up to him, it wasn't his fault that he had so many responsibilities and tasks, she had to understand that she wasn't with just any regular person.

"And just who am I with?" asked Gisela, somewhere between naive and mocking.

Carlos didn't know what to answer until she repeated the question with a slightly challenging tone. Then he started telling her his legend, getting excited and feeling heroic, he moved from the prestige of the past to the responsibilities of the present and the image of a near future when he would be president of the FEU and would speak at great student gatherings; fired up by his own words, he spoke of his role in the destiny of the country, who could know? But for now he had to be loyal to his immediate task, to the confidence of the masses, to the indescribable feeling, which he shared only with her, of knowing himself to be an exemplary revolutionary.

Gisela's singsong laughter sounded like glass breaking in his head, who the hell did she think she was? He directed his most powerful silence at her, but she was still doubled over with laughter.

"A what?"

Carlos took off walking, rage had produced in him an intolerable desire to hit her, which ended up in impotence. Now she was following him, "Hey, hero, wait for me," but he speeded up, to accept all that would have been the limit. "President, Presi," she repeated, with the mocking inflection that was so much a part of her personality, and that he was not willing to tolerate. At two different moments he felt tempted to wait for her, but the memory of her mockery made him keep walking as if he were dragging her through the streets of Vedado, making her pay for her insult. When they got to the Beca, Gisela's tone of voice suddenly changed, becoming almost desperate.

"Carlos," she said, "wait for me." But he went inside without looking back, like a man.

That night he found out what miserable stuff he was made of; he had an erotic dream about Gisela and woke up calling her name. The next day he neglected his duties and like a dog, like a petit bourgeois, he hung around his lover's house. At least he had the courage, as a man and a revolutionary, not to lower himself to asking for mercy. *She* was the one who had been wrong, it was her place to come see him and ask him to forgive her. He would remain intransigent, getting strength and happiness from his work. But once he returned to the Beca, he couldn't even get out of bed. He felt alone and betrayed, without any desire to take care of the dozens of matters that were piling up waiting for a solution. He allowed Benjamín to take charge of everything, listened in silence to the Ghost's little dirty poems, and found out, through Osmundo, that his enemies were taking advantage of his inertia to accuse him of laziness and, like Captain Araña, of getting others aboard then deserting the ship. Desperate, he confessed his story to his friend, who found an ideal answer for the problem: he would tell everyone that Carlos was sick, with a bleeding ulcer attack, and that the awful pain was the cause of his frequent bouts of depression.

That brilliant idea was like a balm in the midst of his misfortune. Francisco stopped making up his little poems, dozens of students he didn't know brought him milk and food, the Peruvian brought all his books up to date . . . But his depression didn't lift until the afternoon when Osmundo whispered in his ear: "She's downstairs, waiting for you." Happiness gave him the strength to get dressed and go down. Gisela was waiting for him in the dining room, drumming incessantly on the bagasse-board table. On seeing him, she went to him and embraced him, crying.

"I love you, coño, I came because I love you."

"It's all right," he responded, kissing her on the forehead, "don't cry."

With their arms around each other they went out to the Avenida de los Presidentes and sat down on a bench. Gisela didn't stop crying while she told him about her loneliness and her love, her desperate nights of insomnia and sadness.

"Maybe I'm stupid, but I, I love you, coño, and I, I'll do whatever you want. I . . . I only wanted to play a little bit."

Carlos dried her tears with his lips and kissed her mouth in silence, because at that moment, he didn't even want to hear his own voice.

He went back to his work with redoubled energy, complaining about the damn ulcer that had taken him away from the fulfillment of his duties. Among the many errors that had been committed during his absence, one was especially grave, having to do with principle: Benjamín was trying to carry out the purge with conciliatory criteria. He masked his objectives appealing to pretexts like caution, tact, and sensitivity; he proposed a legal method belonging to the past, not to accept common opinion (the opinion of the masses, no less) but to abide by the evidence; he spoke openly about not injuring certain professors and students, whom he considered neither revolutionaries nor gusanos (as if such a political expression of his philosophical dualism were possible in life); and to top it off, he was demanding that religious people and homosexuals not be touched, since, he said, those were private matters.

Carlos began his reply by answering the prophetic question he had formulated weeks ago.

"Yes, compañeros, there is a person among us with grave ideological problems: Benjamín Cifuentes, known as el Rubio," and he continued with a demolishing critique of the proposal and of the one who had made it.

But his lapidary intervention didn't have the effect he expected. Benjamín the Fox had conspired disloyally during his absence, to the point of creating a faction of Reflectives that supported him through hell or high water, criticized Carlos for his absurd centralism, his political myopia, and his practice of distributing Chinese propaganda; they managed to get a divided vote and had the arrogance to announce, through their leader, that they would appeal to the Architecture School Council.

"He wants to unseat you," Osmundo told him as they left. "He envies you."

Carlos stayed silent. His illness had served to bring to light his enemies' moral poverty. Osmundo was right, Benjamín envied him, had envied him ever since the masses had preferred him, and now that bastard was conspiring, blinded by a shady thirst for power. Very well, he'd have a war, Carlos knew how to conspire too, he'd reveal in secret to the Hardliners in the FEU who was who in the Architecture School and he'd appeal to the University Council when he had won the fight behind closed doors. He wouldn't stop until he got el Rubio expelled from the association: his current and future enemies had to know what the price of their temerity would be. While he was getting this squared away, he'd continue with his usual activity, he'd distribute Chinese and Albanian propaganda, but he wouldn't criticize Benjamín; his enemies would think he was just a stupid little lamb, and when they finally recognized the tiger it would be too late for them.

But the Hardliners were cautious about his plans, they took note of the problem with the purge, said they'd get back to him and criticized him—they too!—for distributing that propaganda. Arriving back in his room, there was a new aggravation: a group was surrounding Francisco, who avidly leafed through a little book, *Adventures of the Cuban Unknown Soldier*. Carlos couldn't avoid going over and reading, guided by the Ghost's black index finger, ". . . and I slammed him such an awful kick in the balls . . ." Carlos was left stupefied; suddenly he yanked the book out of Francisco's dirty hands, yelling that enough was enough, that he had the proof right there, that now he'd have him expelled from the Beca for sure.

"The proof of what?" asked the Ghost. "Sir, don't you know that this book was written by Pablo de la Torriente Brau?"

Carlos ran his hands over his hair, incredulous, it wasn't possible that a hero, a Communist who had died fighting in Spain could have written that barbarity. And nevertheless it was, his name was on the cover of that obscene little book.

"It's an error!" he yelled, without knowing exactly what he was referring to, and he left slamming the door, amid laughter.

A minute later Osmundo caught up with him in the hallway and whispered in his ear that it had all been planned by the Ghost, who was also sending a little joke around that Carlos was a bugger because he went after fags, what did he think about that? Carlos thought of going back to the room and taking the Ghost by the throat, but managed to control himself, swallowing his rage. He thought it was a provocation, he said, and he wasn't going to fall for it; he had a plan to make them pay at the right time.

More than a month went by before the Hardliners gave him a response, he had so many tasks that he couldn't keep up, and Benjamín made sure to systematically check up on him to have an opportunity for criticism. The master book, functioning since the beginning of the year, hadn't given the results he had hoped for (only he and Osmundo paid their share in a disciplined way, giving the intolerable impression of being the most filthy-mouthed of the floor). The FEU had the nerve to pick someone else to give the opening-day speech at the University Cafeteria, and although it was a Hardliner and he made a pretty radical statement, it was still insulting that he hadn't been picked himself. Even Osmundo began allowing himself a few ironic remarks. Carlos hadn't told Gisela about his setbacks for fear that she'd make fun of him, but the moment came when he couldn't stand it anymore and in one breath he told her about the difficult situation he was in, the shady conspiring of his enemies, both open and concealed, and the envy that his prestige constantly provoked.

He felt sad on confirming that not even his girlfriend understood him, and he secretly harbored the painful suspicion that he was wrong. But two days later Osmundo gave him the most important news of the year: the Hardliners had taken God's name out of José Antonio's testament. It was a sad, shocking necessity of struggle that not even he would have had the courage to carry out. Those who had done it knew why, and they traced out a path for him. The positions he had defended up until then were valid. He should even make them more radical, definitive, and intransigent. If the correct way of thinking could not be stopped even by some aspects of the thought of a hero like José Antonio, how then could he respect Benjamín's vacillations, the Reflectives' doubts? If reality was hard, revolutionaries had to be even harder in order to transform it. He put on his uniform and pistol and looked at himself in the mirror before going out to the 13 March commemoration, at the head of the students of the Architecture School, the school that José Antonio himself had once led.

When he arrived, the wide staircase was full of people. With Osmundo, he worked his way through the crowd to position himself near the podium. Would Fidel know about the testament? Yes, of course, who would ever think of doing something like that without consulting him? Carlos turned around, the multitude was covering San Lázaro Street now, past the stairs, almost down to where they had clashed with the police six years before. Back then they were scarcely a hundred, now they were an entire people; and if he hadn't fled, stabbed by fear, he'd be sitting up on the podium like Mai, whom he had just seen, now a national youth leader; or he would have died and his portrait would be next to José Antonio's, in the Hall of Martyrs.

Fidel began by referring to them, the scholarship students. "Do we want our youth," he said, "to simply limit themselves to hearing and repeating? No! We want our youth to think." Carlos began applauding enthusiastically; he was following the correct line, that of thinking and applying his conclusions through to their ultimate consequences. The multitude kept applauding even when he stopped doing so, in stupefaction. Fidel was reading, above the applause, the words that had been taken out of the testament! "We trust that the purity of our intentions will bring us God's favor, in order to achieve an empire of justice in our motherland." Fidel was lighting into the censors, asking himself could it be possible, compañeros, could we be such cowards; could a way of thinking like that be called Marxism, a fraud like that socialism, a deception like that communism, and repeating "no" to himself, while Carlos fled through the crowd, panting as if he were suffocating. Sometimes the voice reached him from a distance, almost inaudible, and at others it was as if it were asking him right in his ear, what was the Revolution turning into, just a school for domesticated students? When Fidel said that that wasn't revolution, Carlos decided to face words with the courage he hadn't had for bullets, and he returned to hear, standing firm, the rest of the speech. Afterwards he asked Osmundo to leave him alone, and he stayed there until early morning, sitting on the huge, empty staircase.

The general assembly to discuss the speech took place the next night in the school amphitheater. There was a partylike air among the students and professors, but Carlos kept as silent as a zombie, without the spirit to respond to the question from Regüeiferos, the Reflective who was chairing the debate on behalf of the FEU.

"Were there, in this school, any manifestations of the errors that were pointed out in the speech?"

He felt the responsibility, as president, to break the long silence that fell on the room. But he knew he was incapable of threading together a coherent self-criticism at that moment; he didn't understand himself, he needed time and courage, and so he said nothing even when he noticed that Benjamín was looking him in the eyes before saying:

"Yes, there were."

Then he felt better. Now, finally, would begin the revenge that would give him an opening to publicly assume responsibility for the errors he had surely committed. But Benjamín confused him by making a reflective speech, sometimes vehement and at other times slow, almost sad, in which he described a situation where Carlos came out looking like a hardworking sectarian, self-satisfied but striving, a basically good compañero whose enormous errors were due to a personalistic manner of leadership and a colossal theoretical and political ignorance.

"Did the compañero know that José Antonio's testament had been altered?" the dean interrupted.

"No," replied Benjamín, "he didn't know."

"Should the compañero continue to head the association?" Regüeiferos asked the assembly.

Carlos looked at the crowd. During Benjamín's intervention he had felt variously humiliated, sad, grateful, or absent, but his stomach jumped when Emilia Suárez, a slender little dark-skinned girl whom he'd never even noticed, said:

"Well, I don't think he should, because I'm afraid of him." There was a wave of laughter, and the girl sat down, almost scared.

Then Osmundo asked to speak, and Carlos looked at him, wanting to tell him not to come to his defense, to let things run their course, soon he'd get his mind in order and speak for himself. He wasn't able to do that. Osmundo was very far away, in the center of the room, and from there he shocked the assembly by accusing Carlos of being a liar, telling in minute detail a story according to which Carlos had misrepresented his life to seem like a hero, inventing illnesses like the famous ulcer, and hiding decisive information, because yes, compañeros, he *did* know that the testament had been altered, and he was in agreement with it. A wave of murmuring was generated that he heard from far off, as if he were in the bottom of a well.

"Do you have anything to say?" the dean asked him.

"Nothing," he replied.

He felt anesthetized, people's movements seemed slow, their faces distant. He saw Munse stand up as if in a cloud of mist, as if in a cloud of mist he heard him shout that he didn't believe one bit of what the Coachman said, because the Coachman was an opportunist who up until yesterday was licking Carlos's ass, licking his ass, he repeated, and Carlos, he said, was sectarian and self-satisfied but he was a man, and he had demonstrated that manliness in war, facing bullets, and besides that he'd worked like crazy for them, so now they had a cafeteria, books, and a thousand other things thanks to a man who had collapsed shoveling mortar before saying "no" to work, and because of that, because he believed Carlos was mistaken, but had integrity and was capable of rectification, he proposed that he continue as president. The assembly was divided between applause and booing. Regüeiferos called for order and turned to Carlos.

"Compañero," he said, "are you going to speak, or should we vote?"

"No," he replied, with an almost inaudible voice. "Don't vote, I resign."

Only with difficulty did he manage to avoid a fit of sobs, and he left the amphitheater without excusing himself, amid absolute silence. He walked without seeing the streets, guided by instinct, until reaching the home of the Archimandrite, who showed him into the library and listened to his tortured story, asking him please not to forget one single detail. Despondency almost prevented him from getting to his last, devastated question.

"What's the matter with me, Doctor? What's the matter with me?"

The Archimandrite poured him a shot of rum, lit a cigar, and looked him in the eyes while explaining with a grave voice that Carlos was ill, he was suffering from a childhood disease that in adults often had disastrous consequences. And the worst thing was that it had attacked him in its Chinese strain, unfortunately the most virulent and the one that was causing the highest rate of morbidity among us. He was suffering, he said, putting a hairy, somewhat chubby hand on Carlos's shoulder, from the Leftism Syndrome, a psycho-political disease that was common, but very pernicious; luckily, in his case it wasn't accompanied by certain parasitic manifestations such as opportunism, although there was an extremely strong egomaniacal effect that, on the other hand, wasn't the worst thing. Every young man dreamed of being a hero, then life did its work. He paused, and underlined his conclusion pointing at Carlos with the cigar.

"When I say that you're sick, I'm not using a metaphor. You *are* sick, and you suffer, you suffer physically."

Carlos wiped his eyes with the back of his hand.

"Doctor, what should I do?"

"Just give it time," replied the Archimandrite, slowly sucking on his cigar. "That's the only cure."

SIXTEEN

They were dying with laughter about Kindelán's crazy house: crazy swimmers Olympically diving into empty pools, crazy painters hanging from their brushes, crazy journalists who got off believing they were today's paper and suffered thinking about how tomorrow people with diarrhea would use them to wipe their asses; and then the one about the guy who goes to the doctor's office and asks the secretary, ma'am, is the p-sychiatrist in, and the secretary says, yes, sir, but for your information, you don't pronounce the *p*, and the guy goes, Oh no? Well then tell him that Edro Eres's ecker won't oint; and with that Gisela couldn't stand any more, she hung on to the edge of the table so she wouldn't fall down laughing and excused herself to go to the pipiroon, and Carlos said, Wait, wait, what do Brazilian women call the ecker? and Kinde, What? and Carlos, *O Amado Nervo*, and Gisela, Help, help, and Rosa and Ermelinda went with her to the bathroom, and the Archimandrite said, Another Brazilian, another Brazilian, another Brazilian goes to confession desperate, Father, *eu so canalla*, I'm a bastard, I've fornicated with my women friends, my cousins, my sisters, *a meus amigas, a meus primas, a meus irmanas*, and the priest goes, My son! In the dark? *A oscuras?* and the Brazilian says, Yes, *a os curas*, with priests, with soldiers, with peasants, and when the women returned the Archimandrite announced a change of topic, to one that was serious, philosophical, with three morals to the story, and Carlos asked himself how the hell there could be a serious joke. That's a contradiction, he said, but the Archimandrite continued with the sad story of the little bird who was about to die of the cold when a cow took a shit on it and the heat of the shit revived it, it started shaking itself off and a cat, attracted by the shitty movement, began digging, found the little bird, ate it, and that's the end of the story. Carlos and Kindelán looked at each other, What was the joke? but the Archimandrite was wagging his index finger, The first moral: not everyone who shits on you wants to screw you; they all smiled, on hold, waiting for what was coming next, for what they could see was coming, for what came when the Archimandrite announced, The second moral: not everyone who cleans the shit off you wants to save you, and he raised his hand like a traffic cop to stop the laughter and move to The third moral: whoever has shit on him shouldn't move around too much, and then he let his hand fall, giving free reign to the general guffawing while Carlos stayed quiet, thinking how the Archimandrite had closed the circle by telling a serious joke with three pairs: Munse had criticized him to save him, the Coachman had praised him to screw him, and he shouldn't move too much; then he had a drink that turned out to be the good one, the one that relaxed him and allowed him to enter into the fun, to think how all that had happened a thousand years ago, and to see his wife and his pals smiling, digging life, and he started to laugh at the superdupershithead he'd been, to roar with laughter like one of Kindelán's crazies, while the others looked at him without understanding beans, and Kinde asked Gisela, Hey, what's your husband laughing at? and Carlos said, At myself, I'm laughing at myself, and Kinde, Uh oh, bad sign, and Carlos, That once I wanted, I wanted, I wanted, and the waves of laughter kept him from explaining just what the fuck he had wanted, and Ermelinda, Coño! You're worse than Don Rafael del Junco, and now everyone was laughing except Gisela, who wanted to know who was this Don Rafael, and the Archimandrite said, A character in an Egyptian novel about Nasser's right to the Suez Canal, *el derecho de Nasser*, and Gisela, Oh right, go tell it to your grandmother, and Kinde, Ok, so what did you want? and Carlos, To prohibit curse words, pal, just imagine, I was crazy crazy crazy as hell, and then the *chou* started, there was a silence then came the first chord of Froilán's guitar, and then some soft arpeggios that broke out suddenly, abruptly, cutting the air in two, opening it like a curtain of warm affection so that the Señora could enter smiling, Elena Burke smiling at her folks and saying to them *La noche de anoche*, but Kindelán started playing around and said, in a very low voice, From the front, *What a night last night!* sang Elena, and then Kindelán, From behind. Gisela bit her lip so she wouldn't interrupt the counterpoint of *So many things went on*, from the front, *that confused me*, from behind, *I'm so upset*, from the front, *I who was so calm*, from behind, *Enjoying that peace of a love that's over*, from the front, and although Ermelinda pinched him, Kindelán couldn't resist the temptation, and to *What are you doing to me?* he murmured, From behind. *I'm feeling what I never felt!* from the front, *My desire for you is so deep!* from behind, *I swear it to you: it's all brand new for me*, but then, unexpectedly, he said, Liar, and Carlos had to let out a big laugh and Elena said, What? and came over to their table, very much a lady and very much the mistress of the floor, she came over smoothly, as if moved along by the music or by the blue light that followed her, and when she arrived she said, Let's see now, the little one-armed fellow here, *mi negro*, did you want to say something to the audience? and Kindelán, ash-colored under the blue light, doubled over with laughter, I'm in shame, Elena, he said, and Elena, Oh, so he's a poet! What are we celebrating here? and Kindelán pointed at Carlos and Gisela with his only arm, sinister though it was the right one, accusing now, and said, The hitching, and Elena, You mean a horse? and Kinde, That's insane, Elena, and Elena, See? A poet, and Kinde, No, a wedding, a hanging, I mean, and Elena and the light were directed at them, suddenly in the blue circle trying to control their laughter, and Elena, Poor thing, she's still laughing, what's your name, honey? and Gisela said, Gisela Ja, and repeated Ja Ja Ja as if she were joking in slow motion, which provoked huge laughter in the cabaret, and Elena, Hahaha? and Gisela, finally, Ja Ja Jáuregui, and Elena, What's the hangman's name? and he said Carlos, Carlos Pérez, and Elena, Ready for the charge, handsome? and Carlos, You bet, and Elena, Yes? Well just make sure that tomorrow this girl gets up singing *la noche de anoche*, she sang it turning the conversation into music without a transition, her back to Froilán who entered right on the beat, incredibly, magically on the beat, as if it all had been planned to show them that you don't fool around with the great pros. And Elena was great now, huge, pure bolero saying *a marvelous revelation*, making Gisela whisper to Carlos that she had lived, nothing more, she had lived, How? he asked, knowing that Elena would answer for her like a goddess, *Esperando por tí*, waiting for you, and like a goddess would accept the applause, and would continue singing like a goddess, *If I could only tell you how immense* with a high, limpid, crystalline voice that suddenly went down to a low tone, almost guttural, warm, almost hot, close and human like that of a flesh-and-blood woman who at the same time was an immense singer and was biting her man with *From the bottom of my heart, is my love for you*, and that love was truly delirious and embraced her soul and tormented her heart and *Always you*, Elena said suddenly, inventing her own rhythm, improvising, surprising, amazing with her "feeling" ears that were accustomed to fancy stuff, not to the real, whole bolero, and pausing for a rest that the author hadn't put into his song, a rest that Froilán took advantage of to make his guitar sing real sweet, and Gisela to tell Carlos, Always you, making him feel fulfilled and perfect and ready to drink in that voice that suddenly stopped singing and now was talking, saying *You are*, saying *With me*, with a calm, colloquial, tenuous tone, from which it began to go up naturally, effortlessly, softly to the very tips of the palm trees where it set down its sadness, joy, and suffering and took them to the place way up high, secret and blue where it kept the keys to the bolero, of its life and passion and happiness and delirium and he loved it, and when it had them dreaming right there in heaven, it brought them down with a thud to the cabaret murmuring, not singing but murmuring *too*, and smiling and taking away the bolero and the applause just like nothing. Ermelinda said, The bolero's over, and the Archimandrite, That's right sparrow, and he started imitating the song of a bird that was sadder than hell, but Carlos took a big swallow of his drink, I'll go on with my boleros, he said, the Judge's Bolero. No one knew that one, and Carlos sang, very musical and very drunk and very solemn, *You are the guilty one*, and stopped there, accusing Gisela with his index finger. The Archimandrite was the first to laugh, he turned red asking for More, more, and Carlos made a bow before announcing the Cannibal's Bolero and singing *I'll put down the child*. Kindelán couldn't keep from spitting all over his wife, he chomps on chickadees, he said, and Carlos, Coño, Elena was right, this guy's a poet, and now, just for you, the Fairy's Bolero, he said and sang with a high-pitched voice, *Don't be so ungrateful, girl, and come right now*, and over the chorus of laughter, he cried through an interpretation of the Suicide's Bolero, *I'm not afraid to go over the edge*, and the Impotent Man's Bolero, *Today when we can't go on*, and he asked for Someone else, someone else to sing, and the Archimandrite, I'll do the Deaf-Mute's Bolero, and without further ado, in an incredibly out-of-tune bass voice, he sang *Silence* to end the bolero-fest with a flourish, he said, and Kindelán, I'm going to play it'snotthesamething; It'snotthesamewhat? Gisela asked, Thing, Kinde clarified, and Carlos, Sing? You're going to sing? and Kinde, No, it'snotthesamething, it's not the same and it's not written the same, like a bear being in the woods isn't the same as being bare in the woods, or you give me some peace isn't the same as some piece you give me, or as whole isn't asshole, or dickharryjohnsoncametoseefanny'slittlesue isn't the same as littlejohn'shairydickcameonsusy'sfannytoo. A thousand points! cried the Archimandrite. Give them to that nymph, said Kindelán pointing at a chorus girl who was doing the rumba on the runway, almost right over their table, and the Archimandrite looked up, My beard's standing on end, he said, then put on a pious face and began asking God to allow him to redeem that sacred ass, those sacramental buttocks, then suddenly he stopped looking, Women don't interest me, he said. What? asked Carlos, imitating Elena's what, and then the Archimandrite concluded, I'm the one who interests them, and continued to philosophize, All women are *not* alike, he said, Unfortunately, he added, looking at Rosa and then at the chorus girls, They're so lovely that it wouldn't surprise me if they liked each other, he said and Rosa, What did you say? Sex, said the Archimandrite, I mean sense, that is, he said, sex is sense, the groin's in the brain, and he smiled, Balling is so great, he said, and left the phrase hanging in the air, with an ellipsis, and he laughed heartily, as if the laughter were coming from his belly, because it was deep, baritone chortling, Even with your own wife it's good, even with this fat gal it's good, he said, and Rosa, Oh, I was wondering, and the Archimandrite, This woman was so, so fat that when we got married, instead of a floor-length dress hers was wall-to-wall, and he was going to pull another joke out of his joke bag but Carlos interrupted him with the one about the river that was so, so narrow that it only had one bank, and he tried to imagine a river so, so narrow that it would only have one bank and was still doing that, something like ten drinks and one very fun jag later, when the curtain opened again and the Archimandrite said that in the second chou Raúl Chou Moreno was going to sing Chou-gwi, Chou-gwi, Chou-gwi, but a trumpet started tracing a sky-blue circle, started playing, asking, answering, almost conversing, crying and smiling, teasing, until a long golden bolt of lightning suddenly cut the circle of music as if an inexplicable axe had severed the virgin's very source, and now everyone knew that the maestro, Félix Chappottín, had just taken over the floor of the Copa Room, and that the Chinese mulatto who was smiling by his side, testing the microphone with a finger and smiling, was none other that Miguelito Cuní from Pinar, and it was public knowledge that between the two of them they had a lady foursida with four foursideritos and whoever dared touch a foursider would foursiderize himself head to toe, because Chappottín and Cuní could really burn it up. Now it was almost obscene to sit without dancing, without the skin, the smile, the breasts for which Chappottín's trumpet was crying out, bellowing like a bull in the silence of the night, without the magnetic space, sweaty and vibrant, where a hand could be unhooked from the waist to the hips, where it could fall, mold, slide like okra does onto dry yucca; now they went out to the center of the floor because the *son* was calling, it had started slowly, smoothly, naturally free like Miguelito's voice of *ácana*, ebony, and royal palm, that was heating up, cooking the okra with flour and tossing in little dried shrimps and chicken and enjoying the stew that Kindelán was tasting, Soooo sweeet fellows, Miguelito singing the sound, singing the *son*, Kindelán and Ermelinda turning, showing off, and Carlos and Gisela stepping tightly, holding close, and the Archimandrite and Rosa joking around, having fun, and Miguelito hurrying down a swallow of *son* and saying Take it, Arturo, and Arturo coming in, sliding his graceful mulatto fingers over the piano, over the black and white keys of the piano, avoiding some pitfalls in the road, crossing the Habananilla dam or the Cumanayagua bridge until getting to the *son montuno*, where fatally, inevitably, he would have to tell Catalina to buy him a grater; but Catalina wasn't there, she hadn't arrived, maybe she didn't exist, and Arturo set himself to calling her, coaxing her, inventing her on the keyboard in such a way that his fingers melted, merged with black and white of ivory and ebony and everything was mulatto, mixed, interspersed, and suddenly the tumba's ringing started, and the horn's flame and the claves' rhythm and the güiro's cha-cha and the quinto's five-note beat and Miguelito's voice and the chorus of the dancers, who were now a tribe led by Kindelán, Miguelito flaming, exclaiming, Kindelán turning his tribe into a train rolling over the dance floor, Now raise your hand, Now lower your hand, Now stick out your tongue, like an insatiable locomotive, euphoric, crazed, ready to take off and wave around their jackets and shoes following their leader, who held up his stump crying out, *Rumba ñonguito!* giving way to the chorus, *ñonguito!* and Kindelán suddenly changed the cry into Miguelito! and Miguelito called out Catalina! and asked her coño, for the love of her mother, to buy him a grater, that the yucca was dry, ay, Catalina! . . . The tribe euphorically accepted the gift, because the the *son* was inventing Catalina, with hard, flexible buttocks like the drum skin on the tumbadora, dark like the skin of the tumbadora, with legs that were long, shapely, and sweet like the *son*, and now Miguelito was undressing her with his voice, he undressed her until he got all the way to her star-apple sex, then he let her dance, naked amid the quinto and the claves and the tumba, and the tribe wiggling their hips, having a ball, *rayando el guayo, mi negra*, all of them Catalinas and Miguelitos, all the *son*, and then Chappo came in with his golden horn, right on target like the *son* player of

Hamelin, calling to her, and Catalina obeyed docilely, following the beat, lustfully she obeyed, and she began retreating, fading, but suddenly flared up returning to the center of the night, followed by Chappo, Miguelito, Arturo, the quinto, the claves, the tumba, the tribe, the black man, the white woman, the Chinese, and the mulatta, all mixed together, Santa María, San Berenito, San Berenito, Santa María, and the *son* in the lead: Catalina sprawled on the dance floor with her legs spread wide, asking to party, to play, to pull out the stops, and Chappo and Miguelito going at it hot and heavy, charging in unison at that inviolable sex, charging like a pair of oxen in the hills, charging and retreating boastfully, breathlessly, defeated and victorious because Catalina was gone now, the fiesta had ended and now the party was over and the lights would be turned off, like every night. Kindelán wanted to keep the rumba going but Carlos and Gisela were in a hurry, they were steamed up inside like a boiler, and the Archimandrite said Cut it out, *negro*, who in the world on their wedding night, and Gisela, That's right, Archimandrite, and Kinde, Don't jive with me, girl, don't jive with me, and Carlos promised them the Adios Bolero, putting his hands together to pray and singing to God, *A Dios*, and the Archimandrite, Take me away from the strong stuff, and Kinde, I've been kicked out of better places, and he put his stump over Ermelinda's shoulders and his arm over the Archimandrite's, who did the same with him and with Rosa and they went off singing, *Mister watchman, why are you sending me to bed?* and Carlos, *Adios, adios, witnesses of my night*, and he and Gisela started running through the lobby to the elevator, crowded with drunken cabaret-goers who let them through in solidarity, *Please, Pachalsta*, and they answered, *Zenkew, Merci* and the elevator operator said, What floor? and Carlos, Sexth, sexth floor, and the operator pressed six and they were dying of laughter, of the urge to make love and to urinate, and they got to the sixth and there were more *Pleases* and *Pachalstas* and *Gracias* and *Zenkews* and they started running down the hall to the door of six-two-nine, which adds up to seventeen, said Carlos, Moon, my astral mother, he said opening it, Good luck, he said carrying Gisela inside and dropping her on the bed, onto which he then threw himself roaring, A tiger in the bush! A tiger in the bush! But Gisela wasn't there anymore, she was running towards the bathroom and Carlos, Curses! I've been foiled! and he ran after her and stopped at the door, Open up in the name of the law! and Gisela, No papi, I'm getting undressed, and Carlos, Open up or I can't be responsible for what happens!, and Gisela, Don't you *dare*, and Carlos entered and stood there petrified, stunned before the copper-colored thighs, and the thread of honey descending from the dark down which promptly stopped, Because I can't with you here, see? she said, and he answered, Yes you can, yes you can, you'll see, and he started going shshshshshsh and shshshshshsh and shshshshshsh, and she, No! don't be so bad, and he, shshshshshsh and shshshshshsh until she said, Ay! and the golden thread again descended from the down and then it was he who couldn't hold it in any longer and she, What are you doing? No! You crazy! and he let himself go, liberated himself watching the merging of their waters in one beautiful, brilliant yellow liquid that she too was now watching, smiling, laughing, saying My God, I married a crazy! My God, how sweet! while he looked again at the cinnamon-colored thighs and the dark mound that began on the plain of skin next to her navel, and he gave in to the desire to water it, and she gently spread the golden liquid over her hair, and he ended up over the moon, and when he was about to leave he felt her pulling him close, kissing him right there, and making him feel like never before, Mami, like never before, he said, and he let her intone her own private bolero on his member, that mute song that made him hear trumpets of glory while she smeared her face and breasts, and then she suddenly stopped and dragged him to the bathtub, turned on the faucet and he, But I'm still dressed! and she, Into the water, ducks! and he, drenched, Sniff sniff, my only suit, and she, What a shame, and he, Boohoo, my best shoes, and she, That's what you get, and he, That's what you think, you villain, hah! This is a job for Supercarlos! and he took off his clothes and shouted: I've lost all, except for my honor and your love! and fell to his knees and started licking her like a kitten, and she, The telephone, and he, Huh? still kissing her, not caring that she was saying It's ringing, much less that the telephone was ringing, because the motherfucker *was* ringing like a far-off insect, intolerable, inexistent once she gave him her lips and spread her legs in the lukewarm water, and he sat her on top of him and they enjoyed themselves with the lights on, looking at each other and discovering each other and remembering the times they'd been such shitheads that they did it in the dark, a oscuras, With soldiers, with peasants, with workers, said Carlos, and Gisela's breasts shook with laughter and he looked at her belly where their child now was two months along and had married them, and he said, A boy, and Gisela, A girl, and he repeated Boy and Gisela Girl and they kept going like that on a crazy see-saw. Afterwards she bathed him and he bathed her, and they counted each other's moles and delighted in their little tummies, lips and pisses, and he carried her in his arms to the bedroom singing the Wedding March, Da-da-

dadah, Da-da-dadah, and lay her on the bed and got in next to her saying My bonbon and My little turtle dove, and the bastard telephone rang again, Haylooo? he answered, in a playful mood, Entirely devoted to tasks appropriate to my sex, he said, Yes, of course, he said, I'll be right down, and hung up. It was the Ghost, he explained to Gisela, trying to be funny, he told me to report in complete uniform, that the Yanquis decreed a blockade and are threatening us with the atomic bomb, and she, How lovely, at this time of night with a message like that, and Cover your eyes, Papi. He closed them, heard some fabric rustling, soft music on the radio, and the Ready! from Gisela, who had put on a white negligee and was dancing an indefinable dance, between classic and modern and ridiculous, and then the bastard telephone rang again. Yes? he said imitating Gisela's voice, What? No, Carlitos already left a while ago and I'm here lonely in my loneliness, he said, and hung up and called the switchboard operator, Miss, this is Dick Fitzwell, don't put any more calls through to me, I'm dealing with a matter of life and death, he said, and hung up again. Now and for all time, my love! he declared, going towards Gisela, embracing her and heading for the balcony, and she, No! you're in the raw! and he, But ready to cook, and the air was cold and they kissed and began listening to and looking at the sea, which suddenly was illuminated by the very clear, blue light of two huge searchlights: the waves breaking white against the wall, now inaudible, the powerful racket of a military column advancing along the seawall and covering the night. Papi, something's going on, she said, and he, frozen, Yeah, and they went back in and the radio was broadcasting a communiqué they heard holding their breath. Goddammotherfucker! he said, Give me my clothes, quick, but Gisela didn't move, she was collapsed on the bed, crying. Come on! he said, putting on his underwear, and her crying, uncontrolled, turned into long sobs, and he caressed her hair, What's wrong, Mami? and she, not turning over or stopping her sobbing, Those somsabitches, coño, they don't even let you get married. You don't even get to ball in peace, Yanqui shit, coño! and he turned her over and kissed her on the forehead and said, Yeah, but you have to hurry, and she, Yeah, and handed him his clothes and got dressed and started getting everything together, diligently and furiously, and when the suitcases were packed he went over to the radio that again was broadcasting the communiqué, "The nation on a war footing," and turned it off, while Gisela, now at the door, ran her eyes over the room and asked, Nothing left behind?

SEVENTEEN

Right from the start he knew the jeep was going over the cliff, and he managed to shout, "Brake, Lieutenant, brake!" feeling it was useless, that they would keep going downhill and he better hang on to the iron bars, trying to reduce the blows and to figure out if that old jalopy would turn over, breaking their heads against a rock, if it would explode against the eucalyptus trees that were passing by him at a dizzying pace and burn up, making the Bomb Bolero come true, or if the impossible would happen and they would fall into the mud of the river heard far off in the night, that would cushion the crash and the fear and soften the contorted face of the lieutenant, who now had opened the door and was yelling at him, "Jump, militiaman, juuump!" while he kept hanging onto the iron bars amid the violent movement through trees, stones, earth, and night and heard the desperate yell of the lieutenant and saw him leap out, disappearing into the darkness, and he felt alone, helpless, wanting this torture to end in any of a thousand possible and terrible ways, to end once and for goddamn all with the crash against the night that came straight at him when the jeep jumped in a hollow and rolled in the air and smacked against a stone, leaning on its side and throwing him faceup onto the ground, under the very black, starry sky where, for a moment, he felt stupidly happy. He attempted to move and fierce pain stopped him, forcing him to palpate his body, and then he touched his blood, hot and viscous, had an intense, cold perspiration, tried to stand up, and the pain kept him yoked to the ground, yelling, "Over here, Lieutenant, over here!" hearing how the terrible echoed voices sent his fear back to him in the middle of the night, which he suddenly remembered to be inhabited by damned souls, headless horsemen, güijes, shadows of hanged men swaying in the ceiba branches, perpetual fire, daño all along that unknown path that led him to the dark cave where the dead reproduced their voices through ravines and torrents, forcing him to yell, to cry, and to shout out in a useless struggle to overpower the nocturnal screams of death, searching for him with its fire, surrounding him, calling to him, leaving him deaf at the edge of the irreparable emptiness into which he would disappear if he couldn't manage to yell like he was doing now, when the sharp pain stopped him, made him think that death, that whore, had trapped him in that remote grassy place where any effort would be useless, where it was even pleasurable to lie, if one just remained calm, quiet, waiting for her.

Slowly the pain and the confusion let up. The wheels stopped spinning, the jeep was left on its side with the headlights on, lighting up a palm tree and a ceiba in whose huge trunk Chava's soul might be breathing. Carlos touched his head, he felt pain only when he pressed with his fingers. He wasn't going to die, he didn't even need to yell, the lieutenant would be looking for him and would find him, guided by the headlights. Then they'd laugh together and Carlos would invent the Accident Bolero, like he'd invented the one about the Bomb, to kill time, that's what a bitch life is. That morning, bored with watching the sky for the plane with the atomic bomb that would send them all to fucking hell, he had started to sing boleros. He was a spectacular success, all the teams gathered around his cannon laughing like crazy and becoming complete chaos when he announced the Deaf-Mute's Bolero, and sang *Silence*! but just then the lieutenant came running over to the unit and ordered, Silence! and that was really the limit. The militiamen couldn't stop their guffaws. The lieutenant got annoyed in a bad way and was going to sanction half the human race when Carlos took responsibility, "I was singing funny boleros," he said. The lieutenant's face was still screwed up in a fit, and Carlos had an inspiration. "For example," he said, "the Atomic Bomb Bolero," and sang, *Only ashes will you find*. The lieutenant took a second to get it, suddenly broke out in laughter and then said, "The bomb, ashes, that's good, really good," and ran off to sing it to the captain. That night he informed them that the rocket gunners had downed a Yanqui plane, a very modern U-2, and that nuclear war could be unleashed at any moment; he needed a volunteer to accompany him on an urgent mission. The whole unit offered to go, but the lieutenant selected Carlos so he could sing boleros to him and keep him from falling asleep on the road. They had great fun along the embankment, full of slopes and devilish curves, over which the jeep zoomed like a rocket. The lieutenant said he was wiped out, dead tired and sleepy, but he couldn't stop or weaken, militiaman, because the message was absolutely urgent. Carlos felt good, heroic on that special mission, although he was certain that the lieutenant liked danger, liked to provoke, to play with danger while he guided the jeep like a horse asking for more on the hills, yelling at it on the curves, congratulating it on the vertiginous descents, "You're the best, coño, you're the best little jeep, go for it, godammit, the Yanquis want to fuck us over," and exploding with joy on the straights as he threw the jeep against the impenetrable wall of night, infecting Carlos, too, who was feeling taken over by vertigo, "That's it, Lieutenant, that's it!" while he was thinking about his compañeros dying with envy by their cannons, and he dreamed that the jeep was competing with the plane that had the bomb and suddenly he saw the very, very sharp curve and yelled, "Brake, Lieutenant, brake!" feeling it was useless, as useless as attempting to move now.

He had to be patient, wait for the lieutenant to arrive to sing him the Accident Bolero, *It was the night I died, the death of all my hopes*, and although he might have wanted to walk, he *knew* he wouldn't be able to. But the lieutenant was taking too long, he'd had enough time to make ten trips from the place where he had jumped to the one where Carlos was lying, pushing away the fleeting thought that the officer might have gotten smashed on a rock and that he, too, could be condemned to die. The truth had to be different: the lieutenant had climbed up to the road to look for help, and soon he'd come down with more compañeros to save him. He had to keep control of himself, withstand the pain that had returned with rhythmic whiplashes across his face. He started touching it and found it swollen, perhaps deformed, blackened by contusions and blood. Moving his teeth around, he felt them loosen, spit out, counted three in the palm of his hand and began again to yell. He wasn't calling out to anyone, he was yelling with horror, looking at his teeth and spitting blood, trying to get up, suffering from the atrocious pain that left him flat on the grass. He was going to die; he was going to die, lost, bleeding to death, alone; he was going to die, sweet mother, my God; he was going to die, Gisela, without even having seen his newborn child, thinking because he hadn't fallen at Girón facing the enemy, thinking how that death, obscure and without glory, was a just one for a guy like him, who had spent months away from everything with the pretext of his convalescence from the Leftism Syndrome, and that only now, in the hands of the rat and the whore, was he able to recognize to what point he'd been filled with resentment and bitterness at losing the presidency of the school, to remember how hard it had been for him to live as Sir Nobody, how he'd run towards the seawall the night that Munse tore up the book for controlling curse words, and shouted at the sea all the obscenities he had stored up in his soul. He had been a scourge, an ignorant fool, and even a wretch, yes, a miserable wretch, there was no other word to describe his support for the business about the testament or the guilty silence he kept regarding the lie about his legend. Now he reproached himself for not having found the courage to publicly acknowledge those errors, and he asked life for another opportunity, a new chance, just a little chance to perhaps do some of the millions of things that he was still owing: to show, for example, that now he had the courage to be disciplined and to participate as a soldier where he'd been a captain. Munse had accused him of not having that courage, had called him a liberal, proud, and self-satisfied because he ranted against opportunism in the hallways but refused to collaborate with the new leadership of the association, and Carlos had replied with the story of the scorpion that stuck his sting into the back of the frog who was helping him cross the river. But now, his face wet with tears and blood under his last night sky, he recognized that his perverse answer made Munse totally right: not only had he been sectarian, a scourge, a wretch, resentful, and ignorant, but also proud, self-satisfied, vain, and liberal, and he promised from the bottom of his heart not to continue that way, to labor obscurely, humbly, with the courage and the dedication of the most hardworking Communist, if life would give him the opportunity.

Suddenly he heard a noise, a little noise, something that could be coming from the far-off presence of the lieutenant or from a peasant who was looking for him. He felt a primal joy, the certainty that someone would come to take him back to life, and he yelled and yelled until he became hoarse, with the fear that in reality, he had heard the slippery steps of death. Then he was hit by the idea that Grandfather Álvaro could be watching him crying like a coward, and he swallowed his yells, his tears, his blood, as without a doubt the mambís dying in the depths of the swamp had done. That was how he wanted to die. At least his political errors had had a worthy cause: hatred of opportunism, and he felt better repeating in the face of death that he would continue to hate it and would die hating it and would not compromise with the despicable attitude of types like Osmundo the Coachman, corks accustomed to floating in any current, chameleons capable of changing their criteria like a coat, fishing in the roiling rivers of politics, cowards. He became desperate as he understood now, with burning clarity, that his habit of attacking them in the hallways and not attending assemblies or meetings had given them an opening. He should have collaborated with the association to denounce them from within, in an organized, systematic way, as Munse was doing, until they were unmasked and ruined; but he had sworn not to participate in anything as long as Osmundo was still the secretary of that shit, that's just how he said it to Gisela, of that shit, one afternoon when he was on the point of blowing up and she calmed him down with a shoulder massage and she sat on the bed in the cheap hotel, trembling like a little girl, and confessed that she'd counted wrong, that she was pregnant, and that she wanted to have it, and she stayed there looking at him with painful anxiety, reading in his eyes his surprise, fear, and doubt, hearing him say, "But love, we have to think about this," and breaking into tears, curled up into a ball, while he was thinking that this was craziness and she'd get over it, that he didn't want to get married so young, that they didn't have anywhere to live or any way to support it, and he stroked her hair, saying, "It all right, baby, it's all right." Then Gisela pulled her head out from between her legs, as if she were being born from herself, and told him: "I'm going to have it, whether you want to or not," and she kept on crying while she caressed her belly, which he now identified as the place of love and of life, the one where he had finally planted his seed, his credential of manhood. But back then he had tried to reason that it wasn't the right time and found Gisela to be a stubborn wall; she had stopped crying and told him that she wouldn't ask him for anything, that she would grow it and give birth to it alone, she'd nurse it and bring it up alone, and that he could go on his own way. Carlos tried being hard, he told her, "All right," and watched her collapse onto him, moaning like a cat against his chest, then suddenly kissing him with fury, exciting him, sitting astride his sex, looking at him with a gleam of madness, and saying, "You'll never see me again." Offended by the demented nerve of her threat, he shouted, "Shut up!" She slowly caressed her body with the open palms of her hands, from her knees up to her breasts, and softly pinched her nipples while she said, "Take a good look, you'll never see me again." He slapped her, blinded by hate and love, by desire, but he hardly had the time to feel sorry about it. Gisela sunk herself into his neck, making him feel the painful pleasure of a bite that he returned on her shoulder, and they kept on biting and kissing each other, surrendering their blood to each other, making them one like the bodies that finished exhausted. Then Carlos rolled over and fell asleep, and now he was thinking how his desperation, his craziness on awakening alone in the darkness of the hotel had been almost as great as what he was feeling facing death in the darkness of the night; but back then he was able to run to Gisela's house and use his in-laws to try to get her out of her room, from which she refused to come out unless he sent her an answer that he could not give, without insulting his manhood. And then came the disaster: his father-in-law realized that Gisela was pregnant and kicked Carlos out of the house, calling him an abuser and a heel, his mother-in-law attempted to explain that these things happen among young people, and his father-in-law raised a huge scandal; and at that precise moment, Gisela decided to come out of her room, said she was leaving, that they didn't give her a moment's peace, and her father went at her. Carlos got between him and Gisela, his mother-in-law between Carlos and her husband, and they were all yelling at once while the children cried, the neighbors came around, the entire neighborhood learned that Gisela would be getting married in a month, someone brought a bottle, and Carlos endured the toast as the worst moment of his life.

And now, unmoving, abandoned, he blessed the craziness for which his child was breathing inside Gisela, from then on the happiest woman on the planet, who finally destroyed his apprehension through her joy, agreed that he would keep living at the Beca, and only contradicted him on one point: they would have a little girl. Carlos couldn't avoid making a face when she added that, moreover, she'd be a really hot little whore, but Gisela calmed him down, inviting him to practice the national pastimes: highball, swinging pool, basketballing, feel hockey, and now he, feeling fucked on the grass, gave himself over to the memory of the times they had made love in the Havana Forest, and he asked fate that his child would be male, macho, masculine, and he heard his mother's soft voice saying: "Girls love their fathers more," and he saw her, happy for the first time since Jorge went back into exile, sewing the layette of the granddaughter she was going to bring up, she said, "Because we need a child in this house." There was only one tense moment, when Gisela specified: "A little mulatta." His mother kept on sewing, sighed, and said, "A little mulatta." He realized for the first time that his child would not be white, and wished that at least it would be an advancement, that it would *look* white, and suffered from fear that it would come out like Gisela's great-grandfather, a dark-skinned black according to family recollection, to feel ashamed now before the vigilant memory of Chava, perhaps incarnated in the ceiba illuminated by the jeep's headlights, and to have one more miserable thing to regret in the face of death. In his favor, he could only say that in spite of everything he had accepted having it, mixing the blood that was now slowly escaping from his veins into the river of all bloods that were giving the inhabitants of the island their unique and different, beautiful and resistant color of fine wood. And he had done so with the joy, the love, and the hope that filled those happy days in which Gisela's family and his friends, led by Kindelán and the Archimandrite, obtained prodigious quantities of food and beer and organized the first party that had been given in his house since the remote times when the blacks came up the hill from the ravine to drink and pawn their items. Of that he could be proud, in his wedding blacks and whites and Chinese and mulattoes had mixed in a gigantic hubbub while they escaped for the hotel with their witnesses, Kindelán and the Archimandrite, who was drunk and said that his present, a week at the Hotel Riviera, included a night at the cabaret for the wedding couple and their wetnesses, that memorable night in which he and Gisela did wild, outlandish things that now he remembered, feeling perplexed, wondering if their outrageous acts hadn't been excessive, if he should regret having urinated on her and watching her urinate, while the image of Gisela naked, placidly sitting on the toilet, madly happy at receiving the warm shower of his urine, took over as the image of the very beauty of life, reducing the question to its simple stupidity and forcing him to recognize that if he had anything to regret, it was having been such a shithead, so moralistic, as to have divided love into the pure and the impure, leaving so much pleasure, so much craziness, so much life locked up in the dark compartment of what was forbidden, only to yearn for it now, when it was no longer possible to live it, and he raged against the threat of nuclear attack that interrupted his delirium when it had just begun.

He could also be proud of his response, of his desperate race to the Beca, of his joy on seeing the line of trucks and the militiamen conversing on the sidewalks, and to know that he'd caught up with them in time, coño, he'd caught up with them and would have time to change his clothes and joke around a bit before leaving, destination unknown, as the immense billboard of Fidel's image in profile against the mountainside, with backpack and rifle on his shoulder, faded from view: "Commander-in-chief: at your orders!" They were singing, *Soy comunista, toda la vida / bella ciao, bella ciao, bella ciao, ciao, ciao* . . . when he realized that he couldn't take the oath because the Young Communists Union, recently established at the school, had not considered it the right time to study the possibility of admitting him as a militant. "You're a cardless Communist," the Archimandrite had told him during those days, and now he clung to the phrase, convincing himself it was true and wondering how a Communist would die. "Fighting," he told himself, "but against what?" Suddenly the idea of dying horrified him again, and he started touching his chest in a frenzy; he didn't have any wounds there, the pain was coming from his face and legs. And what if he made a tourniquet to stop the blood? If he could gain some time? Maybe someone would pass by there at dawn and then, if he could hold out, he'd be saved. He started dragging himself along on his back by his elbows, withstanding the most intense pain, until reaching the ceiba; there he gathered enough strength to sit up and, moaning, he leaned up against the sacred tree that you couldn't run around twelve times at twelve midnight, where you couldn't urinate. He felt the warm breath of the wood on his back as if it were the pulse of Chava's blood; he took off his shirt, tried to tear it into strips but couldn't, and twisted it to make a tourniquet for his thigh. The effort forced him to close his eyes, dizzy, frozen, and sweating; afterwards he looked up at the sky to ask Grandfather Álvaro for help and felt small and lost in the darkness. Could God exist? Did the dead really keep watch? Would life have any meaning if you died and that was all? He dismissed the answers given by his books, they were of no use to him now; but he felt doubly lost, flanked by fear of abandoning the terrible certainty of atheism, and by repugnance at entrusting himself to an improbable god, in a kind of last-minute opportunism. Then he saw the red lights of a plane shining in the very black sky and had the feeling that he was seeing the one destined to drop the bomb, the final weapon that would incinerate the island, the world, and memory, turning everything into nothingness, dark and without meaning. He felt illuminated by the imminence of the end: the dead existed, and God too, but only in memory, in desire, in imagination, or in the horror of the living; Grandfather Álvaro *was* in his soul like his duty or the daño, like heroes, martyrs, great traitors, and gods in the souls of everyone. He kept watching the plane, asking himself what the last instant would be like and imagining an immense light in which they would grope around like blind people before the earth disappeared, and with it, heaven and hell; *Only ashes will you find*, he thought, realizing that no one would be left to find anything, and that the second line, *of all that was*, was the definitive, implacable end of his last bolero. But then the plane became lost behind the plumes of the palm trees, silence returned, and he concentrated on the horror of his little death.

Reflecting on the holocaust had revealed to him, in a brutal way, that his desire to be a hero wasn't only about disinterest and dedication, but also a longing for power and glory, and even the dark, instinctive need to leave a mark on the memory of others. He had never confessed that to himself, perhaps he had never understood it with such clarity as now, desperate and naked, facing nothingness, when awareness of his failure made his pretensions ridiculous. A nobody was dying there: Gisela would remember him for a year, his child wouldn't even know him, his mother would leave soon and Grand-father Álvaro and Chava would disappear with him when they no longer had anyone to invoke them. He felt a bitter rage against destiny, which had kept him from dying at Girón, giving to a hospital or a school that obscure name that he began to carve with his pistol sight into the ceiba's roots. He had written *Ca* when an atavistic respect stopped him: he shouldn't continue wounding Chava. He caressed the syllable that could continue, Carlos carried on like a comrade *carajo*, gave a hint of a gentle smile, saw how the jeep's headlights went out, and thought how it was true, that all the world's glory fits in a kernel of corn.

EIGHTEEN

When he had spent three hours looking at shop windows and thinking in dollars, his dolorous feet and head became intolerable. He was tired, frozen, and hungry, but he couldn't invest time and money in his own needs. He'd be leaving at dawn, he couldn't return to the island without gifts. How did you say boticas? *Drugstore* was botica, but singular, meaning pharmacy. That dress would be pretty for Gisela. The price? Twenty-four, dove. Impossible, he only had twenty, and he wanted to bring something for his mother, his daughter, his wife, and his in-laws.

"*May I help you, sir?*"

He gave a jump. The mumbo jumbo had been quick and unexpected, and he hadn't understood a thing. The salesman looked at him like a strange bird.

"Nouu," he managed to get out, and he went away rapidly, without looking back.

He couldn't go on like this. He had to get a hold of himself, dare to buy something. An icy gust burned his face and neck. He sunk his chin down and stopped in front of another store. "*Tom is a boy*," he murmured, "*and Mary is a girl.*" His image was reflected in the glass, next to the elegant mannequins, as if in a strange fishbowl. "*Tom is in the classroom and Mary is in the classroom, too*," he said to his reflection, and started to laugh. It was as if Tom and Mary, the old illustrated characters in his English textbook, had grown with him and weren't *in the classroom* any more, but *in the*, how did you say vidriera, escaparate? "*Tom and Mary are in the*," he said and drew a blank. The coat he'd borrowed for the trip was absolutely horrible. He looked like a priest talking to himself. People might think he was crazy.

He speeded up his pace again. His hands ached from the cold. Putting them into his pockets he felt the paper tracing of Mercedita's foot. How would you say it? Zapatoes, like *patatoes*? Zapeti-*ous*? He stopped in front of another window full of smiling Toms and Marys that were looking at each other, as if they were mutually checking out each other's clothing. In forty minutes the stores would close. He had to go in, my God, he had to go in. He filled his lungs with cold air, took sight of the lighted interior, murmured, "Now, coño," and kept on walking like a shot to the next block, cursing his cowardice. Suddenly he burst out laughing. There it was, written right in front of him, on a pair of pointy-toed zapatos that looked a lot like the ones his father had used on Sundays: *shoes*. Cho-es? No, in English the *oe* sounded like *ou*. Ou or u? U or w? It didn't matter. As a last resort he could come outside, point with his finger and grunt like a Cro-Magnon man: "U, u."

On entering, he felt confused. From outside the store looked small, but it was enormous, with many departments, and it was brilliantly illuminated in comparison with the gray, overcast sky.

"*What can I do for you, sir?*"

She was a tall salesgirl, slender, blonde, and freckled. When she talked she showed her teeth, white and even like in an advertisement. Her eyes were a very clear blue. Truly a *beautiful* señorita. Carlos didn't understand her question, but he returned her smile and

"*I one show,*" he said.

"*I beg your pardon?*"

The blonde was confused. He knew something hadn't gone right. Maybe it was his false teeth that didn't do so well with English, and so he decided to take great pains with his pronunciation.

"*I want show,*" he said.

The blonde blinked her eyelashes like Betty Boop.

"*Sorry, sir. I can't understand you.*"

"Qué, qué?" he asked automatically, and added, "*What?*"

The blonde repeated her phrase very slowly. Carlos translated: I'm sorry, I can't understand you, and felt stupid thinking that it sounded like a line from a bolero. Then he decided to eliminate all unnecessary words.

"*Show!*" he shouted.

The blonde looked at him, terrified.

"*Excuse me, sir,*" she said without smiling, and took two steps backward, covering her necklace with her right hand.

Carlos decided to resort to the Cro-Magnon method and approached the blonde, in order to guide her to the window.

"*Don't touch me!*" she yelled, pulling away. She was on the verge of hysteria.

"*What's going on?*" asked a salesman who came over to rescue her.

"*This man is insane,*" said the blonde, starting to cry.

"*Get out!*" shouted the salesman.

"*I want show,*" explained Carlos, touching his own shoe. Then he thought of the plural, and corrected himself: "*Shows.*"

"*Oh, shoes!*" said the salesman, starting to laugh. "*You want shoes, don't you?*"

"*Yes,*" he agreed, with a mixture of joy, amazement, rage, and shame. "Chus."

Some clients had formed a group around them. The salesman looked at them smiling, stroked the blonde's head, and told her:

"*He wants shoes, that's all.*"

"*This man is insane,*" she repeated, looking at the floor.

"*Oh no, dear,*" reasoned the salesman. "*He is just a foreigner.*"

"*An insane, dirty, Latin foreigner,*" the blonde said decisively. "*Tell him to leave me alone, will you?*"

"*Okey, sweetheart,*" said the salesman, giving her a little pat on the cheek. And turning to Carlos: "*Follow me, please.*"

The curious group dissolved in silence. Carlos thought how in Cuba everyone would have said something. But there, not even he had dared to talk, because the dialogue had been too fast and he hadn't understood anything. Only that he had said *chou* instead of *chus* and the shithead blonde got hysterical. His intuition told him to follow the salesman. He needed his chus. His head ached horribly. The man stopped at the men's department with a theatrical, elegant turn.

"*You can choose here,*" he said.

So then, was it chus or chuuus? It didn't matter, he didn't have any business to do in that department.

"Nouu. Soun para *my girl baby,*" he explained, rocking his arms like when he cradled Mercedita.

"*Oh, I see. Follow me, please,*" the man said again, and Carlos followed him again and saw him repeat the theatrical, elegant turn in the layette department, and

"Nouu," he told him.

The employee breathed out as if he were very tired.

"*Let's see,*" he said. "*How old is your daughter?*"

"*Waht?*"

"*How . . . okey? . . . old . . . okey? . . . is your daughter?*" the man repeated, with a scarcely contained anxiety.

Carlos asked him to wait, lifting his left hand, and put the right one to his forehead. *How* was cuánto, *okey* was okey, *old* was viejo. Cuánto viejo? That was okey. And *daughter . . . daughter?* Wasn't *daughter* hija? Of course! He'd been asked cuánto viejo es su hija.

"*He is* grandeicita," he said.

"*He?*" the salesman asked in confusion.

"*Yes,*" replied Carlos. "*Is . . . okey? . . . grandeicita . . . okey?*"

The salesman dropped his head. Carlos touched his own thigh, indicating Mercedita's approximate height, and saw that the man was staring at the sole of his orthopedic shoe. Then he had an inspiration.

"Tri *year,*" he said, showing three fingers. "Tri."

The salesman led him in silence to the children's shoe department and put some boticas on the counter. Carlos pulled out the paper tracing and tried to put it into the shoe.

"*Oh, my God!*" the salesman murmured.

God? Wasn't it gud? The tracing folded over inside the botica. Why had Gisela decided to cut it out in paper, Dios mío, and not in cardboard? He swallowed dryly and put his fingers inside the botica, trying to smooth out the paper and determine if this was the correct size.

"*Okey?*" the salesman asked.

He didn't answer. His fingers were sweaty and it was difficult for him to figure out by touch if the paper reached the tip of the shoe, if it stopped short or if it was still folded over. He was intolerably hot, but he didn't dare interrupt the operation to take off his coat.

"*Is that it?*" the salesman insisted.

Carlos closed his eyes. Could he be feeling at the same point the tips of his fingers, of the paper, and of the shoe? No, it seemed not. He should be safe and buy a bigger size.

"Nouu *god,*" he said.

"*Bullshit!*" muttered the salesman.

"*Big,*" Carlos requested.

The salesman threw a pair of shoes onto the counter and bit off his words.

"*Now, listen. We are about to close. Those ones or none, okey?*"

Carlos didn't understand, but he didn't have the strength to try the size again. He put away the paper, asked God for those damned shoes to fit Mercedita and replied:

"*God.*"

"*Bless you, bastard,*" murmured the salesman with a smile, before leading him to the cash register.

"*Eight dollars, sir,*" the cashier informed him.

He looked at her in confusion. The soles of the shoes didn't have eight, dead man, marked on them, but rather seven thirty-five, spider's ass. Why was that woman asking him for ait? Did she think she could screw him, someone who was a real screwaround?

"Nouu," he said, pointing to the price on the label.

"*Plus tax, sir. Eight dollars,*" the cashier insisted sharply.

He didn't have the strength to argue. He handed her his twenty dollars and received the change, thinking that they'd done a number on him. He went toward the exit, exhausted. There he realized that the salesman had accompanied him.

"Zenquiu," he told him.

"*Good-bye, sir,*" the man replied, smiling once more, "*and never again.*"

He returned the smile. In spite of everything, the guy had waited on him patiently. He had the boticas. But also a colossal fatigue, urge to urinate, thirst, and uneasiness. He looked into the store, saw the blonde, and felt humiliated. He wouldn't do any more shopping. He had been born naked, to hell with things. In the end most of it was plastic.

The street seemed very strange to him, now that he had stopped looking at store windows. It was absurd that at five in the afternoon it should be almost like night. He felt depressed from the lack of light and sea and from the leaden sky and the cutting autumn cold. What was he doing in Canada? If his enemies were right, he'd landed there from pure arrogance. Just that simple. But were they right? Was it just because of arrogance that he abandoned his studies, to wind up by chance, after so many twists and turns, in this stupid situation? Was it his fault that the school refused to let him take his exams in the hospital and made him lose a whole year? His fault that the Young Communists, for a second time, didn't want to process his membership, adducing errors that for him had already been surpassed? His fault that, facing such obstinacy, he began dreaming about going off to join the guerrillas, or that Gisela, after having taken care of him like a child during his convalescence, put his back to the wall because of Mercedita's birth, ordering him to give up his scholarship, to get a job, to assume his responsibilities as a husband and father? No, it hadn't been arrogance, but rather necessity, that had brought him to work at the Center for International Studies, the CEI.

And he had worked well, so well that the CEI director called him a *workaholic* when Carlos dared to criticize his methods. That is, the director translated, he was working obsessively, but from compulsion, not because he understood the task, and while the guy was showing off by laying into him, Carlos felt a little danger light go on inside. He was being advised not to run up against his boss. He wouldn't do it again. He minded his own business. He went out of his way to take care of the valiant Latin American comrades who came from the center of the volcano or were on their way there, risking their hides. It fascinated him to stay in the office until dawn reading, rereading, scrutinizing clippings and translations of whatever news, articles, or essays about guerrilla movements in Latin America were being published around the world. And amid the frequent arguments with Gisela, who continued to reproach him for his lack of involvement—he didn't help her with the housework, he didn't stand on lines, he didn't take care of his daughter, he hadn't even joined the CDR—he started thinking again that his true place was in the Sierra de Falcón, in the Jujuy Forest, or in the Cundinamarca Mountains. But he was in Canada. What the hell was he doing there? When they mentioned a trip to him, he thought about Che, about the guerrillas, about some kind of liaison, contact, risk. Nothing of the sort: he was to attend an event in solidarity with Cuba in Winnipeg, along with Felipe Martínez, and there he was, staring like an imbecile at that automobile that looked like a blind man because its headlights were covered with pieces that resembled eyelashes.

From childhood he had learned to recognize car makes and models, and now after six years of the blockade, he mixed up a Ford with a Buick. The cars turned out to be as foreign as the ads and the language, it was as if at some point in the road, the world in which he'd been born had taken another path, making him lose the code for the one in which he now found himself. How the hell did you say servicio? Luckily the members of the Cuba Solidarity Committee were good people. Really good, really badly informed people. They spent all their time asking timid questions about freedom of expression and of the press and the lack of elections and relations with the Soviet Union. No matter how much he explained it to them, they didn't understand direct democracy or the dictatorship of the proletariat. Pro-Cuban anti-Soviets. The world was fucking complicated. What could that striking iron-and-glass structure be?

He turned the corner at James Street, heading towards the iron-and-glass building, thinking about the people in the committee. In the end he hadn't been able to communicate well with them. They were just wonderful up to the day and hour when the invitation ended, and then they left them all alone, without a translator. Anglo-Saxons. A Cuban wouldn't do that. But they were against the blockade, and they defended and loved Cuba. What more could you ask of them? He stopped in amazement before the railroad station and sadly recalled his old plan of one day building the city of the future. Now he'd never do it. He had learned that first it was necessary to build the man of the future.

He entered the enormous, vaulted waiting room, there had to be a bathroom there. Those people were funny. At the last reception they had collected three hundred dollars and tried to send it to Cuba as aid. When he refused to accept they wanted to give it to him as a personal gift. They couldn't understand why he refused it, also. The man of the past had a dollar sign on his forehead, and reacted with confusion and mistrust to anyone who wasn't branded too. Next to the circular staircase it said *Gentlemen*. He went downstairs following the arrow and read on the door of the bathroom *Water closet.* Closed water? And tightly closed, the little bathroom door didn't give in to his efforts. There weren't any urinals either. He stopped pulling the door for fear of breaking it, or that some kind of bell would ring. He was desperate from the need to take a pee.

"*Plis,*" he said to the employee.

But just then a fat man deposited a coin in the next little door and entered. Charging for a piss. Incredible. He'd have to tell Gisela about it. He stuck the money in the slot and the door immediately gave way. Inside it was white and clean, with the smell of perfume. He opened his fly. He resisted the urge, so as to get greater pleasure from the release, and thought of Gisela. Only when he had her nude in front of him did he let himself go little by little, gently, painfully, greedily, saving up the pleasure until the urine flowed as if from a great pipe, kicking up spume and noise in the little yellow lake. Afterwards there were drops, drops, little drops on his pants and a marvelous feeling of peace.

He pressed a button and the spume disappeared in a white whirlpool. He wasn't meeting Felipe for another hour. It was a crime to have to leave. He felt too good in that sacred place, locked and paid for. He hung his coat up on the door hook and sat down on the toilet. Across from him, underneath the knob, it said *Closed*. He leaned back against the tank, stretched out his legs and closed his eyes. "*God!*" he murmured. The headache gradually went away. He felt his feet and legs pleasantly numb, and a pleasant tickling in his shoulders, freed from the weight of the coat. He was thinking about his return, about how Gisela would meet him at the airport and that night they'd try on Mercedita's new boticas and then they'd make love and would never argue again, when he heard the question:

"*Any trouble, sir?*"

He didn't know whether to answer *yes* or nouuu. Someone knocked softly on the door. He realized his feet were sticking out and pulled them in.

"*Sir?*"

He decided to leave. You never knew with these people. Standing up and putting on his coat, he again felt his whole body hurting.

"*Are you alright, sir?*"

He nodded yes without understanding, went towards the sinks and put his mouth to the faucet. The water was cold and abundant, and it refreshed his throat and ran all over his face and neck.

"*Oh no, sir!*" the employee shouted. "*Don't do that!*"

He opened his mouth wider to drink as much water as possible before they made him give up the faucet. Reflected in the mirror, the guy had a desperate expression.

"*Be careful, sir! You'll get a disease!*"

Two other people were reflected, watching him curiously. He recalled the song about the elephants balancing on a spider's web. When the fourth curious person arrived, he stopped drinking. In the children's song there were infinite elephants. He wasn't willing to support them all. He returned to the main waiting room, checked that the boticas were still in his coat pocket, and went toward a bench. Wasn't that fellow the translator's friend?

"*Hi,*" said Mister Montalvo Montaner.

"Hola," he answered, really happy to be able to talk with someone.

Carlos had seen that chubby, short, olive-skinned man a couple of times. Although the man always greeted him in English, he spoke Spanish correctly, with a bleached-out accent.

"I was just wandering around here," Mister Montalvo Montaner said, vaguely. "How about a drink?"

"Fine," Carlos agreed.

The bar's semidarkness was pleasantly warm. That was different, too, in Cuba the bars weren't pleasant unless they were cold. They dropped their coats on a leather chair.

"What do you want to drink?" asked Mister Montalvo Montaner, sitting down.

"Plain mineral water, sin gas."

"You pronounce the final *s*. In general, Cubans don't pronounce it, and they make a joke without meaning to. Nothing else?"

Carlos shook his head no. Where could that man be from? In all his long experience with Latin Americans, he'd never encountered anyone who spoke in such a colorless way.

"*Scotch on the rocks, and tonic*," Mister Montalvo Montaner told the waiter, and turned to Carlos. "How did your free day go?"

"Bad. Lots of problems with English."

"You should study it," declared Mister Montalvo Montaner. "Such a smart person, it's incredible."

"Not really. I'm no good at languages."

"But I didn't say languages," Mister Montalvo Montaner protested. "I said English."

Carlos took advantage of the arrival of their order and didn't answer. He took a swallow of the tonic water. Its flavor was strange and rather unpleasant to him.

"You could get a scholarship," Mister Montalvo Montaner suggested, and emptied his glass in one gulp.

"I spent three years on a scholarship. I don't want that now."

Mister Montalvo Montaner smiled, understandingly. "A whiskey?" he said.

"Fine," agreed Carlos.

Mister Montalvo Montaner spoke to the waiter in a precise, elegant English, and he returned with a bottle of Chivas Regal and served them two drinks.

"To friendship," said Mister Montalvo Montaner, raising his glass.

Carlos toasted and drank. The whiskey was excellent. A soft, warm, woody tonic. He felt relaxed, happy to be able to speak in Spanish while he waited for Felipe.

"This was a lucky encounter," said Mister Montalvo Montaner.

Carlos smiled. He had figured out the key to the mystery, the guy had no rhythm when he spoke, he didn't sing like everyone who belonged to a place did, that's why his words sounded so plastic. But he was polite, served another drink, said:

"I wanted to talk with you alone."

Carlos looked at him, perplexed. Why alone? Could Mister Montalvo Montaner be a faggot?

"Your friend Felipe isn't very smart."

"Not as smart as you, you mean," said Carlos.

Mister Montalvo Montaner moved his head as if he'd been punched. Suddenly he smiled.

"Touché," he said. "I'm a journalist. Did you have dinner?"

"No."

"Great," he said enthusiastically. "I propose a Cuban dinner as it should be, en regla, no rationing, with a dessert that's divine, made with wine," pausing to laugh at what he considered to be a joke, and continued, "and music and lady friends. Something spectacular, *terrific*."

"Thanks, but I can't."

"So the dessert of divine wine isn't fine?"

"If it were in Regla, I'd accept," replied Carlos, as if he were just following along the flow of jokes, and Mister Montalvo Montaner let out a guffaw. He knew where Regla was. Could he be Cuban? A Cuban faggot, a gusano? "But here I can't, I'm leaving at dawn."

"I know. I can take you to the airport myself."

"How did you know?"

Mister Montalvo Montaner waved off the question as unimportant with a little gesture of his right hand.

"I know a lot of things about you. Shall we go?"

"No," Carlos replied curtly.

Mister Montalvo Montaner drew close to him, murmuring:

"Think it over, there's no rush."

Carlos felt the need to drink something. He did, and ran his fingers over the leather chair, leaving a trail of sweat.

"I said no," he said.

Was this guy a faggot or an agent? Now he was staring into his eyes, as if he wanted to hypnotize him.

"This is your opportunity," he murmured. "Think it over, you're smart."

"Yes," Carlos agreed, staring back at him. "And I'm telling you que se vaya p'al carajo, fuck off."

He felt liberated and secure speaking in Cuban. But Mister Montalvo Montaner didn't look offended. He made a slight gesture of displeasure, as if forgiving him that outburst. Then he softly smiled.

"Someone sends you his greetings," he said in a very low voice.

"Who the hell?"

Mister Montalvo Montaner remained calm. He refilled the glasses, drank, and said:

"Jorge."

"You motherfucker!" yelled Carlos, jumping to his feet.

Mister Montalvo Montaner put his fingers to his lips, calmly, as if that answer were in his calculations.

"He's here," he said. "He wants to see you."

Carlos hit him in the mouth with the back of his hand. Mister Montalvo Montaner didn't try to defend himself. He was disconcerted, wiping away the blood over and over. Carlos grabbed his coat and left the place, asking himself if *here* meant the city or the room, if his brother could have been watching the whole time from the far end of the bar, if he could have been capable of holding back the desire to embrace him that Carlos was feeling now, remembering the photo of the two of them together that his mother kept on her night table, like a relic.

On James Street the neon lights had created a murky clarity. He pulled up the collar of his coat and looked behind him. Mister Mierda wasn't following him. The encounter had had a stupid ending, he hadn't even found out if the guy was a faggot or an agent or both, if he really knew Jorge, if his brother had been part of that dirty business. It was all conjecture, anger, cold, and wishing to go home. At the corner of Main and James he stopped to wait for Felipe. That was where he'd seen the demonstration of young people, bearded and long-haired, against whom he'd felt such repulsion until he'd been able to decipher the meaning of their slogans and their banner: STOP U.S. BOMBING IN VIETNAM NOW!

The world was fucking complicated. He'd rejected the kids because of their extravagant appearance, and he'd accepted a conversation with Mister Mierda because he appeared normal. Suddenly he looked to each side and stuck close to the wall, to watch his back. The sharp yellow of a sign made him look up again. He was underneath a huge photo of a seminude woman advertising Mum Deodorant. From his perspective, her armpit looked like a woman's sex and the tube of deodorant a penis. Almost like in *Swedish Perversities*, the first porn film of his life, a pact made in blood and silence between him and Felipe, because Communists shouldn't see those things, but they had to do it, they told themselves, to confirm just how filthy capitalism was. Although the truth was that he, too, was kind of filthy. Incredible the crazy things that those women did on the screen. In the end, it was lucky that he hadn't been able to touch them and leave the theater with that dirty feeling of guilt. Right then he felt someone poke him in the stomach and he moved backwards, hitting into the wall. In front of him, Felipe was smiling.

"Cut it out," said Carlos. "What's the buzz?"

"Neigho." Felipe paused and whistled at a blonde, who acted like she didn't notice. "You cool too?"

"Ix-nay," he said, looking to both sides. "I had a run-in with an s.o.b."

"Seriously? Coñó, and you were by your lonesome, asere. Spill."

They started walking, and Carlos told him in detail about the encounter with Mister Montalvo Montaner. Towards the end of the story he sensed a strange fellow behind them, wearing a spy hat and with buckteeth. Could he be following them, or was he going the same way? Now he stood out against the reddish, intermittent light of a sign: *Have a Coke! The real thing!* It was fine that the old Coca-Cola had changed its name, but why *the real thing*? La cosa real? The only real thing was that the guy had turned the corner after them, and now he had an ocher light behind him, silhouetting some cowboys and their horses: *Come to where the flavor is, come to Marlboro country.*

Carlos alerted Felipe. They turned completely around and went towards the fellow, who gave them a confused look, almost guilty, stopped in front of a store window, momentarily covering the far-off, yellow *K* of *Kentucky Fried Chicken* towards which they had been walking, and almost immediately started following them again. Carlos felt a savage joy. That bastard was going to pay for it all, for Jorge and for Mister Mierda, for the cold and for English. He restrained his impulse to punch him right there and told himself that life had put a unique opportunity into his hands. Behind him he had a CIA agent, it wasn't about beating him up, killing the goose that laid the golden egg, but about getting information, maybe kidnapping him to the hotel and even to Cuba. Suddenly, the dumb trip had become splendid. They turned into a passageway filled with shops, and the guy followed them and was reflected in the last of the windows. Carlos communicated his plans to Felipe as if he were talking about shirts. They came out onto Parker Street, a secondary street, dark, deserted, and on getting to the first corner, Carlos stopped.

"We'll work him over here," he said.

They took their positions. The man's steps resonated in solitude. Carlos wiped the sweat from his hands onto his coat. He wasn't cold anymore. He was going to find out who Mister Mierda was and what the fuck the CIA wanted and what Jorge had to do with all that. He asked himself what would happen if the guy were armed or if he had a car backing him up. But he didn't have time to answer himself. The fellow reached them. Felipe came out of his hiding place and bent his arms back, immobilizing him, and Carlos grabbed his neck and yelled at him:

"Whoareyamothafucka?"

He let go and started slapping him without waiting for a reply. The fellow was unarmed, contorted with pain, trembling. Carlos grabbed his neck again. Felipe pulled harder on his arms.

"Dropdatude and talk," he told him.

"Soltadme, let me go," the fellow moaned, with great difficulty. "I haven't done anything to you, I don't understand you, no os entiendo."

Carlos shook him by his coat collar, banged his head against the wall, stuck his face into the guy's, and saw him go cross-eyed with fear.

"Who . . . okey? . . . mothafucka . . . okey? . . . are you?"

"I'm from Spain," the man answered, terrified. "Who are you two?"

Carlos smelled strong onions on his breath and banged his head against the wall again, producing a dull sound. He wasn't going to let that somabitch fool him.

"I'm asking, you piece of faggotyass," he said. "Why were you following us?"

"I wanted to speak Spanish," the guy explained, pleading. "I heard you fellows from far off, thought you were speaking Spanish, and, well, that's all, I wanted to talk with you."

"Liar!" yelled Carlos, slamming a knee into his crotch.

The guy was about to double over, but Felipe made him stand up straight. He was breathing heavily, his blue eyes got cloudy.

"I haven't talked at all for three months," he said.

"Why?" asked Carlos.

"Because I don't know any English," the fellow replied, panting. "Because I was thick enough to come to this bloody country to work and I don't know English."

"Liar!" Carlos yelled again.

And he raised his hand, but the man had such an absolutely defenseless expression that he couldn't bring himself to hit him, and he banged on the wall to unload his rage.

"You know Mister Montaldo Montaner," he asserted, "and Jorge."

"No," said the man, with surprised, naive conviction.

Carlos looked into his blue eyes, wide open, still cloudy with pain and fear. The worst thing was that he seemed to be telling the truth. He let go of his coat and turned to Felipe.

"What d'you think?"

"He's just a jerk."

"Let me go," the Gallego begged softly. "I'm stone-broke."

Felipe started to laugh.

"He be missin' a few," he said.

"Sometimes I don't understand you," the Gallego commented.

Carlos felt his rage had dissolved into a strange sadness. He was cold again.

"That means you're crazy," he said. "Talking about rocks."

"Who said anything about rocks?" asked the Gallego.

"Let him go," Carlos ordered.

"Get moving, Gallego," said Felipe, giving him a shove.

The man stumbled and then came back to them, like a battered but loyal dog.

"I want to talk," he said.

Carlos looked at him without hate and found himself thinking that speech, like water, should be denied to no one.

"You two speak jolly strange," said the Gallego. "And you look like a Moor."

"I can speak Arabic," agreed Felipe.

"Oh no you can't."

Now the Gallego was enjoying himself like a little boy who had found some friends in the night. Carlos felt ashamed of having hit him and decided to join in the game.

"He can too," he said. "Felipe, say: the woman wants everything on her sandwich."

"Lady all salad salami."

The Gallego burst out laughing. His loud, uproarious guffaws infected Felipe too, and Carlos silently took pleasure in that laughter, capable of breaking for a moment the silence and the cold.

"And this one here speaks Japanese," declared Felipe.

"Oh, right," said the Gallego.

"Oh no?" challenged Felipe, and he looked at Carlos. "Say dumb ass."

"Kuku inatushi."

"Bloody good!" applauded the Gallego. "But that's not Japanese, or Arabic, or a monkey's uncle. You fellows are cutups."

"Cuntwhat?" asked Felipe.

"Cutups, that you like joking around, vamos."

"Where?" said Felipe.

"Where what?" asked the Gallego.

"Are we going."

"I didn't talk about going anywhere. I said you like joking around, vamos."

"Where?"

"Fuck!"

"Who?"

"As for me, the woman I don't have."

"We screw around with anyone."

"Well, to each his own," commented the Gallego apprehensively, "I mean, in matters of taste."

Suddenly Carlos felt very tired. It was cold and he had to pack his suitcase and that conversation made no sense.

"Chico, we've got to go," he said, but it didn't seem like enough, so he added, "and I'm sorry about hitting you, brother."

The Gallego's face darkened even more that when they beat him up, it was hard for him to find the words.

"Don't leave," he finally begged. "The beating . . . that was nothing. Let's talk. What I said about being stone-broke, vamos, it was just a little white lie, I'll treat you to a nip."

He held Carlos back and blocked Felipe's path. He was anxious, almost desperate. Carlos remembered his purchase of the boticas and felt a rush of sudden tenderness.

"Vamos," he said.

The Gallego led them to a cafe and used three fingers and one word to order them brandy. Then he spent an hour telling them his story. His name was Paco, in Spain he had neither work, a wife, nor children, and he had agreed to come to this bloody country, and yes, he was earning some dollars, but English was a bitch, he just couldn't get it through his head, and he felt homesick, and these jackasses here, damn their mothers, didn't have a clue about Spanish. Goddamn them, no more of his countrymen had come and there he was, working like a dog, missing his aunt, his village, and his wine, and picking up garbage with bloody negros, fuck it all!

For Carlos this was a revelation. The Gallego didn't have a thing to his name and on top of that they'd turned him into a deaf-mute, and he was about to burst from rage. But the guy was just banging his head against a wall. If someone could show him the light he'd stop being a poor devil, his rage would have meaning, he could do everything that was forbidden to him, Carlos, because he was Cuban and had a duty to maintain discipline. He looked at Paco with fresh interest: fate had put a guerrilla fighter into his hands, in the bloody Canadian night.

"Gallego," he suddenly said, "why don't you rise up?"

Paco gave him the dumb look of someone who doesn't understand a joke.

"Rise up?"

"In the mountains," said Carlos helpfully. "In the Andes, the American Sierra Maestra."

"South America?" murmured Paco, with the interest of someone starting to understand.

"Yes," Felipe joined in, "Latin America."

"Hombre," said Paco, now really interested, "and there's work there?"

Felipe let out a big laugh. Paco seconded him, like someone who doesn't know why he's laughing. Carlos ordered silence, the Gallego hadn't understood but he was going in the right direction.

"No," he told him, "there's unemployment, hunger, poverty. A situation up the ass."

"Arse, you mean," Paco clarified. "So then what?"

Carlos tried to control his anxiety and to speak slowly and clearly.

"Rise up against all that," he explained. "Go to war in the mountains."

Paco was tossing down his brandy. He started coughing, the very white skin of his face turning red.

"Well, for me, wars . . ." he said, "it's just, it's just that I don't care about them, vamos."

"But this is a different kind of war, a people's war!" Carlos insisted.

"Maybe so, but it's war."

Felipe nudged Carlos with his elbow.

"Kill it," he said. "He doesn't dig."

"To hell with digging it," answered Carlos, and he started speaking to Paco again. "Che leads this war."

"I don't know that bloke," said Paco, like someone who absolves himself of all responsibility, "and I don't care about wars."

Carlos drank his brandy, disconcerted. Could it be possible that this dolt would tamely put his neck to the blade, that the blows they'd given him had turned him into an ox?

"Gallego," he said to him, "why are you breaking your back like this? What are you hoping for?"

Paco closed his eyes and spoke as if dreaming.

"To save money, go back home, buy some land, find a lass, get married, and have children who won't live the dog's life their father did."

"And nothing more?"

Paco came out of his dream, almost in tears.

"You think that's not much?" he asked, slowly. "And I think it's more than I'll ever be able to get!"

"And the world?" asked Carlos, anxious again. "Wouldn't you like the world to be different, more just, better? Wouldn't you like to change it?"

"Well, sure," murmured Paco, "but the world . . . nobody on God's green earth can change the world."

"Gallego, do you know what Communism is?"

"Of course, everyone knows what it is, it's . . . hell, vamos," said Paco, looking at them as if expecting a joke.

Carlos smiled sadly. Paco imitated him and Felipe let out a resonating guffaw that pulled Paco along. Carlos saw him double over with laughter and when they were about to stop, he started laughing, without knowing why, and he looked at the Gallego's buckteeth and contorted face and blue eyes, sad even when he was laughing, and he remembered his friend Gallego, killed in Escambray, and his brother, and felt his laughter breaking apart on his lips.

"Now we really do have to go, Gallego," he said suddenly.

He called the waiter by snapping his fingers. Paco stopped laughing and reached into his pocket.

"Forget it," said Carlos.

"I invited you," Paco protested.

But Felipe held back his arm, and Carlos paid. Slowly, they headed for the exit. In the street, the wind was howling like a lost dog in the night.

"Galifa," said Felipe, "you'll go right through this life without even know-ing it."

"Well, I suppose so," agreed Paco. "I've got no luck."

They shook hands. Paco held onto Carlos's and asked:

"Can I see you two tomorrow?"

"No, tomorrow we won't be here."

"Oh," said Paco. "And where can I see you?"

"You can't," Carlos explained. "We're leaving for Cuba."

Paco's face darkened, as if he'd heard something awful.

"So then, I won't see you again?"

Now he was a little boy again, on the verge of losing his friends and being left alone in the dark. Carlos gave in to the impulse to embrace him and felt Paco's big hands patting him on the back, and pulling Felipe towards them. For a short while they were together. When they separated, Paco was crying.

"Adiós, Gallego," said Carlos. "Good luck."

And he began walking in silence, a knot of rage in his throat.

NINETEEN

Suddenly he was confused by the feeling of not knowing where he was. He felt the bed to his left, didn't find Gisela there, looked to the other side for Mercedita and saw only the bare wall. He shut his eyes again, wishing he hadn't woken up. Now he could recall that room precisely, the same one where he had lived part of his childhood and almost all his youth, from which he had escaped into the whirlwind and to which he had been forced to return, his own will annulled by hard blows, to turn it into a hospital and a prison. He had been there for days, almost without leaving the bed, without opening the windows or turning on the light, letting himself be coddled by that indefatigable mother who was now entering with his breakfast, like every morning, while he continued to abandon himself to the murky pleasure of reconstructing the history of his disgrace, the conjunction of coincidences, fears, and betrayals that brought about disaster. He spent hours and hours comparing his image—lame, toothless, without a wife, political militancy, or a job— with that of the hero he'd tried to be, of the architect he'd tried to be, of the guerrilla fighter he'd tried to be. But he couldn't manage to unravel why or when reality and desire had grown so brutally far apart. He wasn't a coward, or lazy, or stupid, and yet he was lying there doing nothing while Mai, for example, was fighting somewhere in the world, according to what Héctor had told him when they ran into each other on the street, Héctor himself upstanding, doing fine, plugging away at work, very glad to know that Carlos was general secretary of the Core Committee of the Young Communists and section head at the Center for International Studies, he told him and hugged him and went away smiling, just exactly as he reappeared a few months later, in a photo in *Granma*, alongside the news that he had died fighting for freedom some place in America.

Up to that moment heroes had been huge, distant, inaccessible, but Héctor was Héctor, his classmate and playmate, his equal, his buddy, and now suddenly he was no longer the same age and became young forever. Back then Carlos still cherished the hope of meriting the right to combat, of finding the road to the Andes, and with Héctor's death he redoubled his commitment to the maelstrom that somehow led him to disgrace. Suffering through it now, he began telling himself that Héctor and he were made of different stuff, that they were similar but not equal. The recognition of his inferiority plunged him into a bitter well from which he could escape only by imagining fabulous battles that were decided by his valor and boldness. And then, from the height of exaltation, he plunged down again. He thought about Kindelán, an anonymous hero: he'd lost an arm at Girón, he'd become a widower, but he went on living without complaint; about Pablo, who wasn't a hero but was a leader of the sugar industry; about Munse, a well-known architect, creator of a great plan for affordable housing; about the Coachman, an utter opportunist, a hardened bureaucrat, subdirector for investment at some ministry; and once again about himself, neither hero nor bureaucrat, neither leader nor professional, indefinitely expelled from the Young Communists, his job and salary suspended, and rejected even by his wife.

During the first few days at least he had Mercedita and Gisela in the crazy home of his in-laws, which, through the good grace of his marriage, was his also. He couldn't find the courage to tell his wife the truth, because his mistake was too humiliating for her, and he didn't feel able to face the risk of losing her and giving up his only refuge. He tried to act as if nothing had happened, committing a new error that time would make irreparable. In the mornings he would say he was going to work, he'd head for some park and there he'd pass the day, putting it all back together. If, for example, he hadn't hated opportunism so much; if he'd flatly refused to devote forty-eight hours straight to that damned report; if Gisela hadn't been doing her medical internship; if they at least had had an apartment, and on the very rare occasions when they were both awake at the same time, hadn't found themselves forced to make love halfway, in silence and with the lights out; if Gisela had agreed to move to his mother's house; if his mother hadn't started treating him like a little boy again; if those irrational feelings of jealousy hadn't come up between her and Gisela; if he hadn't had such an obsessive devotion to work; if he had had the courage to wash his own underwear, to get up sometimes at night to take care of Mercedita, to accept and follow the Declaration of Gisela's Rights (that she had proposed to him, half-joking and half-serious, on their third wedding anniversary); if they hadn't argued over and over again; if he had always loved and desired her with the intensity he felt now, or if at least he had had a little luck, things would be different and he wouldn't be out of work in that park, waiting until it was time to pick up Mercedita at her nursery school, with the humble hope that Gisela would never learn the truth.

But things had gone as they did, the director had asked him unexpectedly for the Assessment and Outlook Report, and given him forty-eight hours to hand it in. It was practically impossible to do a good job in that amount of time, but the director insisted, with the pretext of orders from higher up. All he could give Carlos, he said, was an office, a secretary, and a thermos of coffee. Carlos felt the temptation to throw himself into that impossible enterprise, as in his days of being a student leader. He reined it in because now he knew that wasn't the way, for an undertaking like this he needed the help of the Core Committee, where the director's administration and the structure of the organization had been criticized. He called an urgent meeting and the consensus was that some higher authority must have solicited the report; the director was in a bind and was trying to use them, the only political organization in the CEI, to continue on in his post. They had three alternatives: error, caution, and victory. They could make an error if they hurriedly put together a radical report that later on would not withstand analysis by the higher authorities; they could be intelligent and put together a cautious text, that would allow a glimpse of problems subject to further debate; or they could obtain political victory by means of an exhaustive, irrefutable, and devastating work. After long digressions about opportunism and irresponsibility, they advised him to be cautious; a mature leader, they said in agreement, could only throw himself in completely if he were sure of not making mistakes that would lead him to an untenable situation.

Carlos accepted their guidance because it gave him room to maneuver, although that word, used in the discussion by Felipe Martínez, bothered him like a thorn in the side. In reality, he'd been maneuvering for months so as not to lead his compañeros into a face-off with the director. But he knew that in the elaboration of that strategy, besides political savvy, had been present the desire to be promoted to department head, which would bring closer the possibility of someday joining the guerrillas and would permit him, right away, the use of an automobile. In a certain sense, everything depended now on that damned report, and he went into his office asking himself what the limits were between opportunism and caution, between courage and irresponsibility. The director had greased his trap by designating Iraida, his personal secretary, as Carlos's assistant. She was a short, immaculate, olive-skinned woman, who waited with her knees locked together under the typewriter stand, as if on guard. But from the beginning Carlos felt that she was spying on him, wishing for him to fail, that behind that nice, even pretty face, so carefully made-up, she was hiding a mocking, condescending smile every time he tore up a sheet of paper and threw it into the trash. He knew something about her, she was twenty-one, had been chosen as an exemplary youth, but hadn't been awarded party militancy because she lacked sufficient merit: she almost never did work in the countryside, with the pretext of having to take care of urgent business for the director. Suddenly he stopped looking at her and banged on the table, what the fuck was he doing thinking about that informer, he had other work to do. He told her to leave if she wanted to, he wasn't used to giving dictation, he'd call her later on; but she refused, she would be there as long as necessary, compañero, until she did her duty. Carlos threw her an ironic look, bothered by the formulaic little phrase, and decided to ignore her. His intention of honest caution included breaking with the implacable, hollow logic of traditional reports. But that wasn't easy, after three feverish hours he had to recognize that he was writing a dangerously traditional text. He tore up the ten pages he'd written with such enthusiasm and was interrupted by a familiar, unexpected hissing sound. He raised his head, Iraida had gone out. The little noise came from the office bathroom. That was the limit, hearing her urinate he'd never manage to concentrate.

Half an hour later he hadn't been able to formulate a coherent line, and the basket was full of crumpled paper. Maybe he was thinking too hard. After all, formulas existed for everything, and if he used them no one could hold it against him. He moved his hand, searching for the thermos, and Iraida attentively served him a cup of coffee. While he drank, he decided to deal with the report in the most able and least risky manner possible. This approach seemed better to him than honest caution. He would limit himself to making a new version of the reports presented in prior years. A little while later he again heard a familiar noise. Iraida was serving lunch. It was just two pizzas, but she arranged them on the paper plates as if they were lobster. While they ate, Carlos observed her closely. There was something shy, unspoiled, and elegant in the girl. From polite phrases they moved into a friendly conversation and showed each other pictures of their children. When Carlos suggested that Tony could be a good match for Mercedita, Iraida smiled for the first time and he noticed the vague sadness in her eyes. He told her she could leave and come back at night, but she insisted on staying until they did their duty. Meanwhile, she could be working on other things. He went back to his task and kept on writing, encountering little resistance. Four hours later he had finished an assessment that seemed perfect, and he took a rest to give his hand some relief before dealing with the outlook section. Then Iraida asked him for permission to go pick up Tony from nursery school, bathe him, feed him, and put him to bed.

She returned at eleven, embarrassed by the lateness, explaining that Tony had been impossible, he wouldn't let her leave, she was so sorry. He calmed her down, saying that he still hadn't finished, and he thanked her profusely for the egg sandwich she gave him, ashamed that it was so little. While he ate he felt obligated to ask her about herself and learned that her husband was a drafts-man, that they didn't have their own place either, that her father had stabbed her mother to death when she was a little girl. He felt shocked, especially because Iraida had said it as if it were nothing, with the naturalness of some-one accustomed to misfortune. He gave in to the need to share some sad memory and started telling her about his father's death. When he finished he felt a strange peace, as if suddenly he'd been freed from some ghosts. Two hours later he finished the outlook section, gave the report to Iraida and lay down to sleep on the sofa, until she had the copy ready. He was exhausted and happy, he'd done it in less than twenty-four hours. Iraida's legs were straight in his line of vision, he got excited discovering that she had pretty knees, an unusual thing, and he followed the line of her thighs which suddenly widened into round hips and hinted at full buttocks, like moons. Unexpectedly Iraida smoothed down her skirt and Carlos interpreted the gesture as a coded mes-sage: he was offending her, she was too shy to dare to change the position of the stand, he should turn around, please. He did that, and an incalculable time later, heard someone calling him. He didn't have the strength to respond, but a very delicate caress on his forehead made him blink before that face which was saying, "You sleep so restlessly." He looked at her in such a way that she drew back, slightly scared. Only then did he remember Iraida and the job and he got up to go to the bathroom. There he found a towel with her scent, urinated trying not to make noise, and went back to the office. The report was on the desk, next to a cup of hot coffee. He told Iraida to go home; but she replied that it made no sense to leave at five and come back at eight, better just to rest a little on the sofa. He immediately got absorbed in his reading so as not to offend her by watching while she lay down. Soon after someone looked in and excused himself on seeing Carlos, he was on guard duty, said the new arrival, he'd seen lights. Carlos paid him no attention. The report scrupulously satisfied all appearances, seemed impeccable, and exactly because of that it was a disaster.

He felt a sudden overwhelming desire to tear it up. Why, if he had it all ready, if the car keys were tinkling in its wake, if no one could prove that he had been overly cautious? He reread it with a bitter smile; he was getting old, an old hand at this, he knew so much that he'd managed to make invisible the transition from precaution to opportunism, moving between the two with amazing ability, without leaving a trace, as if he'd worked with gloves on. But at least one person in the world existed whom he couldn't fool, and that one he carried inside him. He started pacing the room, if he had the courage he could dare to reveal the links between the malfunction of the center and the work style of the director, bureaucratic, supercentralized, and with no link whatsoever to the base. He knew that style well, it had been his own when he was a leader at the Architecture School. He knew like the back of his hand the opportunists who prospered in his shadow, and he knew that the guy was in a compromised position with them for having celebrated his daughter's fifteenth birthday using state funds. That party, especially outrageous for having taken place in the middle of the zafra, during the two-week tribute to the victory at Girón, when everyone was breaking their backs in the fields, produced a violent wave of criticism in the Core Committee that at the time he hadn't dared to channel, waiting for a more favorable moment. But months went by, the occasion never presented itself, little by little he'd resigned himself to it, and now, suddenly, he had it in his grasp because the director had been obligated to deploy him. And what if he dared to mention errors and those responsible, linking them with the crisis of structure, method, and work style imposed at the center? If he risked it? He felt euphoric, he had a bomb in his hands and he was ready to detonate it.

When he returned to his desk, Iraida caught his attention. She was sleeping on her side, her slightly bent left knee had pulled up her skirt, showing her white thighs, full, covered by a soft hair that started at the back of the knee, the exact point where she stopped shaving, extended up to the edge of her buttocks, and was covered there by pink panties. He sat on an arm of the sofa, stunned by so much beauty, controlling the furious desire to possess her and hear her cry out with pleasure on awakening penetrated. His erection made him close his eyes. He went back to his desk feeling his way like a blind man, and tore up the report. But he couldn't concentrate again until Iraida got up an hour later, the torturous hissing in the bathroom ceased, and he had her before him, her skirt in place, asking why he was going to redo the report. He didn't answer; unfortunately, she couldn't understand why. He submitted again to the intolerable process of smudging and ripping up pages, thinking that if this were about talking, it would be easy. He was brilliant with his tongue, establishing facts, causes, consequences, and all the rest, but writing was as capricious as hell, often he found that what you wrote had a different and even opposite meaning from what you thought. There was only one easy path, to repeat what was done, what was certain, and he couldn't go down it simply because he had decided to say something new. He decided also to run the risk of a clumsy or obscure expression, from which he could get even an ounce of truth. Slowly, stubbornly, laboriously he went along articulating sentences, periods, paragraphs, and he felt that taking the risk had become a source of boldness and sometimes of surprising, unexpected beauty. When Iraida offered him lunch, he asked her please not to bother him, and he didn't reply to the compañeros who looked in to ask how it was going, and he barely nodded his head in agreement when Iraida put a little note on his desk asking permission to pick up Tony and the rest, and at ten, when she returned apologetically, he continued tied up in the task that he finished at twelve, excited, exhausted, feverish.

Iraida brought him fish croquettes, egg custard, and freshly filtered coffee; asked him if he had clean clothes and gently scolded him because he didn't, because the office was dirty, and because he hadn't eaten lunch. Carlos blew her a kiss, he had to work, he said, afterwards he'd have time to eat and bathe, now he was going to dictate to her, with fatigue his handwriting had become incomprehensible. He began very slowly, but Iraida worked professionally, cleanly, silently, and he gained confidence and admired her small hands, with the nails cut very short, and her artisan's love of her work. Almost without realizing it he kept speaking louder and faster while he watched those fingers fly, as if over piano keys. Turning a page, he looked at the floor and discovered her bare feet, unprotected, intimate, and remembered her thighs and buttocks. Suddenly he heard her drumming her nails on the typewriter stand, raised his head, saw her biting her lower lip, blushing, and only then did he become aware of the erection that had turned the fly of his pants into a small circus tent, like when he was an adolescent. He almost turned his back to her, embarrassed, but he continued dictating. Now he was getting into the meat of the thing and that helped his concentration. He went on enumerating errors, with first and last names, until he got to the director, and unexpectedly for Iraida, to himself. Now he was improvising, he heard the tapping of the keyboard like an echo chamber that hammered at his temples with the celestial music of the truth, he understood that he didn't have the right to throw the first stone if he didn't reserve the last one for himself, and the fatigue and the tension were settled in that impassive denunciation of compañero Carlos Pérez Cifredo as complicit in the errors that had been committed, since in his role as a political leader, as a young Communist, he hadn't opposed them with sufficient firmness, hadn't appealed to the base or to higher levels, and he had acted like that from fear, compañeros, from fear that he wouldn't be promoted to department head, fear of political responsibility, and fear of the truth, compañeros, the truth of what he finally had said.

The clicking of the machine over his silence was like an anticlimax. He felt overtaken by sudden worry. What had he done? He didn't have time to answer himself. Iraida stood up, came over to him, embraced him trembling, and told him that she had never, never, never known anyone so brave. Carlos smiled confusedly, Iraida's perfume had made his own sour, sweaty odor seem like an offense to him. But she stayed in the embrace to tell him again, never, and looked into his eyes. They entwined in a kiss while he yielded to the temptation to touch those thighs etched on his memory, that were full and firm as he'd imagined. Iraida took a step back and tried to pull away, but she left her legs spread apart and Carlos caressed her moist sex and dragged her to the sofa, made her pop open the buttons on her blouse and the clasp of her bra, kissed her breasts while she asked him for God's sake to let her go and helped him to take off her panties, went astride him saying no, not that, not now, not there, and he penetrated her smoothly, deeply, and felt her cry out, biting, sinking down to the quick asking, oh God what is this at the same moment that someone opened the door.

Amid the wave of commentary that shook the center, some people said that Carlos had fallen into a trap hatched by the director, that he was a stupid shithead and Iraida a bitch. But he knew that Iraida was a sad, unspoiled girl and that the trap hadn't been set out for him by the director, but rather by life.

The only sure thing, he thought in the parks where time scarcely passed, was that he was a shithead and he had to change. That was why he decided to hide the truth from Gisela. At first he succeeded in pretending with unexpected ease, as if the impact of the disaster prevented him from measuring it. He slept for twenty-four hours straight, hearing his depression in that fatigue. The telephone awoke him, the neutral voice of the administrative sub-director informing him, bureaucratically, that his job and salary had been suspended owing to his scandalous behavior. Flabbergasted, he thanked him; Gisela asked mechanically if he'd gotten good news and he answered yes. He got dressed as if he were going to work and headed for a park where he remembered, obsessively, a phrase learned in childhood: "I am the way, the truth, and the life," and sunk down into a sea of questions about the report, Iraida, the director, opportunism, and fate. That night he suffered through a draining insomnia, made up of the same questions without answers. When Gisela returned from being on call he was still awake, waiting for her, he lied, while watching her undress in the light of the night lamp. They made love in an intense way, so different from the insipid weekly routine into which it had grown that she asked him what kind of bug had bitten him. "Nothing," he lied, "I love you." Then he discovered that the last phrase had become profoundly, unexpectedly true, and he thought about telling her the truth, to tell her about his desperate situation, invite her to the Riviera to relive the unforgettable madness of their wedding night and unravel why their love had died and slipped through their fingers; but he was afraid of the way of the truth or the life, the one that had led him to the report that generated the exultation that produced the embrace that brought him to disaster, and he forced a smile and closed his eyes, thinking it was better this way.

The next day the Core Committee summoned him to a meeting to examine his case. He attended, asking himself if he still had some defense, if having dared to write down what others whispered would serve for something, if truth could also be a shield. But from the beginning he realized that his self-defense was a fallacy. He had literally violated the agreement, his error put the prestige of the organization in danger, made it vulnerable to attacks from the director, the only thing they could do was to proceed in a drastic, exemplifying manner, said Margarita Villabrille, a member of the Ideological Front, and she asked for his indefinite expulsion. Then his buddy Felipe Martínez started the defense, compañero Carlos, whose merit within the Young Communists shouldn't be forgotten, had fallen into a trap, Iraida Meneses was placed in that job to seduce him, and a man, compañeros, is always a man and has to make his manhood clear, all the more so if he is a Communist, and therefore he asked that Carlos be sanctioned with public criticism for having been out of line, and that they move to a discussion of the report, which was the most important thing. The debate heated up when Marta Hernández, after recognizing Carlos's merits, asked what would have happened in the case of a woman, a militant married and with children, who had committed that "error," what would have been the stance of the organization then, what would compañero Felipe's stance have been or that of Carlos himself, whose wives themselves were militants, what, let's hear it, I'd like to know, she said, what would have happened if it had been women and not men being questioned and accused. Carlos saw Felipe go pale and felt himself pale at the thought that Gisela might have, in the hospital, during her nights on call, where there were even beds . . . and he identified with the violent reply of his buddy, who wasn't going to permit in any way, not even for a moment, he said, that the morality of their wives be put in doubt, and in general, to throw some light on the matter, so that compañera Margarita would get some clarity, he wanted to clarify for her that women were very, very different from men, much more so if they were Communist women who had to be examples of morality and decency. Marta got fired up, compañero Felipe upheld the existence of a double standard of morality, could a caveman opinion such as that be allowed among young Communists? Didn't compañero Carlos himself realize that if the organization didn't sanction him, the report would lose all moral force? Don't you realize, compañeros? Rubén Suárez, the convener, asked for the floor, it was obvious, he said, that there ought to be one moral standard for men and women, that the report would lose force if the Young Communists covered up for the error of its general secretary, but it was also obvious that the great attenuating circumstance of compañero Carlos, besides his own merit and his work, was having been the object of a provocation; they would believe his word as a Communist, Carlos, was it true that Iraida Meneses had provoked the incident? Carlos asked that they repeat the question for him to gain time, and he thought it was all so much easier when it was just a matter of hiding the truth, but now it was a matter of shamelessly lying, staining someone as defenseless as Iraida, who hadn't even dared to return to work. "No," he finally replied, "I am the only one responsible." Then Rubén put to a vote Margarita's proposal: to solicit from the Municipal Committee indefinite expulsion, and to help Carlos he asked that the vote begin with those against. Carlos was the first to raise his hand and on doing so realized he was making a mistake, if he'd accepted his responsibility he should have gone all the way, or at least abstained. No one said anything, but an atmosphere of disapproval spread through the room. The proposal was approved ten votes to two. Now they would begin a discussion of the report, but Carlos asked permission to leave.

Going out the door he was struck by the strange idea that he was no longer a Communist. He touched his body as if searching for some wound. He stood standing on the sidewalk, seized by an indefinable astonishment. He tried to find refuge in the concept of a cardless Communist with which the Archimandrite had once saved him, but now the Archimandrite was away on a trip, and he knew too much to be satisfied with so little. He knew that a Communist cannot exist without his organization, just as Cuba couldn't exist without that sea towards which he headed to take measure of the scale of his impotence. It hadn't been easy for him, Grandfather Álvaro and Chava knew that it hadn't been easy for him to win militancy, they knew there was as much strength in his soul as in those waves, and that like that sea, he, too, had ended up exhausted, licking the shore; he turned to them now so they could tell him if there was justice on earth. His dreams of being a guerrilla had broken up like the waves, but the waves would return, the sea always started over again, the dark mass of water became blue and then green and then white, over and over, cleaning and stirring the air that he swallowed in gulps, because it contradicted his sadness.

Clearly Gisela was waiting for him with the hope of repeating the experience of the night before. But he was too depressed to keep everything quiet, and more determined than ever not to risk his only refuge. When she asked him what was the matter, he started stringing together sentences, inventing a story that got more coherent as he recognized he was telling a possible truth. Life was the matter, sweetheart, the director was an opportunist and an exploiter, but he was a clever guy. He'd asked him for a report on the center, insinuating that if he kept quiet about errors he'd be promoted to department head. The big somabitch had tried to buy him off. He had agreed to do the report on very short notice because of revolutionary conviction. But he had done his duty: he criticized the structural problems and the bastard's personal attitude: he lived with his secretary, he had celebrated his daughter's fifteenth birthday with all the trimmings, using state funds, he practiced favoritism, had three cars, always seemed busy but in reality worked very little and badly.

He had set all that out in black and white, counting on support from certain compañeros who had made a commitment to go all the way with him; but at the moment of truth they had chickened out, left him alone, and when the director pressed them, they started stuttering. He had no other proof than his moral conviction, he was pissed off, backed into a corner, and made several mistakes in his argument. The director had suspended his job and salary, and the Young Communists asked for his indefinite expulsion. That was what was the matter with him.

"But you have to appeal this," she said, and offered to help him. They'd write letters, requests, reports, they'd visit all the offices there were in this world or the next until they established the truth. Carlos was surprised, years of a relationship that had become routine had kept him from noticing how much Gisela had changed; he had always considered her a slightly inferior being in terms of politics, a woman, and now he was seeing a cadre lecturing him about the rights and duties of militants, she cited statutes from memory, applauded him for having written the report, criticized him for not having followed through all the way, turned red with rage thinking about the tangled-up mess they were getting him into, and offered advice and assistance. He reacted against her with unexpected violence, would she please do him the goddamn favor of not giving him lessons or shaking her little finger in his face; everything, listen up, everything that she had said he knew from memory; he needed understanding, not harangues; he wanted to talk with a woman, with his woman, not with a cadre. "You're upset," Gisela replied, and Carlos yelled, shaking the house: "Upset my aaaaassss!" He saw how Gisela's face turned into an expression of fear and pity, and perceived in confusion that his father-in-law was trying to enter the room; he was on the verge of telling him to go to hell to end everything once and for all when Mercedita woke up crying. The terrified face of his daughter revealed to him the beast he carried inside. He went to her, said, "Go to sleep," and stayed there stroking her until seeing her smile in her sleep. Then he went back to bed, put his hand on Gisela's belly, and apologized.

He took refuge in his daughter, the only being on earth who made him happy without asking for anything in return. He discovered how very, very much he had lost by not giving more of himself before to that little person with unpredictable questions. He suffered with shame remembering how his disappointment had neutralized his tenderness when he saw her as a newborn, female and almost black. But Mercedita had always preferred him, had bored through his coldness with her innocence, become an indispensable presence of his mornings. He never had enough time for her because he was devoted to the demands of his work and politics, the only things that seemed important to him. And now, when he had nothing to do and didn't think it possible to find repose, he began to rediscover in his daughter's eyes that a rusty can could be something really important, with unpredictable angles and a brownish rough texture that, of course, could let you compare it to a monkey. But no, that's not it, Papá, listen to me, look, the can *was* a monkey. And he relearned how to imagine, to stare, to break with the logic that had imprisoned him, who knew when, and to *see* the monkey with which they wound up laughing and laughing and that soon turned out to be the father of other boy monkeys and girl monkeys and baby monkeys. They were in the middle of Africa, in front of them ran the powerful Amazon, they had to cross the immense Mississippi because Toña was there beyond the Nile, a little girl who had fallen into the hands of the terrible Saquiri the Malay. They had to be careful, Saquiri was very evil and traitorous and didn't allow Toña to go to school, or buy her clothes, or feed her. No, they shouldn't cry about it, they should do something for Toña. Crying would leave them without the strength to join the guerrillas who would defeat Saquiri in a merciless fight. Hurry, get that nest of machine guns! BANG! RAT-A-TAT-TAT! RAT-A-TAT-TAT! BANG! BANG! Watch out, Papá, they're attacking us from behind! Yes, but it doesn't matter, I'll give them SOCK! a punch, POW! another, and hasten to battle, men of Bayamo. To battle, Papá, venceremos! Venceremos, Mercedita! SOCK! RAT-A-TAT-TAT! POW! BANG! BA-ROOOM! CRASH! Sing, my love, sing, we've won! And now what, Papá? Well, now I'll defend Africa and you'll teach Toña to read. Papá, and if she asks me why Martí died in two rivers at once, what should I say?

At night they had lots of fun telling Gisela about their adventures. There were moments when Carlos was thankful for that forced vacation; that was why he was dazed when Gisela put a suitcase with his clothes on the bed and asked him to please leave. Someone had done her the favor of making a phone call and telling her: they had caught him with his pants down in the office, sleeping with a whore. Gisela said all that with a cold, controlled hatred, but suddenly her voice started shaking, what hurt her the most was his lie, what hurt her the most was having believed his story, what hurt her the most was being married to a miserable wretch. She had ended up shouting and broke into uncontrolled sobs. Carlos tried to explain, they were tangled up in a hell of a confusion, the part about the report, the criticism of the director, the expulsion from the Young Communists was true, he swore on his mother's life, it was all true. "And the part about the whore?" asked Gisela. "It's a lie," he said, and tried to stroke her hair. But she backed away against the wall, he disgusted her, understand? Disgusted her. Carlos grabbed the suitcase in a fit of rage, ready to play hardball, when she saw him at the door she'd say his name and then he would concede to having a talk to get things clear and they'd end up like other times, crying, laughing, and remembering. He walked slowly, without her saying a word. Should he turn around, break the golden rule of never lowering himself before a woman by pleading for dialogue? When he reached the threshold Gisela stayed mute and he felt he didn't want to go nor could he stay, and turned around without knowing exactly why. For a moment he thought about apologizing, but an atavistic furor made him challenge her: listen well, Gisela Jáuregui, if he left now, it would be forever.

What hurt him the most at that moment and afterwards, in his mother's house, was that she let him go with a bitter joke: "There's no one holding you up, Carlos Pérez." That phrase gave way to his madness, the desperate stalking that started the next day, when he visited her house to tell her the truth: he'd been unfaithful, not with a whore but with a decent, helpless girl. It wasn't the first time, he'd done it before, she had to understand, men had their needs, that was one thing, and the family, the home, the children, something completely different; he wanted to come back, he was begging her. Gisela had to go to the hospital, she was very tired, it wasn't the right moment, she said, and he felt her expression and words like a slap and he gripped her arm, coño, he was begging her, what more did she want. Then he noticed that she was enduring the pain with a decisive resignation, as if she were feeding her distance with it. He let her go, he was sorry, he was desperate, could they speak later, please? "Yes, no, maybe, I don't know," she murmured; and at dawn he was waiting for her at the hospital exit to tell her, while they headed toward the house, that he had been wrong, he had been wrong, and he recognized it openly and was willing to change, to be faithful to her, to do the laundry and wash the dishes, but she couldn't leave him, coño, because he loved her too much and he couldn't live without her. Up to now you could, Gisela replied, and now it was too late, things had gone cold over time, she was sorry but she felt like something inside her had died. It's not possible, he said, tried to quickly assume a dignified stance, and when they reached the house, he looked at her with all his love and asked her to let him come in. She murmured no, not today, she needed time to think about it.

Carlos thought that time would be on his side. When two or three days went by, she would be the one who would want to get back together, who would hate the miserable person who made the anonymous call as he did, asking himself how, why, who would find pleasure in destroying the lives of other people like that. Seventy-two hours later he approached her in a park near the hospital, what had she decided? "It's over," Gisela replied with a neutral voice, and she looked down on adding: "I was with someone else." Carlos broke into laughter as if he'd heard the best joke of his life, and nonetheless, from the first he knew it was true, that someone, probably a doctor, had kissed the lips, touched the breasts, penetrated the sex of his wife, spilling his dirty sperm there and making it impossible to fix things between them. He didn't feel fury, rather a dull-witted, growing hatred that revolved around the obscene desire to humiliate her, asking her for details: with whom, where, when, and how did it happen; and yes, he wanted her to tell him, he also had a right to know, it was his last right as a husband, his last wish, had she liked it? Answer, cojones! Had she liked it more than with him? No, she shouldn't start crying now, if she'd acted like a whore she should answer like a whore. She was leaving? Did she think he'd let her go like that? Well no, he'd walk with her, run after her, he wasn't going to leave her until telling her that this was what he got for marrying a black woman, because she was black, did she know that? And a whore, did she know that? And yes, he was crazy and what the fuck, crazy and ready to kill her, to rip her to pieces and ruin himself; no, he wasn't going to do it out of respect for his daughter, but he wanted her to know that he hated her and that he'd make her cry bloody tears, that he was going to get revenge by telling Mercedita, "Your mother's a whore, that's why I left her."

When Gisela slammed the door in his face, Carlos suddenly felt the magnitude of the hatred in which he was wallowing. A sudden weakness forced him to sit down on the sidewalk and break into tears. It wasn't possible he'd done what he did, said what he did, found dark pleasure in spilling onto Gisela the slime from the disgusting monster agitating in his head. It would have been better to kill himself or cut out his tongue. Killing himself was a good idea, a sweet idea from which emanated the promise of peace. Only death would save him from the memory (with a doctor, in a cheap hotel, on the night of September 15), would free him from the desire to know more, would redeem him with his dark revenge: he could already see Gisela crying with remorse over his coffin, Gisela crying, paying, feeling sorry. Blinded, he headed for his house, to look for his pistol. Halfway there he stopped. Was he remembering right? Had he called Gisela black as an insult? Had he spit on Chava's memory, making all the world's ceibas tremble with shame? He turned around and started to run. He had to implore her to forgive him, plead with her on his knees, for the love of God, to forget everything. He was panting when he entered the house. His mother-in-law accompanied him to her room, saying, "Love her for me, son, take care of her for me," and he closed the door behind him, and seeing the fear reflected in Gisela's face, looked at her helplessly. He had come to implore her to forgive him, to beg her for God's sake that she let him stay there, with her and his daughter; he understood everything, he forgave everything, he'd forgotten everything. No, she shouldn't tell him it was impossible, nothing was impossible. For love he could even accept, if there was no other way, the existence of the other man. Gisela covered his mouth with her hand, and Carlos started kissing it, knelt down, and looked at her from the floor; he wasn't getting up until she answered him. She sat down on the bed, took his chin, and looked at him through tears, she'd loved him so much, so much, that she didn't recognize him like this, where, oh God, where was her love? Carlos felt overwhelmed by a sweet tenderness and started kissing her tears and her trembling, feverish face and searched for her lips; but she closed her mouth. Then he asked her for pity's sake one last time, promised her that afterwards he would go, and she answered that you don't make love out of pity but because of desire, and also because of hate, as she was going to now, so that he could never forget that his woman was a black whore.

In that agonized coupling, sometimes slow and at other times desperate, they told each other face-to-face about their betrayals, their little miseries, their resentments, and they felt how disgust suddenly lifted them up to the infinite splendor where their best memories were alive, the ones they vowed to save from oblivion, while they consciously bit each other, left teeth marks and saliva on each other feeling how pleasure and pain, disgust and purity, love and hate merged together in the unfathomable sadness of the end. They finished exhausted, silent, spent, and slowly fell asleep. Carlos sank into a nightmare: he was running naked through the streets, provoking laughter like a clown, he got to Gisela's house and tried to enter, but the door was locked and the laughter redoubled at his contortions and his sobs. He woke up sweating, choking on a cry. Gisela lay at his side, naked; the reddish light of sunset filtering through the curtains made her skin glow, coppery, cinnamon-colored, toasted like layers of puff pastry. And what if he killed her? If he gripped that dear neck, fine and slender like a heron's, until giving her eternal rest and following her afterwards into the void? She wouldn't suffer, she'd enter her death asleep, slipping into it as if into a canal. The crime would be an act of love, a limitless offering to that neck that had been kissed by another man. No one could laugh afterwards at their stiff, naked bodies. He got up without making noise and sat down next to her. God, how beautiful she was! He gently lifted her head until it rested on the pillow. Now there was enough space for his fingers around her neck. Gisela slept like a child, why had she done it? Why had she let another male see her naked body? Her pretty little body, my love, her little body, how could he go on living? How could he look his buddies in the face? Didn't she realize she'd left him naked in front of every-one, made into a clown? Didn't she realize, darling, that if he was a man he had to kill her? He lovingly surrounded her neck with his fingers, felt a delicate sensation of pleasure, and knew that he would be aroused when he killed her, aroused like never before, with sublime horror. He began to press, Gisela's face took on an expression identical to Mercedita's when they kissed her while she slept, they looked so alike at that instant that Carlos stopped in terror, jumped off the bed, got dressed, and fled without looking back.

When he got to his house he was in a cold sweat, passed silently by his mother's emaciated stare, and locked himself in his room, asking himself what he had been doing the night of September 15. He couldn't remember. For the first time he bellowed against the times, before the Revolution women stayed at home, knew their place, his mother would never have thought of demand-ing that his father do laundry or wash dishes, she would rather have died than be with another man because things were clear, set, everyone had their place, and there was no room for this chaos that inevitably culminated in deception. Could they have been seen? Could someone know about his shame? Would the gossip already have run through the organization, turning him into a target for the jokes of the director and his clique? He started circling around the room as if that way he could escape his obsession. They'd be mocking him, by now they'd be dying with laughter. He pressed on his temples and banged his head against the wall, that's where his imagination and memory were; to blow it apart, the only escape was to blow it apart. He went to the night table, took the pistol, looked at the telephone, and felt a diabolic joy when he thought about calling Gisela to make her listen to the shot. He could see his own wake with total clarity, his desperation turned into tenderness before his serene face, intact because he had fired in the direction he was aiming: under the left nipple, straight into the heart. Then, from the perspective of death, he discovered his daughter hitting the glass of the coffin, calling to him as he had once called to his Grandfather Álvaro, and he lowered the weapon. He put it on the table, took Mercedita's picture out of his wallet, and placed it on the butt. She would be his saint, his Lady of Mercies, his Tiembla Tierra, she would protect him from death as she had protected her mother earlier. But she would never do anything like that, right? She'd never do that to a macho. The word turned his soul over when he associated it with his daughter. Mercedita hadn't been born to wash underwear or to put up with anyone's cheating. Tiembla Tierra was the name of a goddess, he had learned it in that very room many, too many, years ago, and as payment, punishment, and tribute he had baptized his little girl with it. And if in those dark times Mercedes, the servant in his home, had had to defend her female condition from the shadows, if she had washed the shitty underwear of her masters and of the men in her own family, if she had put up with cheating and drunks, beatings and hunger, she had also inspired the hope that some day, from on high, a river of fire would come down to sweep away that world of shit. And the river had come down, its waters tossing with people and joy, comic-book characters and coffins, dragging it all along to the beat of the huge conga line where he had discovered her doing the rumba, as happy as a freed goddess and giving to him, although neither he nor she knew it then, his daughter's name, Mercedes, Tiembla Tierra, the name of a hot, proud black woman that he pronounced halfway between disappointment and tenderness when he saw her in the hospital, attached to Gisela's tit, female, dark, adorable and defenseless as a kitten.

The earth trembled under the feet of the rumba dancers and night became day in Mercedes's far-off rumba, and it trembled again in Girón, with cannon fire, while during the October Crisis the darkness shone with the terrible fury of gunpowder, and was at the point of disappearing in the death rattle and the definitive light of the atomic mushroom cloud. But by then life was stirring in Gisela's womb, and now his daughter had the power to give him a painful, implacable lucidity. The river of justice that had overflowed wasn't perfect or pure, it pulled along sewage, dregs, heavy ballast, monstrous habits that generated their own pestilence. He knew this all too well, he had suspected that he, too, had a lot of shit inside, but he reacted in horror as he understood, looking at the photo, that he had been on the verge of killing Gisela and committing suicide because of such an embarrassing emotion as egotism. There was no way around it: if he wanted the future to be different, for his little girl to live in a cleaner world, if he wanted to be more revolutionary, he was obligated to accept that Gisela had as much right as he did to sleep with whomever she wanted. He collapsed onto the bed as if he'd reached the limit of his strength. Had he gone crazy? How could you imagine a revolutionary who was cheated on and cheerful? To be a revolutionary was to be a man above all, macho, male, masculine, cocksure to the death. He looked at the pistol and the photo again. Yes, he'd gone crazy, a man's man, a macho who got serious respect, would kill Gisela and the doctor and would brag about his deed saying, asere, a man don't never do himself in over some slut, and he'd go up da river while his bros sang a guaguancó about his honor, washed clean with the blood of a whore. And what the hell did that moral code of garbage have to do with the Revolution? And what did his own have to do with it either, made up of hesitation and lies? He gently stroked the photograph, asking himself if a revolutionary's moral code didn't consist of breaking those miserable standards and accepting once and for fucking all that women were equals, in bed and out, although it might hurt to the quick and rip him apart. That was how Gisela had acted, like an equal, and besides that she had had the blessed ovaries to tell him to his face. Now the truth was so concrete and close that he could grasp it: acting in accordance with her was the only way to recover his wife and his daughter. Did he dare? He swore on his mother's life that he did, closed his eyes, and felt that finally he could fall asleep.

When his mother woke him up twelve hours later, telling him that Felipe Martínez was in the living room, Carlos took a few minutes to understand and to remember, and then everything seemed more difficult to him. He refused to have breakfast and bathe and received his buddy in bed. Felipe came in like a tornado, he was bringing tremendous news, asere, but totally, truly tremendous! Carlos sat halfway up in bed and asked him if he'd seen Gisela. Felipe looked at him in confusion, who the hell said anything about Gisela, the report, my man! The Core Committee had approved it and sent it on up, a few days went by, and, bam, a high-level commission was created to study the matter, and who would have thought, Carlos, that, wham, the commission came down and verified everything, and, shazam, they decided to replace the director, pal, knock him off! That's good, commented Carlos, forcing a smile. Felipe came up so close he took him by the shoulders, what do you mean good, mulatto? It was fucking grrreat, and it was his victory, his, his, his, aren't you happy, my man? "Yes," said Carlos, and Felipe let go of his shoulders and sat down beside him, he had even better news, the Municipal

Committee had lowered his sanction to a year, and he'd found out that if Carlos appealed to the provincial, they could leave it at six months, signed and sealed, was he going to appeal? "I don't know," Carlos replied. Felipe stood up and started walking around the room with long strides, you can't go on like this, pal, you really can't go on like this, he was going to give him the last little bit to see if he'd perk up: he'd worked out a gig for him; a super little job, definitely good, director of personnel at a construction company where he'd have wheels and a secretary; he'd wind up better off than before, mulatto, and his father had always told him it was a lot better to be director than subordinate, fantastic, no? "Fantastic," mused Carlos sadly, and for the first time Felipe changed his approach and with a stealthy voice asked him what was the matter, *negro*, tell me man to man. "Gisela cheated on me," said Carlos, and noticed how his friend's face darkened as if he'd gotten the news of a death. Felipe was a brother, maybe the only one whom he could ask for the favor that he needed like air. "Tell her to come," Carlos told him, "let her know how I am and tell her I need her and I forgive her." Felipe looked like he'd been slapped in the face, what the hell was he saying? Had he gone crazy or fucking what? Carlitos, hell, when I arrived your pura said you were really, really, really bad, but I never thought you'd be such a pansy, do you realize what you're saying? "That I love her," Carlos confessed, and Felipe replied that that was faggoty crap, and got all red as he shouted, "Cojones, better dead than two-timed!" His words were the lash that defeated Carlos's last bit of strength, and left him motionless, mute, nodding to his buddy's philippic on the moral code of a man's man. When Felipe left an hour later, promising to come back, Carlos knew he would have to get a divorce. He imagined Gisela deceiving him as many times as he'd deceived her, or even worse, doing it and telling him about it, and he thought for an instant that she'd slept with a black or a foreigner and felt a sharp pain in his chest. No, he wasn't going to put up with this, it wasn't in his very balls because, thank God, he'd been born macho, white, and Cuban, and for the same reason he wasn't going to be faithful to any woman, either. He'd poke any woman, Chinese, black, or white who came on to him, but his woman, his wife, would have to walk the line, straight and narrow. He wasn't a new man, not a damn, to accept this equality that anyone could confuse with faggoty-assed crap. He would take that job, get to be buddies with the new director, have a ball with the car, keep chipping away until he got an apartment, eat like a beast, and get it on with thousands of girls with whom he'd drink good rum and dance to a good *son*, and he wouldn't have anybody giving him sermons: living was one thing, and knowing how to live was another.

When he stood up he felt dizzy, but drew enough strength from his project to ask his mother for a bath and dinner. She treated him like a king, and he noted that his plan had begun to work. No more lines for the minuscule bathroom at his in-laws' house, or at the pizzeria, or the grocery store; no more fried eggs for lunch and for breakfast; now, instead of giving his quota of meat to Mercedita, he'd get his mother's. She was very happy with his conversation with Felipe and was shooting off sparks against Gisela, that crazy woman who had dared to deceive her son. After eating his full, still sweating from the black-bean soup in the uncertain steaminess of early October, he got back into bed. Years of working at night and on guard duty had created a feeling in him of always being sleepy, and his plan included reimbursing himself for that expenditure that hadn't yielded the least benefit. The sheets were very clean, fresh, starched like they never were at Gisela's house. He felt a placid indulgence, good for dedicating hours and hours to the invention of the brilliant future whose disgustingness attracted him like a whirlpool. The whole of Havana would talk about him, he'd make himself king of la dolce vita, that secret, easy existence that stupid shitheads didn't know anything about. Every night he'd mix with the people at the Wakamba, the most fabulous team of screwarounds of the many that had battered the town. Friendly drunks, fired functionaries, double-edged philosophers who spent their lives drinking and fucking in the Screwaround Contest, guided by their bible, the *Manual of Musical Socialism*, whose first verse, "Man is always and under any circumstances a sensual being . . ." was at the same time their decalogue. And that was where it was at, bro, where it was at, explained the screwarounds to whoever wanted to listen to them in the wee hours at the Wakamba, where they turned up after being involved in really entertaining scandals. Carlos often pulled in there, too, because it was the best place in the Vedado to eat after three in the morning. He had met Mongó, the painter whose masterpiece, according to what the Press—a lady friend of his who'd been in the can—declared, was an accent mark as yellow as a sunflower over an enormous *O*, an emblematic accent, because his own name wasn't Mongo, but Mongó, like Van Gogh; Johnny Fucker, Walker's cousin, who emotionally recited his poem without words, "Numbers"; and his near namesake Juan Carlos Leo, the Gutripper, who called himself a professional pornographer, an amateur philosopher, and a catechumen by vocation, and he often explained to the parishioner to his left, because he was a leftist, that the essence of musical socialism wasn't work, much less sacrifice, merit or effort, but being with it; it was a matter, most illustrious dipsomaniac seated to my sinister side, of being with it, *en la onda*, and la onda, the sorceress, would attract nymphs, astromobiles, *sons*, elixirs, and something to chew on, with which one would arrive at the superior state, or stage, or phase of life: Musical Kommunism. The errrorrr of our politics, the Gutripper then shouted, moving his big mitts around fast, consisted in our not having realized that this country was the biggest producer of asses per square meter on the whole planet; asses, yes, asses, didn't the gentleman like them? Yes? *Equelecuá, quindi*, in the international division of labor we were by definition the screwaround country, did he want to sign up for the contest they were organizing? The first time that Carlos heard the rapid-fire gab he had a great time and asked them to explain to him the code on the blackboard hanging on the cafe wall. The Gutripper immediately did him the honor: Under the *P* were listed the names of the participants in the contest; cs stood for chicks scored, and ja, jag assessment or juicings acquired; reports were made daily to him, the notary, who took charge of scrupulously verifying both the quality of the jags as well as the fact that the piece of flesh taken was different every time, and of assigning additional points for the concurrence of attenuating circumstances: premeditation, nocturnal timeframe, malice afore-thought, height scaled, and advantage; at the end of the month the winner was selected, monarch of the Wakamba, king of la dolce vita, and they bought him as many drinks as he was capable of downing. Carlos considered all this to be a kind of craziness and came to feel sorry for them; but now, recalling the girls that the Wakambans had wakamboed, he felt a terrific envy, growing desires to join the wakamboing, and he wondered where the attraction of the screwarounds lay; they went around drunk, badly dressed, and treated the Wakambettes like dogs, but horror seemed to exercise an uncontrollable fas-cination over a certain type of woman. He could do it, he would do it, he'd drink until he was able to show off his limp and his bare gums, "So what's hap-pening, Gutripper? Kin Charli is here," he'd say while a red-headed Wakam-bette was waiting for him, her breasts dotted with hickeys. At the threshold of sleep he succeeded in getting her, showing her off to his associates, and he went to sleep drunk with joy. But suddenly the Wakambans were laughing in his face and he started running, naked and toothless, and in front of Gisela's house once again suffered the horror of the clown. He woke up with a cry and the room, dark, seemed to him like an extension of the nightmare. He stood in front of the mirror: he was that shadow who had tried to be a hero who had tried to be an architect who had tried to be a guerrilla fighter; that was what he was, someone who had tried to be.

When Felipe returned, three days later, Carlos was still in bed going over the milestones of his disgrace, imagining decisive battles, wondering what had become of poor Iraida, wishing that something would happen in his life. He smiled on seeing his buddy, maybe today he'd take him to the construction company, maybe tomorrow he'd start working. But Felipe arrived really down, his head lowered, and Carlos was thinking there probably wasn't any work for him when his friend halted next to the bed and said: "They say that Che was killed." Carlos stood up, feeling that it wasn't possible to talk about that lie on his back, because it was a lie, right? It was a lie, he said, and grabbed onto his friend to hide his consternation and dizziness. "I don't know," Felipe replied, handing him a copy of *Granma*. "I hope so." Carlos took the newspaper, groped his way over to the window, opened it, and was blinded by the light. When he looked again, the room had lost its sadness. *Granma* didn't say that Che had died, it even made clear that it lacked reliable information, it limited itself to publishing several cables datelined from Bolivia affirming that nonsense. Felipe was waiting for his opinion, had always waited for it, and Carlos felt that his mind was clearing up and recuperating the ability to speculate, Che *could not* be dead, therefore, he was alive, evidently more alive than ever; *Granma* had published the cables for tactical reasons, to confuse the enemy by making them think that we believed their lie was true; when the Granma yacht disembarked the same had been said about Fidel. Felipe finally smiled, coño, compadre, that makes me happy as hell, and he went over to Carlos who had spread out an atlas on the bed and paged through it in a frenzy until he stopped at the map of Bolivia, onto which he started marking the places mentioned in the cable while he improvised a long reflection on the foco theory, on rural guerrillas as a party and *not* a simple armed branch of an urban organization, and on the prolonged popular war as in Vietnam, towards which the process of Latin American liberation would inevitably tend. Felipe was in agreement, as always, but unfortunately he had to leave, could they go tomorrow to the company? Carlos said no, with the pretext of family matters; it would have to be another time. The false news and his political lucubration had revealed to him that he wasn't meant for administrative jobs. He accompanied Felipe to the door and calmed him down, don't worry, he wouldn't get back together with Gisela in a million years, his problem now was to try to get a profound understanding of the operation in Bolivia. The next day, *Granma* published new cables that seemed to confirm the news, but Carlos reassured himself with the tactical-reasons theory, and devoted all his time to drawing a big map of Latin America to mark zones of guerrilla activity and to try to define what was the weakest link in the imperialist chain. He felt personally responsible for events, working as if his own conclusions were absolutely urgent. But he hadn't advanced much when he read in *Granma* that official Argentine sources were confirming the disaster. He went back to his work and was suddenly seized by the conviction that the impossible had happened: Che was dead. And nevertheless, he was still right: there were the volcanoes from which, when things really heated up, would come the fire to make the earth tremble and to change the face of America. Without a doubt that was so, but Che was dead, "Ñancahuazú," "Vado del Yeso," "Quebrada del Yuro" had become part of his vocabulary and of history, and he could not stay shut up in that room.

Going into the living room he told his mother that yes, it was true and that she shouldn't cry, but in the street he felt confused. He didn't have anywhere to go, no one needed his presence or his opinion. He was walking around aimlessly when he remembered that he should do something very, very important: explain it to Mercedita. He went off running towards Gisela's house knowing it would be better to wait for a bus, but that he wouldn't have the patience for it. He went down Twenty-Seventh taking advantage of the slope, crossed Infanta, left the Vedado and, going into Cayo Hueso, heard silence, that unheard-of silence. It was a neighborhood of old houses and heavily populated tenements, and now the streets were full as always, but no one was shouting, or singing, or playing a rumba on the drums. Knocking on the door, he was seized by the fear of having to face Gisela, but she was at work and he took Mercedita by the hand and walked to Trillo Park, wondering how you explain death. No, he told his daughter, Che wasn't in heaven but rather in memory, did she remember him? Well then that's where he was living, watching. "Is he always on guard duty?" she asked, and he replied yes, smiled on hearing her say, "Poor thing," and he explained that Che suffered every time a child was bad, every time a man or a woman forgot their duties. Pronouncing those words, he didn't imagine that he'd be recalling them later, on seeing that *Granma* confirmed the tragedy and the photo of soldiers at Girón with their rifles in the air. In that sea of fists had been his own, now slackened and unable to take the baton. Consternated, furious, he thought about it again during the

Memorial, impassioned on *seeing* the words of the poem; a horse of fire carrying that guerrilla sculpture, amid the wind and the clouds of the Sierra, and he heard himself repeating, "Wait for us. We will go with you," but at the end, for the first time, Fidel's words didn't bring on applause but a shocking silence, and he was seized by anguish, asking himself what to do to achieve the impossible, to remotely resemble that model. Now it wasn't enough for him to hide in the old trick of imagining that he was fighting and achieving victory: he needed *to do* something, and fast. On arriving at the end of Paseo he noted the huge lack of synchrony between his desperation and the concentrated calm of the thousands of people silently abandoning the plaza. He stopped, feeling a tranquil strength overtaking him, he was one among the millions who tomorrow would return to work, without letting their dead die completely. But he wouldn't have anywhere to go, he wasn't willing to accept the comfortable bureaucratic future Felipe proposed. And what if he went far away, very far from Gisela and from himself, to work in the sugar harvest as a cane cutter, a machetero, in Camagüey? He rejected that idea that would separate him from Mercedita, from his mother, and, above all, from the possibility of getting Gisela back. He hadn't invested years of his life training himself as a political cadre to end up beside a cane plant; his limp would impede him from making it through the entire harvest, under the ferocious sun of the cane fields. Suddenly, those same reasons began to work in favor of the idea, it became clear to him that leaving, accepting the challenge, defeating his miseries would allow him to think about Che without shame, like an anonymous soldier in his troops, and he started walking at a calm pace, corresponding to that of the crowd.

He had to draw strength from that decision a week later, when the new director called him to his office, congratulated him for the courage he showed in the report, and apologized for not being able to immediately reinstate him at the CEI; it wouldn't be tactically good, he said, a lot of fuss had been raised about the matter and it was better to let things smooth out; he wanted to inform Carlos that the compañeros on the Core Committee had gone to him, asking that he reconsider the problem; doing without a cadre as able as Carlos really hurt him, but it was just a temporary decision; in six months, a year at most, he would be with them again; but for now, would he accept a job as an analyst at the Ministry of Foreign Commerce? Carlos thought how that was the solution to his problems, but now he didn't have the time or the moral will to accept it. Gisela, Mercedita, his mother, Felipe, and the compañeros of his contingent all knew that he had decided to leave; he had a commitment to them, to himself, and to Che's memory.

"No," he said, "I don't accept." The brusque manner in which he spoke caused a misinterpretation requiring him to explain, his negative answer wasn't the result of resentment or pride, he was aware that he had committed an error, that it had its cost, and precisely for that reason he needed to prove himself in another area. The new director smiled softly and showed Carlos his hands, too large for his body. "Just think," he said, "from the time I was eleven I was cutting cane, then the war came and now I'm here, and you, with those office-worker's hands . . ." Carlos stayed quiet, looking at the director's big hands, until the latter said to him: "OK, when the zafra's over you'll come back with us, agreed?" "Iraida?" he dared to ask, and the director told him not to worry, she was fine, working as a secretary for Pocho Fornet in the Municipal Library, cataloging books, and now at the door he said goodbye with an embrace.

Carlos was calm, with the certainty of having done the right thing, until the afternoon when he signed his divorce papers like a death certificate, and again felt the wish to kill himself in the dusty, desolate notary's office from which he left with Gisela, downcast. He intuited some secret meaning in the fact that his breakup and his leaving had coincided, and it was difficult for him to move forward with the wooden suitcase banging against his knee and the *mocha*, the short, wide machete, under his arm. Until that moment Gisela had been tense, as if pressed by an imperious need for it to be over, but now she was walking in silence while he tried to find something to say, recalled his first love letter, and looked out of the corner of his eye at those hands that this time wouldn't be curing his wounds. On arriving at the train station he stopped underneath the banner saluting the heroic macheteros of the "Che Guevara" contingent, and asked, "Do you remember?" "I remember," she said. A locomotive snorted on the platform, the loudspeakers transmitted the Guerrilla Fighter's Anthem, people were shouting goodbye, and the racket accentuated the silence that again grew between them. Carlos lowered his head repeating between his teeth: "*Guerrillero, guerrillero, guerrillero adelante, adelante . . .*" Suddenly he stopped murmuring and said, "Talk to the girl about me." "Yes," Gisela said in a low voice. After a few, very slow seconds they looked each other in the eyes and by coincidence both said, "Well . . ." Gisela started to smile and her smile broke apart on her lips. Carlos knew he could kiss her and tried to do so, but as he went close he hit her legs with his suitcase, stopped, put the suitcase down, and when he looked at Gisela again something indefinable had changed. "It really was good," she said then, "in spite of everything." Carlos looked towards the tracks: "Can I write to you?" "Of course," she said, and he found hope in her tone, and nurtured the idea of putting his arms around her waist and trying to go back home, but looking at her, he knew if he dared do that everything would fall apart, that he had to leave, and he said, "Goodbye" and heard her shout, "Take care!" while he went towards the train and the suitcase hit his knee again. Alongside him, people were singing.

TWENTY

But from the very first letter, Gisela, you forbade him from talking of love, from using hundreds of words; from writing, for example, *it's a starry night*, although he liked to lie on his back and look at the stars and the moon the color of old gold, and to think about you and imagine going back. When he sat down and wrote the date, he didn't know what to talk about, except for his desperation to see you, and he went blank before the paper until he wrote your name, *Gisela*, with that trembling, uneven handwriting, like a child's. Then, in his first not-love letter, he talked to you about his hands.

They had swollen up so much they seemed to belong to another body. On the right one, the base of the fingers, between the thumb and the index finger and the second and third phalanges, had the skin peeled away. During the first hour of cane-cutting he got blisters filled with sticky, burning liquid that then exploded into reddish sores. What hurt most was closing the hand to hold the mocha or the pen. In contrast, the left hand suffered more gradually, he used it to clear away the plants and little by little it became covered with scratches, wounds, small cuts that the reeds stuck into, burning like a thousand needle pricks. Even so, it was in a lot better shape that its mate. If he'd been left-handed, now he'd have nice handwriting, but on the right, not even the lifeline remained.

In the next letter he talked to you about the rest of his body and about time. The hardest hours were at dawn, when he was awakened by the call "On your feeeet!" in the middle of a damp, blue cold that seemed encased in the very center of his bones; at midday, when a blaze of fire flattened him against the cane field, making the edges of his hat feel like a crown of thorns; and at two in the afternoon, when it took all the courage in the world to go back to the field after the indulgence of the siesta. His arms and legs trembled from the effort, his head exploded underneath the sun and the hat, and the foot he limped with kept folding under him as he misjudged the always uncertain height of the mounds. But the pain was centered in his lower back. That was where it raged when he stood up, bent over the plants, turned around to toss the cane into the pile, and even when he sat down to write. He found relief only at night, when he stretched out in his hammock and counted his aches and pains as if they were virtues or money. That's how he ended the letter, because it was then, at night, when he stroked his sex with his wounded hands, dreaming that he was making love with you, and tortured himself with the jealousy that drove him crazy. And he couldn't talk to you about that, Gisela.

Days later, with his body almost accustomed to fieldwork, he wrote you about the imaginary inventions. Some nights before he'd left the barracks to urinate, and on the way he met Acana leaning up against a liana, looking at the full moon.

"What's up," Carlos said to him.

Acana grabbed him by the arm and without taking his eyes off the sky remarked:

"I was thinking, asere, that if we planted cane on the moon, we wouldn't have to lift it or haul it; cut and toss, cut and toss, and the cane would get into the tippler all by itself, flying."

When he repeated the story, Gisela, inventions became the fashion. Selling cane uncut; telling the Japanese, for example, from here to the sea all this cane is yours, it costs so much, period. Then let them cut it down, let the wind cut it down, let Lola cut it down with her moving around. There were more elaborate ideas, like planting the cane on conveyor belts so that by itself it would hit against a blade placed at the edge. But the invention that won unanimous approval was the planting of sugar trees, which would grow the sugar already refined and bagged. You couldn't deny it, that one was as nice as the idea of being back home.

He would usually invent ideas during the hardest hours of work, and that's what he was doing when he saw it on the horizon. Too large to be a lift, too tall to be a truck, it advanced against the light in such a way that from a distance it looked black, followed by three jeeps that were like fleas next to it. He pulled down his hat to block out the sun and to be sure that he wasn't seeing things;

that those greenish-black lines that the machine seemed to yank out of the earth, split in the air, and pile up in a cart were cane stalks and not an optical illusion. When he was sure, Gisela, he didn't know if he'd gone crazy or if the craziness of their inventions had become reality. It didn't matter, he wrote you that night, what happened was that his compañeros were jumping beside him and he, too, jumped and yelled, and waved his mocha and hat in the air and ran cheering, while the machine advanced like a mastodon able to do the task of forty men without even one blister and with no aching bones. When they got near it, the operator stopped and greeted them:

"*Zdrávstvuite, tavarichi!*"

It amused him to hear Russian being spoken in a cane field, and he felt badly about the awful way the heat punished the Soviet, who seemed to be at the point of dissolving into a pool of sweat. Then he heard applause and cheers, but didn't pay any attention because he had come up close to the machine, painted yellow and red, that shone in the countryside like a coat of arms. He wanted to touch it, thinking it would bring him good luck, and leaned down to stroke its blades. At that moment someone put an arm around his shoulders, asking him what he thought about it. The voice sounded familiar, he turned his head and almost keeled right over. Fidel was leaning over next to him, Gisela, looking at the blades. When he managed to recover, he thought he should make a military salute or something like that, but it was impossible because Fidel kept an arm around his shoulders and repeated the question.

"Perfect, Comandante," he responded in the most serious way he could.

"No, chico," Fidel said to him. "The blades are very high, look how much they left uncut . . . isn't that where most of the sugar is concentrated?"

His hands were pointing now to the stump of cane. They were unexpectedly slender, Gisela, perhaps somewhat small for Fidel's height, and they too showed the tracks of the mocha. It was probably the familiar way in which Fidel contradicted him that made him say impulsively:

"Yes, Comandante, but no. The ground is lower here, so it's logical that the blades would hit higher up."

"The way the ground is prepared is a factor," Fidel admitted, feeling the slope with his fingers, "but the height of the blades is something else, because when the ground gets lower the machine goes down too, isn't that right? And besides, on flat land we have the same problem. What do you think?" he asked, directing himself to the group surrounding him.

A discussion immediately struck up about the virtues and defects of the machine: the power of the motor, the type of steel, the height of the blades, the stony land, the burned cane, the sugar yields . . . Fidel aimed his infinite questions towards the Soviet and Cuban consultants and engineers who were debating and incessantly taking notes. When all of them had given their opinions, Fidel turned to him once more.

"It will be done as I say," he sentenced. "How are things around here?"

"Very good, Comandante. Perfect."

"Chico," said Fidel, "is everything perfect for you?"

He felt himself getting red, Gisela, from the laughter that followed the comment, but the Comandante himself came to his aid.

"Leave your compañero alone," he said, again putting an arm around his shoulders. "Cutting cane is such hard work that you have to take it on like that, with enthusiasm. It's just that I'm always curious. So, all of you, how are you doing here?"

The first concrete answers provoked more questions, now aimed at details, from the average cut, to the quality of the housing and the food, and then Fidel promised to talk with the Municipal Party comrades to see if it would be possible to improve the supply of boots, shirts, gloves, and the frequency of newspaper deliveries. That machine, he told them, was a reality thanks to the collaboration of Soviet comrades, but it would still be many years before they succeeded in completely mechanizing the cutting; meanwhile, the nation's treasury would depend on the macheteros, on their effort, sweat, and conscience. Then, Gisela, when he realized that Fidel was leaving, he tried to explain that the machine had seemed perfect to him because in a way he had dreamed it, and he told him about their inventions. Fidel started to laugh, above all he praised the idea of planting cane on the moon because it demonstrated sensibility, he said, and because it posed a challenge. To plant cane on the moon was a symbol of what was seemingly impossible, but in order to finally end the prehistory of human society, the people had to conquer tasks like that one. He said goodbye to the macheteros one by one, shaking their hands, and went towards his jeep. He had opened the door when he turned around to ask what was the Revolution, compañeros, if not a permanent struggle against the impossible.

That night, Gisela, he wrote you the most intense letter of his life. He was happy, he had done well to come to Camagüey, and he wanted you to admire him a little bit, although he didn't tell you so. He even got to thinking that he'd win your love again, overcome his jealousy, it would be his personal victory over the impossible. The brigade's encounter with Fidel, he wrote you days later, was told and retold around the area until it reached mythic proportions. The supplies improved, annoying the other brigades who got horribly jealous. To calm them, the party's Municipal Committee designated his brigade to cut down some ruined fields that other groups had steered clear of. The men accepted reluctantly, not because they feared the effort, Gisela, but because getting themselves into the *caguazo*, the old, unproductive cane, would lower their average load and their chances to win the regional competition. They left their boarding house while it was still nighttime, making jokes, but when they got to the field their hearts sank, it looked like a field of tall grass where you couldn't see the PPQK stalks, those *Pepecucas* whose only virtues were their enormous resistance to plagues and their fecundity, demonstrated in times when there were no fertilizers or pesticides. On the other hand, they were very difficult to chop, a long, skinny cane, dragging low and hard as iron, pure caguazo. Looking at it, he thought they should refuse and later he admitted it to you, ashamed of himself; but at that moment Heberto Orozco, the brigade leader, raised his mocha and said a silly thing:

"Gentlemen, let us plant the moon."

From the first he adopted the habit of insulting that damned cane while he chopped it. Since the fucker often dragged low and you had to search for the plant among the grass, he called it a majá, a snake, a poisonous serpent, a rattlesnake, a python, a boa constrictor, and from so much thinking that he was killing vipers he really started seeing them, Gisela, in the hours when the sun was making him crazy. Then he offended Pepe, Cuca, and their whole family of bastard children, drunken grandfathers, and smuggler cousins. When Orozco said they had to finish by December 31, Carlos thought he'd gone mad, because too much cane was still standing, but there was no other choice. Orozco was the kind of madman who put his mocha where his mouth was.

At dawn on the thirty-first there was still enough cane for two brigades. He was sure of their defeat and suggested that they ask for reinforcements. Orozco, Gisela, was a tall, strong man, as proud as a ceiba and white as a Gallego: the sun punished him more than anyone. Nevertheless, he was always the first one in and the last one out of the fields. He didn't even respond to the suggestion, looked at his mocha, his arms, and went into the cane field as if he were ready to take it down alone. He had the virtue of leading by his actions, and once more they followed him and worked, truly, more than ever. But it became clearer and clearer that they couldn't finish the task. Under the setting sun, blazing and sad as a fire, they chopped ferociously and when it got dark they put down their mochas with the calm of those who have done everything possible. Then Orozco showed that he was totally mad and ordered that oil lamps be brought in. They carried out the order, Gisela, out of respect for that stubborn delusion. The flickering lights, as they had known would be the case, weren't enough to light the field. But they kept on chopping, slowly now, at risk of severing a leg. They looked like phantoms, the ghosts of dead macheteros, condemned to cut cane forever. Around nine o'clock, the clouds hiding the moon moved away and a spectral light covered the field. Since the heat wasn't bothering them now, they speeded up their rhythm. At ten they started telling themselves that maybe it would be possible, and at eleven they were sure that if they didn't rest for even a minute, if they concentrated that immense strength that can only be born from madness on their work, they would succeed in singing the anthem before twelve, as they did sing it, Gisela, on the clean field, illuminated by the moon.

The Municipal Party honored them and placed them in a field in Puerto Rico Nine Eighty, a pure, beautiful cane, slender as a girl, so that they could recover their lost *arrobas* and try to win the competition. He would never have thought, Gisela, that Heberto Orozco, the leader whom he admired as if he were his father, would be the cause of his most bitter moment in the zafra. He worked, he swore he did, until he was dying. But when they did the quarterly check, his brigade lost by seventy-five arrobas, and it became clear that he, the machetero who came up shortest, was the cause, and Orozco, really upset, threw it back in his face. That night, Gisela, he promised himself that nothing like that would ever happen again. He remembered that the speed of a band of guerrillas was equal to that of its slowest man, and he decided to lengthen his workday to reach the average. The next day he left an hour early for the cutting and worked alone, in the moonless night, by the light of a little oil lamp. When the brigade arrived, Orozco didn't even greet him. Very few times, Gisela, had he felt such rage against a person.

Several nights later the fire took them by surprise. He was writing to you now with singed hands, there had been a moment when he thought he'd never be able to. He was asleep when he heard the shouts and didn't jump out of his cot right away because he thought it was a joke, one of the many that the macheteros played to kill their homesickness. He reacted to the coming and going of people getting dressed and started doing it, too, still dazed by sleep. When he went out of the boarding house he saw in the distance, burning, the fields of Puerto Rico Nine Eighty. A dense cloud of smoke was rising into the reddened sky. Orozco, desperate, was calling to the men from the truck by banging on the roof of the cab with his mocha. Carlos climbed in over the wheel and seconds later the truck, raising up a cloud of dust on the slope, turned into the first pathway and continued on through the fields, bumping along. In the distance the blaze had grown; over the motor's noise could be heard the dull crackle of charred cane. The truck moved forward in jumps and starts over the uneven pathway, making him think they would never get there. Just then the direction of the wind changed, and the fire started coming towards them. They saw, at a crossroads, another brigade crowding into a cart pulled by a tractor, and the shadows of a cordon of macheteros opening a new path.

"Hey, you in the truck!" shouted one of the shadows.

Suddenly, a man jumped up towards the running board, banged against the door, and nearly slipped and fell under the wheels.

"Are you stupid?" Carlos shouted.

The man stuck his head, blackened by smoke, into the cab and said:

"Go back, dern it, go back!"

The suffocating, dense smoke had reached them, clouding their vision. The truck suddenly braked, and the man fell onto the path. Behind them, the flames had jumped the firebreak, the blaze was now rising on both sides. The truck began the torturous maneuver of making a U-turn. Orozco jumped down to help the man stand up. They boarded the truck as it was moving, on the running board, when it had finished making the turn and was heading straight for the fire.

"Floor it!" yelled Orozco. "Floor it, cojones!"

In first gear, pedal pressed to the floor, the truck jumped towards the right edge of the pathway, where the fire still hadn't caught on entirely, and flew past the flames.

"Saints alive, we've been reborn!" yelled the man.

Five hundred meters away they stopped and jumped down to the road, mochas in hand. A group of peasants came over to meet them.

"By Beelzebub!" said Sandalio Oduardo. "It's Orozco! What should we do?"

"Whatever you say," replied Heberto.

Sandalio turned toward the field on fire and said, without raising his voice:

"It's already jumped one firebreak; if it goes past the slope and hits the new cane in Medialuna, the world's gonna go spinning right down t'hell."

"So what should we do then?" asked Acana.

Sandalio didn't seem to have heard him. He was still looking at the field, as if he wanted to measure the distances, the wind direction, and the fire's voracity.

"Orozco," he said, "we have to open up another path right here."

"So far away?"

"It's not far," replied Sandalio. "Fire is a woman; if you back down she'll surround you and fry you."

"And the slope?"

"I'll take care of it," he said, and turning around he left, followed by five peasants.

"Make a path here!" shouted Orozco.

The cordon of macheteros lined up to chop. At first the relative remoteness of the flames and the cool night allowed them to work rapidly, and he wondered, Gisela, what Sandalio was going to do against the fire with only five macheteros. Later, the smoke and the heat turned the path into an inferno, burning smut began flying over the field like shooting stars and the conjuring and shouts of hatred began, "Sparks, your mother!" "Kill the wretch!" and the men set themselves to defending the path they had opened up off a firebreak, killing the fire on the dusty ground, containing the red dragon tongues the next field had turned into, stamping their feet to put out the burning reeds in the middle of the path, dragging the burning plants towards the flames so that fire would consume fire, sweating, burning in their hand-to-hand with the fire, panting, exhausted, they saw how a whirling wind was making the flames spin towards the slope that led to the vast fields of Medialuna.

"Stop, you bitch; stop, wind!"

Now there were only sparks jumping from the side of the path, and Orozco ordered:

"Ten stay here, the rest come with me!"

He followed him, Gisela, running through the path towards the field where the flames had risen up more than ever, setting the sky on fire, and afterwards he wondered how many times the night would have to be turned into day for this country to be able to work in peace.

"Sandalio, coño, where are you?" yelled Orozco.

"Stop, you bitch; stop, wind!" he yelled.

But it was clear that neither a threat, nor conjuring, nor God himself coming down from above could keep the fire from jumping over the slope, hitting the Medialuna fields, spinning down the world, burning Sandalio and his folks to a crisp, and getting to the Tumbasiete mill town, devouring it. When Orozco halted, he did likewise, confused. He knew the brigade couldn't do anything against a fire like that, but it seemed like a faggoty thing to abandon the peasants to their fate.

"What's going on?" he said.

"Look!" Orozco shouted.

Another blaze had started on the edges of the slope. Stunned, he watched it, and thought that now the extent of the disaster would be enough to crush anyone's will, even Orozco's, and he felt powerless. Then it happened: blaze and counterblaze crashed in the air, lifted each other, entwined in a roaring whirlwind, and fire ate fire until it disappeared as if hell itself had swallowed it up. It was a beautiful and terrible spectacle, Gisela, they were still full of hate when they pissed on the ashes to crown their victory.

Orozco decided to chop that cane that very morning, and a small riot broke out. The other brigade leaders had given the entire day off to rest. For the first time, the men of the "Suárez Gayol" threatened out loud not to follow an order. Orozco ordered that breakfast be brought to the field and after drinking a glass of scalded milk and eating a hard piece of bread, said to them: "Goddamn sissies," and went alone into the cane fields.

The brigade leader divided men into the sissics, and the ones who had balls. In the brigade, there was no worse stigma than falling into the first group. But this time it seemed like several of them, led by Acana, were willing to run the risk. The tension was palpable, Gisela, if the men didn't go into the field Orozco would have to resign as leader. He was the first one to follow, tipping the balance, and only to you would he dare confess that, even beyond the hate he had stored up, he felt an obsessive need to gain the respect of that man.

He imagined he'd succeeded, although he didn't know that for certain, Orozco didn't say much. But a lot of people didn't understand, and that day, that day especially, was very hard, until the average of the "Suárez Gayol" jumped spectacularly, and they took the lead in the competition, because of the volume of burned cane that they put into the tippler that very afternoon. The most serious problem that that victory left him, personally, was dirty clothing. Burned cane, without reeds, is easy to chop, but it's as black as a poet's tears when it bursts, and the resin covers you with a greasy coating. No matter how much he washed his pants and shirt, they never got their original color back.

February came in really cold, Gisela, but along with March it was the best part of the zafra. His hands, he informed you as big news, had formed calluses, round, yellow calluses that allowed him to reach the average of most of the brigade, overcome his complexes, and participate in the jokes, almost always innocent, that they played in the house and the roads through the fields. One was so fine that he couldn't resist the temptation to tell you about it. It had to do with a machetero nicknamed the Rooster, because he was the first one awake and he liked to say "on your feet" with a deafening "cock-a-doodle-doo" before leaving to play his joke on the next brigade. He had his own rooster, an old, round alarm clock that invariably went off at a quarter to five. That night, while he was sleeping, the rascals set it for three o'clock. And at three, with the first ring, the Rooster jumped out of his cot with his face puffy from sleep.

"On your feeeet!" he yelled. "Cock-a-doodle-doooo!" he sang.

And he left as always to urinate, wash his face, and bug his neighbors. The next brigade almost killed him, Gisela, someone even slapped him with the flat side of the machete. Meanwhile, in the boarding house, the rascals set all the clocks back, smoothed out the blankets, put on tired faces, and set up a game of dominoes. When the Rooster came running back to his corral, he was left speechless.

"What time is it?" he asked.

"Midnight," said Loose Hips as if nothing were up, and added: "I fold."

The Rooster looked at his watch in silence and tried in vain to verify it: all the clocks said twelve.

"I could have sworn . . ." he started to say, when a spectacular guffawing left his mouth hanging open.

It was probably that very night when he conceived his revenge. Two days later, he was hanging by a noose when they awoke. It was a terrible sight, Gisela, to see him dangling from a rope underneath the center beam of the barracks. Orozco reacted instantaneously, cutting the cord with one slice, and the Rooster fell onto his feet.

"Cock-a-doodle-doooo, I got yooooou!" he sang at the top of his voice.

Yes, February and March, like he told you, were the best months of the zafra. In April the waters came in. Worse than the fire, Gisela, the rain. The fire shouted out its presence, but the rain was a fox; it appeared with a quiet noise that promoted sleepiness and made people cheerful when it got them out of working. But if it lasted, as it was lasting, it brought with it the sparrow, a terribly sad bird that nested in the macheteros' chests during the gray mornings, the ashy sunsets, and the nights without moon or stars. He became accustomed to seeing the river of nostalgia that spilled over the field, and to remembering. When he thought he was going to go crazy, a wine-colored stain started to grow on the wall next to his cot, and to escape the river and the remembering he devoted himself to studying it. At first it was something undefined, but as the hours went by it acquired the form of a child in a woman's belly, and the next morning it was a cloud. He called that little cloud Mercedes, that over time became a ship to navigate through the dark waters of remembrance. There was no way he could avoid it. The dampness had covered everything, the walls and the sheets, the floor and his memory.

The end was nearing, Gisela, and he was feeling better. Regarding that, he wanted to confess a little thing he was proud of to you. On 15 April Orozco called a brigade meeting, following the instructions of the Party Municipal Committee, and asked if by chance there was anyone there who had fought in Girón. When he raised his mocha, there was a second of silence, and then applause. Orozco asked him to say a few words, and he, at first, didn't know what to say. The majority of his compañeros weren't expecting that the slowest one, the clumsiest one during the initial days, would also be an ex-combatant. Such was life. Before opening his mouth he felt afraid. His work had gotten him used to giving talks, to going on in harangues, and he knew those men well enough to know they wouldn't stand for that. He was drawing a blank when Acana said:

"Tell us, pal, go on, tell us."

Then he understood that this was his thing, that he was there to tell the story. He didn't remember what he said in detail. He began by mixing everything up, just as he found it in his memory, and he kept on going like that, without pause or emphasis, giving the same importance to the bombardment and to his fear, to the thirst and the advance, to the dust on the road and the mortars, only paying attention to the uncontrollable rhythm of memory until arriving, finally, at the sea. Then there was no applause. The Rooster said coño, Orozco embraced him, and he was sure that this time, without even trying, he had won his respect. He had to go, goodbye, it was still raining.

It was probably the sparrow and the rain, Gisela, that got him into a mess that almost destroyed the brigade. He was going to tell you about it all in detail, because he still didn't know if he'd acted correctly, and you, although you might not believe it, were his judge, his Jiminy Cricket, his conscience. As you well knew, they had gone to Camagüey for six months and once there had voluntarily given up their leave time. As you also knew, April was the cruelest month, almost lost from the rain. May began the same way. The sparrow grew until it turned into a huge bird. He couldn't even write, he was so sad that it would have been impossible for him to respect certain agreements. He was excited about arriving in Havana on the second Sunday in May and giving his mother the gift of his return. The Wednesday before, the last day of cane cutting according to plan, he packed his suitcase and lay down to dream about the trip. A little while later, Orozco, who was coming from Municipal Party headquarters, entered the barracks and said:

"What a huge mess, we're going on with the zafra."

Immediately an uproar broke out, in which he didn't participate because he felt outside of everything. He'd emotionally left the zafra, and he was determined to leave physically the next day, come hell or high water. And so he closed his eyes and went to sleep in the middle of the scandal, thinking that six months of cane was more than you could ask of anyone. But in the morning the camp was in turmoil. Many men had packed to go, and at breakfast time a spontaneous meeting formed.

"Orozco received an order from the party," said the Rooster. "As long as there's cane, there's a zafra. Any brigade that backs out has no right to the competition, to the refrigerators, to the televisions or the motorcycles. Coño, don't you guys realize what we're losing?"

He was answered by a clamor. Many men tried to speak at once and no one succeeded in explaining himself. He, Gisela, stayed quiet, as if he were absent. He wasn't interested anymore in prizes or medals. He only wanted to confirm, although he never told you so, whether he had won your love once more.

"For me," shouted Orozco, asserting his authority, "none of that's important. The most important thing is not to back down, to keep on having the balls!"

He had thrown his essential, perhaps his only, argument into the ring. After doing so, he always turned around and went off towards the field, confident that he'd drag the rest along. But now the situation was so tense that he stood still in the middle of the house, and suddenly turned to him, pointing at him with his mocha:

"Isn't that right, combatant?"

It was a hard moment, Gisela. But he had no other choice than to respond, as if he were firing a shot:

"No."

Heberto Orozco looked at him with a wounded expression, slowly lowered the mocha and his eyes, and left, leaving behind him a bitter silence. After that no one knew what to do. The ones who had decided to stay didn't leave for the field, and the ones who were going to go kept their eyes down, so as to avoid looking at each other. At midmorning Sebastián Despaignes, from the Municipal Committee, arrived and met with the brigade. He was a very dark black man, almost blue, parsimonious, who dragged his rr's slightly.

"What happened?" he said.

It was difficult to argue with Despaignes, and that, and the uneasiness that Orozco's exit had left behind, inhibited the men. But he, Gisela, needed to go, and since he was sure that that was just, he wasn't afraid of debating anyone.

"We've done our duty," he answered. "We've already been in the zafra for six months and we've done our duty, and everyone here has commitments in Havana, wives, children in Havana, and we want to see them. That's what's happening."

A murmur of approval followed his words. Despaignes himself nodded his head in agreement.

"The compañero is correct," he said. "Anyone else?"

Now would come the counterattack, Gisela. Despaignes seemed meek, but he was a smart bastard. He couldn't let him come out on top, that's why he insisted:

"And now, on the last day, when we've packed our bags and our families are waiting for us, the party, or you, same thing, come and order us to stay. That's a world record for coming in by a nose."

Despaignes didn't answer. Unhurried, he lit a cigar, and from that moment, he realized he was losing ground, that he was too excited and Despaignes too tranquil, and he struggled to calm down, promising himself he'd win that argument anyway.

"The party doesn't give orders, you all know that," Despaignes finally said, looking at his watch. "It's ten o'clock, less than an hour from now, if you want, your transport will be here to take you to the train. Your reasons are correct, will you let me state mine, those of the party?"

He wasn't going to tell him no. But in any case, Despaignes took his time.

"Compañeros," he said, "we've committed an error by informing you about this decision so late. The Provincial Committee also decided late and left us no alternative. Now, think about it, with the cane in the second cutting, what we had left, with luck and little rain, we can still make between ten and fifteen thousand more tons in the mill. A ton is, how many pounds?"

"Two thousand," he automatically responded, and right there he realized that Despaignes had trapped him.

"Uh-huh, two thousand pounds," said Despaignes and asked him, "Start adding this up. How much is a pound of sugar selling for in the world market? Nine cents, no? Two thousand times nine is . . ."

"You know," he replied curtly.

"I know," Despaignes admitted. "Of course I know, let's say one hundred eighty greenbacks per ton, correct?" and he looked at him with all the calm in the world, Gisela, until he had to nod his head in agreement. "All right," he added. "One hundred eighty times ten thousand is, let's see, five zeros . . ."

"One million eight hundred thousand," he said, unable to contain himself.

"Dollars," concluded Despaignes. "What do you say to that?"

He lowered his eyes, Gisela, because he was trapped in that calm, irrefutable logic, and asked about Orozco.

"He resigned," said Despaignes.

The news hit the brigade like a rout, and he, he'd admit it only to you, felt like a traitor.

"Let's go look for him," the Rooster proposed.

They went, Gisela. Orozco agreed to return only when the entire Suárez Gayol committed themselves to winning the competition. Then he greeted the men one by one, except for him, who from that moment on started feeling sick, and that's how he was signing off for today, very sorry about it.

June was a brutal, dreadful month. Slopes and roadways turned into frightful quagmires in which trucks, tractors, and carts jammed up, from which the only ones who managed to pull out were the stubborn, tragic oxen dragging the *rastras*, triangular wedges without wheels, into which very little cane could fit. The Medialuna cane, when wet, was treacherous; its slippery peel could deflect the mocha, producing wounds in the arms and legs. The mud covered their clothes and skin. Whites, blacks, and mulattoes were all the same, the color of the earth. And in the middle of that hell, he and Orozco were going around avoiding each other like enemies, until the day he woke up with a virus, boarded the truck shivering, and Orozco asked him to stay in the boarding house. He couldn't agree to that, only a week was left for the final calculation of the competition and that time, Gisela, the seventy-five arrobas wouldn't wait for him. He felt happy that he hadn't given in despite his cold, and because when the day ended, Orozco said to him:

"Combatant, dammit, I'm dumber than a doornail. And you . . ."

"Cut it out," he answered.

That was all that was necessary, Gisela, Orozco didn't talk much. In the final stretch he felt renewed and that awful effort became beautiful to him, maybe because it took him to the very limits of his dedication. It was, he didn't know how to explain it otherwise, as if he were gathering strength from the earth. The best part was what happened in the Santa María de Sola movie theater, when Despaignes proclaimed the Suárez Gayol absolute winner of the competition and the macheteros of the Che Guevara contingent started to chant:

"O-roz-co! O-roz-co! O-roz-co!"

Orozco waved from his seat in the orchestra. But the shouts grew, Gisela, because the men wanted to see him up on the platform. He went out into the aisle trembling like a little kid and when he got up there, the shouts increased wildly. He moved in confusion from one side of the stage to the other. Despaignes led him to the podium, and there was a silence that Orozco couldn't manage to break. Applause burst out. Then Orozco raised his fist and shouted:

"Patria o Muerte!"

Now the zafra really had ended, Gisela, and when he got to the house, the Rooster sang for the last time and he looked for the last time at his wine-colored stain, which was now a bird with its wings spread wide, and for the last time he said goodbye to you, Gisela, until very soon, without daring to ask you to be there to meet him, because he needed it too much.

TWENTY-ONE

When they brushed on the last stroke of paint and *América Latina* could be read down the length of the imposing smokestack, the sugar mill's siren whistled three times, like that of a huge ship about to sail. From the top, where he'd made the mistake of climbing up under pressure from those peculiar Gallegos, Carlos looked at the ocean of cane and the gray structures of the factory and felt an awful fear. Beside him, on the extremely narrow ring at the top, the Gallegos had just finished roasting a suckling pig amid delirious balancing acts. Now they were eating, drinking straight from the bottle, singing *Unha noite na eira do trigo* with all the homesickness in the world. Carlos closed his eyes, imagining he was going through a nightmare, but now Manuel, the brigade leader, was offering him a chunk of meat and a bottle of beer while he sang *Pábilu, pábilu, pábilu* and did a tap dance on the edge of the tower, more than a hundred meters high. Carlos had no choice but to eat and drink, and found the pork hot and the beer cold. That delirium was as real as him being named administrator of the América Latina mill. To win over the workers he'd accepted the dare of the Gallegos who were the builders of these towers and who, by tradition, celebrated each newly finished smoke-stack with a party on the top, and now he was wind-battered, ringed by a cloud, flanked by a void of light on the left and another of darkness on the right, promising himself he'd kiss the ground three times if he managed to stand on it safe and sound.

He wasn't able to do that because when he got back down, dizzy and trembling, the Gallegos lifted him up on their shoulders and started parading him around the mill town to the sounds of their music. Happy to be alive and to have proven his courage, he went around greeting the workers who were celebrating the end of construction by singing country music. The sounds of *tiples*, güiros, and *bandurrías* mixed with that of bagpipes, and the overlapping voices created strange variations: *Unha noite na Guacanayara, ay Palmerito do trigo*. Gallegos and guajiros joined in a demonstration suddenly crossed by the sounds of banjos and a defiant anthem, *We shall overcome, we shall overcome, we shall overcome someday*, sung by the North Americans from the Venceremos Brigade, who were milling around the administration building waiting for the Vietnamese from the Ho Chi Minh Brigade, ten combatants who had come from the war to the zafra with little canvas hats and their songs, as graceful as reeds. Behind them the red flags of the Leninist Konsomol were raised, along with the airs of balalaikas and a chorus dominated by bass voices, *Kalinka, Kalinka, Kalinka moya, hej*! From the other side entered a fire-breathing dragon and the strange, atonal, and fascinating music of the Korean brigade, the Chullima Horsemen. And then a tumbadora could be heard, guiding along the construction workers' rumba, *Aé, aé, aé los constructores, que nos quitamos el nombre o hacemos los diez millones*, and it swept all the other brigades along with it towards the mill as it passed by, while the beating of the goatskins fused in the afternoon air with the sound of cornets, tiples, bagpipes, bandurrías, basses, and balalaikas in a crazy bedlam that made the English and French technicians come out, enveloped them in the bash like a ball of fire, incorporated their anthems into the pandemonium, *Unha noite we shall enfants de la patrie god save los diez millones Kalinka Guacanayara aé*, while Carlos sang *aé*! at the top of his voice because the entire world had met at the América Latina, a nowhere place in the Camagüey plains, to celebrate the beginning of the greatest sugar harvest in history.

But at night, when the international brigades had left to join the cutting and he was alone before the huge, lighted mass of the sugar mill, he felt a fear as bad as his vertigo. He had agreed to be the captain of that ship in its most difficult crossing, but he didn't know how the hell to guide it. At that moment there were serious problems with the tandems, and he wandered around the area like a ghost, because he didn't have the slightest fucking idea of what he should do. His appointment had been an agreement, a lions' pact between "el Negro" Despaignes, from the Party Regional Committee, and Pablo Fernández, his old buddy the Nose, now the provincial representative of the Sugar Ministry. They had spent days rejecting each other's proposals until one night, with the zafra about to begin and their leaders demanding an agreement, Pablo said:

"Appoint your assistant."

Carlos smiled, trying to follow his drift, and then got serious when he saw el Negro was looking at him. They had become friends during the '69 zafra, when he had worked as chief of the regional brigades, promoted by Despaignes himself, who now it seemed was asking him who his boss would be if he were appointed administrator of the América Latina mill.

"You can't do that either?" Pablo said ironically.

"Yes," el Negro said suddenly, and turned to Carlos. "Congratulations, Administrator."

Carlos smiled again and said that was nonsense, craziness, but Pablo and Despaignes were euphoric about having reached an agreement and they guaranteed him the support of the Sugar Ministry and the party, he'd have an extremely able, though politically erratic deputy, and he should feel proud, because the Ten Million Ton harvest was going to be a war and they were naming him a captain. The América Latina was the biggest mill in the country, meaning the world, did he realize that? And it was receiving tremendous investments that would turn it into a key piece of the gigantic effort with which the island, finally, would break the back of poverty. Besides, after three years in the zafra, he knew something about sugar, didn't he? And we'll say no more about the subject, Administrator, the rest is just a simple matter of luck and balls.

And now, heading towards the tandems, he told himself that at least tonight the solution seemed to depend on luck. The problem was so serious that it would free him from responsibility, although not from anxiety. Everything was ready for the América Latina to try out its capital investments the next day, but the English technicians couldn't get the new electric tandems to start up. The old steam equipment had been dismantled to send it to the "Argentina" mill; if the English couldn't get it right, the América Latina wouldn't be able to operate, and without that colossus, planned to mill 1.3 million arrobas a day, it would be totally impossible to reach the ten million tons to which the country's honor and future had made a commitment. The English manufacturers, whose money and prestige were on the line, were inspecting the enormous mechanism with a desperate meticulousness. Carlos climbed up an iron staircase and stopped on the bridge next to Pablo, over the huge hammer mill of the shredder. He didn't say anything to him, everybody was in a terrible mood that night. At the level of the fifth mill, Captain Monteagudo, provincial coordinator of the zafra, incessantly came and went, arguing with the engineer Pérez Peña, the sugar minister's representative;

behind them, heads down, were el Negro Despaignes and Ortiz Quintana, from the National Construction Group. The workers stood in their places, arms folded. Carlos watched, hypnotized, the double pair of magnets that came before the crusher, when someone grabbed him by the shoulder. Startled, he turned around and smiled on seeing Happy, the mill town's mascot, a young lunatic who always wore a blue cap with a scorpion on the front.

"Administrator," said Happy, "I'll fix it."

"Oh, hell, get that idiot out of here," complained Pablo.

"Loco, not an idiot," Happy clarified.

Carlos put an arm around his very skinny, sharp shoulders and gently took him all the way out to the tippler yard. Happy had the virtue of making him feel good because he was almost always there, doing honor to his nickname. He was the son of a worker who had died from being electrocuted and a madwoman who had killed herself after the accident. From then on he lived with his grandmother in an old wooden shack, and had very little schooling; people said that he carried the electricity that killed his father in his blood.

"Go home to your grandmother," said Carlos, "get going."

"I'll fix it," Happy insisted.

Next to the huge tippler, recently completed, a line of cars full of cane was waiting.

"Tomorrow," Carlos murmured, looking at the train, and he returned to the factory.

Nothing had changed there. The new machinery was shining like a useless exhibit.

"Up the ass," said Pablo. "A disaster."

He saw that Pepe López was coming over and leaned on his elbows over the handrail, his back to the bridge. López passed by him in silence, as if he hadn't seen him, and greeted Pablo.

"What's happening?"

"Waiting for you," said Pablo ironically. When López kept going, he turned to Carlos. "You have to say hello, my friend."

"That guy is a somabitch," he said.

"Perhaps, but he's the construction leader here, and cadres have to talk to each other. This isn't some game of . . . Coño, look at that!"

Happy was talking to el Negro Despaignes and Ortiz Quintana. Captain Monteagudo and the engineer, Pérez Peña, were walking towards the group. Carlos started running, trying to keep the loco from interrupting them. Halfway there he slowed down, the captain and the engineer, absorbed in their discussion, had stopped. When he passed by them, Monteagudo was saying, "I can't tell Fidel that . . ." He would have liked to have kept on listening, but didn't dare. A little further on, Despaignes was giving the grate little kicks.

"I'll fix it," Happy was saying.

"Excuse me," he interjected, gently grabbing him by the arm.

"Make him disappear," Ortiz Quintana ordered.

Once again he put his arm around Happy's shoulders and took him out to the tippler, wondering if he should ask the grandmother to lock him up. He decided not to do that, it was too cruel. The old woman, desperate because of the constant, unpredictable movement that drove the loco to run away to other towns, and sometimes to other provinces, often attached a slave shackle to his right ankle, with an iron ball and chain.

"Go on to your grandmother's," he told him.

Happy looked at him with clear stubbornness.

"I'll fix it," he insisted.

"I'm going to get mad," Carlos threatened him, and shouted, "The shackle!"

Happy shook his head and arms, as if attacked by St. Vitus's dance; fear clouded his eyes and he ran, disappearing into the darkness. Carlos returned to his post, downcast. Maybe he'd been too hard, but he had no choice. Being administrator of the mill implied a kind of civil authority over the town, and it was his duty to exercise it. Three hours later, with nothing having changed in the tandem section, he cursed himself for having been so soft. The disaster was in front of his eyes, Pablo was calling him a shithead, Pepe López was laughing, el Negro Despaignes was holding his head in his hands, and Happy was interrupting the conversation between Captain Monteagudo and Pérez Peña, with no one able to stop him.

"What's this?" the startled captain asked.

"I'll fix it," said Happy.

"Just what we needed," Pérez Peña remarked. "An idiot."

"No, a loco," Happy clarified.

"Excuse me," said Carlos, and again grabbed him by the arm, this time taking him to two workers who would deliver him to his grandmother.

Luckily, the captain and the engineer kept on with their discussion as if nothing had happened. But Carlos had to take a chewing out from Pablo and Despaignes, until the Englishmen left their work at the controls and came up to the bridge. Everyone followed, at a distance, the conversation between

Monteagudo, Pérez Peña, and the technicians, as if it were a silent film, and they came to the conclusion that a catastrophe had occurred. The captain was beside himself when he summoned the cadres to an urgent meeting.

"The English say," he informed them in the office, "that they don't have a solution to the problem. They want to consult and their consultation will take a month. We, compañeros, *cannot* wait that long. Who here has an idea for getting us out of this predicament?" He left the question in the air and looked at the cadres one by one. "No one? Very well," he said then, turning to Carlos. "Administrator, go look for the loco, find out what his plan is, and bring me the answer right away."

Carlos started to smile, as if he hadn't understood the joke. But Monteagudo was looking at him seriously, challengingly.

"I think it's useless, Captain," replied Pérez Peña. "Useless, and . . . just useless."

René Monteagudo stayed silent. Carlos pushed back his chair, and the noise of the wood against the floor sounded to him like a sacrilege. Slowly he went towards the door, hoping in vain that the captain would order him to stay. Celso Couzo, the machinery chief, went out with him. He was a man of unpredictable character, familiar with every screw in the mill from the times when it was called Sola, and now he was going around in a daze from the new investments.

"You . . ." Carlos started to ask him.

"Yes, me," Couzo interrupted him.

"You, what?"

"Me too."

"You too, what?"

"Am going crazy, chico."

Carlos followed his path under the carob trees bordering the main road, wondering if Monteagudo could be pricking the sugar makers' pride to force them to resolve the problem, or if desperation had brought him to actually trusting in madness. They began to cross the neighborhood of the Americans who had been the owners of the mill, mansions that now were a hospital, a daycare center, a school, and that reminded him of Tara, of Twelve Oaks, from the film *Gone with the Wind*. He told himself that life in the mill must have been terrible before the wind. The town was built with a sinister perfection. Social classes, sectors, and strata had their occupations, their clubs, the places they shopped, the size, location, and even the color of their houses preset for them forever in that place, totally isolated from the rest of the world by seas of cane. The Americans used a plane to fly out; but the workers had no alternative other than the Sola Sugar Company trains, and that, other than for exceptions that because of their rarity had become part of the town's mythology, was strictly forbidden.

Imagining that bleak uniformity, Carlos blessed the wind that engendered the disorder he was caught up in. Since nationalization, everyone painted his house whatever color he liked, a highway was built on which many people realized their dream of leaving for the cities, and the name of the mill was changed. But something of the immobility of those times must have been left during the years when *América Latina Sola* was still being written on the bags of sugar. The great wind arrived with the remodeling of the mill for the Ten Million Ton harvest. Thousands of construction workers; millions of rubles, dollars, pounds sterling, and francs in equipment and pieces; dozens of buildings, boarding houses, and cafeterias; technicians and internationalists from many different latitudes came together in Sola to reconstruct the América Latina in only a year, introducing a dizzying movement and making that place as delirious and happy as the loco to whose hut they had, finally, arrived.

But Happy was sad now, melancholy as always when they shackled him. Carlos calmed down his grandmother, asked her for the key, and made his way through the intricate tangle of useless cables, condensers, radios, irons, buzzers, telephones, and televisions that the townspeople had been giving Happy as gifts to calm his insatiable hunger for electronic garbage. The loco was sitting on top of the rusty structure of a refrigerator, like a king imprisoned on his throne. Carlos knelt down in front of him, freed him from the irons, and stroked the wounds on his ankle.

"What should we do?" he asked him.

Happy's eyes gleamed as soon as he started talking. Carlos didn't understand anything, but once again he felt good. From the day he was named as administrator, Pablo and el Negro insisted that he had to spend part of his time attending to the townspeople, and from that duty had grown his habit of listening to and protecting Happy, who now was speaking with inspiration about fields, diodes, and alternating currents while he drew sketches on a dirty scrap of paper. When he finished, Carlos thanked him and handed the drawings over to Couzo.

"Are you going to do it?" asked Happy anxiously.

"Of course," he said, while he did a balancing act walking through the junk.

"Should I tie him down?" asked the grandmother, by the filthy wooden door.

Carlos looked at Happy, who had put his head inside the shell of a television set and was sticking his tongue out at him.

"No," he said, and turned to the loco. "Don't you move until the siren blows."

Happy imitated the mill whistle. The door creaked as it opened. In the street, Carlos started to laugh.

"Did you understand anything?" he sighed.

"I don't know beans about electronics," replied Couzo.

While they were going back to the office, he thought that some English or Cuban solution must have come up and no one would even ask him what the loco had said. But on arriving he found extremely strong tension between Monteagudo and Pérez Peña, which reached the limit when the engineer refused to evaluate Happy's plan, saying that he would never go so low as to work with madmen, and he held fast to the opinion that they should make the English pay a fine and wait. Then Monteagudo took drastic action, ordering Carlos to copy Happy's sketches onto linen paper and to deliver them to the English, because what could be lost from trying?

The Brits were known as the Four Horsemen of the Apocalypse. Their work habits clashed so much with the reigning disorder that they always created a special tension. They never raised their voices, drank their gin calmly, and the only thing that drove them wild was black women's asses. When Carlos handed the folder over to the group leader, christened in Sola as Perfidious Albion, he thought that the Horsemen would whinny with rage at the joke. But Perfidious maintained his calm, tranquilly examined the sketches and asked:

"Who did this?"

"Well . . ." said Carlos.

"It's absurd," commented Perfidious. "There's not a calculation done right, or a proportion correctly determined. It's practically impossible to accumulate so many mistakes in just one diagram."

"Forget it," Carlos murmured, putting out his hand to take the folder.

Perfidious Albion kept on looking at the sketches, paying him no attention.

"Typical of you people," he said finally. "A brilliant idea, riddled with stupid blunders."

Carlos wondered if he'd heard right, but didn't dare interrupt Perfidious who now, bent over the diagram and talking in his jargon with the other Horsemen, was writing down numbers and figures next to the sketches. Although it seemed they were working mechanically, you could notice unusual excitement in them. When they finished half an hour later, Perfidious Albion ceremoniously handed over the folder to him.

"Build it like this," he said. "*And God save the tandems.*"

In spite of the fact that Carlos followed Captain Monteagudo's rigorous instructions and ordered the operators of the electronics shop to work in the strictest secrecy, all of América Latina found out that the Four Horsemen of the Apocalypse had ordered the building of Happy's plan to get the tandems to start up. Hundreds of workers and townspeople crowded around the workshop's fences, and Carlos had to call out the volunteer firemen to control them. The primary-school principal made a formal complaint to him about the terrible example he was giving her students, who now wanted to be crazy and inventors and cut class to run around the fence like they were in an asylum. The traveling priest, a polyglot Belgian who served the churches of five mills in his brand-new vw Brasilia, warned from his pulpit against the consequences of fanaticism. The Seventh-Day Adventists predicted that a holocaust, a local Armageddon-like death would sweep away the América Latina for having dared to challenge the Lord's plan, and dragged its few followers away to live on the outskirts of town in improvised tents.

Almost no one got to see the small piece of equipment built thanks to Happy's delirious imagination and the cold British calculations. But almost all the inhabitants of América Latina, concentrated around the outskirts of the mill, were waiting for the results of the test. The Four Horsemen of the Apocalypse oversaw the assembly with exhausting meticulosity. When everything was ready Carlos stuck close behind Perfidious Albion so as not to miss one detail of that historic moment. The long, thin, freckled finger of the Englishman stopped as if in doubt in front of the wide red button. Carlos swallowed hard thinking about Happy, about Grandfather Álvaro, Chava, and Kindelán. Monteagudo closed his eyes. Perfidious pressed the button. A soft purring of motors filled the air, and everyone exploded with joy while the first pieces of cane fell with a crash onto the conveyor belt, the machines chopped them, shredded them, extracted their juice, and the siren announced to the world that the América Latina had started milling.

"The loco!" shouted the captain in the midst of the scene.

Carlos went off running after him. At the tippler they were wrapped in a cloud of dust and reeds, the crash of a bin as it overturned against the buffers, and the sharp yells of the grabbers. Carlos felt elated by the sound and the fury of the harvest, and his eyes teared up with gratitude thinking about the loco. The crowd on the platform had improvised a party, dozens and dozens of couples were dancing to the sound of a barrel-organ that someone had brought in an oxcart. To avoid the dancers they ran in a zigzag and wound up by a chorus. They said they couldn't stay to sing and kept on running through deserted streets until they reached Happy's shack, where his grandmother met them in tears.

"He left," she told them. "He was scared."

Carlos didn't hesitate. He knew the place where Happy often hid in his panic attacks and he invited the captain to return to the mill so they could go there in a jeep. Once again they neared the lighted factory, went around the party, and got into Monteagudo's car, which started up, making the tires squeal, and gained a dizzying speed, while Carlos remembered the very friendly lieutenant who killed himself and almost killed him during the October crisis. But he swallowed his fear. Monteagudo was solid, short, Indian-looking; he was known for having fought in combat on his feet, and it wasn't Carlos's place to tell him to be careful. When they got to the Hanging Slave exit gate it started to rain. The captain slowed down and looked at him, singing, *There are four roads in my life, which of them will be the bessst?* Carlos pointed to the highway that connected the América Latina with the rest of the world, wondering if it could be true that the captain, besides the zafra, also led an orchestra that played Mexican music. Monteagudo charged up the railroad embankment and the jeep jumped over the tracks and again hit the asphalt. On the right side, the wind had made the Adventists' tents fly away. Carlos yelled, "Armageddon!" and the captain started singing "Bed of Stone" with slightly desperate emotion. They entered Marverde, the unending sea of cane that surrounded the América Latina, and with the last Ay-yay-yay! they halted by the gray wall at the pathway.

"So much blood," murmured Monteagudo, stroking the blackened stones.

"Happyyyyyyyyy!" shouted Carlos.

The loco didn't respond. They started searching for him in the openings of the wall. The downpour had lessened, but a cold breeze cut through the cane field. Suddenly, in a ruined hut, two little blue eyes shone like a cat's. Happy, holding a skull in his hands, was shivering. He lowered his head and backed up against the wall asking to be forgiven, saying he didn't know, that he'd never thought, that they please not shackle him. The captain stretched out on his stomach with his ear to the ground. For a second Carlos looked at him in confusion, but had the hunch that he should do the same. At ground level there was a very strong odor of manure. Happy stretched out, too, cautiously.

"The earth trembles," the captain said then, with a very quiet voice. "It's the mill."

Carlos observed, fascinated, the transfiguration of the loco's face, which went from fear to doubt and to joy and to peace, and he smiled at the skull and placed it to his side on the ground.

"It that your friend?" asked the Captain.

Happy nodded. His little eyes got smaller when he smiled at the skull.

"Did you hear? We did it," he said.

It seemed to Carlos that the loco's face and that of the dead person had some family resemblance, he looked intensely at the empty sockets and the perpetual smile, and thought about his grandfather and his father on feeling how the earth transmitted regular beats, like those of a warm, palpitating heart.

On the way back to the mill, the captain decided that Happy should go to Havana so that psychologists and engineers at the university could study his case, and the loco designated Carlos as custodian of his skull.

"Talk to her at night," he told him. "She understands."

Carlos didn't dare discourage him, and he hid the skull in the little wardrobe of the bare hotel room where he was living. That afternoon the commission, presided over by Monteagudo and Pérez Peña, decided that the state of the capital investments in the América Latina would allow it to continue with the zafra, and they continued their inspection tour by heading for the "Peru" mill. Carlos had gone more than seventy-two hours without sleeping, but he was pulled to the mill as if it were a sick child. In the control room and the laboratory they informed him that everything was going great, the cane was fresh and pretty clean and the factory was tip-top, although of course they were working at a very low rate, only two hundred fifty thousand arrobas.

"Mill on high," he said.

Immediately he realized that that instruction, handed down by the commission, would just be so much bagasse if he didn't decide something concrete, and he asked what would happen if they tightened up and doubled or tripled the rate. Jacinto Amézaga, his deputy, flat out opposed it because there were too many things in the factory to be tested. The commission, he said, had been hasty in deciding that they should continue the milling. Couzo was in favor of tripling; in his opinion this baby would run like clockwork, but even if it didn't it was best that the problems came out now, when there was time for everything. Carlos looked at them in silence, Amézaga's point of view was safer, if he adopted it no one could reproach him for that, but the ten million wouldn't be reached by being so careful. Not for nothing had Lenin said what he did about audacity, audacity, and more audacity.

"Step it up," he ordered. "Seven hundred fifty thousand arrobas, and what will be, will be."

The Horsemen of the Apocalypse greeted the decision with all the enthusiasm they were capable of expressing, because it would allow them to test the tandems at half their capacity. Perfidious Albion personally operated the equipment, which responded as Couzo had predicted. When the great rollers increased the speed of their rotation and the little stream of juice grew in the canals until it turned into a golden river, Carlos felt like a true captain on the ship's bridge, and he ordered that the province and the country be informed that the América Latina had tripled its rhythm.

Then he felt dizzy with fatigue and had no choice but to go to bed. The little hotel that the Sola Sugar Company had built for unmarried technicians depressed him terribly. It was made of wood, painted the color of the ochre earth, and the awful lighting suggested frustrations and miseries. In his small room there was a narrow iron bed, a little night table with chipped paint, a pitcher, and the small wardrobe. Opening it to hang up his shirt, he saw the skull.

"That's the limit," he murmured, "living here with this thing."

He fell asleep before he could take off his boots and after a while sank into a nightmare. The mill had no electricity, he, Couzo, Amézaga, and the Horsemen were wandering around the dark premises like lost souls. He started shouting and sensed he was dreaming, but no one came to wake him up. When he succeeded in opening his eyes, he was hoarse and disconcerted, and leapt to the window. He wasn't able to see a thing. The bits of bagasse had been falling for years on the wire mesh like an inclement rain of ashes. He went out to the hallway, bounded down the thirty-nine steps, and started to laugh; the mill was illuminated.

Returning to his room, hearing the gloomy sound of his own steps on the old, dusty wood, he was overcome by sadness. He lay down on his back, desperate to see Gisela. Suddenly he decided to write her, tell her how much he loved her, and ask her, please, that sometime, if she could, to come visit him. Among the many failures of his life, she was the greatest one. Never again, since the divorce, had they been able to get along. When she was far from him he felt capable of the greatest resignation, but on seeing her he went back to his reproaches, as if he were reciting, against his will, a role he had learned. That was what happened at the end of the '68 zafra, when she went to meet him at the station and he didn't know if he had the right to kiss her until they were face to face and looked at each other and she broke into tears. He thought then that everything was resolved, and afterwards, in the house, he couldn't understand why she was afraid and was asking him, please, to really think about this, because they had already suffered enough. And since he had thought about it for whole months, during the zafra, he looked humbly into her eyes as he asked her if he could stay, forever.

With their savings they went to the Riviera, repeated the craziness of their wedding night, and invented more, without being interrupted this time by the Yanquis. Carlos even made a joke: they had two October crises, one historical and the other personal. In the mornings his mother-in-law brought Mercedita over, and he taught her to swim in the pool, told her stories about the zafra, heard her laugh. But one night Gisela said hello to a doctor in the elevator and when they got to the room, Carlos asked her if he had been the one.

"The one what?" she said.

"The one who slept with you," he calmly replied.

Months later, well into the '69 zafra, while he suffered through his loneliness like a dog, he was amazed to recall the sinister calm with which he managed to yoke her to the logic of his madness. They had to talk with civility, like adults, he had said, getting back together meant knowing everything about each other, being in agreement about certain basic points, for example, she had cheated on him, correct? Gisela tried to avoid that conversation, but for weeks he went about fencing her in, like a mouse, no, love, he didn't want to argue, only to have a rational conversation, now why was she *afraid* to talk about *that*? When she accepted the challenge and told him that she *hadn't* cheated on him, that the incident had happened *after* the separation, he felt his face burning as if before a fascinating bet, *please*, sweetheart, to call that an *incident*, when it happened the divorce hadn't been final. That was only a piece of paper, she sobbed, he was with that girl too, what did he want, what was he hoping to get with this harassment. Nothing, he would say, retrenching himself in a silence that lasted for days, until she gave in and caressed him and he went back to his game, fencing her in, making her contradict herself and cry and he sucked in her tears and aroused her and possessed her in a blurred, luminous way. The night he won his victory, making her recognize that, yes, she *had* cheated on him, he felt a bitter taste of ashes because he hated her and loved her more than ever. And when she noticed his desperation, or a minute later, when she told him he was the man of her life and begged him for pity's sake that they get remarried, Carlos confessed that once he'd been on the verge of killing her.

And that Monday, without thinking about it twice, he escaped for the zafra where he was going to ponder his solitude to the point of delirium. He wasn't able to confess the reason for his bitterness to Orozco, or to Acana, or to the Rooster. When Despaignes promoted him to workforce chief he came to love the endless embankments where he took apart the mechanism of his madness while he went from camp to camp. All he wanted was another chance, another couple of months to show Gisela he had forgotten. But the country was in the Year of Decisive Effort, there was almost no break between those two zafras, and only with difficulty did he obtain seven days of leave. He used up three to get from Camagüey to Havana getting rides on carts, trucks, jeeps, and in that train, very slow and dark as sadness, that made every station and every whistle stop. When he got to the house, Gisela wasn't there. His mother-in-law informed him that she'd gone to serve with the cane-cutting camp "Daybreak," in Unión de Reyes. Carlos took Mercedita to the zoo that morning, and in the afternoon resumed his odyssey.

Under that scorching August, Havana looked like a cemetery. On the closed doors of barbershops, bars, offices, repair shops, and restaurants, there were little signs: "Gone to the Zafra." The streets were as deserted as the dusty slopes of Sola. But the bus terminal was an anthill, hundreds of people were swarming around the platforms struggling to board, and many more were waiting seated on the ground, on pieces of newspaper. When Carlos asked for a ticket to Unión de Reyes the employee at the information window laughed in his face and told him he'd get there faster by walking, he had 762 people ahead of him on the waiting list, and the next bus was still being fixed. Right then a mulatto with gold teeth offered to take him for two hundred fifty bucks. It was a month's salary. Carlos was about to punch him or curse out his mother, but thought the better of it, and now, half-asleep on the hard old bed in his hotel, he had moments of enduring the nightmare of being on the suffocating highway again, crossing strange towns like Bolondrón and Alacranes, or lost in the reddish streets of Unión de Reyes where no one seemed to know where the goddamned Daybreak or anything like it was. His anguish was short, because now he was pursuing Gisela atop a cart of fertilizer, arriving at the camp where he saw her joking around with a guy, and he wasn't making the stupid jealous scene that he made that night, by the carob tree where they loved and she confirmed to him that, yes, unfortunately, he was the man of her life, even in that brief encounter that he obsessively recalled now that he was falling asleep, maybe he'd be lucky and dream about it.

He didn't. He woke up in a bad mood and, sitting up on the bed, saw a copy of *Granma* under the door. Mechanically, he picked it up and felt his pulse rise: *The "América Latina" triples its milling rate*. Underneath there was an article where the cadres of Sola were congratulated for their aggressiveness and were held up as an example. At the end, his secretary had tacked on a note: a journalist was waiting for him at the office. He sang as he bathed, and singing he headed for the building where that short, fat young man who wanted to interview him was waiting. He smiled, flattered; at one time, as a child, he had appeared on television, and on another occasion, when very young, *Revolución* had published his picture carrying a coffin. But they had both been coincidences, while this had to do with a personal interview about the country's most important activity. He smiled thinking that his name in the paper would be, in addition, a message in code for Gisela.

"Go ahead, compañero," he said.

The reporter cleared his throat while he wiped off his sweaty hands with a handkerchief already stained by dirt.

"Compañero Administrator," he said in a tone too high for his stature, "it is undoubtable that you, the heroic sugar men here at the América Latina, have achieved a productive deed by getting the factory started and tripling the milling rate in such a short time. We would like to know how you have done it, and what obstacles you had to overcome to attain such lofty goals."

When Carlos was getting ready to reply, Jacinto Amézaga entered the office, went over to the desk, and whispered in his ear:

"Friend, in three hours that baby is going to shut down."

"What?" he exclaimed.

"Did something happen?" the reporter asked.

"No," said Jacinto. "Internal affairs."

Carlos asked the reporter to excuse him for a few minutes and then Jacinto explained that a ridiculous thing was happening, without precedent in the history of the sugar industry: the mill would shut down because the bagasse house was full, since there was no equivalence between the rate of the new tandems and the size of the old storehouse.

"Solution?" asked Carlos.

"Slow down to one hundred thousand arrobas for three days, until the new house is finished."

He shook his head while he listened to Jacinto's lecture on the terrible damage the mill would suffer if he allowed the system of bagasse distribution to overflow. His deputy was right, it would be a disaster, but he couldn't allow himself the luxury of slowing down the rate and confusing the country after having stimulated it; there *had* to be another solution.

"No," Jacinto insisted, "slow down now or shut down later, who knows until when."

He felt his shirt stuck to his back with sweat. He was about to make a big fool of himself as an administrator for the first, and perhaps also the last, time. The line of responsibility was so clear that he would surely be replaced as soon as the mill shut down or slowed. Suddenly he wanted the disaster to have happened already and to be once again chopping cane, with no more responsibility than raising his arm and bringing it down onto the defenseless plant. It would be easy to promote that sort of civil suicide by waiting until time passed, like someone waiting for poison to take effect. But it would also be cowardly. He needed to attempt something, although he didn't have the slightest fucking idea what to do.

"Let's go," he said.

Jacinto followed him like an automaton. The reporter was leaning against a column in the entryway of the office.

"May I go with you?" he asked.

"No," Carlos replied sharply.

"But compañeros, the readers . . ."

Carlos kept going. He didn't give a damn about the readers. That shithead couldn't have picked a worse moment to stick his nose into the mill, he had to be kept on a short leash. Luckily the factory was milling normally and a terrific smell of syrup was floating through Furnace Street, down which they went all the way to the bagasse house. Silently they stopped at the edge of the disaster; the site, a rough wooden shed, was about to burst. Carlos asked what would happen if they destroyed the front wall with an axe and let the bagasse accumulate in the street. Jacinto put his hands on his head, that would be madness, he said, bagasse was abrasive and combustible, on the one hand the wind would drag it inside the factory and there it could damage a lot of equipment; on the other, spread around in the street and dry, it would be an invitation to sabotage; the only way to resolve the problem was to compact it.

Then Carlos conceived a desperate solution: to ask Pepe López for a motorized grader. He had to overcome many scruples to stoop to calling him, because his differences with Pepe covered an enormous list of problems and touched on the whole social structure of the town. For more than half a century Sola was a closed community of sugar workers, but for months now it had been shaken up by thousands of builders coming from remote cities, whose mere presence was a threat to tradition and a seedbed of problems. Over that buzz of daily misunderstanding grew the struggle between builders and investors, and leading the two forces were precisely Pepe López and him, at war. With his hand on the telephone he thought that surely the bastard would refuse with some kind of excuse, and immediately he took it back, in spite of everything the guy was a revolutionary and he should understand, had to understand, was going to understand that this foul-up was part of the common struggle for the Ten Million. And if he didn't? Because Pepe López was a somabitch, there was no way around that. But could you be a revolutionary and a somabitch at the same time, say, a somablutionary? The logical thing was to find out, to call Pepe, to tell him without reserve that he, too, was responsible for the mess, for having gotten behind on the finishing of the new bagasse house. He did so and felt hopeful because Pepe López listened to him without getting upset, he was in agreement that they should understand each other as compañeros, but finally he said he could not lend him the equipment exactly because bagasse was abrasive and could render it useless, and imperceptibly Carlos went from reasoning to yelling and when he realized it Pepe had hung up, leaving him full of arguments and fury until he ran out towards the jeep, while Jacinto asked him what the hell had happened. He turned the corner, making the tires squeal, entered like a shot into the baseball field that the construction group had taken away from the sugar-ministry workers to turn it into a parking lot for equipment, and he braked over the third-base line, next to a brand-new Komatzu grader.

"Get going for the bagasse house," he said.

The operator refused, alleging that he only carried out orders from construction, and Carlos pulled out his pistol, put it into his ribs muttering, "You're going to go, brother, you're going to go," and the guy went pale and got going. They crossed the town in that apparatus as tall as a tree trunk and arrived at the bagasse house, where Carlos ordered him to go inside, destroying the wooden planks, and to start compacting the bagasse. "That's it, brother, that's it, again, again," until the mounds curled with yellow shavings were turned into bales, and there was room to keep receiving bagasse for three days, at least.

Then he returned to the office asking himself what the fuck he had done. Now Pepe López would have proof to be able to get him fired, and show that the somabitch was him, Carlos, who would have no defense facing Monteagudo and would make his buddies Pablo and Despaignes look bad. Nevertheless, the mill hadn't shut down, that was all he could say. But that would be later on. The problem now was that journalist, stuck on talking about achievements, obstacles, and goals. What to tell him? About Happy, the pistol, that somabitch, and the bagasse house . . . ? No, not in a million years; those, as Jacinto had well said, were internal affairs. What was important was the heroic effort they were making; the achievements, compañero, had been obtained by working day and night; yes, there were obstacles, difficulties, that was true, how could there not be in a task of that magnitude; but he wanted to tell him, compañero journalist, that there would be no problem, barrier, technical or natural obstacle that the sugar workers and cadres wouldn't be capable of overcoming in that decisive battle against underdevelopment; and now, if he would please excuse him, he had urgent obligations to take care of, if he needed anything else, please see his secretary. The reporter finished taking notes, closed his little book, and looked at him with a mixture of admiration and disenchantment. Carlos held his gaze, although he wasn't seeing him anymore; now his problem was to defend himself against the riposte, because he didn't know when, how, and from where Pepe López would attack him. He spent four nights going over the construction workers' unmet duties and although he was able to put together a voluminous, detailed file, he felt a shock go down his spine when they told him he had an urgent call from the ministry. He never thought Pepe would attack from so high up, he'd probably gotten support at the national level and it would be a tremendous scene. Answering, he noticed that the sweat on his hands had covered the telephone.

"Watch out," a voice whispered. "Because I'm going to fuck with you."

He was left stunned, thinking how that was no way to treat a cadre.

"Wh-what?" he babbled.

"Now I'm high up," the voice said. "And I know all about you."

Then he recognized Happy and started to laugh, relieved, what the hell was he doing using that phone? The loco told him he was visiting all the nice places in Havana and that the National Zafra Control Room was the prettiest, with electronic computers and red telephones; soon he'd come back to Sola with a box full of photographs so no one could call him a liar, would he let his grandmother know? Of course, said Carlos, and let the loco go on telling him about his visit to the university while he got lost again in his problem.

Pepe López made a thorough attack on December 23, at a meeting presided over by the captain. While he listened to the accusations of the abuser, thief, and bandit, Carlos realized that his opponent had picked a bad day. At 11:10 in the morning, six hours earlier than planned, they received the news that the country had produced its first million tons, and they interrupted the meeting to join the workers' explosion of jubilation and to hang up a gigantic number one under the immense red and black banner hanging at the entryway to the mill:

THE TEN MILLION GO FORWARD!

Carlos sensed that Captain Monteagudo wasn't in the mood for internal complaints, and when they resumed the meeting and his turn came, he limited himself to saying that he was there to keep the factory milling and that was what he had done. Never had he gotten so much effect from so few words. Monteagudo agreed, satisfied, looked at Pepe López and ordered him to resolve his differences with the ministry fraternally. And now they could move to the most important point: the need to create conditions for what he termed an attack on the second million. It was as if he'd lit a fuse under Pablo and Despaignes; they were on edge with the contradictions between agriculture and manufacturing. The América Latina was supposed to start milling, the next day, 1,200,000 arrobas, and Pablo and Depaignes didn't coincide on their estimates of the quantity of cane, or on the structures of the cane stocks and their variations, or on the organization of the cutting, or on the yield levels planned for the mill. When Carlos needed to intervene in the polemic he did so from the perspective of agriculture, because that was all he knew, and then Pablo attacked him with unexpected violence, asking him if he was with the lion or the hunter, and accused him of being irresponsible and a coward for having allowed Despaignes to take twenty-five men away from him for the cutting. Carlos pounded the table, shouting that he didn't accept being called a coward from Pablo or from anyone, he was the administrator, it was his responsibility, and if they didn't allow him to make decisions then they could remove him right now. Monteagudo called for calm, was able to get an agreement on the plan for the cutting, said that time would take care of proving the truth of the estimates and added that both the yield levels as well as the norms for milling could not be changed, because the contribution of the América Latina to the Ten Million depended on them.

Carlos knew that his prestige as a cadre depended on million-arroba millings, and that Despaignes, as much as he might try, wouldn't send him enough cane to attain them. Weeks later, under pressure because the América Latina was the only one among the country's colossal mills that hadn't gone over six figures even once, he decided to slow down the rate of milling and accumulate cane in the bins to attempt a spectacular workday. That day he had a caustic argument with Jacinto and finally understood why Despaignes had termed him politically erratic. Jacinto was opposed to any risky decisions on the basis of the very conservative concept of keeping the milling stable, without valuing the psychological effect that a record would have on the masses. Carlos had no alternative other than to ignore his deputy's opinion and to personally take over supervision of the process. He was in the mill for forty-eight hours without leaving, followed around by a high-level commission made up of members of the party, the Young Communists, and the Workers' Union, visiting all the work stations during each shift, from the tippler to the bagging floor and impressing upon the workers their responsibility through repeated, quick meetings. When everything was ready and the line of bins reached nearly to the Hanging Slave junction, and the whistle blew and the América Latina started to mill at full speed, he couldn't leave to go to sleep. He was certain that his presence in the factory was crucial, that there was a strange, obscure, essential connection between his gaze and the positive outcome of events. He dismissed the commission, whose members were exhausted, and continued with his perpetual pilgrimage from the tandems to the vacuum pans and from the tippler to the centrifuges. Every half hour he was informed of the quantity of milled arrobas, but when the factory reached eight hundred thousand he reduced the interval to every ten minutes, and one hundred thousand arrobas later he went into the control room to follow the growth of the number with the anxiety of an old miser. Scarcely five thousand arrobas were left when he headed for the ceremony that the Communist Family Association had organized at the mill entrance. He calculated the pace of his steps and appeared before the crowd just at the moment when the whistle began blowing and the base radio, after a flourish of cornets, announced that the América Latina had milled, for the first time in the zafra, a million arrobas of cane in less than twenty-four hours. He was in his glory when the boys of the Young Communists carried him on their shoulders up to the platform, from which he said that there was no problem, barrier, technical or natural obstacle that the sugar workers and cadres weren't capable of overcoming in that titanic struggle to produce the Ten Million.

When the ceremony concluded he felt that Jacinto Amézaga's time had started to tick. His deputy had predicted serious problems after that display, and he was ground down by fatigue, but felt unable to leave the factory. He thought that if he stayed there, with his eye on the machines, asking Grandfather Álvaro and Chava to help him in that battle that, this time for sure, was the last one the island would wage to achieve wealth and happiness, no kind of mishap could occur because, beyond fatigue and sleepiness, the obsession for triumph that had built up in his soul would become a material force, capable of prevailing over all obstacles. And so he began again his tour from the tippler to the tandems, from the kettle room to the bagging floor. In the fresh darkness of the storehouse there was a strange peace; the noises of the factory reached it muffled, at regular intervals, and the ground trembled slightly, almost as the earth had trembled at the Trocha, as a boat at full speed would tremble in a calm sea. He lay down on the sacks intending to get up in fifteen minutes. Two hours later he was awakened by the tragic certainty that the ground had stopped trembling. He went off running through the factory, dead and dark as in a nightmare, telling himself he should calm down, that he was dreaming, but the workers who were wandering around in astonishment through the gloomy premises all said the same thing: the mill had lost power, how or why was unknown. At the electric plant, he found Jacinto, the chief engineer, and the Horsemen of the Apocalypse totally disconcerted, searching for the cause of the disaster in the wavering dawn, and he told himself he was the one responsible, for having fallen asleep.

But first he had to see a commission made up of members of the local Popular Power, the CDRs, the Women's Federation, and the administrators of the pasteurizing plant, the hospital, the bakery, and the ice factory. He was very sorry, he said, he too was desperate, it was a tragedy that thousands of liters of milk would spoil, pounds of bread, 100-kilogram blocks of ice, it was anguishing to know that there was a doctor helping a woman give birth with flashlights, but what else could they do, he told them. Someone replied that

Happy had returned to town, and Carlos ordered them to bring him fast to the electric plant, with the hope that the loco would again get them out of danger. Perfidious Albion gave the hint of a disdainful smile when he saw Happy looking over the control panel with a lamp. Carlos forgave him the look, because the image of the loco, set off against the trembling light of the gas lamp, was truly grotesque. The blue hat with the scorpion, the bony cheeks, the little sunken eyes, and the hooked nose made you think of a scarecrow. But Carlos also thought that behind that erratic appearance there lived a genius, mutilated by the conditions in which he'd been born. It would be his turn to laugh when the Englishman's jaw fell with surprise at the unexpected solution to the problem the loco would give him. Happy finished looking over the controls, sat down on a stool stroking his chin, and suddenly started to run away. Carlos managed to catch up with him by the fence.

"Wait," he shouted, "what should we do?"

"I don't know," Happy replied.

He looked at the factory, dead as a ghost ship, heard the loco's steps, and began to kick the fence shouting obscenities; if at least, coño, he could do something, cojones, put his pistol to the head of some somabitch, crush the balls of some . . . Just then they urgently called him back to the office, he was being phoned by the regional, provincial, and national committees. When he arrived at his desk he stopped in confusion, looking at the three telephones. Finally he stuck one receiver between his jaw and shoulder, answered the others, informed them that he was listening and heard the same question three times: What the hell was going on?

"We have no electricity," he said, "and we don't know why."

A stream of voices came through the receivers: doing dumb things, lack of foresight, responsibilities, they're beating us, exemplary measures.

"Correct," he said.

Despaignes informed him he was leaving for the mill, Pablo that he'd keep on calling every fifteen minutes, and the ministry that they would do so every hour. When they hung up, Carlos let the phones drop.

"Why don't you rest?" his secretary asked him tenderly.

"Because I won't!" he yelled. "Tell Roberto to meet me at the electric plant."

Suddenly he felt very tired and thought about apologizing to the girl, but he was alone, downhearted, she reminded him intensely of Iraida and he didn't want to get mixed up in another mess. He headed double-time to the electric plant. Roberto, responsible for security in the mill, was waiting for him in the office. He didn't suspect anyone, it had been more that five years since they had dismantled the last and only counterrevolutionary network there ever was at the América Latina.

"Well," said Carlos, "maybe you rested on your laurels and they gave it to us in the ass, so start finding out."

"Okay," Roberto responded. "I'll leave now."

Just then they heard cries of "A rat! A rat!" and Carlos looked out the door, irritated: it was the limit that they should be crying like little fairies about a motherfucking rat. He almost crashed into the chief engineer who was approaching nervously, with the electrocuted animal in his hand. It's incredible, compañero administrator, but this little thing had been the cause of the disaster, the scoundrel had stuck itself in between two cables, making a bridge and bringing about a short in the master control.

"I can't believe it," Carlos murmured.

Theoretically it was impossible, said the engineer, because the register where it had entered *should* be sealed with porcelain, but the porcelain was broken; nevertheless, it was still impossible, because the cables it had grabbed onto *should* be covered with insulation, but they were peeled bare.

"All right," said Carlos in a very low voice. "How much time do we have now?"

"Minutes," replied the chief engineer, "minutes."

Back in the office, Carlos found on the table a copy of *Granma* with a headline highlighted by his secretary: *The "América Latina" joins the list of sugar mills reaching a million.* He read it with a weak smile, the reporter wasn't as dumb as he looked; he had captured the tense atmosphere in the mill and although he praised it, between the lines he complained about the lack of attention paid to the press and ended by insinuating a terrible doubt: "Will the men of the 'América Latina' be able to maintain the level of their historic responsibility?"

"Depends on the rats," Carlos murmured, clenching his teeth.

At 1:32 in the morning, a day after what was stipulated in the plan, the country produced its second million and Carlos presided over the ceremony, where the number two was hung under the banner of the Ten Million. He was annoyed because he felt responsible for that delay, small but unjustified at a point when the yields and the millings had to be optimal, to gain time over the rains of May and June. The rat incident had gotten the América Latina into a trap, when the mill shut down the cutting was stopped so the raw material wouldn't get old, and when the factory was ready to start up there wasn't enough cane. In addition, the sugar yields were almost two points below what was planned, and Despaignes, who attributed this to deficiencies in the manufacturing sector, was giving it more and more hell at the zafra staff meetings. Jacinto, on the other hand, pointed to the shocking level of foreign material that the agricultural sector was sending into the tandems. Carlos didn't know what to do. With Couzo's help he found the problems in manufacturing: lack of uniformity in the cane blanket, excess imbibition of water, imbalance in the grinders, irregularity in the alcalinization of the juice, bad operation of the vacuum pans; but he also discovered, with a migraine drilling into his brain, that almost all of them originated in the errors the agricultural sector was making: brutal alterations of the plan for cutting, an unacceptable level of impurities, systematic irregularities in the supply, dreadful loading in carts, bins, and trucks . . . And all this proved, he shouted at the staff meeting, that it was agriculture that first had to put its house in order; respond, compañero Despaignes, he was giving him a summons. Despaignes became livid, and Carlos felt glad. El Negro exerted an insufferable authority over him, recently he'd been enduring him like a scolding father, and now he had freed himself and for the first time he felt the cadres from manufacturing were pleased, that finally they recognized him as a leader. Because of that he decided to keep on punching and turned the summons into a challenge, manufacturing would commit itself, he said, to resolving its problems in two weeks and to maintaining the million-mark millings, and he wanted agriculture to say right then and there if it was capable of resolving its own, and of supplying sufficient cane. He finished exultant, but by then Despaignes had recovered and was saying that the problems of the harvest, with a nonexpert labor force, were too serious for making a commitment to resolve them in such a short time; he made one of his very astute pauses, then he congratulated manufacturing for the commitment it had publicly assumed, which would be checked on there, in the meeting, and he promised that there would be cane, there would be cane even if the factory shut down and even if it rained so hard the sky fell, he was the one responsible for that.

Carlos was left voiceless after meeting with all the heads of the factory at every level, but for some reason that escaped him, being conscious of the problems wasn't enough to resolve them. He was desperate when the country reached the third million, two days late, with scarcely twenty-four hours left before the América Latina had to stop because the cavity underneath the tippler was overflowing. A totally absurd reason, Jacinto had said; never in sugar manufacturing had anything like this happened, he could look through the books of all the mills from every era and verify that. Carlos responded enraged that now they had to get done with shame and balls what used to be done from desperation and hunger, which wasn't the same thing, did he understand? And he left, leaving Jacinto before he had a chance to speak. He knew very well that it was his fault, for having allowed Despaignes to move the twenty-five men who should be keeping the motherfucking cavity clean out to the cutting field, and he repeated over and over to himself that he hadn't done it because of irresponsibility or cowardice, but ignorance. The cavity under the new tippler was immense, he would never have thought that it could overflow in three months, threatening to jam the conveyor belt to the tandems, or that the pump meant to keep it down would be broken and unfixable. And now Despaignes refused to give him back the brigade. The worst thing was that he, in Despaignes's place, would have done the same. Besides being ignorant he had been a stupid shithead, and incapable of maintaining the authority of the manufacturing sector with which Pablo had entrusted him by proposing him for the job. Something like that was what Pedro Ordóñez, secretary of the Workers' Union, said to him when Carlos proposed forming a brigade with men who were now having time off, to clean the cavity. It was very difficult, compañero administrator, to convince workers about things like that, the secretary added, they had given up pay for overtime, they were willing to do double shifts and to die producing sugar, but could Carlos please tell him why they had to steal hours of sleep and rest from them to pay for a mistake that wasn't theirs? Carlos stayed mute and dropped his head. He had a nice little speech prepared about proletarian honor, but felt incapable of saying it. Perhaps that saved him, because Pedro Ordóñez seemed to be expecting a harangue and was disconcerted and suddenly murmured, all right, he was going to talk to his people.

Against Jacinto's judgement, Carlos put himself at the head of the brigade that was going to clean the cavity. Pedro Ordóñez's question about the mistake had shaken him, and although he could understand that perhaps an administrator shouldn't use his time or energy doing a peon's job, he felt the moral need to pay. At first the work was disgusting, but bearable. The accumulated waste reached street level and they went about putting into sacks the rotted cane, reeds, and rats that they then moved to a truck. They worked standing up in that filthy muck, and as they went on pulling it out, they sank more and more into the cavity. From the bottom rose an unbearable stench of dead animals, sewer water, and rotted slime. Their gloves, clothing, bodies became impregnated with a pestilent magma. When it was no longer possible to move the sacks directly and they had to be tied to a rope to hoist them up, Carlos decided to rotate the men every five minutes. But no one could stand so much time amid moldy cane, rotted cats, and sulfuric gases. The men prepared themselves above to submerge into that putrid mass, ran down the ladder, worked until they felt their lungs about to burst, and came up dripping with a thick, black liquid like tar. Preparing himself for the plunge Carlos thought how ironic it turned out to be that as you advanced you sank down, filled his lungs with fresh air, closed his eyes, and started to descend on the wet, rusty ladder towards the territory of shit, cockroaches, and rats' snouts. He felt like he preferred war or death to that torture and decided that one sack was enough. But he couldn't manage to fill it. He was ashamed to go up with it empty, calculated that he could stand it for a minute, and made the mistake of kneeling down on the dark putrid mass to shorten the task. Then he felt that he was choking, swallowed a mouthful of stinking air, thought he saw the antennae of a cockroach twirling in his nose, and fainted.

Up above, surrounded by workers to whom Pedro Ordóñez was shouting to give him some air, he managed to stand up, vomited, and decided his task was finished. After burning his clothing he got under the shower, with soap and a brush, but the stench plagued him for weeks, like a punishment. That horrible effort had an unexpected compensation, his prestige among the workers increased so much that they came to consider him a local. Thus harbored by the town, his life became easier. Families argued over the privilege of inviting him to lunch, old ladies made him desserts with delicious flavors, were constantly concerned about his health, and made him infusions of white morning-glory flowers when they noticed he was nervous. One day he received a report from the University of Havana where it was stated that compañero Ireneo Salvatierra had been subjected to several tests whose result was definite: mental health, unrecoverable, of which he was being informed for his knowledge and for all other intents and purposes. He took a moment to realize that Ireneo Salvatierra was none other than Happy. Then he concluded that he had behaved like a scoundrel with the loco and decided to give him the apartment that came along with his position of administrator and that he had dreamed of moving into with Gisela. She hadn't even written to him, she wasn't going to come now or ever, and it was all the same to him whether he had a room or a bunk. His efforts to lead the mill seemed condemned to go in a sinister cycle: million-arroba milling—breakdown—suspension of the cutting—lack of cane; or else the latter on account of early rains, a low average for the macheteros, or because it was Sunday. His relationships with Pablo and Despaignes were very tense, and he wondered what would happen when the agricultural sector got reinforcements and was able to change the balance of unmet goals that now favored manufacturing.

The fourth million was produced on March 5, exactly five days after what was planned, and although as always there was an enthusiastic ceremony, Carlos was feeling the impact of an awful calculation. He had figured it out as a game, because despite everything five days seemed like an acceptable delay to him. But thinking about it, he realized that the unmet goals had been growing in a geometric progression and if it continued that way, or even increased only by five each time, the tenth million would be achieved on July 45, with good weather. For the first time he thought an unutterable word: *never*. By that date—August 19 by the calendar—the cane would be in the inverse phase of its vegetative cycle and wouldn't produce a drop of sugar. He went towards the platform feeling upset, but on seeing the crowd accused himself of being self-satisfied and skeptical; that misfortune *couldn't* happen, there *had* to be a solution, surely *already* there was one, and only skeptics like him would make room for the germ of dissolving doubt. When he hung the number four under the slogan he trembled from the ovation and began to talk against his own thoughts: there were those who gave themselves the luxury of doubting, he said, but the people didn't have time for those parlor games, because they were meeting their goals, as that four proved, just one more point in the heroic road of the zafra. He joined in the crowd's chorus of *vivas*, and soon his doubts seemed like the hesitations of a stranger. He had been able to exorcize them in communion with the people who had been struggling for happiness since the time of his great-grandfather, and who now, more than one hundred years after having gone to war, were at the point of winning their noblest battle. He was happy feeling that he had confidence and believed more than ever in his own words: the island would sink into the sea before failing in this commitment, patriaomuerte, compañeros, venceremos.

The next two weeks brought about his reconciliation with the América Latina. Watching it mill the sugar, Carlos reaffirmed his faith in victory and in future yields, above all now that the cane was guaranteed by soldiers, recruits, and students, besides the usual and the volunteer macheteros. On March 20 a technical commission came to the factory to install the most modern of machines, the hydrocyclone, able to separate impurities, thus facilitating the manufacturing process. He felt radiant on seeing his predictions met, but at five in the afternoon he was informed that there was a very strange problem with a train in the tippler yard. He walked down the line stepping on *every* nail, but it didn't do him any good; it was a god-awful mess. The train belonged to the phantom district, a special area created by Despaignes in an attempt to break the vicious cycle that went from stoppage due to breakdown to suspension of the cutting to stoppage due to lack of cane. There they cut phantom cane, a reserve that any of the six mills in the region could avail themselves of if they urgently needed raw material. The América Latina had milled that cane several times, grateful to Despaignes for such a brilliant idea. But during those days, with the entire region milling at speed, the phantom cane had accumulated and when the district's men took some action, stopped the cutting, loaded that train, and sent it off with an unknown destination, the raw material had begun to decompose. That was why Epaminondas Montero, chief of production at the América Latina, refused to accept it. The phantom engineer insisted on speaking with the administrator and was about to create a bottleneck in the traffic through the yard. On principle, Carlos usually supported his subordinates, but the phantom engineer impressed him with his odyssey. He had rotated in vain through four of the six mills, had been riding that old heap for thirty-two hours, his head felt like a watermelon, and, after all, cane was cane. The engineer was right. Besides, he would avoid problems with Despaignes, and although the yield went down a little, perhaps the hydrocyclone would compensate for the loss.

"Weigh it," he ordered.

"Señor Administrator," the voice of the chief of production was very nasal and came out high and sharp like that of a *son* singer, "if you do such an atrocious thing, I resign."

Carlos turned around, furious, with the intention of telling him to go ahead and resign; Epaminondas Montero wasn't a revolutionary and that public challenge to his authority had an undisguised political tone. Suddenly he decided to have a discussion, he hadn't been leading the mill for months just for fun, he knew as much about sugar as anyone, and he felt capable of teaching him a lesson.

"And what do we do with this cane?" he asked.

"Throw it out," said Epaminondas.

"Aha," Carlos murmured sarcastically.

The nut had been cracked, who would think of throwing out a trainload of cane in the middle of the zafra except a gusano? Fat Epaminondas, as chief of production, was responsible for the low yields, and perhaps for much more.

"And doesn't that," he said, "seem like sabotage to you?"

Epaminondas Montero was ruddy-faced and asthmatic and he got red, as if on the verge of collapse. When he recovered his speech he said, Señor Administrator, he had been the chief of production at Sola for thirty years and he loved those machines like his children, did he have any idea what would happen if they milled that cane? Carlos replied, yes, the yield would go down and that was a calculated risk. But Epaminondas didn't let him go on; I can't believe this, he said, and swallowed some air, and said, no, Señor Administrator, it would produce a process of acidulation, which as everyone knows destroys the sucrose molecule and splits it into glucose and fructose, reducing sugars capable of spoiling *all* the production that right now was in the belly of the mill and amounted to trainloads and trainloads of cane; and that, Señor Administrator, that really *was* sabotage, and now he was going home because it was impossible to work like this.

"Take the train away!" yelled Carlos, torn between his authority and his ignorance.

"Where to?" asked the engineer.

"To wherever you like," he replied, running off after Epaminondas Montero.

He wasn't sure whether to call to him and apologize, to ask Pedro Ordóñez for advice, or to order Roberto to investigate the case. A moving train forced him to stop. The bins, empty and all alike, passed by like in a movie. Another locomotive whistled: the phantom train resumed its mad pilgrimage. He watched it feeling guilty, about what he didn't know, and suddenly he waved goodbye. From the high-up cab, the engineer gave him a sad look. The thirty-two cars went by, clickety-clack, clickety-clack, and became lost in the distance, under black thunder clouds.

Pedro Ordóñez told him not to worry, Epaminondas Montero lived longing for the order of Sola Sugar, but he wouldn't lift a finger against the mill, tomorrow he would be at his job. So it was, and when Carlos plucked up his courage and apologized, Epaminondas replied reluctantly that an administrator had to know how to act accordingly. Carlos didn't know if he was referring to the incident with the train or the apology, nor did he try to find out, he thanked Epaminondas for saving him from an irreparable mistake and that was enough. He was almost happy, that March 26 the fifth million had been reached and in his own very personal calculation of probabilities, that was a triumph. Now the accumulated delay was nine days, it hadn't increased in geometric progression or by five, as he had come to fear. Nevertheless, his dark side insisted on reminding him that April was the cruelest month and May the most terrible, how could they decrease the delay with the rains?

During the first week of April the América Latina reached three million-level millings and was going after the fourth when it had to stop running because of lack of cane. An untimely downpour had forced a halt to the cutting, and Carlos reacted with terrifically intense fury, and went out to rant against the somabitch, traitorous rain. Just then he saw a very long train coming, remembered the phantom district, and began jumping for joy. Suddenly he stopped, mouth hanging open. It was impossible, totally, completely, absolutely impossible. He started running in the rain telling himself that a hallucination or the gray sky, clouds, and air were making him see gray cane, a leaden, ashy, funereal gray that wrapped like a mist around the phantom train which now had halted, with the engineer sending him from the cab an imploring, unreal look, and inviting him to hear the sad story of the Wandering Screwed who went rolling along, wrapped in a cloud of flies and gnats. When he had sent him away from the América Latina he went to the "Brazil" mill, where they wouldn't let him unload either; he kept roaming to the "Peru" and the "Venezuela" and he even made it to the "España" and the "Africa Libre." And since they always told him the same thing, he realized that his fate was to transport that damned cargo to nowhere, for all eternity. He wasn't afraid anymore of the insults or the mockery. He simply ceased making stops at the mills. He traveled. In the fresh mornings and the nights he enjoyed the trip, but he suffered under the glare of the sun and tortured himself with useless questions in the crushing solitude of the oceanic cane fields. Then he would pull in at some whistle stop, next to the cranes, where merciful hands would give him water and food so that he might continue his pilgrimage. Several times he tried to throw out the rotted cane, but no crane operator wanted to be an accomplice to such waste.

"Why didn't you talk with Despaignes?" Carlos, moved, managed to say.

The engineer smiled sadly while he stroked the beard he had grown during the trip. He didn't dare, he said, the mistake of not halting the cutting had been made by the administrator of the phantom district, a brother of his to whom he had sworn on his mother's grave that he wouldn't return until he'd gotten the cane milled. Now he didn't know what to do, where to go, when to stop. Now, with the rain, the bugs were hiding, but when the sun came out a horrendous swarm of flies and gnats would come down again on the fermented cane and over his head. Could he do something, not as an administrator, but, say, just as a Christian?

Carlos permitted him to pull the phantom train into a dead-end track and had Despaignes come. El Negro went gray, ashen like the cane on hearing about the tribulations of the Wandering Screwed, said that the administrator of the phantom district was going to spend ten zafras as a machetero, so he'd know what it was like to get the full treatment, and ordered that they pull the train out of the dead-end track and take it to the last crane to finally throw all that garbage out. The phantom train went back on the road for the last time, but it was traveling in Carlos's imagination until the end of the zafra.

The provincial meeting of the sixth million was celebrated at the América Latina; by then, April 16, the accumulated delay was thirteen days and Carlos had reasons to feel optimistic. For the first time the lag had been equal to that of the preceding million, four days, and that could mean that they had begun a downward curve. If they were able to reduce by one day the delay for each of the remaining millions, they'd produce ten before July 26 and the country would have consolidated the necessary material base for simultaneously building socialism and communism. True, they would have to attain that feat in terrible months, but there was no other alternative. And so he suffocated those damned interior voices that insisted on talking to him about rains, low yields, failures in the hydrocyclones, and all the rest. They were in the waiting room of his office, waiting for Captain Monteagudo and the engineer Pérez Peña, gathered in private with the foreign technicians after their goodbye party. Carlos was trying to explain the operational complexities of the hydrocyclone to Pedro when the captain made his entrance, crossed the area with long strides, head down, and in silence reached the door of the office. Then Happy stopped him, tugging on the sleeve of his shirt. Carlos asked himself where the hell the loco had come from, he must have been there from before, without a doubt, but no one had seen him and now the damage was done. Monteagudo was in a nasty mood and reacted violently when he felt himself pulled, but controlled himself and tried to smile on seeing the loco.

"Hey, Captain," said Happy, "say hello, you know? Because if you don't, you'll be like me, with no friends, and that's bad, baaaaad."

"What's up, Happy," Monteagudo replied, putting his hand on his shoulder, with an unusual gesture of tenderness. Then he turned toward the group. "Afternoon, compañeros."

During the meeting Carlos was thankful for Happy's craziness, somehow it had relaxed the atmosphere and softened the many contradictions that emerged. But Monteagudo was not optimistic as he gave the summary. The phase of decisive effort, he said, had begun; to attain the Ten Million it was essential to reach the seventh in April, reducing the delay by three days and not by one, as compañero Carlos had said; and even so, between May 1 and July 26 three more millions would have to be produced, and that, with the rains, would be little less than a miracle. He stopped talking, surprised by his own words, to which he immediately gave the correct response: the people, he said, were capable of doing miracles in circumstances like this; in the province there was sufficient cane and courage, but that was only half the problem, the other was knowing if manufacturing, even if it were receiving in its tandems a high proportion of foreign materials . . .

"Yes," Carlos interrupted him.

"Why yes?" the captain answered.

Carlos went mute as he realized he had spoken with his heart and not his head; he wasn't able to explain it, but he *felt* in the deepest part of his soul that so, so very much effort couldn't be left undone, that force of will could prevail even over the laws of that complicated manufacturing process, that even they would have to submit to justice because the people had spilled too much sweat to have victory denied them. Carlos couldn't decide whether or not to speak, Monteagudo was expecting another kind of answer, and it wasn't his place to try to inspire his confidence. He felt better when Pérez Peña took the floor and said that manufacturing would be capable of that achievement, although not for miraculous reasons, but scientific ones; next week equipment with nuclear technology would be installed in the mills, capable of reducing by one to four hours the process of cooking the syrup in the vacuum pans, increasing productivity incredibly. Carlos gave in to the temptation to pat Pablo and Pérez Peña on the back, but Monteagudo murmured a pensive I hope so before standing up.

In his sixth-million speech Carlos referred to an atomic solution, making the word and the expectation widespread in Sola. When the ceremony ended he had to accompany Monteagudo to Happy's house. The captain was truly interested in the loco, and although he was pleased that Carlos had given him an apartment, he couldn't hide his irritation with the conclusions from the university. They weren't crazy, and they had seen the loco do wonders, he had to be given confidence, a job, and of course a salary, he said before entering the apartment that Happy had already packed with old pieces of electronic junk. Behind the bedroom door was a motor that sounded like it was about to make the building fly away. When they entered, led by the grandmother, they were met by a furious gust of wind. They stood there looking at a large fan with very wide yellow blades, and Happy explained that the heat made him nervous and he'd built the machine with the motor from an abandoned truck. Monteagudo started to laugh and attempted to steer the conversation to the needs of the América Latina. But Happy didn't give him a chance, it made him nervous that children fell, he said, it made him feel sorry, he never understood why they couldn't fly like birds; in Havana they had explained it to him and now he was inventing the Graviton, a machine able to overcome the effects of the Law of Universal Gravitation and allow children to fly like finches. Like that, little by little, scientifically, he'd resolve all the problems that made him nervous and he wouldn't be crazy anymore. Carlos walked over radios and mixers until he sat down on the big shell of a television against the wall, where he could avoid the blast of wind that was drilling through his head. Monteagudo seemed not to feel it, he was sitting on top of a tangle of cables, his hair like a windmill, and asking Happy why, then, had he made the tandems start that day. The loco sighed; always, ever since he was a boy, he'd gone to sleep with the noise of the tandems, and that year they hadn't sounded although they were nice and new, and that made him nervous and everyone in Sola was going around nervous, like children when they can't fly. Carlos smiled at that irrefutable logic, but made a sour face when Monteagudo asked Happy about his friend; he felt a little like a thief about that skull, that in spite of everything made his room more human, and with which he'd gotten used to talking. Happy threw him a conspiratorial smile, his friend had moved, he said, he was living with the administrator, where he was needed more. Monteagudo nodded, showing no sign of surprise, and when they said good-bye, he invited Happy to the installation ceremony for the nuclear device. The loco flatly refused.

"It makes me nervous," he said.

After meeting with the Provincial Commission, Carlos returned to his office intending to look over the laboratory reports. Sitting down in the old revolving chair, he was stunned: on the desk there was a letter from Gisela. He reached for it: was it a honeycomb or a hornet's nest? He couldn't open it there, unable to control his reaction, and he ran to his room panting, between excitement and despair. He put the skull on the night table and asked it why Gisela had taken five months to answer him, maybe because she'd decided to get remarried and she felt bad about hurting him, or because she'd gotten tired of the other man, or because there wasn't any other man, but just him, only him, with his love and his craziness. He closed his eyes and fumbling, tore the envelope open, and covered the paper with his hand to keep his desperation from making him read ahead. He uncovered the sheet of paper slowly, feeling that he was betting his happiness on a card, that card. Finally he decided to look. He felt a happy palpitation, he had an ace, it was dated in February, it wasn't Gisela who had taken so long but the mail, that miserable entelechy, how was it possible that his love, his fate, his life could have been imprisoned for so much time in valises, trains, dark offices? Not even the skull could answer him. He had to go on, dare to read the first line, had she written *Love*, another trump, or just *friend*, a poor hand? *Carlos*, she had written *Carlos* and that could mean so many things that he decided to break the rules of the game and read in one blow that disconsolate letter, that at times took refuge in anecdotes and messages from Mercedita, and at others opened up with anxious questions that involved both his love and the zafra, could they, did he think they could?

He responded yes with a decisiveness that would have surprised Monteagudo again. He felt that over the despair and the delay and the inability and the craziness and the mistakes and the doubts, both they and the island had won through struggle the right to happiness, and that there could be no force in this world or the next capable of blocking it. But another answer, tortuous and gloomy, pounded at his skull: no, they couldn't, neither the two of them, nor the country. The afternoon when, finally, the atomic device was installed, Carlos had arrived at an absolutely unstable equilibrium. Enrique Martiatu, the specialist from the Nuclear Commission, inspired in him a profound mistrust; he was too sure of himself, too aware of his intelligence, too distant from the real country. Watching him operate, Carlos told himself time and again that this must be what physicists were like, those modern wizards, clean, immaculate, so wise that they were thousands of kilometers from people like him, who had no other horizon than the zafra.

Martiatu had climbed up the first vacuum pan and addressed himself to the group looking up at him from below, their mouths open.

"This," he said, pointing to a metallic, bright blue wrapper, that he held with some nickel-plated tongs, "is a radioactive isotope of cobalt 60 contained in a sealed dish, which in turn is introduced into a hermetic capsule, absolutely secure against radioactivity, all right? Good, now we introduce the isotope into the cooked mass"—and he let the wrapper fall into the pan—"in such a way that it will move with it for the whooole process. The isotope, compañeros, emits gamma rays, all right? Now let's go to the outside of the pan. Here, as you see, we have eight detector devices"—he moved the tongs toward some metallic crustaceans attached to the body of the tank—"that follow through the gamma rays the movement of the radioactive dish, and therefore of the cooked mass, determining the form and velocity of the circulation. Each detector device traces, through electronic impulses, a graph of its area, so that at the end of the cooking we will have eight graphs that, together, reproduce the process in the whooole pan, allowing us to determine the real velocity of the mass and the dead areas inside the machine, all right? Good, with that we can optimize operations, always using the best pans and repairing the worst ones, reducing the cooking time by several hours. Until today you have been working blindly; the atom, compañeros, will allow you to *see*, to scrutinize the insides of the process, all right? Good, any questions?"

Carlos felt that the men of the boiler room were looking at him blankly. He himself hadn't understood a damn thing either, but Martiatu's explanation was so coherent, so solid, so persuasive that maybe all that stuff really was true. The workers would feel hurt because he had called them blind, which was tactless; but it wasn't a matter of clashing, but rather of allying with science. The compañero had to understand, he said, that there in the América Latina they didn't have, on the average, a high level of schooling, and therefore that they preferred to learn through practice; he, personally, was sure that in one or two weeks, the workers, determined not to be left behind in the technical-scientific revolution, would learn under Martiatu's direction all the secrets of atomic optimization of the pans, would contribute in that way to the growth of productivity, and with that, would make the América Latina recoup what it had lost and advance much more.

"It would be great if it were possible," Martiatu replied, "but the country has 126 mills and only three atomic physicists, therefore I have to take care of forty-two. That means I have to leave. The device is installed and functioning; the rest is your responsibility."

Three days later, in spite of the fact that Carlos, Epaminondas, Couzo, and Jacinto ruminated like oxen over those indecipherable diagrams, the atomic solution was discarded, April ended, and the seventh million was not made. Carlos couldn't unlink the fate of his love from that of the zafra, and when, with eighteen days of now unrecoverable delay, the seventh million was finally attained, he had no strength to talk at the rally. He couldn't lie or say the truth either, his frustration was so great that he harbored the fear of ending up in tears on the platform. He did the ritual duty of putting the number under the banner and responded to the applause with a succinct patriaomuerte.

On May 11, Jacinto interrupted his insomnia to inform him that mercenary launches had sunk two fishing boats and kidnapped their eleven crewmembers. It was the second attack in less than a month, on April 18 a landing in Baracoa had occurred, the mercenaries were captured, but five militiamen died in combat. This time a general mobilization was decreed, and Carlos put himself at the head of civil defense for the América Latina, thinking that those actions could be the prelude to another Girón. The Yanquis had spies, analysts, computers; they probably knew about the imminence of failure and had thought it was the moment to strike. The people responded with an effervescent frenzy, and he forgot his depression in the midst of the double battle, following day by day the unequal pace of the factory and the defense preparations. Opening the sealed envelope with instructions on how to proceed in case of an attack caused a unique excitement in him. There was a detailed plan for the evacuation of children and old people, the order to defend the town house by house, another to burn it down if there were no alternative, and another to escape the mill and withdraw into the mountains to continue fighting down to the last man and the last bullet. That apocalyptic decision gave him spirit during the nine feverish days in which the people stayed in the streets of cities, hamlets, and mill towns, ready for anything, and finally attained the liberation of their brothers. Then the whole country exploded into a party that became suddenly very, very sad, because when he met with the fishermen, Fidel said that they would not make the Ten Million Tons, and Carlos thought about Gisela and wondered why, and recalled the instructions for war and decided that he, too, would take on the motto of turning setbacks into victory. But he scarcely found the strength to stand in the midst of the overwhelming silence that fell on the office when Fidel's speech was over. He went out into the street downcast, telling himself that in spite of everything, they had performed quite a feat, that by now they had produced more sugar than the companies in their greatest harvests and that they had done it with a large dose of craziness, but without hunger or the whip. Mechanically, he turned to the left and suddenly found himself enveloped in the fast-paced atmosphere of the tipplers. The base radio was transmitting the last chords of the anthem. The workers, who were working with a kind of molasses-like stubbornness, greeted him in silence. He returned the greeting and, swallowing hard, went into the factory.

W hy? he repeated, feeling like his mind had gone blank at Margarita's question. They'd have to forgive him, he said, they might think he was improvising everything, but no, he'd stayed up all night, conscientiously reflecting on the form, the *tellmeyourstory*, and scarcely two hours ago . . . The silence stopped him. He had thought the informal little expression would cause laughter, would alleviate the tension, and now, with his compañeros' expectant eyes on him, he asked himself again if it wouldn't have been better to refuse that debate, exercising his right to voluntary participation, and immediately answered, no, that he had done well to agree to it, that above all else in the world he needed to know how much his life mattered, and no, compañera, he went on, breaking the silence, the matter of the vouchers wasn't so simple, if he hadn't sold them it wasn't *only* out of fear, there were other factors he didn't mention so as to simplify things, because . . . what else could you do in a summary? Now, if this was about *telling* his life story, truly telling it, then he'd have to start with his grandfather, because that was the first important memory he had, and with a little illiterate girl named Toña, with whom he'd fallen in love, although . . . He stopped, panting. If he continued down that path, avoiding the outline of questions, he'd end up in a labyrinth. What the hell did it matter that he had fallen in love with Toña? What did that have to do with his *political* trajectory? They'd have to forgive him again, compañeros, he was a little nervous. What was certain was that after that, there was a war, that is, something kind of like a war, an eviction in the neighborhood where he was living. They should understand, he didn't mean that in those days he had a political consciousness, not at all, just that those events had made an impression on him, the same as his grandfather and an old black man named Chava. Of course he wasn't going to get into those stories, they weren't relevant, but about the vouchers . . . yes, compañera, it had been out of fear, the same as at the demonstration, in '56, when the police opened fire and he turned his back on his compañeros and ran away and didn't get involved in politics again until '59. He wanted to make clear that he considered that act an error, a serious error, which he would never regret enough, but he was grateful that his compañeros hadn't made him pay for it, because thanks to them, after the Revolution, he served as press and propaganda secretary on the slate of the United Left at the Instituto. In those days, he wasn't trying to hide it, he had prejudices against the Communists, but life itself and the right had taken care of refuting and dissolving them. The left won, he devoted himself to his work and frankly, he thought he'd done it well, until his brother came back from the North, in '60. Then, because of family reasons and his profound ideological weakness, he distanced himself from political work, he spent months distanced from political work. It was incredible, he said, and shook his shoulders, as if freeing himself from that memory. In his favor, he could say that in November he joined the militia, walked the sixty-two kilometers, and left home. He also met the woman who would become his compañera, finished boot camp, and participated in the January '61 mobilization. Then he had a problem, his father had been sick for a while, the truth is that the Revolution had done him a lot of damage, and during those days he had a heart attack, and he decided to leave to go see him in the hospital, there was an inspection, and they sanctioned him with the loss of his command.

"You left before or after the break off with the United States?" asked Marta Hernández.

Carlos closed his eyes, he didn't remember, but suddenly he saw as if in a dream the headline in *Revolución* with the news, and he said, oh, yes, after, after the break.

"Don't you think that's a *very* serious error?" asked Jiménez Cardoso.

No, Carlos replied looking him in the eyes; at that time, compañeros, things were different, it was another kind of discipline, people left and went back and he had been sure he'd have time enough to return before the battalion moved out. Soon after he decided to accept a scholarship, he recognized that having been sanctioned bothered him a lot, but he wanted to make clear that the most fundamental reason was that he didn't have anywhere to live and in the Beca, at least, he'd find a refuge. Maybe that need was what led him to enroll in Architecture School, he couldn't say for sure, but at that time he dreamed about building houses and cities. Oh, wait, he had forgotten something, he hadn't participated in the Escambray Clean-up because he wasn't in the combat unit, or in the Literacy Campaign because he was a university student. That gave him something like a complex, no? A dissatisfaction with himself. The fact is that when his father died, he was just a student. Months later Girón happened. He participated in the war, to be entirely frank, almost by accident; but he fought correctly, normally, and that was an important moment in his life, because it allowed him to overcome his complexes and his fear. He believed, if they'd forgive him, that a man, besides having a child and planting a tree, should prove himself in war. When he returned to the university they elected him president of the FEU of his school. It was a dark period, no? He worked hard, but he became sectarian, extremist, a sort of Red Guard or better yet, red priest. He had a kind of halo, he said, and his voice trembled slightly, he knew it was ridiculous, but he came to think that he was a hero, yes, compañeros, since childhood he'd had that illusion. Well, he was over the edge, totally nuts, and among other things he would give orders and impose his opinions, and, well, he made life impossible for people. And so when the . . .

Jiménez Cardoso had raised his hand.

"A clarification," he said. "How was it that you made life impossible for people?"

Well, he said, looking down at the floor, that was what he was trying to explain, no? That his compañeros would come and tell him, for example, that they were going to put up an exhibition of paintings, and if he didn't like the pictures then he'd prohibit them, that's all, he'd prohibit the exhibition, or better said, he tried to prohibit it, and the same thing, let's say, with curse words, he prohibited curse words . . . Someone let out a snort of laughter behind him; Carlos smiled, uncomfortable, and things of that sort, he said, like he'd see a strange fellow, a little soft, who seemed a little too soft to him? Well, that would stick in his craw, as the vulgar saying goes, he wouldn't leave him in peace . . . He wiped the sweat off his temples, with a feeling of relief, and imagine how crazy he was, he added, he'd been in agreement with the altering of Echeverría's testament; he'd gotten to that extreme, compañeros. That was in '62, and Fidel shocked him with his speech on March 13. The student general assembly removed him from the presidency; he was left in a bad way, confused and hurt, and again closed himself off between March and October, like in '60, months and months without doing anything, without saying boo, as they say, without . . . His voice trickled off and with a movement of his head he thanked them for the glass of water they handed him from the table. He drank, wiped his eyes, and said that he had been saved, compañeros, by the October Crisis. It was, he'd never forget it, his wedding night. Thanks, sorry, he said, returning the glass. During the crisis he had an accident in which he was left lame and lost his teeth, because of that and being nervous he had some difficulty speaking.

"You know, compañero," the chair of the assembly interrupted, "I'm sorry to go back, but I've got a question: after March 13 you distanced yourself from political activity, is that right? Well, did that mean that you didn't understand Fidel's speech, or that you didn't agree with his criticism of sectarianism?"

Carlos asked him to repeat the question for him, afraid he'd lose the thread of his thought again, and, no, compañero, he said, not at all. Fidel showed him how far down someone can go into . . . Yes, he had understood, he was in agreement from the beginning . . . But other things happened, in the assembly there was a guy, an opportunist, and he . . . He couldn't explain it, he was very confused.

"And couldn't it be, compañero, that your wish to be a hero was still evident in gestures of self-satisfaction?"

Carlos was stunned as he recalled his own monologue facing death; now he had the same lucidity, the same obsession for truth and he said that, yes, the compañero was right, he had been self-satisfied. Then the chair suggested a recess but he refused, he preferred to keep going if the assembly didn't mind. Silence prodded him to continue, he took up the thread at an earlier point, when the UJC didn't think it opportune to put through his membership and he, compañeros, in one more manifestation of his self-satisfaction, didn't understand that decision. But after the accident they didn't put it through either and that, both then and now, seemed to him an error of the Core Committee. Well, he lost a year at the university because the school refused to give him exams in the hospital, and when he went back to his classes he felt discouraged and soon after he left his studies. Several voices asked why and Carlos put up his hand asking for silence before saying for several reasons: his daughter had been born, he needed to work, and besides that, compañeros, perhaps as part of the illusions that had always been with him, he dreamed of joining the guerrilla movement. He closed his eyes to avoid some mocking expression, because he wasn't willing to let anyone play games with what had been his highest hope. Because of that, he continued, he had gone to work at the center. He opened his eyes and looked around the room as he said that there, as almost everyone present knew, they had awarded him militancy in the Young Communists, he had become general secretary of the Core Committee and section head. He paused before asking the assembly if it was necessary to refer to the incident. "Only in its political consequences," replied the center director from the table, and Carlos remained silent while he tried to discern which exactly had been the political consequences of the deed that had forever disrupted his life. He didn't have them clear; he didn't even know how to refer to what had happened with Iraida; he didn't dare say that they were *making love*, much less that they were *balling*; he simply said that they had been caught by surprise in the office, which had been an error, a lack of respect, an outrage on his part. So then they had expelled him indefinitely from the UJC and suspended his job and salary. Around that time, compañeros, Che died, and he, out of work, decided to go cut cane. "Go back to the UJC," Margarita suggested, and he said: Oh, yes, the Municipal Committee of the Young Communists lowered his sanction to a year, wasn't that right, Rubén?

"Yes," Margarita replied, "and I need for you to explain, Carlitos, why you didn't appeal or petition when the period was over, that is, why did you almost expel yourself from the organization?"

He felt perplexed, actually he hadn't thought about that even doing the *tellmeyourstory*, and now he felt disarmed. He tried to explain, without having it seem like a justification, how differently things looked from the cane fields, Márgara, for a machetero, a workforce chief, or the administrator of a mill during the '70 zafra. Then Felipe asked for a point of order, and Carlos had the hunch that his old buddy was going to launch an in-depth attack.

"I'm going to go back," Felipe announced, "it's an issue, well, ugly, upsetting, but we're here for that, to clarify—" He stopped talking as if anguished by the gravity of the problem, and suddenly added, in an almost confidential tone, "Carlos, look, I think it's better if you present it yourself, it's cleaner."

Felipe's tension had created a growing expectation in the room, and Carlos, all eyes on him, felt like he'd been slapped in the face; it wasn't possible that Felipe could be so low, it wasn't possible that he could be referring to *that*, but, what else could it be then? He didn't understand the compañero, he said, they'd have to forgive him but he didn't know what he was talking about.

Felipe made an annoyed face, as if Carlos had forced him to say, to his regret: "Look, when you got into the jam about Iraida, you got divorced, right? Why?"

The expectation in the room turned into a wave of murmurs, over which Carlos shouted that he refused to answer that question or in general to discuss his private life.

"For me it's a question of principle," Felipe replied, "because later you got married again to the same woman."

Carlos had shouted that that wasn't anybody's business when the chair demanded silence.

"The compañero," he said, "has the right to refuse, and you"—he directed himself to Felipe, who was asking to speak again—"to present your opinions, later, in the debate."

He nodded at Carlos to continue and asked again for silence. The assembly calmed down. Carlos, his head low, ran his fingers through his hair, disconcerted, and asked what he'd been talking about.

"About the Young Communists," Marta Hernández said helpfully.

Yes, about the UJC, he said, he knew it was hard to explain, but between '68 and '70 he had only two leaves, one for a month and a half and one for a week, and during that time, truthfully, he didn't think about appealing or petitioning. It was an error, *another* error, and, well, what could he tell them? He'd already explained about the zafra, three campaigns, machetero, workforce chief, and administrator; he thought, honestly, that he'd done the best he possibly could.

"Isn't there anything you regret about those years?" asked Margarita.

He tugged at his hair again, let me think, regret, regret, what you could call regret, no, truthfully, he didn't regret anything; or maybe having accepted responsibilities for which he wasn't ready, but to refuse under those circumstances would have been a greater error, and then, how could he explain? After the last zafra he got married again to the *same* woman who'd been with him for most of his life, he said, looking at Felipe, and returned to the center with the aim of going through the party process if he was chosen as an exemplary worker in that assembly. He went silent as he felt the relief of someone who has said everything, and added that that, more or less, had been his life.

The assembly started to relax. Carlos saw Rubén give him a look of solidarity. For the first time he asked for a cigarette. His hands shook as he lit it, and he wondered if he'd managed to escape the temptation of the labyrinth.

At the table, the chair was discussing something with the director before saying that even though the compañero had been quite exhaustive, perhaps someone wanted to ask some other question to clarify things for the debate. There was a silence full of whispering until Ruiz Oquendo, the administrative subdirector, asked for the floor.

"Just very briefly," he said, "two important matters you didn't refer to, perhaps because you overlooked them. What was your activity in the CTC and the CDRs?"

Carlos started coughing, his eyes filled with tears and he threw away the cigarette, wet with saliva. He'd been a member of the union, he said, since he began working; he had a medium level of activity, on two occasions he'd been a leader of voluntary work brigades and he always was part of the Vanguard Movement. The CDRs were something else, actually he'd never had a home, he was on scholarship at the university for a long time and then, well, then at the zafra. During the years he lived with his wife he'd had a lot of work, guard duty and meetings, and the truth was he hadn't joined the committee, he never found the time.

Ruiz Oquendo sat up with his eyes popping.

"You mean you're not a member of the CDR?"

No, said Carlos and tried to explain, actually, he'd been thinking, now that he was more or less stable, about talking with the chairwoman of his block to . . .

"Compañero Chair," said Ruiz Oquendo, interrupting him, "I don't think there's any sense in going on with this case. The committees are one of the pillars of the revolutionary process, and someone who isn't even a CDR member . . . how can he hope to be an exemplary worker? Therefore I propose we move to another case, period."

Carlos breathed again when he heard the chair reject the proposal and ask Ruiz Oquendo to calm down and control himself.

"We're not in a rush, compañeros. This task *also* has an educational purpose. It's not correct to kill the discussion of a case that, from what I see, is *quite* complex. After the debate, each person can express his opinion by voting. Any more questions? None? All right, opinions then. Margarita."

Margarita Villabrille stood up, smoothing down her miniskirt. She was very confused, she said, looking at Carlos with an almost painful anxiety; on the one hand, how could a person who had fought at Girón, been left lame in an accident during the October Crisis, and done three complete zafras not be an exemplary worker? But on the other, how could someone be exemplary who wasn't a member of the CDR, who had failed the Young Communists, and besides that, committed errors of self-satisfaction? She didn't understand, compañeros, they'd have to forgive her, but she didn't understand. Jiménez Cardoso stood up to explain. The problem, compañera, was to find *the* line through all those contradictions. For him, he was going to be as ugly as he was frank, it was ideological weakness and recurrent error. Carlos looked at him, attracted by that devastating confidence, and from then on Jiménez spoke to him. He meant to say, he pointed out, that that life started with one error, not daring to sell the vouchers, and it continued with another, *running away*. "Around how old was he then?" Rubén interrupted. "Sixteen," said Carlos, and the chair asked them, please, not to start personal conversations. Then Jiménez added that the running away was repeated in '60, the year of nationalizations and the most intense class struggle, when the compañero was already twenty. It isn't until November that he leaves home, and please, don't tell me that he was still a little boy. All right, what did he do in January? *Absent himself* from a military mobilization at a time of war. "For three hours," murmured Carlos, and Jiménez replied, for however many, compañero, and looked straight at him and said that even more, what did he do when they sanctioned him? *Abandon* the combat battalion, on account of which, later on, he could not participate in the Escambray Clean-up. He goes to Girón, accidentally, as he said, because he's honest, but he does go, and that has to be noted to his credit. Nevertheless, what happens when he returns to the university? He thinks he's a hero! Jiménez Cardoso spread his arms apart, consternated by that pretension, and Carlos lowered his head and was about to cover his ears, but Jiménez's question, what was he, in reality? led Carlos to continue hearing an extremist, a sectarian, as he himself just admitted, dictating ukases, persecuting those who *seemed* inverted, an unacceptable sign of subjectivism, because if he had persecuted those who actually were and had antisocial behavior, now the assembly would be looking at a merit and not at an arbitrary act. All of this, compañeros, was even worse if you took into account that he was talking about someone who less than a year before had *distanced* himself from all political activity; someone, compañeros, capable of a politically, humanly, and historically monstrous deed: agreeing with the altering of the testament of a true hero like José Antonio Echeverría! The accusation fell like a tombstone onto Carlos, who pulled out his handkerchief and twisted it with sweaty hands; he would have liked to believe that Jiménez was a somabitch, a scoundrel, an enemy, and not the hardworking, intelligent man who now had just taken a swallow of water and was asking, what happened, compañeros, when Fidel himself reestablished the truth? What did Carlos do then? *Abandon* the struggle, like in '56 and '60. But there was more: until today, nine years later, he hadn't come to understand that his reaction was one more sign of his self-satisfaction. Yes, he reintegrates at the time of the October Crisis, and that too has to be noted to his credit; he has an accident that amounted to a war wound, with all the merits that implies, that he wasn't going to diminish in any way. But note that afterwards he *abandoned* his studies, when he was already almost an architect, a technical expert, with the illusion of joining the guerrillas because, it seems, he never resigned himself to being a normal person, a rank-and-file revolutionary. At the center, it was only just to recognize this, he was a magnificent worker, a man who uprightly opposed the immoralities that once were committed there, a good militant, and also a good secretary for the Young Communists. However, he wrecked it all by being the protagonist, at a key moment of internal ideological struggle, of a lamentable incident, a sign of his immaturity and weakness. Then, he was expelled from his job and from the UJC, and he went to cut cane, without doubt a laudable thing, although it was also true that, as he himself said, at that moment he was completely out of work. At this point, compañeros, he wanted to make a parenthesis to criticize compañero Felipe for having introduced a private problem into a political process; that also explained why he wasn't going to refer to the issue of the woman and the rest. He supported Carlos's position in that sense and wanted to return to the case, where, again, his tendency to error manifested itself. The Young Communists at the center asked for an indefinite expulsion and the Municipal Committee lowered the sanction to a year. What should a militant have done? Appeal, wasn't that right? Well, Carlos *did not* appeal. Now he wanted to invite the assembly to suppose, for the benefit of the doubt, that the compañero was completely convinced of his error and didn't appeal because of that. But then, how to explain that three years later he still hadn't presented himself before the organization to clear his case? He left the answer to the assembly and reminded it also of an extraordinary fact, that the compañero *wasn't even* a member of the CDR. To conclude, he wanted to make it clear to Carlos that he had said all of this for his own good, that he considered him a friend and was giving him his hand.

Carlos saw Jiménez Cardoso coming towards him with his hand stretched out as if in slow motion, felt that the assembly was waiting for his reply and that what he did was going to affect the vote, that he *should* shake his hand as proof of his maturity and sense of self-criticism, but a sort of atavistic pride caused him to return Jiménez's look in silence and to cross his arms. Then a wave of commentary broke out, an impenetrable mixture of approval and reproach, and the chair gave the floor to Rubén Suárez, who was snapping his fingers, dying to express, he said, his total, complete, absolute disagreement with Jiménez Cardoso's intervention, because for him, Carlos's life had been a desperate and sometimes pathetic struggle to be on a par with his times. He wanted to begin with the matter of the vouchers and the demonstration. About that he disagreed even with Carlos himself, who in spite of everything *was at* the demonstration, being almost a boy, in '56, compañeros, when *very* few people in Cuba were politically active. That he ran away? He did run away, but how many people wouldn't have done that in the face of police fire? And even though he didn't remain in the struggle afterwards, that fact should be interpreted as a merit, as proof of political sensibility, and not as an error. That, he wanted to remind the assembly, was how Carlos's compañeros at that time saw it, rather than reproaching him they asked him to be part of the slate of candidates for the United Left after the Revolution. A united left, that was the key to class struggle in '59–'60, and Carlos, whose father had land, money, and buildings and had been affected by practically *all* the new revolutionary laws, was on the strategically correct side at that defining moment. That later, for some months, he distanced himself from the process? True, but it was necessary to recall, compañeros, that his family was splitting in two and that he found himself in the middle of an awful mess. What was impressive was that he had been able to resolve it in the most radical way, walking the sixty-two kilometers, leaving home, and finishing one of the first militia camps Cuba had with battalion, what was the number? "113," said Carlos, with the strange sensation that Rubén was alluding to another person as he repeated the number, added, among the first ones, and asked, how could they criticize him for having gone to see his sick father? How could they stuff their mouths full and say "abandonment of a mobilization at a time of war," if he had returned voluntarily two or three hours later? Then, the Beca, another classic example of damned if you do and damned if you don't, it turns out that they were criticizing him when, in '60, he stayed at home, and also in '61, when he accepted a scholarship, as if to have autonomy he hadn't been practically forced to do that, gentlemen! Girón, the war, he said quickly to himself, that was risking his hide and what more could you ask of someone? Rubén paused, searching for Jiménez Cardoso's eyes before continuing, to go to one of the most delicate problems, the compañero believed he was or wanted to be a hero. That was just in the air, and the models were Fidel, Raúl, Che, Camilo, and so many others. We were living in a heroic time and it was understandable that someone would feel that temptation, or more precisely, that vocation. Very well, Carlos, of course, wasn't a hero, he was wrong, he became intoxicated and committed errors that he had recognized before the assembly and that Jiménez Cardoso lamentably amplified. He wanted to remind them, compañeros, that Carlos was not the only prosecutor or the only extremist at the university at that time; he, Rubén, was harassed many times for his mane of hair, simply because he damn well liked to wear his hair long. But what was important was that Carlos had overcome those errors long ago, and what was paradoxical was that at this late stage Jiménez Cardoso himself would insinuate that there could have been merit in prosecuting the taste or the private life of others. No, compañeros, that motherfucking mania, if they would pardon the expression, was something he himself had suffered through, and he wanted to make it very clear that, from his point of view, it could not imply merit either before, or now, or ever, because . . .

"A very debatable opinion," Jiménez Cardoso interrupted. "Under certain . . ."

"Then let's debate it!" exclaimed Rubén.

A growing murmur spread across the room and the chair asked for silence, for them to please not start a personal conversation, and urged Rubén to continue but to keep himself to the case and the facts. Rubén murmured of course, of course, although he obviously had lost his train of thought, which he seemed to recover only when he looked at his opponent again, and once more sure of himself, said that he wasn't going to refer to the October Crisis because even someone as hypercritical as Jiménez Cardoso recognized a merit, a true merit, a military merit, in the wounds that had forever marked the compañero. About the center he was going to say something, Carlos was the best general secretary that the Core Committee had had there, the most hardworking, the most courageous; he, who had replaced him in the position, knew what he was talking about when he said this, and in addition, it was his opinion that he had been treated too harshly when the business with compañera Iraida happened. What was his answer? To go to the zafra, to devote three years of his life to that, if they would excuse what he was going to say, heroic task. He didn't appeal to the UJC and that was an error, without a doubt, but the assembly should remember that all he had was the two months of his first leave to do it, and at that time he was *devoted* to the zafra, where he must have worked very well, because the Municipal Party of Sola promoted him twice. He was going to end now, he only wanted to ask, if the errors of a revolutionary were something like the original sin, if there were any better place to overcome them than in the bosom of the party.

Someone applauded at the back of the room. Carlos wasn't able to figure out who because when he started to turn around, the director took the floor and he interrupted his movement anticipating the intervention. Compañeros, the opinions expressed by Jiménez Cardoso and Rubén Suárez suffered, according to his way of seeing things, from the same defect: an inability to face the complications of life. Both of them had stuck to *one* line, but it just so happened that there were always two or who knew how many, and that was how you had to see this. That was the same problem that confused Margarita, because, deep down, we all yearn for a movie that's easy to figure out: the good guys here, the bad guys there. The trouble was that it wasn't like that and so to give an opinion was also to commit yourself, *to take a risk*. Very well, he wouldn't beat around the bush, he was going to take his. For him, Carlos, the same one who went to Girón and didn't appeal to the UJC, the one who wasn't a CDR member and went off a cliff during the October Crisis, the one who slept with Iraida in the office and did three zafras, certainly *was* an exemplary worker; first, because he went to war, and the man who puts his hide on the line has put everything; second, because he had political courage and right there, in the CEI, he went head on with opportunism and defeated it; third, because he went to cut cane with smooth hands and came back with calluses. The director said thank you, and, from behind, timid applause could be heard again. Carlos turned around in time to see Margarita Villabrille clapping. Just then the chair's voice startled him. He was going to take his turn, compañeros, he was totally in agreement with the *type* of risky approach that the director proposed, but not with his conclusions. For him, Carlos Pérez Cifredo, even with his many merits and virtues, *was not* an exemplary worker, and he was going to explain why. They were in the process of *building* the party at the center, searching for the best among the good, and the compañero had committed cardinal errors. To start with, he wasn't a member of the CDR, and that was a very grave problem: how could someone who didn't even form part of a mass organization be a source of the vanguard? It was simply unacceptable.

Besides, the compañero had seriously failed the Young Communists, the source of the party, and that *should* have consequences. Lastly, all through his life he had shown a tendency to overvalue himself, a tendency incompatible with the modesty that should characterize a mature revolutionary. That was his opinion, and he had tried to express it with total frankness. Nevertheless, he wanted to remind them that the assembly was sovereign, and his was only one more opinion. If Carlos turned out to be chosen as an exemplary worker, he would begin the process in the party, where a more profound assessment would be done and all the details would be scrupulously verified. Very well, more opinions.

Felipe stood up and was silent for a few seconds. This was very difficult for him, compañeros, because he knew Carlos well, they had been buddies, they'd even been together abroad. He didn't agree with anything Jiménez Cardoso had said, nor with the chair's conclusions. Why? Because all the errors they had pointed out were the errors of a man, and a man, in life, commits errors, as the director said. But there was *one* error that you could not commit, compañeros, and that was to know that your wife had said certain things and to stay with her, or even worse, to go back to her *afterwards*. Felipe was silent again, as if it had been very hard to speak, and Carlos felt devastated, unable to object, with the dark suspicion that in spite of everything Felipe was right: he had violated a sacred law of the tribe and it was fair that he pay the price for it that Felipe demanded, as he added, maybe in Sweden or in Denmark, but not here, not in Cuba, because here a man who would do that loses prestige, compañeros, the masses won't respect him, how could they respect him? And therefore, compañeros, he could not be exemplary. That was his opinion, he was very sorry, it was very unfortunate, he concluded, waving his hands in front of his eyes, as if he needed to exorcize some ghost. Marta Hernández started talking without being given the floor. How long would they have to put up with that moral standard full of tricks and lies? Tricks and lies! she repeated, seeing Felipe with a scornful expression. Because when Carlos had that incident with Iraida, the same compañero Felipe who now wanted his head said at a Young Communists meeting that a man was always a man and much more so if he was a Communist, and that, compañeros, was something she would never forget. Of course, for the big handsome machos it was all just good girls and bad girls, like in the movies the director had talked about. But life was complicated there, too, and compañera Gisela Jáuregui, Carlos's wife, was a militant in the Young Communists, a very accomplished doctor, and she hadn't done even one hundredth of what Carlos had done to her. Did they want to know something else? The best decision Carlos ever made in his life was to go back with her because he was *never* going to find another woman like her.

"Compañera," the chair interrupted her, "you may be right, but I think it's best to leave those personal problems aside, not to take them into account."

Marta shook her head no, they *had* to take them into account, but in a positive sense: by doing that, Carlos proved he was brave and sensitive, because in this country, only a man who had both of them right where they belonged would do what he had done, for love; and thank you, that's all.

Marta dug into her purse and pulled out a cigarette; Margarita turned her head and said something to Jiménez Cardoso, who shrugged his shoulders; Felipe looked at the floor and cracked his fingers one by one; someone in the back started coughing. The chair ran his eyes over the assembly, asked if there was some other opinion, some other question, and Carlos felt suspended in a void when he heard him say:

"Very well, compañeros, then we are going to vote by a show of hands: first all those in favor, then all those against."

EPILOGUE

I

Critics in Cuba have yet to agree on which of Jesús Díaz's novels is his finest, some arguing it is the one the reader holds in his hands, from 1987; others that it is *Las palabras perdidas*, published five years later. I refuse to join in such parceling out of cups and medals—literature, as Faulkner said, is not a horse race—but I've never hesitated to affirm that *The Initials of the Earth* is an emblematic novel of the Cuban Revolution, and the most significant of those set in the Cuba of the 1960s. I'm not sure to what degree readers outside Cuba may be able to partake in this assessment, as they will likely lack not only relevant points of comparison but also the experience that would permit evaluation of the text's referential merit. But I can assure such readers that few works managed with more imagination and spirit to capture the complex internal dynamics of the era from the perspective of a young participant in the revolutionary process. Authenticity is, indeed, one of the novel's principle merits. The author bears witness to his reality and times with the boldness and expressive command he had already exhibited in his first book of short stories, and which secured for both works foundational status in contemporary Cuban narrative.

I will return to this matter, but first wish to offer a personal testimony of my own, which may help the reader understand the difficult and contradictory personality of a man who was first one of the most impassioned supporters of Cuban Revolution, and later, during the last ten years of his life, one of its harshest critics.

2

Supported by a grant from a German cultural institution, Jesús Díaz moved with his family to Berlin in early 1991, intending to return to Cuba when his funding ran out. He never went back. But that didn't mean we stopped seeing each other; indeed, we met abroad on several occasions after 1991, the first time at a writer's congress in Mérida, Venezuela, during the summer of 1993. There it quickly became clear to me that our friendship—precisely because so profound—could only be sustained in a manner bordering on schizophrenic. Our personal relations remained as before, but when it came to political matters we were cleaved in two, or better, doubled into two different times and personalities. And since for him—and for me, too, I wasn't long in realizing—the personal and the political were intimately related, the simple personal relation became increasingly conflicted the more it was staged in a public arena.

Despite our difference in age (I was almost ten years older than Jesús), our friendship was too solid, too sturdy, was based on too many shared tastes, experiences, and aspirations to brook such a fracture, a split, which yet could not fully threaten the integrity of the whole. Like Siamese twins, we had forever been fused at the spine of that igneous couple—Literature/Revolution—whose explosion illuminated the social and cultural atmosphere of the era. It was in this atmosphere that I first met Jesús; he was still very young and had just ushered in an entire new narrative turn with *Los años duros*, his first collection of short stories, which had been awarded the 1966 Casa de las Américas prize. Jesús exuded talent, acumen, and energy from all his pores: he wrote fiction, was a dramaturge, an essayist, a professor of Marxism, a spirited performer of guarachas and guaguancós, a formidable polemicist . . . Already in these years, and with the arrogance of a musketeer, he blasted aspiring aesthetes on the one hand and die-hard populists on the other, excesses for which we alternately praised or pardoned him out of admiration or reciprocity, for we knew his passion was sincere and that he possessed the supreme virtue of being a true friend to his friends.

For me and many others like me, Jesús, often accused of being "self-satisfied" and authoritarian, was, despite this—or perhaps because of it—a *natural* product of his time. He was the prototype incarnate of the young writer we never were nor could have been, because such a specimen quite simply could not flourish in the arid terrain characterizing the years of our own youth. He was master of his world, a political animal in the strictest sense, boldly thrusting himself on the polis, brandishing with full awareness his rights as a citizen. All this was not, to be sure, the product of sheer spirit, but owed much to the opportune opening up of real possibilities. At a crucial moment a certain young man from a modest background decided to become a professor and was awarded a post, wanted to publish and succeeded in finding publishers, wished to found journals and encountered the necessary resources, desired to travel and circled half the globe, and when, finally, driven by circumstance, he turned to cinema, he was able to make both feature films and documentaries within and outside Cuba.

None of this, of course, took place in a vacuum or via a magic carpet, but amidst a tumult of contradictions and conflicting interests where Jesús, as much as the rest of his cohort, served at some times as hammer and at others as anvil, facing down or carefully skirting obstacles, squeezing out an opposition or repairing to lick his wounds. The latter was the case during a period I have elsewhere termed the *quinquenio gris*, the Gray Five-Year Period, which began in 1971 and during which mediocrity and dogmatism aspired to build a world in their own twisted likeness, absconding with Cuba's cultural might. Vital art and literature were to be passed over in favor of a mass-produced culture whose parts, recently imported and lacquered with local color, were to be hastily assembled in the rusting factory of socialist realism.

It was then that Jesús, having sought refuge in the Cuban Film Institute (ICAIC), a space free of dogmatism, collaborated as screenwriter on the films *!Viva la Republica!* (Pastor Vega, 1972) and *Ustedes tienen la palabra* (Manuel Octavio Gómez, 1973). Jesús directed his first shorts (*Cambiar la vida* in 1975, *Canción de Puerto Rico* in 1976) during the same period, and as secretary general of the Cuban Communist Party (CCP) for the ICAIC, succeeded in fostering intense political activity between 1976 and 1980, a moment which also saw the production of his two great documentaries (*55 Hermanos*, 1978, and *En tierra de Sandino*, 1980).

I don't know how he managed simultaneously to continue writing prose fiction, but it was during these same years that he finished the first version of *The Initials of the Earth*, whose ingenious structuring conceit—the framing of the novel's action by the standard questionnaire given those aspiring to join the CCP—condemned him to the limbo of a tacit censure that dared not speak its name; the conceit was considered heresy, particularly coming from a *militant* (the Cuban term for someone belonging to the party). Here, however, the old adage about silver linings obtains, for when the undeclared censure was at last lifted—in 1981, if I'm not mistaken—Jesús, rather than dashing off to the publisher with his novel, as impatience must surely have dictated, had the composure and professional sobriety to sit down and rewrite the novel from scratch, yielding the incomparably superior version we have now. (I was so close to this process I can still plot the action of *The Initials* chapter by chapter, corresponding breaks included, as must have been the case in the past for readers of serialized novels).

3

I noted above that our first reencounter occurred in 1993. Jesús's decision of the previous year had unexpectedly cast us into opposing ideological camps, but we both knew how fruitless it would be to delve into political discussions. He explained his decision as the result of a dawning awareness—whether gradual or sudden I don't know—about the political situation in Cuba. Perhaps the decision might be conveyed in words he himself used some time later when referring to the 1971 "Padilla Case": he would write that in those times "many, I among them, were fascinated by the Cuban utopia, blind to the dictatorial reality already hiding behind it." What for me rendered this claim untenable was not the invocation of blindness itself, but rather that the alleged blindness would last for Jesús *twenty years more.*

Objections will be raised that surely a person has the right to revise his views, that anyone might have reached such a conclusion, that Jesús was not the first Cuban intellectual to mark his distance, openly break with or abjure, as the literary magazine *La Gaceta de Cuba* put it in its rather elegiac treatment of the case, "the cultural and political project of the Revolution." Anyone might have done the same, it's true; many had done so before and others will likely do so in the future. But the matter is at once more simple and more complicated: Jesús was not *anyone.* For me, Jesús Díaz was *Jesús Díaz,* palpable evidence of the existence of the Revolution, and his political trajectory, writing, and films were there to prove it. No one, not a single one of the other exiled authors had said and done the things he did and said over the course of thirty years; no one had participated in so many battles and skirmishes, nor served as visionary for a generation, nor written those short stories, articles, novels, and *testimonios,* nor conceived and directed those films (to the documentaries named above were added the feature films *Polvo Rojo,* in 1981, and *Lejanía,* in 1985). Jesús was Jesús, and it was for that reason that I decided—

there, on the spot in Mérida, during our first reencounter—to assume as the basis for our future relations a kind of schizophrenia, which seemed to me the only means, however paradoxical it may sound, of maintaining a healthy relationship. I couldn't stop being his friend, but neither could I fully recognize my friend in the Jesús I had before me—or rather I *could*, so long as the conversation didn't veer towards more perilous terrain; that is, so long as it didn't "devolve" into politics.

But this self-imposed silence—perfectly serviceable for conversing with aunts and cousins in Miami—was no good between Jesús and me, since neither of us had ever refrained from "talking politics" in private or public, and since I, anyway, kept abreast of what he published in newspapers or declared to news agencies, reading the pieces sometimes with sadness, sometimes with irritation. As we say in Cuba, *no era fácil*; it wasn't easy: if the Revolution was indeed as he said it was at that point, then I, who supported it—who *still* supported it—was a miserable ass. On the other hand, if what he said was not true, or was only a half-truth . . . No, it was not at all easy. And even less so in an international climate in which the disintegration of the great socialist simulacrum was followed by the heralding of the end of history, and with it the likely end to that utopian experiment Che Guevara had once described as the intimate, dynamic exchange between man and socialism in Cuba. We were walking a knife-edge in those days, and depending on one's own expectations, anything—miraculous solutions as much as imminent catastrophes—seemed possible. But I didn't believe in miracles, so I had to prepare myself for the worst. In Cuba it was understood that Jesús was also preparing himself for such an outcome, but crowing victory with the satisfaction of having jumped a sinking ship in the nick of time. Had I shared this opinion of Jesús as vulgar opportunist I could not have continued to be his friend. To put it simply and with candor, I never understood—I still don't, I perhaps don't *want* to understand—why Jesús assumed the mantle of mouthpiece for an exile that was not his, and to which he arrived decidedly too late. I do know that wherever he went he was destined to play the role of protagonist: he was genetically programmed to be a captain, never a mere grunt. But this protagonism could have taken a different form outside Cuba, similar to that which indeed it had taken within: namely, that of an intellectual whose critical stance is taken up on behalf of, not against, a cause.

In any event, it's not my task here to imagine that history that did not come to pass. What *did* happen was that, when we least expected it, Jesús suddenly popped up on the other side of the trench, and that about this unusual event a web of speculations, tergiversations, and legends began to be spun. It was said that in 1991—in the wake of the debut and subsequent censorship of the film *Alice in Wonder Village*, an unequivocal satire about bureaucratism—a high-ranking official in the Cuban government had "warned" Jesús that he ought not dare return to Cuba. The director and the screenwriter of *Alice*, both friends of Jesús, were adamant that though a most helpful advisor he had not contributed a single line to the screenplay. And although it is true that Jesús's enemies (who, as good doctrinaires, tended also to be enemies of his friends and of anything that smelled of *ideological deviation*) thought they discerned his pernicious influence in the film's unabashed proposals, in none of the debates about the film between ICAIC cineastes and government officials was Jesús so charged.

The 1992 article in which Jesús made public his break with the Revolution, "*Los anillos de la serpiente*" [The serpent's rings], was reproduced in the *Gaceta de Cuba* and elicited a scathing response from the then-minister of culture, whose *moral* censure Jesús converted—I don't know whether seriously or in jest—into a fatwa, as if the metaphorical rings of his argument were so many satanic verses meriting a death sentence from a criollo ayatollah. One day Jesús went to Miami in his capacity as a journalist, and we were shocked (and pained) not so much to learn that he had met with members of the Cuban-American far right, but that, after having flown with pilots from the organization Brothers to the Rescue, he should, on return to Madrid, publish an article titled "*Al rescate de los Hermanos*" [Rescuing the brothers], which already in its very title seemed to seal the bonds of a new friendship from which we, his true brothers all his life, were excluded. At least, that's how we felt. In short, we would have liked things to have turned out very differently, but Jesús always did what he did with full awareness, before as much as after he chose exile, and he doesn't need us to reconstruct his biography here.

4

I had assumed that with Jesús's decision not to return to Cuba a chapter had closed on our ongoing exchanges of work and critique, but then one day Jesús sent me the manuscript of *La piel y la máscara*, his first novel written in exile, that I might give him my opinion on it. I confess I was rather upset with him, and, to prick his amour propre, I wrote back that his vision of Cuban reality had suddenly become so coolly critical and distant that the novel might have been written by a Swiss (this an insult to someone who understood himself to be so deeply criollo). Some time later he again sent me the novel, now published, "with the hope," as the manuscript's dedication read, "that it not appear to you too *Swiss,* and [with] the commitment to forge ahead." To "forge ahead," I wondered, in the *same* direction? To my mind such a path led straight to the formulaic "anti-Castro" novel, a subgenre that had flourished between 1965 and 1971 and that was experiencing something of a revival in these later years, thanks to circumstance and the urgent and lucrative exigencies of the market.

Such a literary end, it seemed to me, awaited Jesús. All the passion, the wit, the poise, and verbal dexterity, the search for meaning, the humor, the imaginative struggle with a dynamic, changing reality—indeed the entire summation of talent and courage which seethed in *Los años duros,* in *The Initials of the Earth,* in *Las palabras perdidas*—was it all, in the end, to be poured into novels whose greatest merits would be political (in)correctness and flawless technique? Were all his glories to be shrunk, as for Shakespeare's slain Julius Caesar, to such little measure? Jesús continued to send me copies of each new book, which bore dedications by turns generously intimate or simply courteous, attesting to the passage of time and attendant changes in sentiment ("For my *maestro* . . . with admiration and nostalgia from . . ." in *Dime algo sobre Cuba;* "For the *maestro,* this distant history and affection from . . ." in *Siberiana;* "For my *maestro* . . . this non-fiction from the hard paths of Europe and a greeting from . . ." in *Las cuatro fugas de Manuel*). I read the books with interest—the last one, above all—but always with the disquieting feeling that Jesús was putting into them more officiousness than passion; that all of them, so well, indeed *too* well, constructed, remained beneath his talent and his own creative potential.

5

And then one day I found out, via a phone call from Miami, what had happened. What had happened was that Jesús no longer existed. I had the shocked impression that the order of the universe had been altered, that a flagrant injustice had been committed, that something was occurring that ought not *yet* occur, as when, in times of war, the world is turned on its head and parents bury their children. But memory is voracious and egoistic. Mine, stimulated by a *horror vacui,* immediately shot out in all directions, attempting to recuperate time spent together without ceding room to depression and confusion. What this strange response may be I don't know; something connected with nostalgia, certainly. In any event my memory suddenly seized on a photo I have about my house and which periodically disappears, only to resurface in the odd perusal of old files. It is, as far as I can remember, the only photograph in which Jesús and I appear together: it is 1979, the first time we served together as judges for the Casa de las Americas literary contest (there would be a second time, ten years later). Neither of us yet has gray hair.

But nostalgia, or whatever it was, continued to feed its insatiable appetite, grasping at mental snapshots and evanescent moments. I conjure the moments and images as chaotic flashes, fragile like memory itself, knowing that they cannot resist for very long the inexorable passage of time. There is Jesús in my living room, while the rest of the family sleeps, smoking like a chimney and talking a blue streak about literary figures and concerns, local and international; and there he is making a polemical intervention at a packed assembly of ICAIC workers convened in the Chaplin Cinema towards the end of the 90s; there he is again in a cluttered souvenir shop in Times Square, posing, amused, before a poster whose script reads WANTED above his impassive face. There he presents a talk on Alejo Carpentier in a seminar at the Havana Film Festival; there, in a small bar in Santa Cruz de Tenerife, Canary Islands, not far from the city's only detestable spot—the Valeriano Weyler Plaza—he assures me that despite the late hour I am sure to get a bus back to my hotel in La Laguna; and there he is engaging with hundreds of students, eager readers of *The Initials of the Earth,* at the University of Havana. There, in his brand-new Madrid apartment, ever the good host, he offers a succulent lunch to the Argentine screenwriter Jorge Goldenberg and myself, proudly introducing to us his daughter Claudia, already grown into a lovely teenager. And there he is bringing me books, attempting to keep me more or less up to date with current prose. He would invariably return from trips or reunions with friends with some trophy with which he would immediately present me: *Artificial Respiration,* by the Argentine novelist Ricardo Piglia; Rushdie's *Midnight's Children*; *Juegos de la edad tardía,* by the Spaniard Luis Landero (a copy which had, in fact, previously been given *him* by the Peruvian novelist Alfredo Bryce when the latter was in Havana, in 1990).

At almost the same time that I was again chancing on Jesús in these explosions of memory I was made aware, in receiving numerous phone calls and messages from mutual friends, of what one might call the public image of our friendship, an image of which I, quite honestly, had been ignorant, and which moved me profoundly. I suddenly realized that in the eyes of others I was *the* friend of Jesús in Cuba, the person to whom, in such circumstances, one had to offer condolences. The map of this mourning had Havana at its center but radiated halfway about the world; the messages arrived from Miami, Chicago, Barcelona, London, and were likewise being composed, I found out later—as tacit condolences, as nostalgia for old times—in Boston, San Juan, New York, Monterrey . . .

6

I fear having abused the reader's patience and I turn now immediately to *The Initials of the Earth* and its significance for post-1959 Cuban narrative. In those years—the sixties—everyone both within and outside Cuba wondered when *the* novel of the Revolution would appear; when the saga or cycle would arrive that would depict, in all its dramatic intensity, the greatness and violence of that process which had, with a single blow, changed Cuban history. A radical transformation, long-anticipated throughout Latin America, was taking place where it had least been expected: only ninety miles from the United States, a country whose government had systematically opposed anything that smacked of revolution in its southern backyard. Alejo Carpentier, considered the most important Cuban novelist of the century and the great chronicler of Caribbean revolution (see *The Kingdom of this World* and *Explosion in a Cathedral*), had by then announced his intention to write a trilogy that would capture the epic feel of the Cuban Revolution, which he finally addressed in the 1978 autobiographical novel *The Consecration of Spring*. But what Carpentier recounted there was less a specific moment in Cuban history than a variety of significant twentieth-century events, as they bore on the lives of men and women who either assumed or rejected political engagement during such critical junctures as the Russian Revolution, the Spanish Civil War, or the Cuban Revolution itself . . .

This last event furnished Carpentier with a new historical perspective and the conviction that individual lives are closely linked to collective destinies. Like Death for the hapless gardener in Ispahan, the epoch inevitably met up with the individual, no matter how much the latter sought to evade it. *The Consecration of Spring*, however, did not elaborate on but instead ended just short of 1960s Cuba, concluding with the moment of military victory at Playa Girón (which North American readers will likely know as the Bay of Pigs fiasco). It was with this spectacular victory that the new regime, already declared socialist, was consolidated. The Revolution would not face a similar trial until the following year—and now on a global scale—with the Cuban Missile Crisis, known in Cuba as the October Crisis. *The Initials of the Earth* is the novel that gives voice to the ways in which Cubans—and particularly young revolutionaries—experienced these years of epic change and crisis. It is entirely fictional, but it could well be accompanied by a chronology that would mark for the reader the history through which the characters advance, both in the time of the *fabula*—that is, Carlos's memories—(including the flashbacks which remit to a pre-Revolutionary period) and in the novel's real time (that of its action).

7

In the 1987 blurb penned for the first Cuban edition of *The Initials*, I wrote: "It is a singular novel of apprenticeship, the baldest *Bildungsroman* of contemporary Cuban literature. But unique among other examples of the genre, here the formative process for the young hero is also a *collective* process, the unleashing of class struggle and of the great revolutionary transformations. This fascinating synthesis of drama and epic, nourished by currents of popular culture, makes of the novel—as the title indeed suggests—both a political and aesthetic challenge, the foundational act of a new collective consciousness and of a language able to express itself in all its complexity." The novel's title is borrowed from Chilean poet Pablo Neruda's book *Canto general*, considered one of the literary manifestos of Latin American cultural identity. Did *The Initials of the Earth* also aspire to be a literary manifesto? Was this *the* novel of the Cuban Revolution the world had been waiting for?

The question, I think, only served at the time to obscure the existence of a broader spate of novels (between 1959 and 1970 sixty novels were published in Cuba) boasting their own traits—a group that included the above-noted *Explosion in a Cathedral*, by Carpentier, and *Paradiso*, by José Lezama Lima, to cite only a couple of the more notable examples. In those years, moreover, the focus of critical debate had been shifting from the novel to the short story—and it was Jesús Díaz, precisely, who helped spark this shift with the publication of *Los años duros*. The volume's stories were characterized by fresh thematic and stylistic elements, including a rigorous focus on the present day. What in these stories was perceptible as *revolutionary* was the atmosphere of the times: the human, social, and political features that delineated the horizon of a collective experience in which the readers, too, felt involved. The dramatic elements that made up the volume's wager were the bravery, the violence, the chaos, and the crisis of traditional values—that is, of bourgeois ideology. Some of these features would subsequently become even more sharply defined with the 1968 publication of two similarly themed books—*La guerra tuvo seis nombres*, by Eduardo Heras León, and *Condenados de Condado*, by Norberto Fuentes—where the violence was rendered, if I may put it this way, in its purest form, amidst the thunder, gunpowder, and truces of combat. The three authors—all of whom were under thirty at the time—situated Cuban narrative squarely within a literary vanguard. The Uruguayan critic Ángel Rama defined their work as models of a new realism, "a vertiginous, expressionist, dramatic realism."

In 1969, pondering the relative novelty of the Cuban short story, I indicated that two extreme positions then jockeyed for final word on the issue: one held that revolutionary literature must be epic, given that it had to capture that colossal collective force that is a socialist revolution in an underdeveloped country, while the other alleged that a literature of revolution could only be experimental, since all authentic revolutions presuppose a revolution in form, or, as it is often put, a revolution at the level of language. Both positions seemed tacitly to assume a dichotomy between form and content, which disqualified them as equally reductive. I attempted to avoid these extremes by appealing to more pragmatic criteria; that is, to the materials I had before me. "Is this or is this not," I asked myself, "a *new* literature?" "Is this or is this not *the* short story of the Cuban Revolution?"

There existed, as it turns out, a satisfactory formula palatable to all, whose very simplicity has made it a classic: namely, that it was no longer the old literature, it was not yet the new: it was a literature of transition. But what a literature of transition has over any other kind, epic or experimental, is the advantage of existing. It is a concrete fact. Not what *ought* to be, but what *is*; not the demonstration of a thesis but rather a spontaneous antithesis. The new Cuban literature had, up to that point, only been defined in the negative terms one critic reduced to four fundamental elaborations of what it was *not*, namely: 1) the baroque style of our two greatest writers, Carpentier and Lezama; 2) the mystical and introspective current of 1950s Cuban poetry; 3) a vernacular, populist, and folkloric local color; or 4) socialist realism. But these negations in fact added up to an affirmative position: that the new literature was doubly "contemporary" for being both epic in its content and innovative in its formal resources. Yet it was precisely such traits that seemed to be lacking in the Cuban novel (which, moreover, was then flourishing): that is, the organic fusion of those elements that had come to be, in the minds of critics and readers, the defining features of the new literature, and, by extension, of the revolutionary literature.

Los años duros had also begun with an epigraph by Neruda, "*I am here to tell the story,*" the nucleus of a poetics that would reach its full realization in *The Initials of the Earth*. We realized, once the latter appeared, that the novel had in fact been anticipated, not merely for being long-awaited, but because it quite literally had been heralded. For in effect its protagonist Carlos Pérez Cifredo—rather a poor devil, who doesn't believe himself to possess a single merit he could "call his own rather than shared by all, or due to circumstances"—discovers for himself one 15 April 1969 (according to the time of the fabula) what the author of *Los años duros* had discovered in Neruda three years prior. In the cane cutters' camp where Carlos seeks to resuscitate not the power of epic but his own strength (the better to stave off a more general collapse), the brigade celebrates the eighth anniversary of Playa Girón. They ask whether anyone of the group actually fought in the battle, and, to widespread surprise, Carlos raises his hand. They ask him to speak.

> Before opening his mouth he felt afraid. His work had gotten him used to giving talks, to going on in harangues, and he knew those men well enough to know they wouldn't stand for that. He was drawing a blank when Acana said:
>
> "Tell us, pal, go on, tell us."
>
> Then he understood that this was his thing, that *he was there to tell the story*. He didn't remember what he said in detail. He began by mixing everything up, just as he found it in his memory, and he kept going like that, without pause or emphasis, giving the same importance to the bombardment and to his fear, to the thirst and the advance, to the dust on the road and the mortars, only paying attention to the uncontrollable rhythm of memory until arriving, finally, at the sea.

This simple fragment sums up, I think, the poetics of *The Initials of the Earth*: its objective, its tone, its discursive strategies . . . But this is not to suggest that the novel's greatest merit lies in its testimonial nature, as my insistence on that virtue might suggest. It is a complex text precisely because of the tense relationship it establishes between the historical space of social experience and the symbolic spaces of individual and collective consciousness. It is worth dwelling for a moment on this secret dialogue between fiction and reality.

8

One of the first things literature professors teach their students is that in analyzing a work of fiction one must distinguish clearly between what one might call the work's theme and its subject; the theme being the meaning of the work, and the subject the stuff of anecdote. The reader will forgive my didacticism, but I want to be sure to make myself understood. In the case of *The Initials*, the theme occupies the narrative present (e.g., the introduction and conclusion) while the subject corresponds to the twenty-one numbered chapters structured as a vast retrospective. Everything within the novel's real time occurs during this protracted, reflexive, evocative, and difficult span that begins when Carlos sits down to the questionnaire and continues up until that moment during the assembly in which he is summoned before the panel of colleagues who are to decide whether or not he is an "exemplary" worker, and therefore whether he has sufficient merit to opt for admission into the Cuban Communist Party. The blank questionnaire is, to employ the jargon of criticism, a metonymic displacement of the blank pages on which the novel is written. The narrated past cannot, then, be judged independently of the present, nor vice versa, because the novel does not take place in either time but rather in the fusion, and fatal collision of, past and present. To put it more simply, the questionnaire is the key to both the novel's subject and its theme, since it sets in motion the character's history, and yet—and herein lies the paradox that "explains" the existence of the novel—it is a personal history whose multiple dimensions no questionnaire could encompass, for the simple reason that life does not fit within the parameters of forms or schema. If the questionnaire demands, in effect, a confession—hence the mocking phrase *tellmeyourstory*—it implies at the same time an experience of a frustration that can be overcome only by profound self-contemplation. The novel attempts just such a study in consciousness, understood as a rescue operation of the nuanced, the singular, the quotidian, the lived and felt, of flesh-and-blood reality.

And it is this contradiction (that *first* contradiction, whose poles are the asphyxiation and plenitude of memory) that is made dramatically manifest with the commencement of the assembly, and that suddenly becomes a conflict between being and appearance, intention and act, comprehension and intolerance, private and public morality, opportunism and conscience. In other words, the questionnaire—quite clearly a mute dialogue—begins by proposing an epistemological problem (Is it possible to know reality via data taken out of context?) and ends up presenting an ethical problem (Is it possible, based on such data, to judge the degree of social responsibility or moral integrity of a person?). This further turn of the screw is a decisive factor in the success of the novel's theme, because without that false conclusion that is the assembly—without the open ending after which the voting is to take place, abruptly involving the reader in the debate, for he, too, must decide either "in favor" or "against"—*The Initials of the Earth* would be a good novel, certainly, but not a great novel.

9

The Cuban reader who had lived through situations similar to those of Carlos Pérez Cifredo might have had the impression that *The Initials of the Earth* was an autobiographical novel, or even a chronicle of the era. Indeed, Carlos participates in almost all the events which, in the popular imagination, characterize the social and political life of 1960s Cuba. But this is merely the expression of a narrative strategy that would underscore the fact that Carlos is a person typical of his milieu and time. His vicissitudes are the same as those of millions of Cubans who were then between the ages of fifteen and fifty, and who grew accustomed to plotting their daily episodes against the measure of a collective time, since in those days public and private life could not be neatly separated. Thus one person married, another lost his grandmother, a first child was born; elsewhere someone finished her studies and someone else met the woman who later became his wife "during the Literacy Campaign," "a bit before Girón," "after the October Crisis," "during the 1970 zafra." People then spoke in these terms, and many do so still without realizing that they are dividing their life into what we might call "historically significant segments," without realizing that they are creating possible novelistic structures. Life itself furnished these segments and structures. Jesús Díaz did nothing more than render them in black and white.

Often, moreover, there was something almost natural or automatic to this structuring process, because if in 1960 or 1961 one had committed oneself to the project, one most likely became a militiaman; and if one became a militiaman one likely passed the first test of walking sixty-two kilometers; and if one passed that test one's chances improved for training in a boot camp; and if one graduated from such a camp one might at any moment be sent to trenches anywhere in the country . . . It was all a chain. Neither historically nor literarily could these situations be considered "contingent" or "forced"; historically, for the reasons stated, and literarily, because all literary history from

Homer to the present has depended on just such "chance" connections that nonetheless appear inevitable and realistic when they respond to a story's internal logic and generic conventions. Not for nothing did Balzac observe that chance was the greatest novelist. But since numerous Cuban short stories already had dealt with these same themes, one critic essayed that with a work of this nature Jesús risked "telling us once again what we already all know" (one imagines an Athenian spectator at the premiere of Euripides's *Electra* exclaiming with irritation: "Surely they're not going to tell me the same story *again*?!").

Jesús ran no such risk, it seems to me, for the simple reason that he was telling the story of a singular figure involved in an adventure at the time not yet rendered in Cuban fiction. In *The Initials of the Earth* the quantitative— the panoramic, almost exhaustive vision of an epoch—makes for a notable qualitative difference, inasmuch as the novel encompasses a variety of media and genres, from the newspaper chronicle to the epic. The lion, Valéry once said, achieves his form by assimilating sheep; here such accumulation serves an aesthetic end. The events we allegedly "all know," moreover—the militia-man's march, life at boot camp, the zafra, etc.—become something else entirely the moment in which they are articulated within a larger system of relationships and tensions within the text, and again when they fulfill a symbolic function: for they are also part of the "tests" the hero has to pass in order to win the princess. The hero of fantasy fiction has to traverse a forest, ford a river, elude evildoers, and, finally, slay the dragon to rescue and conquer the princess; destiny—that is, history—submits modern heroes to other trials. As Propp so sharply observed, those earlier intrepid paladins without a past were less characters than narrative functions; lacking proper lives, they were forced to rehearse immutable roles while only their garb varied. When the literary hero enters into a *dynamic* relationship with the medium, by contrast, he enters into the domain of history and begins to be transformed along with it: he is obliged to become, as Bahktin put it, "a new kind of man, previously nonexistent." It is no coincidence that the predecessor to the modern hero should appear in moments of crisis or that his first steps be situated not "within an epoch, but on the limit of two epochs" (Bahktin cites as examples *Gargantua and Pantagruel* and *Wilhelm Meister*).

I am not attempting here to force a literary kinship, but rather to substantiate my claim that the literary heft of *The Initials*, derives from its secret link to a narrative tradition erected, on the one hand, on the supports of the oral tradition, and on the other, on those of the novel of formation and apprenticeship—the bildungsroman to which I referred earlier. *The Initials* is, finally, further strengthened by an intertextuality sporting fully postmodern roots: like Valéry's lion, the novel swallows and assimilates all the codes and languages it happens across: comics, cinema, popular music, Afro-Cuban mythology, jokes, slogans, slang . . . Thus we arrive again at our earlier point, ready to admit that, yes, *The Initials* is also and perhaps above all the literary testimony of an era.

10

How is the book's referential value registered? In its infallible and meticulous linking together of characters, contexts, and their respective development: the characters are defined—*must* be defined—through the same process by which the Revolution comes to define them. This seems, in principle, to be the idea: to narrate how a revolutionary comes into being—or better, to narrate how someone who was not previously a revolutionary becomes one. In this, *The Initials* contributes to the bildungsroman a dimension not found, as far as I am aware, in other instances of the genre, for at stake here is again both an individual and a collective process of learning, the "formation" of a character and the "formation" of an entire people. This idea is not, to be sure, manifested as a passive reflection of history but instead as the symbolic expression or "transfigured reflection" of the real—that is, via linkages set up between reality and its artistic representation. The most obvious such nodes are the protagonist and his family; the former embodying a subject of potential change, the latter, the guardian of immutable values. Family relations indeed are presented as the only thing that cannot change, come what may; they share with bourgeois property the status of being "sacred." In such a context—in which the family as institution appears as the last bastion of individualism and tribal ethics—the domestic conflicts reproduce, in microcosm, larger social contradictions, which is to say that they are revealed to be simple dramatic variations on class struggle. But what counts aesthetically are precisely these variations, not their ideological referents, for it is only the former, with their emotive and symbolic charge, that are able to function as legitimate links to reality.

11

It should be clear that these links are expressed not in allegorical or conceptual terms but in strictly narrative and poetic ones. Something always seems to be happening or a new development brewing, a feature that on the face of it would seem to belong more to the territory of adventure films, but which in fact is borrowed from the most ancient of oral traditions. It was the mastery of narrative strategy that saved Scheherazade a thousand times over, and it is this strategy that may also partially explain the success enjoyed by *The Initials* on both sides of the Atlantic. Narrativity—that trap for the unsuspecting, long the purview of the jettisoned traditional novel alone—was rediscovered by certain avant-garde authors after a half century of suspicion and criticism (to only varying degrees justified) aimed at its alleged complicity with bourgeois order and the machinations of the market. But is there really anything essentially bourgeois or servile about the art of telling a story? Neither Scheherazade, nor the chivalrous knights, nor the African griots, nor the hoary Mayan who rescued from the depths of time the inaugural heroes of the American imagination knew a thing about capitalism or marketing. We are, then, clearly dealing here with something else, something we might term, for lack of a better phrase, a new sense of modernity.

The reencounter between oral literature and the modern novel—I'm thinking of Latin American examples such as Juan Rulfo's *Pedro Páramo* or *The Devil to Pay in the Backlands*, by João Guimaraes Rosa—began on a discursive level with the incorporation of popular speech culled from multiple sectors of the populace, and continued, on a diegetic level, with the vindication of plot-heavy narrative structures. It was a return to the starting point, but now at a higher level of the spiral, concerned with rescuing the story's traditional mechanisms while at the same time conserving and reformulating the expressive innovations of the vanguard (for example, such techniques as free indirect discourse, which allowed an author to suture the omniscience of the narrator to the consciousness of the character). Theory and criticism, for their part, would respond to these devices of authorial practice with a renewed interest in the "pleasure of the text" and with the reader himself as center of diverse textual strategies. It was as if, suddenly, overwhelmed by an excess of jargon and logocentrism, we remembered that novels are written to be read, not studied.

I mention all this because I was struck that several Cuban critics recognized the thematic and stylistic merit of *The Initials* but not the modernity of its proposals. Modern is that which presupposes a quest. But as questing, in the arts, has itself gone on for millennia, it might be more appropriate to say that the modern writer or artist is he who finds new questions in old answers, and his own way of answering them. I won't appeal to the hackneyed metaphors of the relay race or of dwarfs on giants' shoulders, but there is something to the claim that the great avant-gardes always depend on great traditions, and for that very reason are obliged to go beyond them. One of the tasks of the critic is to identify and document new trends that they may be incorporated into the theoretical consciousness of each new artistic or literary movement. This is not easy, to be sure—trends are established not by chronometer but by consensus—but it would be more difficult still if we didn't so rigorously track artists' every experiment and innovation. Certain critics' take on *The Initials* was similar to that of the common reader: lulled by the style and smooth plotting of the novel they failed to take notice of its artifice, innovations, "technique." That the novel manages to occlude its devices is, to my mind, precisely one of its formal strengths. We might say the form has become invisible or better, transparent; for the form, working slyly and unconditionally on behalf of the content, dissolves into it. I suspect that the great boon yielded by this strategy is a language whose rendering of popular speech manages to erase its own traces and to achieve a level of spontaneity Roland Barthes termed "degree zero." But if we examine at any length the mechanism by which certain effects are realized, we quickly discover surprising, or at least uncommon, formal solutions.

What, for example, is the nature of the text about the 1969 zafra which constitutes chapter 20? It is a love letter—or a summary of the love letters Carlos would have liked to have written Gisela, but which, honoring Gisela's request that he not speak of love, Carlos turns into simple *cartas de relación*, the daily recounting of life in the field. Indeed, this arduous renunciation manages to lend to Carlos's repressed passion a certain charge of tenderness and veracity one otherwise looks to the amorous epistolary writings of earlier eras to find. But who is the true recipient of the text? Not Gisela, for Gisela is the apostrophic addressee to whom the epistolary discourse is directed, not actually the intended reader of a recounting that would, in any case, make little sense to her. To whom, then, does the narrator appeal? What does such a plea mean for Carlos? What function does it serve?

Our puzzlement begins to subside when we notice that the address presumes a bifurcation, a dialogue of people and masks involving *four* characters: on one side, the virtual Gisela and the real Gisela who, in no uncertain terms, forbids talk of love; and on the other the real Carlos and the one who once accepted such terms but who cannot now contain himself. The words, directed to the virtual Gisela, have for Carlos the symbolic function of re-establishing the equilibrium between reality and desire. We are witness to the love letter never written, but over which Carlos cannot stop mulling in his fevered state of waiting; the game recalls Poe's tale of the letter hid in plain sight. I wonder whether what Díaz achieves here is not in fact an innovative rendering of his character's crisis, by which we find ourselves obliged to share in Carlos's need to daydream. We see a letter that doesn't exist because the mirage created by the narrative technique compels us to believe in its existence.

Another example: the internal structure of the novel. The action unfolding in the numbered chapters develops chronologically in irreversible time; that which occurs first comes first, and that which happens later, later. But this progressive and apparently linear external structure does not coincide exactly with that of the internal structure. In fact, nearly all the chapters begin in medias res, and then at some point the action gives way to a "retrospective" in which the loose ends of the preceding chapter are tied up, before the current chapter returns to its respective subplot. In other words, each chapter is designed as an incomplete dramatic structure whose action, carried to its climax, achieves resolution only in the subsequent chapter. The internal structure thus develops in a kind of spiral, not a straight line; the impression of absolute linearity is another of the novel's mirages. But the most innovative formal solution, I would argue, is the structuring of the text into three narrative blocks permitting a bold reflection first on the novel's theme and then on the very nature of the genre. This simple move, it seems to me, exemplifies better than any other the manner in which Jesús, seemingly without effort, devised strikingly creative solutions to certain technical and structural problems of the modern novel. I have to backpedal a bit to explain how this all works.

12

The introduction and conclusion are two sides of the same coin. Both remit to the problematic identity of a protagonist desirous of a social recognition he himself doubts he deserves. Indeed, what has he done to merit it? Has he performed exceptionally in the "tests" that earn him revolutionary accreditation? Has he, throughout a difficult process, maintained an honest and consistent attitude? Answers can be offered from the perspective of either insider or outsider, with the eye of one who is both judge and participant or of one who judges solely. In either case the risk is great: both tend to operate in that slippery zone of individual and collective consciousness where it is all too easy to take the apparent for the real, and vice versa. The solution, given this dilemma, is to be the questionnaire: the search for the precise datum, the objective event, the concise piece of information. But it is precisely here that Carlos feels attacked: the form's questions "disconcert him in their simplicity"; they do not encompass, as it were, the totality of his being. He himself would not be able to say of what such a totality might consist: his life appears to him more labyrinth than sphere. Still, he has discovered one of the great contradictions directly linked to the text's structure, whose poles, as I mentioned above, are the asphyxia and plenitude of memory, or the dramatic opposition between brute fact and the infinite, unforeseeable modulations of memory. Carlos now responds to or impugns the questionnaire, evoking all that is left out—in a word, his life. In contrast with the questionnaire's stale truth, the numbered chapters are, I repeat, an attempt to rescue the vibrant truth, flesh-and-blood reality. That reality, contradictory by definition, reinforces the idea of the labyrinth—except that now the reader has his Ariadne's thread, and for him the labyrinth has ceased to be a mystery.

Not so for the other characters . . . and here we encounter the novel's second great contradiction, which is intimately bound up with its sandwich-like structure, and which becomes salient with the conclusion's return to the present. Carlos arrives at the assembly after having weighed his life with implacable honesty: it is obvious that his errors, vacillations, and blunders have not, ultimately, prevented his passing the tests with some measure of success. Obvious, that is, to us. The participants in the assembly, however, do not know the labyrinth from within; they lack the memory with which to orient themselves inside it; their judgments will be based, inevitably, on the data in the questionnaire and on personal experience; they have no other means of decipherment; they have not read, as we have, the numbered chapters of the novel. In steering themselves towards a decision they will call on only those primitive instruments of analysis readily at hand, and on varying degrees of good or bad faith.

Again we are struck by the novelty of the book's structure: because it permits us to follow the assembly proceedings from the privileged position of some supreme tribunal, assessing the proceedings' every fluctuation with the benefit of full knowledge, we discover that there is something irremediably pathetic or malignant in this obsessive search for an objectivity that nowhere is to be found—because it is not there, in the terrain of the datum and the abstraction, that concrete truths, crucial elements of social experience, or what we might rather vulgarly term the reality of life are made manifest. In other words, the book's organic structure facilitates the conclusion's reactivation of the function of the introduction: the reader's reaction to the assembly is the same as Carlos's before the questionnaire. If to this functional mirroring we add the temporal, thematic, and expressive links between the conclusion and introduction, we see that the two form a unit—the text's "analytic" block—in contrast with which the numbered chapters constitute a narrative block presented as the paradigm of authenticity, as the *true* novel. In between the codified tensions of the introduction and conclusion, the numbered chapters describe a voltaic arc all along which the sparks showering forth from action or imagination illuminate the vast, riotous, evasive complexity of life.

We are, then, before a structure that locates the self-reflexive character of the modern novel on the plane of content, not form. If it is true that the recursive nature of the modern novel, with its assiduous calling of attention to its own devices, has provoked a sustained and systematic reflection on the nature of the genre, such reflection has rarely gone beyond formal analysis. *The Initials* is a self-reflexive novel of another kind: by signaling the authenticity of its narrative block from the antipodal perspective, it proposes a reflection on the peculiar aptness of the genre as a medium for knowledge, as a uniquely privileged space of concrete truth. When human and social relations flow through narrative discourse in accord with their own dynamics and without passing through the filter of false consciousness, we find ourselves before the most authentic representation of reality language can offer. This was something readers already faintly discerned in the picaresque and emphatically announced in the nineteenth century. At least two statements now classic within the Marxist tradition serve as examples: Marx's claim that British novelists such as Dickens, Thackeray, and Charlotte Brontë "revealed to the world more truths" than all the ideologues of his time, and Engels's confession that he had learned more from Balzac about French Restoration society "than from all professed historians, economists and statisticians of the period together." It seems to me truly a formal accomplishment that *The Initials*, through its simple sandwich structure, manages to thematize these issues on a narrative level.

13

By counterposing narrative to analytic discourse and by asserting that only one is authentic, does the author perhaps insinuate that all criticism is, by definition, superfluous? The reader who has followed me thus far may feel my

analysis leaves out—among other things—the imaginative force, the drama-
tism, the humor, the irony, the scrupulous intensity with which the author
recreates characters, situations, and conflicts both encompassing and tran-
scending an era, in order to concentrate, with debatable success, on other
aspects: issues which surely pertain to, but are not, the novel proper.

Tolstoy once said that the only way to do a novel justice is to retell it
completely, word for word, and this remains true; true anyway for writers and
illiterates. Criticism, on the other hand, primarily intended for the reader,
draws strength from the paradox that though it cannot but be a simplification,
it is also the sole means of leading the reader, via successive approximations,
towards a fuller enjoyment of texts. It works to forge on the one hand a certain
sensibility and on the other a system of values that would make of each
successive reading a new experience.

In revolutionary Cuba *The Initials* was, in its moment, considered to be an
invitation to active commitment and social participation, particularly by the
youth. When the novel ends and the reader finds himself obliged to vote, he is
indeed aware that he is voting not for an isolated instance but for a project. It
is often said that the only past we can change is the future. *The Initials* makes a
similar claim: that human beings, simply by virtue of being human, are not
condemned to stumble twice over the same stone.

14

I hope the reader of this edition—and of this epilogue—may have arrived at
some of these same conclusions, or at least that he may now feel stimulated to
corroborate or revise his own.

To my own personal testimony I must add that after receiving that unfathomable phone call from Miami it took me days to fully comprehend that
Jesús no longer existed, and for that very reason would not disappear. I'm not
referring here to his legacy of novels and films, though it is clear enough that
the history of Cuban culture since 1959, or that of its first thirty years anyway,
could not be told exempting his substantial contributions as a narrator and
filmmaker. His spectral presence has rather to do with something at once
more complex and more simple: it has to do with the contradictory and totally
unpredictable entity that is the human being, the human soul. I am certain of
this; I am keenly aware of it. The problem is that I don't want to establish the
schizophrenic relationship with my own memory that in a certain moment,
purely out of friendship—or convenience—I established with Jesús. The Jesús

Díaz I remember and whose image I wish to preserve is of a single piece and wears a luminous face. Others will attempt, from their respective positions, to render more or less objective portraits and evaluations of him. I wish merely to preserve the conviction that the great ground we covered together was, for both, a splendid adventure, one that allowed us to inscribe the earth's initials in the grip of a friendship that continues still. And to preserve as well the conviction that no one can take away the grief within me, because that adventure, though uncommon, was a real, earthly experience, deeply significant, and having nothing to do with paradise, hell, hallucinations, or nightmares.

AMBROSIO FORNET

HAVANA, WINTER OF 2005

TRANSLATED BY RACHEL PRICE

AFTERWORD

What I would like to explore in these pages is what I know intimately: the special problems presented to a translator rendering Jesús Díaz's *The Initials of the Earth* into a North American idiom, to be read by a North American audience. For the historic relationship of Cuba and the United States is so close, so fraught with ambivalent emotions, and since 1959 so mired in violence and ignorance that no attempt at communication, including a literary translation, can steer entirely clear of that difficult environment. Bringing the novel into English thus poses unique challenges, some of which I will describe in this brief reflection on practice.

CONSIDERING HISTORY

If Cuba and its Revolution—as portrayed through the coming of age of the novel's protagonist Carlos Pérez Cifredo during the decades of the 1950s and 1960s—are at the heart of this epic novel, U.S. politics, power, language, and culture are never more than ninety miles away. They are present in every chapter, whether it be through Carlos's identification with comic-book heroes as a boy, his adolescent erotic fascination with a blond *americana*, the political and geographical divisions within his family after the Revolution, or U.S. aggression at the battle of Playa Girón (Bay of Pigs) and its aftermath. In chapter 18, Carlos must struggle through conversations in English during a visit to Canada as the guest of a local solidarity organization, trying to think in that language and to make himself understood despite his anxiety and fear. At all these points in the narration, the North American reader will find familiar words, places, and characters. In some ways, then, the task of the translator is made easier, for many references will be understood without requiring too great a leap in imagination.

But this apparent advantage also presents certain hazards, for *The Initials of the Earth* in its essence is a Cuban novel, wholly identified with the Cuban context. While the North tantalizes the young Carlos, after the Revolution it becomes everything Cuba is not, or should not be: capitalist, racist, individualistic, humorless, cold. Moreover, English most definitely is not Spanish, a playful instrument Cubans use creatively on a daily basis through poetry, rhyme, rhythm, humor, and word games more or less elaborate, but the common birthright of all. When, in chapter 15, access to authentic Cuban language is denied through the banning of obscene words, Díaz makes clear the futility and absurdity of such an action, and the foreign (in this case Chinese) doctrine behind it: how can Cuba be Cuba without these words and the power of imagery and emotion they evoke? It is language and the limits bureaucracy imposes on it—a topic explored in more detail by Ambrosio Fornet in his epilogue—that takes us into the very center of the Cuban revolutionary process, of its ideals, triumphs, and hypocrisies, as Jesús Díaz understood them.

How, then, to make this Cuban novel intelligible for the North American reader of English and not lose the joy, the play, the rapier wit, the eroticism of a Spanish so intrinsically connected with national liberation? Friedrich Schleiermacher wrote in the nineteenth century about the key choice to be made by a literary translator: to bring the writer to the reader, or the reader to the writer.[1] The former approach implies putting the foreign into a familiar, domestic idiom, easing the reader's way, while the latter requires the reader to accept the text on its own foreign terms, making the journey more of a challenge. My translation of *The Initials of the Earth* takes the second approach, with the goal of preserving the heart and soul of a narrative so concerned with what makes Cuba Cuban. The novel itself asks how to translate Marxist-Leninism into Cuban, and how that enterprise, more than a decade into the process as the narration ends, can succeed. Each reader must decide for him or herself the conclusions to this question; thus it is crucial that the English-language reader join to the fullest extent possible in Díaz's quest to interrogate, from within the process, the combination of Cuba and Communism.

However, the contemporary U.S. reader faces special obstacles to understanding such a work. Cuba, in the 1950s exotic yet so close, is today almost entirely unknown, not only foreign but forbidden. There is almost no point of reference for the everyday, the local, things that constitute a person's life story in a place now demonized as completely other. While a German or French reader of *The Initials of the Earth* might easily grasp the protagonist's ambivalent relationship to North American culture and the English language, the U.S. reader, paradoxically, has a more difficult task. Though details from North American culture in the novel might seem familiar, they must be understood as a Cuban living through the revolutionary process would see them, through the prism of Carlos Pérez Cifredo's experience, mind, and emotions.

Thus as I have endeavored to bring the reader to the writer in this translation, I have remained aware of the nature of my work within a specific historical context. My primary goal has been to capture the vitality of Díaz's language, which operates in so many different registers that each chapter introduces entirely new and different problems. I have tried to preserve the pathos of some moments and the sharp humor of others; I want my reader to have as much fun with parts of this novel as someone reading the Spanish would. But the reader, in my view, should always be aware that this book is considered by some to be *the* novel of the Cuban Revolution, and that it was originally written in Cuban Spanish. As Fornet explains in his epilogue, many Cubans who lived through those same years feel that *The Initials of the Earth* describes the trajectory of their own lives. While most North American readers cannot identify on that kind of experiential level, my goal is that they might imagine, in a new and empathic manner, historical events veiled by decades of ignorance and lack of information. With that accomplished, Díaz's complex political stance can be judged and evaluated on its own terms.

CONSIDERING HUMOR AND PROFANITY

The translation of humor and that of profanity have long been recognized as especially difficult challenges for the translator, and even as untranslatable quantities. This novel overflows with both. The Cuban *choteo*, the constant banter, joking, and wordplay that form a much-studied cultural phenomenon, presents a particularly notable case, being identified as it is with a national way of being.[2] One approach is to translate the gist of the humor, its tone and essence, into a cultural milieu closer to the reader's own frame of reference. Suzanne Jill Levine, the translator of works by the recently deceased Cuban writer Guillermo Cabrera Infante, has argued persuasively for this method, drawing parallels between Cuban and New York Jewish humor as a vehicle for translation of complex wordplays.[3]

In *The Initials of the Earth*, where humor functions as a commentary on Cubanness in the revolutionary situation and the jokes are often political in nature, I have made distinctions between wordplay for language's sake and jokes that cannot be disconnected from the local context. I have translated the former more freely than the latter, where I usually stick not only to the sense but also to the words of the original. At the same time I have attempted to preserve Díaz's vividly funny portrayal of Cubans thriving and surviving through the creative use of language. Thus, while the Archimandrite's description of his wife's wedding dress as "wall-to-wall" instead of floor-length in chapter 16 is a free translation of *en vez de vestirse de largo tuvo que vestirse de ancho*, the Ghost's play on the words *polyclinic* and *Polinesio* in chapter 15, with its specific reference to an actual, elegant, Havana restaurant, cannot be translated into a North American cultural reference without losing the nuances entirely. The interested reader will find commentary on many other examples in the endnotes.

Profanity and obscene words present an entirely different situation. Humor is about the shock of the new, the juxtaposition of the familiar with the unexpected. Obscenity is about the old, about the deepest wishes and fears from our early years of life making their way from repression to speech. The Hungarian psychoanalyst Sandor Ferenczi, a contemporary of Sigmund Freud, wrote about the power of obscene words to evoke almost hallucinatory moments of feeling, combining past and present, in the person who pronounces them.[4] Of course, the definition of obscenity and its form of expression varies from culture to culture. While some bodily functions translate quite easily between Spanish and English (*mierda* and *shit*, for example) the closest analogues to etymologically sexual words used in Cuban profanity often involve references to religion or blasphemy in English (*carajo* translated as *goddamn* being a prime example). I have aimed to evoke an emotional response to obscene words in the English-language reader similar to that experienced by the reader of the Spanish original (a matter of degree) while trying to keep the sense of what the original means. My solutions are varied depending on context; numerous examples, again, are to be found in the endnotes.

The translation of obscene words, however, takes on additional, crucial meaning in chapter 15. This chapter in its entirety discusses questions hitting at the heart of Jesús Díaz's experience as a writer in 1970s Cuba: What kind of language is Cuban? What kind of language is permissible in a revolutionary culture? What can be said, what can be written, what is art, what is treason? When Carlos Pérez tries to ban slang and obscenity from his university residence hall, words are divested of humor and play, and made into counter-revolutionary acts, more Chinese than Cuban. Díaz, through the Archimandrite's diagnosis at chapter's end, makes clear his own view: such censorship is a neurotic, if not psychotic, affliction. The inability to respond to (Cuban) obscene words with sensuality and humor is a cultural sickness of external origin, resulting here in Carlos's own internal repression and suffering as it combines with his desperate wish to be a hero.

Not wishing to commit further treason in the translation of all this to English, my goal has been to communicate the original Spanish word's force and capacity for inspiring feeling; the image evoked by the word to the Cuban reader or speaker; and a similar, or parallel, emotional response in the English reader. Above all, the absurdity of censoring words, whether spoken or written (as captured by Carlos's reaction to Cervantes's use of *hideputa*) must never be lost. We would do well, in the United States of the early twenty-first century, to reflect on Díaz's condemnation of such narrowness of ideology and its consequences. If hearts and minds are opened by this translation, I will have accomplished my task.

KATHLEEN ROSS
DECEMBER 2005

NOTES

Sources used have been identified by the following abbreviations.

DMC   José Sánchez-Boudy, *Diccionario Mayor de Cubanismos* (Miami: Ediciones Universal, 1999).

HPC   Argelio Santiesteban, *El habla popular cubana de hoy* (La Habana: Editorial de Ciencias Sociales, 1997).

TITLE, EPIGRAPH, INTRODUCTION

pp. iii and vii *The Initials of the Earth*: The title and epigraph of the novel are taken from Pablo Neruda's *Canto general* (1955), a classic work of Latin American poetry that narrates a sweeping history of the continent from 1400 forward. The lines of the epigraph are found in the second stanza of the first section of the poem, "Amor América (1400)," which offers a description of indigenous men before the arrival of European conquerors. This translation is taken from *Canto General*, translated by Jack Schmitt (Berkeley: University of California Press, 1991). The entire stanza reads: "Man was dust, earthen vase, an eyelid / of tremulous loam, the shape of clay— / he was Carib jug, Chibcha stone, / imperial cup or Araucanian silica. / Tender and bloody was he, but on the grip / of his weapon of moist flint, / the initials of the earth were / written" (13). *La tierra* in Spanish also means "the land," with political and/or patriotic connotations of "country" or the Cuban *patria* (motherland, also fatherland or homeland) that is integral to Díaz's novel. But in Neruda's poem *la tierra* is unambiguously "the earth," physical in both the elemental and planetary senses.

p. 3 *Tellmeyourstory*: Carlos calls the bureaucratic form or questionnaire a *cuéntametuvida*, literally "tell me your life", or more loosely translated, "tell me all about it" or "what's going on with you."

p. 3 *Zafra*: The sugarcane harvest, la zafra, became synonymous with revolutionary Cuba's will to economic survival, especially in the 1960s and early 1970s when it attracted international brigades of sympathizers. Díaz develops this fully in later chapters of the novel.

p. 4 *Compañero*: *Compañero* (or *compañera* in its feminine form) cannot be captured by any one term in English. In its leftist political sense, as here, it comes close to *comrade*, but often implies a much more personal and intimate relationship, more like *partner* or *mate* (as in roommate or classmate). It will be left in Spanish throughout this translation, except in exclusively political or military contexts where *comrade* is more appropriate.

CHAPTER I

p. 5 *Tarmangani*: *Tarmangani* is part of the ape language created by Edgar Rice Burroughs in his Tarzan novels and in subsequent movies based on the novels. It means white man.

p. 5 *Ride, Vaquero; Shane; Durango Kid*: *Ride, Vaquero* (dir. John Farrow, 1953; Spanish title *Una vida por otra*) starred Robert Taylor, Ava Gardner, and Anthony Quinn. *Shane* (dir. George Stevens, 1953; Spanish title *Shane, el desconocido*) starred Alan Ladd, Jean Arthur, and Van Heflin. The Durango Kid was the central character of many Westerns starring Charles Starrett, made between 1940 and 1952.

p. 6 *No-Do Newsreel*: No-Do was a Spanish cinema newsreel put out by the Franco regime and shown as a propaganda tool before the main feature film.

p. 7 *Kreegor; bundolo*: *Kreegor* (scream) and *bundolo* (kill) are more words from Tarzan's ape language.

p. 7 *Saquiri the Malay*: Saquiri el Malayo was a character in the 1940s and 1950s Cuban radio serial "Los Tres Villalobos"; he was the nemesis of the three Villalobos brothers, who were do-gooders.

p. 7 *Daño*: The daño is a curse, a supernatural power that can overtake one's soul, as will become clear later in this chapter.

p. 7 *Ceiba*: The ceiba, or silk-cotton tree, is one of the trees venerated in Afro-Cuban Santería or synchretic saint worship, a belief system that will be explained more fully in chapter 2.

p. 7 *Weyler*: Valeriano Weyler (1838–1930), Spanish general, was installed as governor of Cuba by the Spanish in 1896 with powers to suppress the rebel insurgency. He enacted a policy called *reconcentración* in order to separate the rebels from the civilian population, placing 300,000 civilians in camps. Over 30 percent died of starvation, disease, and poor sanitary conditions, generating great anti-Spanish feeling in Cuba.

p. 8 *Jinx*: *Ñeque* is the Afro-Cuban word translated here as *jinx*; when a person has bad luck owing to an evil eye or spell cast on him, he is said to have ñeque.

p. 8 *Mambí*: *Mambí* refers to Cuban rebel fighters in the wars against Spain.

p. 8 *Máximo Gómez*: Máximo Gómez (1836–1905) was born in Santo Domingo and went to Cuba in 1865 to command troops for Spain but changed sides in the struggle and became a patriot for Cuba's cause. Gómez was named chief general of the Liberation Army by José Martí in 1895 and led a victorious campaign against the Spanish.

p. 9 *Blackhawks*: The Blackhawks were comic-book heroes first introduced in 1941. They were an international band of volunteers whose mission was fighting the Nazis. Their leader was Blackhawk, a Pole until the United States entered the war, at which point he became an American. The Blackhawks continued to fight Communists and later super-powered criminals until 1992.

p. 9 *Niño Alvaro*: *Niño* or *niña*, literally little boy or girl, is the respectful manner in which black slaves addressed their masters' children, somewhat akin to *miss* and *master* in English.

p. 10 *Guajiro*: A guajiro is a Cuban peasant.

p. 11 *Rodolfo Villalobos*: Rodolfo Villalobos was one of "Los Tres Villalobos" of the radio show, as noted above.

p. 11 *Raffles*: A. J. Raffles was a character originated by E. W. Hornung in his 1899 volume *The Amateur Cracksman*. An upper-class thief supporting his lifestyle through crime, Raffles was a Victorian gentleman. There were several collections of Raffles stories; films and radio programs were later based on the books, notably the 1940 film *Raffles* starring David Niven.

p. 13 *The Crimson Pirate*: *The Crimson Pirate* (1952) starred Burt Lancaster; Spanish title, *El Pirata Hidalgo*.

p. 13 *The Black Corsair*: *El Corsario Negro* (1944) was a Mexican film directed by Chano Urueta, based on the Italian novel of the same title by Emilio Salgari.

p. 13 *l'Olonoise*: François l'Olonoise was a seventeenth-century pirate who sacked Maracaibo and Gibraltar (present-day Venezuela). The governor of Havana sent out a warship to find and kill him but l'Olonoise murdered all aboard.

p. 14 *Coño*: *Coño*, literally "cunt," is used frequently in Cuban Spanish as an expletive that generally has no overt sexual connotation, usually to express surprise, admiration, annoyance, or another strong emotion. It could be translated, variously, as "Damn!" "Wow!" "Shit!" "Fuck!" etc., but since none of these retain the underlying female sexual imagery, and the word is used repeatedly throughout the novel, it will be left in Spanish when grammar and style permit.

p. 14 *Ciguaraya; rompesaragüey; abrecaminos*: The ciguaraya, rompesaragüey, and abrecaminos are tropical plants and shrubs valued for their medicinal, curative, and magical properties by the Santería tradition.

p. 15 *Shazam*: *Shazam* comes from the *Captain Marvel* comic books. When Billy Batson, an orphan boy, uttered this word he would become a superhero.

p. 17 *The timid tar-tar-tar*: Díaz makes an untranslatable play on words here, since the Spanish for *stutterer* is *tartamudo*; thus, *el tímido tar tar tar de un triste tartamudo* (attempting to say Tarmangani).

pp. 18 *André; Olaf; Chop-Chop; Dr. Strogloff; Dr. Walter*: André and Olaf were members of the Blackhawks. Chop-Chop was a Chinese character who served as a kind of sidekick to the team. Dr. Strogloff and Dr. Walter, however, did not appear in these comics.

p. 23 *My mama loves me*: "My mama loves me" (*Mi mamá me ama*), is a typical first sentence learned in a Spanish primer.

p. 24 *Saloon*: *Saloon* is in English in the original text.

p. 25 *The End*: *The End* is also in English in the original text.

p. 25 *The occupation*: The occupation (in Spanish, *la intervención*), refers to the military occupation of Cuba by the United States, begun on 1 January 1899 and ending in 1902, formally inaugurating the Cuban republic.

p. 25 *Mister Leonardo Wood*: "Mister Leonardo Wood" was General Leonard E. Wood. As a cavalry commander he fought alongside Teddy Roosevelt and the Rough Riders with Cuban troops against Spain. During the 1899–1902 U.S. occupation he became military governor of Cuba.

CHAPTER 2

p. 26 *Vedado*: The Vedado was a middle- and upper-middle-class neighborhood in pre-revolutionary Havana.

p. 27 *Bembé*: The bembé is an African, and Afro-Cuban, religious ceremony celebrated with music, drumming, and dancing. In Cuban Spanish the word can also have sexual connotations, stemming from the vigorous movements of the dance (DMC 81).

p. 27 *Santeros*: Santeros are performers or ritual priests in the religious practice of Santería, a syncretic Afro-Cuban cult of worship that continues to thrive today, both in Cuba and the Cuban diaspora. In Santería belief, the *orishas* (gods and goddesses of Yoruban origin) are each identified with images of Christian saints (*santos*), as will be seen in detail later in this chapter.

p. 27 *Shola Anguengue*: Achola Anguengue is a warrior goddess in the Santería pantheon.

p. 29 *Tonight is Christmas Eve*: The *villancico* (Christmas carol) reads in Spanish: *Esta noche es Nochebuena/vamos al bosque, hermanito.*

p. 30 *Hey, you people!*: *Gente* (people), in this context, is a pejorative term specifically applied to blacks; in the era of slavery in Cuba, the term for a group of blacks working at a sugar mill was *gente* (HPC 192).

p. 30 *Goat*: The goat is an important sacrificial animal in Santería rites.

p. 30 *A la cholandengue!*: The phrase is a corruption of the Afro-Cuban chant *Shola Anguengue.*

p. 30 *White boy talking black*: The Cuban word for black, i.e., Afro-Cuban, dialect is *lengua*, literally "tongue."

p. 30 *Toque*: *Toque* refers to the *toque de santos*, another term for the bembé, i.e., a public ritual drumming ceremony.

p. 32 *Chilindrón*: *Chilindrón* refers to a whole goat, seasoned and roasted.

p. 33 *You break it, you pay for it*: In Cuban Spanish, the expression is *chivo que rompe tambor con su pellejo paga*, literally, "the goat who breaks the drum pays with his hide" (goatskin being a common covering for a drumhead). Thus Manolo makes an untranslatable joke in reference to the actual goat he has killed. The expression itself comes from a popular song: *Chivo que rompe tambor/con su pellejo paga/y lo que es mucho peor/en chilindrón acaba* (the goat who breaks the drum/pays with his hide/and what's even more/ends up as *chilindrón*) (HPC 146).

p. 33 *Abairimo; fiñes; guaguancó*: *Abairimo*, a word of African origin, means goodbye or so long. *Fiñes* are children. A *guaguancó* is an improvised Afro-Cuban musical composition, where the rhythm is made with whatever is at hand (in this case, the bottles of rum).

p. 34 *Jorge the Pilot*: Jorge el Piloto was a character from the Cuban comics who was nicknamed Manteca (lard) because of his fat belly, which caused him to keep losing buttons from his shirt (DMC 428).

p. 34 *Barbarito Diez*: Barbarito Diez was a lead singer with the Antonio María Romeu Orchestra for twenty years, beginning in the late 1930s. He was renowned for his melodious voice and made many records with Romeu in the danzón and bolero styles, becoming one of the most famous singers of his time.

p. 34 *Virgin of Regla*: The Virgin of Regla is one of several important incarnations of Mary in Cuban culture; another is the Virgin of Caridad del Cobre, the island's patron saint, who will be mentioned in another song.

p. 34 *Papá Montero*: Papá Montero is a representative character of the black underworld—pimps, prostitutes, emancipated slaves, and secret societies—that thrived in the areas on the outskirts of Havana during the nineteenth century. The character, celebrated in popular song, was immortalized by the Cuban poet Nicolás Guillén in "Papá Montero's Wake," from his volume *Sóngoro Consongo* (1931). *Canalla y rumbero* describe Montero's low-life ways of betrayal and carousing.

p. 34 *Antonio María Romeu Orchestra*: Antonio María Romeu (1876–1955), composer and bandleader, wrote more than five hundred danzones and led his orchestra for almost fifty years.

p. 39 *Kisimba; Insancio; Luleno; Tiembla Tierra*: Kisimba, Insancio, Luleno, and Tiembla Tierra, like Achola Anguengue, are all *mayombé* (Congo) gods, associated in Santería with Christian saints. Mercedes says she is Tiembla Tierra's daughter because the warrior goddess is identified with the *Virgen de las Mercedes* (Our Lady of Mercy).

p. 40 *Lucha Libre*: *Lucha Libre* is Mexican-style wrestling, popular on television throughout Latin America.

p. 41 *Antonino Rocca*: Antonino Rocca was a world-famous wrestler of the 1940s and 1950s.

p. 44 *The Mulatto*: The Mulatto refers to Fulgencio Batista, the general who led a movement against Machado's dictatorship in 1933. He served as president from 1940 to 1944, and returned to power through a coup in 1952. In 1958 he was overthrown by Fidel Castro's revolutionary movement.

p. 45 *Que llueva, que llueva, la Virgen de la Cueva*: "Let it rain, let it rain, Virgin of the Cave." This is the first line of a children's rhyme.

p. 45 *St. Isidro*: St. Isidro is the patron saint of agriculture.

p. 45 *Victims of the flood*: The Spanish word is *damnificados*, implying condemnation by a force of nature in biblical terms.

CHAPTER 3

p. 48 *Antonio Guiteras*: Antonio Guiteras y Holmes, born in Philadelphia to a North American mother and a father from a prominent Cuban family, was a militant who founded the Young Cuba movement. During the short-lived government of Grau San Martín in 1933, he served as minister of government, instituting many far-reaching popular reforms. He was killed by Fulgencio Batista's army in 1935 while trying to escape into exile at the age of twenty-eight.

p. 48 *Instituto*: The Instituto referred to here, and in later chapters, is the Instituto La Habana, one of several public preparatory schools in the capital in the 1950s.

p. 48 *Chinese charades*: The term here is *charadita*, from the *Charada China*, a kind of lottery game brought to Cuba by the Chinese. The game is played with a drawing of a Chinese man whose head and body are covered with thirty-six drawings, mostly animals, each associated with a number; the person running the game gives players a riddle or enigma in order for them to guess the winning number by association.

p. 48 *Smartasses*: In Spanish, *los Cabrones de la Vida*. *Cabrón* (literally, either a male goat, or a cuckold) as a vulgar expression has different connotations all over the Spanish-speaking world, usually implying some degree of badness; in many instances the translation could be "bastard." In Cuba it can also signify cleverness or intelligence. Here the term is adopted by a group of white adolescents using black or hipster language and identifying themselves as a kind of brotherhood.

p. 48 *From a rat it turns into a monkey / seated on his throne*: The riddle rhymes in Spanish: *Del ratón al mono / está sentado en el trono.*

p. 48 *Johnny Crime*: In Spanish, *Juanito el Crimen*; among the boys in the group, some have nicknames taken from underworld figures.

p. 49 *M-26-7*: The *Movimiento 26 de julio* (26th of July Movement) was founded in 1955 by Fidel Castro and other members of revolutionary groups.

p. 49 *The Naked City*: *The Naked City* (1948), directed by Jules Dassin, was an important and influential detective film (Joseph Cotten did not appear in the cast, however).

p. 49 *My man*: The Cuban slang here is *consorte* (literally "consort"), taken from underworld argot where it means "partner in crime."

p. 49 *You be crazy, asere!*: In Spanish, *Tas loco, asere*! Here black speech is imitated by Pablo. *Asere*, which has come to mean friend or buddy in Cuban Spanish, is a word of African origin used in religious rituals of the Abakuá secret society. Literally it means, "I greet you."

p. 50 *The wide staircase*: The *escalinata* is a wide staircase that is an emblem of the University of Havana, leading up to its main entrance.

p. 50 *Carlos Verdugo; Rubén Batista*: Carlos Verdugo was a Cuban medical student and patriot shot by the Spanish in 1871. Rubén Batista Rubio was the first student martyr in the struggle against Fulgencio Batista; he died in February 1953.

p. 51 *José Antonio*: José Antonio Echeverría was president during the 1950s of the FEU, the Federación Estudiantil Universitaria (Federation of University Students), founded in 1922 by Julio Antonio Mella. Echeverría was killed on 13 March 1957, during an attempted overthrow of Batista's dictatorship. This will be explained in more detail in later chapters.

p. 51 *Trejo*: Rafael Trejo, a student at the University of Havana, was killed in the struggle against the dictator Machado in 1930.

CHAPTER 4

p. 53 *Koch's Bacilli*: A pun runs through this chapter, playing with the identical sounds in Spanish of *Bacilos* (literally, bacilli, specifically Koch's bacillus, which causes tuberculosis) and *vacilar*, Cuban slang meaning "to ogle" in a sexual manner (*bacilo* also sounds identical to *vacilo*, the first-person singular form of the verb). The young men in chapter 4, and later in chapter 5, refer to themselves as *los Bacilos*, and the verb *vacilar* is used in conjunction with their actions at the whorehouse. The pun is approximated in English with "Koch's Bacilli" and "catch that." (Note also that the German pronunciation of Koch sounds like *cock*.)

p. 53–54 *San Isidro; Colón; Los Sitios; La Victoria;*: These are all Havana neighborhoods associated with marginal populations, and, in pre-revolutionary Cuba, prostitution and underworld activities.

p. 53 *Ñico Membiela*: Ñico Membiela (b. 1913) is a famous Cuban singer of boleros.

p. 53 *Combed through*: The Spanish is *con el peine pasado*, also Cuban slang for sexual intercourse (DMC 531).

p. 53 *Papaya*: Papaya, or *frutabomba* as it is called in parts of Cuba, is a slang term for the female genitals.

p. 54 *Vertigo*: *Vertigo* is a classic 1958 Alfred Hitchcock thriller, starring James Stewart and Kim Novak.

p. 55 *The Dance of the Millions*: *La Danza de los Millones* refers to a period of prosperity in Cuba around the time of World War I when sugar prices skyrocketed worldwide. The prosperity ended with a fall in prices in 1920.

p. 55 *Yarini*: Alberto Yarini was the playboy son of a well-to-do Havana family and a famous pimp. He died in 1910 in a shoot-out with his French rivals; crowds of women showed up to mourn at his funeral, as described in Alejo Carpentier's *Ecué-Yamba-O!* (1933) and Miguel Barnet's *Canción de Rachel* (1969).

p. 55 *Guayabito*: A guayabito is a kind of mouse, and by extension a cowardly person (DMC 342).

p. 55 *Big Fella*: El Gallo, literally the Cock. *Gallo* is a common term in Cuba meaning guy or fellow, but in this instance the word is capitalized as Yarini's nickname.

p. 57 *t'Yunai*: *Yunai* is the Cuban pronunciation of *United*, meaning United States. *Que me voy pa'la Yunai* is a phrase from a popular song (DMC 712).

p. 57 *Dark girl*: The Spanish here is *mora*, literally a Moorish woman.

p. 57 *What a catch; partying it up*: *Un vacilón*, another play on the sounds of *vacilar* and *Bacilos*.

p. 58 *His honeythewhore*: The composite word in Spanish is *putasunovia* (and later in the chapter, *putaminovia* and *putamichulo*). Since *puta*, or *la puta*, is often used as an epithet to indicate anger, there is an aggressive tone to the Spanish.

p. 58 *"A Man's Tears"*: "Lágrimas de hombre," composed by the Cuban band leader and composer Orestes Santos, was recorded in the 1950s by the band La Sonora Matancera with Leo Marini, a well-known Argentine singer of boleros, as vocalist. The words are: *lágrimas de hombre / que son más amargas / por estar condenadas / a nunca brotar.*

p. 58 *Otto, the matron*: Normally the word in Spanish is feminine, *la matrona*; here it is masculine, *el matrón*, indicating Otto as a biological, though effeminate, male.

p. 61 *If in this, in this, in this beautiful Havana*: The Spanish of the guaguancó reads: *Si en esta, si en esta, si en esta preciosa Habana, León, donde yo la conocí.*

p. 62 *Quinto; güiro; vacunao*: These are terms from Cuban music. The quinto is a type of conga drum; the güiro is a percussion instrument made from a dried gourd with ridges carved into it, played by being scraped with a stick. The vacunao is a pelvic thrust made in the rumba by the male to indicate his conquest of the female.

p. 62 *Yoyi*: "Yoyi" is a common nickname for Jorge.

p. 64 *Strong*: In English in the original text.

p. 64 *Turn up the juice until they fry*: *Candela al jarro hasta que soltara el fondo*, literally, put the pitcher on the fire until the bottom breaks. A saying that implies force carried out to the limit without mercy, it was used by Batista's henchmen; thus, here Pablo means it ironically, since anti-Batista revolutionaries have presumably set off the bomb (DMC 139).

p. 65 *Caballito de San Vicente, tiene la carga y no la siente*: Literally, "the little horse of St. Vincent, that's loaded up but doesn't feel it." A rhyme from a children's game that has come to signify, in Cuba, a person who does not realize what is happening, and in particular, a husband who puts up with a domineering or cheating wife (DMC 113).

p. 65 *Barroso*: Abelardo Barroso, a famous Cuban singer of the 1950s who sang with the group Orquesta Sensación, as will be seen further in chapter 5.

p. 65 *Castillo; Campanario; La China*: These are different types of Cuban lottery games.

CHAPTER 5

p. 71 *Orquesta Sensación; Barroso*: Orquesta Sensación and its singer, Abelardo Barroso, were famous in 1950s Cuba, as already noted in chapter 4.

p. 71 *The Rueda*: The Rueda (or Rueda de Casino) is a type of salsa dancing, done with at least two couples and usually many more, where the couples form a wheel (*rueda*) and the movements are done as a group, with passing of partners in time to the music. There is a leader who sings out the moves. The Rueda has a mixed ancestry of French forms and Afro-Cuban rhythms.

p. 72 *Montuno*: The montuno is part of various types of Cuban musical compositions, here a *son* (DMC 459).

p. 72 *"Moonglow"*: "Moonglow," a song from the 1930s that was a hit for Benny Goodman, was part of the soundtrack for the movie *Picnic* (1955), starring Kim Novak and William Holden. The song accompanies a scene where Novak and Holden do a dance of seduction.

p. 72 *Give it to me mama!*: *Rúñeme, mamá*, which could also be translated "love me, baby." *Ruñir* is Cuban slang for having sex (DMC 607).

p. 72 *Roberto Faz; Benny Moré*: Roberto Faz and Benny Moré were two famous Cuban singers who had their own popular bands in the 1950s.

p. 72 *Ay, mama, mama, mama, mamacita de mi vida!*: The double meaning alluded to here is between the words *mamá* (mama, mother) and *mama* (suck it, from the verb *mamar*); as the sounds are repeated and the words run together the accent is lost and the meaning becomes blurred.

p. 73 *Mamá me lava ropa con Fab*: "Mom washes my clothes with Fab," a commercial jingle. The conga line runs together the syllables and changes the accent to result in *mamelá*, another version of "suck it."

p. 77 *So-so; Bye*: In English in the original text.

p. 77 *Skinny son of a bitch*: Carlos's nickname is Flaco, or Skinny.

p. 77 *We sell lots of chamber pots*: *Vendemos tibores en colores* (we sell chamber pots in different colors), from the Cuban expression *para gustos se han hecho colores y para nalgas tibores* (colors were made for taste and buttocks for chamber pots), roughly translatable as "to each his own" (DMC 203).

p. 78 *Chuchero*: A Cuban figure of the 1950s somewhat like the Mexican *pachuco*. *Chucheros* dressed flashily (typically with pegged pants, knee-length jackets, a wide-brimmed fur hat, and a long chain) and were associated with delinquent behavior, drug use, and a slang of their own (DMC 186).

p. 79 *Orquesta Aragón*: Cuban band founded in 1939 and still immensely popular today.

p. 80 *Summertime*: The famous ballad from the Gershwin opera *Porgy and Bess* (1935), as sung by Ella Fitzgerald.

p. 81 *Hi*: In English in the original text.

p. 81 *What are you talking about . . . Go to hell*: These two lines spoken by Gipsy are in English in the original text.

p. 82 *Vicentico Valdés*: Vicentico Valdés (b. 1921) was a singer with the Sonora Matancera group in the 1950s. He later went to New York and continued his very successful career.

p. 82 *Orlando Vallejo*: Orlando Vallejo was a great singer of boleros, or romantic ballads. Born in 1919, he moved to Miami in the 1960s and continued to record and perform.

p. 82 *Chano Pozo*: Chano Pozo (1915–48) was a percussionist and Afro-Cuban jazz musician who moved to New York in the 1940s, where he was later murdered in a bar. He played and recorded with Dizzy Gillespie.

p. 82 *Pérez Prado*: Pérez Prado refers to Dámaso Pérez Prado (b. 1916), pianist, composer, and bandleader, who combined elements of North American jazz with Cuban melodies.

p. 83 *Hermanos Castro Orchestra*: The Orquesta Hermanos Castro was a well-known high-society band in existence from 1930 to 1960.

p. 83 *I painted a hazy Matanzas*: The poem Carlos recalls is attributed to Antonio Eugenio Hernández Alemán (1856?–1936?), a poet from Mantanzas known as "Seboruco." Abelardo Barroso and Orquesta Sensación included these popular verses in "Tiene sabor," a 1950s hit song. (Enrique del Risco, personal communication.)

p. 84 *Chupa la caña, negra*: Literally, "suck the sugar cane," with obvious sexual connotations.

p. 86 *The attack at the palace*: In March 1957 the leftist group Directorio Revolucionario

(Revolutionary Directorate), led by José Antonio Echeverría and others, simultaneously attacked the Presidential Palace and took over the station of Radio Reloj. The assault failed and Echeverría was killed, as noted above in chapter 3. More detail on this episode will appear in chapter 15.

p. 88 *Oh John, John, go to hell*: In English in the original text.

p. 90 *Radio Rebelde*: A clandestine radio station set up by Fidel Castro and his forces in February 1958.

p. 91 *The 26th of July Anthem*: "El Himno del 26 de julio," battle song of the Cuban Rebel Army. Written by Agustín Díaz Cartaya in the early 1950s and first clandestinely recorded in 1956.

p. 91 *Banda Gigante*: La Banda Gigante, founded in the 1950s, was Benny Moré's own band.

p. 92 *Was fine; very nice; a many splendored thing*: Phrases in English in the original text.

p. 92 *La sitiera*: "La sitiera" is a frequently recorded Cuban bolero.

p. 93 *Pero qué bonito y sabroso*: A mambo composed by Benny Moré.

p. 95 *Pa que tú lo bailes, mi son Maracaibo*: A *son* composed by Benny Moré.

CHAPTER 6

p. 96 *Bacán*: *Bacán* is Cuban slang for good, great, excellent (HPC 51).

p. 97. *Bela Kun; Rosa Luxemburg; Karl Liebknecht*: Bela Kun was a politician who founded the Hungarian Communist Party in 1918. Rosa Luxemburg and Karl Liebknecht were cofounders in 1918 of the Spatacus Party, the precursor of the German Communist Party. They were both murdered in 1919 after the Spatacist uprising.

p. 97 *The smoky slum*: La Cueva del Humo, literally the cave of smoke, Cuban slang for a poor neighborhood, or an otherwise bad place to live (DMC 229).

p. 97 *'68; '95; '30*: The references to 1868 and 1895 are to wars of independence against Spain; 1930 refers to student demonstrations against the dictator Machado.

p. 97 *Batista in '34; Grau in '44*: These names and dates refer to different upheavals and coups in Cuban political history.

p. 98 *Ring boy; flower girl; honeymoon in Mexico*: All in English in the original text.

p. 98 *Diario de la Marina*: The *Diario de la Marina* was a conservative newspaper of the Cuban upper class; it was seized by the Castro government in 1960.

p. 99 *High Sierra; The Big Sleep; The Maltese Falcon; Casablanca*: *High Sierra* was a 1941 thriller starring Humphrey Bogart and Ida Lupino. *The Big Sleep* was a 1946 film noir, starring Bogart and Lauren Bacall. *The Maltese Falcon* was a 1941 film noir starring Bogart and Mary Astor. *Casablanca* was a 1949 drama starring Bogart and Ingrid Bergman.

p. 99 *Casa de Usher*: *The Fall of the House of Usher* was a 1949 British film.

p. 99 *Las Casas; Kazan; Casaus; Kasabubu; Casona; Martínez Casado*: Father Bartolomé de las Casas sailed to America with Columbus in 1493; during the sixteenth century he became famous as an advocate for the human rights of indigenous peoples. Elia Kazan directed such award-winning Hollywood films as *On the Waterfront* (1954). Víctor Casaus

(b. 1944) is a Cuban poet and filmmaker. Joseph Kasabubu was president of the Republic of Congo in 1960 when Patrice Lumumba was arrested and later killed. Alejandro Casona was a well-known twentieth-century Spanish playwright. Ana Margarita Martínez Casado is a Cuban actress and singer now living in the United States.

p. 99 *casatenientes*: This is an archaic term for homeowners and heads of household.

p. 99 *High Noon; Gunfight at the OK Corral*: *High Noon* was a 1952 Western with Gary Cooper and Grace Kelly. *Gunfight at the OK Corral* was a 1957 Western with Burt Lancaster and Kirk Douglas. Its Spanish title is *Duelo de titanes* or "Duel of Titans," as will be seen later in the chapter.

p. 99 *La Manzana de Gómez*: La Manzana de Gómez is a famous block of commercial buildings in Havana.

p. 100 *26th of July Movement; Revolutionary Directorate; PSP; Auténticos*: As already noted, the 26th of July Movement (M-26–7) was founded by Fidel Castro and others. The Revolutionary Directorate was the Directorio Revolucionario, a leftist anti-Batista movement. The PSP was the Partido Socialista Popular, the name the Cuban Communist Party (PCC, founded 1925) adopted in 1944; in 1965 the PSP was reorganized as the PCC. The Auténtico Party (Partido Revolucionario Cubano), founded in 1934 after the fall of Machado the year before, was carried into power by Grau in the 1944 elections.

p. 100 *3:10 to Yuma; The Hanging Tree*: *3:10 to Yuma* was a 1957 Western with Van Heflin and Glenn Ford. *The Hanging Tree* was a 1959 Western with George C. Scott, Gary Cooper, and Karl Malden.

p. 101 *José María Heredia*: José María Heredia (1803–39), great Cuban Romantic poet and patriot, lived in exile in Mexico and the United States. One of his most famous poems, written in the neoclassic style, takes as its subject the sublime inspiration of Niagara Falls.

p. 101 *The Damned Lie*: This is the Spanish title (*La mentira maldita*) for the 1957 dramatic film *Sweet Smell of Success*, with Burt Lancaster and Tony Curtis.

p. 102 *Winchester '73*: *Winchester '73* was a 1950 Western with James Stewart and Shelley Winters.

p. 103 *The Man with the Golden Arm*: *The Man with the Golden Arm* was a 1955 drama directed by Otto Preminger, starring Frank Sinatra as a drug dealer obsessed with jazz and poker; it also starred Kim Novak and Eleanor Parker.

CHAPTER 7

p. 107 *Mikoyan*: Anastas Mikoyan, Soviet deputy premier who arrived in Cuba in February, 1960 with a trade delegation. Several weeks later Cuba and the Soviet Union resumed diplomatic relations, suspended since 1952.

p. 111 *Amor bajo cero*: *Amor bajo cero* (Sub-zero Love) was a 1960 Spanish romantic comedy, set in Barcelona at an international skiing competition.

p. 112 *The Fable of the Shark and the Sardines; The New Class*: *The Fable of the Shark and the Sardines* was written by Juan José Arévalo, Guatemalan writer and politician. *The New Class: An Analysis of the Communist System* was published in 1957 by the Soviet author Milovan Djilas.

p. 114 *Villanueva University*: Villanueva University was a Catholic institution in Havana operated by the Augustinian order, related to other such institutions including Villanova University in the United States.

CHAPTER 8

p. 121 *Gusanos*: Literally "worms," a common term within Cuba for Cubans who left the island after the Revolution.

p. 122 *Lata*: *Lata* means tin or tin can.

p. 126 *Shit; mierda*: *Shit* is in English in the original text. *Mierda* is *shit* in Spanish.

p. 127 *Explosion in the harbor*: The explosion described here happened on Friday, 4 March 1960. At three o'clock in the afternoon the French freighter La Coubre, loaded with munitions for the rebel militia, blew up in Havana harbor. A second blast sometime later killed many of the police, firemen, and troops who had rushed to the scene. After many more explosions, the ship sank. Castro blamed American sabotage; the U.S. government, in turn, blamed the explosion on careless handling of the cargo by Cuban dockworkers.

p. 130 *Patria o muerte*: *Patria o muerte* literally means "Motherland or death." It fast became, and still is, the best-known slogan of the Cuban Revolution's resistance to U.S. power.

p. 130 *Siboneys*: The Siboneys were the aboriginal inhabitants of Cuba from 1000 B.C.E. They were displaced from all areas of the island, except the westernmost extremities, by the Arawak (Taíno) tribe.

p. 131 *A little book*: The book referred to here is Marx's and Engels's *Communist Manifesto*, originally published in London in 1848.

p. 132 *Roa*: Raúl Roa, Cuban foreign minister under Castro in 1960.

p. 133 *Cuban Telefón Compani*: The Cuban Telephone Company, an affiliate of ITT, was nationalized in March 1959. In January 1960, land owned by U.S. companies, including United Fruit, was expropriated. Eisenhower responded by shutting off Cuba's sugar quota; it was cancelled completely in July 1960, following Cuba's nationalization of U.S. oil refineries and U.S. business and commercial properties.

p. 133 *Done gone*: *Se ñamaba*, a Cuban expression meaning "he (she, it) died." The actual expression is *se llamaba*, literally, "he was named"; *se ñamaba* imitates the black speech of the negrito, a character on the radio show of the actor Alberto Garrido (DMC 404).

CHAPTER 9

p. 137 *Bob-bob-bobbin' along*: *En el tíbiri tábara*, a phrase originating with a popular song, expressing that one is getting along, in response to the question, "How are you?" (DMC 653).

p. 138 *Revolución*: The official newspaper of the 26th of July Movement, founded in May 1957.

p. 139 *Creampuffs*: *Casquitos de dulce guayaba*, a conserve made of guayaba peels. Under Batista, untrained new recruits were called *casquitos* because Castro's guerrilla movement ate them up, i.e., beat them (DMC 159).

p. 142 *Cojonudo*: *Cojonudo* is a vulgar expression for great, amazing, or gutsy, based on the word *cojones* (balls). Carlos turns his condition of *cojo* (lame) into an asset by adding the word *nudo* (knot).

p. 144 ***Turquino Peak***: Turquino Peak (Pico Turquino), in the Sierra Maestra mountains, is the highest point in Cuba.

p. 144 ***Ten Days that Shook the World***: *Ten Days that Shook the World* is the title of American journalist John Reed's firsthand account of the Russian Revolution.

p. 146 ***Cunagua Sugar Mill***: The Cunagua Sugar Mill was controlled by Chase Bank prior to 1960.

p. 148 ***Hydrochloric acid***: Carlos tells Jorge to wash his mouth out with *salfumán*, a commercial acid used in many cases of suicide in Cuba (DMC 541).

p. 149 ***Negrito***: The negrito (little black) is a traditional character in Cuban comic theater along with the Gallego, explained below.

p. 153 ***Gallego***: *Gallego*—literally, a Spaniard from the region of Galicia, in the northwest corner of the country—is the standard Cuban term for all Spaniards, regardless of origin. In the theater, the Gallego is the target of the negrito's mocking jokes (HPC 188).

p. 153 ***Lumumba and Gallego, shadows which only I see***: The reference here is to Nicolás Guillén's poem "Balada de los dos abuelos" (Ballad of the Two Grandfathers) whose first line is *Sombras que sólo yo veo*. The poem tells of two grandfathers, one black, the other white.

CHAPTER 10

p. 163 ***He hasn't got the goods . . . he was a no-good***: The pun in the Spanish text is between the slang expressions *gao* (pad, digs) and *singao* (i.e., *singado*, damned, fucked, from the verb *singar*, to fuck). In common Cuban Spanish the *d* is aspirated, forming the syllables *sin* (without) and *gao* (a home) (DMC 320, 626).

p. 165 ***The Bayamo Anthem***: The Bayamo Anthem, now known as the National Anthem, was composed in August 1867 by Pedro Figueredo. It was first sung on 20 October 1868 (now celebrated as Cuban Culture Day) when the Independence Army forces entered the city of Bayamo. The anthem, a stirring march, was modeled on the French Marseillaise.

p. 169 ***FAL***: Fusil Automatique Leger, or Light Automatic Rifle, manufactured in France during World War II. After the war it was redeveloped and became a classic battle rifle.

p. 172 ***Panfilov and the Volokolamsk Highway***: General Ivan Panfilov led a famous division of twenty-eight Soviet soldiers, who in November 1941 held back advancing German tank troops on the outskirts of Moscow along the Volokolamsk Highway. All twenty-eight were killed and are recognized as important war heroes, since ultimately the German invasion was stopped.

p. 174 ***I'm yours because you taught me how to love***: Lyrics from the bolero "Tuya soy": *Tuya soy porque tú me enseñaste a querer.*

CHAPTER 11

p. 179 ***Chan Li Po***: "Chan Li Po" was the title, as well as the name of the protagonist, of a popular Cuban radio series written by Félix B. Caignet which began to air in the 1930s. The character was a Chinese detective noted for his great patience (DMC 169).

p. 179 *Camilo*: Camilo Cienfuegos (1932–59), who along with Fidel Castro and Ernesto "Che" Guevara commanded the Rebel Army during the struggle leading up to the Cuban Revolution.

p. 180 *The Spanish deck*: The Spanish deck of cards (*naipes* or *barajas*) consists of four suits: *oros* (gold coins), *bastones* (batons), *copas* (cups), and *espadas* (swords). Each suit has both picture cards and numeral cards. The Spanish deck is commonly used in Latin America as well as Spain.

p. 181 *Venceremos*: Literally, "we shall win" or "we shall overcome." "Venceremos" became the slogan corresponding to "Patria o muerte" in a call-and-response pattern; thus Gisela's reply to Carlos.

p. 182 *Get behind me, virus!*: Díaz's phrase is *Vade retro, catarrás*, a play on the Latin biblical phrase "Vade retro, Satana" (Mark 8:33, "Get behind me, Satan!"). *Satanás* is Satan, *catarro* is cold, thus the combination resulting in *catarrás*.

p. 183 *Pepechá*: A Pepechá is a Soviet-made submachine gun.

p. 183 *Journey back to the source*: In Spanish, *viaje a la semilla*, the title of a well-known story written in 1944 by the Cuban Alejo Carpentier.

p. 184 *Momish-Uli*: Momish-Uli or Momishuli, a Kazakhstani name, was presumably a figure in the 1941 battle led by General Panfilov, as noted in chapter 10.

p. 184 *Put a bullet in the punch*: *Tener una bala en el directo* is an expression that means one is ready for anything (DMC 253–4), a directo being a straight punch.

p. 188 *They broke off*: The United States officially broke off relations with Cuba in January 1961. The daily newspaper *Revolución*, as noted in chapter 9, was the organ of the 26th of July Movement until 1965, when it was discontinued and the newspaper *Granma* was established.

CHAPTER 12

There are no notes for Chapter 12.

CHAPTER 13

p. 195 *The Beca*: The "Beca," or university residence, is so named because the students living there are *becados* or *becarios*, that is, with scholarships or *becas*.

p. 195 *The war*: The Bay of Pigs invasion (known in Cuba as the Battle of Playa Girón) began on 17 April 1961. Within forty-eight hours the invaders had been defeated by defending Cuban forces.

p. 195 *The Dude*: Carlos's nickname, *el Ruta*, is slang for a flashily dressed, usually lower-class, male, akin to "dude" or perhaps "zoot-suiter" among Chicanos.

p. 196 *Cochero*: The constellation known in English as the Charioteer is called Cochero in Spanish, meaning both charioteer and coachman, Osmundo's nickname.

p. 196 *Chullima*: Chullima, or Ch'llima, was a legendary flying horse in Korean myth, said to have galloped a great distance (i.e., with great speed) in a day. In 1958 North Korea initiated the Ch'llima Work Team Movement, an economic production campaign modeled on the Chinese Great Leap Forward.

p. 196 *Yuri Gargarin*: Yuri Gargarin (1934–68) was a Soviet cosmonaut who, in 1961, became the first human to fly in space.

p. 196 *El Encanto*: El Encanto was Havana's largest department store. It was burned down in an act of sabotage just before the Bay of Pigs invasion, and never rebuilt.

p. 199 *Escambray*: Escambray refers to the Sierra del Escambray, one of Cuba's main mountain ranges, where anti-Castro guerrilla groups were concentrated after the Revolution. A military campaign known as the Escambray Clean-up defeated these groups in 1960–61.

p. 199 *Cuñada*: *Cuñada* means sister-in-law. It is common in Spanish for the girlfriend or boyfriend (*novia* or *novio*, terms also signifying bride and groom) of a family member to be addressed in this manner even before marriage.

p. 200 *Seafront promenade*: This is the Malecón, the boulevard running along the Havana seafront.

p. 202 *Conrado Benítez*: Conrado Benítez was among the first volunteer teachers in Cuba's huge Literacy Campaign, which began in 1960. He was murdered in January 1961 in Escambray, reportedly by counterrevolutionary forces. Brigades of literacy teachers thereafter were named for him.

p. 202 *Pura*: *Pura* is chuchero slang (explained in the notes to chapter 5) for mother. What the Ghost says is: *Ruta, tu pura está daun* (i.e., down), also using English as slang. *Pura*, literally, is the feminine form of the adjective *pure*.

CHAPTER 14

p. 208 *Pintos*: *Pintos* refers to the invading guerrillas. One can assume they are dressed in some kind of mottled camouflage.

p. 210 *No matter how far the buzzard flies, the kingbird will always bite it*: *Por mucho que el aura vuele, siempre el pitirre la pica*, a saying indicating that those who are ahead will never get far, if those behind run better (DMC 58).

CHAPTER 15

p. 214 *José Antonio's testament*: José Antonio Echeverría, president of the Cuban Federation of University Students (FEU) in the 1950s, as already noted, was also one of the leaders of the Revolutionary Directorate, an anti-Batista political movement. On 13 March 1957, Echeverría was killed during an attempted overthrow of Batista by the RD. Echeverría was with a group that occupied the studios of Radio Reloj and read a statement declaring that Batista's regime was ended. Afterwards he was killed trading gunfire with the police. Although the Revolutionary Directorate and the 26th of July Movement were not allies in the struggle, since the revolution the events of 13 March have been commemorated each year with a speech by Fidel Castro, as will be seen later in this chapter.

p. 214 *Top secret*: In English in the original text.

p. 217 *La Rampa; La Zorra y El Cuervo Jazz Club*: In Havana, "La Rampa" is the name given to the portion of Calle 23 from its intersection with L down to the seafront promenade (Malecón). La Rampa is known for its clubs, restaurants, and nightlife. The La

Zorra y El Cuervo Jazz Club, still a prominent musical venue today, is located on La Rampa.

p. 218 *Pequeño Larousse*: The *Pequeño Larousse* dictionary contains a section devoted to the arts, letters, and sciences with capsule biographies of famous figures, works, etc. Thus, to have a cultural knowledge based on the *Pequeño Larousse* is the opposite of being well-read; it signifies someone who is only superficially learned, and probably not interested in more than that.

p. 220 *Rationing; the CDR*: Food rationing was imposed in Cuba in March 1962. The "CDR" refers to the local Comité de Defensa de la Revolución (Committee for the Defense of the Revolution), a system set up in September 1960 by Fidel Castro. Each block has a CDR that oversees local community and political activity. The CDRs have been both lauded as a uniquely Cuban system of grassroots empowerment, and bitterly criticized as a method of government control over all aspects of daily life.

p. 222 *You ain't nothing but a hound dog*: In English in the original text.

p. 223 *On Contradiction*: *On Contradiction* (1937), as well as *On Practice* (1937) mentioned below, are famous texts of Mao Zedong.

p. 224 *There's a lot of self-satisfaction here*: The note reads in Spanish, *Aquí tienen mucha autosuficiencia, pero no tienen autocrítica ni automóvil*, a playful repetition impossible to recreate entirely in English.

p. 228 *Cowboy*: In English in the original text.

p. 228 *The Polinesio*: El Polinesio is an elegant Chinese restaurant located in the Havana Libre Hotel. Thus the cries of the students and the Ghost are, respectively, *Al Policlínico!* and *Al Polinesio!*

p. 229 *Manco del espanto*: Miguel de Cervantes was known as the *manco de Lepanto*, a reference to his crippled arm, a war wound received in the Battle of Lepanto (1571). The Ghost plays with this phrase, rhyming it into *manco del espanto, espanto* meaning fright.

p. 230 *Xinhua; Yenan forums*: Xinhua is the Chinese government news agency. The Yenan forums on literature and art in the Chinese revolution took place in 1942; Mao Zedong's talks there were later published as a volume.

p. 231 *Lam, Portocarrero, Antonia Eiriz*: Wilfredo Lam, René Portocarrero, and Antonia Eiriz are all world-renowned twentieth-century Cuban painters.

p. 231 *Al Mamarte*: *Alma Mater*, as explained in the text, is the official publication of the FEU. Francisco turns the title first into *Al Mamarte* (literally, "when sucking on you") then *Alma Marte* (*Marte* being Spanish for Mars).

p. 235 *Captain Araña*: The expression "to make like Captain Araña" means to induce others to perform a difficult task while one personally does not get involved. The phrase is of unknown origin (http://www.arcom.net/belca/index.htm).

p. 237 *Pablo de la Torriente Brau*: Pablo de la Torriente Brau (1901–36), born in Puerto Rico but educated in Cuba, was a journalist, writer, and political activist who died fighting for the Republic in the Spanish Civil War. *Aventuras del soldado desconocido cubano*, his only novel, was left unfinished at his death and was first published posthumously in 1940. Many of his writings were reedited in Havana by Ediciones Nuevo Mundo in 1962, the year in which the action of this chapter takes place (http://www.cubaliteraria.com).

p. 238 *13 March commemoration*: As noted above, the commemoration of the death of José Antonio Echeverría and the failed assault on the Presidential Palace is observed each 13 March with a speech by Fidel Castro, often on the wide staircase (the escalinata) leading up the main entrance to the university. The text of Castro's speech of 13 March 1962 has not been transcribed in any archives. However, the text of the speech one year later contains references to the events described here by Díaz: Castro's criticism of the suppression of Echeverría's references to God in his testament (http://lanic.utexas.edu/la/cb/cuba/castro/1963/19630313).

p. 241 *That's the only cure*: The Archimandrite's phrase is *No hay otro remedio*, which is also a common expression of fatalism meaning "there's no other choice" or "there's nothing else to be done about it."

CHAPTER 16

p. 242 *O Amado Nervo*: Amado Nervo (1870–1919) was a Mexican modernist poet. *Amado nervo* literally means "beloved nerve" in both Spanish and Portuguese. The jokes made here add on the articles *o* and *os* to make a fractured Portuguese sound authentic.

p. 242 *A oscuras*: The joke here puns between the Spanish *a oscuras* (in the dark) and the Portuguese-sounding *a os curas* (with priests).

p. 243 *Don Rafael del Junco*: Don Rafael del Junco was a character in a popular Cuban radio drama of the 1940s and 1950s, "El derecho de nacer" (literally, The Right to Be Born), written by Félix B. Caignet, and later adapted for television soap operas throughout Latin America. Don Rafael was the family patriarch, paralyzed and confined to a wheelchair, who became mute and thus could never divulge the many secrets he knew. *Nasser* and *nacer* are pronounced identically in Spanish.

p. 243 *Elena Burke*: Elena Burke (1928–2002), known as la Señora Sentimiento (Lady Feeling), was a prominent Cuban vocalist who first became famous in the 1940s when she was identified with the *filin* (or "el feeling") movement in Cuban song. This group, influenced by North Americans such as Ella Fitzgerald, made their contemporary interpretations of boleros and other traditional ballads expressive and emotional. "La noche de anoche" is one of the best-known of all boleros.

p. 245 *The Judge's Bolero*: The Judge's Bolero and the other boleros made up in jest here give punning titles to verses from actual boleros, for instance "you are the guilty one" (*usted es la culpable*) from "Usted," and "silence" ("Silencio"), the title of another bolero. Some create plays on words impossible to translate exactly; for example, what I have translated as the Fairy's Bolero, a line from the bolero "Amapola" which reads *no seas tan ingrata y ámame*, in the novel turns into *no seas tan ingrata, Yaaamaaméeee*, where *y ámame* means "and love me" while *ya mamé* means "I already sucked."

p. 246 *Sex is sense*: There is a word play here between *el sexo* (sex) and *el seso* (brain) which are pronounced identically in Spain and some parts of Latin America.

p. 246 *Raúl Chou Moreno*: The Archimandrite puns with the sounds of the words *show* (*chou* in Cuban Spanish), the name of Raúl Shaw Moreno, a famous Bolivian bolero singer and member of the well-known Trio los Panchos, and *changüí*, a style of Cuban music that preceded the *son*.

p. 246 *Félix Chappottín; Miguelito Cuní; the Copa Room*: Félix Chappottín (1909–83) was a renowned trumpeter and leader of the *son* group Conjunto Chappottín y sus Estrellas (Chappottín and his stars), founded in 1950. Miguelito Cuní was a famous vocalist who sang with this group as well as with others. Conjunto Chappottín still exists and records, now featuring Félix Chappottín's grandson. The Copa Room is a prestigious cabaret in the Hotel Habana Riviera.

p. 246 *A lady foursida*: There is a nonsense tongue-twister here: *tenían una cuatratrepa con cuatro cuatratrepitos y que quien se atreviera a tocar un cuatratrepo se cuatratreparía todo.*

p. 247 *To tell Catalina to buy him a grater*: The song being sung here is *Dile a Catalina que te compre un guayo / que la yuca se me está secando* (Tell Catalina to buy you a grater / cause my yucca is getting dry) (DMC 343). The *guayo* is also a percussion instrument.

p. 247 *Rayando el guayo*: *Rayando el guayo* (scraping the grater) is an expression for dancing.

p. 248 *Take me away from the strong stuff*: The Archimandrite's phrase in Spanish is *Esa que es fuerte fuerte sepárala*, a slogan from a Cuban cigarette company advertisement (DMC 309), used to indicate "I'll stick with what I've got."

p. 248 *Pachalsta*: *Pachalsta* means "please" in Russian.

p. 248 *A tiger in the bush*: Carlos says *El palo del tigre*, *palo* being slang for the sex act, and *echar un palo de tigre* indicating the accomplishment of something very difficult (DMC 306).

p. 250 *The Yanquis decreed a blockade*: This refers to the Cuban Missile Crisis of 16–28 October 1962, known in Cuba as "the October Crisis."

p. 250 *Dick Fitzwell*: Carlos calls himself "Tomasín Galindo," an invented name that plays on the verb *singar*, to fuck (as noted in chapter 10). Thus the syllables separate into: Toma/singa/lindo, or "Tom fucks great."

p. 250. *You're in the raw . . . But ready to cook*: *Estar en cueros y con las manos en los bolsillos* (To be naked and with your hands in your pockets) is an expression indicating financial hardship. Additionally, a party given *en cueros y con las manos en los bolsillos* indicates a gathering with no sexual limitations on the participants (DMC 427).

CHAPTER 17

p. 252 *Only ashes will you find*: *Sólo cenizas hallarás*, a line from the famous bolero "Cenizas" by Wello Rivas. The second line, which appears later in this chapter, is *de todo lo que fue* (of all that was).

p. 253 *It was the night I died, the death of all my hopes*: *Fue la noche de mi muerte, murieron mis esperanzas*, from the bolero "Boda gris" by Plácido Acevedo.

p. 256 *Highball, swinging pool, basketballing, feel hockey, and now he, feeling fucked on the grass*: The puns here on names of sports are *el jaibol, la nadación, el vaciloncesto y el joder sobre el césped*, the last one referring to field hockey (*el hockey sobre el césped*), but meaning "screwing around on the grass." The pun continues with Carlos being *jodido sobre el césped*, literally "fucked on the grass."

p. 257 *The wedding couple and their wetnesses*: The Archimandrite puns on the words *testigos* (witnesses) and *testículos* (testicles).

p. 257 *Soy comunista toda la vida / bella ciao*: "Bella Ciao" is a famous World War II song of the Italian partisans. These lyrics come from the Spanish Communist version.

p. 257 *Young Communists Union*: The *Unión de Jóvenes Comunistas* (UJC) was established in 1962.

p. 259 *Carlos carried on like a comrade carajo*: *Carajo* is an expletive (literally a vulgar term for the penis) that can be rendered into English in a number of ways depending on context, such as "fuck," "hell," or "goddamn," as it has been all along in this translation. What Carlos says to himself, repeating the first syllable *ca* is *Carlos carajo caíste camarada*, or "Carlos goddammit you fell a comrade."

p. 259 *All the world's glory fits in a kernel of corn*: This is a well-known quotation from the great Cuban writer and patriot José Martí (1853–95): *Toda la gloria del mundo cabe en un grano de maíz.*

CHAPTER 18

p. 260 *Drugstore*: Throughout this chapter, English is used in the original text. I have not changed any of the English words and have kept the same spelling in almost all cases, as well as the original italics. In some parts of the dialogue I have left Spanish words, which are not italicized as they normally would be, such as boticas. This allows the translation to make sense, and also gives the English reader a sense of what the Spanish reader experiences reading the bilingual text.

p. 264 *Screwaround*: *Screwaround* is an approximation of the Cuban term *jodedor*. *Joder* literally means "to fuck," but in Cuba the verb refers as much to joking around and enjoying oneself as to sex, as was noted in chapter 17. A jodedor is a man whose approach to life combines both womanizing and a carefree, irreverent, carnivalesque kind of humor. *Joder* will appear again later in this chapter, and *jodedor* in chapter 19.

p. 264 *They'd done a number on him*: The Cuban expression is "they'd done a number eight on him" (*un número ocho*), punning on the eight-dollar charge.

p. 265 *Sierra de Falcón, Jujuy Forest, Cundinamarca Mountains*: These are located in Venezuela, Argentina, and Colombia, respectively.

p. 267 *Elephants balancing on a spider's web*: This refers to a well-known children's song that teaches how to count. When the first elephant sees that the spider's web will support his weight, a second elephant joins him, and so on.

p. 267 *Mister Montalvo Montaner*: Carlos's dialogue with Mister Montalvo Montaner (as he is called in the original text) is all in Spanish, except for the English words in italics which have been preserved.

p. 268 *Sin gas*: *Sin gas*—i.e., still, not sparkling water—would typically be pronounced *sin ga* by Cubans, who often drop the final *s* from words. Thus it would sound like *singa*, from the verb *singar*, which as noted in chapter 10 means "to fuck."

p. 269 *En regla*: *En regla* literally means "by the rules" or "in good order." Regla is an industrial suburb of Havana.

p. 270 *Mister Mierda*: *Mierda*, as noted in chapter 8, means "shit."

p. 271 *What's the buzz*: The dialogue between Carlos and Felipe is written in *chuchero* slang, approximated here by 1950s hipster language.

p. 272 *Soltadme . . . no os entiendo*: The use of *vosotros*, the second-person plural, familiar form of address, immediately identifies the fellow as a Spaniard (thus called "Gallego" by the Cubans), since this verb form is not used in Latin American Spanish. The entire dialogue from here to the end of the chapter plays with the differing vocabulary of Spain and Cuba, as the Spaniard uses many typical expressions from his country. In places I have given the Spaniard's speech some Britishisms, to indicate that his words are not ones that Cubans would use and that would sound strange to their ears.

p. 273 *I'm stone-broke*: The Spaniard's phrase for having no money is *no tengo ni una perra gorda*, where a "perra gorda" (literally, a fat female dog) means a ten-cent coin. Carlos then tells him he is crazy, talking about dogs.

p. 273 *Lady all salad salami*: The "Arabic" phrase is *la jeva jama la jama*, where *jeva* means woman and *jama* means food or to eat (both Cuban slang expressions); Carlos tells Felipe to say "a woman eating." Since the Spanish *j* is pronounced like an English "*h*," the phrase creates a sound imitating Arabic.

p. 274 *Kuku inatushi*: The "Japanese" phrase is *sekome sukaka*, sounding like *se come su caca*, literally "he eats his poop"; Felipe tells Carlos to say *comemierda*, Cuban slang for a coward or shithead.

p. 274 *Vamos*: *Vamos*, meaning "let's go" (and the root of the expression "vamoose" in English) is commonly used in Spain as an interjection roughly equivalent to "I mean" or "anyway" or "you see." Here the Cubans joke with the literal meaning of the word to tease the Spaniard.

p. 274 *We screw around with anyone*: The dialogue plays with the Spaniard's use of joder as an expletive meaning "fuck," while for the Cubans it means having fun or joking around.

p. 275 *Up the ass/arse*: Carlos says the situation is *de pinga*, where *pinga* is Cuban slang for penis; *de pinga* can mean something is very good or very bad. Paco corrects him using the term *pija*, the equivalent term in Spain.

p. 276 *Galifa*: *Galifa* is a Cuban expression for a person from Spain.

CHAPTER 19

p. 290 *Hasten to battle, men of Bayamo*: This is the first line of the Cuban National Anthem, or Bayamo Anthem: *Al combate corred bayameses*.

p. 290 *Martí died in two rivers*: José Martí died in a battle against the Spanish royalist army at Dos Ríos (two rivers) on 19 May 1895.

p. 291 *There's no one holding you up*: Gisela's phrase is *Nadie te está aguantando*, where the verb *aguantar* means variously to physically support, to bear or endure, and to hold back.

p. 298 *The Wakamba*: The Wakamba, named for a Kenyan ethnic group, is a cafe in Havana's Vedado district. It opened in 1956 and became the first restaurant in Cuba to offer a self-service menu. Today the Wakamba caters to tourists paying in dollars.

p. 298 *Screwarounds*: As noted in chapter 18, *jodedores* in Cuban Spanish.

p. 298 *Mongo; Johnny Fucker*: *Mongo*, short for mongoloid, is Cuban slang for idiot. Johnny Fucker is in English in the original text.

p. 299 *En la onda*: Slang term, literally "in the wave," meaning to be where it's at or with it, with good vibes.

p. 299 *Equelecuá, quindi*: *Equelecuá* is an expression meaning "very well then." *Quindi* means "therefore" in Italian.

p. 299 *Kin*: *Kin* is the Cuban pronunciation of *king*, as in "Kin Kón."

p. 300 *They say that Che was killed*: Ernesto "Che" Guevara was captured in Bolivia on 8 October 1967 and executed the following day.

p. 300 *Granma yacht*: The *Granma* was the motor yacht in which Castro, Che, and others traveled from Mexico to Cuba in 1956 to start the insurrection which eventually led to revolution.

p. 300 *The foco theory*: The "foco" theory (*teoría del foco*) of armed revolution held that a small group of guerrillas (the "foco" or center) could begin an insurrection in rural areas by sparking off rebellion among the peasantry, without first building a mass movement among urban workers.

p. 301 *Ñancahuazú, Vado del Yeso, Quebrada del Yuro*: These are locations in the Bolivian mountains where conflicts occurred between Che Guevara's guerrilla forces and the U.S.-backed Bolivian army. Che was captured at the last of these sites.

p. 302 *The Memorial*: The memorial service for Che Guevara (*La Velada Solemne*) took place on the evening of 18 October 1967 in Havana's Plaza de la Revolución. Hundreds of thousands of people attended. Fidel Castro read a famous eulogy, "Hasta la victoria siempre" (Ever onward until victory), and the poet Nicolás Guillén read a poem composed several days earlier, "Che Comandante." The references here are to several lines from the poem: *un caballo de fuego / sostiene tu escultura guerrillera / entre el viento y las nubes de la Sierra* and *Espéranos. Partiremos contigo.* As described here, for the first time ever no applause followed Castro's speech.

p. 303 *Pocho Fornet*: Ambrosio "Pocho" Fornet (b. 1932) has been a prominent figure in the world of Cuban literature and cinema since 1960. He has edited several anthologies of Cuban literature and written screenplays, notably that of the 1980 *Portrait of Teresa*. In 1967, the time of this chapter, he was codirector (along with the writer Edmundo Desnoes) of the publishing house Arte y Literatura.

p. 303 *Guerrilla Fighter's Anthem*: The "Himno del Guerrillero" or "Marcha del Guer-rillero" was played at Che Guevara's 1967 memorial, and again in 1997 when his remains were sent to Cuba and interred there.

CHAPTER 20

p. 306 *Let the wind cut it down, let Lola cut it down with her moving around*: This is part of a refrain from a popular song originating during the post–World War I Cuban sugar boom: *Yo no tumbo caña / que la tumbe el viento / que la tumbe Lola / con su movimiento.*

p. 307 *Zdrávstvuite, tovarichi!*: This means "Hello, comrades!" in Russian.

p. 309 PPQK: PPQK (phonetically spelled pe/pe/cu/ca) is a type of sugarcane plant, introduced into Cuba in the 1940s.

p. 310 *Arroba*: An arroba is a Cuban weight of about twenty-five pounds.

p. 313 *Suárez Gayol*: Jesús Suárez Gayol, known as "El Rubio," was an anti-Batista student leader who later became a captain in the Revolutionary Armed Forces and vice minister of the Cuban sugar industry. He joined Che Guevara's guerrilla army in Bolivia and died there on 10 April 1967.

p. 315 *15 April*: U.S. bombing of Cuban airfields began on 15 April 1961, leading up to the invasion at Playa Girón two days later.

p. 316 *Jiminy Cricket*: Jiminy Cricket, in his Spanish version, is called "Pepe Grillo."

CHAPTER 21

p. 320 *Unha noite na eira do trigo*: "Unha noite na eira do trigo" (One night in the threshing barn) is a well-known Galician ballad written by Manuel Curros Enríquez, a Galician poet and journalist who emigrated to Cuba at the end of the nineteenth century and died in Havana.

p. 321 *Tiples, güiros, and bandurrías*: These are Cuban folk instruments. The *tiple* is a stringed instrument strummed like a guitar; the *güiro*, as already noted, is a percussion instrument made from a dried, hollow gourd with notches carved into it, played by rubbing a stick up and down the notches; the *bandurría* is akin to a lute.

p. 321 *Bagpipes*: Bagpipes (*la gaita gallega*) accompany traditional music in Galicia, a legacy of the region's Celtic heritage.

p. 321 *Guacanayara, ay palmarito*: "Guacanayara, ay palmarito" is a famous example of the *punto guajiro*, improvised ten-line songs (*décimas*) sung by Cuban country singers.

p. 321 *Konsomol; Kalinka, Kalinka, Kalinka moya*: The Konsomol was the name of the Communist Soviet Youth League. "Kalinka, Kalinka, Kalinka moya" is a well-known Russian folk song.

p. 321 *Los diez millones*: *Los diez milliones* refers to the 1970 Cuban sugar harvest, la zafra de los diez millones. Fidel Castro set a goal of a record ten-million-ton harvest for that year. As will be seen in the course of this chapter, the effort required the compulsory participation of Cubans from all walks of life in the cane cutting. Nonetheless the goal was not reached, causing serious economic difficulties.

p. 329 *Barrel-organ*: The barrel-organ referred to here is the *órgano manzanillero* or *órgano oriental*, used since the late nineteenth century as part of traditional dance bands in the eastern provinces of Cuba.

p. 329 *There are four roads*: "Cuatro caminos" (Four Roads) and "La cama de piedra" (Bed of Stone) are well-known Mexican mariachi songs, written respectively by José Alfredo Jiménez and Cuco Sánchez.

p. 331 *Audacity, audacity, and more audacity*: "Audacity, audacity, and more audacity" was a phrase originally stated by Georges-Jacques Danton (*De l'audace, et encore de l'audace, et toujours l'audace!*) and picked up by Lenin through Marx.

p. 331 *The thirty-nine steps*: *The 39 Steps* (1935), a spy suspense-thriller, is one of Alfred Hitchcock's early masterpieces.

p. 333 *Bolondrón and Alacranes; Unión de Reyes*: Bolondrón and Alacranes are towns in Matanzas province. Their names mean, respectively, "big stone" and "scorpions." Unión de Reyes is also located in Matanzas.

p. 338 *The Ten Million Go Forward*: *Los Diez Millones Van*, the omnipresent slogan of the 1970 zafra.

p. 340 *The Trocha*: The Trocha was a system of fortifications built by the Spanish from north to south in Camagüey. It was the scene of many important battles in the Ten Years' War for national liberation.

p. 349 *The Wandering Screwed*: The Spanish here is *Jodío Errante*, where there is a pun made between *jodío*, a peasant's pronunciation of *jodido* (fucked or screwed), and *judío* (Jew).

p. 355 *Fidel said they would not make the Ten Million Tons*: Fidel Castro made a speech on 19 May 1970, welcoming back the kidnapped fishermen, and saying publicly for the first time that the ten-million-ton goal for the sugar harvest would not be met. In the end 8.5 million tons were produced, a record harvest.

CONCLUSION

p. 359 *Having a child and planting a tree*: A Spanish refrain holds that every man should have a child (*un hijo*, also meaning a son), plant a tree, and write a book.

p. 359 *Red Guard*: A reference to the Red Guards, radical young people who between 1966 and 1968 created social and economic turmoil through censorship and arrests during the Chinese Cultural Revolution.

p. 360 *UJC*: As noted in chapter 17, the Unión de Jóvenes Comunistas or Young Communists Union.

p. 363 *The CTC and the CDRs*: The CTC is the Confederation of Cuban Workers (Confederación de Trabajadores Cubanos); the CDRs, as noted in chapter 15, are the local Committees for the Defense of the Revolution.

p. 364 *Persecuting those who seemed inverted*: A reference to the persecution of homosexuals in revolutionary Cuba for "antisocial behavior," particularly carried out in the 1960s and 1970s.

AFTERWORD

1: Friedrich Schleiermacher, "From 'On the Different Methods of Translating'", trans. Waltraud Bartscht. In *Theories of Translation: An Anthology of Essays from Dryden to Derrida,* ed. Rainer Schulte and John Biguenet (Chicago: Univ. of Chicago Press, 1992) 42.

2: Such as in Jorge Mañach's well-known 1928 work *Indagación del choteo*.

3: Suzanne Jill Levine, "Translation as (Sub)version: On Translating *Infante's Inferno*." In *Rethinking Translation: Discourse, Subjectivity, Ideology*, ed. Lawrence Venuti (London: Routledge, 1992) 75–85.

4: Sandor Ferenczi, "On Obscene Words." In his *Sex in Psychoanalysis*, trans. Ernest Jones (New York: Basic Books, 1950) 132–153.

GLOSSARY OF SPANISH WORDS

Entries are ordered alphabetically. The interested reader will find more detailed descriptions of these words in the endnotes.

Abairimo Goodbye or so long.
Arroba Weight of about twenty-five pounds.
Asere Friend or buddy in Cuban Spanish.

Bacán Cuban slang for good, great, excellent.
Bandurría Cuban folk instrument akin to a lute.
Bembé African and Afro-Cuban religious ceremony, celebrated with music, drumming, and dancing.

Carajo Expletive (literally a vulgar term for the penis) that can be rendered into English in a number of ways depending on context, such as "fuck," "hell," or "goddamn."
Casatenientes Archaic term for homeowners and heads of household.
CDRs Committees for the Defense of the Revolution, local block organizations charged with monitoring counterrevolutionary activity.
Ceiba Silk-cotton tree, one of the trees venerated in Afro-Cuban Santería or syncretic saint worship.
Chilindrón A whole goat seasoned and roasted.
Chou *Show* phonetically spelled in Cuban Spanish.
Chuchero Cuban figure of the 1950s somewhat like the Mexican *pachuco*, i.e., a flashily dressed man associated with delinquent or morally questionable behavior.
Cojonudo Vulgar expression for great, amazing, or gutsy, based on the word *cojones* (balls).
Compañero/a Person with whom one shares a close relationship that may be political (akin to *comrade*) or more personal and intimate in nature.
Coño Literally "cunt"; expletive used frequently in Cuban Spanish that generally has no

overt sexual connotation, usually to express surprise, admiration, annoyance, or another strong emotion.

CTC The Confederation of Cuban Workers (Confederación de Trabajadores Cubanos).

Cuñada Sister-in-law; commonly used to address the girlfriend or boyfriend of a family member even before marriage.

Daño A curse or supernatural power that can overtake one's soul.

En la onda Literally "in the wave;" slang meaning to be where it's at or with it.

Equelecúa Expression meaning "very well then."

Fiñes Children.

Gallego A Spaniard from the region of Galicia, in the northwest corner of Spain; standard Cuban term for all Spaniards regardless of origin.

Guaguancó Improvised Afro-Cuban musical composition, where the rhythm is made with whatever is at hand.

Guajiro A Cuban peasant.

Güiro Percussion instrument made from a dried gourd with ridges carved into it that is scraped with a stick.

Gusanos Literally "worms"; common term within Cuba for Cubans who left the island after the Revolution.

Lata Tin or tin can.

Mambí Cuban rebel fighters in the nineteenth-century wars against Spain.

Mierda Shit.

Montuno A component of various types of Cuban musical compositions.

Patria o muerte "Motherland or death,"the best-known slogan of the Cuban Revolution's resistance to U.S. power.

Pura Chuchero slang term for mother.

Quindi *Therefore* in Italian.

Quinto Type of conga drum.

Rueda Type of salsa dancing, done with at least two couples and usually many more, where the couples form a wheel and the movements are done as a group.

Santeros Performers or ritual priests in the religious practice of Afro-Cuban Santería or syncretic saint-worship.

Son Cuban musical composition of African origin.

Tiple Cuban folk instrument, stringed and strummed like a guitar.

Toque *Toque de santos*, another term for the *bembé*, i.e., a public ritual drumming ceremony.

UJC The Unión de Jóvenes Comunistas or Young Communists Union.

Vacunao Pelvic thrusting movement made in the rumba by the male to indicate his conquest of the female.

Vamos "Let's go"; commonly used in Spain as an interjection roughly equivalent to "I mean" or "anyway" or "you see."

Venceremos "We shall win" or "we shall overcome"; slogan corresponding to "Patria o muerte" in a call-and-response pattern.

Zafra The sugarcane harvest.

BIBLIOGRAPHY/FILMOGRAPHY

Title translations in brackets indicate unpublished work (translations by Kathleen Ross).

Books by Jesús Díaz (alphabetically by title)

Los años duros [The hard years]. La Habana: Casa de las Américas, 1966.

Canto de amor y de guerra [Song of love and war]. La Habana: Letras Cubanas, 1979.

Las cuatro fugas de Manuel [Manuel's four escapes]. Madrid: Espasa, 2002.

De la patria y el exilio [On exile and the homeland]. La Habana : Unión de Escritores y Artistas de Cuba, 1979.

Dime algo sobre Cuba [Tell me something about Cuba]. Madrid: Espasa, 1998.

Las iniciales de la tierra. Madrid: Ediciones Alfaguara, 1987.

Lejanía = Parting of the ways. New York: Center for Cuban Studies, 1992.

Las palabras perdidas [The lost words]. Barcelona: Ediciones Destino, 1992.

La piel y la máscara [The skin and the mask]. Barcelona: Editorial Anagrama, 1996.

Siberiana. Madrid: Espasa Calpe, 2000.

Screenplays written with the participation of Jesús Díaz (alphabetically by title)

Barroco. Dir. Paul Leduc, 1989.

Clandestinos (Living Dangerously). Dir. Fernando Pérez, 1987.

El extraño caso de Rachel K (The Strange Case of Rachel K). Dir. Oscar L. Valdés, 1973.

Mina, viento de libertad (Mina, Wind of Freedom). Dir. Antonio Eceiza, 1976.

Otra mujer [Another woman]. Dir. Daniel Díaz Torres, 1986.

Ustedes tienen la palabra [It's your turn to speak]. Dir. Manuel Octavio Gómez, 1973.

¡Viva la república! [Long live the republic!]. Dir. Pastor Vega, 1972.

Films directed by Jesús Díaz (alphabetically by title)

55 hermanos [55 brothers], 1978

Cambiar la vida [To change life], 1975.

Canción de Puerto Rico [Song of Puerto Rico], 1976.

Lejanía (Parting of the Ways), 1985.

Polvo rojo [Red dust], 1981.

En tierra de Sandino [In Sandino's land], 1980.

Critical work on books and films by Jesús Díaz (alphabetically by author)

Brotherton, John. "Rewriting the Revolution: Jesús Díaz's *Las iniciales de la tierra*." *Journal of Iberian and Latin American Studies* 1, no. 1–2 (1995): 69–81.

Cachán, Manuel. "*Los años duros*: La Revolución del discurso y el discurso de la Revolución cubana." *Explicación de Textos Literarios* 19, no. 1 (1990–91): 84–94.

Collmann, Lilliam Oliva. *Jesús Díaz: el ejercicio de los límites de la expresión revolucionaria en Cuba*. New York: Peter Lang, 1999.

Fernández, Enrique. "Parting of the Ways: A Cuban-American View." *Cineaste: America's Leading Magazine on the Art and Politics of the Cinema* 15, no. 4 (1987): 23, 29.

Fornet, Ambrosio. "A propósito de *Las iniciales de la tierra*." *Casa de las Américas*, no.164, September–October 1987.

Fornet, Ambrosio. "Simplificando." *Casa de las Américas*, no. 168, May–June 1988.

Georgakas, Dan, and Gary Crowdus. "Parting of the Ways: An Interview with Jesús Díaz." *Cineaste: America's Leading Magazine on the Art and Politics of the Cinema* 15, no. 4 (1987): 22.

Kozak, Gisela. "*Las palabras perdidas* (Jesús Díaz) o del lugar de la literatura." *Revista Iberoamericana* 68 (October–December 2002): 1041–65.

Nieves, Dolores. "Cronotopo y lenguaje en *Las iniciales de la tierra*." *Universidad de La Habana* 233 (1988): 11–26.

Ortega, Julio. "*Los años duros*, de Jesús Díaz." *Cuadernos Hispanoamericanos: Revista Mensual de la Cultura Hispánica* 260 (1972): 391–99.

Padura, Leonardo. "*Las iniciales de la tierra:* a favor o en contra." *Casa de las Américas*, no. 164, September–October 1987.

Rodríguez, María Cristina. "Jesús Díaz, un director que no teme enfrentarse a lo controvertible." *Imágenes: Publicación Semestral de Teoría, Técnica, Crítica y Educación* 2, no. 1 (1986): 25–27.

Rodríguez-Vivaldi, Ana María. "Jesús Díaz: El cine como texto y pretexto para la literatura." *Atenea* 21, no. 1–2 (2001): 125–36.

Smith, William. "Personajes, lenguaje, y temática en *Las iniciales de la tierra*." *Revista de Estudios Hispánicos* (Rio Piedras, Puerto Rico) 25, no. 1–2 (1998): 227–39.

Vera-León, Antonio. "Jesús Díaz: Politics of Self-Narration in Revolutionary Cuba." *Latin American Literary Review* 21, no. 41 (1993): 65–79.

Journal issue dedicated to Jesús Díaz.

Homenaje a Jesús Díaz. Encuentro de la Cultura Cubana 25, summer 2002. (Issue dedicated to Jesús Díaz following his death.)

Jesús Díaz (1941–2002) was a prominent Cuban writer, filmmaker, and intellectual. His novels include *Las cuatro fugas de Manuel, Dime algo sobre Cuba,* and *Las palabras perdidas.* He wrote screenplays and directed movies, including *Lejanía* and *Polvo rojo.* Díaz was the founder of the influential cultural magazine *Encuentro,* which publishes the work of Cuban writers on the island and in exile.

Kathleen Ross is a professor of Spanish at New York University. She is the author of *The Baroque Narrative of Carlos de Sigüenza y Góngora* and the English-language translator of *Facundo: Civilization and Barbarism* by Domingo F. Sarmiento.

Library of Congress Cataloging-in-Publication Data
Díaz, Jesús.
[Iniciales de la tierra. English]
The initials of the earth / Jesús Díaz ; translated by Kathleen Ross ;
foreword by Fredric Jameson ; epilogue by Ambrosio Fornet.
p. cm.—(Latin America in translation/en traducción/em tradução)
Includes bibliographical references.
ISBN-13: 978-0-8223-3829-1 (cloth : alk. paper)
ISBN-10: 0-8223-3829-7 (cloth : alk. paper)
ISBN-13: 978-0-8223-3844-4 (pbk. : alk. paper)
ISBN-10: 0-8223-3844-0 (pbk. : alk. paper)
I. Ross, Kathleen. II. Title. III. Series.
PQ7390.D5715S13 2006
863.'64—dc22   2006010434